THE CASEY GRIMES SERIES

THE MOSTLY INVISIBLE BOY, TRICKERY SCHOOL, CROOKED CASTLE & THE GHOST OF CREEPCAT

AJ VANDERHORST

The Casey Grimes Universe
stories in order...so far

CG#1
CG#2
CG#2.5
read anytime after CG#1
CG#3
CG#3.5
side stories

www.ajvanderhorst.com

The Mostly Invisible Boy (Casey Grimes #1)/AJ Vanderhorst. - 2nd ed.

Trickery School (Casey Grimes #2)/AJ Vanderhorst. - 2nd ed.

Crooked Castle (A Twisty Thriller from the Casey Grimes Fantasy Universe)/AJ Vanderhorst. - 1st ed.

The Ghost of CreepCat (A Sylvan Woods Short Story)/AJ Vanderhorst. - 1st ed.

PRAISE FOR CASEY GRIMES

★ **2020 Wishing Shelf Book Awards Silver**
★ **2020 Readers' Favorite International Awards Contest Bronze**

"A steppingstone path of small mysteries and action scenes. Sylvan Woods is a splendid conception...fast moving and exuberant, packed with imagination." – *Kirkus Reviews*

"The Mostly Invisible Boy excels, venturing into unpredictable territory, combining the feel of a fantasy with a treasure hunt." – *Midwest Book Review*

"A true adventure, where the stakes are high, the danger real, and the goal is almost impossible to reach." – **Bookworm for Kids**

"The Mostly Invisible Boy is a gripping book from start to finish...riveting." – **LitPick**

"Brimming with intrigue, danger and humor." – **Book Craic**

"Original and inventive, full of courage and heart." – **Amy Wilson**, author of *A Far Away Magic, Shadows of Winterspell*, and *The Wild Way Home*

"Fun, funny and imaginative, The Mostly Invisible Boy is a rollicking good adventure." – **Andrew Chilton**, author of *The Goblin's Puzzle*

"Perfect for middle grade—not too scary but enough to keep you flipping the pages. Surprises at every turn keep the plot moving at a quick pace." – **Always in the Middle**

"Vanderhorst has created a character in Casey Grimes who is so relatable, and so tangible...a must-read fantasy novel for middle grade readers." – **Frank Morelli**, author of *No Sad Songs* and the *Please Return To* series

"A gripping fantasy adventure." – **Wishing Shelf Book Award**

"Incredibly imaginative and fun."– **Book Pipeline**

"Likable characters, clever plot, and unexpected twists and turns." – **Indie Reader**

"Vanderhorst connects to the deep feelings many middle school children deal with day in and day out." – **Reader's Favorite five-star review**

"Enchanting and unusual...the story entertains from the first page to the last." – **Story Sanctuary**

"A once-in-a-lifetime adventure. The characters are all so witty and eloquent, and yet the dialogue feels so natural and flowing. The story itself is fast-paced and fun, it doesn't ever get stuck on anything or leave you bored." – **The Artsy Reader**

"AJ Vanderhorst has the most beautiful imagination. The way he puts this world in your mind is nothing short of brilliant. The journey to Sylvan Woods had me on the edge of my seat, and I wouldn't have it any other way." – **Bookish Bliss**

CONTENTS

THE BOOKS...A QUICK INTRO

The Mostly Invisible Boy (1)

Casey Grimes thinks his invisibility is permanent until he finds a secret forest society in charge of monster control.

Trickery School (2)

Monster-control academy starts for Casey & Gloria, but there's one little problem: A secret enemy who's playing for keeps.

Crooked Castle (2.5)

When Brook is dumped on a deadly island by a beast that shouldn't exist, she's haunted by a past that stays just out of reach.

The Ghost of CreepCat (Novella)

When Lila Banks takes a hike, she doesn't expect to be stalked by the ghost of her recently-deceased cat.

Into Thin Air & The Pencil Killer (Short Stories)

These tales with a twist feature Casey Grimes characters and were written by sons Aidan and Asher—with editing help from me, AJ.

Twisting Trails (3)

Casey and Gloria finally have a chance to carve out a home in Sylvan Woods. But something is terribly wrong with the forest itself.

Dark Sky's Ashes (3.5)

When Conley moves to the Kansas City Dragon District, he gets an ancient house with a secret that might roast him alive.

HOW 'BOUT?

Want a free Casey Grimes story?

Sign up for *The Sylvan Spy* at **ajvanderhorst.com/invisible.**

AJ VANDERHORST
Wishing Shelf
WINNER
CASEY GRIMES
THE MOSTLY INVISIBLE BOY

To Lindsay, Aidan, Asher, Ezra, Miles, Flannery and Gwendolyn. You were all part of the great escape.

STRENGTH AND HONOR, FRIEND.
WITHOUT STRENGTH, HONOR IS
FRAIL. WITHOUT HONOR,
STRENGTH IS CRUEL.
THE ONE WHO GUIDES, PROTECTS
AND DEFENDS CIVILIANS
—WITH STRENGTH AND HONOR—
WILL ALWAYS BE WELCOME IN
SYLVAN WOODS. A FELLOW
CHAMPION IN OUR NEVER
-ENDING FIGHT AGAINST THE

(HERE THE PAGE ENDS.)

CHAPTER 1
EVERY LAST IDEA

CASEY GRIMES WAS INVISIBLE. At least most of the time. He jogged in place as his school bus sped down the street. It slowed to roll through a stop sign, and Casey sprinted alongside, smacking the door. Sound and movement gave him a fighting chance to be seen. For a few seconds, anyway.

"Open up!" he yelled.

The driver squinted through the smudged glass, and Casey banged harder, until the brakes squealed and the accordion doors whooshed open.

"Where'd you come from?" The driver peered at him.

"Same place I always come from." Casey jumped into the bus.

The driver shrugged and floored the accelerator.

It didn't always go this well. Maybe the addition of the safety vest was actually helping. He stood in the aisle, straightened the ugly lime green mesh, and waved to the other kids, but they kept right on talking. *Ok, no problem. Didn't actually expect it to work.*

Casey took his usual seat by the window, pulled out his battered notebook, and flipped to the very last page. Grabbing his pencil, he crossed out the top item on his list: ~~HIGH VISIBILITY VEST~~. Last day of sixth grade. Time to check off every single idea.

Even the stupid ones.

Inside Vintage Woods Middle School, Casey opened his locker, and waited. A minute later, a girl walked over, opened her locker... and Casey smashed the steel doors together.

"Ah!" She jumped and gave a little shriek, her eyes darting right and left until they found Casey. "Um, do I know you?"

"Of course you do," Casey said. "You're Lydia, we sit next to each other in–"

But she'd already started talking to someone else. Casey frowned, and mentally crossed out: ~~SMASH LYDIA'S LOCKER~~. *Another long shot, I guess. But this next idea...*

As if on cue, Manuel walked past. Back in March, they'd had a five second conversation, as long as he'd ever talked to anyone at Vintage Woods. It was a big deal.

He took a deep breath.

"Hey Manuel!" Casey jogged alongside, feeling like a total idiot. *But who cares? No one can see you.* He waved his arms over his head as he ran. "Manuel, hey, hey, hey!" And then...

The boy paused for a millisecond. His eyes widened—and Casey held out his hand for a shake or a fist bump, anything to make contact.

But then Manuel blinked. His eyes slid away. He strolled off.

Casey's face grew hot as he came to a stop. Slowly, he slid out his notebook.

~~MANUEL~~.

He wished the kid hadn't looked up at all. A few seconds of hope only made things worse.

When Casey had first arrived in Vintage Woods, Oregon, halfway through the semester, he'd taken every snub and missed connection personally. Teachers stopped calling his name on roll. Cafeteria ladies didn't serve him. No one held his feet for sit-ups in PE.

This is just a snobbish, stuck up place, he'd told himself. But after three months, he'd realized the horrible truth. He'd been about to shove his Biology partner, who always ignored him, when the awful realization struck home:

This kid doesn't see the hands reaching for his shoulders.

Vintage Woods wasn't a snotty social club. He was really invisible.

It was like bad magic, a windshield wiper cleaning his memory from the minds of everyone around him. When he looked in the mirror, he saw a boy with wide blue eyes and a handful of freckles. Not a flickering hologram or a blurry ghost.

During lunch, Casey did what he always did. Sat in a group of chattering kids who bumped him and said things like, "Oh, didn't see you," and, "Dude, where'd you come from?" He glanced down at his notebook, but there was nothing left to cross off. He'd tried every single idea. And no one had noticed.

"Not their fault," Casey said through gritted teeth. "They can't help it." It was a mantra he repeated often, to avoid losing his temper, but it always raised a troubling question.

Whose fault was this?

Today, the answer was deafening, like someone screaming in his ear. *You're the problem. And there's nothing you can do to solve it.* Falling off his seat. Rustling papers like a poltergeist. Swiping chocolate milk. Nothing made him more...obvious. It had been this way since last October, ever since his family moved to Vintage Woods. Before that—he didn't remember.

In History, students whispered and passed notes while the teacher watched a romantic comedy set in the age of Shakespeare. Casey could feel his temperature rising. He kept busy to stay calm. Today, that meant crafting a paper crocodile by folding old homework. By now, he was very good at origami. The zoo in his locker kept growing, the creatures more and more lifelike.

With a few minutes of class left, he got up, shouldered his pack, and walked out the door. In the hall, the monitor didn't ask him for a pass. Casey yanked his locker open, grabbed his paper menagerie, and stuffed them in his pack. He stared into the empty locker.

Then he tore open his pack, pulled out his beat-up notebook, and threw it inside as hard as he could. *Clang!* A few pages fluttered loose. He ripped off the safety vest, balled it up, and threw it after the notebook. With all his strength, he slammed the locker door.

The last bell rang, and kids flooded the halls. Casey wove his way through the happy crowd, dodging larger kids, shouldering past smaller ones. It was over, totally over. Now he just wanted to go home.

Outside, he stepped onto his bus. The driver raised a hand. *Weird.* Casey hadn't shouted, thrown his pack or kicked the door. Maybe it was the heat. Maybe it was extra caffeine. *Who cares?* He had no idea what caused his invisibility to fluctuate. *Unless...* Casey's heart missed a beat, then hurried to catch up. *At the very last second of the very last day, could it be happening?*

"Wrong route, buddy," the driver said.

Casey couldn't help himself. He said, "Excuse me, sir. Can you really see me?"

Another kid turned in the aisle.

"Go on, look at me!" Casey hadn't meant to shout. "Sorry," he said. "But come on, I'm just a few feet away, right here."

The kid stared. He opened his mouth.

Casey couldn't believe it.

"Weird," the boy said. "For a second, I thought someone was standing there."

The driver shrugged. "Whatever, kid."

Casey stumbled off the bus as fast as he could, chest throbbing like he'd been punched. *Of course he couldn't see you. You* knew *he couldn't see you.*

Laughing kids jostled past. Doors whooshed shut.

Buses rumbled away as he sat on the curb.

Casey rubbed at his stinging eyes. "At least now I'm done with this...with this..." He didn't have a bad enough word. "Gotta get out of here," he said.

Eyes hot and heavy, it took him forty-five minutes to walk home.

He wanted to grab a brick and throw it through glass. He wanted to slump against a tree and think about nothing. He wanted to—he couldn't decide *what* he wanted.

On his front porch, he took a deep breath. The Grimes house was a rock and timber A-frame surrounded on three sides by forest. High ceilings, big picture windows. Set down somewhere else, it would have felt like a get-away cabin. Not in Vintage Woods.

Summer break was here though, that was something. Maybe his family would take a vacation. Escape to a mountain, a lake, or an ocean. He'd even take a prairie or desert—anywhere but here. At least once a day, he caught Mom standing in the kitchen, holding a feather duster, staring at nothing in particular. Most mornings, he found Dad stirring his coffee with a pen or pencil—whatever was close to hand. They could all use a break.

As his fingers touched the knob, the door flew open. Mom pulled him inside and gave him a squeeze, ruffling his brown hair.

"Welcome home, honey!" she sang out.

Casey took a half-step back, tripping on a dusty moving box. She hadn't had this much energy in...months? Years?

She waved a colorful letter. "We just got some amazing news."

As if by magic, Dad appeared, sloshed down a pint-sized mug of coffee, and did a basic dance, stomping and throwing his fists in the air. "Don't ask me how, but we've won an instant vacation to Jamaica. We're leaving today!"

Casey stared. So often, Dad was fighting to keep his tired eyes open.

"We've already started packing." Mom clapped her hands and laughed. "Easy, since we never finished *un*packing."

"You've got to be kidding me." A kaleidoscope of butterflies took flight in Casey's gut and soared toward his heart. "We're actually getting out of here?"

Six-year-old Gloria skipped into the hall, dodging a toaster oven on top of a tv on top of an armchair. Glitter dotted her face and her blonde ponytail bounced. "We get a super special babysitter—and Mom and Dad will bring us *presents*."

"Ohh." The butterflies in Casey's chest turned to dust and cobwebs. "Oh, wow. Dad and Mom, that's great..." The space behind his eyes boiled. He wished he could fade, disappear from his family like he did from everyone else. His parents grinned at each other like they'd eaten too much sugar. Casey slipped up the stairs and collapsed on his bed, pressing his knuckles to his eyes.

He imagined them giggling as they leafed through tour brochures and dive schedules. "It's not their fault," he said. "They can't help it." Then he caught himself. His parents were tired—miserable even—but they *could* help it. He wasn't invisible to *them*. If they paid attention, they'd know he was miserable, too.

Casey punched his pillow, but his tears just came faster. As he drew long, uneven breaths, a tree brushed his window. He sat up, wiping his face. Twigs tapped the glass like knuckles.

"Great timing," he choked. "I'm on my way." He held his back-pack upside down over his bed, shaking out every last paper animal and book and sheet of homework, then headed to the garage to fill it with more useful things.

Casey'd climbed every tree in his yard, especially the ones by his bedroom. High above the ground, his heart felt less heavy and his tight shoulders relaxed. He wasn't invisible, close to birds, squirrels, and the trees themselves. Sycamores, beeches, elms—the names of friends. They didn't say much but they knew he was there. When he stood on the shoulders of leafy, wind-tossed titans, life seemed like it could be different.

Today, the scalding tightness in his chest said nothing would ever change.

In the backyard, mist snaked the ankles of the forest giants. Branches bent like muscular brown arms, wooden hands grazing the roof. Taller trees towered over the murk, deep in the hollow behind the house. For a moment, sunlight burned away the haze. Casey spotted a tree that stretched higher than the others, right before the mist swirled back in.

"You're the climb I need today," he said. "As far from the ground as possible."

Dad and Mom got a free vacation. The least he could do was get away.

He stomped into the woods, ignoring the paths—too knotted and looped to keep track of anyway—and marched deep into the forest, toward the giant tree. It wasn't easy. Thanks to the ravines and brush, Casey hiked further than he ever had before. Further than he meant to, really. *Where is that tree?* The ground sloped away like the inside of a huge bowl. He came to a stop, sweating under his backpack, surrounded by old growth timber.

Nothing looks familiar. This is getting stupid.

He'd climb whatever was close by.

Casey turned in a circle, looking for the tallest and twistiest tree. Mist streamed overhead like a shifting gray ceiling, making it hard to see. Suddenly, sunlight broke through in a rush of gold. The forest soared skyward. Enormous branches framed the blue sky like a thousand fingers.

Casey's shoulders gave a jerk.

All the branches came from the same trunk...

His eyes and mouth became three wide circles.

An ancient oak. Unthinkably huge. His whole sixth-grade class, holding hands, wouldn't be able to wrap their arms around this monster. The bark made deep ridges like dinosaur skin. Casey touched the tree and flinched away like he'd grazed a hot stove. The trunk felt warm.

"Are you for real?" Nervousness scraped his gut and rose to his heart where it transformed into something with wings. *Do it. Climb it.* He flexed his fingers. The oak seemed too big to climb. Too big to exist. But here it was. Waiting.

He reached for a whorl of bark and hung there, ready to jump if the tree—did what? Burnt him? Threw him? Roared, GET OFF ME?

Casey snorted. But he still waited a few more seconds.

Nothing happened—*of course not, dummy*—so he grabbed another knot, and another, and wedged his feet in. Hand over hand, he scaled the bumpy hide until the bark got brittle. Maybe he needed a rope. As he hung there, deciding what to do, metal gleamed in the shadows—silvery metal, shaded by vines. He leaned closer.

"No way." A whole line of metal prongs—hammered into the oak. Like railroad spikes but bigger. Flecked with rust, they twisted up and out of sight.

One corner of Casey's mouth tugged up. "This isn't possible."

The spike ladder rose into leafy shade.

Casey squeezed his eyes shut, counted to five and opened them.

The ladder was still there.

"Let's see what you've got to show me." He scrambled over and put a foot up.

Bluish steel tingled his palms as he climbed.

CHAPTER 2
LEMUR SPEED

CASEY SCRAMBLED AND GRABBED, breathing hard. *Take your time*, he told himself. *It's not like it's going to disappear.* Puffy clouds glowed orange, reflecting the sunset as he caught his breath. *Then again—who knows what rules apply to this tree?*

The higher he got, the more sure of himself he felt. Things didn't usually go well for him on the ground, but the upper stories were his playground. Under his hands, a timber heart pumped sap through woody veins. He shook his head in disbelief.

"So cool. So crazy cool."

Exploring a tree this big might take days—a thought that made him hum. Dozens of living walkways twisted into the gathering dusk. Branches faded from grey to black.

"Maybe I'd better stop taking my time." He tugged his pack-straps tighter and moved up the trunk at raccoon speed. Possibly even lemur speed. Casey always believed he'd be able to find the next handhold when he needed it, and so far, he'd always been right.

A pale moon glowed through clouds. A breeze tugged his hair. He looked down and gave a low whistle. He was higher than the highest metal power lines. Sleepy squirrels squeaked as he moved past.

Ten rungs later, Casey slowed to a koala pace. He'd never been this high before. He couldn't see past his outstretched hands. But something was up there, waiting.

Another ten spikes, and the breeze turned to a wind that jostled him. Casey moved like a three-toed sloth, climbing by touch in the dark. An owl called far below.

Suddenly, everything was pitch black, like the moon had drifted into a cave.

Branches creaked and groaned. Maybe the tree was about to shrug him off like a flightless bug. How long would he be airborne? How many branches would he bounce off before he hit the ground? Heart pounding, Casey leaned into the trunk and took a shuddering breath. *Get a grip, man.* He felt around for his pack, but taking a hand off the ladder made him nervous. He'd have to do without his flashlight.

"Just ten more spikes," he said. "Then I'll quit."

Maybe the moon would come back out.

He rolled his shoulders, relaxing as much as he could. Up he went in the windy night. One spike. Two spikes. Three spikes, four. Five spikes, six spikes, seven... As he reached for number ten, his face smashed something hard. He jerked away.

Casey teetered backwards, clawing at the ancient oak. *Find a grip, please, please, please.* But his fingers didn't obey. Black sheets of wind rushed over him.

He screamed and fell into the darkness.

CHAPTER 3
A PECULIAR BABYSITTER

THE HOUSE GOT CHAOTIC, even before anyone realized Casey was missing.

"It's go time!" Dad yelled, gulping his coffee. "We need to be at the airport in an hour."

He and Mom threw last minute stuff in their suitcases—sunscreen, flip flops and sunglasses. In a flurry of splashes and squirts, Gloria created a huge piece of glittery, pastel artwork that smelled like watermelon. A limousine pulled up at the curb and an oldish woman stepped out—grey hair, nice nondescript face, wire glasses perched on her nose.

"Thanks so much," Mom called across the lawn. "Your references are incredible."

"I'm ready to play games!" Gloria squealed.

The babysitter smiled as her chauffeur tugged a big, battered suitcase out of the trunk. Everyone collided on the front porch, shaking hands. "Nice to meet you." "Take care." "Bye!"

Mom and Dad hugged Gloria and ran across the lawn, dragging their luggage. They were halfway into the limo, struggling to stuff in Gloria's farewell poster, when Mom paused. She looked at Dad with a pleasant, perplexed expression, like there was something she was trying to remember.

"Oh my goodness," she said, "where's Casey?"

Gloria and the babysitter stopped waving. Everyone froze.

Dad sprinted inside and reappeared, throwing his hands in the air.

"What should we do?" Mom wailed.

She and Dad looked at each other helplessly.

"Go on, shoo!" Ms. Jones, the babysitter, waved them away. "I'm sure he's up a tree, just as advertised. Escape while there's still time, dears. Gloria and I will pass on your goodbyes."

That broke the spell. Dad sprinted across the lawn and dove into the idling limousine.

"Tell Casey we'll miss him," Mom yelled out the window.

"Tell my right hand man, good things are coming!"

The limo hurtled off down the street.

Ms. Jones and Gloria looked at each other and smiled.

"Well, that was exciting," the sitter said.

"I was wondering," Gloria said, "if maybe you'd like to play Uno?"

"Of course I would, dear," Ms. Jones said. "Games are an important part of my resume."

They stepped into the open, high-ceilinged house. Light streamed through huge windows onto randomly placed furniture and cobwebs.

"Oh my," Ms. Jones said. "Maybe I'll just tidy up the kitchen first."

That had been several hours back.

As Ms. Jones washed the dishes and wiped the counters, Gloria explained her plan for the week—to have fun and play games. They played several rounds of Uno and when Casey didn't appear, the babysitter examined his room. She noted the scuff marks on his windowsill and the branches grazing the roof, and felt better. He seemed like the kind of boy who could handle himself in the woods.

"Casey is the world's best climber," Gloria said. "He *never* falls."

But as they grilled cheeseburgers on the deck, they were getting worried. For a while, they took turns guessing which tree Casey was climbing. As the sun faded to glowing ash, they stopped talking and looked at each other. Gloria had a little crease above her eyes.

"Do you know where we could find a flashlight?" Ms. Jones said.

By the time Gloria found Daddy's light, the woods were huge dark cutouts, full of whispers and small screams. She took the babysitter's hand.

"Let's go find your brother." Ms. Jones patted Gloria's head and stared into the murky forest, blinking. "My goodness, this is unexpected," she murmured. "Don't worry, dear, I won't let the Razor Wings or Bog Creeps or Tree Shrieks get you."

Gloria gave her a small, confused smile.

Ms. Jones' mind was racing. She was barely aware of what she'd said. With a few rare exceptions, her jobs involved watching ordinary children who threw temper tantrums and tried to make messes they didn't clean up. She couldn't remember the last time someone had disappeared. Much less vanished into the wild.

As the sun went down and the forest came alive, she felt the unpleasant sensation you get when you're forced to deal with something nasty—vampire bats, for example—in a place you didn't expect, like your vacation cabin in the Rockies. Ms. Jones wondered how to follow Casey through the woods, full of dirt paths and maybe other things.

What kind of child was he? Did he know what he was doing? If he was wearing some kind of beast deterrent, no one had mentioned it. All indications were that he and Gloria were quite normal. She could call him home (there was a bullhorn in her luggage), but given the nature of these woods, it was asking for trouble. She didn't have a bloodhound and it was after sunset.

None of her options were very good, but she had to take action.

Hand in hand, she and Gloria walked into the forest.

CHAPTER 4
DEAD OR NOT

WITH A SCREAM, Casey plunged into the dark. He hunched his shoulders, waiting for the first horrible *crunch*—then his scream was cut short. Air rushed from his lungs. His heels knocked the oak. Nylon straps cut into his armpits. He dangled from a ladder rung, held up by his backpack.

"Oooow," he gasped.

A ripping sound came from overhead.

Casey reached as high as he could, grabbing air until his hand found a metal spike. His pack ripped again. Then he was hanging from one arm. Wheezing, he swept his feet back and forth until they smacked metal. He put one foot on the spike, then the other. *Safe. I'm safe.* Tears and sweat streaked his face. He tasted copper. Casey pressed his forehead against the tree.

"Thank you," he croaked.

He didn't want to climb all the way down. He wasn't sure he could. But he couldn't spend the night on a spike. So he gritted his teeth and inched toward the hard, flat structure he'd smashed his face on. Five rungs later, the light changed. The moon and stars were out again.

Casey's eyes widened. "What kind of crazy tree are you?" He

staggered off the ladder, fell to his knees, and pressed his face to a wide and solid floor. Heat from the long-gone sun brushed his cheek.

"I made it," he gasped. "I'm all right."

But no one else knew that.

After a minute of gulping air, he shrugged off his pack, and dug around until he found what he was looking for. A collapsible kite and a sharpie. Better than nothing.

CHAPTER 5
TWISTED TRAILS

GLORIA AND MS. JONES shoved through sticky webs. Tiny feet scuttled in their hair, but they brushed them off and kept going. Gloria beamed the flashlight right and left. They took turns calling, CASEY!

When they came to the first **Y** in the trail, Ms. Jones knew her plan had failed. There were no broken twigs or gum wrappers, no signs of an eleven-year-old boy.

She took a guess and followed the right-hand trail. A little later, their path crossed another, forming an **X**. One prong of the **X** headed back. The righthand trail was overgrown with toadstools. They turned left, and twigs snapped nearby.

Gloria squeezed the sitter's hand.

Ms. Jones opened her mouth, then closed it. She'd been about to say, "Don't worry about that, dear." Because she saw things moving in the dark. Some of them were imaginary, like Casey's body hanging upside down, his neck at an odd angle.

But other things were not imaginary. Things with teeth and claws, that didn't appear in any suburban guidebook. The Bog Creep, with its flaming eyes, was especially troubling. It clearly hadn't eaten for awhile. Ms. Jones was doing her best to keep Gloria from noticing.

After a while, the path sloped down. Their shoes made slurping sounds and Gloria swept the light around. Behind them were two sets of footprints. A lady's sensible shoes and a small girl's tennies. Ahead were two other sets, but they weren't Casey's. One moved lazily from side to side. They might belong to a heavy cat. The others could have been made by a bird with very large claws.

Ms. Jones glanced over her shoulder. She waited, then tugged Gloria around. "Let's head back the way we came, dear." Her voice shook, but only slightly.

Another set of clawed bird tracks had appeared in the trail.

Gloria stepped right over them as if she didn't notice.

"What I wouldn't give for a dark lantern right now," Ms. Jones murmured.

They walked fast, except when they had to get their bearings. Once, they came to a **K** in the trail that neither of them remembered, but Ms. Jones was not fooled. Another time, the trail made a **&** and they missed their turn and started down the dark double loop. Gloria tugged the babysitter's hand, and Ms. Jones gave a start. "Oh, let's not go this way."

Something snarled nearby.

"I'm not scared," Gloria said. "We have to find Casey."

Finally, they found the very first Y. Starlight reached them through the trees. Ms. Jones removed her glasses and wiped her forehead. "I'm so sorry, Gloria." She took a breath to smooth the panic from her voice. "We've done all the searching we can tonight."

Gloria sniffled. "I hope Casey is all right."

"My goodness, so do I." Ms. Jones dabbed at her eyes. "I wasn't ready for this forest, not in the least. If I'd known we'd be in a place like this, I would have packed very differently." She looked curiously at the small girl. "I must say, you took everything in stride."

"I saw the killer bird," Gloria said. "Its feathers looked like knives. But I didn't want to worry you."

"That would have been the Razor Wing," Ms. Jones said. "You were very thoughtful."

"I saw the murder cat too, growling like a tiger."

"The Bog Creep was a rather close call," Ms. Jones said. "You just might have saved us."

They walked toward the house.

"I'm so confused right now," the sitter said. "I must admit you are not what I expected."

"What do you mean?" Gloria said.

They stood in the small backyard and watched a wind sway the trees. Ms. Jones was about to answer, but a multicolored kite sailed through the air, gliding back and forth until it landed at their feet. In the moonlight, written on the kite in large letters, they read:

I HAD A SMALL ACCIDENT BUT I'M SAFE NOW. I'M SPENDING THE NIGHT IN A TREE. I HOPE YOU SEE THIS BUT IF YOU DON'T I'LL SEE YOU TOMORROW. LOVE, CASEY

"Thank goodness." Ms. Jones said. "No, not at *all* what I expected."

CHAPTER 6
THIS ISN'T A TREEHOUSE

THE UGLY SONG of a crow woke Casey. His back ached and his neck was cricked, but he jumped to his feet, turning in a slow circle.

"It's real," he said. "I wasn't dreaming."

The sun bubbled over the edges of the world, changing the woods from gray to yellow-green.

"Unbelievable," Casey said.

Yards and fields and forest spread out like a map, rolling into hazy distance. His house no bigger than his thumb.

He stood on a wide wooden floor, the one he'd smashed his face on the night before. The deck made a rough octagon. The oak grew through the center and twisted overhead. On four of the deck's eight sides, short ladders led to higher decks. Carved railings, like very old bannisters, circled the platform. The railings on the higher decks were made of blueish metal.

This wasn't a hideout. Not a treehouse. Casey had seen pictures of ancient ships. The fortress looked a little like that. "Who built you?" he breathed.

For a second, he waited for an answer.

The fortress smelled like earthy dust. When the wind blew, the floors creaked but barely moved. Every few steps, Casey glanced over his shoulder, looking for a security guard, or the tree's owner—but no one came.

He climbed each of the four lookout spots, heart pounding. He was trespassing but he didn't care. There weren't any signs posted: KEEP OUT. PRIVATE TREE FORTRESS. So who could blame him? The views were even better from the upper decks. Carved compass letters marked each one: N, S, E and W. The wind parted on the compass decks, leaving muffled silences.

So quiet it was peaceful. And creepy.

On his way down from the western lookout, Casey saw a door behind the ladder. It opened on a closet full of shelves. Candles and matches, a black metal lantern, a picnic basket, a football, a zippered pouch, two flannel bathrobes, musty blankets, some books... *The Horse and His Boy, A Sylvan Handbook,* and *You'll Never Walk Alone So Be Ready: Self Defense for Woodland Travel.*

Casey laughed. Self defense against what—rabbits and chipmunks?

The pouch held two brittle toothbrushes, crusty toothpaste and a bottle of shampoo. In the picnic basket, he found a tablecloth, glasses, plates, and an ancient jar of Greek olives. A small, confused spider crawled from one corner.

Casey's stomach growled, and that made him think about his family. Would Dad and Mom be relieved or mad? He hoped they'd found his note. Now that he finally had some excitement in his life, was he about to be chained in his room for summer break?

He stepped out of the closet and shrugged on his pack. At the top of the ladder, he looked down and remembered how it felt to plummet into darkness. Almost dying kind of put things in perspective. What was the point of going to school? Turning in homework? What was the point of any of it? This couldn't go on. Wouldn't go on. It was time for a better plan than *Try harder* and *Keep your head up.* Big Changes. He didn't know what they were yet, but he would.

Casey threaded rope through a pulley and let the ends fall, thudding on branches and whipping through leaves. He flexed his fingers and started the long descent.

CHAPTER 7
MYSTERIOUS MS. JONES

BURRS AND LEAVES stuck to Casey's clothes like forest confetti as he came out of the woods. Gloria and a grown-up were sipping drinks on the deck. They cheered as he ran across the lawn. Casey's smile faded as he took in an older lady. Sharp eyes, kind face, neatly dressed—except for one of Gloria's ribbons threaded through her gray hair.

"Who are you?" he asked as Gloria threw her arms around him. "Wait a minute." His eyes widened. "You can see me?"

"Of course I can, dear," Ms. Jones said. "I'm Ms. Jones, an extremely well-qualified traveling babysitter. Technically, I'm part of your parents' vacation package. Practically, I'm happy to meet you, Casey Grimes, and very glad to see you in one piece."

She held out her right hand. Casey eased his hand out from behind his back and inched it forward. The sitter gave his shaky fingers a brisk, warm squeeze.

"Seriously," he said. "Mom and Dad left?"

"Of course they left," Gloria said. "We told them not to skip their vacation just because you went for a walk."

"Oh...that's good." He'd been about to say, "They didn't even say goodbye..." But then he thought, No lecture, no being grounded. No telling about the Oak.

"Between the three of us," Ms. Jones said, "Your parents desperately needed a vacation."

Casey smiled weakly. The babysitter's eyes were like magnifying glasses. He shifted his weight from one foot to the other and rubbed a sudden itch on his nose.

"How about some breakfast?" Ms. Jones walked inside.

Gloria put her mouth to Casey's ear. "You'll never guess what happened to *us*."

"Same here," Casey whispered. "You won't believe what—"

"Let's talk about it over bacon and eggs," Ms. Jones called from the kitchen.

Gloria's eyes widened.

"You're such a loud whisperer," Casey said.

"No, *you* are."

When they sat down to breakfast, Ms. Jones said, "We were so happy to find your note, dear. Of course, now you simply *must* tell us about this tree you slept in."

Casey's gut twitched. "Um, right. Sure."

"And just so you know," the sitter said, "I am absolutely, most definitely, in the pro-climbing camp. The bigger the tree, the braver the kid, I say."

Casey glanced up to see if she was being sarcastic. She caught him with a smile. He almost choked on his toast.

"Let's see..." In his mind, Casey edited the mostly-true story he'd prepared for his parents. "I found an oak that was so huge and twisty, I had to climb it. But I lost track of time, and the sun started going down. Then I had a...a little slip, and I decided the *safest* thing would be to spend the night."

"Hmm." Ms. Jones raised one eyebrow.

"Where did you spend the night?" Gloria asked.

Casey licked his lips. "Um, a deck sort of thing, at the top of the ladder."

Uh oh. He hadn't meant to say that.

The babysitter leaned in. "How intriguing. Tell us more."

Panic rustled Casey's insides. But Ms. Jones couldn't erase what he'd found. Even if she didn't approve, the tree would be there, waiting.

"It was super safe," he said. "With railings...a closet...and climbing equipment."

Ms. Jones' eyes widened behind her glasses.

"You've got to help me get up there," Gloria said.

Casey shot her a look.

"No, I won't be quiet."

The sitter rested her chin on one hand. "Vintage Woods *is* a border city..." she murmured. "I wonder..."

Casey eased his chair away from the table, but the legs squeaked.

The sitter blinked. "Let me just say, Casey, you deserve an extraordinary amount of credit for climbing this tree." Her forehead made rows of wrinkly lines.

"I do?"

"If you don't mind me asking, have you found anything like this before?"

He shook his head no, then froze. Had it been a trick question? He probably should've said, Yes, all the time.

"Astonishing," Ms. Jones said. "Unheard of..." She gave her head a small shake. "Here's an idea, Casey. Maybe you shouldn't tell your friends about this tree. The oak could be your little—well, your *big* secret. Not everyone can climb like you and–"

"It won't be a problem," Casey said.

"What a relief." Ms. Jones breathed out. "Why not?"

"Um." Casey counted dots of pepper in his egg yolk.

"We don't have any friends," Gloria said. "Kids act like we're invid—invidsible."

"Shh," Casey said. "Wait, what?" He swiveled to face her.

Gloria sipped her orange juice. "It's why me and Casey are best friends."

Casey stared. "But everyone likes you, Gloria."

She giggled. "No they don't. They hardly even notice me."

"Are you serious?" He wished he'd paid closer attention. Gloria was always so bright and cheerful. He thought of all the paper animals guarding his locker, more than enough to share. He reached over and gave his sister a squeeze.

When he looked up, Ms. Jones' expression was soft and pointed at the same time. "When you say invisible, dears...do you mean people truly can't see you?"

Casey didn't answer.

Gloria nodded.

Ms. Jones' eyes grew big enough to hold goldfish. "For the first time in years," she said, "I have to admit I have no idea what is going on." She pushed her chair back and stood. "Maybe I'll do some more cleaning."

Casey got Gloria's attention and pointed his eyes toward the door.

Ms. Jones paused on her way across the kitchen. "Excuse me if I seem to be prying, but have either of you seen a doctor recently, or had any blood work done?"

They shook their heads.

She stuck her head under the sink. Her voice sounded muffled. "Whatever happened, it's not your fault. Quite the opposite. So run along. Enjoy the weekend."

Something unfolded its wings and shook itself in Casey's chest —the feeling you get when you're about to escape.

"Let's go, Gloria."

She followed him downstairs and into the garage.

"We've got to move fast," he said. "I didn't just find a deck—I found a fortress. It's ours now, and we're taking a vacation."

"Oh goodie!" Gloria picked up a pair of roller skates.

"Probably not a good idea. Let's pack some basic stuff and sneak out."

"Sneak out?" Gloria said. "That's silly, Ms. Jones is our friend. I was trying to tell you what happened last night in the woods..."

She explained how the paths changed shape, and about the bog creep and Razor Wing. Casey became a statue of a Boy Staring at His Sister While Holding a Campfire Waffle Maker.

"And I didn't *see* a Tree Shriek, but there was probably one close by," Gloria finished.

She had her faults, such as being overly optimistic and obsessed with glitter glue, but Gloria was not a liar. It didn't even occur to Casey to question her.

"Monsters," he said.

"At least three kinds," Gloria said. "And all of them eat kids."

Casey frowned.

"We'll be extra-special-careful," Gloria said.

"Plus..." Casey said, "it's day time."

At the back door, Gloria handed Ms. Jones one of two walkie-talkies they'd found in the garage. Casey stood on the deck stairs, waiting to see what would happen. If there were *really* monsters in the woods, would Ms. Jones let them go back? If she said no, elderly people weren't known for their sprinting abilities. He and Gloria could run for it.

"Very good, dears." Ms. Jones took the walkie-talkie. "Let's be in touch."

It had almost been *too* easy.

"Just a minute," Ms. Jones said.

Casey's toes tensed in his running shoes.

"Casey," she said. "Don't let Gloria free-climb any huge trees."

"Er, right, of course not."

Ms. Jones certainly knew more than a normal sitter.

Their supplies sloshed and rattled on Casey's back as they rushed across the lawn. Gloria had looped a coil of rope over one shoulder, but it kept unraveling, so she skipped every few steps to avoid tripping. Casey felt like skipping too, but at the same time there was a thin, unsettled feeling at the bottom of his stomach.

CHAPTER 8
GHOST'S DOORBELL

GLORIA STARED UP, sweeping back her golden hair. "It's so huuuge." Next to the giant oak, she looked doll-sized. *Ant-sized.* Hopefully this was a good idea.

As Casey watched, his sister circled the trunk, oohing and aahing. "What's in the closet?" Her voice came from the other side of the tree.

"What closet?"

He found Gloria standing between two roots taller than she was. It took him a moment to see the low, dirty door in the side of the tree.

"I guess you didn't know about *this.*" She folded her arms and smiled.

"It looks like an old basement," Casey said. "Hey wait, don't—" but she was already tugging. The door creaked open in a flurry of cobwebs. Gloria stuck her head into the spidery darkness. She leaned forward. With a little yelp, she was gone.

"Gloria!"

Casey lunged inside, where it was almost too dark to see. Hinges creaked behind him and he whirled as the door slammed shut like it had a grudge. The opening was only a crack when his shoulder knocked it wide. Gasping, he wedged the door open with a rock and rushed back into the dark. Something scuttled overhead. *Somethings.*

"Gloria!" He pitched his voice lower. "Where are you?"

His sister sniffed. "Right over here, around the corner."

"What corner?"

A small hand took his. "This way, dummy."

She tugged him forward.

"Um Gloria, I'm supposed to be keeping *you* safe..."

The air smelled sticky. They turned left, and the walls of a narrow hall glowed yellow-green. It didn't *look* like a deathtrap. A few steps later, they stood at a dead end washed by soft light. They stared at a tarnished silver button, etched with a lightning bolt and a leaf. It gleamed in the wall like a ghost's doorbell.

"Ok, this is pretty cool," Casey said.

Gloria looked pleased with herself.

"Wait, you didn't push it, did you?"

"Of course not." She stuck out her tongue.

Casey felt an urge to push the silver button himself, like it was a strong magnet and his fingers were made of iron. *What danger could there possibly be in—*

"Um, what do you think you're doing?" Gloria said.

Casey snatched his hand back guiltily.

"Right," he said. "Let's be safe. We barely even know this tree, and we definitely have no idea what's going on down here. Let's get out."

Maybe I can sneak back later and ring the doorbell.

He headed back down the passage. When he slowed, Gloria bumped into his back and giggled. Outside, they stood in ferns and sunshine.

The door in the tree vibrated on its hinges. Casey rolled away the stone doorstop, and the cellar slammed shut angrily.

"Did the oak grab you?" Casey said. "How did it suck you in?"

"It didn't." Gloria smiled. "I jumped in. I wish my whole room glowed like that closet. One. Big. Nightlight. The special rocks were nice too, I guess."

Casey closed his open mouth. "Wait, what special rocks?"

"Like this one." Gloria toed the stone he'd used to wedge the door. Smooth, maybe polished by a river. A hole had been drilled through its middle. Painted on one side in white letters was the word *Pomeranian*. After that, in smudged chalk: *Tom-Tom*.

This was no ordinary rock.

"Pom..Pom-er..." Gloria sounded out.

"A Pomeranian...is a small dog." Casey said slowly.

"I guess its name was Tom-Tom then," Gloria said. "Just like the other rocks. Names of kids and words, like *small boy, medium girl, big boy*. And then there was *really big boy*." She laughed.

"Wait..." Casey felt ridiculous. "You're saying they're inside the tree? I guess you found a storage closet."

Gloria beamed. "*My* discovery."

"I was too busy saving you from the spiders." Casey stared into her big eyes, violet with amber flecks. She was sure observant for someone her age. And very hoity-toity.

"I win," Gloria said.

"Ok, ok," Casey said. "I guess it's time to climb this tree."

They walked to what he thought of as the front of the oak. His rope from that morning dangled by the spike ladder. Casey took one end of the rope, wrapped it around Gloria's waist, and tied his best knot. He did the same thing with the other end of the rope and his own waist. As soon as he finished, she started up.

"Pace yourself," he said. "It's a long way to our secret fortress."

Casey hadn't seen her climb for weeks. Maybe even months, the last time they'd sneaked out on the roof together. She crawled up the trunk like a squirrel, loose rope dangling. He tugged the slack through the pulley far above. As Gloria got higher, more and more rope looped at his feet. She reached the first branches and he yelled, "Take a break, Gloria."

He followed her up, undid the knot around his waist, and tied a new one, pulling the extra rope through so they were connected tightly again.

"Ok, up you go," he said. "No rush."

Gloria rubbed her hands together. "Up I go," she sang.

As she climbed, Casey wondered if her sharp eyesight would make heights better or worse. He had the feeling Gloria was a somewhat strange six-year-old. That made him wonder how weird he was himself, and if *that* was why he was invisible to most people. Or was it the other way around, and he was weird because he'd been see-through for so long?

He was thinking about it, reeling in Gloria's slack, when she screamed. The rope jerked in his hands. Casey clenched his fists and her scream ended. She kicked and grabbed, spinning in the air twenty feet overhead.

"I've got you," Casey yelled.

Gloria sagged into her rope. "Help meee," she groaned.

"Hold on." Casey kept his voice calm. "I'll move your feet down." He fed rope back to the pulley, and Gloria sank. She hooked one ankle over a spike. A second later she was on her feet, face shoved against the oak. Casey sighed out a long, steadying breath. His palms were raw and the rope was streaked with blood.

"Do you want to come down?" he called.

Gloria didn't say anything, so he climbed after her.

"This is more scarier than I expected." His sister hugged the tree trunk—the tiny patch of it she could reach. Her face showed some very light freckles you usually couldn't see. Casey helped her onto a sidewalk-sized branch.

"I thought this would be fun." Tears made trails down her cheeks.

"You know what?" Casey said. "I used to fall all the time when I was your age. But unlike you, I wasn't climbing hundred-foot trees."

Gloria blew her nose on a pink shirt sleeve. "Well, you didn't have a big brother to help you. Are we almost there?"

Casey ran a hand through his hair. "Maybe it's time for a change of plan."

CHAPTER 9
MACE VERSUS SWORD

CASEY PACED THE FORTRESS DECK, groaning and pretending to be in pain. It was tough, with sun-warmed boards creaking under his feet and wind ruffling his hair.

"Oh stop faking," Gloria said. "I weigh as much as Tinkerbell."

Gloria was a slip of a girl. No one would ever call her big or meaty. Maybe she even had hollow bones. She'd laughed and tapped the ladder spikes, *ding-ding-ding,* as Casey hauled her up. Standing at the eastern rail, she held her arms up like she might take flight. A summery breeze ruffled her shirtsleeves and flipped her ponytail.

"What a beautiful place," she said. "It's as good as a story."

Casey gave up trying to sound serious. "Isn't it amazing?"

"Perfect for summer break," Gloria said.

They pulled out the picnic basket. Casey spread the tablecloth and loaded it with plates and glasses. Gloria set a checkers game on one side. By the time Casey was done unpacking, she'd weighed each corner of the blanket down with a smooth black stone.

"Where'd you find the climbing weights?" He poured lemonade.

"In the closet." Gloria fitted an apple slice into her mouth so she had a one-piece smile trimmed with red.

Casey smiled back. "With the picnic stuff?"

She chewed up her smile and swallowed it. "No, the other closet."

"What other..." He tried to stop, but it was too late.

"Ooh." Gloria raised her eyebrows. "You didn't know about that, did you?"

"Darn it," Casey said. "How many closets does this tree have?"

Gloria's closet was well organized. Ropes and harnesses hung from hooks in the ceiling. Rows of climbing weights lined a wall. Drawers contained carabiners, O-rings, and boxes of chalk. On the final wall...

Casey's shoulders twitched.

Swords. Spears. Bright, oddly-shaped weapons. Cold traced his spine as he took a spiky mace down from the wall. "This is unbelievable," he said. "Feels totally real. Heavy...and, ouch! Sharp points —these *are* real." He put the barbed club down and sucked one finger.

"Thought you'd like it," Gloria said.

"I do," Casey said. "But...why do you think they stockpiled weapons? An enemy, say a rogue knight, would have to climb a long way to attack you. It would be easier to drop a rock on his head."

"Tree Shrieks, maybe?" Gloria stood on tip-toe and grabbed for a blade, but she wasn't tall enough.

Casey reached down a sword for her. "We'd better trade closets."

"Fine," Gloria said. "But I want this sword and a climbing rock. I already picked one out." She pointed. The stone said, *small girl.* Written after it in chalk: *Gloria.*

"Were you afraid another small girl would take it?" Casey said.

"Hmph. I tried to find a rock for you, but I couldn't find one that said...'very big dum-dum.'"

"Very funny."

They played checkers and staged bouts of Mace Versus Sword on the main deck.

"I challenge you to single combat," Casey announced.

"Challenge accepted," Gloria squealed.

After she sliced a hole in his t-shirt, right over his belly button, they added a new rule:

Mace Versus Sword would always be played in slow motion.

Looking for an even better view, they climbed the north lookout. The peaceful calm, walled off from wind and bird cries, gave Casey space to catch up with himself. He felt happy. On top of the world. And...

"I'm getting hungry," he said.

"Me too," said Gloria.

He dug through his pack and found the walkie-talkie. Maybe the elevation would help the signal.

"Climber King Casey checking in," he said. "We're thinking about heading home for lunch...a very *quick* lunch and then back out the door."

Gloria leaned over. "I'm here too. In case you're wondering, this is...Green Queen Gloria."

Casey raised his eyebrows. "Let us know what you think, Ms. Jones. Over and out."

They leaned against the railing, looking over the woods.

"I hope this isn't a mistake," Casey said.

Something metallic buzzed far below.

"Asking someone to make lunch is never a mistake," Gloria said.

Their walkie rattled. "Lunch is served," Ms. Jones said. "Come down when you're ready." Tinny feedback crackled up from the forest floor.

"Oh no." Casey sat bolt upright. "She's down there, waiting. She found the oak."

CHAPTER 10
WHAT'S GOING ON WITH THIS BABYSITTER?

CASEY'S SCALP tingled as he strapped Gloria into a harness, attached a rope and ran it through a pulley. He clipped her *small girl* climbing weight to the other end, and pulled on his own equipment.

"You first, Gloria," he said. "I'll keep an eye on you."

Gloria squealed as they bounced down the tree. When they let go of the ladder, their ropes hummed through the pulley. Slowed by their climbing weights, it was like falling through molasses. Casey barely noticed.

Why did Ms. Jones follow us? How did she find us?

"LOOK AT MEEE!" Gloria glided to the ground, hands and feet spread like a ballerina.

"Outstanding, dear," the sitter said. "You're such a brave climber."

Casey didn't meet her eye as Ms. Jones unpacked a stack of bacon-lettuce-tomato sandwiches. "I must say, this tree is bigger than I imagined," she said. "Its roots must touch half the forest."

Now was a good time to change the subject. But Casey was too late.

"I found a secret room that glowed in the dark," Gloria said.

"And then I found *another* secret room, with lots of very sharp swords and, um, *vases*..."

"Maces." Casey groaned.

A quiver moved over Ms. Jones' face—or maybe it was his imagination, because the next second, she seemed quite relaxed.

"Are you sure you've found all the closets? In cases like this, it's best to be sure they are all empty. You wouldn't want anyone jumping out."

Casey was pretty sure this was not how babysitters were supposed to behave. On the other hand, Ms. Jones seemed very on top of things. Spending time around her, with her energy and pointed questions, made him wonder if Mom and Dad were totally ok.

"Ms. Jones," he said. "Who are you?"

She hesitated, then the corners of her mouth tugged up. "A certified traveling babysitter, dear. Possibly the world's best."

It sounded impressive...but she hadn't really told him anything.

"You *are* the best," Gloria said. "And we're having *soo* much fun, we thought we might spend the night in the tree, except I don't have my teddy bear."

Casey put a hand to his forehead. So much for their secret plan.

Ms. Jones sighed. "To be honest, I'm beginning to feel a bit uneasy. I'd hoped the tree was smaller. However..." She looked up at the oak. "You've already proved you can climb it. And it is summer break, after all. You can sleep in the fortress, er, hideout, just this once." She pulled a teddy bear from her picnic basket and handed it to Gloria.

"Ooh, you're magical," Gloria said. "But how did you–"

"You left your dresser drawer ajar, dear." Ms. Jones winked. "It was obvious you'd packed your pajamas."

Casey stared. Who was this woman?

"I brought some dinner too," she said. "Make sure you are inside the railings by sunset. Nothing will bother you up there."

"You're a great sitter, Ms. Jones." Casey felt dazed.

"Casey?" Ms. Jones tapped his shoulder. "I'd like your solemn oath that you'll take no chances in the woods tonight."

"You've got it," Casey said.

Ms. Jones had secrets, no question. He'd make a point of finding out about her later. As soon as he'd figured out what was going on with this tree.

After their late lunch, Gloria tried to persuade Ms. Jones to climb the tree while Casey made shushing motions.

"I'm a little old for free-climbing," the sitter said. "But you go ahead."

Phew. Casey strapped on his harness, and helped Gloria with hers. She stuck her hips out and clipped herself to her rope. Casey gathered their supplies.

"Happy climbing," Ms. Jones said. "I'll just watch you up and out of sight."

"Ready, Gloria?" Casey said.

"Of course."

He slid her O-ring free, and her harness tugged her upward. She moved in little hops, like a tree frog.

Ms. Jones smiled. "Take good care of her. And Casey—try to enjoy this extraordinary event for all it's worth. It won't last forever."

Casey nodded. "I'll do my best."

As he climbed, he wondered what she meant. He'd found the oak twice now. What could stop him from finding it again and again? He shrugged as branches flickered past.

Climbing with weights was like being pulled by unseen hands. If he jumped, his *medium boy* stone whirred through the pulley, and he covered four or five rungs at a time. No shaking fingers, no salt in his eyes. The Old Oak's climbing system was rock solid.

On the catwalk below the fortress, Gloria was unclipping herself.

"You did great," Casey said. "I barely even saw you."

"Climbing is more fun when you know you won't become a pancake."

They hung up their harnesses and climbed the last few feet. The sky was turning lava gold.

Safe for the night, he thought. Just wind and starlight and mysteries. No smashed faces, no dangerous climbs. And definitely no monsters.

CHAPTER 11
STRENGTH & HONOR

FOR DINNER, they ate roast beef sandwiches in a pile of pillows and blankets. As the sky turned navy blue, Gloria changed into her pajamas, covered in unicorns.

"Who do you think made this fort?" she said.

Casey leaned back, stretching his legs. "Inland pirates, probably. Later they died in a river battle and never came back."

"But there aren't any skeletons or gold."

"Hmm."

Gloria put her head on her pillow. "Maybe it's a secret clubhouse."

"What kind of club stores weapons a thousand feet in the air?" Casey caught himself. *Whoa. No need to be so serious.* "Maybe Peter Pan used to live here."

"He's made up, silly." Gloria yawned. "Maybe...a watch tower?"

"Could be," Casey said. "Although there's nothing obvious it's watching."

"Except the stars and moon." Gloria snuggled into a blanket. "Which are very nice."

When she said the fortress might be a stable for flying unicorns, Casey said she was probably right, and she fell asleep.

But he couldn't.

What if they weren't alone?

Calm down, Grimes. Look at this place, dusty and forgotten.

He got up and pulled the metal lantern out of the closet. As he struck matches, he thought about their unusual babysitter. She'd acted like his invisibility was all a big mistake. Like someone had put an X in the wrong box, and *whush*—transparent Casey.

The antique lantern flared to life, making him jump. He grabbed a stack of books from Gloria's closet and sat on the floor, flicking pages. There weren't many left in *A Sylvan Handbook*. Yellowed and brittle, stained with water-ruined ink. Blue and black streamed over the paper like blurry mountain ranges.

THE SYLVAN PLEDGE topped one page...but the rest was torn away. Casey finally found an undamaged sheet. A towering, leafy tree, covered in swirling flames. Under the tree, in strong, flowing script, he read:

STRENGTH AND HONOR, FRIEND.

WITHOUT STRENGTH, HONOR IS FRAIL. WITHOUT HONOR, STRENGTH IS CRUEL. THE ONE WHO GUIDES, PROTECTS AND DEFENDS CIVILIANS—WITH STRENGTH AND HONOR—WILL ALWAYS BE WELCOME IN SYLVAN WOODS. A FELLOW CHAMPION IN OUR NEVER-ENDING FIGHT AGAINST THE–

Casey turned the page. Another mess of runny ink, except for one word. MAGIC. Dim light from the moon and stars silvered the main deck. He frowned, blew out the lantern, and walked from rail to rail, looking out across the darkness.

"Who built you?" he whispered. "Where's Sylvan Woods? Why all the weapons?"

The tree didn't answer. He hadn't expected it to. Well, maybe he had, a little.

Casey climbed a compass deck to get closer to the stars. He felt sleepiness sneaking up. The rail seemed a lighter shade of grayish blue. Maybe it was the moonlight. He ran a hand along the railing, and it didn't *feel* any different, but it was certainly glowing.

He gasped, as a voice spoke in his ear.

A girl's voice, but it wasn't Gloria.

"Hubba hoy!" the voice said. "Done polishing the stars yet, Fire Ducky?"

CHAPTER 12
PERSON UNKNOWN

CASEY JERKED UPRIGHT, looking right and left. He was alone—except he wasn't. Was the Oak talking to him? It didn't sound like a tree's voice. At least, not what a tree would sound like in his imagin–

"Umm, hello?" the girl said. "Come in, Fire Ducky."

He squeezed the glowing rail with white knuckles.

"Uh, hi," he said. "I—I'm here."

"Did you catch a cold?" she said. "I hate those summer colds, they can last for weeks. Even though they're *probably* contagious, you can't hide from people that long, so on top of all the snot, you feel guilty."

"I hate summer c-c-colds too." Casey's face tingled as the conversation stretched beyond five seconds. Did trees catch colds? Of course not. Which meant.... Another kid. Was talking. To him. He stepped back and wiped sweat from his forehead, trying to think of something to say.

"I had—I had a cold last year that lasted most of summer."

So dumb.

The chatty voice in his head was silent.

He slumped against the railing, breathing out through his nose.

"Hey, where'd you go?" the girl said.

Casey almost shrieked. Instead...he squeaked. And vowed that he would never, ever make that sound again.

"New pet?" the girl said. "Sounds cute. What were you saying?"

"Umm," Casey said. "*I* had a summer cold last year."

Intriguing stuff, Grimes. Definitely worth waiting for.

He pressed a hand to his forehead and kept the other on the rail.

"You did?" the girl said. "That's awful. Hey, wait a minute, no you didn't. You're not Fire—ahem, you're not who I thought you were. Who is this? Which compass point am I on?"

Casey didn't say anything. Suddenly the night felt shivery. He stared into the dark as if the stars might blink out a message that would keep him from saying idiotic things.

"East...north...south...west," the girl whispered.

Casey imagined her turning around, getting her bearings. Discovering he was no one she wanted to know. Stepping away.

"Very tricky," the girl said. "I sneaked out for a while, just making the rounds, with my mind on the battlefront, you know. But I'm in the South so you're East, in the abandoned Old Oak. Who is this? Robert, it's you, isn't it?"

"Uh, no," Casey said. "No, it's not." *Say something interesting. She has a tree too. This is someone you should know.*

"Jake, then. I always knew you had a tricky side."

"Nope, not Jake." He knuckled the side of his head.

"This is getting ridiculous. I guess it's the part where you tell me you're some dark, horrible thing, and jump out of the night to grab me with your tentacles."

"No, not at all!" *Quick, think.* He gulped air. "Er, this is Casey."

Silence.

"I don't think we've met," he said.

Still nothing.

"I don't have tentacles," he added desperately.

"If that's some kind of code name, I don't get it," the girl said. "Who are you really?"

Why was she dragging this out? Suddenly, he wished she'd leave him alone.

"Casey Grimes is really me." He leaned into the dark and closed his eyes.

"But why don't I know you? And how did you get in that oak?"

"I...I climbed it. Obviously." He felt a spark of anger in his chest. Too many questions. Somehow, he'd already failed, and she was about to–

"Fine," the girl said. "How long will you be there?"

"Um, what?" Casey blinked. "I'll be here all night, but–"

"I'm coming straight over," she said. "May as well, since we can stay up as late as we like. I don't believe you, by the way, so you'd better have a good excuse for being in that off-limits Sentry tree. Remember my grades in Personal Woodland Defense? I'll be mad if you run off before I get there. How's the treeway in your direction?"

Casey's head spun and the stars became silver blurs.

"Never mind, I guess I'll find out soon enough. Bye."

The railing's glow faded. He slumped to the deck, knees to his chest. What had just happened? Well, he'd proven he had no idea how to talk to other kids. However fast or slow the girl arrived, she'd look right through him when she got here.

Maybe that was for the best.

"It's my oak," he said. "I found it, and I'm not going anywhere." The force in his voice surprised him—like he was about to fight someone. Well, maybe he was.

CHAPTER 13
DARK, HORRIBLE THING

CASEY PACED THE DECK, gripping his mace like a baseball bat. He'd thought of something else. Something he should've thought of instantly. Maybe the person he'd talked to wasn't a girl at all.

Gloria said there were monsters in the woods. Maybe when the girl had said, "dark, horrible tentacled thing," she'd been describing herself. Teasing out his location...in a lonely fortress in the middle of the night.

What kind of a girl would do that?

A very strange one, to say the least.

Or more likely, a girl with tentacles.

Casey wished he'd taken self-defense classes or even batting practice, but that was hard, when you were invisible. As he paced, forcing himself to take deep breaths, something awful caught his eye. A kind of hovering, milky glow, floating over the tops of smaller trees. Moving toward the oak.

So the monster-girl could fly.

Casey ran to the armory and tore weapons off the walls, as many as he could carry. He dumped the swords and spears and maces in a gleaming, deadly pile. Tentacles usually came in sets of eight. He'd need every weapon he could get.

The ghostly glow reached the oak. It rose quickly up the trunk.

Casey's arms quivered as he hefted a mace.

If the flying octopus was dumb enough to take the ladder, he'd get it right in the squishy face. He raised the mace, and stood to one side of the hatch.

Pale, spectral light shone into the fortress. A dark shape rose from below.

"AAAAH!" Casey yelled and swung at the ugly, nightmarish body.

Except, that's not what it was.

"AIEEEE!"

He checked his swing and put a dent in the tree. A girl hung on to a spike for dear life, feet kicking the air. Her eyes were shut and her mouth hung open, the last bit of a blood-curdling scream coming out. Some kind of glowing light hung around her neck.

Casey's mace hit the deck. He dropped to his knees and reached down to grab her wrists.

"Is that you, God?" the girl said. "Am I still falling or am I already dead?"

"Put your feet on the ladder," Casey said.

She opened her eyes and looked up. They were brown, then they were angry. Her mouth snapped shut and her feet stopped kicking. She brushed Casey aside and climbed up. Slumped on the deck, she glared at him, breathing hard. The necklace lit up her face and her wavy dark hair, pulled back with a headband. Some of it had tugged loose and was swirling around in the breeze. Her skin was light brown, and blood streaked one of her cheeks, but Casey didn't point that out.

"Sorry," he said. "I had no idea who you were and I thought you might be a monster. Plus I had to protect my little sister."

"What little..." snapped the girl, then she saw Gloria. She stood and brushed at her black t-shirt and khaki shorts. "I ought to punch you," she said. "Or at least slap you in the face."

"Well, maybe," Casey said.

"Don't be so reasonable." The girl stretched her arms and wriggled her fingers around, making sure they worked. "That makes it hard to hit you."

Casey shrugged. He waited for the girl's eyes to slide off to the side, gaze into the middle distance, stare right through him. Instead, she touched her face, glanced down at her fingers and gasped. Then she slapped him.

"Ouch!" Heat rushed to his cheek, probably in the shape of a girl's hand.

She took a deep breath. "For ripping my face open with a mace."

"It's only a scratch." Crazy laughter tickled Casey's throat, fighting to escape. This couldn't be happening. Could the girl actually see him? His burning face proved it, right?

"Don't forget, you almost fell to your death," he said wildly, just to see what would happen.

"That's right!" Her eyes narrowed. "I owe you another."

She raised her hand again. Casey adjusted to the new reality and jumped back.

I'm visible! Seriously visible!

"Hmph." The girl looked around, stepping over the pile of weapons. "You really were expecting a monster." One corner of her mouth quirked up. She looked at Gloria, who was snoring gently. "Well, your sister's a cutie."

"Can you see all my fingers?" Casey held up one hand. "I'm not blurry or anything?"

"Why would you be blurry?" The girl put her head on one side. "Wait, did someone sell you one of those fake invisibility t-shirts?" She laughed. "You'd have to be a total sucker. The real ones are ancient, more holes than a spider-mole den."

"I would never pay money to be see-through," Casey said.

The girl darted her eyebrows. *Yeah, right.* Her hands slid to her hips. "Beautiful view. I hate to admit this, but it's closer to the stars than my favorite tree. I didn't know anyone came here—so close to the Civilian edge, you know. We've been missing out." She dabbed at her cheek. "Well, Casey Grimes, sorry for hitting you, although you kind of deserved it."

Besides Gloria and his parents, and all of a sudden Ms. Jones, no one ever said Casey's name. His heart thumped wildly. He folded his arms over his chest to muffle the sound.

"Luciana West," the girl said.

"What?"

"That's my name. Let's stop fighting, ok? We didn't get off to a great start, but I guess we could still be friends."

Luciana held out her hand.

The bottom dropped out of Casey's stomach. He felt like he was falling through the deck into space, while standing still. *Friends* were something other people had. Something he could never earn, no matter how many names he memorized or how wide he smiled. You read about friends in *books* along with talking dinosaurs and outlaws in green and–

"Don't you think you're being a little stubborn?" Luciana said.

Casey shook himself.

She was looking at him strangely.

"I'm in," he said. "Friends, absolutely. You've got yourself a deal."

They shook. Casey's head spun and a little blood from Luciana's face smudged his fingers. Somehow, this was really happening.

CHAPTER 14
Q&A

OK, MY TURN." Casey leaned back, playing it cool. The pinks of his fingernails, pressed into his palms, were turning white. "Can you...really fly?"

He and Luciana sat cross-legged on a blanket next to sleeping Gloria. He was happy the glow from Luciana's pendant didn't reach his face. She tilted her chin at the stars and laughed.

"That's funny. You were pretty freaked out, weren't you?" She touched the scratch on her cheek. "Never mind, dumb question. The dark night, the treeway, the element of surprise..." She smiled. "You should've seen it coming, though."

"Yeah. Absolutely." He wiped sweat off his forehead.

"Let me guess, you're one of those kids who slept through Sylvan 101."

What the heck was Sylvan 101?

He cleared his throat. "I've been known to take naps at bad times."

"My turn." Luciana narrowed her eyes. "How come I've never seen you before?"

"Umm, because we've never met?"

The dark didn't dull her pointed look.

"I've never even heard your name. What classes are you taking?"

Finally, a question he could answer. "Math, History, English, Biology–"

Luciana stared. "Casey," she choked. "You don't even belong here!"

His spine wilted like a plant stem. "What do you mean?"

"I mean, you're a Civilian! You're not supposed to get from there to here." Lit by the pendant, her eyes were huge. "You discovered the Old Oak, right? And climbed it by yourself? That's a crazy feat for one of your kind. So I've been talking to a Civilian all this time?" She jumped to her feet. "Holy creeps, if anyone hears about this..."

Civilian. No, it couldn't be possible. Now there was something *else* wrong with him? Wait, he'd seen that word earlier. On the page in the *Sylvan Handbook.* STRENGTH and HONOR and MAGIC. WHOEVER DEFENDS CIVILIANS WILL ALWAYS BE WELCOME IN...

"Luciana." He got to his feet. "Are you from Sylvan Woods?"

Her eyes darted to the pile of weapons. "How do you know about that?"

"You just told me," he said. "Sylvan 101, remember."

"That makes sense...I guess." She wrapped her arms around herself. "What is going on?"

"Maybe you could tell *me*." Casey had the feeling she was about to turn him off—*click*—like a channel she could switch. Bye, Casey Grimes.

Instead, she turned her dagger-sharp eyes back on.

"You don't *seem* like a spy. No dangerous slimy feel. That makes you a woods-wise Civilian, which should never happen, or..."

"Or what?" Casey pressed a hand to his chest. *Calm, calm.*

"Is it possible...you're Sylvan?"

In the silence, a dark shape droned by, high overhead.

Something bubbled up in Casey like a freshwater spring. He wanted to blurt, YES, MAYBE THAT'S THE ANSWER. Instead, he forced himself to wait.

Luciana held up her hands. "I don't see how you could be."

Casey's eyes felt wet. It was the most ridiculous, stupid thing. Ok, so he was a Civilian, whatever that meant. Why should he care? *It means you're still the one left out.*

Luciana's face softened. "You deserve a lot of credit, though. I've never heard of someone climbing a Sentry tree at night without a rope. Or ambushing a flying octopus with a mace."

Casey grunted. He knew she was trying to make him feel better, but it wasn't working. "Tell me one thing," he said. "What is Sylvan Woods? Why is it so dangerous? Where is it?"

Ok, so three things.

Luciana stopped smiling. He didn't think she was going to answer.

"It's very close by," she said finally. "Right here, really. Where you've been living for the past year, without even knowing it."

CHAPTER 15
CIVILIANS NOT ALLOWED

MORNING LIGHT WARMED Casey's eyelids and he sat up. He'd dreamed he was in his room, putting his pajamas away. Double-checking his perfect homework before chasing down the bus. When he saw oak leaves instead of an off-white ceiling, a weight fell from his shoulders. Then he remembered his other bad dream.

A flying ghost-squid who'd changed into a girl.

A girl who'd made him feel totally alone.

A door creaked behind him.

Luciana stood in the closet entrance, brushing her teeth and patting down her wild hair.

"Goob moornfing." She walked to the rail to spit.

Casey squeezed his eyes shut, trying to sort his thoughts into the right order. The girl was real, and she could see him, and they were friends, sort of—or maybe not, since she was Sylvan. And he was...he had no idea.

"Morning," he said with an effort. "Do you...have any idea how old that toothbrush is?"

"I was hoping it was a spare you kept for guests, but now that you mention it..." Luciana ran her tongue along her teeth. "Kind of musty. Thanks for the extra blankets, by the way. This was a cool way to start sleepover week. Now I've got to be on my way before I get a detention."

"You're welcome," Casey said. "Oh, you're leaving?"

"I've got to," she said. "But I'll come back sometime, ok?"

He found he didn't quite believe her.

"Uh, wait." He bent over Gloria, nudging her awake. "We'll climb down with you."

Luciana hovered by the hatch. "I guess I could spare another minute."

Gloria yawned, smiled at Casey, and looked past him.

"Oh, hi," she said.

"Wow, pretty eyes." The Sylvan girl drifted over. "I'm Luciana, but my friends call me Luci."

Funny how she hadn't mentioned that last night.

"Casey invited me to your slumber party," she said, "after he almost killed me with a mace. Now we've got to climb down fast or I'll be late for class."

Almost killed, really? Casey rubbed his racing heart with a closed fist.

Gloria laughed and sat up. "I'm Gloria. And my friends call me, um..." She licked her lips. "My friends call me...Glo."

"That's lovely," Luciana said. "Would you mind if I helped you down the tree?"

"Sure." Gloria stretched. "I just need to put my clothes on." She disappeared into the storage closet.

Luciana paced. Eager to be on her way.

"Wait a minute," Casey said. "It's Sunday."

She made a face. "It's the worst, isn't it? But that's what happens when our parents are on the battlefront. Plus it's finals week. Extra security, you know, so total chaos..." She took in his blank expression. "Oh, sorry. I forgot who I was talking to."

He shrugged as his face got hot.

Gloria danced out of the closet. "Ta-daaa," she sang.

Luci smiled at her and Casey ducked away, stuffing gear into his backpack, whatever came to hand. He pulled on his bulky, sharp-cornered burden and followed the girls to the ladder.

"Here, write your name on this *medium girl* rock," Gloria said.

"You're adorable," Luci said.

They headed down.

Casey noticed Luciana climbed carefully. She liked to have her toes on the spike below before she let go up top. So as cool as she might be, and as much as she might know, Casey was still a better climber. At least that was something.

"Nice old-school ladder," Luci said. "More dangerous but really popular."

Casey pictured kids with grappling hooks, laughing fearlessly. He was probably giving them too much credit. *I bet I've spent as much time in trees as any of them.*

Halfway down, Luci said, "Off on the right, along that jumbo-sized branch, there's the treeway I came on. Can't take it now, not direct enough."

Casey picked out a thick ropewalk stretching away over the forest. The twisting, leafy path could easily have led to Mirkwood or Robin Hood's lair. Instead, it went somewhere even more mysterious. Sylvan Woods.

At the bottom of the tree, they unclipped themselves.

Luci and Casey played an awkward game of tag with their eyes.

"It's been fun," Luci said.

"Hang on." Casey did his best to sound casual. "How about me and Gloria tag along, hang out with you for the day. You could show us around..."

Luci rolled her eyes. "Believe me, that's a very bad idea."

"Why?" Casey frowned.

"Yeah, why?" Gloria bounced on her toes.

"I really don't have time for this." Luci gazed into the woods, like even the trees could understand how dumb these kids were.

"You can't even give us a reason?" Casey crossed his arms.

"Ugh, ok." Luci took a step away. "High security. Military culture. Aggressive creatures—just to name a few." She seemed proud of her list. "You wouldn't last a minute, not to mention the trouble I'd get into when they caught you. Do you have any idea how hard I've worked to—holy creeps, I've got to go."

She turned and headed down the trail. "Goodbye," she called over her shoulder. "Enjoy your Sunday *without* combat classes." She disappeared around a bend. Her voice floated back. "I'll try to visit but it's really hard...to get on the same side...of the border..."

Sunlight glimmered. Birds trilled and warbled.

The sun seemed murky and the birds were out of tune.

Gloria sighed. "She was nice."

"Really?" Casey said. "You thought so?"

He took Gloria's hand and shuffled a few steps toward Vintage Woods. Toward a bunch of kids who'd ignored him for a whole year while he shouted and waved. Kids who didn't climb trees. Who were supposed to become his best friends.

He stopped in his tracks.

"Who cares what Luci says. We're following her anyway."

CHAPTER 16
CREEPS & SHRIEKS

CASEY AND GLORIA ran down the path, carrying swords. Protection had seemed like a good idea, but the swords kept snagging branches. The dark lantern clanged Casey's shoulder. The path grew fainter as it drifted downhill. Then, without warning, it was gone.

"Uh oh," Gloria said.

"Luci," Casey called. "Wait up!"

They slowed to a walk. Moss hung from trees like streamers. Wisps of mist crawled over soggy ground and cattails blocked the way.

"Maybe you should light the lantern," Gloria said.

"Why?"

"Um, it just seems like a good idea." Her eyes darted right and left.

Casey stuck his sword in the mud. He searched his pockets for matches.

"Ok, I'll tell you." Gloria hugged his knees. "There's a murder cat hiding behind that log. Up there's probably a Tree Shriek. We've got to get out of here."

There weren't any matches in Casey's pockets. "But it's day, we're supposed to be safe." He patted his shoulders for backpack straps that weren't there.

"It's not very sunny down here." Gloria grabbed his hand and tugged him into the cattails. Mud sucked Casey's sword as he pulled it free. A bristling orange house cat stalked down a hollow log. A shadowy raccoon crouched on a branch.

But wait.

His eyes were playing tricks, because the cat was three times bigger than normal, with tiger stripes and blazing eyes that said, *I hate you, even though we've just met*. The shadowy shape in the tree wasn't a raccoon. Deep eye hollows darkened its bony skull. Long white tusks stuck past its chin. It threw back its head and let out a hungry wail.

Casey had seen something similar in a nightmare.

"It's hunting us," Gloria whispered.

"We're—we're armed," Casey said loudly. "Don't make us hurt you."

The Bog Creep grinned horribly, ears plastered to its head. The Tree Shriek ground its tusks, calling dibs on them. Casey hung the dark lantern over his sword arm and scratched at his empty pockets again. *Wait, he had back pockets too*. Water sloshed his sneakers as he finally found a match. He struck it on the metal lantern. Once, twice —dropped it—caught it with trembling fingers...

The Tree Shriek climbed higher, tensing its long back legs.

The Bog Creep crept closer. Its eyes were flaming slits.

The match took light. The lamp flared to life.

Gloria gasped. "Look, a path."

Casey fumbled with the lantern, and rays shot toward the water's edge. At the same second, the Bog Creep sprang. It screamed and threw up its paws, twisting to avoid the light. *Kersplash*. It plunged headfirst into the swamp. Casey brushed cat hair from his t-shirt with shaking fingers.

An eager wail came from the tree.

"Quick." Gloria tugged his elbow.

Holding the lantern high, he shuffled down a narrow trail. Their feet crunched wet gravel. Hidden by the rushes, the Tree Shriek wailed in disappointment.

"It feels nice to be alive." Gloria looked pale.

"It really does..." Casey turned an attack of shivers into a stretch, shaking his hands, flexing his arms, rolling his shoulders.

"*You're* not scared though," Gloria said.

"Of course not." He gave a hollow laugh. "Luci made this place sound horrible, but we've got nothing to worry about." He gave Gloria his best fake smile. "Did you see that cat's face right before it hit the water?"

She giggled. "*Eek, sploosh!*"

"Dumb Bog Creep."

Casey wished he could stuff Gloria's ears with cotton and let out the wild, strangled yell building in his throat. Instead, he swallowed it. That gave him time to notice how quiet the marsh had become. *Weirdly* quiet. No birds, no insects...nothing.

He cleared his throat. "I wonder if Luciana heard us calling."

"I think she likes us, so I'll bet she's—"

But Casey never found out what Gloria thought, because an ear-splitting roar shattered the stillness. A shadow fell on the path. Wind gusted down, flattening the cattails. They saw the far shore. They saw the huge shape hurtling through the air.

The wild scream in Casey's throat came rushing out.

"OOOHNOOO!"

He and Gloria plunged into the bog, tripping over hidden stones, choking on muddy water, trying to escape.

CHAPTER 17
DOOM IN THE SWAMP

RUN GLORIA!" Casey tried to shout, but it came out, "Ruuungl!" because a stone rolled under his foot and he plunged underwater. He flailed to his knees in the shallows, choking and spitting. Mud dripped off his face. More water rolled over him with a thunderous splash, and his sword jolted in his hand.

He blinked grit from his eyes. *Where's the shore?—oh no.* Fierce gold eyes the size of floodlights stared into his. A hooked beak as big as his arm prodded the sword. The creature's upper half was covered in brown and white feathers, like a bald eagle. A bald eagle the size of an elephant.

It was over. But maybe he could buy some time for Gloria...

Casey lifted the dark lantern, his muscles seizing up. Incredibly, it hadn't gone out, but the creature didn't care. It might even have smiled. The beast twitched its tufted, ten-foot tail and snapped its beak on Casey's sword. With a shriek it tossed the broken shards away. At least his death would be quick.

The thing opened its beak again...

A shrill whistle came from the shore. The monster growled. Another whistle, and it reared on furry hind legs and roared. A third whistle—and the thing bounded away. Leaping into the air, it circled once, and soared into the dim marsh on twenty foot wings. Gold eyes flashed at Casey. *See you next time.*

He pushed himself to his feet and stumbled ashore, feeling light-headed. Gloria teetered on the muddy bank with her mouth open, sword in her hands. Behind her stood an old man—but *stood* might have been an exaggeration.

He sagged over a walker, clutching the metal frame like it was keeping him alive. The senior citizen spit a gold whistle from his lips. It bounced against his sunken chest and dangled from a chain. His mouth sagged in a frown.

"Curse you both with wood rot, making me come out here. And if I *hadn't* heard screaming and *hadn't* sprinted through the orchard, what then?" He scowled at the children. "What the dervish would I report if the gryphon bit your head off? They like skulls you know, love the way they crunch. Not to mention the cleanup. Can you imagine the cleanup?"

Casey swallowed. He couldn't imagine the old man sprinting through the orchard.

But he could imagine the cleanup.

The oldster scooted a step forward and squinted. His eyes almost disappeared. "Sebastien Drooce, isn't it." He jabbed a finger at Casey.

"Ugh, erck." Casey spit out swamp.

The grandpa nodded. "I may be as old as Methuselah but I'm not easily fooled." He jerked his walker toward Gloria. "That would make you, let's see...ah yes, young Tonya Cortland. Thick as thieves, you two."

Gloria hung her head.

"I don't need to tell you I'll be sure to write this up. Skipping class at a time like this. Playing in the swamp—while we're at *war*? Boneheads." With surprising agility, he set off, hunching and scooting through rows of trees.

They looked at each other. Sopping wet, dripping muck, eyes like baby deer. Gloria pushed soggy hair out of her face. Casey coughed, trying not to swallow any more brackish water.

For a second, he thought he was about to let out another unearthly howl. Instead, he snorted. Chuckled. Started laughing. Gloria joined in, and Casey decided insane laughter was better than wild screaming. By the time they stopped, gasping and wiping their eyes, the old man had disappeared in the orchard.

Casey brushed mud off his arms and legs. The laugh attack had left a small core of heat in his middle. One thing for sure, he wasn't going to sneak home now.

"We still haven't died, Gloria," he said. "So we'd better follow that angry senior citizen."

CHAPTER 18
DANGEROUS-LOOKING KID

CLOTHES DRIPPING, shoes sloshing, they shadowed the old man through rows of fruit trees. He disappeared through a gap in an ancient stone wall, and they hurried to catch up. A wide green field opened ahead, flat and well cared for. A gravel path ran along the wall in two directions. The old man was gone. But across the field...

"Do you think that Luci's school?" Gloria said.

Casey shaded his eyes. Across the field, the forest began again, but the trees seemed organized. Buildings soared between branches. Wisps of smoke drifted skyward. The complex was right in the middle of a forest. A soaring, ancient forest.

Casey's stomach felt unsure of itself.

Was he afraid or excited?

"Should we go say hi?" Bits of dried swamp flaked off Gloria's face.

"Cross the field? I don't think that's a great idea." Casey folded his mud-blackened arms. "We need to find Luci before anyone else sees us. Or any*thing* else."

He felt irritated just saying her name.

Gloria took his hand. They strolled down the right hand path, mud-skins crumbling in the heat. Casey's back burned where he'd hit the bottom of the marsh. The dark lantern felt heavy. He was thinking about how good it would feel to sit in the shade and eat something (maybe), when they rounded a bend in the path.

There was a blur of movement.

Casey and Gloria stopped mid-step.

A fierce-looking boy crouched in front of them. His dark eyes were narrow under spiky black hair. He clenched a red and chrome spear, ready to stab.

"What are you?" he muttered.

Casey let go of his sister's hand and put down the lantern. Maybe he should put his hands in the air. Then again...

Gloria didn't seem to notice when he tugged the sword from her fingers. She was probably admiring how clean the stranger was and how good he smelled. A smell Casey couldn't quite place but liked, even though he didn't want to. Oh, that was it...pancakes.

"Drop the sword." The boy tensed in his trail shoes.

"We're looking for Luciana West. She's a...a friend." Casey's face warmed up like a toaster.

"You know, *Luci*," Gloria said. "We had a little bitty accident and almost died. Is breakfast over?"

"Oh, you're human then." The boy wiggled his spear. "Why are you covered in mud? And what are you doing out here? Wait..." His eyes flashed. "I've never seen you before in my life. That means you've got to be spies. Or Civilians. Or *Civilian* spies." He spat out the C-word like it tasted bad.

Casey blinked away muddy sweat. "We're—we're her cousins."

The boy's eyes gleamed. "We'll soon find out. Line up and march, straight to the security station. I'll come behind in case you try anything."

For a long time, Casey hadn't had any friends, but he also hadn't been bullied. As he stood in Sylvan Woods, holding a very sharp sword, he realized he didn't like the feeling at all.

"Not a chance, buddio," he said, and instantly remembered he wasn't good at talking to kids his own age.

The spear came back up. "Buddio? I don't think so. That counts as resisting arrest."

"Hey, wait," Casey said. "I don't want to–"

The kid jabbed and Casey tried to block, but somehow his sword hit empty air. The spear cracked his side. Casey gritted his teeth. The spear swayed back and forth. Left, right, left, right—Casey sliced down, hoping to cut off the point. Instead, he got another crack in the ribs.

"Ouch!" Now he was really angry. But the boy was too quick. On top of that, he'd stopped frowning to give Casey a very annoying smile.

Heat rose off Casey in waves.

Gloria gave the boy her worst frown.

"Ok, you've seen what I can do," the kid said. "Now put down that sword before you get hurt, waving it around like a magic wand."

Casey took another swing. He couldn't help himself.

"Incredibly stupid move, Civ-brain." The warrior-boy's grip shifted. Suddenly it occurred to Casey how fast the spear could fly through the air, and what might happen when it did. The kid drew back his arm. Gloria screamed and Casey got ready to dodge.

Something small and white shot past and hit the boy in the eye.

"Ouch!" One hand flew to the kid's face and his spear point dropped.

"Got him," Gloria said in a surprised voice.

Casey froze, panicky thoughts whizzing through his mind. *The fight's over now, right?—Of course it's not over, idiot—But his eye is hurt, he'll give up—No, you've got to get him now—*

"Get him, Casey!"

Gloria gave him a push and he rushed forward and flopped on the other boy. He grabbed a handful of spiky hair—that's what you did in a fight, right?—and dug in with his elbows, hoping he wasn't being too rough.

"NOO!" Casey yelled as the warrior-kid aimed a punch at his

throat. They rolled back and forth, scraping their knees and doing their best to hit each other.

"Go Casey, go Casey, go!" screamed Gloria.

There was a satisfying *huff* as Casey managed to punch the other kid in the stomach. *Maybe now the fight's over—oof.* The boy kneed him in the kidney. Casey winced and grabbed more spiky hair, but his arms were getting weak. His breaths were ragged gasps. He couldn't hold out much longer.

"Casey, Gloria!" someone yelled. "What in the beast-woods are you doing here?"

CHAPTER 19
COUSIN LUCI

LUCI WEST STOOD in the path, hands on her hips, eyes flashing. Casey and the fierce kid pushed away from each other, breathing hard. They got to their feet, brushing at their clothes, although for Casey, there was no point. His mind raced as he stared back at the irritated Sylvan girl. *Now what?*

"Luci," he rasped. "*Cousin* Luci...you finally got here."

Gloria picked up his cue. "My favorite cousin!" She ran to give Luci a hug.

Luci's mouth dropped open. She picked at Gloria's muddy hair as her eyes stabbed Casey through the heart. "Hello, *cousins*," she said through gritted teeth. "Hello, Robert."

The other boy touched his face, where his eye was beginning to swell. "Seriously? They look like mud golems."

"I *told* you not to cross the border on foot," Luci said.

"You did?" Casey said. "We got a little turned around."

Her eyes stabbed him some more.

"You may as well be a Civilian, you're dumb enough." Robert picked up his spear. "If Luciana hadn't shown up, I would've poked you full of holes."

"No way," Luci said. "Not appropriate, Pierce. You owe Casey an apology."

"Not a chance," Robert said.

She folded her arms. "Shake hands, or I'll report you to Old Knock—you too, Casey, even though you're my *cousin*. No one should be out here on the border, fighting."

Robert Pierce groaned and extended his right hand. Casey had no idea who Old Knock was, but he'd been knocked around enough that morning. They shook. Casey's knuckles cracked.

"Watch yourself," Robert said. "Maybe next time you won't have *girls* to save you."

Casey massaged his fingers as the other boy jogged off.

Their pretend-cousin stood in the path. Her expression was hard to read...was she about to give him a high five? Or another slap in the face?

Luci let out a low whistle, shaking her head. "Number one, you have no idea how much trouble you're in. And number two, wow, what a bad time for you to be here. We're at war, everyone's on edge." She tried not to smile. "But seriously, you navigated the swamp—no map, no entry charm—and got past Bones? I'm impressed. Not *crazy* impressed, so don't push it. But how did you do it?"

Gloria gave a little sigh.

"First of all..." Casey caught himself. "It's quite the story," he said. "Very exciting. How about we get cleaned up, and we can talk about it over breakfast. What was the idea anyway, disappearing in thirty seconds?"

"Trying to follow me was your first mistake," Luci said.

Casey tried his own version of the murder stare. "Once we're not like *this*"—he gestured to himself and Gloria—"you can tell us what you've gotten us into."

"What *I've* gotten you into, that's nice." Luci started down the path, walking backward. "When Bones came into the cafeteria, complaining about kids fooling around in the marsh, I had a bad feeling and I headed right out. Good thing, too. Pierce would've beat your head in."

"I was on top," Casey said.

"He let you *think* you were on top," Luciana said.

Casey grunted. Gloria patted his elbow.

The path left the orchard wall and twisted uphill through a grove of trees.

"So let me guess," Luciana said, "Did something try to drown you in mud?"

"You could say that..." Casey trailed off.

She could wait. He had questions of his own. Lots of them.

"Look, Casey, you owe me." Luci smoothed her hair back under her headband. "Baths straight ahead, boy on the right, girls on the left. Glo and I will meet you outside in fifteen minutes." She tapped her foot. "Got it?"

Wait, was this a joke?

Luci kept talking, something about lost and found, but he didn't catch it. The white path forked. One side ran through sunny woods. The other fork, the one they were standing on, ran straight into an enormous, shadowy cave.

CHAPTER 20
WELCOME TO THE BATH CAVE

CASEY TIPTOED OVER POLISHED ROCK. He turned a corner...and light filled a cavern, glowing through a haze of mist. The glow reminded him of Luciana's necklace. There were no lamps or candles—the *cave* was glowing. He was pretty sure, from Biology, it was what you called phosphorescence.

Rows of waterfalls gurgled over rocks, spraying a blue-tiled floor. Red or blue stones stood by each fall. The red falls steamed in the cool cave air.

"Hot springs," whispered Casey.

It got even better. A huge waterfall rushed down the back of the cave, filling a long rectangular pool. Behind all the splashing, he heard its low, crashing rumble.

It made his Vintage Woods locker room look like a jail cell. Casey stood in the entrance, waiting for a tour guide or lifeguard to yell at him. No one did, so he peeled off his stiff clothing and ran to the nearest red-stone waterfall. The hot water turned brown as it hit his skin. His shoulders began to unknot. His hands shook, and he couldn't make them stop.

Monsters. A maniac soldier kid. Fake identities. It seemed like he'd rolled out of his sleeping bag just five minutes ago. Now he and Gloria were in this secret, dangerous place.

Sylvan Woods.

"Strength and Honor...and Magic," he said out loud.

It sounded good in the *Sylvan Handbook*. But up close and in person, it gave you bruises and made your hands shake. All before breakfast.

Ms. Jones was probably scouting the woods right now. If he and Gloria could get back over the border, their very qualified babysitter could get them safely home.

What an embarrassing thought. How old are you, six?

Pale, knobby stalagmites rose from the floor, hung with brushes, sponges and bottles.

One thing at a time.

Casey chose orange soap and green shampoo, hoping for the best. He scrubbed himself off, and took a running jump into the pool. Cool water tingled on his skin. The tiled bottom sloped away and he began to swim. At the crashing falls, he took a deep breath and paddled under. Water pounded over him.

The falls massaged his scrapes and bruises like liquid hands, and he came up, gasping and laughing. Maybe things weren't so bad. What if he and Gloria actually were *Sylvan*, and there was some list or roster with their names on it...

"Hey, did you drown in there?" Luci called. "We don't have a lot of time."

"Oh, right." Casey swam to the side and took a fluffy white towel from a rack. His old clothes leaned against the wall like they were made of cardboard.

"I left some clean clothes around the bend," Luciana yelled.

Casey pulled on a pair of very tight boxers, neon green running shorts and a scary "Manticore-Man" graphic tee with cut off sleeves. Yellow flip-flops completed his outfit. He looked in a wall-length mirror and frowned.

Not ideal for a day when kids could actually see you.

Oh well. One thing at a time.

Casey ran his hands through his hair, tossed his towel on the floor, and glanced at his old clothing. Maybe he'd pick it up later—with a pair of gloves. Better yet, maybe someone else would. He shrugged his warm, clean shoulders and headed out of the cave.

CHAPTER 21
TRICKERY SCHOOL

LUCIANA'S EYES WIDENED. "Sorry Casey, I did my best, but those clothes were in lost and found for a reason. At least you smell..." She sniffed. "Like minty orange."

For someone terrible at picking clothes, she looked very pleased with herself.

"Don't worry about it," Casey said. "The flip-flops kind of match the Manticore-Man logo." He didn't mention the too-tight boxers.

"Good attitude," Luci said. "Just go with it."

Gloria looked fairly normal in dark jean shorts, glittery flip-flops and an oversized unicorn tank top. "Weren't the falls amazing?" she said. "Like a waterpark."

"Absolutely," Casey said. "I'd shower three or four times a day."

"My record is thirteen," Luci said. "Oops, probably shouldn't have told you that. Let's talk about your extraction plan over breakfast." She frowned. "I'm already tardy, thanks to your romp in the swamp."

They headed downhill, zig-zagging around trees and rocks. The forest pulled Casey's eyes in all directions. Pretty Dogwoods, bristly Catalpas, snaky Willows... dripping with sap and shadows and very, very big. Surely it couldn't be an accident that Sylvan Woods was, well...*in* the woods. Built right into the trees. He'd never seen anything like it.

The trail bottomed out and they shoved through towering evergreens. Casey's muscles slowly tensed up after his waterfall massage. *Relax*, he told himself. *This won't be anything like* your *school.* But he was clueless and wearing awful clothes. *What if being visible only made things worse? What if kids saw him and still–*

"Welcome to the heart of Sylvan Woods," Luci said. "Trickery School."

Casey looked up. His whole body stiffened. *This can't be real.*

"Let's talk strategy," Luci said. "Don't speak, but don't act all secret and mysterious either. Keep your heads down, but act like you belong. Relax, but don't slap your flip-flops on the trail, it looks unnatural..."

She faded to background noise. Casey's eyes pinned themselves to the sides of his face.

Trees enfolded the campus like leafy guardians. One building scraped the sky like a gothic church, high enough to hold clouds. Another hung in a web of cables, hive-shaped and mysterious. Sun shone right through a tower made of amber. Stairways and ladders arced the upper air, linking elevated halls and platforms.

Casey's hands fell to his sides. His heart pounded—*yes, yes, yes* —like a cheering crowd, far away. He pictured people scratching plans on scrolls and building them by hand, with total disregard for gravity and heights. It was the most beautiful thing he'd ever seen.

Luci cleared her throat. "Um, this is probably a lot to take in. We can't just hang out, though. I'm supposed to be in my first class, Survival Sewing, and you have no documentation, so if anyone stops us, we're toast."

Casey shook himself. "Survival Sewing. Like sewing a sleeping bag?"

Luci smirked. "No, Casey. Like closing up a nasty laceration."

He forced himself to stagger after her. Voices drifted out of windows, high overhead. A group in the transparent amber tower stopped mace-fighting to point and wave.

Kids having a mace fight. Why not?

Gloria raised her hand and Luci yanked it down. "Don't wave back, they might decide to take a recess. That Advanced Dueling class is always looking for a fight." She led them to a staircase that spiraled up a giant maple. "I hope you're not afraid of heights."

"That's funny." Casey smiled, trying to wake up his paralyzed face. "But Luci, why does everyone carry weapo—"

"Shhh, no time to waste."

The stairs climbed higher than chimneys, higher than lightning rods, higher than flying crows. At the top, thick brown ropes and narrow catwalks wove through the canopy. *Treeways.* Casey's eyes and mouth froze again—in a very stupid expression, judging by how smug Luci looked.

There was nothing he could do about it. He didn't even care.

Their wooden footpath twisted along. Just normal kids. Walking to breakfast. At the height of flying hawks. *It's over,* Casey thought. *Whatever horrible secrets I discover, human sacrifices or whatever, I'm gonna have to stay here.*

It took all his self-control not to climb the ladders, swing on the ropes, sprint along the leafy edges of Trickery, shouting with joy.

This is my place. I've found it.

A white marble hall rose from the shadows, cedars supporting the roof. Behind the proud trees stood an atrium full of sculptures.

"Mythic History," Luci said as they walked past. "Pretty quiet this period, but it gets lively later."

How did she stay so calm?

By the time they reached a clearing full of sunbeams, Casey was sure his eyes were bugging out like a dragonfly's. Gloria's certainly were. Wooden walkways circled open space, falling earthward like sports stadium exit ramps.

"Ok wait," Casey said. "This is too much. You're super secret and everything, and we're not supposed to talk, but where did all this come from? Who built it?"

"Was it bears?" Gloria whispered.

"We did, obviously." Luci smiled, like that explained everything. "Cafeteria down below. You've got lots of routes, for traffic control, but people still get trampled at breakfast."

Was she being infuriating on purpose? Casey decided it was pretty likely.

They paced in wide circles as the ground got closer. On the forest floor, a building soaked up sunlight with wide windows and a grassy, flowering roof. Blue and yellow blossoms trailed over the gutters.

"It's so pretty," Gloria said.

"Unfortunately, the cafeteria is closed." Luci made a sad face. "But the back door, probably not." She flashed a smile, enjoying her power *way* too much.

They circled the building, getting their ground-legs back. A trail threaded through a vegetable garden on a sunny cliff. Far below, a wide blue river rushed through rocky banks.

"I didn't know there was a..." Casey started. Then he stopped, because it was clear he knew absolutely nothing about Sylvan Woods, the strange and wonderful place he'd been close to, all this time, without even knowing it.

CHAPTER 22
CAFETERIA CATASTROPHE

LUCI DUCKED and ran past a bank of windows. She waved them through a yellow door, carved with flowering vines. Casey's stomach rumbled. Bacon and eggs, herbs and cheese, hot bread and spices…all in one whiff of kitchen air.

The room was big and dimly lit. Light from the windows gleamed on polished wood, stone counters and huge copper pots. Their noses pulled them in all directions.

"Toast and jam?" Luci said. "Steak and eggs? Corned beef hash with breakfast pizza?"

"I'll eat it all," Casey said. "But where is it?"

She laughed. "Just sit down."

He and Gloria pulled stools to a butcher-block table. Luci disappeared in the shadows. Cupboards creaked, metal clinked and plates clattered. She staggered back with her arms full. "I forgot how much this bacon weighs."

Casey helped himself to still-warm cinnamon bread and the thickest bacon he'd ever seen. Gloria started on scrambled eggs and ham. Luci set down a tray of mugs as Casey ate medium rare steak. They drank orange juice, milk and cocoa so good he didn't mind it being lukewarm.

"Soo good." Gloria looked like a chipmunk, cheeks stuffed with breakfast pizza.

"Glad you like it, Glo." Luci picked at a croissant. "Let's talk about my plan to get you home."

Casey swallowed. "There's no rush."

"Actually, there is." Luci shoved her pastry away. "I like you two, but things are just starting to go well for me, after a whole year, and if Trickery security catches me harboring illegal Civilians–"

Casey didn't like where she was headed. "We could be Sylvans, you said so yourself."

Luci held up a hand. "That was just wishful thinking. I shouldn't have said it. Things aren't that simple."

"And *if* we're Civilians," Casey said, "your own handbook says you ought to help us. 'The one who guides, protects and defends Civilians,'" he quoted, "'with strength and honor, will always be welcome in Sylvan Woods.'"

"How do you know that?" She sounded irritated.

He folded his arms. "If you're too scared to help us, just say so."

"Shh," Gloria said.

"Too *scared?*" Luci glared at him. "I'm not gonna just sit here and–"

Hinges creaked nearby.

Luci stiffened. "Uh oh."

Feet stomped over a floor, followed by a low, tuneless whistle.

Luci shoved them toward the door. *Go, go, go!* she mouthed. Casey might've been scared if he hadn't been so irritated. Luci eased the yellow door open. She slipped outside. Gloria sucked in her cheeks and followed. Casey stood alone in the shadowy kitchen.

Something stomped closer. Something that frightened Luci.

Ok, *now* he was scared.

He dove after the girls, but his elbow hit a broom, which knocked a giant mixing bowl.

CLONG!

"Stop right there!" snapped a gravelly voice.

The door banged the outside wall as he ran. Luci and Gloria were sneaking through the garden, and Casey bumped into them, looking over his shoulder. "Run for it!"

They bolted around the corner. Casey grabbed Gloria's hand and pulled her, flip-flops slapping. They didn't stop until they'd crashed through a line of fir trees and dropped behind a tangle of willows. Casey hoped the thicket was dense enough to hide his neon shorts and garish t-shirt. Not to mention Gloria's sparkly unicorn outfit.

"You didn't tell us," he said, "that even breakfast is dangerous."

Luci pretended not to hear him.

Gloria squirmed and coughed, swallowing her pizza. "What was that weird whistling?"

"We've got a rhyme for it," Luci whispered. "To sort the security force." She peered through the underbrush. "High and clear, Bones is near. Flat like a rock, you're about to be—oh no!" She ducked down and whispered. "He's after us. Old Knock is on our scent—and we definitely don't have hall-and-trail passes."

The fear in her voice sent a shiver down Casey's spine. They plunged into the trees. His flip-flops twisted on his sweaty feet, doing their best to trip him. Luci grabbed Gloria's other hand and they tugged the small girl along.

"Old Knock is fiendishly good at tracking," Luci gasped.

Gloria panted, becoming more and more dead weight.

"Don't you know any good hiding places?" Casey said.

Luci leaned against a birch tree, stealing glances around the trunk. Loose strands of hair stuck to her forehead. "Believe it or not" —she gulped air—"I'm not usually running through the woods, trying to escape a crazy teacher swinging an axe handle." She sucked in several quick breaths. "If he catches us...oh creeps, let's not even go there. There will be detention for sure, and my grades...ooh." She looked slightly sick. "Even worse, he'll want proof you're my cousins. He'll find out who you are, and Knock is violently anti-Civilian. This will become a—an espionage case." She groaned. "During a war."

"Just tell me where to run," Casey said.

Luci's eyes darted right and left. "He's coming up the hill."

A tall, hairy figure pushed through the trees, head bent toward the ground.

"My legs are tired of running." Gloria sighed.

"Climb on my back." Casey bent down, she jumped up, and he grabbed her knees.

"Giddy-up, horsey," she whispered.

Gloria bounced on his spine as he ran, and pain radiated from his bruised tailbone. Leaves rustled behind them. It was hard to say exactly where Old Knock was, but there could be no doubt he was getting closer.

"I don't want to get thwacked," Luci gasped. "This can't happen." Eyes a little glassy, she doubled over, breathing hard.

"What about treeways?" Casey wheezed.

A hollow crack rang out down the slope...the sound of an axe handle clearing a path.

Luciana's head snapped up. "Treeway, treeway, where's the nearest treeway?" She put a hand on her forehead and groaned. "Think, think."

"It's up there." Gloria slid off Casey's back and pointed.

Forty or fifty feet overhead, so slim it was hard to see, a ropewalk stretched through trees. And behind them, forty or fifty feet back, Old Knock yelled, "I KNOW YOU'RE OUT THERE, KIDDIES! RUN ALL YOU WANT, ONCE I GET A LOOK AT YOUR FACES, YOU'RE DONE FOR!"

CHAPTER 23
OLD KNOCK

IF THEY'D BEEN SQUIRRELS, the kids could've climbed faster than Old Knock walked. Instead, Casey shrugged Gloria back up. His knees wobbled, but he had to keep going. If Old Knock caught them, it was goodbye Sylvan Woods. And that was a best case scenario.

"Sorry sir, we got lost," Luci murmured. "No, no, no. Um, these two are new hires on the kitchen crew, and I was helping..." She groaned. "Mr. Knock, we were getting apples for our teachers..." She put her face in her hands. "Nothing I say can possibly explain this."

"Giddy-up," Gloria said. "Everything's gonna be fine."

With the last of his strength, Casey took off, craning his sweaty neck. He crushed plants and tore through brambles. Luciana crashed along behind. The treeway led uphill, and soon his chest was heaving. At the top, he fell to his hands and knees. Behind them, feet pounded the earth in a sudden burst of speed. An eerie whistle floated through the air.

"I'M...STILL...COMING!"

"He's...crazy," gasped Luci.

"Gloria...down...rest," Casey choked.

Maybe he couldn't run forever after all.

"Good horse, good horse." Gloria patted his back.

He wanted to throw himself in the shade, cover himself in pine needles, and pretend he was invisible again. Instead, he leaned against a cool rock, wiping salt from his eyes. Any second, Old Knock would crest the ridge and put him in handcuffs.

Somewhere nearby, a mouse squeaked. And kept squeaking.

It was probably laughing at him.

"Come on, lazybones," Gloria said.

Her voice came from overhead.

†

Sun beat down on them, but the wind fought back, whipping their hair and cooling their flushed skins. Casey had seen ski lifts, and this was the same idea. They stood on a moving ropewalk as thick as their ankles, clutching tight guide wires. Below, the hill dropped away, giving them more altitude as the rope swayed along.

No one said a word. Back on the ridge, the rope squeaked through a massive wooden pulley. Out here in the treetops, it glided.

That was a good thing, because Old Knock was hiking up the slope with long, angry strides. He swung an axe handle, snapping the heads off flowers. His flannel jacket and wild black beard were an odd contrast to his gym shorts and headband.

The kids held their breath as the rope carried them into a stand of walnut trees. If it was possible to be pale and sunburned at the same time, that's how they looked.

"I don't know where this treeway goes," Luciana said. "Didn't even know it was up here. But if we end up on the third floor of Advanced Dueling, I'm going to start crying."

Five minutes later, they stepped onto a platform near the columns of the Mythic History building. On the far side, kids practiced archery with targets shaped like Razor Wings, gryphons, and huge tentacled moths. Other lifts connected to the platform, but no one else was arriving or departing. Luci put a hand up to shield her face and the Grimes kids did the same. They got some strange looks as they hurried to the three-story stairs and down.

"*Now* we mingle," Luciana said.

Casey's skin tingled and his knees felt weak. The terror of Old Knock was leaving his body. But something else was coming in.

"It's so weird they can all see me," he said.

Luci gave him a tight smile. "You picked the wrong day to stop being invisible."

They quick-walked around a corner, slipped down an ivy-covered alley, and entered a courtyard. At the center was a large fountain, full of kids with goggles, snorkels, and tridents. They stopped their splash-and-stab exercises to stare.

Casey rubbed his sun-baked neck. He tried to let their glances slide off him like the sweat trickling down his back. "Why do people hate Civilians?" he said.

"We really don't have time for that," Luci said.

A frail-looking lady sat in a wheelchair, waving her own trident at the snorkelers. She gave them a hard look as they left the court-yard. Luci led them up long, skinny stairs, through a hanging rose garden, up a rope ladder, and over a high bridge that clattered under their feet.

"Let's see Old Knock follow *that* trail." She smiled, her eyes still big. "Can you believe it? We actually escaped. I'm not sure how...but yeeesss!" She pumped a fist.

"Teamwork?" Casey suggested.

She laughed. "Listen, I already missed first period, and after that disaster, I've got to run or I'll miss my my next class too. I can't just drop you in the middle of campus. I guess we'll have to pretend you're my cousins a little longer. Man, this is crazy."

"It's super crazy," Gloria said.

"Maybe insane," Casey said.

Their shaky bridge shot out of the trees and swayed toward a building like a Viking hall on stilts. Several trees grew through its thatched roof.

"Land Creature Defense," Luci said. "I don't have an attack scheduled today and it's not a lab, so we can finally relax. Good news, right?"

"The best," Gloria said.

"What's Land Creature Defense?" Casey said.

It didn't *sound* very restful.

"It's a lower level class, but essential to everything we—oh, there you go again, trying to get me talking." She put a finger to her lips. "No more Civilian silliness."

Casey's eyes did backflips as they pushed through a hulking wooden door, reinforced with spiked metal bands. It groaned menacingly on its hinges.

CHAPTER 24
LAND CREATURE DEFENSE

THE BUILDING SMELLED LIKE A ZOO. A central hall stood empty except for lockers and a few animals on leashes. A large gray cat flattened its tufted ears and snarled.

"Bloodhounds, mostly," Luci said. "A few domesticated lynxes. We get to use them on tests. Last week someone brought in a feral pig, but it didn't end well."

From behind a door came yells, roaring, and applause.

"Sounds like someone passed her final," Luci said.

"Fighting a wild animal?" Casey asked.

Luci gave him a side-eye. "Of course not."

"Luci," he said. "You chat your head off, except when I ask a—"

"Shhh."

Casey fumed as they climbed stairs so steep pickaxes would have been handy. The second story looked much like the first. Halfway down the hall, Luci stopped.

"Ok, keep a low profile," she whispered. "With all the excitement, hopefully no one will ask why you're there, but if they do..." She sighed, smoothed her t-shirt and reached for a door knob. "Let me handle it."

Twenty-some kids sat at desks in a room the size of a barn. They wore shorts and t-shirts in browns, greens, black, and several types of camouflage. Clearly, earth tones were in. Casey glanced down at himself and shuddered. Maybe no one would look at him closely.

He and the girls took seats in the back.

"...and somehow crossed the marsh, activating the border alarm," the teacher was saying. "Until the warrior is apprehended, assume the worst. Adult and dangerous. Be careful out there."

Heads nodded. Fists smacked open palms.

People here are always spoiling for a fight.

Luci was mouthing words at him. *Fat as woo.* No...*That was you.*

What was that supposed to mean?

"And now, some good news," the teacher said. "Your parents are in position and poised for action. As always, the Civilian population is in the dark about the imminent war."

Mumbles and snorts swept the classroom.

"Stupid Civilians."

"Skivvy Civies."

Casey glanced at Gloria, who looked confused.

"I realize you may be stressed," the teacher said, "since your regular teacher isn't here for finals. However, I'm quite sure that Miss, er, Miss..."

"Miss Smithson?" Someone said.

"Yes, Miss Smithson—has carefully prepared you for what you're about to face in this, er..." He glanced at a stack of papers on his desk. "This...Land Creature Defense final."

"Better and better," Luci muttered. "How in beast-guts did we get Carrots?"

The teacher was tall and thin with orange-red hair and a patch over one eye. His long fingers twitched as he waved his hands about, and they seemed to be covered in dried mud. After the swamp, Casey knew what that looked like.

"Hello, you in the back," the teacher said.

Luci plastered a smile on her face. "Luciana West, present and accounted for."

Carrots marked something down. "And your guests, Miss West?"

Casey held his breath.

Luci groaned soundlessly. "These are my cousins, sir. Casey and Gloria Grimes, visiting for a few days from, um, Woodlandia." She darted a look at Casey. "My very dear cousins," she whispered, "one of whom will shortly die."

Chairs scraped the floor as students turned to stare. Casey felt eyes brush his face like dozens of tiny spotlights, darting away to his torn and mismatched clothing. His chest twisted up like his heart and lungs were wrestling. So this was what it felt like to be solid... and out of place...in very weird clothes.

The teacher tapped his pencil. "Very good, Miss West. Let's deal with their paperwork afterwards. For now I'll put them down as present." He scribbled a note.

Casey stared at the side of Luci's head. After five seconds, she stopped ignoring him.

"What?" The points of her dagger eyes were getting dull.

"Thanks," he said.

"Don't thank me yet." She shook her head.

Carrots cleared his throat. "It appears this class begins each period with the Sylvan Pledge. A bit dated, with its archaic emphasis on magic, but it still has historical value. Shall we?" He raised a hand, swept it down, and the students chanted:

"We'll never stray from trees and sky.
An urban life? We'd rather die.
Our friendships happen face to face
with feasts thrown in on special days.
We fight the monsters in the woods
to keep them from Civilian 'hoods.
We'll guard the magic of the border
to keep our bloodlines in good order.
Fields and rivers we will tend,
forgotten trades and arts we'll mend.

We build, we brew, we craft, we defend!"

Gloria looked at Casey with big eyes. Her mouth formed a silent *Wow,* and he nodded, wishing he could hear the pledge again and take notes. Trees, friends, feasts...the bit about guarding borders was worrying. Maybe it explained the obsession with fighting. But it didn't explain why everyone hated Civilians. Sylvan Woods ought to be *protecting* them.

Carrots scanned his notes. "Hmm, my instructions were a little vague..."

Stone tiles covered the front half of the barn-classroom, rising up the walls. There were no windows in the tile-shielded side.

The teacher stood, shrugging his thin shoulders. "Well, let's see what we've got." He opened a door behind his desk and shut it quickly. Cracked it. Took a longer look, slammed it.

"Oh dear." He ran his fingers through his hair. "I volunteered to oversee this class because I heard 'Land' in the title, and thought, logically enough, *dirt*, soil, gardens. Of course, I must've taken this class, back in my youth." He gave a nervous laugh. "How much can things have changed in twenty years?"

The class buzzed uneasily.

"He's a botanist," Luci whispered. "His real name is Mr. Garret."

"Garret, Carrots, I get it."

"And this class was introduced last year." She frowned. "It's *very* hands-on."

Carrots rubbed his palms together. "Er, how do the buttons work?"

A student hurried forward. The teacher's face brightened. "That makes perfect sense. I suppose the only other thing I need to know is how many."

Luciana raised her hand. "Thirteen, Mr. Garret. Everyone else has already taken their—"

But the wild-haired botanist was already pushing buttons. Without warning, his desk shot into the air. His head disappeared between high rafters. Whirring and clanging sounds came from the closet. Students exchanged glances. A girl in the front row climbed on top of her chair. "Mr. Garret? Excuse me, Mr. Garret? Who's first?"

Under someone's desk, a napping lynx woke up and snarled.

Then a lock clicked, and the door swung open. Casey's feet jerked against the legs of his desk. A smallish Bog Creep leaped out, shading its face with a paw and growling. It was followed by something wooly with snapping teeth—then another and another. A stampede of bumpy hides, darting eyes and scratching talons. Was this some kind of 3D projection? Kids screamed and piled out of their desks, pushing toward the back of the room.

"Um, Luci..." Gloria said.

"Is this normal?" Casey asked.

Luci appeared to be in shock.

"Push the barrier button—the orange one, the orange one—like your hair!" someone yelled, but Mr. Garret did not reply. With his head crammed between the rafters, he might not have heard. It was impossible to say.

Casey's stomach felt squishy as he realized something painfully obvious. *People here fight monsters. This is a monster-fighting class.*

More beasts poured out of the retaining pens. A warty toad the size of a dog jiggled its fat chin, threw back its head, and let out a bellowing laugh. "Noo, not the hyena toad!" someone shrieked. The entire class stampeded for the door, overturning desks, tripping over backpacks. Screams and loose papers filled the air.

Luci's hand landed on Casey's shoulder, breaking his horrified trance.

"Quick, we've got to–" she began, but a wailing kid ran right over her. Her shocked face disappeared in a swirling cloud of paper.

A flying chair crashed into Casey's shins. Staggering, he shoved Gloria behind him, grabbed the chair and waved it around as a rabbit-shaped creature with fangs jumped at him. Without thinking, he swung. The killer bunny sailed over the crowd. Near the front of the room, a lynx bounded into the air, caught it like a football, and disappeared.

Just keep moving, he thought. *Do the next thing.*

Some of the class had escaped out the door, which made things even worse for the kids stuck inside. Casey waved the chair, fending off another fanged rabbit, as Gloria clutched the waistline of his shorts. Luci sat up and looked around with a glazed expression. Casey batted the second rabbit away, grabbed her arm and pulled. She slid across the polished floor.

Pull-slide, pull-slide—they reached the door.

He dropped his chair and reached for the knob. A throaty chuckle boomed behind him.

RHAW, RHAW, RHAW.

Casey shoved Gloria into the hall and whirled as the enormous toad hopped forward. There was no time to think. He swung Luci's limp arm and smacked it across the face.

Tears welled up in its eyes.

Casey didn't wait to see if the toad's feelings were truly hurt. He dragged Luci into the hallway, slammed the door, and leaned against it, panting.

CHAPTER 25
TRAIL CRED

KIDS WITH BLOODHOUNDS and lynxes on leashes rushed past as Casey, Gloria and Luci slumped against a row of lockers. The classroom door opened, students with cuts and torn clothing spilled out, and the rescue team hurried in.

A wild din of baying and snarling reached them through the wall.

Luciana stared at the Grimes kids, blinking. A shoe mark smudged one of her cheeks.

"Sorry I had to drag you," Casey said.

She looked at him blankly.

"Do you remember who we are?" Gloria said.

"Um, *yeah...*" Luci scrunched up her face. "How could I ever forget? You're...you're my missing hamsters!"

"Uh oh," Gloria said.

Luci smiled at Casey and petted his head. "Where have you been hiding, honey-buns?"

The Grimes kids exchanged looks.

"I think she needs help," Casey said.

"Holy creeps, I'm kidding!" Luciana blinked several more times. "Of course I know who you are—Cloria and Gacey... I mean, Gloria and Casey. Oh, my brain is still echoing." She put a hand on her forehead.

Casey took her other hand out of his hair.

"We're on lunch break now," Luci said. "But maybe we could just sit here awhile…" Her eyes gained focus. "Casey, did you…drag me to safety…past that hyena toad? Did you save us?"

"He really did." Gloria's ponytail flipped up and down as she nodded.

Casey shrugged. "Maybe. Well. Yes."

Luci's mouth fell slightly open. "That toad has been the bane of our existence all semester. And you wouldn't believe the chunks those baby skrabbits can take out of you." She stretched her legs and rotated her feet. "Not a single bite. Casey, thanks so much."

"Anyone would've done the same." He sat up straighter.

A line of serious-looking kids filed out of Land Creature Defense, leading their animals. Two unhappy children with mops and buckets disappeared inside.

"Does that…happen often?" Casey pictured the fanged rabbits snarling.

"Not even close," Luci said. "Final Attacks are supposed to happen one kid at a time, in a controlled environment. But look on the bright side. Now everyone thinks you're my cousins. And after that fiasco, no one's going to look at the paperwork carefully."

"If there's any paperwork left," Casey said.

"It's possible, um…" Luci tugged at her headband. "Maybe I underestimated you and Gloria a little bit. And just so you know, I don't hate Civilians. Even though the two of you can't be more than half-civ at best." She smiled.

Casey stared. "Wait, so now you're not going to kick us out?"

She wriggled her fully-functional feet. "At least not until after lunch."

"How thoughtful." Casey didn't want to smile, but he couldn't seem to help himself.

Luci levered herself upright. "If we happen to run into Old Knock, just act normal."

If that meant remembering to breathe, maybe he could pull it off.

They made their way over the rickety bridge, back to Trickery central. Students shoved by, snickering at his ludicrous outfit.

"Luci," Casey muttered. "Why is no one else wearing flip-flops?"

"Oh...um...well." She didn't meet his eye. "Last year, someone smuggled a bunch across the border and everyone wore them, until we realized how ridiculous they look, and how worthless they are when you actually have to do something. Typical Civilian gear." She caught a glimpse of his face. "Sorry."

"And you *picked* these for me?"

A smile ghosted her lips.

"You've got to be kidding me."

Sunlight and good smells filled the cafeteria. Picture windows opened on the river and woods. When they found a table, Casey's plate was piled with smoked chicken and ribs, potato casserole, and bread pudding. He hoped his stomach would play along. Gloria had several slices of leftover breakfast pizza.

"Do you always get to eat like this?" Casey said.

Luciana took a bite of jello. "The kitchen staff never gets called to the front, even though some of them are physically fit. Our parents want to know their kids are being taken care of, and that means lots of healthy, soul-nurturing food." She raised her eyebrows and ate an apple slice.

"So your parents are out there...fighting monsters?"

Heavy footsteps echoed through the cafeteria. Chatter died down as Old Knock walked the aisles, eyes sweeping from kid to kid. Casey, Gloria and Luci bent over their plates. Knock stalked past, stood glaring in the door, and was gone.

Breathe, Casey told himself.

"Whew," Luci said. "Normally, I'd be pretty nervous about the war, but this is a code vermilion, which means something land-bound. It's late in the season for banes, so I'm thinking Death Dogs or a migrating herd of skrabbits. No Shadow Lords or Murklurkers. Nothing especially horrible."

"What counts as especially horr—"

Leaf-shaped speakers crackled in the corners of the room. "Happy Sleepover Week, Trickery!" an energetic voice said. "It's time for a battlefront news update. Sylvan Woods' monster squad, our moms and pops, reached the edge of the kingdom this morning. Soon they'll be joined by military detachments from, um, other places. A very large herd of skrabbits has been spotted, trying to make a surprise flanking movement. You know skrabbits, they're not the brightest..."

"Am I good or what?" Luci said.

A few tables over, Casey caught a familiar icy stare coming from a black and blue eye socket. Robert Pierce raised a fist.

Casey shook his head. *I don't think so.* One corner of his mouth tugged up.

Pretending to be cool felt good.

"Other beasts may be lurking nearby, but that hasn't been confirmed," said the kid reporter. "And that's all the *verified* news we have today. However..." He paused, then sped up. "There's a word-of-mouth report that two deceptive, ugly Civilian kids have infiltrated Sylvan Woods and we can't be too—"

There was a *beep* and dead air.

Casey clenched his napkin. Luci looked worried.

"How...who?" he whispered.

The radio crackled back to life.

"Just to be clear," the reporter said with less energy, "this is only a rumor. Don't get your weapons harnesses in a bunch. Back on the topic of *real* news, I'm sure our parents are up to the challenge of all those skrabbits. Hey, someone's gotta keep those clueless Civilians safe. For Trickery News, this is Jake McGusty reporting. Over and out."

CHAPTER 26
THE SECRETS OF LUCIANA WEST

THE SPEAKERS DIED and the room buzzed. "Idiot Civilians," someone said a table over. "You know they'd sabotage us if they could, even though all we do is protect them..."

Casey's mouth felt dry.

Luci frowned. "Sebastien Drooce."

"What?"

She lowered her voice. "The guy Bones mistook you for in the marsh. Drooce is a piece of work. Plus there's Tonya—they're always together."

"Tonya was me." Gloria smiled.

"What am I missing?" Casey's neck prickled as he imagined all the eyes on his back.

"Bones must have given Drooce detention, so Drooce knows other *kids* were in the swamp—not him.. Let's just hope he doesn't connect the dots to you and Gloria...and me." A shadow crossed her face.

"Hey, I've been meaning to ask," Casey said. "Civilian warriors— do people here really think that's a thing? All we have in Vintage Woods is a small police force. No one knows this place exists."

"No way. Are you serious?" Luci paused with a spoonful of applesauce halfway to her mouth. "I always thought Civs were competent, but too lazy to deal with their monster problems. You're saying the average Civilian knows nothing about us? Monster control? Guarding your borders for hundreds of years?"

Casey looked at her blankly.

"I can't believe this." She turned her spoon over, and the applesauce slopped down. "I mean, we get government subsidies, so someone must know. Don't you keep track of what your taxes pay for?"

"Um..." Casey would've sworn Luci's eyes couldn't get any wider.

"I guess I don't know much about the safe, ordinary world at all," she said. "Apparently no one here does."

"But you think of us as enemies." Casey no longer felt hungry.

"Oh no, not enemies," Luci said. "That would make us equal. It's more like looking after spoiled little siblings who take you for granted. At least, that's the general idea..."

What a mess, Casey thought. *No wonder everyone hates Civilians— if that's what we are. We're supposed to be lazy idiots...but also dangerous and hostile. Worse and worse. And stupider and stupider.*

"It's hard to have your parents gone." Gloria rested her chin on her hands.

Luci licked her lips. "Oh you're right, Glo, it really is."

Casey gulped down some juice, hoping it would cool his temperature. It looked like Kool-aid but tasted earthy, like roots. Nothing around here could be trusted.

"Hey, is Robert one of your friends?" He tried to pull his thoughts together.

"Sort of. No. Not really."

"That's a relief. But at least there's what's-her-name? Your friend from the oak."

Luci looked at him blankly.

"You know, um...Fire Ducky?"

"Oh right." Luci stared into her milk. "She's around somewhere.

Usually we just talk at night, from our trees." She looked away. "I'm the only one who can see her."

Casey's shoulders jerked. *Figures.* On top of being sarcastic and bossy, Luci was starting to seem...very strange.

"I have a friend like that too," Gloria said. "She can fly."

Casey sighed. Luci looked out the window.

Their table became an island of quiet in the loud hall.

Gloria patted Luci's hand. "I'm happy *we* get to be your friends."

"Aww, me too." Luciana gave the little girl a squeeze.

"So. Have you lived here long?" Casey said.

"Just over a year." Luci's face turned rosy. "It's been great, everything's gone well. I mean, nothing bad has happened. No big accidents or anything."

"Cool, cool. Sounds like a good first year."

Something glimmered in her dark eyes. Casey winced. He'd seen that look before, many times. In the mirror. It had a way of leaking out. That sad, hungry gleam.

Luciana mopped her face with a napkin.

Casey looked down, sweat dotting his back. He'd wanted to ask, Why are you hanging out with us, Luci, when everyone hates Civilians? Why are you helping us sneak around?

Now he had an answer.

Luciana West was lonely.

It wasn't always your fault. Casey knew that. But it didn't make him feel any better.

Because none of this made sense.

Luci was smart, and nice-looking, and good at climbing. She had her faults—man did she ever. But it didn't add up. She ought to have friends. There had to be something she wasn't telling them. That made Casey nervous.

CHAPTER 21
RELUCTANT GOODBYE

A BELL RANG and kids streamed out of the hall. Luciana passed a hand over her eyes. "All of a sudden, I'm not feeling great."

That makes two of us.

"It takes a while to recover from being run over," Casey said.

She slumped in a patch of sun on the cafeteria steps. "Maybe I'll go see the nurse. A bath...and a nap...would feel really good."

"Mmm," Gloria said. "Yes they would—if I wasn't too old for naps."

"You could tag along," Luci said, "but the nurse might get curious. Or I can show you the way home and we could maybe see each other later."

"How much later?" Casey glanced right and left as kids hurried past, clattering up ramps. He wouldn't mind a break. But without Luci, it would be hard to get back into Sylvan Woods. Well so what? *People here hate me without even knowing me. And they fight constantly. And there are monsters. So if I never come back, no big deal.*

But it wasn't good enough. People here could see him. He couldn't leave. Not without finding out more about this amazing... deadly...place.

Luci wrapped a hand around her stomach. "How about I come

get you when I feel better? There's another sleepover tonight. We can go over together."

"Hooray," Gloria said. "I love sleepovers! I mean, I *think* I do..."

"Deal," Casey said. "But what if you..." There was no easy way to say it. "What if you, um, forget to come find us?"

Luci gave him a strange look.

Casey took a breath. "How do we know you won't ditch us?"

"I'm *not* a liar." Her head drooped, like she didn't have energy to be upset. "Fine, take this." She tugged off her pendant and handed it to Casey. "My favorite necklace. It's a light source and beast deterrent. You won't need it, but you'd better believe I'll come get it." She frowned. "Happy?"

"Thanks." Casey hung the pendant over his tattered t-shirt.

Maybe she actually likes you. Or maybe she has a whole closet of them at home. Or maybe the necklace has some kind of magical hex...

Watching him, Luci shook her head. They walked into the deep shade of trees and old-world skyscrapers. Feet thudded high overhead. In a treetop arena, metal clashed and kids shouted as a weapons exercise began. "Parry and cut, parry and—ouch, you got my fingers!"

The instructor sounded mad.

When they reached Trickery's front edge, the yelling faded. Casey's skin felt less tingly. No more sharp eyes, pricking his face.

"Follow the trail past the baths," Luci said. "Just before you reach the orchard, take a left. That trail leads back to your oak. Your house is behind the tree, right?" One finger traced her bare neck. "Maybe I'll sneak a few steps over the border."

"Goodie," Gloria said.

"Sounds great," Casey said.

You do want to get back into Sylvan Woods, right?

"One more thing." Luci hesitated. "Sylvan alarms probably aren't real, right? The ones that hurt our sensitive ears? Or people traps? You know...the ones that catch Sylvans?"

She didn't seem to be kidding.

"We just gave ours a good cleaning," he said.

Luci put a hand to her mouth.

"Just kidding." Casey felt a little better.

"Ooo." Her sickly face took on color. "Of course you are. Ok, bye!"

Before Luci could escape, Gloria hugged her. Casey forced himself to shake her hand. He and his sister hiked off. When he looked back, Luci stood in the meadow, watching. She seemed to be swaying slightly, but she didn't take her eyes off them.

CHAPTER 28
MS. JONES
KNOWS BEST

CASEY AND GLORIA followed the trail past the baths, circling boulders and thickets. A small trail twisted away on the left. Summer sun beat down and grasshoppers whirred. Puffy clouds floated overhead. The clouds looked very normal.

"What if this is a dream?" Gloria said.

"You know what," Casey said. "I was thinking the same thing. But look at my clothes. These are too ridiculous to be made up."

Gloria laughed and took his hand. He squeezed, and they kept walking. The trail wound along a ridge, dry and hot. Before they knew it, they reached the Old Oak. Casey looked up at its shady branches and sighed. They couldn't hide from Ms. Jones forever.

The world's best certified traveling babysitter was stomping back and forth across the backyard, raising her feet high, as Casey and Gloria walked out of the forest.

"Hallo, adventurers." She didn't seem surprised to see them.

"What are you doing to the yard?" Gloria asked.

"I noticed the grass could use some aerating." Her shoes looked like medieval track cleats. "That means poking thousands of holes in the turf to make it grow. And luckily, I accidentally packed my ice crampons—they happen to double as aerating shoes."

"My birthday is getting close." Casey liked how the sun glinted off the metal spikes. He also liked how the conversation was going. The less said about where they'd been, the better.

Their sitter sat on the deck stairs and pulled the crampons off. "Once, but only once," she said, "I wore these back inside my house. That's the kind of mistake you don't make twice."

"Why don't you let me take a turn," Casey said.

Ms. Jones handed the crampons over and smiled.

Casey's chest tightened.

Her smile said, I know exactly what you're up to and we'll talk later.

He caught Gloria's eye and zipped his lips. She rolled her eyes as he buckled on the crampons. Out in the yard, the spikes worked like small daggers, slicing the soil like butter. *I'm not invisible.* Stomp. *I might be Sylvan.* Thump. *I just need to...* He finished the backyard and the front and sides, trying to complete his sentence. When Ms. Jones called him inside for lemonade, he slumped in a chair.

Gloria snored softly, her head on the kitchen table.

Ms. Jones sat down. She folded her hands like the roof of Trickery's great hall. "You've been busy, dear."

He sighed. "Those crampons wear you out."

"I'm just happy you survived the gryphon."

His head jerked up.

"And that murderous boy." Her kind eyes hardened. "And a whole zoo of monsters."

You could never trust Gloria to keep her mouth shut.

"It...happened very fast," Casey said.

The sitter waited.

"We didn't have to come home, but we did...because we—we like you," he said. "Please. You've got to let me go back."

She gave him a sad smile. "Technically, dear...I don't. You have no idea how complex my contract is. And what would your parents say?"

"Maybe they'd be happy for me." His throat felt gritty. "I fought off monsters. And I kept Gloria safe, and I...made a friend."

Ms. Jones sighed.

"Kids can actually see me. And the treeways, the woods... You can hardly imagi–"

"Very well, dear."

"–hardly imagine how huge the trees are, with the buildings built right into–"

"I *can* imagine, dear."

"–right into the forest, so please, please...what did you say?"

Her eyes looked shiny. "You can go back."

A feeling like cool, clean water washed over Casey. "Thank you." He swallowed down a wet, uneven breath. "But why?"

She gave him a half smile. "Because I'm a traveling babysitter, dear, and a good sitter lives in at least two different worlds at once. As a result, she sometimes faces impossible, insane decisions...and is forced to choose."

"Oh," Casey said.

"Besides, I think your heating and cooling system needs a good cleaning. May as well keep you two out of the way." She took their empty glasses and stood.

Casey watched her hum and scrub. Was she crazy? Was he? Were both of them? A minute later, his tight underwear reminded him how dirty and uncomfortable he was.

He got up to take a shower.

CHAPTER 29
MIXED FEELINGS

CASEY SCRUBBED SCRAPES he didn't remember getting. It gave him something to do as his brain ran jittery laps. What had Luci done, *really*, to prove they could trust her? Everything she'd done to help also saved her own skin. She was acting friendly now, but why? *Maybe you should let this go.* His head ached, just thinking about it. And there were other things to worry about.

Everyone in Sylvan Woods hates Civilians. And you'll probably get attacked by something in the next twenty-four hours. Maybe the hate didn't matter, because he was a lost Sylvan, like Luci said. Maybe he could win his place with Strength and Honor, like in the *Handbook*. Or he could fail and be prosecuted...or worse.

As Casey dried off with shaking hands, he knew one thing, and one thing only. He wanted to return to Sylvan Woods. But he had no idea what he'd do when he got there.

He dressed in his most forest-colored clothes and put Luci's necklace under his t-shirt. Maybe the woods would help him relax. They always had before. He made his way through the trees to the Old Oak and collected his pack. The oak seemed restless. Leaves tossing, limbs creaking, like there was something it wanted.

Oh wait. That was *him*.

He climbed the eastern compass deck, where he'd first talked to Luci, and let the wind rush across his face and arms and the back of his neck. It smoothed away his worries while it made a mess of his hair. But he couldn't stay here forever.

"I've got so much to tell you," he said to the oak. "Talk to you, later, ok?"

Finding this tree had turned his life upside down, but it still had a calming effect.

If only the calm would last.

Back home, Luci waited on the deck stairs with her legs crossed, a high-tech trail shoe looping the air. Her wavy hair was pulled back in a ponytail. Casey noticed a thin swoop of turquoise at the collar of her fatigue v-neck. Probably a daring Sylvan fashion statement.

"Hubba hoy, Casey. That's an ancient Sylvan greeting, by the way. I'm trying to bring it back. So..." She smiled and looked away. "You were right about the people traps. I guess they were just legend."

Seeing her on his deck felt like Sylvan Woods stretching its twiggy fingers into his home. But at the same time, warmth traced his chest. "So you crossed the border and risked the traps and everything."

Luci touched her ears. "Luckily your Sylvan alarms are low on batteries."

Casey cocked his head. "Uh..."

Luci laughed. "I guess those are made up too."

She's really not so bad.

"Are you feeling better?" He sat down next to her.

"So much better." She pressed imaginary wrinkles from her black shorts. "And I've had time to think. I was thinking...maybe I could help you and Gloria stay in Sylvan Woods. I mean, if you want to." She twisted her t-shirt. "That is, if you're Sylvans. And you're thinking about wanting to stay. And if you really want to belong, maybe I could help. Help you, you know, belong." She passed a hand over her face. "Wow, that came out funny."

Casey felt a smile split his face. "That sounds amazing."

Whoa, play it cool, man. He flicked at some pretend dirt on his sleeve.

"I mean, it was really hard to understand." He cleared his throat. "But...I accept."

He looked up at the same second Luci stopped tugging at her shoe laces.

Their eyes met and darted away.

"Ok, cool." Luci tucked her hair back. "First things first, the sleepover. A good opportunity for you to see what Sylvan Woods is all about."

"Right," Casey said. "Of course."

"You won't need food or a sleeping bag...but the school doesn't provide other essentials, like, you know, toothbrushes."

"Right." He walked indoors.

In the kitchen, Ms. Jones was peering into an air vent with a feather duster.

Luci actually likes us. She came back. So she actually likes us.

Upstairs, he set his pack on his bed. Most of his equipment screamed *Civilian*. What should he bring, a flashlight? But kids in Sylvan Woods didn't use them. He'd left the dark lantern and sword in the bath cave, stupidly enough. Finally, he took his toothbrush from the bathroom and stuck it in his pocket. At the top of the stairs, he paused. Over the hum of the air conditioning, he heard voices.

"...know absolutely nothing," Ms. Jones said. "Keep them safe..."

"Like a babysitter, you mean." It was Luci.

"...basically defenseless..."

Casey inched closer.

"Wait. Shh."

He frowned, and creaked down the stairs. Luci sat the kitchen table across from Ms. Jones, twisting a lock of hair around her finger.

"Yep, things are really great in Sylvan Woods," she said. "Much better than the Cumberland Chasm."

"Wonderful to hear," Ms. Jones said brightly.

"I'm ready." Casey gave them a look. "Where's Gloria?"

Gloria tottered in from the living room, yawning. "I wasn't asleep, I was just resting." Her eyes were unfocused, hair in tangles. A pillow print marked one cheek.

"Come along, Gloria," Ms. Jones said. "Casey can pack for you while I brush your hair."

He stomped upstairs, found a pink toothbrush, and stuck it in his other pocket.

Know absolutely nothing...defenseless. Really? After I dragged Luci to safety and scared off that Hyena Toad? There's no way I'll let her babysit us, not a chance. Why couldn't they give me a little credit for getting off to a good start?

When he returned, Gloria's hair was in neat pigtails. Her pupils were smaller and she looked more like herself.

"We'll see you later, Ms. Jones," Luci said. "Safe and sound."

"I'm counting on it, dear." The sitter watched them out of sight.

"We've had pretty good luck with treeways today," Luci said. "I thought we'd take one to the Big Beech, even though no one is chasing us with an axe handle."

It was a joke, Casey knew that. After what he'd overheard, he didn't find it very funny.

CHAPTER 30
VALLEY OF THE SHADOW OF MONSTERS

READY FOR YOUR FIRST SYLVAN SLEEPOVER?"
Luci said. "I hope you like monster charades."

They were climbing the Old Oak, Gloria first, then Luci, then Casey.

"Um, I'm not really–" Casey began.

"Just kidding." He heard the smirk in her voice.

Way to be gullible, Grimes.

At the treeway, Luciana took a guide line in each hand, and stepped on. She moved into space, Gloria right behind, and Casey followed. They hovered over tree tops, slipping through upper branches. Twigs scraped the soles of their shoes. A flock of swallows darted past. Creeks and dirt paths twisted below, powerless to help or slow them. Walking through thin air felt amazing, unlike some other things.

"Hey Luci," he said. "Will there be a lot of kids at the sleepover?"

She looked back, wind flipping her dark ponytail.

"Lots and lots," she said. "I'm not sure who, but kids like the Big Beech. Let's hope Old Knock isn't in charge, right?"

"Right," Casey said.

Just do your best. Don't let her babysit you.

The ropeway ran uphill toward an enormous white tree that glowed in the setting sun.

"Kids say it's haunted." The breeze blew Luci's words back.

Gloria froze on the rope. "It is really?"

"Beeches shed their bark," Casey said. "They get that ghostly white look."

"Spoiler," Luci said.

They pushed through outer leaves, and gnarled branches closed in. Voices and laughter fell from overhead. An enclosed metal ladder led up the central trunk.

"I can't wait!" Gloria tossed her pigtails and started climbing.

Casey followed more slowly. *Strategy, think strategy. Stay on Luci's good side, at least for now. Avoid Old Knock at all costs. And Robert, same deal. And Sebastien Drooce, ditto.* Man, that was a lot of avoiding. Then there were Ms. Jones and his parents—wildcards. *Treat them with respect. But they're not here now, so you don't need to think about them.*

He frowned and tried to slow his breathing. Becoming visible had not solved his problems. He was walking a very thin line. A slippery treeway made of thread that stretched across a valley full of monsters.

CHAPTER 31
MS. CRAKE

GLORIA DISAPPEARED through the Big Beech's hatch, Luci right behind. Casey took several quick breaths and followed. When he stepped off the ladder, flames blinded him.

His first time here, the tree *would* be on fire.

"Don't worry." The shape next to him was Luci's. "The fire pit is lined with stone and that trough is full of water. The next ring out is sand, and the floor is painted with fire retardant, so it's safe. It freaked me out the first time I saw it."

Casey's eyes adjusted to the light. They stood on a platform the size of a gym. Metal bleachers stretched down two sides, and a bonfire blazed in the middle, kids clustered around. Most of them held ten foot skewers, long enough to reach over the rings of sand and water.

Gloria tugged his arm. "Casey, can you believe it? All these kids with no moms or dads or babysitters, just...a big fire."

"Is that you, Luciana West?" The voice sounded accusing.

Luci looked up. "Yes Ms. Crake, it's me."

Casey followed her eyes. The beech's ladder continued up the trunk to a second platform. A woman stood at the rail, fading sun at her back. Her blonde hair was short and spiky and her shoulders hunched. Shadows hid her face as she scanned a clipboard.

"These are my cousins, Casey and Gloria Grimes," Luci said. "We checked in earlier, in Land Creature Defense, with Mr—"

"More than enough detail, Ms. West." The woman scribbled notes. "I heard about the chaos in LCD. Some of your classmates needed stitches. A few had broken bones. I hope it was worth it, making a total hash of final attacks."

"I'd already passed *my* final." Luci tossed her head. "Anyway, Carrots, I mean, Mr—"

"Silence, Ms. West." The woman's eyes moved to Casey. "*You* chose a strange time to visit. Sylvan Woods at war, Civilians causing trouble on the border. A *dangerous* time. What brings you here..." She glanced at her clipboard. "Casey Grimes?"

"Um, plans were made in advance," Luci said. "We didn't know—"

"Silence." Ms. Crake stabbed her clipboard at Luci. "I'm sure your cousin can speak for himself."

Casey's body temperature dropped under her stare. He felt more like a Civilian than ever. "I've always wanted to visit Sylvan Woods, ma'am, because...it's so magical."

In the shadows, it was hard to read Ms. Crake's expression. "Hmm," she said. "An unusual answer, but not a bad one, Mr. Grimes."

Luci gave Casey a sidelong glance and rolled her eyes.

"Run along," the teacher said. "And *Lu-ci-an-a?*" She drew out each syllable.

Luci took a quick breath. "Yes?"

"Keep that evil eye to yourself."

Luci's mouth hung open for a second. "Yes, Ms. Crake."

She grabbed Casey and Gloria and tugged them away. Halfway to the bonfire, she whispered, "She's kind of a monster. Very different from Old Knock, but even scarier in her own way. And she doesn't like me. By the way, thanks for not mentioning how you were looking forward to seeing your favorite cousin." She darted Casey a look.

"Very funny," Casey said. "Is Ms. Crake alright?"

Flames snapped and crackled ten feet high. Heat washed their faces.

"Your guess is as good as mine." Luci chose an open bench. "She used to be one of Trickery's best and brightest. They said she'd end up leading an army, managing a forest, or something even bigger. But then she had a really bad fall in a cliff battle, and she's never been the same."

"Just because you get hurt doesn't mean you have to be mean," Gloria said.

"I totally agree," said Luci.

They sat down by the fire. Kids glanced over, but no one seemed to recognize them. Casey grabbed a skewer, trying to look like he knew what he was doing.

"By the way," Luci said. "Even though Crake liked your answer, magic is not something you want to talk about around—mmf!"

A hand clamped her mouth and dragged her off the bench. At the same moment, someone shoved Casey from behind and he crashed to the floor.

CHAPTER 32
FIRESIDE FIGHT

A BOOT THUMPED Casey's chest. An angry face glared down. "A week of detention from Bones, are you kidding me?" The face was tanned, green-eyed, and framed with plastered hair. The boot was wet, heavy, and covered in bumps. "When I'm done with you, you'll wish you were back in that swamp."

Bones...the swamp... Arms flailing, Casey tried to connect the dots. It wasn't easy, with his lungs being squeezed like an accordion. Someone squealed on the other side of the bench, and his attacker's eyes darted away. Casey grabbed the boot with both hands, and yanked. The other boy crashed to the deck as Casey lurched to his feet, sucking air.

Here we go again. Why are people always trying to kill me?

The mean kid yowled and jumped up. He pulled a large splinter from the seat of his desert camo shorts. "Now I'm really going to hurt you."

Casey took a step back. "Could we just say we're even?"

A few feet away, Luci struggled with a scratching, clawing stranger. It was hard to say what the girl looked like because Gloria was sitting on her head.

"Don't let Casey fool you," Luci gasped. "He may seem innocent, but he'll break you in half, Sebastien." She looked pale.

Sebastian. Sebastien Drooce. The piece of work.

"This is just a misunderstanding," Casey said as the boy closed in. "Back in the swamp, I didn't actually–"

"Drooce, help meee!" screeched the girl Gloria was sitting on.

Drooce's eyes narrowed to wild slits. He took a step toward the girls, growling. It was the growl that did it. Sebastien Drooce, snarling at his sister. Casey's stomach became a bubbling volcano. Molten rage surged through his body.

"HEY YOU!" he shouted.

Sebastian whirled and Casey erupted.

Drooce was a head taller, but Casey jumped several inches in the air as he slammed his knuckles forward. There was a meaty crunch, a moment of shocked silence, and a horrified wail. Blood gushed from Sebastien's nose. The lava in Casey's chest flowed away, and he took a step back. *Did I really do that?*

Off on the side, the girls stopped scuffling.

Sebastien roared and lunged at Casey, metal gleaming in his fist. Casey backpedaled, throwing out his hands, but he was too slow... He shut his eyes.

Crack-crack!

How was he still standing?

Kids began cheering and clapping. Casey opened his eyes. He didn't seem to be hurt, apart from his throbbing knuckles. Sebastien whimpered, rolling on the deck. The crowd of students surrounding them seemed happy...none of it made any sense.

Icy fingers clenched his shoulder.

"Casey Grimes?" Ms. Crake's gaze was as cold as her grip. "We don't tolerate unscheduled fights, whether in Sylvan Woods or...*where* did you say you were from?"

Casey's mind froze like a cantaloupe on ice.

"But wait..." Crake's fingers fell away. "It's Sebastien Drooce. And you've saved me the trouble of searching for contraband."

Casey's opponent groaned, holding his bloody nose and rubbing his kneecaps. A dagger gleamed on the deck beside him. Ms. Crake snatched the weapon and straightened—as straight as her crooked shoulders allowed.

"Mr. Drooce, you look terrible. Did Mr. Grimes do this to you?"

"I tripped over a bench," Sebastien said. "Grimes, are you kidding me? That little Civ-scat couldn't hurt a–"

"That's enough," Ms. Crake snapped. "Keep talking and you'll be mucking out gryphon pens for weeks."

The crowd muttered appreciatively.

"Fighting without permission is of course a punishable offense." The teacher turned to Casey. "But in light of Mr. Drooce's testimony, and his contraband stiletto..." She narrowed her blue eyes. "My hands are tied."

The circle of kids buzzed.

"But half the puzzle is missing." Ms. Crake folded her arms. "Where's Tonya Cortland?"

There was a flurry of pushing and shoving. The crowd parted and a girl staggered out, straight blonde hair swinging in her chilly eyes. It didn't hide the good-sized lump on her forehead.

"Aha." Ms. Crake paced the circle, firelight gleaming off the pearl buttons on her shirt. "Would you like to tell me who did this to you, Cortland?"

The girl glared at Casey.

"Ahem," said a small voice. Gloria stepped out from behind a boy twice her height. She clasped her hands and looked at the floor. "I'm Gloria," she said. "*I* did that. Sorry, but she was, er, *they* were, trying to beat up me and my brother."

Ms. Crake stared. At the back of the crowd, someone giggled. Someone else started clapping. Others picked up the rhythm. A few seconds later, the whole crowd was chanting. "GLO-RI-A! GLO-RI-A!"

Gloria smiled shyly.

Casey felt proud.

Ms. Crake raised a hand and the chants died away. She shook her head in disbelief and motioned at Cortland and Drooce. The sulky gang of two joined her, and the crowd parted.

"You'll pay for this, Grimes," Drooce hissed as he walked by.

Ms. Crake brought up the rear. As passed, she put her mouth to Casey's ear.

"You owe me."

CHAPTER 33
BOOTMAN

CASEY TRIED to scrape the boot-print off his shirt, but it was too late. The bonfire had baked it into a decal. Kids swarmed over to congratulate him and Gloria—Frank and Devontae and Angel and Grace and Gabriella and a bunch of other names he couldn't remember. They thought the boot-print was pretty cool.

"You gave Drooce the boot, man!"

"Three cheers for Bootman!"

Casey didn't mind the nickname. The kids had questions, though. "Are you new here? Where are you from?" Luckily, the crowd was big enough he could just nod and smile. Hopefully he looked confident and humble, instead of how he felt—slightly sick.

Gloria was even more popular. After Ms. Crake left, the kids picked her up and carried her around the bonfire, cheering. Everyone wanted to give her a high five. About twenty girls stopped by to say how adorable and brave she was. Knowing how his little sister liked to talk, it made Casey nervous.

When the crowd had wandered off, Luci reappeared and Casey let himself relax. She had a fat lip and a cut on her chin—but he didn't point that out. The stars were out and the camp was quieting down.

"I would've spoken up," Luci said, "but with Crake in charge, I would've hurt your chances. She likes you, it's kind of creepy."

Casey gave her a tired smile.

"That punch was shocking." Luci sat down next to him. "I didn't realize a Civilian could stand up to a Sylvan kid. Oops, that came out wrong..."

"Do people here care about anything besides fighting?" Casey said.

"Well, yeah..." Luci propped her skewer in the sand, and slid roast pineapple and salmon onto her plate. "Boxing is popular too. But I'm not gonna lie, that fight got everyone's attention." She wiped pineapple juice off her chin and winced. "You two are really something. You know so little about, well, *everything*, but you don't let it stop you. Lots of kids tiptoe around Drooce and Cortland. After tonight, I don't think I will anymore."

Casey sighed. *The secret to my courage is my fear of being invisible.*

"I've been meaning to ask you something," he said. "It's kind of important."

Luci leaned closer. So did Gloria.

"So, no one here likes Civilians—I mean, except you—but a Civilian who's really good at this Trickery stuff, or at least a person everyone *thinks* is a Civilian, he could probably earn a place here, right?"

Luciana put her head on one side.

"The Sylvan Handbook says people are welcome here if they show strength and honor. And something about magic." He swallowed. "Is that still true?"

Luci put a knuckle to her chin. "Strength and honor sound familiar. Magic—don't even get me started on how last century that is. No one talks about it, except in a casual way, like, Hey, that party was totally magic. Wow, did you practice that move, or was it magic?"

Her smile faded. "The sciences are where it's at now. Dendrology, metallurgy, things you can test in a lab and control. And personal combat, obviously. I hate to say it, but maybe that handbook is out of date. We don't use them in class anymore. We need to find another way to give you an inside track."

She made a sad face.

Casey felt himself deflating like a party balloon. "That doesn't even make sense. Sylvan Woods is the most magical place I've ever seen."

"You'd better keep that to yourself." Luci hesitated. "I guess I was hoping we'd find out you really *are* Sylvan. Like maybe you had a bad accident, and it would all come back to you. But there aren't any Grimeses in the Sylvan Woods registry, Casey. I sneaked in and checked after my nap."

See, she really does care. But it doesn't make much difference, does it.

"What if we were switched at birth?" He immediately felt bad, because what would that make Dad and Mom?

Luci wrinkled her forehead. "Anything's possible. But on the bright side, if there's some forgotten path to citizenship, you're off to a great start. People here love combat and toughness..."

She trailed off.

"What?" Casey studied her worried face.

"Just...be careful. They like you now but that doesn't mean they'll like you later."

"Oh, there's no question about that." He threw a marshmallow in the blazing fire. "I'm not good at fighting. I don't even like it. If we keep hanging around, it's just a matter of time until someone finds out who we really are..."

"Maybe we could visit on the weekends," Gloria said.

All of a sudden, Casey had a lump in his throat.

"So you really do want to stay? I thought you might..." Luci grabbed their hands and squeezed. "I'll try to help."

Metal clinked as someone sat down next to them.

"How cute," the person said. "What a sweet little family."

CHAPTER 34
PIERCE MAKES A MOVE

GET OUT OF HERE, ROBERT." Luci's eyes got hard.

The boy's face was still puffy from Gloria's rock. His blue-black bruise had taken a greenish hue. If things went on this way, he'd soon be wearing a rainbow. Robert Pierce stretched one arm along the bench. "What's your secret, Grimes?"

"My secret?" Casey blinked. "What secret? Where did you come from?"

"Everyone has one." Robert grinned. "But you don't have to tell me. I'm just making conversation while I wait for someone to thank me."

Luci gave him a cold stare. Gloria tossed her pigtails.

"Did you plan this in advance?" Robert said.

"Um, no," Gloria said. "We don't do very many plans."

"That's right." Luci darted a smile at Casey. "We live in the moment."

"Living in the moment has been rough on your face," Robert said.

She touched her fat lip.

"Don't listen to him." Casey's gut began another awkward dance.

Robert frowned. "I realize I moved fast, but hell's bells. I just kept Bootman from becoming a colander. I'm the reason he's famous."

"A cool-ander..." Gloria said. "Is that what you cross out until it's your birthday?"

"A net, a sieve, a person full of holes." Robert huffed. "I saw Sebastien coming at you"—he tapped Casey's shoulder—"and you had a stunned look on your face. After that punch, I couldn't just stand by and watch, so I grabbed a piece of firewood, cracked Drooce's kneecaps, and down he went. You're welcome, Macey. Thanks to me, you still have a large intestine."

"Gross," Luci said. "You're making that up."

"My name is Casey," Casey said with a sinking feeling. "And thanks."

"Don't thank him," Luci said. "He just wants attention."

"I hate to say this," Casey said, "but he's telling the truth."

"*Finally.*" Robert threw his hands in the air.

"There's no way Ms. Crake was quick enough," Casey said. "It was Robert."

The dangerous boy pretended to buff his knuckles.

"Fine." Luciana sat up straighter. "Congratulations, Robert, you did something considerate for once in your life, which is surprising, since all you care about is looking good and showing off. Oh wait, that's kind of what you're doing right now, isn't it? My cousin *Casey* thanked you, so now you can go irritate someone else."

Casey's eyes widened.

"This guy can't be your cousin," Robert said. "His combat IQ is way too low. Plus he's too polite."

"Bye," she said.

Robert shrugged and got up. "Hey Bootman," he said over his shoulder. "You should find some better company." He sauntered off.

Luci breathed out through her teeth.

"You really ripped him," Casey said.

"He is the *most* irritating kid," she said. "Whenever I'm nice to him, I end up regretting it. Seriously, I don't know why he hangs around."

"He's super, what's the word, aggressive," Gloria said.

"He's very good at combat," Luci said grudgingly.

"I'm glad he doesn't like Sebastien Drooce," Casey said. "Otherwise, I might not have a large intestine." He smiled.

"Stop it," Luci said.

The moon was high. Kids were pulling sleeping bags out of storage lockers. Gloria yawned, and Casey realized how exhausted he was. They dragged their gear toward the fire and chose a spot of open deck. Luci unzipped her pack and took out a toothbrush. Casey pulled two crushed ones from his pockets.

"Seriously," she said. "I know those are really heavy, but I could have carried them for you."

They brushed at the rail, careful not to spit into the wind, and walked to their camp in the moonlight. The Big Beech was quieting down. Gloria slumped on her sleeping bag, unconscious in seconds.

"Good night, Casey." Luci's shadow swirled.

"Good night, Luci."

Finally. Time alone with his thoughts.

I'm here. In Sylvan Woods. I'm still alive...

Casey caught himself snoring. *Wait, you can't sleep yet. Plans, important plans...* He jerked awake again when Ms. Crake moved past, yelling, "Get out from under those bleachers right now or so help me I'll burn your grades in the bonfire!"

Thoughts of Luci, Ms. Crake and the elusive path to citizenship whirled behind his eyes. It was too much. He surrendered to the darkness.

CHAPTER 35
THE NIGHTMARES

AT FIRST, Casey's dream was good. He and Gloria and Luciana were on a treeway. Far below, Old Knock, Sebastien and Tonya shook their fists and brandished weapons. Backing them up were a Bog Creep, a Tree Shriek, and a pack of fanged rabbits. The treeway climbed higher, and everything disappeared. It became a skyway.

Luci looked at him and smiled.

"We're safe." Casey said. "There's no way they'll catch us now."

He turned to Gloria, but like the birds and branches, his sister was gone.

"Just you and me." Luciana's smile got bigger. In the wispy clouds and wind, her shadow came to life and grew. Her eyes pulsed with hungry green light. Tentacles writhed and twisted. Snakes streamed from her head like hair. Then Luci became her shadow.

"They're all gone," she whispered. "There's no one left to hear you scream."

Casey shot upright, sweating and gasping for breath. His t-shirt glowed, and it took him a second to remember he was wearing Luci's pendant. The fire was out, the moon behind clouds. Was it his imagination, or was the Big Beech tossing uneasily?

A terrified scream split the night. Casey rubbed his ears.

It was real. And it wasn't him.

Luci jerked to life in her sleeping bag. "Casey, Gloria, are you ok?"

"Not really." He squirmed away.

Gloria didn't reply. The flap of her sleeping bag was folded back and there was no one inside. Casey's blood froze, then the bag moved. Gloria crawled out from under it, blinking.

Another scream. "Help, someone help me!"

Casey jumped to his feet. The terror from his nightmare crawled along his bones. Anything was better than sitting in the shadows next to Luci. The shrieks came from the far bleachers. He took two steps that direction, turned and rushed to the fire.

"One of those poky things," he muttered.

He grabbed a skewer from the embers, orange tip glowing. Confused kids sat up, rubbing their eyes, as he ran by. Luci's bare feet smacked the planks behind him, and he ran faster.

On the top bleacher, in the farthest corner...a girl hunched on the metal bench, twisting and kicking. She seemed to be wrestling the night.

The night hissed. It had writhing black arms and legs. Casey charged up the bleachers, clanging from bench to bench. He yanked the pendant from his shirt, and milky light shone on dagger teeth, flat black eyes that swallowed light...a wicked-looking stinger. The monster's spindly, sharp-edged body was like a blend between a scorpion and a wasp.

Another nightmare. But in this one, he wasn't trapped.

Better yet, the monster wasn't Luci.

Silvery wings swept the air. The struggling girl hooked an ankle under a bench and screamed as the thing dragged her skyward. Casey drove the skewer forward. The glowing tip caught a wing and sizzled. The monster shrieked. It tore free, hurtling down the benches. Straight for Luci and Gloria—who stood there, paralyzed..

"NOO!" Casey yelled.

The wasp-thing launched itself, all its legs clawing.

Something shot through the darkness with a dry crunch, and the creature fell. Black blood splashed the deck. For a moment, everything was quiet and still.

Casey felt painfully awake.

His skewer clanged the bleacher. The nameless girl began to cry, muffled sobs that stuck in her throat. Ms. Crake appeared, carrying a second javelin. She drove it through the monster's spine, pinning it to the deck.

"Hell's bells." Her uneven shoulders shuddered. "Did anyone die?"

CHAPTER 36
GRIMES THE FIGHTER

THE WHOLE BIG Beech was awake. Carrots arrived, red hair standing on end, and took the hurt girl down the tree with help from student volunteers. Once they left, Ms. Crake ordered everyone to the fire, even though everyone was already there.

Bleary-eyed kids crowded close like it was winter and not a summer night. Crake authorized a huge pot of hot chocolate, climbed onto a bench, and shouted at them while the cocoa bubbled.

"No wandering off to stargaze," she yelled. "No climbing the bleachers. If you need to use the bathroom, take someone with you —even if you're a boy." Boys groaned. "If you'd prefer to be stung and dragged into the night, do as you like." The groans stopped. "This was a freak accident, but we'll take precautions. Have a cocoa and try to go back to sleep."

"What was that thing?" someone said.

One corner of Ms. Crake's mouth turned down and she put a finger to her chin. It was a thoughtful, girlish gesture for someone so dangerous.

"You may as well know." She sighed. "It was a Butcher Beast. Something we haven't seen for a long, long time..." Her eyes became distant. "Well, sweet dreams." As whispers spread around the bonfire, she crooked a finger at the Grimes kids and Luci.

They fell in line without a word.

Why couldn't I just be asleep, really asleep, Casey thought. His sweat had dried cold and clammy. The feeling of escape was gone. He kept seeing the monster's flat black eyes.

The teacher's crow's nest had carved metal compass points like the Old Oak. A telescope was bolted to one rail, overlooking the bonfire and bleachers. Ms. Crake led them inside a tent with billowing curtains.

An army cot stood on one wall, a tufted leather sofa on another. A small fire burned in a wide stone bowl. Crake pointed to the sofa and they sat.

"Ms. Crake, will that girl be all right?" Luci hugged a pillow.

"Shhh. We can only hope." Crake paced the tent with her slow, ungainly walk, black cloak swirling. "It all depends on what I can find...in here." She pressed her temples, eyes shut. "It means something...terrible," she whispered.

The children stared.

Her eyes flicked open. "Why are you here? Oh that's right." Her glance pinned Casey to the couch. "I sense a pattern with you, Mr. Grimes, and it's a little concerning. Perhaps Ms. West has been encouraging you, God knows she's had her issues."

Luci studied the weatherproof ceiling.

"You seem to be always spoiling for a fight, Grimes. Good at it, too."

Casey's shoulders twitched. "Really, I'm not very–"

"Don't get me wrong," Crake said. "I'm grateful. You stopped a monster—some would say two." She smirked. "Consider this a friendly warning. There's more to Sylvan Woods than fighting. Take the trail less traveled. Discover the magic." She raised her brows. "Right, Ms. West?"

"Um. Sure." Luci inspected the fire. The furniture. Everything but Ms. Crake.

"Now, that glowing skewer, Mr. Grimes, those thin wings—perfect combo." The corners of her eyes creased up. "Like a hot knife through butter. Of course you didn't know a Butcher Beast was waiting, so let's give luck its due. Do you *feel* lucky, Mr. Grimes?"

Casey swallowed. "A little, I guess?"

"Fair enough." Ms. Crake held up one hand. "Here's to good luck."

Casey stared at her.

"High five," whispered Gloria.

"Oh." Casey slapped the teacher's palm, and they stood.

"I'll see you get commendations," Ms. Crake said. "Mr. Grimes stopped the butcher in its tracks. Ms. West, Ms. Grimes, your supporting roles were also valuable." She shooed them from the top of the ladder. "Think about what I've said."

The Big Beech creaked under their feet. Casey rubbed his aching knuckles, feeling numb and slightly dizzy. "I can't believe she thinks I'm good at fighting."

"She really seems to like you." Luci looked baffled.

"Every fight I've been in," Casey said. "There was someone to bail me out. I'm not a *little* lucky, I'm a lot lucky."

"Well, you did defeat the hyena toad," Luci said.

"I escaped," Casey said.

"You smashed those baby skrabbits," Gloria said.

"Exactly," Casey said. "*Baby* skrabbits."

"Don't be so hard on yourself." Luci touched his elbow. "Other things matter besides fighting. For example...umm..."

"What did Ms. Crake mean about magic?" Casey said.

Luci glanced right and left. "She's one of the few teachers who talks about magic like it's important, something beautiful and strong, like a dance, that connects us to ancient, wild things." She threaded hair behind one ear. "Everyone knows that's silly."

"Is that you, Bootman?" A mushroom cloud of springy hair jounced as a boy moved toward them. Even with the hair, he was just a head taller than Gloria, which made him pretty small for his age. The moonlight shone on dark skin and curious eyes.

"First the Drooce face-punch, now the Butcher Beast," he said. "You don't run from a fight, do you, Grimes?"

Casey groaned. "Actually, I–"

"Nice work with that skewer. Did Crake tell you her plan to stop the *bugs*—they look a lot like insects, don't you think? I'd like to have something for the Trickery News."

"Hey Jake," Luci said.

"Hey Luciana." The boy stayed focused on Casey.

"Oh..." Casey said. "You're the one on the intercom."

Jake smiled. "Trickery News, always on the job. Got anything for me?"

"Let's see," Casey said. "I'm not sure Ms. Crake has a plan yet."

Jake looked disappointed. "So just the improv strategy for now. By the way, which battle school are you enrolled in, Grimes? They do a good job, teaching those sick skewer moves."

"Well...I..." Casey rubbed his nose.

"It's kind of prestigious," Luci said. "He prefers not to make a big deal about it."

"Gotcha." Jake raised one eyebrow. "No worries, at least not until I'm ready to run a profile. How 'bout an exclusive on your next stunt? We could do a full-length interview in the *Trickery Times*." He punched Casey's shoulder and walked away.

Casey stared at the stars, trying to calm down.

"He seems nice," Gloria said.

"You've gotta keep me away from him," Casey said. "An interview would ruin everything...it would be the end."

Luci frowned. "Yeah, we're gonna have to keep an eye on him. And you know who else?"

Everyone?

"Ms. Crake. I haven't had Air Creature Defense, but I've skimmed the curriculum, and Butcher Beasts are not covered. If she's our only hope, we're in trouble." Luci sat down on her sleeping bag and touched her swollen lip.

Casey pulled a blanket over his face.

Maybe Ms. Crake *was* trouble.

But what if she knew about the old ways of strength and honor... and magic?

CHAPTER 31
DAYLIGHT PROBLEMS

FOR THE FIRST time since he'd started sleeping in trees, Casey didn't rise and shine. As the sun got hot, he put his pillow on his head. It only made him sweat.

He kicked off his blanket and sat. His tailbone ached, his right hand was swollen, and one hip creaked. Casey stared into space, feeling cranky. He'd been thinking about something hopeful as he fell asleep, something that would probably seem stupid now...

That was it. Ms. Crake. Yeah, stupid.

Fingers snapped near his face. "Are you asleep sitting up?"

Luciana sat in her sleeping bag, pulling back her wild hair. Her bottom lip was less fat and her cuts were scabbing, but she looked like Casey felt—a little worse for wear.

The sleeping bag between them wriggled like a caterpillar.

"I can't get out," said a muffled voice.

"You're at the wrong end," Casey said.

The caterpillar bulged in the middle, and Gloria's head appeared.

"Phew," she said. "It was getting hot."

All around, kids were stretching, yawning, folding up blankets and sleeping bags. Casey, Gloria and Luci joined a crowd that streamed toward the storage lockers. Standing in line, Casey felt eyes on his back. He turned. Robert held a finger to his lips and mouthed, *Talk later.*

Casey nodded groggily. What could they possibly could have to talk about?

Ms. Crake stood at the front of the line, checking names on her clipboard. "Mason...Graham...baby girl Grimes, hi there, sweetie... West...slightly-lucky Grimes..."

"I'm starting to feel a little jealous," Luci said.

A few minutes later, Ms. Crake limped to the crow's nest. At the top of the ladder, she cleared her throat.

"Listen up!" she yelled. "I know you're all worried about Kimmie Blake and the monster attack. Good news from the infirmary! Kimmie is paralyzed..." Kids gasped and groaned. "But she'll recover use of her arms and legs in a few days. Good news from the battle-front, too. A vanguard of..." Crake glanced at her clipboard. "...one hundred and eighty-four skrabbits was decimated last night. No casualties."

Kids pumped their fists and cheered.

"Unfortunately," Ms. Crake said, "other skrabbit detachments are maintaining their positions on the Civilian border, so your parents won't be coming home quite yet. But they're doing a great job." She lowered her clipboard. "Breakfast in an hour."

Crake has clout, Casey thought. The kind of person who could help him and Gloria if she wanted. But asking her for help would mean admitting who he was. What if she hated Civilians? What if she hated cousin impersonators?

Casey shook his head to clear it. He needed a break from thinking.

He started down the ladder behind Gloria and Luci. Snatches of conversation drifted through the leaves.

"Clueless Civilians..."

"We fight the monsters, they just live their lives."

Casey focused on the Big Beech's swaying limbs. He pictured new arms grabbing more of the sky. His vision swirled green and brown—leaves unfolding, waving, fading when he looked away. But something seemed a little off. Too much brown, too many bare branches. Was the tree sick? He reached out to touch an imaginary limb and caught himself.

Get a grip, man.

He stepped off the ladder, rubbing his eyes. This was what happened when you got a horrible night's sleep, and people thought you were a great fighter, when actually you were an illegal Civilian who didn't know who to ask for help.

They stood in a sunny clearing. A dirt path curled away through the woods.

"Know where you are?" Luci said.

"Um, maybe," Gloria said.

"No idea," Casey said.

"Good." She edged toward the path. "That means I'll be the first one to the baths. Last one there's a rotten hag!" She laughed and ran down the trail.

"Did she just say, 'rotten *hag*?'" Casey said.

"Yes." Gloria pointed. "Look, there's a hag behind you!"

Casey looked. Gloria ran away giggling.

He gave her a decent head start.

Being a rotten hag was the least of his worries.

CHAPTER 38
TOO MANY SECRETS

KIDS SCRUBBED in the waterfalls and splashed in the pool. Voices bounced off the cave walls. "...bet my Pop killed twenty skrabbits by himself... you can chop them up for stew, after you defang them... Mom fought a king once, skrabbit the size of a kangaroo..."

Casey wondered what his parents were doing. Reclining in beach chairs? Sipping drinks with tiny umbrellas? Definitely not fighting fanged rabbits. He wondered what they'd think of this place. Maybe they'd be energized. More focused. With dozens of things to do (like stay alive) to keep them from being distracted.

Today was Tuesday, so he had three more days before they came home. Hopefully they were having a wonderful time...and would be in a great mood.

Casey found an open shower. He draped his boot-stamped shirt and smoky shorts over a stalagmite. Why would anyone think he belonged here? He couldn't even pack clean clothes.

He washed, jumped in the pool, and paddled toward the falls. Blurry kids splashed him through a curtain of mist, and he dove below the surface. The shouting and laughter faded. Warm and cold torrents rushed over him, rubbing his scalp, soothing his muscles.

Casey stayed down as long as he could. When he rose to the surface, Robert Pierce was waiting.

Casey's calm evaporated.

"Hey Boot." Robert held out a towel. "Can we talk?"

"I guess." Casey dried off, keeping tabs on Robert. His eye was a messy watercolor. Yellow had joined the black, blue and green.

"I just wanted…" Robert trailed off. "What I mean is…"

Casey finished drying his hair. "Thanks for the towel."

"Hell's bells." The fierce kid smacked the floor. "I'm just…" He gritted his teeth. "I'm…sorry. I was a jerk earlier. I…apologize." He seemed to be in physical pain.

Casey stared. If the boy had gut-punched him, he wouldn't have been surprised. But this was shocking. "It's ok," he said. "We didn't have the greatest start."

"Thanks," Robert said. "I appreciate it."

Casey retrieved his shirt and shorts and shoes. Wincing, he put them on. The baked boot-print scraped his chest.

Robert nodded at the shirt. "I was planning to get even, you know, but after that punch on Drooce, I had to like you." He grinned. "Plus you went right at that butcher bug—not pretty, but you got it done. *Tactics*. I love that stuff." He tapped his head. "Unconventional weapons, grit, plans of attack. Who needs magic?"

"Thanks," Casey said. "I try to keep it simple."

There it was again. No magic. In Sylvan Woods, the most magical place he'd ever been in his life. Acting like he agreed with Robert was maddening.

They walked through mist and wet kids to the cave opening. Casey checked for his crusty swamp clothes, and was happy to see they were gone. But he had the feeling he was forgetting something…

They walked down the path toward the campus.

"Where did you say you were from?" Robert said.

Casey ran a hand through his damp hair. What had Luci told Carrots in Land Creature Defense? All he could remember was the huge toad, throwing back its head and laughing. An answer popped into his brain. "Cumberland Chasm."

"Really?" Robert looked impressed. "What was it like, growing up around lava lizards?"

"Uh, a little weird," Casey said. "But you get used to it after a while."

Robert chuckled. "You're not a very good liar."

"Ohh..." The warmth from the baths left his skin.

"It's ok, I get it." Robert nodded. "You're embarrassed about your hometown. At least, that's one explanation. No big deal, everyone has a secret."

Jake thought he went to a big name school. Robert assumed his home was a blip on the map. The lies were getting hard to keep track of.

"Everyone has a secret?" Casey said.

"Well, just about."

Casey wondered what Robert's secret was. Even more important...

"What about Luci?" he tried to sound casual.

Robert smiled. "Oh, especially Luci. Her secret is kind of a big one. I'm surprised she hasn't told you."

"A big one, huh. Cool." Casey felt jittery, like he'd been drinking cola on an empty stomach. Suddenly he pictured hungry green eyes, snaky hair... *Get a grip, Grimes. You're a little old for nightmares.*

"Man, I'm starting to get hungry," he said.

"Me too." Robert gave him a sidelong glance. "Love that corned beef hash."

They pushed through the pines into Trickery. The leafy skyscrapers and gleaming amber tower stole Casey's attention. But only for a moment. Something kept rustling in his stomach.

"Er, could tell me Luci's secret?"

Robert stopped walking. "No, I really can't." He crossed his arms. "One of my rules is, No telling other people's secrets. If she hasn't told you...maybe she doesn't want you to know."

Heat rushed to Casey's face. "Good point," he said. "Sorry I asked."

"Maybe there's another explanation." Robert watched from the corner of his eye. "Are you really her cousin?"

Casey snorted. "Hah, puh-leaze. We just haven't seen each other in awhile."

He stuck his sweaty hands in his pockets and kept walking. Robert was right. Casey was not very good at lying. Unfortunately, Robert was very good at prying. Was there *anyone* he could trust?

CHAPTER 39
ROBERT HANGS AROUND

CASEY WALKED OVER TO THE GIRLS' table, Robert right behind him. He slid in across from Gloria and rubbed his sweaty palms on a napkin.

Robert hovered. "Mind if I join you?"

Luci shot him a look.

"I was just telling Casey..." Robert gripped a chair with white knuckles. He spoke through gritted teeth. "I was...a jerk yesterday and..." He squeezed his eyes shut. "I'm...sorry."

It looked almost as painful as it had in the cave.

Luci stared. "Is this really happening?"

"If you stop being mean," Gloria said, "you can sit with us."

Robert dropped into the chair next to Casey.

Why did his sister have to be so forgiving?

Luci rapped a fork against her mug. "Don't push your luck, Robert."

A bell tolled loudly. The cafeteria erupted in shouts and clatter, and they hurried to grab trays. Once again, Casey found himself stuck with Robert.

Try to act natural. Like you don't have a secret.

"I'm not sure Luci likes you very much," he said.

"You noticed, huh." Robert frowned. "Well, you may have heard, I can be a bit of a show-off. Hey, not so fast!" A kid tried to cut in front of them, but Robert grabbed his shoulders, spun him around and shoved him out of line. The boy stumbled and fell backward into a cart. It rolled into a table and flipped over. The kid lay in a pile of knives and forks, groaning.

"Cheater," Robert muttered. "What was I saying? Right, maybe I show off sometimes. Then again, Luci is just an unpredictable girl..."

Casey forced himself to look away from the flatware disaster. "Watch what you say about my cousin."

"Don't tell me she's never been mad at you."

Casey licked his lips. "She, uh, tried to beat me up a day ago."

Robert laughed and Casey joined in, only a second late.

They filled their plates. In the middle of the crowded hall, they stopped at a tree trunk table, ten feet wide. Pitchers of juice, pots of tea, and shining silver urns covered its surface. Casey poured himself a coffee. Maybe it would speed up his reaction times.

"So you really are her cousin?" Robert said at his shoulder.

Casey's hand jerked. Coffee sloshed the floor. "Will you quit with the cousin stuff? How many times do I need to answer that?"

"Ok, I'll lay off." Robert raised his hands. "I just like things out in the open, especially when we're at war. So where are you actually from?"

"Tell you what, Robert." Casey took a sip of steaming coffee, pretending it wasn't burning his tongue. "Since everyone has a secret, you tell me *yours* and I'll tell you where I'm from."

For a long, horrifying second, Casey was sure Robert would speak right up. Maybe he was afraid of high dives. Maybe he'd been dropped as a child. Instead, Robert shrugged.

"Fair enough," he said. "Let's go eat.

CHAPTER 40
RISING TENSIONS

EVERYONE TRIED THE BREAKFAST SPECIAL, even Gloria. Cooked in honor of the battlefront victory, it came with laurel leaves and toothpicks shaped like spears.

"I didn't expect roast skrabbit to be this good," Casey said.

Luci darted her eyes at Robert.

"In the past I've only had it fried," he added.

"Very tender for such a murderous animal," Luci said.

"Even better with gravy," Robert said.

"The best on breakfast pizza," Gloria said.

They were finishing up when a face appeared, a few inches higher than the table. A pencil stuck out of a cloud of high-flying hair.

"Morning, all," Jake said. "That skrabbit's not bad, is it? I was just wondering, Grimes—or do you prefer Bootman?—if you've come up with any new defense tactics. I'd like to put out a special news bulletin."

"Umm..." Casey felt his body tensing up. *Think, think, don't blow this.*

Jake held up a paper napkin. Sketched in pencil was a very realistic drawing of a Butcher Beast swooping toward a screaming stick figure.

"Good at creatures, not so good at people. Skewering the wings is brilliant, but what if you can't reach the wings, or you don't have a skewer handy. Soft underbelly, you think?"

"I...I'm working on it," Casey said.

Jake stuck the napkin in his pocket. "Maybe I'll check after lunch."

"I wouldn't count on a soft belly." Robert banged his mug down. "Judging by its anatomy, a butcher bug isn't much more than skin and bone. I bet the spine is a weak point. A spear to the neck, *shnick*, or a nice sharp sword to the eye, *sploosh*, that would do the trick." He stabbed a fried potato with his fork as the other kids stared. "What?"

Jake scribbled feverishly on his napkin. "What do you think, Grimes?" he said. "Does that check out?"

"Absolutely," Casey said. "Couldn't have said it better."

"Excellent," Jake said. "All right, catch you beast-killing kids later. Gotta get to class." He and his gravity-defying hair disappeared into the crowd.

Casey groaned silently.

"He's right about class," Luci said. "But what *are* we going to do about the butchers?"

"I'd suggest concealed weapons." Robert got to his feet.

Casey only had one idea, and he was beyond caring if it was stupid. "What about Ms. Crake? Maybe we could help her out."

Robert slid a blue-handled dagger from under his tray. "The Craken, are you insane? She's one of those magic-schmagic weirdos that can't let go of the past."

Luci eyed the knife as Robert walked away. "He has good taste in weapons for a crazy person." She turned to Casey. "Relying on Ms. Crake is not a great idea. Were you paying attention last night? She barely knows what a Butcher Beast is."

"But she saved you and Gloria," Casey said. "It can't hurt to talk to her."

"You're infuriating." Luci stood up. "C'mon Gloria, can you believe this guy?"

Gloria raised her hands, smiled, and shrugged.

Chairs screeched and trays clattered as kids packed up. Casey grabbed a spear toothpick and followed the girls out. If Ms. Crake was off limits, what was he supposed to do? Stand on a table and shout out to everyone who he was?

"We don't even know where the butcher bugs come from," Luci said, "or what they want, or why they've been gone for—oh creeps, if we don't hurry, I'll be late for Public Storytelling." She smoothed her hair as they quick-walked down the path. "I'm right about this, Casey." She tucked in her t-shirt. "We need a plan. The *school* needs a plan. With our parents gone, we need to be prepared."

"Right," Casey said. *But the plan needs some remotely possible outcome where Gloria and I don't end up dead or in a cage.*

"Can I count on your help?" Luci said.

"Hell's bells!" Casey snapped the toothpick in half as her mouth dropped open. "I've never even *seen* a monster until yesterday, remember." He flung the tiny broken spear into the woods. "I'm just *lucky*, so I'm not sure why you need my opinion. EVERYTHING IS A MYSTERY TO ME."

A few other kids looked over.

"Ok," Luci said. "No need to overreact."

"Fine. Great." Casey crossed his arms. "By the way, if Robert asks where we're from, don't answer."

"I won't tell that kid a thing." She fought a smile. "And even though you're mad, I hear what you're *not* saying. Thanks for helping us, Luci West. I'm so grateful for your assistance."

"Ugh." Casey tried to flick her arm but she dodged easily.

"I *am* right about the Butcher Beasts," Luci said. "Just wait and see."

CHAPTER 41
LESSONS FROM THE WILD WEST

AND SIR RAFAEL threw himself off the balcony, falling three stories onto Jeffrey, his waiting horse."

Luciana stood in front of the class, hands behind her back. "Goblins swarmed after him, screaming in rage. Arrows filled the air as Sir Rafael galloped toward the castle gate. A spear grazed Jeffrey's backside, urging the stallion to greater speed. Unfortunately, an indestructible drawbridge barred the way. They flew across the courtyard faster and faster, straight at the steel-reinforced door.

"'We'll break through or die trying!' shouted Sir Rafael.

"But the goblins were careless. A stray arrow ricocheted off the bridge's pneumatic release valve. With a hiss of escaping air, the enormous bridge thundered down. Sir Rafael galloped into the sunny mountain pass, shouting in victory. The goblins gnashed their teeth. After so many awful misadventures, their nemesis was free. The end."

Luci bowed.

The class clapped politely as she returned to her seat.

A mustachioed man with his leg in a cast stumped forward. "Thank you, Miss West. Seven minutes on the dot. Extra points for details about modern drawbridges. High octane ending. Constructive criticism..." He stroked his mustache. "The dungeon scene was a bit gruesome. Also, I question Sir Rafael's physical state after falling onto his horse. The story wobbled a bit between realism and fantasy. But overall, nicely done."

"Thank you, sir." Luci smiled.

"All right, Mr. Giddens, you're next..."

Luci turned to Casey and Gloria. "How was it?" she whispered.

"Yours was the very most amazing," Gloria said.

"It was great," Casey said. "I loved the dungeon scene."

Luci's face took on color. "Thanks, I think stories can be realistic as well as—oh, shhh."

Actually, Casey had missed most of the dungeon scene. It had involved an over-confident troll jailer, a goblet of poison, and a meat cleaver. It made him think about the Butcher Beast, all fangs and talons and stinger.

Luci's second class, Lessons from the Wild West, met on the fifth floor of the amber tower. The filtered light gave the room a golden glow. They pushed through swinging doors and crunched across a transparent floor dusted with sand and peanut shells.

"Do we get snacks in here?" Gloria said.

"Those are from our lesson on bar fights." Luci flicked a cashew off a stool and sat down. "Today I'm not sure *what* to expect." She took a compass, pocket knife and pliers from her backpack and lined them up on a wooden bar table. "This class has been very unpredictable, and just so you know, the teacher is kind of scary."

"I feel like you've said that before," Casey said.

The swinging doors banged open. "Good morning, heroes and desperadoes." A wrinkled old lady in a leather vest sauntered down the aisle. She seated herself behind a massive saloon-style bar. Beady eyes glittered under a black fedora.

"Good morning, Ms. Steele," a few kids said half-heartedly.

Her prickly gaze swept the room. "Who are the extras?"

"My cousins, Casey and Gloria Grimes," Luci said. "Just visiting."

"Nice day for a visit." Ms. Steele wrote down their names. "You tenderfeet don't know this, but final exams in the Wild West are legendary. No magical mumbo jumbo, just cold hard reflexes and skill. I hope you've absorbed your lessons. If not...well, it won't be pretty." She smiled like an elderly shark. "Equipment below your seats. Good luck." The teacher leaned back and crossed her ankles. Her boots tapped the dented bar as kids fumbled around.

"You've both got one too," Luci said.

Casey's fingers brushed a cardboard box. "Oh, ok. May as well join in."

He dug at the flaps, tearing them open. Shredding and ripping sounds filled the air.

"Oh my." Luci held up a boxy metal slingshot. "Uh oh..."

"ON YOUR MARKS," Ms. Steele shouted. "GET SET, GO!"

"Umm..." Luci gripped her slingshot and glanced around. Across the room, kids were doing the same. "There's no ammo in the box, so maybe it's already loaded?"

"Watch out!" Gloria squealed.

The double doors banged open. Three tall kids in black hats and bandanas jumped through, slingshots ready. "Welcome to the not-OK corral!" Laughing, they opened fire. *Sproing, sproing, sproing.* Shouts and splashes filled the air.

Green goo splattered Casey's stool.

"Crawl for that corner," Luci yelled.

Shots whistled overhead, drumming the walls like green rain. Luci shoved a bar table over with a crash. She dragged a stool against the legs, and they ducked behind the barricade.

Kids returned fire, but several were already dripping like swamp creatures. Luci sighted over the barricade and thumbed her sling. *Sproing.* One of the bandits yelled, spun in a circle and went down, clutching his heart. A round of return fire exploded over their fort, spraying them with emerald mist. Casey thumbed his sling release, but nothing happened.

"Turn off the safety," Luci gasped. "And be careful, you only have six shots."

"We see you in there, missy," a black hat shouted. "Just you wait!"

On the far side of the room, a kid rose from behind a stool, but she was too slow. Goo splashed, and she stumbled backward with an angry yell.

"These guys are *too* good." Luci fired again, elastic whizzing forward and back, but her paintball smacked a wall. The two remaining desperados fanned out. Crouching behind desks, they picked kids off. Only a few were left.

Gloria sighted down her sling. "Splash! Splash!" she yelled, but nothing happened.

Casey found the button he guessed was the safety. He clicked it to red.

One of the outlaws dove for a new stool, and Casey thumbed the trigger. Ooze splattered a chair three feet from his target. The masked kid stuck his head out, and Casey flicked again. This time he hit a backpack. "I'm terrible at this."

"Four shots left." Luci mopped her forehead. "Wait until he takes aim at Isabella over there...now!" They shot and missed at the same time. Across the room, Isabella took a goo-grape in the gut and went down.

"They're ruthless!" Luci said.

Two kids were holed up against Ms. Steele's bar, shielding themselves with stools and school supplies. One of them slid a notebook aside and fired.

"When the bad guys move in, one will be in our crossfire," Luci said.

A tall, bandana-wearing kid scrambled across the aisle on his hands and knees. Casey's shot zinged down the row and burst against the teacher's bar. Luci did better—the outlaw howled and went down, grabbing his rear.

"I ain't dead yet, you yellow-bellied cowards!" He dragged himself up the aisle.

Casey took careful aim and thumbed his sling.

Mist showered the fort by Ms. Steele.

"Ouch!" A kid yelped and flopped around inside.

"You shot one of our allies," Luci said.

"Holy creeps," Casey said. "How is that even possible?"

The disabled outlaw in the aisle started laughing.

Luci groaned, sighted, and shot his hat off. "One paint ball left. We're in trouble."

The surviving kid crawled under the bar, trying to escape, but that left him vulnerable. He slumped in a green puddle, shaking his head.

"Is it over?" Gloria whispered.

"Not yet." Luci crouched even lower. "He's got unlimited ammo and he knows we're almost out. That means he'll attack any—ack!"

Green goo dripped from fingers. "I'm not a very good shot with my left. Here, take it."

Casey grabbed the slippery slingshot.

The outlaw jumped out of cover and sprinted up the aisle.

"NOOO!" screamed Luci.

"Get him, Casey," screamed Gloria.

Casey's shot whistled between the boy's legs. Then he was leaning over their hideout, chuckling nastily. He stuck his sling inside, right at Luci's nose. "Time to pay for defying us, you little—"

Sproing.

"Hey!" Green goo trickled down the outlaw's chest. "Holy creeps," he muttered. "I was sure you were out of ammo."

Slow clapping rang out from the front of the room as Casey, Luci and Gloria stood up, rubbing their knees.

"Thanks, Casey," Luci whispered. "I've been taking too many hits lately."

Ms. Steele stood behind her enormous barrier. "Looks like we have three survivors. So if the Grimes-West gang would lower their weapons and step forward..."

"Yesss!" Luci said.

Paint-splashed kids clapped weakly as they pushed the fort

apart and came out, smiling. Outside the windows, a crowd had gathered. Students shoved their grinning faces through the greenery, waving and smiling at the students in the amber room.

Ms. Steele smiled too. Her toothy grin got even bigger as she raised a triple-decker slingshot from behind her bar.

"Trust no one," she snarled.

"AAEEII! NOO!" Kids shrieked in horror, but none of them as loud as Casey and Luci. A flood of lime gook blasted them backwards.

Ms. Steele snickered, then a shocked expression appeared on her face. Ooze splashed the wall behind her. On the right. On the left. A third shot got her between her eyes. Paint dripped off her chin. Her black fedora floated to the floor.

"I win!" Gloria stood at the back of the room, slingshot raised. "It took me a while to, um, turn it on."

The spectators burst into wild applause.

CHAPTER 42
MYTHIC HISTORY

OUTSIDE THE WILD WEST, a student assistant handed out icepacks and wet rags.

"Best last stand I've ever seen." He gave Gloria a fist bump. "Everyone's supposed to die, you know."

"We figured that out," Luci snapped.

She and Casey looked like they'd taken a bath in lime jello. The triple-decker slingshot blast stung...but the injustice felt even worse.

"If I didn't score an A, so help me..." Luci said. "C'mon Casey, let's raid lost and found again. Would you care to come with us, little hero?"

"Of course I'll come," Gloria said. "Just don't touch me."

Casey made a grab for her as she ran down the hall, laughing.

The selection at Lost and Found had gotten worse. After a shower, Casey pulled on polka dotted red swim trunks and a striped purple shirt. *Your basic court jester outfit.* No flip flops, though. Never again. He rinsed off his tennis shoes and they faded from jade to mint.

Luciana didn't look any better. She tugged at an oversized blue blouse, trying to make it less billowy. Encased in tight yellow jeggings, her legs looked like pencils under a lampshade. She'd probably never worn so much color in her life. They looked at each other and shook their heads. He handed over her pendant, mostly clear of streaks.

"What a stupid final exam," Luci said.

"Designed to punish the winners," Casey said.

"I thought it was amazing," Gloria said.

Casey wished he was still covered in ooze so he could grab her.

At lunch, they ignored the stares of kids around them. Jake McGusty's voice crackled over the speakers.

"Good afternoon, students," he said. "We've got an update on Kimmie Blake's condition: Now she can move her fingers and toes, and form short sentences like, 'No more soup.' Well done, Kimmie! Hopefully you'll be able to eat solid foods again soon. Jake for Trickery News, over and out."

Casey's mood improved as he ate a half-pound cheeseburger with skrabbit gravy. "When's the next time we're going to see Ms. Crake?"

"We'll see her soon enough," Luci said. "But if you take my advice, you won't say a word."

In Luci's next class, Medicinal Flower Arrangements, students collected blossoms, leaves and herbs from a ground-level garden. The only excitement came when a girl confused cayenne pepper for saffron. Her partner ran to the creek, gagging, and ducked his head underwater. Otherwise, things went smoothly.

Casey was wondering if he could talk to Ms. Crake without giving himself away, feel her out a little—when something grazed the back of his neck. Cool, crisp, *big*. He slapped, expecting a super-mosquito. Instead, an oak leaf rustled in his palm.

Suddenly, he had an idea.

In Luci's last class, Mythic History, they sat in a cool, echoey room. Dozens of sculptures lined the walls. Ms. Crake stood up front, checking off names as students took their seats.

"Hey, it's *her*," Casey said.

Luci rolled her eyes.

He could say something to Ms. Crake right now...except she looked like she meant business.

"Put your notes away. Take out your pens and paper." Crake sat in a high-backed sculpture that looked like a throne. Dressed in black, she was a human-shaped hole in the white marble. "I've got eyes all over this classroom. Asking your characters for help will not be tolerated. Three pages minimum. When your assignment approaches, please begin."

She tapped a small silver bell on one arm of her throne. Silence filled the room. As second and third notes chimed, sculptures started moving...

A beautiful woman wearing a wreath glided down an aisle. A huge wolf-dog turned from a window and showed its teeth. A warrior leaned on a spear, wincing and favoring his left heel. Casey couldn't keep track of all the movement. A massive, long-bearded man with a trident strode toward them.

"I'll take Neptune, I'll take Neptune," Luci whispered, but he lumbered past.

Instead, she got a tall, curly-haired man with a silly grin. He stopped by her desk and struck a pose. "Of course, I get Paris." Luci glared at the statue and picked up her pencil. "Idiot who started the Trojan War, he *would* choose me."

The Paris sculpture flexed its biceps.

"Is this magic?" Gloria said.

"Shhh, not so loud." Luci licked her pencil. "Of course it's magic, Crake doesn't care about trends. It's probably the only good thing about her." She started scribbling.

This back and forth about magic was so confusing.

Casey felt glad a marble character wasn't looming over him. Time passed very slowly under the gaze of those unblinking eyes...

When Luci smacked her pencil down, he jumped. At the front of the room, she handed her essay to Ms. Crake. One corner of the teacher's mouth curved up when she saw Gloria and Casey.

"Hi Ms. Crake." He pictured Luci rolling her eyes.

"Hey there, a-little-lucky," Crake said. "Hope you're staying out of trouble."

He was a second away from spilling his guts right there. "I'm trying my best," he wanted to say. "But I'm struggling and I could really use your advice. Do you have a minute for a serious question?"

But more students were lining up behind him, and it was too quiet, under the eyes of stone villains and heroes. Later, maybe that evening.

He'd talk to Ms. Crake then.

CHAPTER 43
ONE MORE PAGE

THE AFTERNOON WAS MOSTLY GONE when they said goodbye to Luci. "See you in a couple hours?" she said. "I'd invite you home, but I don't have any clothes that would fit you."

She and Casey looked at each other. Their lost and found outfits were more hideous side by side than apart. She wrinkled her nose and he snorted. They said goodbye, and Casey and Gloria followed the trail to the Old Oak.

"What about visiting Ms. Jones?" Gloria said.

"She's busy cleaning our house. Let's not bother her."

Casey clipped them in, and they climbed to the fortress.

At the top, Casey slipped into the housekeeping closet. Just as he'd hoped, he found a change of clothes, folded on a shelf. Neatly creased. Clean-smelling.

Remember when you were that person?

Ever since he'd met Luci and become visible, his life was total chaos.

When he came out, Gloria was snoring on a blanket in a patch of shade. She'd changed out of her perfectly clean outfit into another one. Her tee said, I Dream of Unicorns.

Casey believed it.

He returned to the closet, and scanned the cluttered shelves. The mess was intricate. And ancient. He stacked and shifted, trying not to break anything. After an hour, the tiny room looked even messier than before. He'd found a few small weapons, a sewing machine, a box of flares...

Maybe if he threw everything over the railing.

He kicked the flare box, and something rustled underneath. Casey pushed and shoved. On the floor, half crumpled, lay a single page. Just one. Dusty and brittle, stained with blueish ink. One side was blank, but on the other...

...APPLY TO THE GUARDIANS, KEEPERS OF THE OLD WAYS, CHAMPIONS OF THE MAGIC. LET THEM WEIGH THE PETITIONS, AND THOSE JUDGED WORTHY WILL BE SYLVAN, NO MATTER BIRTH OR BLOOD. FOR WHAT MAKES ONE SYLVAN BUT A LOVE FOR ALL THINGS WILD AND ALIVE?

Casey read it again. And again. A smile spread across his face.

After a blur of ink, at the bottom of the page, he read:

...YET WOULD DO WELL TO FEAR THE SYLVAN WATCH, FOR IN THIS AS IN MANY THINGS, THEY AND THE GUARDIANS ARE OPPOSED.

Well who cares? He'd found his answer. There was a way in. A way to belong. Which raised the question, who in Sylvan Woods was a guardian? The answer was obvious.

"Ms. Crake," he breathed.

Heart racing, he slid *A Sylvan Handbook* off its shelf. He placed the missing page inside. A tattered, ink-stained piece of hope.

As he stood there holding the handbook, a strange smell drifted through the closet. Musty, even rotten. He and Gloria should've been more careful with their picnic basket. But there'd be time to clean later.

"Hubba hoy, anybody home?" Luci called. "Oh, hello Gloria."

Casey stuck the slender *Handbook* in his back pocket and hurried out the door.

Time to make his move.

CHAPTER 44
STRIKE ONE

SEVERAL STORIES BELOW, the woods swirled with shadows. They'd left the Old Oak and headed over the treeway toward the Big Beech. A side trail led them over the hollow as the western sky shimmered. They stood at a tangle of treeways, arguing.

"If you're so sure Crake's a bad idea," Casey said, "why haven't you suggested any other ones?"

"Look." Luci tossed her head. "When my parents get back, I'll ask them how we can make you a Sylvan. And the regular teachers—someone must know about the old path to citizenship."

"I already told you, someone does," Casey said. "And it's Crake. Besides, you don't like any teachers. And I'll be gone by the time your parents get back. Gone for good."

Luci frowned. "There are reasons I keep my head down. Besides, I don't know which sleepover Ms. Crake is supervising. The teachers probably toss coins. She might have the night off. Of course, she's pretty mobile, even with that limp, so she probably doesn't get to. Creeps, I don't know why I said that."

"It's because you think out loud," Casey said. "Let's go find her."

Luci's necklace lit up her displeased face, giving her an unusually wild shadow. "If you have to interview that harpy, let's check the

Pavilion," she said. "We'll take the aqueduct through the Mudlands."

"Perfect."

They followed a ropeway that angled down like a gigantic strand of spider web.

What if Crake turns you down? Casey thought. *No, that's not an option.*

"Hey Luci, how do you keep your bearings?" He had to distract himself.

"We'll get you a map eventually," Luci said. "*If* your crazy idea works."

Great, so much for being distracted.

"What's on the map?" Gloria said.

"Glad you asked, Glo." Luci stopped glaring at Casey. "You've got Lesser and Greater Trick 'n' Trap Woods, Thistle Fort, the Legbreak Slopes and of course the Mudlands, where the gryphon almost got you. Speaking of, let's hope Sebastien and Tonya aren't set loose anytime soon."

"I keep meaning to ask," Casey said, "what happens to kids who break the rules?"

"Oh, whatever horrible task needs doing most urgently." Luci shrugged. "Mucking out beast enclosures is a big one. Once there was a tiger rat infestation in the sewers and kids got sent down for detention...now that was unpleasant."

Sometimes it was hard to tell if she was joking.

Their treeway touched down by a high stone bridge. It jutted from the hillside into the gloom. "It's an aqueduct, an old water channel," Luci said. "I spotted a Razor Wing up here once, but monsters mostly leave it alone."

Mostly? When Casey tossed a pebble off, he counted one-thousand, two-thousand, three, before it splashed. The aqueduct arched through the murk like an old, cracked sidewalk. Finally, they stepped off in a dim corner of the orchard. Through the gap in the stone wall, the green field blazed with light. Luci's shadow streamed and curled behind her.

Casey jabbed at it with a finger and felt very silly.

Focus, Grimes. Keep it together.

"What a beautiful tent!" Gloria said.

A red and gold big top stood in the center of the field. Wind gusted its three-story peaks. Kids moved in and out under its embroidered flaps. Casey imagined knights sitting around a fire, polishing armor and roasting a wild boar.

They crossed the field and ducked inside. Kids slouched in bean-bags, playing board games. A few flicked through textbooks, desperately taking notes.

"Cramming for finals." Luci shook her head.

"Hey look." Casey pointed. His hand shook, just a little.

A figure dressed in black leaned on a tent pole, scanning the field.

Luci frowned.

This is it. Be smart. Be honest...if it's possible to be both.

They started forward, circling a ring of beanbags, and the person turned. A tired-looking man in black jeans and a hooded sweatshirt. His dark skin didn't hide the circles under his eyes.

"Oh, it's a *different* teacher dressed in black," Casey said.

"It's Mr. Chandler," Luci said. "Just off bed-rest. Poor guy, he doesn't look very good."

"Great, where now?" Casey felt irritated...and relieved.

They circled back around the beanbags.

"Didn't you just come this way?" someone said.

"Hey, it's that little girl who plunked the teacher."

"That was awesome, let's say hi."

Beans crunched as kids floundered to their feet.

"Sorry Gloria." Casey tugged her away. "Gotta keep moving."

"Couldn't I just say hi?" Gloria looked back and waved.

"We're running out of daylight." Luci took her other hand and pulled.

"See you later," Gloria called.

The sky above the field was charcoal, streaked with yellow.

"I guess we could try the Sighing Sycamore," Luci said. "I have the feeling you may not like it as much."

"As long as Crake's there," Casey said, "I don't even care if it's haunted."

CHAPTER 45
STRIKE TWO

THEY CUT across Trickery's empty campus. Pitch black shadows loitered under arches. Fireflies floated like dying sparks.

"The Sighing Sycamore's a bit of a hike," Luci said. "It's not as popular as the Big Beech, don't ask me why."

"Why?" Casey said.

She flashed a smile. "It's kind of a tree-monster hybrid—don't worry, not a bad monster. I like it."

"Because?" Casey said.

"It's one of a kind." A branch skimmed her face, and she tugged her headband back in place.

"Hey, look at all the frogstools," Gloria said.

"Toadstools, you mean," Casey said.

But she was right. An army of pale green mushrooms poured over the trail and through the forest as if following an invisible stream bed.

"Strange." Luci knelt and brushed one with her fingertips. "I can't remember seeing these before." She smelled her hand and made a face. "Remind me not to eat them."

The trail twisted through leaning slabs of rock. In the glow of

Luci's pendant, they stepped into a clearing. The Sighing Sycamore towered overhead.

"Holy creeps." Casey hated to admit it, but the tree was even taller than his oak. Knotted roots made a base like a satellite tower, and there was something...unsettling...about the tree. He wanted to climb it. At the same time, he wanted to back away. A heavy chain dangled, creaking through a pulley on the ground, rattling up through bent limbs. Dim lights hung far overhead.

"Totally harmless," Luci said. "I'm not sure why kids are scared to touch it."

"I'm not scared." Gloria hugged herself.

"How does this work?" Casey stared at the escalator-chain.

Luci picked up a wooden slat that looked like a very short broomstick. "Slide it through the chain...step on...and up you go."

She floated into the night. In a few seconds, all they could see was the pendant's glow, rising through the darkness.

Gloria didn't move. "This is kind of creepy."

"Want to ride with me?" Casey said.

"Yes."

He kept a hand on her shoulder as they stepped onto their ride. Wind gusted through crooked branches. Gloria hugged his waist.

"No wonder kids are scared of this tree," she said. "*Other* kids."

Murky lights got closer. They swayed through a metal frame and stepped off, their half-broomstick clattering to the floor. The deck was rusty woven metal. Steel saplings formed the railing, small carved creatures hiding in their branches.

But no one was there. No kids, no sounds. Not even a fire, just the pale glow of tiny lights. Casey jumped as someone touched his arm.

"Um, sorry guys," Luci said. "I thought there was a sleepover here, but it must have been last night. We could stay a few minutes if you like. It's a great place for studying...and thinking...and being alone at night."

Casey's throat felt dry. "We'd better keep trying to find Ms. Crake."

"Well sure." Luci raised her eyebrows. "I just thought you might want to rest a minute. The view of the moon is really nice."

Gloria took Casey's hand. "Let's go back down."

The tree groaned and Casey's scalp tingled. Was the Sycamore speaking? If so, it was saying something frightening. He shoved his free hand in his pocket, not sure what he was hoping to find. Matches, maybe. Or courage.

"Looking for something?" Luci said. "You can use my pendant if you get a little closer."

A switch clicked in Casey's head, and his body tensed up. *Warning, warning, something's not right.* He backed away, pulling Gloria with him.

"Boys can be so stubborn." Luci's shadow twisted behind her.

Metal bit into Casey's back as he hit the railing. He raised a hand as Luci stepped forward. "Stop."

Her dark eyes widened. "What's the matter?"

"Um. Well, everyone has a secret, right?" He swallowed. "What's yours? You could get expelled for helping us sneak around, but you keep helping us. Are you—are you..." He had no idea exactly what he was trying to say.

"Am I what?" Luciana froze, one hand touching her hair.

He had to say something. A sliver of nightmare flashed through his mind.

"A...a monster?"

Luci's mouth fell open half an inch, then her face tightened up and her hands balled into fists. "How could you say that?" She took a step toward him. "How could you?"

"The dark." His words jumbled out. "The empty tree, the ghost lights, nobody here."

All of a sudden, Luci was in his face. "*You're* the one who said we were related. Now *I'm* in trouble for being nice?" She pushed at his chest.

Casey's shoulders sagged. "I don't get it," he said. "It doesn't make sense. Why are you being so nice to us? Why would you want to be friends with *me*?"

Gloria squeezed his knees.

Luci took a step back. Casey had the strange, silly idea she was about to cry. If anyone should be crying, it was him.

"I really am sorry," he said.

Luci looked down. "I like you and Gloria, it's that simple." She tucked a curl behind one ear. "Can't we be friends without checking lots of boxes?"

"We *are* friends," Gloria said.

"I'd love that." Casey swallowed. "But I just don't understand how—"

"Shut up," Luci said. "You can be so stupid. I guess we both can."

Gloria chose that moment to give Luci a hug. Casey had no choice but to follow. Her hair tickled his ear. Nothing bad happened. The hug was actually nice. Far away, a hollow crack rang out over Trickery. It could have been an axe handle, smacking a tree trunk or a kid's dense skull.

Luci glanced at the starry sky. "We've got to check into a sleepover pronto, before we get picked up for straggling."

CHAPTER 46
KNOCK KNOCK

CRICKETS CHIRPED and toads croaked as they hiked toward Trickery.

"Woooo, woooo." Luci glided her fingers through the dark, haunting them.

"Very funny." Casey pretended his skin wasn't still tingling.

On the campus, they paused in an empty square. "I wonder where the other sleepovers are," Luci said. "Obviously I memorized the wrong schedule."

A fountain bubbled nearby. Tuneless whistling came from an alley off the courtyard.

"Oh no." Casey knew that sound.

They ducked behind the fountain as Old Knock strolled into the square, scratching his back with his axe handle. He looked right and left, then sauntered down another alley.

"Thank goodness he didn't smell us," Luci whispered.

"Now what?" Casey inched his head over the fountain.

"Do you think they have s'mores at that campfire?" Gloria said.

They followed her outstretched hand. A patch of flame blazed to the north. Smaller dots burned nearby.

"The campsite on Legbreak Slope," Luci said. "You're a genius, Glo."

Casey had climbed the ridge with Gloria on his back and Old Knock on his trail. It wasn't an experience he wanted to repeat, especially after dark.

"Let's take the moving treeway," he said.

"Good idea." Luci stood. "We should be safe if we're quiet..."

They hurried across the square and into another alley. Halfway down, flat whistling reached them from the other end.

Casey's heart revved up a notch. "How many places can he be at once?"

They doubled back and down another path, between higher buildings. This one was darker. They slowed to a walk, feeling their way.

"Kind of cluttered," Luci whispered.

"Watch out," Gloria breathed. "That looks like a big mousetra—"

Snap!

"Ow, ow, my toes," Luci whisper-shrieked.

"WHO'S THERE?" Old Knock's shape appeared. "Ready or not, here I come!"

He bounded into the shadows.

Suddenly, Casey knew exactly where he was going. They rushed in the opposite direction, hands outstretched, Luci whimpering. Behind them, pottery crashed and Knock cursed. They came out on a wide moonlit path and Luci collapsed, prying at a tiger rat trap on her toes.

"Wow, that really hurt." She blinked away tears.

"Quick." Casey pulled her up and they limped away.

The trail branched left, through a grove of saplings.

"There's Mythic History," Casey said.

"DON'T THINK YOU'VE GIVEN ME THE SLIP!" Knock shouted.

Gloria's violet eyes got huge.

"Just leave me," Luci gasped. "I'm slowing you down."

"Not a chance." Casey took her arm. "The rope lift is straight ahead."

Gloria grabbed Luci's waist and they hobbled like contestants in a five-legged race. Sprint-limping past cedars and marble, stagger-dashing to the platform.

"YOU THREE AGAIN? YOU'RE DEAD SKRABBITS!"

At the stairs, Luci's eyes darted right and left. She shrugged free, took a deep breath and charged. "Ow, ow, ow, ow, ow!"

Casey winced. He and Gloria ran after her. When they reached the top, Luci was limping onto the lift. The creak of the rope was music to his ears. As they glided away over the treetops, a dark figure shook his fist at the bottom of the tower.

"THIS ISN'T OVER!"

"If he ever sees our faces…" Casey ran a hand through his hair, thinking about tiger rats, sewers, or worse. But what could possibly be worse than… Better not go there.

"I'm sorry, poor little toes," Luci groaned.

"Why are you wearing sandals?" Casey couldn't see her face in the dark. He didn't have to. It was The Night Casey Grimes Says Everything Wrong.

"Because they're pretty," she snapped. "And I never get to wear them and we're supposed to be relaxing on a sleepover, not running for our lives. Also, my feet needed air after all that green goo."

Suddenly, they were laughing.

"This has got to be some kind of record," Luci gasped. "We've escaped Old Knock twice in forty-eight hours. I don't think it's ever been done."

They sailed through the sky, brushing pine needles under the stars.

"We're artists of, um, escaping." Gloria giggled.

"Terror is inspiring," Casey said.

"You know what sounds good?" Luci lifted her swollen toes off the lift and frowned. "A mug of cocoa, a blanket and a board game."

Casey opened his mouth to agree—but the screaming began.

They jumped—a dangerous reflex, forty feet above the ground. Gloria floundered into a guide rope. Casey see-sawed on the main cable. Luci came down on her black-and-blue toes with a little shriek.

The screams were wild and desperate. On the ridge, small forms ran back and forth like terrified ants. Casey saw a shape he recognized. The waspish shadow hovered over the bonfire and darted after a child. Another dove from the sky, swooping past the flames.

"Oh no," Gloria said. "Butcher Beasts."

"What do we do?" Luci shivered.

"I knew I should've packed a real weapon," Casey said.

"We can't get off," Gloria whispered. "We can't get away."

The lift swayed higher and higher. It was like watching a disaster unfold, far away on tv. But the distance was shrinking fast. Casey unzipped his pack and pulled out his mom's weed digger, stuffed in days before. All of a sudden, there was a dead weight in his chest.

I hope you're having a good time, Mom. I hope we get to see you again. He clutched the metal shank with its orange plastic handle.

Up on the slope, the bonfire was total chaos. The closer they got, the more horrible and *real* it looked. Dark forms hovered and dove. A sharp voice shouted, "Take cover under the trees! They don't like the—" The voice was cut short.

A kid yelled, "Skewers! Skewers!"

The lift rose higher, level with the ridge, and evergreens hid the campsite. The pulley *squeak-squeaked* nearby. They'd reached the end of their ride.

CHAPTER 47
STRIKE THREE

WHAT IF WE *just climb back on?* For a few seconds, there was nothing in the world Casey wanted more. But being caught on the lift by butchers would be awful. Besides, he couldn't just run. Sylvan Woods was no place for cowards.

"Gloria, stay close to me," he said. "We've got to help."

"Right." Luci took a deep breath.

Ashes floated to earth as they stumbled up the ridge. The air smelled burnt. Whimpering kids ran past. "Get out, they're coming!"

"The lift's not safe," Casey yelled.

But the students crouched on the rope, creaking into darkness. Crashing sounds came from Legbreak Slope. Kids were running for it, escaping any way they could.

Casey tried to think of what Robert would do. He'd find a weapon, of course. Casey picked up a bare white branch under a tree. He tossed it to Luci and scanned the ground for another.

A droning buzz filled the air. Part of the sky disappeared, stars blacked out. Moonlight gleamed on a hungry face and dead black eyes.

Oh no. Casey waved his tiny weed digger. "Stay away!"

He hit the ground and rolled as the butcher dove. Bony talons tore the earth. When Casey jumped up, claws dug into his shoulder, dragging him toward a jagged mouth. There wasn't even time to scream. He closed his eyes as something ripped. Hot liquid splashed his face. *Now* someone was screaming—a hair-raising wail—and Casey fell.

The ground jolted his eyes open.

Luci stood next to him, black blood dripping from her stick.

Shrieks came from overhead.

"They have...weak eyes," she gasped.

I'm not dead. It's not over.

The monster spun in circles above them, scratching at its face. It veered sideways into a tree and crashed like a broken helicopter.

"Take this." Luci held out her branch. "I'll find another." She slipped away.

Gloria threw her arms around him, sniffling.

"I'm ok." Pain leaked down his arm from his shoulder, and he wondered how mangled it was. Blood splotched his shirt. "We just need weapons before—"

Dzzzzzz. More black shapes whirred across the stars. He shoved Gloria under a pine tree and threw himself after her. They huddled under velvety needles as two more butchers circled. A third hovered by the tree, jabbing the air with its stinger.

Gloria's whole body was shaking. He put an arm around her, a hand over her mouth. The monsters flew downhill, following the lift. Overhead, the dying wasp thrashed in the tree. Its blood dripped down, turning the needles black.

"C'mon, Gloria." He crawled out, tugging his sister. Luci shoved her way out of the woods, dragging a long, forked stick. They looked at each other, breathing hard.

"You saved me," Casey said.

"Thank me later."

They moved along the rocky hill. Spilled backpacks and broken branches marked the scene of the attack. Casey wished he could look away.

No bodies. Not yet.

Kids huddled by the bonfire, holding skewers and torches.

"Hey, it's Grimes." Jake McGusty stepped over. "Bootman, where you been?" His shirt was splashed with black blood, and his voice sounded different. The energy was gone.

"Didn't plan on actually fighting these things," he said. "I just wanted to write about them. Guess we should've known better, right? High altitude, another huge bonfire. So much for investigative reporting. Wish you'd got here sooner, man."

Six dead butchers littered the camp site. Two had smoldering wings, and one sizzled in the bonfire. The others appeared to have broken spines.

"The hurt kids are under the trees." Jake pointed. "That's what Ms. Crake said to do before she...well, see for yourself."

Silent kids stepped aside. On the ground, Ms. Crake's body looked more twisted than usual. Staring into the night sky, she shivered.

"Oh no." Casey's knees hit the dirt. "It's me, Casey Grimes. Can you hear me?"

Her shoulders twitched but her eyes stayed far away.

"I'm so sorry," Casey said. "I wanted your help. I didn't know..."

Didn't know you needed help from me.

"Not many kids liked Crake..." Jake shook his head. "Man, that'll change now. She killed a bunch of wasps, before we saw 'em coming. Then one of them grabbed her while a second one..." He shuddered. "I just hope they didn't...that she's not..."

Cold fingers snatched Casey's wrist.

"Grimes..." Ms. Crake's gaze burned his face. "The lucky one... finally here."

"It's me." Casey forced himself to look at her.

"You seem...have a knack..." Her voice faded in and out. "Kill... stop them...find...bones..." Her breaths got shallow. "Bones...in the woods." Her jaw relaxed. Her face looked surprisingly young. Her fingers fell from Casey's wrist.

CHAPTER 48
ON OUR OWN

MS. CRAKE'S eyes froze like sapphires. She didn't say another word. Casey's insides felt frozen too.

"Oh no, oh no..." A girl next to him sobbed.

"We've got to get her off the hilltop," he said.

"Why, she's barely old enough to be someone's mom." Luci hung her head.

Jake swallowed. "Uh, most of the hurt kids can move." He motioned to the skewer-carrying crowd. "C'mon, let's get 'em." He and his crew moved away.

"We'll have to carry her." Casey's voice sounded strange in his own ears.

"Nothing is moving in the sky." Gloria stood with her back to the fire, searching the night. Casey jumped to his feet and hugged her. Gloria took a sobbing breath, and the ice in his chest turned to water.

A few minutes later, a crowd of kids moved toward the lift. The skewer patrol walked on the edges and the injured kids stumbled along inside. They had cuts and gashes and clothes splashed black and red. Everyone could move, but not without lots of wincing and groaning. Everyone except Ms. Crake.

Casey and Luci carried her, hands locked under her back. Gloria held her feet. Wobbling and staggering, it seemed like they'd never reach the lift. Everyone else was gone, creaking away down the slope, by the time they figured out how to keep Crake upright. Their awkward human chain lurched right and left.

"Hold on! Look out!"

"Please, no more wind," gasped Luci.

On the platform, Jake was standing guard with a skewer. They stumbled off and lowered the teacher's crooked body.

"Have a good sleep," Gloria whispered.

Casey didn't have the heart to set her straight. He slumped on the deck, pressing a hand to his bloody shoulder.

Down the path from Trickery, lights moved closer. Feet clattered on the metal stairs and the tall, dark shape of Mr. Chandler bounded up, holding a torch. He threw back his hood and put a hand to his side, panting. His face was tired, but his eyes flashed. "You kids ok?"

"We're fine..." Luci said. "But Ms. Crake..."

Chandler knelt by Ms. Crake. He handed his torch to Casey and lifted her gently.

"Infirmary's open," he said over his shoulder. "Cafeteria's open. Everyone sleeps in the pavilion tonight, get there as soon as you can." He ran back down the stairs, carrying Crake's unmoving body.

Jake sat down, clutching his ten foot skewer. "What in creeps is going on? Monsters falling from the sky, kids getting torn up, teachers going down."

Luci massaged her swollen foot. "Oow." Her toes were black and blue and twice their normal size. "We're on our own now, with no clue what to do."

That killed their conversation. They were halfway down the stairs before Casey remembered it wasn't exactly true.

CHAPTER 49
THE TRAIL GROWS DARK

AT THE MYTHIC HISTORY BUILDING, Jake said goodbye and hurried after his friends. "Gotta help them get their heads right," he said. "They're pretty shaken up..."

They winced their way through Trickery. Teachers waited at intersections, identifying each kid who passed.

"Which way to the infirmary?" Casey said.

Luci made a face. "I feel like such a wimp, but it really does hurt. And you're hurt too."

He touched his aching shoulder.

The infirmary was a long stone hut with a tile floor and a hearth. A woman in a smock and mask opened the door, leaning on crutches. Sharp black eyes and a tied-back pouf of curly hair were all they could see of her.

"Come in, I'm nurse Diaz." She motioned them to chairs by the fire. "Have some tea. I'll just finish up this bit of sewing..."

A kid groaned on a padded table. A hanging lamp shone on a rather gruesome wound across his chest. Firelight danced off a needle as Nurse Diaz leaned in. "There, there, let's get this over with..."

"Survival Sewing." Luci shuddered.

Casey's shoulder began to feel much better. Probably just a scratch. He got up and poured himself some tea. Luci grabbed the mug from his hands.

"Maybe I don't need medical attention." She gulped the greenish liquid. "There's not much you can do for toes. And others have worse injuries. I'll bet you're in a lot of pain."

"I'm feeling much better," Casey said.

Nurse Diaz turned, brushing her gloved hands together. Her eyes darted between Luci and Casey. They held their breath.

"Let's have a look at you, miss."

Casey sighed in relief.

"It's just a little bruise." Luci tucked her foot behind one leg. "I realized I'm being a baby, so if you don't mind, I'll just—oh help!" She lost her balance, plunging face first into an armchair.

"Aha!" Nurse Diaz grabbed her ankle. "Why, this is seventh degree swelling. You're not leaving my infirmary with toes like cucumbers."

"Let ee oh please!" The chair muffled Luci's voice.

Gloria tugged the nurse's smock. "The two of us aren't hurt at all."

"If you don't mind, we'll just wait outside," Casey said.

They hurried out before she could argue.

"What do you think Mom and Dad are doing right now?" Gloria sagged against the doorframe.

Casey looked down at her tired little body, scuffed up and bleary-eyed. "I bet they're having a great time on the beach," he said.

Gloria gave a small smile, as if his answer made things ok. She was a spunky kid. But things weren't really ok, were they? He'd come close to killing them both, trying so hard to make this work.

When Luci joined them a few minutes later, a splint wrapped her foot. She held a hand to her belly. "Stuck me with a needle...five times. Now I can't even *feel* my toes. And she made me drink a quart of turmeric-cayenne tea for the swelling."

The air smelled spicy.

"At least now you can walk," Casey said.

"Oooh." Luci shook her fist. "I'll begin by walking straight to a bathroom."

By the time they reached the cafeteria, dinner was mostly gone. Battered students straggled down the stairs. Casey, Gloria and Luci split a steak-and-mashed-potato pie three ways. A tired one-armed chef watched them finish.

They left the empty hall and hiked across Trickery. Mist curled the ground. Nightbirds called deep in the woods. Gloria's head slumped, and Casey put a hand on her shoulder. Halfway across campus, she stumbled against his knees. He picked her up.

"I'm...not...sleepy..." She sagged in his arms.

Tiredness washed over Casey. Tiredness, and something heavier. A dark, dusty feeling pressed his heart.

"What are we going to do?" Luci's watery eyes reflected starlight. "Things keep getting worse, and all the grown-ups are a couple days away."

They stood at the edge of the Pavilion field.

For a second, Casey thought about lying, but he was tired of that.

"I think it's time for us to go home," he said.

Luci froze.

"Strength and honor and magic." He forced the words out. "That's what you need. If you didn't have to keep saving me and...*babysitting* me, you could focus on protecting yourself."

"Oh, I see." Luci's hands slid to her hips. "That's how you're playing this?"

"It's the truth." His heart felt heavier than ever.

Luci's brown eyes darkened. "You're just as selfish as everyone else."

"You don't understand." Casey shifted Gloria's weight, trying not to drop her. His shoulder flared with pain. Something rustled in his back pocket, flaky and brittle. *Oh no.* He pulled out a handful of ink-stained shreds.

"The Sylvan Handbook," he groaned. "It's ruined."

"Who cares?" Luci turned away. "You're leaving anyway."

The moon went behind clouds. Luci stalked toward the pavilion, taking her pendant with her. Gloria mumbled in his arms, and Casey stood there, frozen, until Luci glanced back.

"C'mon. You can't leave in the middle of the night."

He followed her glow across the field. It was like walking down a long, dark tunnel into a refugee camp for students stalked by monsters. And for Civilian kids without friends.

CHAPTER 50
A HEALTHY DAY'S DREAD

YOUR FACE HAS BEAN-PRINTS ON IT," said a blurry figure.

Casey rubbed his eyes, wondering why he felt so awful. The beanbag under him rustled. Oh, that was it. He'd been bitten by a Butcher Beast. Luci hated him. He was going home.

Robert Pierce sat on a stool with his legs crossed. Over his black t-shirt, he wore a camo vest with dozens of pockets. "Thought you'd never wake up."

Grey light filtered into the Pavilion. The morning smelled like mist and damp grass. Here and there a few kids stirred, but most everyone slept on.

Casey sat up and rubbed his neck. "Ow. What time is it?"

"Six-thirty." Robert held out a mug. "I don't recommend sleeping in beanbags. Coffee?"

Casey took it.

"No classes today." Robert watched him slurp. "The last round of finals is being postponed. I listened in on the teachers' meeting an hour ago, and the second butcher attack has everyone scared. They should be, kids could've died last night. If I hadn't been on that tree-way, they would have."

"What treeway?" Casey rolled coffee grounds on his tongue. For once, he didn't mind Robert monologuing. The less talking he had to do, the better.

"Going up Legbreak," Robert said. "While you were about to come down. Three wasps were tracking the lift and the lower they got, the slower they got, but then they saw the kids. Luckily, I had my bow and arrows."

"Wait." Casey stopped mid-sip. "You shot them?"

Robert nodded. "Got the first one in the eye. Second one too. The last one flew at me, and my arrows kept bouncing off." He shook his head. "Had to shove a spear down its throat. Seeing those fangs so close...man, it shook me up a little." He shrugged. "I'm ok now though."

Casey choked down the coffee along with the grounds.

Robert leaned in. "Everyone knows Crake was a dark-ager, but no one knew more about monsters than her. She's gone, but apparently she passed on some advice."

"Dark-ager?" Casey put down his mug. "Is that an insult?" He remembered Ms. Crake's surprisingly young face. Her blind eyes staring up at him.

Robert shrugged. "Anti-realist, magicker, dark-ager, it's all the same. Almost as dumb as Civilians. But there's a rumor going around." He uncrossed his legs. "You know what I'm talking about, right Grimes?"

Casey's breaths came in gulps. He rolled free of the beanbag and fought the impulse to kick Robert's stool out from under him. Instead, he stuck a finger in the boy's face.

"Never. Ever. Insult Ms. Crake again."

Robert leaned forward, a hand on his weapons belt.

"And shut up about Civilians, too," Casey said.

"What's gotten into you?" Robert laughed.

Casey kicked Robert's stool and tumbled him into the grass. Unfortunately, the kick had too much force. Casey landed on his back with a *whuff* as air left his lungs.

Robert smirked. "Is it crazy I feel sorry for you?"

Ancient parchment crumbled to even tinier bits in Casey's back pocket.

"Bones," he spat out. "'Bones in the woods' is the clue. Have fun with it."

Luci groaned and rolled over. "What's going on?"

Robert rubbed his chin. "Wonder if the bones are human or bestial."

"Wait, what?" Luci sat up, her hair wilder than usual.

"He's good at killing things," Casey snapped. "Exactly what you need."

"You told him?" She jerked her headband into place. "You should've asked me. Especially since you're leaving—you kind of lost your vote."

If she'd been sitting on a stool...

"Calm down, kids, let's talk over breakfast." Robert looked amused.

Luci shot Casey a dirty look. He shot it right back.

How long had he been up, ten minutes? Hard to imagine this day could get any worse.

On their way out, a teacher stopped them. Finals were postponed. Students were to stay on campus, at low altitudes. No news from the battlefront, although a message had been sent about the monster threat. Further instructions would come at lunch.

"Told you," Robert said.

Except for a group of chattering girls, they were the first ones in the cafeteria. On their way to the breakfast counter, Luciana lagged back. She caught Casey's eye. He braced himself.

"Why did you do this to me?" she whispered.

"He can help."

"I don't trust him."

"Why not, you've known him long enough."

Her face turned cloudy.

"Hey, aren't you hungry?" Gloria stood on tip-toe, piling pizza on her plate. Robert towered behind the little blondie.

"Be there in a second." Luci fake-smiled. "Knowing people *isn't* just about time going by, Casey. It's about going *through* things and helping each other and...and not being scared away." She crossed her arms.

"Thanks for the lecture," Casey said.

In half a week, he and Gloria had nearly died or been disabled numerous times, all as a result of meeting Luciana West. It had been exciting—even the awful parts, once they were over. But now Sylvan Woods seemed like a place you could die. A place where he was useless. A place they couldn't stay.

A crowd of kids shouldered past, eager to get in line.

"What are you thinking?" Luci narrowed her eyes.

Casey swallowed. "I'm wondering when we should leave."

Luci hissed out a breath through her teeth. "Fine." She spun away before anyone else could cut, splint clunking the floor. Halfway to the counter, she looked over her shoulder and stabbed holes in Casey with her eyes. It was a feeling he'd almost forgotten. The beginning of a healthy day's dread swirled in his stomach.

That meant it was time for breakfast.

CHAPTER 51
WEAPONS WISHLIST

ROBERT SHOVED his plate across the table. Bowls, mugs and shakers clinked like dominoes. He drew a map from his vest and smoothed it out.

"Where's the best place in Sylvan Woods to find a skeleton?"

The rainbow colors around his eye were fading. Some of the new skin was a brightish pink. It made him look, just a little, like a comic book character.

"Nice map you have there," Luci said.

Robert looked at her suspiciously.

Trickery School was drawn at the center, surrounded by the Mudlands, Legbreak Slopes, and several sections of Trick 'n' Trap Woods. Different colored lines crisscrossed everywhere. Buildings and places were labeled in tiny script.

Luci jabbed her finger down. "If *I* was looking for mysterious bones, I'd start here."

Casey leaned in. *The Beast Woods.*

Robert nodded. "If there's someplace a body could lie and rot, that would be it."

"The...Best...Woods." Gloria smiled. "Sounds like a nice place."

Casey forced himself to smile back.

"We'll have to be armed to the teeth." Robert drummed his fingers on the table. "But how do we find a skeleton in a forest the size of a county?"

"A bloodhound," Luci said.

"Possibly..." Robert tossed a strip of bacon in his mouth.

"Would a lynx be better?" Casey asked. It seemed like a fair question.

"Nope." Robert crunched his bacon. "Better claws, worse sniffer."

"Why should you care?" Luci said. "You're running home to Aunt Jonesie."

"We are?" Gloria said. "But I'll miss Luci. Of course, I *do* miss my room and my glitter glue..."

Robert raised an eyebrow. "Really leaving, Grimes?"

"Maybe. Not sure. Probably." Casey frowned at Luci.

"Family feud, huh," Robert said. "Can't help you with that. But what I can do is set us up nicely with weapons. What do you want?"

"Oh wow, let's see." Luci rubbed her hands together. "I'd love a scythe-staff and a bow and arrows, if you've got them."

"Absolutely."

She beamed. "Thanks so much, you're the best."

Casey fought down a sick, bubbly feeling.

"Oh, I don't suppose you know where to find the new stilettos? The Femme Fatale model, anti-static with the rubberized grip?"

Robert scoffed. "You've got it."

Luci's mouth made an excited O.

Casey made a mental note to stop looking at her.

"How about you, Grimes?" Robert said. "I mean, hypothetically, in case you and your cuz get on the same page real quick. How about a sword?"

"Uh...sure," Casey said.

Luci sniffed. "That basic, huh?"

Casey didn't look at her. "And a mace."

"A sword and a mace." Robert gave Casey's shoulder an encouraging shove.

Gloria tugged Robert's sleeve. "Could I have a very big knife, please, Pink-Eye?"

"Pink-Eye?" Robert laughed. "One K-level sword, sure thing."

"I knew he'd say yes," Gloria whispered to Casey. "He has that lovely pink eye."

She sounded jealous.

Robert folded his map, slid it inside his vest, and stood. "What supplies are you all tracking down?"

Casey leaned his head on an elbow so he wouldn't have to look at Luci.

"I can get a bloodhound," she said. "Mr. Collins is on the battle-front, so he can't sign them out, but luckily I interned at the Hound Hole last semester, and he never changes lock combinations."

What a show-off.

"Great," Robert said. "A hyena would be even better, but you can't have everything. Grimes?"

Casey studied the table. What did he have that could be of any use?

"Casey!" Gloria squealed. "The black night light."

Robert's eyes brightened. "That dark lantern you were carrying when we met."

Casey sighed. "Right."

Robert rubbed his palms together. "Pretty rare. Any Sylvan worth his salt would love to have one."

Casey didn't look up. "I left it...in the baths...with my sword."

The table got quiet.

This was where Luci would usually say something to keep him from looking like a Civilian fool. Instead...

"It was *my* sword." Gloria patted his arm. "I'll help you look for it."

Casey tried to ignore Robert's look of disbelief as they headed for the door. Was it his imagination, or was Luci sticking her nose in the air? He shouldn't have trusted her. She didn't care about him and Gloria at all.

"Try to avoid teachers," Robert said. "They'll want us back at the tent."

"Meet at the baths?" Luci said. "Then we can jump on the orchard path–"

"Straight to the BeastWoods," Robert finished.

"Hey, great minds!" She flung up a hand, smiling.

Robert shrugged as he gave her a high five.

"Sure," Casey said. "Whatever."

CHAPTER 52
STANDOFF

THE BATHS WERE DESERTED, everyone still at breakfast. They were also very clean. Gloria checked the girls' side, just to be sure, but no use. The dark lantern and sword were gone.

"Great." Casey scuffed his feet on the path. "I should've come back sooner."

He joined Gloria on a mossy boulder.

"Are we going home soon?" she asked.

He bent his head forward to get a good look at his toes. "It's not safe for us anymore, Gloria. I'm not good at this Sylvan stuff."

"Silly." She smiled. "Of course you are."

As if that settled it.

"What about Luci?" she said.

That was a tougher question.

"She's tired of us. The sooner we leave her alone, the better."

"Umm." Gloria laughed. "She wants us to stay."

"That's ridiculous." Casey smiled at his little sister. "When you get older, you'll understand this stuff. Luci is safer with Robert, plus she likes him lots better. I've taken too many risks for you and me." He ripped at a patch of lichen with his thumbnail.

Gloria watched a hawk circle overhead. "Sylvan Woods can be a little scary," she said. "But I don't mind. Whatever happens, you'll keep me safe."

"You know what?" Casey hugged her. "You're the best little sister in the world."

Snuffling and clinking came from around a bend. Luci held the leash of a drooling, sad-eyed bloodhound. Robert wore a metal frame on his back. Handles and blades stuck out in all directions.

"No one even tried to stop me." Luci smiled.

"No one even *saw* me," Robert said.

He handed her a bow, arrows and a wicked-looking staff.

"Wow, these are *really* nice."

Robert pulled a glittery knife with a pink grip from his vest. "Don't forget your Femme Fatale stiletto."

"I've always wanted one, ever since they came out!" Luci turned the blade in her hands like she was holding the keys to a castle. "Such a pretty little dagger...I'll take good care of *you*."

You could've iced a cake with all the fake frosting in her voice.

"Here you go, Grimes." Robert handed a gleaming mace and sword to Casey.

"Thanks, these are...good looking."

He buckled on the sword belt and clipped the mace to his backpack, so it wouldn't destroy his kneecaps.

Gloria belted a sheath around her waist. "It's a little sword!"

"Grade-school kids deserve real weapons too," Robert said. "The Combat Department much have a slim budget where you come from." He winked at Casey.

Luci slung her scythe-staff across her back. She put the bow and quiver over one shoulder. Her Femme Fatale stiletto had disappeared, and the weight of her new weapons made her stand taller. "No dark lantern?"

"It's gone." Casey's sword chafed his leg. His lack of Sylvan sense on display. *Look at me, I don't know how to look after awesome weaponry.*

"Maybe we could check Lost and Found," he said.

"Too rare." Luci watched the bloodhound snuffle Gloria. "No, it's good as gone."

"What are you talking about?" Robert said.

"Security," Luci said.

Casey didn't have an answer to that.

Gloria giggled as the bloodhound snuffed her cheek.

"What's the problem?" Robert looked from face to face.

"Old Knock," Casey said. "He's chased us twice this week."

"Whoa," Robert said. "Running from Knock is like going in the woods alone at night. It's like playing with unquenchable fire."

Casey turned to Luci, who looked away. "I *want* that lantern back," he said. It came out more snappish than he'd planned.

Luci's head jerked up. "We don't have time."

He glared back, hoping she'd blink and say, Creeps, what are we doing? Cousins shouldn't argue—and maybe flash a tiny smile. But she didn't say a word.

"Hell's bells," Robert said. "Stop it, you two. But lucky this came up—it made me think of something. We need to stop by Security, to get an upper level trail pass. Otherwise we'll set off the BeastWoods' motion alarms."

"Perfect," Casey said to the side of Luci's face. "Then we'll walk you to the edge of the BeastWoods...before we say goodbye."

She still didn't look at him.

Robert tapped one of his many weapon hilts. "Shall we?"

They headed down the trail to Trickery, Robert and Gloria leading the way.

Casey and Luci followed in icy silence.

CHAPTER 53
SECURITY BREACH

YOUR T-SHIRT IS HILARIOUS," Robert said.

Gloria giggled. "Unicorns are so amazing."

"Nice sense of humor for a kid your age."

Casey didn't smile. He didn't think he could.

The security building stood among boulders and pines. It looked like it belonged in Alabama or South Carolina. Rocking chairs sat on a porch under spinning ceiling fans. It seemed too pleasant to be Security, but Casey pictured Old Knock in a rocking chair, gripping his axe handle, and changed his mind.

"Just remember, we have every right to be here," Luci said. "We haven't done anything wrong."

"At least not yet," Casey said.

She ignored him and creaked up the steps. "Anyone home? We're here about some missing property."

Robert nodded. "She knows how to work it."

"She's good at bending rules," Casey said. "And eventually breaking them."

They followed her up the stairs.

"I don't think anyone's here," Luci said.

"Look." Gloria pointed through a window.

Chairs circled an open hearth. On the wall next to the fireplace hung the dark lantern. Gloria's sword dangled below it, with lots of other gear. Weapons, harnesses, dangerous-looking equipment.

"There's a trail pass next to the Death Dog trap," Luci said.

It looked like a shiny arm band.

Robert cracked his knuckles. "Should I break the window?"

"*NO.*" Luci whispered so loudly she squeaked. "There's sure to be some kind of alarm. They're probably just waiting for someone to break in."

The front door creaked, and everyone jumped.

Gloria stood in the doorway, looking pleased.

"You've got to be kidding me," Luci said. "How is that unlocked?"

Casey stepped forward. He'd go out on a high note. Show Luci she'd misjudged him. And he wanted the dark lantern.

The interior of Security smelled good. Casey sniffed the air as he crept over a cowhide rug. Cinnamon? Oregano? He grabbed the trail pass and lifted the gleaming lantern from the wall. Maybe Old Knock enjoyed cooking. Robert appeared next to him and took down Gloria's sword. They moved stealthily toward the door.

Someone whistled outside. The whistle sounded horribly familiar.

They jostled onto the porch and ran for the stairs as the girls watched wide-eyed.

"Close the front door!" Luci hissed.

Casey skidded to a stop and doubled back. A figure turned the corner as he sprinted down the porch, swung the door shut, and flung himself off. Branches scraped him as he crashed into a large bush.

The whistling stopped.

"What can I do for you boneheads?" said a leathery voice. "Did a spider squid crawl out of the swamp and bite someone? No need to fill out a form."

Casey pushed aside a branch digging into his stomach. His skin felt raw in several places, but at least he hadn't landed on the mace. He pulled a twig out of one ear and peered out.

Luci, Gloria and Robert stood in a row. Gloria shook her hair around her face. Robert held the recovered sword behind his back. Luci stood in front of the borrowed bloodhound, shifting back and forth.

"Well, speak up, I haven't got all day," said the leathery voice.

"Um, three dead Butcher Beasts," Luci said. "On Legbreak Slopes under the lift."

"We've already recovered those," the voice said. "Nasty poisonous stingers. My theory, they paralyze you, then carry you off to eat you alive. Awful way to go. So run along, find a safe tunnel."

Footsteps stamped across the porch. Luci waved frantically at Casey's bush, and he shoved his way out and ran to join them.

"Thank goodness it wasn't Old Knock." Luci yanked the bloodhound's leash.

"Be a good doggy and mooove." Gloria shoved it from behind.

The door swung open, and Casey dove behind a tree. A stooped figure hunched over a metal walker. He shut the door, locked it and fumbled in a shirt pocket. Bones put on a pair of glasses.

"Goodbye, sir," Luci said. "We're just leaving."

The old man muttered down the stairs and disappeared into the woods. Casey stepped out from behind his tree. He held out the trail pass. Luci took it, and their eyes met.

"That's a nasty scrape." She winced. "Hold the dog, Glo. He likes you better anyway."

Gloria tickled the bloodhound's ears. "It's because I know his secret name, don't I, Old ThunderSnot?" She giggled.

Luci licked her ring finger and dabbed a spot under Casey's eye.

"Ouch!" He jerked his face away.

"Don't worry, spit is like antiseptic."

Robert appeared next to them, holding Gloria's old sword. Sunlight glinted off its perfect blade. "Nice little sword, Grimes. You actually left this in the bath house?"

"Eh…" Casey tugged his belt, which always seemed loose. "I can take that."

"I don't know, can you?" Robert said.

Luci frowned. "Knock it off, Robert."

"Oh, now you two are friends again?"

"Stop being mean, Pink-Eye." Perched on the bloodhound, Gloria stuck out her tongue.

Robert handed the sword over grudgingly.

In Casey's hands, the weapon felt light as air. Its edges shone. Maybe it was his imagination, but the blade seemed sharp enough to slice through atoms.

"Good job, Pink-Eye," Gloria said. "Now that Mr. Bones walked into the woods, *we* can go look for bones in the woods. Hey, isn't that funny—wait, Old Thundersnot, stop!"

The bloodhound snapped to attention, snuffling the air. He let out a hoarse bellow, and dashed off into the trees as Gloria hugged his neck, bouncing like a sack of potatoes.

CHAPTER 54
BONES IN THE WOODS

CASEY BOLTED AFTER HIS SISTER. She and the bloodhound were a loud combination. He caught up with them in a sunny clearing, Robert right behind him. Luci brought up the rear.

She knelt, pulled off her splint, and threw it into the woods. "Ugh, I hate this thing. Hey, why is everyone so quiet?"

Sun gleamed on an aluminum walker.

The kids looked at each other.

"We were dumb," Luci said.

"Crake wanted us here," Casey said.

Butterflies and bees flew from flower to flower. A crystal-clear creek bubbled through the grass. Other then the walker, there was no sign of the old man. They crossed the creek and entered a ring of standing stones.

"Now what?" Luci sank into the grass.

A fountain trickled down a stone slab and into a pool where rainbow-colored fish swam lazily. A hummingbird hovered, squeaked at them, and darted away.

Robert scowled. "It's classic. Subterfuge 201, and really well executed."

"What do you mean?" Casey said.

"Perfectly landscaped." Robert turned in a slow circle. "Everything in place, like a jigsaw puzzle. So many details, you never notice the one piece that doesn't belong. Fish, plants, birds, stones...it could take all day to find the key."

"I hope you're pranking us," Luci said.

"Look at that cute little frog." Gloria leaned on Old Thundersnot's ribs, her head moving up and down as the hound panted.

Robert rubbed his forehead. "I've never seen a hidden gate this good."

"How can you tell, since you *don't* see it?" Luci snapped.

Gloria looked very tired. Casey didn't want to leave, but the adventure had stalled out. Maybe now was the time to say goodbye.

His sister stuck her head under a fern. A small, gray frog made a clicking sound when she petted it. It didn't blink or move a muscle —but the kids did.

The ground shook, and they were falling into darkness.

CHAPTER 55
BOOKS AND BONES

EVERYTHING WAS quiet and pitch black. Casey felt a weird sense of relief. Now he could stop torturing himself about what to do. At least until they escaped.

"Gloria, are you ok?" he said.

"Old Thundersnot's hugging me," Gloria said. "I think he's scared."

"What is this, an underground jail?" Luci said.

"I bet we need a password," Robert said.

They waited in the dark.

"Um, is someone going to push the button?" Gloria said.

Luci held up her pendant. In the wall, a carved stone serpent curled around an apple. Luci pressed the sculpted knob. The wall grated open. Light flooded the cave and stepping stones rose from the pool. They walked across and stood in a bright hall, making a puddle on the floor.

The wall slid shut behind them.

Straight ahead, a white-haired woman sat behind an ivory desk. She reminded Casey a little of Ms. Jones.

"Why hello," she said. "You must be new here." She slid a bookmark in *The Rise of Magical Barriers*. "I'm Ms. Aello, and congratulations on your library privileges. Step forward, it's been a while since I've been able to do this."

The kids moved closer, glancing at each other.

"Right hands up," the librarian said.

Casey braced himself, waiting to be shocked or stung. Maybe even branded. Instead, Ms. Aello put something in his palm.

"Your entry charms and memory aids." She smiled. "Non-transferable of course."

They held small stone frogs, like the one in the elevator garden.

"They'll automate the lift for you," the librarian said. "And they're able to memorize a page at a time. The important words are 'memorize,' 'recite,' and 'forget.' They're just starter frogs but I'm sure you'll enjoy them. Now, what are you researching today?"

No one spoke. Then Luci said, "Butcher Beasts, ma'am."

"Oh, I'm glad to hear it." The woman held up a finger. "Not that Mr. Bones isn't adequate, but we've got to get these monsters sorted." She pointed to a stone arch. "I'm sure he'll be happy to see you. Just leave your dog with me, please."

"Thank you, Ms. Aello," Luci said.

In the stone corridor, they stopped by a suit of armor. Ceiling-high rows of books stretched away on both sides, marked by scripted signs. The kids spoke in hushed voices.

"This isn't what I expected." Robert stuffed his frog into his vest.

"You could spend weeks down here," Luci said.

"What's our play?" Robert said. "Snatch the books and run...or overpower Bones and tie him up?"

"Both sound horrible," Luci said.

Something fell into place in Casey's mind. "Wait a minute," he said. "Don't you think Ms. Crake and Bones know each other? Don't you think they're kind of on the same team?" No one answered. "I think Crake probably wanted us to *help* Bones...not attack him."

The others stared.

"He's finally lost it," Robert said.

"Do you have any idea how ridiculous you sound?" Luci said.

Gloria smiled at him.

So this was how it was going to go. Casey spun on his heel and marched down the passage.

"Casey, don't!" Luci sounded panicky.

The rows opened into a high hall with marble columns, woven rugs and rows of tables. Sun shone through skylights. Bright pennants hung from the ceiling. The hall could have held fifty students easily, but only one person was there. Bones sat in a patch of sunlight with a stack of books towering over him.

Luci darted in front of Casey, waving her hands like she was trying to slow a runaway horse. "Casey, stop, it's a bad idea."

"I'm tired of running and hiding," he said.

And lying, he thought.

Luci frowned. "No one put you in charge," she whispered.

Bones turned to face them, levering himself out of his chair. "What are you doing here?" He tried to snatch a book off the top of the leaning pile.

"Let me help you with that, sir." Luci smiled. "We're here to do a little research ourselves." She held out the book. "Ms. Aello sent us right in..."

When Casey stole a glance at Robert, the dangerous kid was reaching for a couch pillow, probably to muffle the old man's shouts. Next to him, Luci tensed up, her fingers fluttering. What was she gonna do, disappear the entire stack of books?

Bones stiffened, sensing the tension in the air.

Casey elbowed Luci out of the way. "MR. BONES!" He found himself shouting in his rush to get a word in. "Ms. Crake sent us to find you. We're here to help *you*—to help stop the butchers."

"What's that?" The old man froze, a heavy tome held high, about to smash Luci's head. "Crake, you say? She sent *you*? Hell hash, could've sworn you were up to no good." His coal black eyes bored into Casey and drifted away. "Gets straight to the point, doesn't he? Kid has spunk. Hmm, maybe he's not lying." His gaze flicked back. "What did you say your name was, boy?"

Luci shook her head. *No, no, no.*

Robert looked furious.

Casey sighed. "Casey, sir. Casey Grimes."

Bones put his glasses on and squinted. "Grimes, you look familiar. Maybe you took one of my classes." He grunted. "Well, I'm as stubborn as a junkyard goat, but I know a good argument when I hear one." He waved the children forward. "Grab a book, don't be shy. We're about to be eaten alive, what are you waiting for?"

CHAPTER 56
BOOK OF BUTCHERS

STACKS OF BOOKS cluttered their table. The hall echoed with the *flick-flick* of pages.

Luci frowned and set aside *A Brief History of Sylvan Woods: The Magical First Century*. It was four inches thick. Casey's book, *Trickes f'r Quelling Sky Monsters*, had fewer pictures than he'd hoped.

Luci plunked open *Woodland Fauna and Flora, Including Rare and Extinct Species*. A cloud of dust enveloped her and she burst into a coughing fit.

Casey scooted his chair further away. Across the table, Gloria paged through *A Golden Guide to Bad Beasties*. Robert had snatched all the available books with *fighting, combat, war,* or *death* in the titles. He sat next to Gloria, glowering.

Shadows moved across the floor.

Casey felt like they'd been snatched out of Sylvan Woods, and dropped in a parallel universe where everything was safe and clean. No blood, no Butcher Beasts, no dead teachers. Knowing it was a lie made the library creepy.

"What if there's nothing here?" Luci opened the third massive volume of Sylvan Woods history. She sighed, shut the cover and stole *Ancient Dendrology* from Casey's pile.

"Hey, that's mine," he said.

Hundreds more pages flicked past, then thousands.

Robert smiled as he read *Shadow Death: The Untold Story of Secret War.* Gloria opened *The Nasty Night Book,* covering her eyes. Casey leaned back in his chair, blinking away dust. He was reaching for one of Luci's histories when his sister squealed. "I found it!"

Everyone rushed to look. A drawing of a Butcher Beast covered two pages. Notes surrounded the menacing picture.

"Poisonous stingers," Bones muttered. "Prehensile claws, armored hides, knife-sized teeth...tell us something we don't know."

"Parasitic," Luci read. "Originally thought to have hunted Faeries. Advance guard seeks out a hive location, then summons the swarm. Ugh, how disgusting."

Casey pointed to a footnote. "Rarely seen after the 1800s, when anti-magics were developed."

"Anti-magics?" Robert snorted. "Give me a break."

"Hush, boy." Bones's finger traced the page. "Thin spines, soft eyes...drawn to open flame." He pressed his lips together. "Turn the page, girl, there must be more."

Gloria turned the page. They stared at a drawing of a Leopard Alligator.

Bones huffed. "Go back."

They read and reread every note on the Butcher Beast.

Bones spit on the floor. "We *already* know more than this. Keep reading, kids." He limped back to his chair.

They slumped at the table, shuffling their books.

"Wait a minute," Casey said. "When was Sylvan Woods founded?"

Luci stared at him. "Before the 1800s. So why haven't I read about *that* century?" She unstacked her volumes. "*Here's* the third century, and it covers the 1800s. I should've read this hours ago."

"You stole my book on trees instead," Casey said.

Luci palmed her forehead and flung the book open. The others crowded around. They skimmed through a blacksmith expansion, a bounty on Bog Creeps, an alliance with Misty Gulch, a record-setting plum harvest, a marauding ogre...

"Here it is," Luci breathed. "The Butcher Beast Attacks of 1886."

Everyone leaned closer.

"At first, the poisonous flying creatures were easily dispatched," Luci read. "But their numbers increased to dozens and then to hundreds. They filled the trees and marshes of Sylvan Woods like pestilence."

They looked at each other.

"Treeways were abandoned," she read. "Houses boarded up. Tunnels dug under the forest. When Sylvanites went above ground, the cost in life was high.

"It appeared Sylvan Woods would be wiped off the map of settled lands. Families fled to neighboring kingdoms and many died, trying to escape. A last group of Sylvanites barricaded themselves inside the Great Hall. As wasps gnawed the roof, they made a desperate plan. Powerful anti-magic was brewed. The magic that would save Sylvan Woods."

Robert coughed. "Can we skip to the good part?"

"Shut up, boy." No one had noticed Bones standing behind them. "Go on, young lady."

"Great stores of elixir were brewed," Luci read. "The Sentry Trees were chosen for strength and location. Then came the last, desperate attempt. Carrying the elixir, the Butcher Brigade fought their way to the Sentries. They soaked the roots with bright elixir—and human blood. Half the war-party never returned. But the deliverance of Sylvan Woods had been accomplished." Luci swallowed. "I don't think I can keep going."

Casey took the heavy book. He followed her finger down the page:

"The mighty Sentries grew.

They branched the magic web.

The wasps could not fight through.

The butchers withered and fled."

He took a deep breath.

"The surviving Sylvanites came out of caves and tunnels. They kindled their hearth-fires and mourned their dead. They dug the reservoirs and stored the magic. The Sentry Trees would never die, and they would never be forgotten. Guardians would be trained and treetop watches kept. Every half-century, their roots would be renewed. In this way, the wasps, those killers of the woodland races, would never trouble Sylvan Woods again."

Luci looked over his shoulder. "Don't read the list of Sylvanites Who Gave Their Lives. It's too long and awful."

The story sucked light from the library.

Bones slid the book from Casey's weak grasp. "She's right. That's a lot of names." He grimaced, rubbing his chin. "It's too bad, ain't it... that history don't come with an instructions manual."

CHAPTER 57
BUTCHER BRIGADE

THE SENTRY TREES *WERE* FORGOTTEN," Casey said. "The history said that would never happen." He thought about the Old Oak, and felt his throat tighten.

"No one ever talks about maintenance," Luci said. "Renewing their roots or anything."

"That's because history was basically fiction back then." Robert buckled on his sword. "Trees that act as guardians, thanks to magic —no thanks, that's bedtime story stuff."

Casey'd had enough.

"What's your problem?" he said. "Every time someone mentions magic, you become a stupid jerk."

Robert stiffened. "Only losers talk about magic, Grimes. Kind of surprising I need to spell this out for you. Like Civilians, magic is useless. People have moved on for a reason."

Casey jumped to his feet.

Luci put a hand on his arm.

He knew he should stop, but he couldn't. "What's the matter with you? You live in this amazing, magical place, and you're afraid to admit it. People here *used* to care about magic and honor and the trees, and they were right. That's the Sylvan Woods I care about. You're no better than Drooce and Cortland."

The others stared.

"Is there a problem?" Bones creaked toward them.

"Um, no problem," Luci said brightly.

Robert yanked straps on on his weapons frame. "I've heard enough," he growled. "Don't try to run off, Grimes. We'll talk outside." He swaggered down the hall.

"Casey…" Luci's voice shook. "Why'd you do that?"

Casey balled his fingers into fists. "Because I *hate* what Sylvan Woods has become."

She stared at the marble floor. "Robert will try to turn you in, and I won't be able to stop him. But…there's something you should know." She looked up and took a breath. "It doesn't make you popular, but some kids still believe in magic. Some people think *magic* is the whole point of Sylvan Woods." She swallowed. "I'm one of them."

Inside Casey, a dry, hot desert cooled to swirling mist.

"I guess that makes two of us," he said.

Luci took his hand and squeezed.

Gloria grabbed his other hand. "Three of us!"

"If only you could get past Robert." Luci bit her lip. "Then you could go home."

Casey's laugh sounded like a frog croaking, but he didn't care. "Not a chance. If we can get out of here, I'm helping you fight the Butcher Beasts."

Luci's face glowed, then she hung her head.

Behind them, someone started clapping.

The kids froze.

"Some people think I'm as deaf as a wall," Bones said. "Can you believe that? Now if I was ten years younger…hell's bells, even five years younger, I'd do this myself. Crake gone, Old Knock a bonehead…who does that leave? Oh, that's right. A strange kid who cares about magic and trees."

"I'm here too," Luci said.

Bones' eyes pinned Casey in the doorway. "How much do you love Sylvan Woods?"

Casey swallowed. "It would be my favorite place, if it was how it used to be."

Bones tapped his forehead. "No wonder Crake liked you."

They looked at each other.

"Go on, git." Bones said. "I'll pull things together here. If the mean kid tries to stop you, tell him you're in charge of the Butcher Brigade." He held up a wizened fist. "Bones says so."

"Yes sir." Casey felt himself drifting backward, and around a corner. *What had just happened?* Luci and Gloria appeared next to him.

"Yay!" Gloria said.

Luci's eyes gleamed. "Let's get this straight. I'm *on* the Butcher Brigade. As far as you leading it, we'll see, but..." A smile lit up her face. "Can you believe that just happened?" She threw her arms in the air and squealed.

"No." Casey's head spun. "I really can't."

His stomach lurched as they tramped down the corridor, past the suit of armor, up to Ms. Aello's desk. Old Thundersnot lay at her feet, snoring.

The librarian looked up. "Did you find what you were looking for?"

"Everything," Casey said.

"And more," Luci added.

"Mr. Bones must be so pleased." The librarian waved them through.

The walls of the lift slid shut, and they rose through flower-scented darkness. Casey clenched his fists and breathed in through his nose. They shot into daylight. Bees buzzed, birds chirped. Robert waited, arms crossed.

"Casey Grimes." He half-slid a sword from its sheath. "I hereby arrest you for most likely being a Civilian spy. I'm taking you to Security for further questioning."

"Don't plan on it," Luci said.

"What about me?" said Gloria.

"You're not taking me anywhere," Casey said.

Robert's face darkened. "By the power vested in me as a member of the Sylvan Watch—"

"You?" Luci's eyes widened. "The Sylvan Watch?"

Eyes throwing sparks, Robert swept a battle hammer from his back.

She gave herself a shake. "Doesn't matter. Casey's on the..." She swallowed. "He's *leading* the Butcher Brigade. If you don't like it, talk to Bones."

"What?" The hammer drooped in Robert's hand. "That's impossible."

"Only if you don't believe in magic." Luci tugged a shiny object from her pocket. Bones' golden whistle swung from her fist.

Casey stared. Robert passed a hand across his eyes.

"He tried to toss it to you," Luci whispered. "But you were kind of spacey."

She handed it over.

He looped it around his neck, trying to pull himself together. "Ok, Butcher Brigade...let's head to the Old Oak, the nearest Sentry Tree...I think."

"Right," Luci said.

They started across the sunny clearing.

"Pink-Eye, aren't you coming?" Gloria called.

Robert moved after them, muttering. "Dark-agers...anti-realists..."

Casey slowed, trying to think of something to say.

"Ignore him." Luci rapped his shoulder. "We don't have any time to waste."

CHAPTER 58
THE SCENT OF LONELINESS

THEY STOOD under the Old Oak, wrinkling their noses. Colonies of pale toadstools swirled everywhere, following the tree's roots.

"I can't believe it happened so fast..." Under Casey's hands, the oak felt as tough as ever, but the smell of rot hung in the air. His heart sunk. "He's been suffering a long time."

If only I'd noticed sooner.

"Pure coincidence." Robert frowned. "Trees die all the time, especially old ones."

Casey took off his backpack. "Gloria—remember what we found, your first day?"

"Ohh..." Gloria said. "When you were afraid of the dark."

"Right," he said. "We're going back inside."

Luci unstrapped her own pack.

"Seriously, you're following Mr. Magic into a tree?" Robert laughed.

She didn't bother to reply.

Casey lit the dark lantern. Toadstools exploded under their feet and Old Thundersnot whined. They stopped in front of the weathered door.

"What are we looking at?" Luci shaded her eyes. "These roots look impenetrable. I don't see how we can possibly—oh!"

Gloria pushed the dirty portal open.

The bloodhound snuffled uneasily.

"Here, boy," Robert said. "I'm not going in that smelly hole."

Gloria handed him the dog's leash. "You two can take a little break, *this* time." She disappeared through the door. Casey and Luci followed.

Under the oak, the lantern and pendant pushed back inky blackness. A rack of climbing weights leaned on a wall. The bottom row had cracked, spilling stones like flattened bowling balls. The smell of mold grew stronger.

I'll do whatever I can to help you, Casey promised.

The room made a T with a thin top line. On the left side, they crowded into the glowing corridor. Phosphorescence flickered like dying fireflies. They looked at the oak's mysterious button. A silver lightning bolt and leaf.

"Push it," Casey said.

Gloria shoved with two hands. Clunking and dragging boomed through the tree. The kids huddled closer. Gloria hugged her brother's waist and shivered.

At the far end of the hall, a dark arch stood open. Rings of age scraped their shoulders as they ducked through. Stairs twisted into darkness thick enough to taste. An awful smell swirled from below, and something else. Carried in the air, whispering through the wood. Loneliness, exhaustion...sap hardening into death.

Casey took Gloria's hand. Luci wrapped hers on top.

"We can do this," he said. "We've got to."

"Stay close." Luci's eyes were wide brown pools.

At each step, Casey wanted to turn and run, pulling the girls with him. But he couldn't. He wouldn't abandon the Old Oak, his very first friend in Sylvan Woods.

They stood in a cellar that swallowed their lights. Gloria's fingernails dug into Casey's palm and Luci slipped her arm through his. He saw the reason he wanted to run.

CHAPTER 59
IN THE BELLY OF THE OAK

ROTTEN TIMBERS HELD up a sagging ceiling. A low stone circle made a bump on the floor. But the floor was black. The walls were black. The ceiling was black. Midnight mold covered everything. It smelled like death.

"I'm scared." Gloria shook against Casey's knees.

"Me too." Luci touched the little girl's hair.

"So am I." Casey held the lantern higher.

Rotten roots twisted overhead. Empty spider webs dangled.

"The oak is dying from the inside out," he said. "No one has come here forever."

"Don't stir up the dust," Luci whispered. "Don't breathe too deep."

Casey tiptoed across the room. Inside the ring of stones, darkness fell away.

"I think it's a well." He looked back at the girls. "But where's the...the magic?"

Luci bit her lip. "The history said they dug reservoirs and stored the elixir." Her pendant seemed to light up less and less of her face. "Don't you think we're standing in the reservoir? The elixir should be right here."

An echoing boom rolled down the stairs.

The blood left Luci's face. "The door..."

Stale air swept down the staircase. Black dust rose in clouds, powdering their skin. Gloria coughed. Luci held her close.

If the elixir was here, why couldn't they find it?

Dust slid over the girls like hungry black snakes. Their horrified faces disappeared a bit at a time, eaten by the dark. Casey felt the death-dust coating his nose and mouth, swirling in his lungs. The room plunged into choking darkness.

Gloria, I'm so sorry.

He stumbled over the rough stone ring, and something jarred loose in his brain. He fell to his knees, brushing at the well. Under the swirling black powder, the stones glowed faintly. He read the message chiseled in the rock:

THESE ROOTS RENEW—WITH MAGIC'S DEW. TURN ME. ⤜

Casey drew a deep, horrible breath and threw his arms around the well. Stone grated as he wrenched the enormous dial around. Liquid gurgled far below. Splashing, rushing. Casey collapsed, his chest on fire. Gloria's sobs had stopped. He tried to say her name but he couldn't speak.

The hidden chamber exploded. Liquid surged through Casey's mouth and nose, washing him from the inside out. The elixir tingled when it touched his skin. It sank down through his muscles and soaked him to the bone.

He felt happy. Joyful. Buoyant.

When he opened his eyes, wet strands of golden hair tickled his lashes. He chuckled and hugged Gloria back. They got up, dripping.

"We're alive!" Luci laughed and shook her head, spraying silvery-green drops.

"The tree gave us a bath." Gloria giggled.

The room smelled like young wood and blue sky and fresh, clean dirt. Under their feet, the floor gleamed rosy-brown. A dripping, mossy ceiling rose higher than before. In the well, light gleamed on silvery liquid far below.

"Your scrapes are gone!" Luci pointed to Casey's face.

"So are yours," he said, "even that nasty one on your chin."

"Hey, that's rude." She laughed and poked a fist at him.

Casey took a silly boxing stance. Luci laughed so hard she snorted.

"We don't have to put up with this, Gloria," she gasped. "Get him."

Casey swayed back and forth, pretending to struggle. He felt so fresh and strong, he knew he could defeat the girls at any time, just by flexing his little finger. Little did he know, they felt the same way. They double-teamed him to the floor, laughing.

A green vine twined around his wrist. Another circled his ankle.

Gloria stopped poking his ribs. Luci stopped twisting his arm. They jumped up, pulling creepers from their hair. Vines darted up the walls like leafy millipedes. The plants soaked up puddles of elixir, twining between the floor and ceiling.

"These vines need room to dance!" Luci clapped her hands and shimmied up the stairs.

"We'll get you later, Casey." Gloria followed, spinning in circles and giggling.

He skipped after them, swinging his lantern and sword. As he sped up the corkscrew stairs, humming a tune, he tried to remember why they'd come down in the first place.

CHAPTER 60
WAKING FROM A DREAM

THEY LAUGHED and busted moves in the upper hall, each better than the last. Casey felt as if he could climb the highest tree, walk the thinnest wire. Gloria felt as if she could make the most beautiful, glittery work of art. Luci felt as if she'd be able to find exactly the right words, whenever she needed them.

They strutted, they clapped, they pirouetted. They whirled out into daylight, panting for breath. The trees had long shadows. Their wrinkled clothes felt uncomfortable.

Luci passed a hand over her forehead. "How long were we...in there?"

"Good question." Casey shook himself. "Hey, look at the Old Oak."

The tree towered straighter and taller than before. At its roots, green toadstools were crumbling into dust and disappearing on the wind.

"Did all that really happen?" Gloria blinked. "The horrible dirt, the tree splashing us..."

Luci covered her mouth. "We...we almost died."

Twigs crunched. "Well, it took you long enough," Robert said.

"After an hour, I got tired of waiting and I..." His mouth dropped open. "What happened to the cellar?"

The ugly door in the tree had changed. Ten feet high, it swayed on gold hinges, shining like spun honey. Robert stuck his head inside. "How'd it get so bright in here—and so big?"

Casey tried to focus. "We found the reservoir. We renewed the Sentry's roots, but don't worry..." He smiled. "We didn't use the slightest bit of magic."

The bloodhound's leash fell from Robert's limp hand. Old Thundersnot crept over and sat down next to Gloria.

"Didn't we have a dance party?" She crinkled her eyebrows.

"Um, maybe," Luci said.

Casey rubbed the bridge of his nose.

"You see, Pink-Eye?" Gloria held up a finger. "Even though we almost died, it was wonderful, and you missed it. *That's* what happens when you don't come along."

Robert stared a moment longer, then disappeared.

"I wonder..." Luci licked her lips and looked down at her damp clothing. "Do you think humans are supposed to, you know, drink elixir...and take baths in it?"

"I feel pretty good." Casey touched his glossy hair.

Luci smiled. "So do I, like waking up from a nice dream..."

"Which also happens to be true," Casey said.

"Are you dark-agers coming or not?" Robert called.

"Oh right." Luci tucked back her hair, loose ends flying. "We've got more work to do."

Casey strapped on the lantern, clipped on the mace, tightened his sword belt, and picked up his second sword. It was a lot to keep track of.

Robert moved away. "This one's our last freebie."

Gloria and Old Thundersnot jogged after him. "What do you mean, Pink-Eye?"

"After this it gets *dark*." He glanced over his shoulder. "When it gets dark, paths move around and monsters come out to play. No more fun and games."

Robert lengthened his strides as the shadows did the same.

CHAPTER 61
ANCIENT RELIC

THEIR PATH SWERVED LAZILY, wiggled back and forth and shot between two boulders.

"Whoever blazed this trail really enjoyed himself," Casey said.

They circled a hill and the Big Beech rose ahead. Fading light shone on its patchy skin. Toadstools streamed away in all directions.

"There's that gross smell again," Robert said.

"It's not haunted," Gloria told the bloodhound. "So you can go first." She jerked Old Thundersnot's leash. Skin piled up at his saggy neck and he didn't budge. She whispered something in his ear, and ran to join them.

"Stupid dog," Robert said. "He's done nothing to help."

"He's tired of that smell," Gloria said. "But it was nice of you to keep him company last time, Pink-Eye."

Robert grunted. They climbed through knobby roots like elephant knees.

"Where are you hiding, magic door?" Gloria said. "Oh, there you are." Something clinked in her hand. "Uh oh."

She held an off-white combination lock. It hung from a slender cream handle.

"Painted so students won't see it," Luci said. "But where's the door?"

They stepped back, looking for edges.

"It's got to be here," Casey said. "Why else would the tree be locked?"

Robert smirked. "So no one would break in while the owners were out."

Casey wrapped his hands around the lock and yanked.

Robert made a face. "Let's see how it likes my diamond-edged blade." He raised his longsword, yelled, and swept it down. *Crack!* Sparks flew everywhere. "What? A notch? You're kidding me!"

"Are you carrying anything sharper?" Luci glanced at his weapons rack.

"There's not a sharper sword in Sylvan Woods," Robert said.

"Maybe it's time for double swords." Gloria nudged Casey's elbow.

"Double swords? Oh." Casey held Robert's loaner next to Gloria's old sword.

Get ready to look like an idiot.

"Sorry Grimes," Robert said. "The one I gave you is just titanium."

"Ugh." Luci groaned. "A padlock is going to defeat us?"

Casey put the titanium sword back in its sheath. "Any other ideas?" He flicked the old sword at the lock. *Clink.* Sparks flickered. "Oh great, I put a notch in this one too."

Except he hadn't. The silver-blue edge gleamed straight and bright. The padlock dangled like a chunky metal candy cane.

"You did it." Luci gasped.

"I barely even swung." Casey reached a finger toward the blade.

"Wouldn't do that if I was you." Robert crossed his arms. "Where did you steal it, Grimes?"

"What are you talking about?" Luci pried the broken padlock away and handed it to Gloria. Gloria tossed it over her shoulder.

Robert raised one finger. "First, he shows up carrying an ancient

Sylvan blade worth a fortune. Seriously, you haven't noticed the engraving on the hilt?"

Casey tilted the sword, blade-down. Sure enough, an SW marked the metal.

Robert held up two fingers. "Second, he leaves it in the bath house—along with an indestructible dark lantern. And finally..." He lifted a third finger. "He's totally clueless about how to use this relic." Robert stared Casey down. "At best, you're a thief. Obviously, you're not Sylvan."

The Beech creaked overhead.

Casey shrugged. "Good thing I'm leading the Butcher Brigade, isn't it."

"Shhh," Gloria said as Robert opened his mouth. She turned the tree's handle and a section of the trunk disappeared.

"Creeps!" Robert tripped over a root and fell, weapons jangling.

A tall, dark doorway loomed in the Beech.

"No wonder they locked it," Luci said. "Who could resist doing that over and over?"

CHAPTER 62
AWKWARD DANCE

THEY MOVED THROUGH THE ARCH, fingering their weapons. Robert's mouth hung open, eyebrows stuck halfway up his forehead. The high, shadowy space smelled like rot—the hidden kind that multiplies in attics.

A sunken hole gaped in the floor, wide enough to hold dolphins. When they leaned over the edge, glazed blue stone shone under their fingers.

Luci slid one leg over. "Guess I'm the one with the light."

"Hang on." Casey pulled off his pack and rummaged around. His rope slapped the side of the dry pool. "We'll hold this end."

"Much better." Luci grabbed the rope and swung over.

Her glowing shape descended, hand over hand. "Deeper than I thought, but bone dry." She took a few steps, twenty feet below. "*Literally* bone dry. Fish skeletons everywhere—and a rotten old ladder." Her shape moved away. At the center of the pool, she knelt. "This looks like a fountainhead. And here's a lever..."

She ran back, face glowing. "Why couldn't all the reservoirs work the same? It's a little irritating. There are two numbers, fifty and one-hundred, with an exclamation point after the hundred. They're labeled 'Maintenance' and 'Midsummer's Eve.'"

"It *is* summer," Gloria said.

"More important, the numbers are probably years," Robert said. "The history said the trees were supposed to be renewed every half-century—every fifty years."

"Look who was paying attention after all," Luci said.

"It's been a long time," Casey said. "So I vote one hundred."

"Makes sense." Luci looked around her sunken prison. "Based on what happened last time, this could be explosive. How do I get out?"

"Um, run really fast?" Casey held up the rope. "And then we pull you out?"

"Afraid you'd say that." Luci took a deep breath and pumped her fists, jogging and jangling in place.

"Better throw us your stuff," Casey said.

"Oh, right."

Her pack came sailing up and Robert caught it.

"Scythe-staff, handle first," she called.

Shielding his face, Casey grabbed it.

"Bow, heading your way." It made a hollow twang as Robert snatched it.

"Lots of arrows!"

"Look out! Duck! Ouch!" Arrows clattered to the floor.

Robert sucked his wrist and Casey checked the side of his face for blood.

Luci's voice moved away. "Get the rope ready." In the center of the pool, she did several jumping jacks and bent over the lever. "Here I GOOO!"

"Hand me the rope, will you Robert?"

Robert jerked his wrist from his mouth. "Thought you had it."

"HELP!" The ground vibrated and gurgled like a pod of whales clearing their throats. Luci stared up at them. "Bad time to joke around, guys."

Silvery, foaming liquid misted everything. Waves crashed the bottom of the reservoir.

A wet rope end hit Casey in the face.

"I'll get you for this," Luci screamed.

He wrapped the rope around his shoulder and Robert and Gloria grabbed on. They backed away, straining, as a very wet Luciana West scrambled over the edge. She pulled the dripping quiver off her back and dumped it on Robert, who dodged away too late. She shook her hair in Casey's face and pinched his arm, hard. "I expect better from you!"

"Ouch!" Casey blinked. "It was because of–"

"Hush." Luci touched his mouth. "Not another word." She turned to Gloria, who backed away. "It's ok, Glo-baby, I know you weren't part of this."

Elixir roiled and churned, surging up the pool walls.

Luci bounced on her toes. She jumped on the bright blue rim and balanced on one leg. "Actually, I don't feel so bad. We should all go for a swim."

Robert's hand fell on Casey's shoulder. "My head...dizzy."

Casey shrugged him off. "Luci, I'm not sure you're ok."

She spread her arms. "Hubba hoy, Grimesy. I feel wonderful, although just a little bit irritated with you."

Casey glanced at Robert, who was sneezing violently.

Luciana bent her knees, arms pointed at the gurgling pool.

"Do something, quick," Gloria said.

Casey held out one hand. "Luci. Um." He hung his head. "Would you like to dance?"

Poised on the edge like an Olympic diver, Luci's eyes lit up. "That's an amazing idea!"

"Quick Gloria, grab our stuff," Casey groaned.

Luci took his hand. She pranced around him, snapping her fingers. She swept away, curled in close, and sent him spinning. Casey tripped and Luci caught him. She spun them both in a circle. The dance went on forever.

Gloria came running. "Everything's outside, even Robert."

Casey nodded as Luci reeled in an invisible rope, gliding closer and closer. She shut her eyes, flung her arms in the air and threw herself at him.

"Holy Bog Creeps!" He fell to one knee and caught her, pushed her arms over his shoulder and staggered to the door. Outside, the sky was pink and purple. He spilled Luci to the ground. She rolled over, opened her eyes and smiled.

Casey leaned against a tree root, breathing hard.

Robert was sharpening his diamond-edged sword. "She's definitely *not* your cousin."

Casey felt his face turn red.

Once again, the Beech was blank and smooth. Mushrooms crumbled to dust and the air smelled clean. They collected their things, strapped everything on, and took the path toward Trickery and the Sighing Sycamore. Robert led the way. Casey and Gloria came next, side by side, with Old Thundersnot.

When Casey looked over his shoulder, Luci was skipping.

CHAPTER 63
DOUBLE THREAT

THE SKY DARKENED as they hurried through campus. One street over, someone ran past, breathing hard. Dry leaves blew under their feet.

"Wonder where everyone's hiding." Luci seemed back to normal.

On the forest's edge, Old Thundersnot stiffened, looking back.

"Someone there?" Casey called.

The woods were silent, no nightbirds or crickets. Fireflies stayed out of sight. They heard the rattle of the Sycamore's chain long before they could see it. A carpet of toadstools spread under the forbidding tree.

"Come on, Old Thundersnot," Gloria said.

The bloodhound followed, huffing and shaking his paws.

"He's getting braver," Casey said.

"Maybe he got a whiff of elixir," Luci said.

"He still won't be a bit of good," Robert said.

Gloria stamped her foot at him.

"Oh for crying out loud..." He rolled his eyes.

Parting huge ferns, they circled the tower of a tree.

"Maybe this sick-of-more tree is not so bad," Gloria said. "Look."

Casey held the lantern high. Vines climbed the ancient bark.

Behind the leafy curtain, a brick patio hugged the trunk. A pointed gate barred a dark doorway.

To Casey's surprise, the gate creaked open but the hinges stuck halfway. He sucked in his ribs and squeezed onto narrow stairs. Gloria slipped after him, then Old Thundersnot, then Robert. Their feet smudged grimy blue and white tiles.

"It's filthy in here," Robert said.

Outside, something thudded into the Sycamore.

Luci parted the leafy screen. "Who's out there?"

"Do you think she's ok by herself?" Robert's fingers twitched on his sword.

"Probably one of us should—"

Luci screamed.

Casey lunged after her, but his sword wedged itself through the spiky, rusted gate. The hilt bit into his hips, pinning him. He twisted back and forth. Robert shoved from behind. It only made him more stuck.

"Let...me...go," Casey gasped.

Laughter came from outside. A low snicker, a high cackle, none of it nice.

"...all by yourself in such a perfect spot..." someone sneered.

Metal rang as it slid from a sheath.

"You should really pick better friends," a girl said.

Casey knew those voices. Drooce and Cortland.

"Get away from me or you'll be sorry!" Luci yelled.

"We're coming," Casey tried to say. With the gate pressing his chest, it came out as a whisper. "Robert," he rasped, "Pull off my sword belt."

Metal crashed outside. Old Thundersnot barked and Gloria cried, "Luci!"

"Hell's bells!" Robert rattled the gate. "There's no room."

Weapons rang and Tonya squealed.

"I warned you," Luci yelled.

Robert took a running jump, grabbing for the top of the gate.

Metal screeched on metal, and Luci hissed in pain. Silence, then a horrified yell. Piercing shrieks. Crashing sounds moved further and further away.

Casey stopped struggling. Robert cursed.

The vines parted and Luci stepped through, hair flying madly. Blood dripped from a slash on one cheek. "Seriously?" She looked around with glassy eyes. "I guess that's just how it goes sometimes." She unfastened Casey's sword belt and he struggled free. The metal screamed in protest.

"How'd you beat them?" Robert stared at Luci. "Drooce is dangerous."

"Got lucky I guess." She looked down. "Give you the play-by-play later."

Gloria hugged her. Robert turned to climb the narrow stairs.

"That cut looks deep," Casey said.

Luci touched her face. "Let's get this over with."

They creaked up the stairs and onto a balcony. Bead necklaces glittered, dangling from lamps and bannisters. Tables and chairs lined a wide floor below

"Looks like a King Midas Day party," Luci said. "That holiday when everyone dresses up and pretends to be fabulously rich."

Their feet left dust prints as they tramped downstairs.

"A tavern and *dance* floor." Luci winced. "Where's the reservoir?"

Under the balcony, stools crowded a copper-topped bar. Dusty bottles and glasses filled long shelves. They looked at themselves in a smudged mirror. Luci dabbed at the blood on her cheek and looked away. Gloria stood on her tip-toes and waved. Then she pointed.

"Look, a switch."

Casey followed her gaze, and flicked it. With a *whoosh*, lamps flared to life. A crystal chandelier flashed overhead. Fire roared in a grate below their feet.

"Super cool," Casey said. "But we want elixir, not fire."

"Here's something." Robert stooped behind the bar. "A dial with three settings. Renew, Cleanse, and Ambience. It's got to be elixir, right?"

"Set it to renew," Casey said.

"Do it, Pink-Eye," Gloria said.

"Hold on a second." Luci inched toward the stairs. "Is everyone ready to run?"

CHAPTER 64
FINAL MESSAGE

THEY STUMBLED OUTSIDE, sneezing and rubbing their eyes. Old Thundersnot turned in circles, woofing. Clouds of silver steam billowed out, rising through the branches.

"Should've turned out the torches." Casey coughed.

"Who knew it would vaporize?" Luci put her face in her hands, feet jittering the ground. "Ooh, I've definitely had enough for one night..."

Robert held a truncheon in one hand, a war hammer in the other. "We are the champions!" His eyes gleamed madly. "We'll take all comers!"

Gloria's eyelids drooped as she leaned on Casey.

He felt as if he had wings on his shoulders, tugging him skyward. At the same time, his head swam like a bowl of goldfish. "It's over, right?" He threw his fists in the air. "We did it! Three cheers for the Butcher Brigade!"

Robert let out a happy yell and sneezed.

"Hooray!" Gloria laughed woozily.

"Victory parade!" Luci's pendant lit up her queasy smile.

High overhead, branches crashed and snapped. The sounds got closer. A heavy branch cratered the forest floor, showering them with wreckage. Thin screams pierced the night. Waspish shapes darted across the moon.

"Wait." Casey couldn't believe his eyes. "This can't be right."

"I...I don't understand." Luci's voice trembled.

"Maybe they're leaving," Casey said.

"But there are more," Robert said. "At least two dozen. There are supposed to be less."

Gloria hugged Old Thundersnot's neck.

"Let's get out of here," Casey said. "Let's go home." As they stumbled away, he thought about his dad and mom and Ms. Jones and the popcorn ceiling in his boring bedroom. Was that home or was this?

Butcher Beasts followed them, shrieking and throwing branches. Once, Robert tackled Gloria out of the way as a treetop smashed the path. Butchers flew lower and lower as Old Thundersnot howled. Robert and Luci strung their bows under the leaning stones. Arrows whistled into the night and a monster fell, screaming. Then another.

What had they done wrong? This had to be some awful mistake. But the butchers kept coming, and nothing they'd discovered had prepared them for this. Not Ms. Crake, not the history. None of their fighting techniques were enough now.

On the edge of Trickery, they sprinted from the woods and dove into an alley. Wings whirred overhead. Roof stones came crashing down. Robert clutched multiple weapons and tears shone on Gloria's cheeks. Nothing Casey could say would make this better. Luci hid her face in her hands. It seemed too horrible to be real.

Torches flickered down the alley.

"Grimes, is that you?" Jake McGusty yelled. "We've been looking all over for you, man. The Skewers aren't going down without a fight. Most important, Bones told me to say, What's taking so long, kid? And he said to give you this."

Jake held out a wrinkled, black-streaked parchment.

Casey took it with shaking hands.

"Sorry," Jake said. "Got a little blood on it."

It was a very basic map of Sylvan Woods. Trees were triangles. Hills were squiggles.

Someone threw a torch in the air and a Butcher Beast crashed down. Casey moved his finger over the map as kids rushed forward, stabbing with their skewers.

"Oh no," he said.

Luci and Robert leaned in. Gloria hugged his knees.

"There's another Sentry tree," Casey said. "In the BeastWoods."

CHAPTER 65
SKEWER SQUAD

BONES TOLD us about the Sentries, super serious stuff," Jake said. "How about an armed escort?" Three carcasses popped and hissed in the street. Dozens more butchers swarmed overhead, clicking their claws but staying out of reach.

"The trail to the BeastWoods is unprotected..." The gash on Luci's cheek had faded to a pale twist. "How can we keep them off us?"

"What about the bath house tunnel?" Jake said.

They looked at him blankly.

"Can't believe you haven't used it. Maybe you're never late for class."

He put two fingers to his lips and whistled. Kids came running down the alley, skewers clanking. "New assignment," Jake yelled. "Get Grimes and the Butcher Brigade to the BeastWoods. They've got crazy important stuff to do."

"Death to the butchers!" someone yelled, and skewers rattled.

Jake pumped his fist. "Let's go."

The forest of skewers marched through Trickery. Butcher Beasts screeched overhead. Whenever the kids crossed open spaces, stones and branches hurtled down.

"Move faster," Jake yelled. "Horsetail formation!"

The crowd dissolved into lines and started jogging. Helping Gloria, Casey could barely keep up. His breath came in gasps.

"Take a break, Grimes." Robert grabbed Gloria's hand.

Casey didn't argue.

Weapons clashed and torches guttered as they sped through Trickery. The Great Hall was boarded up. Light shone through cracks. Butchers scratched and tore at the moonlit roof.

They swept through the towering pines and up the winding trail. The monsters shrieked like angry witches and the formation crumbled.

"Don't stop moving," Jake yelled.

They ducked and ran, scrambling up the rocky hillside. Butchers dive-bombed them, fangs and talons glinting. A girl rolled through the brush, screaming, as a monster clawed at her. Others ran to help, skewers slashing.

"Get underground!" Jake stood by a gaping hole in a pile of boulders. He caught Casey's eye and waved him past. "Catch you on the other side, Grimes."

Casey stumbled underground, Gloria right beside him. They scraped through darkness, kids bumping them from behind.

"Watch it," Robert snapped nearby.

The elbows went away.

Where was Luci?

Casey's sword kept snagging the walls as his feet scuffed downhill. Fur brushed his knee and a wet nose snuffed his arm.

"Let me squeeze past, would you?" It was Luci's voice, several kids back.

"She's with us, let her through." Robert sounded ready to punch someone.

Milky light from her pendant glowed around them.

"I'll try and stay in the middle," she said.

The tunnel was dirty and cramped, but at least it felt safe.

This could still end well. Casey rubbed his eyes. *We'll find the last*

Sentry Tree, and the magic will wake up. Everyone will be safe. Gloria, Luci, Robert, everyone.

He did his best to believe it.

They walked for what seemed like a long time. Roots poked through the sides of the tunnel, just one or two, then more. The floor sloped upward. Heavy air swept their faces.

They climbed into the watchful silence of a wild, ancient wood.

CHAPTER 66
OLD THUNDERSNOT EARNS HIS KEEP

A HALF CIRCLE of skewer-carrying kids hunched in the clearing. Casey glanced at Bones' map. It was very short on detail.

"It's so nice and quiet here." Gloria yawned. "Can we take a little nap?"

"Wish we could." Casey smoothed her hair. "We've got to keep moving."

He walked to the circle of waiting kids. "We're heading in, looking for green mushrooms. They'll lead us to the Sentry tree."

"We'll be right behind you," one of them said. "Once Jake gets here."

On the edge of the BeastWoods, Casey lit the dark lantern. Robert pulled out a bludgeon. Luci gripped her scythe-staff. The forest closed around them, dense and dark. It smelled like rotting leaves and bitter herbs, with the occasional harsh whiff of monster. Casey held the lantern high. They slashed through vines and branches.

"They say Bog Creeps get as big as bears in here," Robert said.

"Razor Wings the size of pterodactyls," Luci said.

"That's great," Casey said. "Thanks."

"Let's be really, really quiet," Gloria whispered.

Green eyes gleamed in the darkness. Ten feet off the ground. Casey lifted the lantern, heart pounding. Something small and high up bounded away. He pressed a hand to his chest.

"Shh," Luci said. "Where there's a baby, there's often a protective–"

RAWR! Something crashed through the thicket. The ground shook and trees whipped the air, closer and closer. Robert swept an arrow from his quiver.

"It's too big," he muttered.

He stuck his arrow into Casey's lantern, and the dry wood whooshed into flame. Robert sent the arrow whistling away. The forest stopped shaking—and shook in reverse. The enormous beast chased the flame as the kids rushed deeper into the night.

Creatures circled behind leafy curtains, just out of sight. Trails died away to nothing.

The woods are toying with us, Casey thought.

Robert kept his bludgeon raised. "We must be almost a mile in."

Gloria leaned on Old Thundersnot, who shifted nervously.

"If only we could put him on the scent," Luci said.

"He's just a useless old...hey, wait." Robert unlaced a hiking boot. He raised the tread and sniffed. "Disgusting. If that dog is honest, toadstools are the strongest smell." He stuck the boot under the bloodhound's nose.

Old Thundersnot stiffened and jerked away.

"Now's not the time to think of yourself," Gloria said.

The dog grunted, raised his head, and snuffled. A low roar rumbled in his chest.

"Good boy." Gloria picked up his leash. She looked over her shoulder with bleary eyes.

She can't take much more of this, Casey thought.

The hound led them over a ridge. Through a thicket. Into a clearing. For a moment, stars gleamed overhead. A bird with ten foot wings glided past, and they hit the ground. When they looked up, they all noticed the same thing.

"This clearing stinks," Luci whispered. "He's done it."

Green mushrooms puffed through spiky grass.

"He's not good for nothing after all," Robert said.

"We knew that all along, didn't we?" Gloria rubbed the bloodhound's head.

Fungi twisted away into the woods like frayed ropes.

"Good luck to anyone trying to find us." Starlight shone on Luci's face as they followed the rot-loving toadstools back into the dark.

CHAPTER 67
SIX-LEGGED DEATH

THE SENTRY WAS huge enough to hold a climbing gym, but the tree no longer brushed the sky. It leaned over the BeastWoods, supported by lesser trees. Roots twisted in the air like dead octopi. They stared in horror.

"We're too late," Robert said.

"You can't even tell what it is." Luci hung her head.

Casey held up the lantern. In its yellow light, the tree looked even worse. A jagged crack split the trunk above the roots. If only there was the slightest sign of life...

High overhead, something screamed. The scream floated closer, joined by other screams. Dark shapes blacked out the stars.

"Oh no," Luci breathed.

They scrambled through the Sentry's gaping crack. Inside the crumbling wooden tower, the air smelled like sawdust and sulphur. A Butcher Beast landed in the opening. Then another. They crowded the night with dagger teeth and evil button eyes.

The children backed into the center of the tree.

Through Casey's tiredness, it felt like a horrible dream—until he looked at Gloria. He set down the dark lantern and dragged his

Sylvan sword from its sheath. *This is it. Now you fight, the best you can.* He drew his second sword.

"Weak spines," Robert snarled.

A Butcher Beast darted forward, and his arrow found its open mouth.

Two more took its place.

"Weak eyes," Luci gasped. She slashed with her staff and a monster fell.

"Take that and that and–!" Casey lashed out with his swords. One missed everything, but the Sylvan blade sliced off a butcher's arm.

Robert bludgeoned the snarling monster to the dirt.

"Found it," Gloria cried.

Casey couldn't take his eyes off the monsters.

More launched forward, teeth clacking, stingers jabbing.

Rusty metal creaked behind him. What was Gloria doing?

Dead eyes and hungry teeth flew at them. Robert smashed one but the next one tore the bludgeon from his hands. Casey's Sylvan sword sliced through its face as Robert pulled out a war hammer. Luci screamed and sliced. Black blood dripped and spattered.

Twitching butchers stacked the ground.

"Hurry!" Gloria screamed.

Casey spun. His sister hovered over a dark opening in the floor, Old Thundersnot growling and snapping beside her. More butchers boiled inside, clinging to the walls.

"Climb down, Gloria!" Casey shouted. "Luci, follow her!"

Robert threw a javelin and a butcher fell. Casey's titanium blade broke off in a monster's eye. Another ran itself through on his Sylvan sword, biting and spitting. Robert killed the next one with a spear. His weapons rack was almost empty. A monster snapped at his throat and he hammered it to the dirt.

"Go, Casey!"

The butchers crawled the walls like six-legged death.

Casey jumped, grabbing at metal rungs. Robert's boots crushed his fingers as they half-fell down the ladder. The last thing they heard was Old Thundersnot, howling.

CHAPTER 68
UNDERGROUND GRAVEYARD

MILKY LIGHT GLOWED at the bottom. Gloria sobbed in Luci's arms. They stood on the skeletons of leaves, fighting for breath. Inky blood dripped from their clothing.

Casey pulled his sister into a tight hug.

Robert's face was dark. "Filthy bugs."

The tunnel was as quiet as a cemetery at midnight. Then... Casey's scalp tingled. They weren't alone. Something was watching. Enormous and almost dead, but still holding on...with the last weak roots of its hope.

"We can't stop," Casey said. "We've got to keep going."

His friends looked ready to collapse, but no one argued.

Ghostly roots brushed their faces. With the lantern gone, they walked slowly, staying close. The air changed. The dirt walls disappeared into open space. Luci held her pendant high.

The stood in an earthen cave. A chasm split the ground, too wide to cross. Dead roots clutched empty air. When Casey stumbled to the edge, his eyes couldn't find the bottom.

"No," he said. "No..."

Then he saw the one last living root.

Stretching over the darkness like a gnarled rope. The last trace of the great tree's life.

Casey thought about the Old Oak. How it had caught him that first night, a hundred feet in the air. How it had needed his help. He took off his pack and handed his sword to Robert.

"What are you doing?" Robert said. "Save the heroics."

Luci grabbed Casey's wrist. "Not a chance."

"Casey," Gloria said. "Don't."

The air was heavy and dead, the way a graveyard might feel underground. It pressed Casey's skin. Tugged his eyelids. He kicked off his shoes. All of a sudden, he laughed.

"Heroics," he said. "That's funny, Robert. We're the Butcher Brigade. What do you think we've been doing all this time?"

A smile squeezed out through Robert's gritted teeth.

"No way," Luci said. "None of this tough boy stuff. I know you're good with trees, but we're tying a rope to you at least."

"Sorry." Casey stood at the edge. "You're Sylvans, so I shouldn't need to tell you this, but this tree has been used and forgotten. It needs to *trust* me."

"Nooo." Luci stretched out her arms.

He put a foot down, testing the root's strength. If it was dry and brittle, he wouldn't be able to cross, and whatever happened next, it would happen to all of them together. But he felt the tiniest movement, like a weak old earthworm waking up and stretching.

"I know you're still alive," Casey whispered. "I want to help." He closed his eyes, held out his arms, and breathed. The root stretched rough and hairy under his toes. Holding still. Waiting. Or had it heard him at all?

Hands flung wide, he stepped into space. The root wobbled, but he'd expected that. The tree was so tired, it couldn't help itself. One foot in front of the other, he moved over the deep ravine. No stopping, no looking down.

"Don't let me fall," he whispered. "I'll find the elixir and help you..."

The far edge was six feet away. Casey wanted to lunge for it, but he knew better. One step closer...and the root twisted.

The tree doesn't believe me.

His hands clawed the air as he staggered sideways—one step, two steps—and fell toward the bank. His arms and chest hit soil. His fingers found rock. He pulled himself to safety as his friends shouted. He waved to them shakily across the deep chasm.

"Casey!" Luci's pendant flew across and landed next to him.

He gave them one last look, and moved away. The tunnel twisted, soil rustling from the walls. It ended in a small room with a timber ceiling. Luci's pendant shone on a table covered with playing cards and tobacco pipes. On the wall, a painted sign said *Butcher Brigade ~ we never forget.*

Casey sighed. In the center of the floor stood a gleaming metal pump.

"The brigade is back," he whispered.

CHAPTER 69
THE TRAP SPRINGS SHUT

CASEY GRABBED the pump with both hands and pulled. His shoulders shook. The silver handle swung open. Liquid gurgled and roared under his feet.

He turned and ran.

The floor softened to mud. Dirt slid off the walls. The cliffs of the chasm shook, chunks breaking off. His root bridge drooped into shadow. He was trapped.

"The gap is getting smaller!" Robert yelled.

Luci dug through Casey's pack. Gloria clasped her hands over her heart. The cliffs lurched and everyone stumbled. Then a coil of rope snaked through the air. Casey wrapped the rope around his hands. *Don't think about it, just do it,* he told himself. He took a running jump.

The rope tore his fingers as he hit the opposite wall. Foot by foot, his friends pulled him to safety. Gloria hugged his knees, Luci threw her arms around him, and Robert shook both his hands, pressing the Sylvan sword into them.

They splashed through an underground swamp. Water lapped the rungs of the ladder.

"Maybe we can climb halfway and wait," Luci said.

But the silty flood kept rising.

"It's at my shins," Robert said.

Casey pushed Gloria higher. Her head brushed the rusty hatch.

Behind him, Luci took a deep breath. "We fight the butchers or we drown."

Robert squeezed by in the dark, a dagger in his teeth. He punched Casey's shoulder. The door creaked open. He was gone.

"Haven't used this scythe-staff nearly enough." Luci tried to smile.

Gloria closed her eyes as Luci disappeared. Water lapped their heels. Casey hugged his sister and felt her tears hot on his neck. He pressed his face into her dirty golden hair.

"I'm sorry," he said.

She squeezed his hand. He pushed the hatch open and they climbed out.

Into something impossible.

The inner tower of the tree was empty. Robert and Luci waited in the shadows, confusion on their faces.

"Are we dreaming?" Luci said.

An ear-splitting groan shook the tree. The ground vibrated as its roots grabbed acres of dirt, struggling to make itself right. The trunk jerked straighter. The jagged opening in its trunk shrank as glowing fibers knit it back together.

"Wait!" Casey yelled. "That's our door!"

Robert ran forward, slashing with his longsword. "I'll hold it back!"

Casey got a running start and dove, pulling Gloria after him. Luci's head and shoulders slid out, but splinters snagged her pack.

"Casey, help!"

He grabbed her hands and pulled. Fabric ripped, and she jerked free.

"Robert!" Casey yelled.

The dangerous boy's eyes met theirs, wide and startled, as the tree sealed itself shut. His sword twisted in the thick gray bark and stuck. The giant Sentry towered over them.

"No." Casey slumped against the roots. "Not Robert."

An angry hum rose from the woods. Starlight glinted on waspish bodies as hundreds of insect eyes crawled over them, picking at their skins like knives and forks.

So the magic had failed. After all they'd done.

An enormous butcher flew forward. Its high forehead and curved mouth seemed vaguely human. Its jaws opened...and Casey shuddered. The monster spoke. Hard, metallic words.

"We-claim-you. Feed-my-young. The-swarm-will-take-you..."

Luci yelled. Her arrow glanced off the butcher's head. She sent her last ones whistling at the monster, but not one found a mark.

The butcher queen sneered.

Casey raised the Sylvan sword in both hands. He'd fight as long as he could.

The queen raised a talon and her swarm surged forward.

CHAPTER 70
THE BUTCHER QUEEN

THIS WASN'T RIGHT. Where was the magic, the rescue? Casey felt very strong—or very angry. He jabbed his sword at the queen. "I CHALLENGE YOU TO SINGLE COMBAT!"

The advancing swarm hovered. The butcher queen gnashed her teeth, and Casey realized the grinding sounds were laughter. He sheathed his sword.

"YOU COWARDLY BUG!"

Something Robert would have said.

The queen stopped laughed. She shot forward.

Casey dove for the Sentry, scrambling up the trunk. *Don't let me fall, please,* he begged. Wings whirred behind him. A cold breeze fanned his back. *Now!*

He turned and jumped. Surprise twitched in the queen's eyes as he flew past. Casey's bare feet hit her spine—narrow as a rooftop or a sapling. But that was nothing new to Casey.

She snarled, lurching right and left. Trying to throw him. They rose into the air. The forest fell away. He slid out his Sylvan sword with a silvery ring.

"I wish I was better at this," he said, and swung down wildly.

His sword glanced off the queen's armor, slicing off a foot.

He swung again and her whole leg spun away. Wings flailing, the queen twisted and shrieked, but she didn't know Casey. He locked his knees around her spine. His sword came down again. High above the forest, clinging to a butcher's back, Casey smiled.

I'm going to win.

But the wasp queen realized the same thing. Suddenly, they were falling, her wings pinched back. Two tiny figures stood in a halo of light far below. Closer and closer they rushed. Casey saw the horror on Luci and Gloria's faces. The butcher's wings flared out as she struck.

Casey hit the ground, rolling through dirt and leaves. The girls were pinned beneath the monster's talons. "YOU'RE A LIAR!" he shouted. "A COWARD!"

With a shriek, the queen leapt on him. Black blood splashed him, lots of it—then teeth like knives sank into his shoulder. He screamed as a thousand fireflies danced overhead. His heels kicked the air. Time slowed down for Casey then.

His sword fell from his hand and spun away.

Somewhere, Gloria wailed.

Blood, real red blood, gushed from his shoulder.

Dark wings flick-flicked.

They lifted away.

Luci bounded from a root, rising after them. Her eyes flashed green. Snakes coiled around her head like wild hair. The butcher jerked aside, but Luci caught it. A stiletto sparkled...once, twice, three times. His friend fell away, hands snatching, eyes wide.

"Luci..."

The monster rose into the night, half-blind and screaming.

Her stinger jabbed Casey's belly.

Overhead, the heavens blazed blue and purple. Silver lightning split the sky. Brilliance washed the forest with an electric hum, brighter than the moon and stars.

One of Gloria's blurry watercolors.

Casey's toes brushed treetops. Numbness stole over him but he forced his eyes open.

One last time.

The Sentry towered ahead, forked hands reaching. Gold lights sparkled in its branches, darting together in a whirling blaze. The magic exploded. It tingled Casey's skin, lighting the woods like sunrise. Brightness wrapped the butcher queen, eating her to dust as she screamed. Her evil face collapsed and a rushing wind washed her away.

We did it. Casey shut his eyes. *The magic is real...we set it free.*

Then he was falling.

CHAPTER 71
RETURN TO VINTAGE WOODS

THE ROOM WAS WHITE, too white for Sylvan Woods. Machines hummed and beeped. Voices mumbled. Instruments clinked. All very far away. Casey couldn't move his arms or legs, but he didn't mind. He closed his eyes against the painful glow.

Later, the lights went down. People left the room.

The dark was warm. No one to fight. Nowhere to go.

After awhile, a door swung open. A dangerous-looking boy leaned over the bed.

"Not supposed to be here, but I had to check on you." Robert shook his head. "You did really well for a Civilian kid. Actually, better than really well..."

Light pooled like spilled milk. The room began to blur.

"Gloria..." Casey rasped.

"She made me ask her permission to visit," Robert said. "Can you believe it? Don't know when I'll see you again, but... I hope things turn out." He pressed something into Casey's palm. "Take care of yourself."

Casey tried to wave, but his arms were too heavy, so he closed his eyes.

When he opened them, a girl sat in the corner, holding a bunch of wildflowers. Her wavy hair was tied back with a ribbon. He sat up a little on his pillows.

"Casey!" Luciana West jumped up. "You really scared us. If it hadn't been for that pine tree..." She shuddered. "I never want to see legs bent like that again. Thank goodness Bones showed up with the Skewers—they're an official club now—and summoned a gryphon. Otherwise, you never would've made it out of the BeastWoods."

Her words rushed over him, making his head spin.

"I told the front desk I was your cousin, remember how we used to say that? Getting here was kind of difficult. I sneaked across the border into Vintage Woods and took a taxi. Getting inside the hospital was a little tricky, but they didn't have a Sylvan detector, luckily."

She gave him a small smile.

"Thank you," he said. A memory flitted through his head. Green eyes...a knife...snakes. "When the Butcher Beast got me..." He trailed off. Their eyes met.

Luci looked away, pushing at her hair. "I was hoping you wouldn't remember that."

Somewhere out of sight, a machine beeped like an alarm clock.

She clasped her hands in her lap. "It's not common, but it happens sometimes, when I get really angry or scared and I...I didn't want you and Gloria to know. It's why my family moved to Sylvan Woods, to get a fresh start." She blinked several times.

"*What* happens?" Casey fought to focus as the room swung back and forth.

"It was a long long time ago." Luci's eyes swam. "My great-great-grandma was a...a gorgon or something, and it kind of hangs around in your DNA. You were right, Casey." Her voice crumbled to a sob. "I've got a little monster in me." She hung her head. "Just a little."

Casey sank back in his pillows.

Luci buried her face in her hands.

Stars hovered around his head, but he squinted until he found

Luci, halfway to the door. "You should have told me sooner," he croaked. "Then I could have said...who cares?"

She froze.

His mouth felt full of cotton. "I mean I don't care, Luci. You're my friend."

He felt her arms around him, cautious of his cast. "Thank you, that means a lot." She wiped her eyes. "I'll miss you, Casey."

"I'll miss you too," he said, but the room was already empty.

After awhile, he found himself staring at Gloria and his parents. A diamond-tipped throwing star had imprinted itself on his palm. Wildflowers and a small stone frog sat on his bedside table. He realized he was wide awake.

His head ached and his eyes became puddles.

Gloria hugged him. Mom held the fingers that stuck out of his cast. "It's good to see you with your eyes open, honey." Her voice caught. "It must have been quite a fall, but the doctors say you'll be walking again soon."

Dad squeezed Casey's non-bandaged shoulder. "You must have been really high when the yellow-jackets came after you. Thank God you'll be ok."

Casey found himself crying. He couldn't think of anything to say.

†

A week later, Casey left the hospital. His family drove home down the curvy Civilian road on the safe side of the forest. He limped around the house for about a month. By the time summer ended, he could move slowly, without crutches.

He hid Robert's throwing star under his pillow.

He kept Luci's wildflowers until they were dead and dry.

Every day, he told the stone frog to "recite," and in a bass voice, it would speak the poem from Sylvan history: "The mighty sentries grew. They branched the magic web..." After a few weeks, he couldn't listen to it anymore.

Gloria spent hours with him in the sunshine, sitting on the roof.

They decided when he was better, they'd take their parents into the woods and show them things, like the Sentry Oak, and the changing paths, and maybe a Bog Creep. Then Dad and Mom would stop smiling and saying, "Oh, Casey, Oh Gloria." They'd believe their stories.

Ms. Jones sent Casey a postcard from the beach. It didn't say anything much, just something about purging old Sylvan *invisa-fade* from their lawn and air ducts, so no more invisibility to worry about —and have a happy school year, dear. It didn't make a whole lot of sense, but she'd always been obsessed with cleaning.

No one else came to visit.

Really, who else was there?

A week later, Casey went back to school. He was ok if he moved carefully and took his time. He stood in the front yard as the clean yellow bus rolled up.

The driver nodded at him. "Grimes, right?"

Casey didn't say hello. When he reached Vintage Woods Middle School, it hit him. People could see him. Whatever Ms. Jones had done to their house had worked. But it wasn't a big deal.

"Are you new here?" Lydia asked.

"No, not really." He walked away.

In the cafeteria, students offered to sign his cast. He told them thanks, but he didn't have a sharpie. During Chemistry, he folded homework and made Gloria a Razor Wing. He wasn't sure, but he thought it was her favorite monster.

The next day was his twelfth birthday. Casey decided he'd take a sick day and sleep through it. "Oh sweetheart," Mom said. "I'm sorry. You still need all the rest you can get."

He closed his eyes and told his spine it might as well heal faster. Sometime later, Gloria woke him.

"Get up, birthday boy."

"Shouldn't you be at school?" He rubbed his eyes.

"I took a sick day too." Gloria smiled.

Casey let her tug him downstairs. "I made you coffee," she whispered. "Drink it right away before Mom notices."

Several presents waited on the dining room table. Hot, roasty smells filled the kitchen. But something else filled the kitchen too.

People.

Casey stopped and stared.

"SURPRISE!"

Luci and Robert and Jake jumped out, laughing. Ms. Jones clapped by the sink. A wrinkled old man let go of his walker and whooped. Mom and Dad stood in the middle, handing out drinks. They looked surprisingly full of energy. A bent figure dressed in black leaned by the coffeemaker. Her blue eyes shone and her spiky blonde hair stood on end.

"Am I dreaming?" Casey said.

"No way, man!" Jake pounded his back. "Just took us a while to get our act together."

Luci gave him a hug. After an awkward pause, so did Robert.

"Your paperwork finally came through," Ms. Jones said. "I'm sorry it took so long, dear."

"And what a mountain of paperwork it was." An unhappy man in a light blue suit slumped against the fridge. "Everything is in order, but as long as I live, I never want to see a case like that again." Mom handed him a glass of wine and his expression brightened. "Thank you so much," he said. "Legally, I have to be here."

Ms. Crake straightened, as much as she could. "In the presence of these witnesses, and by the power vested in me as Headmaster, I hereby declare the Grimes family lawful residents of Sylvan Woods."

Clapping filled the kitchen.

Ms. Crake smiled at Casey and Gloria. "Welcome to Trickery School—and in case you're wondering, the buggers only paralyzed me."

The small crowd cheered some more. Everyone held wine and cocoa and coffee.

Gloria put a mug in Casey's shaking fingers.

Dad raised a toast. "Here's to a better school for you and Gloria —and some new friends. If I can say this, it's about time!"

"CHEERS!" everyone said.

"And here's to this lovely forest community," Mom said. "It sounds so unique, and we've all been dying for a change."

"HEAR, HEAR!"

"They have no idea what they're in for." Jake smiled at Casey.

"Not to worry." Bones thumped his walker. "Things actually *happen* in Sylvan Woods."

"We build, we brew, we craft, we defend..." Ms. Crake said grandly.

"We spy, we fight, we run for our lives," whispered Luci.

Everyone sipped their drinks, beaming at Casey. His heart floated up his windpipe to the back of his throat so he couldn't speak, even if he wanted to.

"In all my days of trans-communal work, I've never handled a situation this complex," Ms. Jones said. "We fought tooth and nail to get you transferred off Civilian books—very secretly, too. The system seemed determined to keep you. It was a sneaky uphill battle, but I pulled it off with lots of help from Trickery. Not to boast, dears, just so you understand why it's taken so long. But now you're free."

The whole room cheered and clapped some more.

Casey looked from face to face.

"This is too good to be true," he said. "I can't believe it."

"C'mon, man." Robert cuffed his shoulder. "Have a little faith."

"Have some cake." Mom handed him a plate. "Let it sink in."

"But not too slowly," Robert said.

Luci smiled. "Trickery School starts tomorrow. Don't worry, we recovered your sword—and the dark lantern, after Robert hacked his way out of the tree."

"And some of those birthday presents will help." Jake pointed.

"No way." Casey shook his head. "It's too much, I'm not ready."

"Oh, you'll be fine." Luci tossed her head. "Although...back at Trickery, people are arguing about magic again. There's a huge debate about Civilians too—what they are, what they're good for. Some of them blame you for regressing us a couple hundred years. Others say you don't even exist, that the Sentries were a publicity stunt. Can you believe it?"

Butterflies swirled in Casey's stomach. He did something he'd be doing a lot in the days ahead. Inside a circle, looking out, instead of outside, looking in...he smiled.

THANKS FOR READING THE MOSTLY INVISIBLE BOY.

If you're wondering what to read next, the adventures of Casey, Gloria and their friends continue in *Trickery School*.

For all the inside stuff on the Casey Grimes universe—including book news, tips on fighting monsters, and a free story—sign up for *The Sylvan Spy* at **b.link/MostlyInvisible.**

ACKNOWLEDGMENTS

My wife, Lindsay, gets number one billing, not only for being supportive, but for metamorphosing into an excellent beta reader with an eye for character arc. My kids are a wonderful local critique group and give me reliable feedback while laughing out loud at the funny parts (usually).

Thanks to my extended family for not viewing me as any more strange than usual when I announced I wanted to write kids' fantasy books. Special thanks to my brother Peter who remained interested through the many ups and downs of the road to publication. That ain't easy, folks.

Finally, in an over and under and behind everything way, I thank my Creator, Jesus, for walking with me through hard times, keeping me on my feet, and making my own life story weird and good with lots of plot twists. So let us always go on and on this way...why not?

ABOUT THE AUTHOR

AJ Vanderhorst (that's me) has had many jobs, including journalist, paramedic, escape artist, and baby whisperer. One time in fifth grade, I built a traffic-stopping fort in a huge oak tree, using only branches and imagination, and slept there for a week.

Now my wife and I live in a woodsy house with our proteges and a ridiculous number of pets, including a turtle with a taste for human toes. This makes me an expert on wild, dangerous things—invisibility spells, butcher beasts, hungry kids, you get the idea.

I'm the only author in the world who enjoys pickup basketball and enormous bonfires, preferably not at the same time. My family has drawn up several blueprints for our future tree castle. Visit me online at **ajvanderhorst.com**

And hey, if you enjoyed this book, would you do me a favor? Head over to **b.link/ReviewMIB** on your phone or laptop and leave a review. Casey, Gloria and their friends sure appreciate it!

AJ VANDERHORST

The Wizning Shelf
book award
WINNER

CASEY GRIMES
AT TRICKERY SCHOOL

Dedicated to my generous local critique group.
You're the best at toasts and creative chaos.
Thanks for making it fun.

The Sylvan Pledge

WE'LL NEVER STRAY FROM TREES AND SKY—
AN URBAN LIFE? WE'D RATHER DIE.
OUR FRIENDSHIPS HAPPEN FACE TO FACE
WITH FEASTS THROWN IN ON SPECIAL DAYS.
WE FIGHT THE MONSTERS IN THE WOODS
TO KEEP THEM FROM CIVILIAN 'HOODS.
WE'LL GUARD THE MAGIC OF THE BORDER
TO KEEP OUR BLOODLINES IN GOOD ORDER.
FIELDS AND RIVERS WE WILL TEND,
FORGOTTEN TRADES AND ARTS WE'LL MEND.
WE BUILD, WE BREW, WE CRAFT, WE DEFEND!

CHAPTER 1
WORST CASE SCENARIOS

CASEY GRIMES BENT OVER HIS claw-marked desk and stared down at the test that would determine his future. This was a big deal—A REALLY BIG DEAL. So why was he struggling to focus? He flicked the side of his head. "Elixir, Butcher Beasts, scythe-staffs," he whispered. "Get a grip."

Sylvan Woods was a wonderful place where trees towered higher than low-flying satellites. Sky-high paths twisted everywhere, leafy treeways that tied the forest together. You could walk to your friend's house, or Trickery School campus, or the Sylvan Shops without ever touching the ground. It was beautiful.

You could also die or be mangled in an endless number of ways including monster attacks, weapons classes, and unauthorized student duels. It was horrible.

Casey's mind flicked back two months to when he and his little sister Gloria had plunged into the woods behind their suburban Oregon home. Once they'd discovered the secret forest society of Sylvan Woods, they'd ended up fighting for their lives against an invading swarm of Butcher Beasts. In the final moments of battle, as the magic of the Sentry trees flared to life, he'd thought they were about to die.

Actually, there'd been a lot of moments like that.

But against all odds, they'd survived—and for the past forty-eight hours, he'd been a genuine Sylvan citizen, enrolled at Trickery School. It hardly seemed possible.

A chair scraped the floor and Casey jerked himself back to the present.

Around him in the battle-scarred Land Creature Defense classroom, dozens of kids circled answer after answer on their Trickery School placement tests. Incoming students like him, having an easy time. Or maybe he was giving them too much credit. Maybe he knew more about weapons trajectories than he thought. After all, he'd used several weapons—and hey, he was still alive.

Unlike the characters in these Trickery math problems.

Casey blinked several times, scanned the next scenario and circled E: *The spear misses the Bog Creep and shatters the oil lamp, causing an inferno.*

Optimal Pathways of Weapons (OPOW) was an upper level math class. Like everything else at Trickery, it was all about fighting monsters. Back when math involved apples and oranges, Casey still hadn't been great at it. Now he was mostly guessing where the swords and maces would connect. Choosing the worst possible outcomes. In his real-life experience, those were the most likely.

C: The arrow ricochets off a shield and stabs the archer in the rear.

E: The rapier snags the clothesline, allowing the spider-squid to bite the swordsman.

B: The slingshot rebounds off the gryphon's beak and hits the shooter's eye.

Classes like OPOW reminded Casey how bad he was at Sylvan things. Things like fighting, combat, and—attacks. The Sylvan approach to monsters and life in general was *Get them before they get you.* But for once, he felt ok.

After all, he was good at staying alive. That counted as a skill, right?

One of the most important ones.

You never knew when something might try to get you.

Casey's worst experience had happened in the sky. He'd been alone under distant, icy stars, dueling the butcher queen. When he'd plummeted from her spiny back, high over the woods, he'd felt his life slip through his fingers like wind. The fall had almost killed him. *Almost.*

Sylvan Woods was scary all right. But also amazing. *Amazingly scary. Scarily amazing.* For Casey the amazing won, hands down, because he was also good at trees. His pen hovered over the quiz. *Good at trees.*

There had to be a better way to put that. Let's see...he had a special connection with sappy, growing things. That didn't sound quite right. But it was true. Yesterday he'd tested straight to the top of Forestry and Climbing. If you boiled everything down, his love for trees and climbing was one big reason he was in Sylvan Woods, enrolled at Trickery School, sitting in the drafty Land Creature Defense barn. Of course there were other reasons, even better ones.

Luci, Robert, Jake—Sylvan kids who'd fought side by side with him and Gloria. Kids who liked them enough to risk their necks. For the longest time, friends had been something other people had. Not anymore.

Casey smiled. And circled D: *The javelin will fly between the willow's branches, straight into the heart of the maddened marsh hag.*

It couldn't hurt to be a little optimistic.

Because there was another reason, maybe the most intriguing one. *Magic.* Ancient and mysterious, ignored and unexplored for years, moving just below the surface of Sylvan Woods. Flowing in the roots of the Sentries. Unlike the kids obsessed with weapons and test results, Casey couldn't ignore the shimmering beauty of the forest. He couldn't un-see it. And surprisingly, he seemed to have a knack for tapping into the deep, quiet power of leaves and roots and branches.

Good at magic.

He liked the sound of that.

Of course, "open to magical options" or "saved by magic at the last second" would be more accurate... A trumpet blast rang through the woods. Casey quickly circled the final three worst outcomes he could find and jumped to his feet, grabbing his things as kids spilled down the aisles.

"How'd that test treat you, Grimes?"

A thin girl with short, tousled black hair stared at him as she shrugged on an oversized pack that threatened to pull her over backwards. Icy eyes flashed in a face that hadn't seen much sun that summer, maybe ever.

"Um, it went great," Casey said. "How do you know my name?"

"Written on the top of your test, obviously." She stuck out her hand. "Nice to finally meet the infamous Casey Grimes. Fiera Laurent."

"Famous? I'm definitely not—oww." Casey's knuckles cracked.

"*Infamous*," Fiera said as she squeezed.

Her grip was dry and talon-like. Not surprising. Sylvan kids viewed handshakes as little battles. Fiera flashed a quick, chilly smile. "If you don't mind, I'd like to–"

A low rumble came from the front of the room as the teacher cleared his throat. Casey turned quickly, before Fiera could finish. Best not to know what she wanted. He doubted it would be anything nice.

The teacher raised a plate-sized palm to slow the flood of kids. His fingers gleamed like they'd been dipped in metal—maybe a tight-fitting silver glove. The hand was attached to a tall, craggy man with a face like sandstone cliffs. He wore a black vest and crisp, neatly rolled shirtsleeves that would fray any second under the pressure of his rocky biceps.

"Head straight to the cafeteria," the teacher thundered. "Your presence is required—required, got it?—for an important announcement. Don't skip, even if you're done testing." His black eyes rolled up and down the rows, paused on Casey, and moved on. "I'm Mr.

Kawkazi," he added as an afterthought. "Some of you will have me for Fireside Cookery."

Kids shuffled in the aisles. Someone snickered.

"Ok, get moving." Mr. Kawkazi dropped his bruising gaze and students surged forward.

Casey dove into the river of kids, handed over his test, and ducked outside. The greenish light of Sylvan Woods washed over him.

"Hey, Casey," someone yelped behind him. He'd only known her for five seconds, but there was no mistaking Fiera Laurent's voice. Sharp and bratty, as if she expected you to do exactly as she asked. Well, he didn't have time to be interrogated.

Casey hurried onto the crowded, rickety bridge that left Land Creature Defense. When he glanced back, Fiera was struggling to follow. Her backpack dragged her shoulders back and her chin up, like she was snubbing everyone around her. She kept bouncing off other kids, eyes darting right and left from under her lids.

Casey sped up. Everything seemed better in the open woods.

Maybe the placement test had gone well after all.

CHAPTER 2
SHORTEST SYLVAN DISTANCE THEORY

CASEY COULD'VE STAMPEDED TO THE cafeteria with all the other starving kids. Instead, he took a shortcut and almost didn't get there at all.

He clattered up a wooden stairway, circling the trunk of a towering maple. On his right and left, kids rushed along the popular treeways, eager for lunch. Their pounding feet and chatter faded as Casey corkscrewed higher and higher.

Trees hid the Land Creature Defense building, a towering barn that resembled a viking hall on stilts. Since it housed dangerous beasts for classroom use, the hall was located on the edge of Trickery's campus. That meant Casey had some ground to cover before lunch. But there was more than one way to cover ground. In the two days since he'd been granted citizenship in Sylvan Woods, he'd spent as much time mapping the treetops as he had sleeping—maybe more.

He rubbed his eyes.

Lying awake in the small hours of the night, he'd come up with a scheme. He called it Shortest Sylvan Distance Theory, and he was kind of proud of it. The idea was, the shortest distance between any two points in Sylvan Woods was at the highest altitude. So by climbing higher, he'd reach lunch sooner. At least, theoretically. Trickery's treeway system was huge. There was still a lot of testing to do.

Wind rustled and swayed the enormous maple as Casey stepped onto a weathered platform that looked like a dance floor. Surrounded by green-gold sprays of leaves and lanterns on carved columns, it stood open to the indigo sky, far above the more popular paths.

"Hellooo Sylvan Wooods!" Casey shouted.

A tossing green sea surrounded him, brushed by clouds. It concealed miles of trails, loads of ingenious architecture, and Trickery School itself. Standing here at the top of the world, you'd never guess how close you were to safe, boring neighborhoods like Vintage Woods, Oregon—and that was kind of the idea. Sylvan Woods was meant to be hidden, a secret society on the edges of the map, created to protect those who remained blissfully unaware in the suburbs. Because the monsters weren't gonna police themselves.

Casey ran a hand through his wind-ruffled hair. He traced the top of his spine, down past his shoulder blades. No longer bent. His body was mostly back to normal after his terrible fall from the butcher queen's back. His stamina wasn't great, but he was getting his strength back, a day at a time.

In Sylvan Woods. His home.

He was totally ready for a fresh start. But he had to keep moving.

Rope walkways swept away in three directions. Casey chose the most cafeteria-pointed path and plunged into the forest. The rope bridge shot from trunk to trunk like a strand of wire strung on a giant fence. It descended slowly, heading north.

"That's what I'm talkin' about," Casey said.

The cafeteria hunkered by the Roaring River on the north edge of campus.

Then the bridge twisted sharply left. Casey frowned. This was unexpected, since pretty much every location in Trickery connected to other important ones—and what could be more important than lunch? He raised a hand to shade his eyes. The ropewalk showed no signs of veering back on course.

Great. So much for his Shortest Sylvan Distance Theory.

He stood at owl height, fifty feet above the ground in an aspen colony with pale green leaves and silver trunks. Glancing around, he found the metallic glimmer he was looking for. High-stepping over the guide rope, he moved onto a ladder bolted to a rocket-straight trunk. Seconds later he was on the ground.

The aspens ringed a clearing surrounded by toadstools, a circle within a circle. Casey smiled. Another magical place, but then...most of Sylvan Woods was magical.

His stomach rumbled.

"Don't go anywhere, ok?" he told the clearing. "I'll come back and visit."

He half-closed his eyes to get his compass bearings. North was through the hollow and over that stone wall. Bog Creeps, now he had his work cut out for him.

Casey took off running.

CHAPTER 3
TRICKERY SPIRIT

ALL CASEY WANTED WAS A HOT skrabbitburger with gravy and pickles—those killer bunnies were surprisingly tasty. Instead, he was ambushed by a beast with a thousand eyes.

He shoved out of the underbrush, picking burrs off his clothes. Straight ahead, smoke rose from the cafeteria's chimneys. Wildflowers trailed from its garden roof. Casey bounded up the wooden stairs, and the carved yellow doors gave way at his touch. He took a step into the sunny hall—and froze. The doors swung shut behind him with a hollow boom.

Every table was full of kids, parents sprinkled in here and there. Dozens of Trickery employees sat up front. Casey had never seen such a big crowd of people wearing earth and forest-colored clothing. He smoothed his black t-shirt nervously and flicked a leaf off his camo shorts. At least he had the apparel right.

So why is everyone staring at me?

A thousand eyeballs examined him from head to toe. Casey'd been mostly invisible for a year, due to a weird invisa-fade accident that made him blurry in the Civilian world. He'd hated it, but he'd also gotten used to being unnoticed. As a result, when people stared at him, he felt like a ghost being shredded by sunbeams. A few seconds passed, but to Casey, they felt like hours. He took a slow step backward, feeling for the door. If only he could slip away...

On the right, a pair of brown eyes said, *Hey, hello, right here!*

Casey's shoulders sagged in relief.

He staggered through the crowded room, weaving around backpacks and lynxes on leashes. Finally, he reached Luciana West. Her dark, wavy hair was pushed back with a headband. Her khaki and fern-green outfit complimented her tawny skin perfectly. Had she started ironing her t-shirts? It was hard to believe someone so fiery could be so pristine.

She gave him her trademark glare but it weakened to a smile. "I know you lose your bearings sometimes, but c'mon." She shoved books off a chair. "Luckily I saved you a seat."

On Luci's left, Casey's six-year-old sister Gloria gave him a wave. Her blond hair was pinned back neatly with a glittery butterfly clip. Her *I Vote Unicorns* t-shirt was a rosy brown that came dangerously close to pink, but she looked so fresh and well-prepared, no one would ever complain.

A dark figure loomed next to her. Black spiky hair, black clothes, black weapons harness, black everything—except for his bronze skin, which he sometimes hid with black camouflage paint. Robert Pierce was one of the most dangerous kids in Sylvan Woods and probably the world. He gave Casey a well-practiced smirk that said, *A year older but no wiser, eh Grimes.* Or more likely, *What an idiot.*

Casey sighed and dropped into the empty seat.

At one end of the long room, someone resumed talking. Casey sat up straighter as he recognized Ms. Crake's voice. She was his favorite teacher—although technically he hadn't taken a class yet. And after her role in the Butcher Beast War, she was the acting headmaster of Trickery. Crake stood on a platform in front of the huge stone hearth. As she spoke, she limped from side to side, a dark cloak swirling around her crooked shoulders. The rumor was she'd fallen off a cliff in a battle years ago.

"...in light of everything I've told you," Crake said, "Don't even think about missing Back to School Night. We'll talk all sorts of magic and mayhem once your parents join us." She paused, a hand to her chin. With her spiky pale-blond hair and blazing eyes, Crake had a way of making you forget how young she was—hardly old enough to be someone's mom—until she made a girlish gesture like that.

"What did she just say?" Casey whispered.

"You won't believe it," Luci whispered back.

"Something you shouldn't have missed," Robert added.

Casey gave them a dirty look. In some ways Luci and Robert had been easier to work with before they'd started speaking to each other.

"She talked about the magic trees," Gloria breathed. "And the butcher bugs and you and me!"

"What?" Casey looked at his friends.

Luci nodded, eyebrows raised.

'It's true," Robert said.

Ms. Crake's cold blue eyes flickered over the crowd, resting a second on Casey's table. He wished he hadn't wasted his time on the shortcut.

"And now, the moment you've all been waiting for," Crake said. "Please keep in mind what you've heard as our student reps come up...to help us with Trickery Spirit!"

Students clapped and stomped their feet.

It was weird to hear Ms. Crake say *please*. "Move your lazy hind-parts" was more her style. She was making an effort to be pleasant.

Casey leaned toward Luci. "What's Trickery Spirit?"

A half-dozen students moved toward the stage.

"Didn't the courier reach your house?" Luci glanced over. "The invitation should've got there yesterday at the latest." She touched her chin. "Weird, I kind of thought The Craken would ask you to be a student rep...guess it's too late now."

Up front, the students were sitting down on stools. A hush fell over the cafeteria as they squirmed around, getting comfortable.

"All right, Trickery, listen up!" Crake called. "It's time to choose our virtues for the year. In true Trickery fashion, we've got six excellent options—but only three will survive." She smiled. "Student reps, take a minute to make your case. Then we'll vote on the virtues that will define our school year." She swept a hand toward the first kid in line.

"Hey, there's Jake," Casey said.

Jake McGusty, the vertically-challenged reporter for the *Trickery Times*, sat on the end of the row, waiting his turn. His mushroom cloud of dark hair gave him a few extra inches of height, making him almost as tall as the other student reps—as long as they were sitting down.

"Jake's good with crowds," Robert said.

"He'll do his best," Luciana added. "But it won't be easy..."

"What are you talking about?" Casey said.

But the first student had started talking.

"I'm Camille Graham, and I've got an easy job," said an energetic girl, tossing her curly, caramel-colored hair. "I invite you to cast your vote for the Trickery virtue of..." she glanced around dramatically. "*Fighting*! What could be nearer and dearer to our Sylvan hearts? I know *I* love a good round of combat!" She placed one hand on her heart, then raised it in a triumphant fist pump.

"She's a shoe-in," Robert said.

"True," Luci said. "She's cute, and quite dangerous." She dug an elbow in Robert's ribs. "Stop smiling."

"So what's the big deal?" Casey said as the applause died down.

"It's not *just* a popularity contest," Luci said. "Trickery Spirit voting is also a student mandate to decide what virtues are most important to us—and this semester, it really matters."

"She has a point," Robert agreed.

The next student rep was up.

"I'm Matt Rhiannon," a relaxed, reddish-haired boy said, "here on behalf of all us incoming students." He played to the crowd with a smile and wave. "It makes total sense that I'm representing the spirit of Adventure. Everything here is new to me, and I'm thrilled to be a part of it. If you didn't love Adventure, you wouldn't be here either!"

"Bravo! Yeah! Bring it!" the crowd shouted.

"There are a *lot* of new students," Luci said. "Houses are flying off the market, even one-room studio treehouses with swamp views. Trickery is trending up."

Casey still didn't see what the big deal was.

The next presentation was for Preparedness, and parents scattered through the crowd gave it a nice hand. After that came Secrecy, which was only moderately popular, although Robert did his best to make some noise. Then came Courage, which got plenty of applause.

That left Jake.

"Hey everyone, great to see ya." Jake flashed his trademark grin. "I'll look forward to meeting you newbies, but let me tell you why I'm here. In the past, I've voted for great Trickery virtues like Curiosity, Integrity, and of course, Investigative Method. But this year I'm representin' a dark horse, a super important one. Not a standard vote-getter, but we're ok with weird, experimental stuff here, right?"

A few kids screamed.

"I want you to join me in something kinda wild," Jake continued, "something brand new on the curriculum, something that saved our butts last semester. Please vote for the Trickery virtue of...Magic!"

He stuck both arms in the air.

Scattered applause broke out. A few people cheered but quieted down when they didn't get much support. Casey, Gloria and Luciana clapped like crazy and yelled their lungs out. Robert reluctantly joined in. The only other person who matched their enthusiasm was a wrinkled old man, leaning on a metal walker near the door.

Good old Bones, Casey thought. His belief in magic is legendary.

"Beast-guts, this is gonna be close," Luci whispered.

"Well done, representatives." Ms. Crake joined the kids on stage. "Time to fill in our ballots. As always, the top three vote-getters will determine our Trickery Spirit themes."

"Why do you keep looking at me like that?" Casey asked Luci.

"Sorry." She glanced away. "I can't help feeling it should've been you up there." She picked up a slip of paper off the table and started writing.

Casey stole a look over her shoulder:

Magic

Courage

Preparedness

That was Luci all right. She liked to feel like she had a handle on things, but she didn't scare easily—that was for sure—and she'd been a closet magic-lover for years. Of course, with her history she could've voted for Secrecy as well.

Gloria and Robert were scribbling on their ballots.

"Where's mine?" Casey said.

"The door warden handed it to you on your way in," Robert said.

"No he didn't," Casey said.

"Oh creeps." Luci folded her ballot neatly in half. "You're right, you got here so late, the balloting process had ended." She shrugged, one corner of her mouth turned down. "Sorry, Casey. With a little luck, it won't matter."

Robert folded his ballot, shielding it protectively.

Secrecy, one hundred percent, Casey thought.

"How do you spell Unicorns?" Gloria said.

"How cute, Glo, a write-in vote." Luci reached across to help. "Last year I wrote in Emotional Intelligence. No one else did, but I was happy I gave it a try."

Teachers moved from table to table, collecting ballots. Casey told himself he shouldn't feel left out. "So what did Ms. Crake say before I came in?" he asked.

"She introduced the new magical classes, and then..." Luci lowered her voice. "The Craken told the *whole* story about the Sentry

Trees. I could hardly believe it. She laid out the Butcher Beast War as solid fact."

"Which it slashing well is," Robert muttered.

"Of course it is," Luci said. "But that's not what people have been saying. When you think about it, exposure to the Butcher Beasts was pretty limited–"

"Thanks to us," Robert said.

"–and lots of people–"

"Absentee cowards," Robert said.

"–have claimed it was a fake publicity stunt. Ms. Crake said it *really* happened and that Trickery would've been wiped off the map and she mentioned you and Gloria by name." Luci's eyes were big.

"Oh wow," Casey said.

"West and I got a shout-out too," Robert said.

It was hard to tell if he was pleased or ticked off, and Casey *felt* like Robert looked. Of course the butchers were real, and so was the magic elixir that had saved them, and everyone should know it. On the other hand, he wasn't sure he wanted all this attention.

"It was amaaaazing." Gloria beamed at him.

Casey forced himself to smile back.

"The votes have been tallied," Ms. Crake called from the stage, and the buzzing cafeteria quieted down as she held up her clipboard. "First, in a landslide...Fighting!" Applause filled the hall and Robert joined in. "Next, by a healthy margin...Courage!" More clapping and shouts. "And finally..." Ms. Crake shuffled her papers. "By just *one* vote, I'm slightly surprised to announce that our last Trickery virtue is..."

The room held its breath.

"Adventure."

The room erupted once more and Ms. Crake joined in, but Casey could tell her clapping was polite. Her chin drooped and he had a pretty good idea why. He felt disappointed too—at the very first Trickery gathering of the new semester.

"If Magic came in fourth, I'm gonna be sooo mad," Luci said through her teeth.

Casey thought about the vote he *could've* cast and felt a twinge of guilt. After what had happened last semester, Magic absolutely should've won. This was an unfortunate accident...but life had to go on. His stomach rumbled.

"C'mon guys, let's get something to eat," he said.

CHAPTER 4
A WILD, BEAUTIFUL DANCE

GLORIA WASN'T HUNGRY. She'd already eaten two skrabbit sliders and a side of breakfast pizza.

"You've gotta be kidding me," Casey said.

She rubbed her tummy. "It was sooo good, Casey."

He couldn't believe it. Lunch was over.

While he'd been sweating in the forest, the extra guests had devoured everything except a fresh Chicken of the Woods salad. That would've been fine, except Chicken of the Woods was a fungus that looked like a ruffly, orange sea creature. Casey groaned, poured himself a lemon-lime spritzer and returned to the table. Luci didn't seem to notice when he slid an untouched drumstick off her plate.

"Did I miss anything else?" he asked to create a distraction.

"Crake's talk was solid," Robert muttered. The Craken was not his favorite person. "She said something about extra security and a UWA representative or two. You can never have too much security."

UWA meant Unified Wilderness Alliance. Casey still had to piece the acronym together. He wasn't sure he agreed with Robert, though. There could definitely be such a thing as too much security. He'd spent his first week in Sylvan Woods running from Trickery's fearsome security force. Of course, Robert *would* think differently. It wasn't public knowledge, but he was a member of the deadly Sylvan Watch. At the horrifyingly young age of thirteen.

Casey took another bite of chicken, hoping Luci wouldn't notice. She seemed busy frowning at the table.

"Why so bent out of shape?" he asked.

Her eyes flicked over. "Give me that drumstick right now."

He tore off another chunk.

"Just kidding, I don't want it, so you can stop scarfing it like a Tiger Rat."

Casey let himself relax. He preferred to chew his food more thoroughly.

"You know how I feel about magic," Luci said.

"Me too—!" Gloria said.

"Putting it on the curriculum was a risky move, but getting the Trickery Spirit vote would have really helped. Now there's gonna be backlash. Kids are catty enough around here as it is."

Robert snorted. Casey knew what he was thinking, but it would be a mistake to call Luciana catty. She was more a snaky type of girl.

"The Sentry Trees stirred up all kinds of gossip," Luci continued. "Most kids still think magic is *so* last century. They don't understand the wild, beautiful dance of magic at all."

Her eyes got a far off look.

Robert groaned. Casey winced. Not because he distrusted magic like Robert but because he'd been forced to dance with Luci before.

"Not to mention," Robert said, "lots of kids still don't think Casey exists."

"Wait, what–" Casey said.

"Or me!" Gloria rolled her violet eyes. "But I'm right here!"

"Those crazy flip-flop brains are missing out!" Robert's voice got all bouncy when he talked to Gloria. It was weird, like a clown's voice coming out of a gargoyle. When they were together, you could almost believe Robert was a nice guy. Which would've been his worst nightmare.

He turned to Casey, clearing his throat. "Anyway, I think The

Craken expected you to make an appearance today. Now kids are gonna keep saying you're not real. And once they *do* find out you exist *and* you're enrolled in Trickery *and* you're the one who started all this magic stuff, well...let's just say you'll have a target on your back. Hanging out with you is going to be exhausting." He tried and failed to hide a smile.

"Nice," Casey said. "You're looking forward to it."

Honestly, that was kind of a relief. Because even though Casey was pretty sure he'd never swung a weapon until that summer, he had a reputation at Trickery as a lethal kid, always ready to rumble. Even Ms. Crake thought he could handle himself in a fight. Luckily, that rep was limited to a few dozen people who knew him on sight. The truth was, his victories had come against baby monsters...with help from friends...assisted by his little sister.

Then there were the Butcher Beasts.

He'd actually done that, but it had been terrible. The magic of the Sentry Trees had flared to life just in time, and he'd almost died. A few people might think he was a hero—especially Gloria—but he couldn't laugh about it. He remembered the numbness, and the piercing cold, and the nightmarish fangs too well.

Anyway. This semester, he would try to get good at weapons. Hopefully *before* everyone found out he really did exist.

CHAPTER 5
PEEPS AND SQUEAKS

THE GRIMES HOUSE COULDN'T SEEM to decide if it was Civilian or Sylvan. At least now it felt like a home instead of a dusty obstacle course. Casey and Gloria's parents were waiting when they crossed the backyard and slid open the glass door.

"Hi honeys!" Sitting on a stool at the kitchen counter, Mom looked up from a copy of *The Sylvan Woods Shade*. She wore a nice grass-green top over a black skirt.

Very tasteful, Casey thought. Mom had figured out Sylvan clothing quickly.

Dad, on the other hand...

"Hey kids!" Dad appeared from his home office, sporting a desert camo shirt with jungle camo shorts and—oh no. Casey touched his forehead. Were those urban camo flip-flops? He hadn't known such awful things existed.

"Our schedule opened up and we tried to make it to your Trickery Spirit lunch," Dad said. "But I think we took a wrong turn."

"Several wrong turns," Mom agreed. "We stopped when we came to a sunken marsh–"

"With glowing eyes in the shadows," Dad finished.

"Probably bog peeps," Mom said.

"Or tree squeaks," Dad said.

"Well, thanks for trying," Casey said. "Next time, let's figure it out so we can go together." It was kind of cute his parents thought the monsters of Sylvan Woods were something you'd find in an Easter basket. They needed a little help before they were ready to handle the forest on their own. Or Sylvan society, for that matter.

"Hey Dad," Casey said. "About those flip-flops."

"Too much?" Dad said.

"I told him it was too much," Mom whispered.

Just a couple months back, everything had been too much.

His parents had wandered around their open A-frame house like zombies. He and Gloria hadn't been much better. After a very qualified traveling babysitter, Ms. Jones, had cleaned some old Sylvan invisa-fade from the air ducts, everyone began to feel more healthy.

Dad stopped drinking coffee by the pint and started finishing his remote work ahead of schedule. Mom no longer looked like there was something she wanted to say that she couldn't quite remember. In fact, if Casey's hunch was correct, she'd been scanning Help Wanted ads in *The Sylvan Woods Shade*.

Boxes had been unpacked, furniture rearranged. An armchair no longer lurked in the foyer. The toaster no longer lounged on the couch. You could use the bathroom at night without stubbing your toe on the blender. All they needed now were weapons cubbyholes and Sylvan artwork on the walls. Except those were probably the same thing.

It was hard to believe their life had been a confused, slow motion blur, just months ago. Casey still couldn't remember much before they'd arrived in Vintage Woods, just snatches of color and sound, but he didn't really care. Sure, he'd lived someplace and gone to school someplace, but he didn't have a single friend to show for it. Maybe he'd been mostly invisible even then. The only old memories he cared about included Dad and Mom and Gloria.

"Hey," Mom said, "we're attending Back to School Night, right?"

"Hmm," Casey said. "Maybe we could take a few warm-up hikes and talk about, um, clothing and stuff before–"

"Nice try, bud." Dad held up a postcard, black with silver Sylvan lettering. "Back to School night…"

"Is tonight!" Mom swung a fist cheerfully like she just couldn't wait to hit the trail.

Casey chuckled uneasily. Kind of crazy his parents hadn't visited Trickery yet. Or maybe not, since Sylvan Woods wasn't a place you just strolled into, and he'd only been enrolled forty-eight hours.

"We'll have to be extra special careful of monsters." Gloria looked worried.

Dad smiled at her. "Tell you what, you bring your swords, or whatever they gave you for fencing practice, and I'll bring, hmm…"

"A weed whacker?" Mom suggested. "And I can bring a frying pan."

"Right," Dad said. "Together we'll deal with all the peeps and squeaks."

"Ohhh boy," Casey said.

CHAPTER 6
WELCOME TO THE MAGIC

THE GRIMES FAMILY SLID INTO THE back row of Trickery's Great Hall. Casey's antique dark lantern jangled under his seat, attracting some annoyed glances.

He'd never been inside the hall before, but he could barely take in the glowing chandeliers, stained glass windows and arched ceiling miles overhead. He did a quick breathing exercise.

Deep inhale, down to your gut...hold it...aaand out, one inch at a time. There it goes, all that stress leaving your body. Floating up, past the candles, out the windows, into the night...

He was still hyperventilating.

Mom and Dad looked pale, holding hands. Dad's shorts had a badly-placed rip that made them look like a kilt. Mom was missing a trail shoe. Gloria's smile was frozen in place. Her ponytail was a couple inches shorter than it'd been when they'd started down the trail.

Casey didn't want to know what he looked like.

He'd *wanted* to leave earlier, before it got dark, but it took time to persuade Dad to change his outfit, and then Mom insisted on everyone eating a good dinner. Well, they wouldn't make that mistake again.

The shrill cries of the attacking Tree Shriek rang in his ears. A dull clang as Mom connected with her frying pan…a puttering roar as Dad's weed whacker chugged to life. The Tree Shriek hadn't stood a chance.

Unfortunately, monsters flocked to Civilian sounds and smells like moths to light. He and his mace and Gloria with her K-level sword had got quite a workout. They'd been lucky to escape with their limbs intact. Somewhere in the woods, a mangled weed whacker rested near a well-chewed frying pan and a pile of monsters.

Casey counted his fingers. All there. Ok then.

We did that. We survived, and with no Sylvan help.

He forced his face into a painful smile.

"Hey." It was Luci, half-turned in her seat, eyebrows lifted. "The restrooms are in the foyer, to the right of the armory." She turned back around.

Whatever. Casey focused on her neat, wavy ponytail. Luci's hair was legendarily troublesome. If she could create order from chaos, so could he.

The enormous room slowly came into focus. Someone was droning away up front. Casey made out a trim shape with a splash of red makeup across her face. Thanks to the amazing acoustics, he heard every word.

"I'm certain you share my excitement as I say, welcome to Trickery."

She didn't sound excited. Neither did the polite applause.

So that was it.

Luci tilted her head far enough for him to see one eye rolling back.

Apparently he hadn't missed much.

Now a familiar black-clothed figure walked crookedly onto the stage. Casey had never been happier to see someone who looked like the angel of death.

"Oh, it's that nice young lady," Mom whispered. "Ms. Cake."

Nice young lady? Ms. Cake? Well, at least Mom was capable of speech again.

Crake did a lopsided spin, hands held high, as she reached center stage. You couldn't fake enthusiasm like that. "IT'S A MAGICAL NIGHT!" she shouted.

"HOORAY!" Tossed hats and foam battle axes filled the air.

Darn it, we missed the door prizes.

"These are exciting times," Crake called. "Trickery School has always been top shelf, but now it's a destination school in the Unified Wilderness Alliance. Enrollment is rising...so give yourselves a pat on the back and shake some hands. You're an up-and-coming Sylvan district!"

The crowd roared its approval.

"Even better," Crake said, "Sylvan Woods is once again protected by Sentry Trees. Maybe you've heard the rumors. Earlier this year, we were almost slaughtered by the Butcher Beast horde. In the eleventh hour...magic saved us."

A hush fell over the packed hall.

"That's right, I said *magic*. Some have suggested the story is fabricated but I'm here to set the record straight. Those suggestions...are total hell hash."

Parents in the crowd winced but Ms. Crake plunged on.

"The UWA investigated, and the result of their investigation is this." She paused before belting out a single word, like it was a team name and she was the mascot. "MAGIC! Magic came to the rescue, everyone!"

Cheers rang out here and there, disappearing in the hall's cavernous echoes. Casey's mouth felt dry, but he put his hands together. His claps rustled like dry leaves.

"Trickery is piloting magical courses." Crake yelled louder to fill the silence. "In consultation with the Alliance, we've determined it's a mistake to bury our past, unless we want to be blindsided by monsters and, you know...get eaten alive."

Gasps rose around the room. Parents covered small children's ears.

Oh come on, Casey thought. *Let's be real here.*

"Sometimes," Crake said, "you have to fight to be who you're supposed to be."

Casey nodded. So true.

"Let's see...fine print." Crake smoothed a lock of hair behind one ear, and Casey felt sorry for her as she glanced down at her notes. "We don't expect everyone to agree on the importance of magic at first," she said, "or for everyone to take the magical classes, but at the very least, please show kindness as we reclaim our history."

Please. She'd said it again. That showed how hard she was trying.

"And now," she said brightly, "let's introduce our new, highly-qualified teachers!"

The great hall began to show signs of life as she raised an arm and a line of figures paraded across the stage. Wow, there were quite a few. Hard to say what they looked like, but one was tall, built like a tank. Light gleamed off his raised fingers as he scanned the crowd. Casey had the weird feeling Mr. Kawkazi was staring right back at him.

"The UWA sent extra funding and a Golden Wolf award our way after *last* semester." Ms. Crake smiled, and Casey could tell she was trying to regain her enthusiasm.

"As a result," she yelled, "Trickery is becoming bigger and more dangerous than before! Thanks for being part of it. And welcome to the future of Trickery!" She paused for applause and excited squeals, and Casey felt relief as the audience warmed up.

"Welcome to the future of the Unified Wilderness Alliance!" Crake shouted.

Whoops, whistles and clapping.

"WELCOME TO THE MAGIC!" Crake threw her arms in the air.

Casey's heart did a backflip and he jumped to his feet, screaming with everyone else as a huge green banner unfurled behind Ms. Crake, thirty feet tall and as wide as the stage.

OUR WOODS
OUR ROOTS
OUR WAR
OUR MAGIC

Hooray, Ms. Crake had done it, she'd managed to–
Casey's hands stopped clapping. His body went limp.
In between the big script letters, written in a thin, spidery scrawl
—words that made his heart jump in a different way.

Casey Grimes
is a
traitor.

CHAPTER 7
ARMED ESCORT

MUTTERED QUESTIONS FILLED THE great hall, and Casey stiffened like someone had doused him with ice water. He passed a hand over his eyes as they got to their feet.

"I don't get the joke." Dad squeezed his arm.

"I mean, who is there for you to betray, honey?" Mom smiled at him.

Casey tried to smile back, but his face had that numb feeling. His parents were babies when it came to Sylvan Woods. They didn't understand the deep distrust for Civilians. The us versus them ways of thinking. Hard to say what his parents *did* know about Sylvan Woods and Trickery. Maybe they thought it was a weird private school...with a heavily wooded campus...and mutant animal species.

Suddenly, he felt very nervous, moving down the aisle with his Civilian parents.

"Hi, Mr. and Mrs. Grimes." Luciana pushed through the milling crowd, her hands balled into fists. "I can't believe someone would do that. Not after everything we—oh, sorry, these are my parents." A well-dressed, dangerous-looking couple stood behind her. Casey's dad and mom stepped over to say hello.

"Drooce, do you think?" Robert Pierce materialized at Casey's shoulder. "My parents let me step away for a sec."

Sebastien Drooce was Trickery's most-feared bully. He'd never forgiven Casey for the previous semester, when an accidental case of mistaken identity had landed Drooce with several weeks of detention—along with other indignities.

"But we already beat Drooce up." Gloria had a small crease in her forehead.

"Technically, *I* did, Glo," Robert said.

"If you *really* want to get technical, I did," Luci said.

"You both did, ok?" Casey said. "About that banner, should I be–"

A heavy hand fell on his shoulder. He felt like a cardboard cutout squeezed in a vise.

"Superintendent Crake has asked me to escort your family out." Mr. Kawkazi looked even taller and craggier close up. Above his white collar and crisp black tie, sharp eyes glittered in his stony face.

Robert nodded. "Yep, that's smart. Good call by The Craken."

"Since when do you compliment Ms. Crake?" Luci said.

Robert shrugged as Kawkazi turned to Casey's parents.

Casey massaged his shoulder. His neck made tiny popping sounds.

"Don't worry about the banner," Luci said. "We'll figure out who did this."

"And we'll get them," Robert said.

A minute later, they were crossing the foyer in Mr. Kawkazi's mountainous shadow.

Gloria, Mom and Dad looked confused. Casey felt the same.

"Hey, is that him?" someone said.

"That kid is sneaking out!"

Robert shoved his way to Casey's side, shooting dark glances right and left. That quieted things down, but chatter filled the air as they stepped into the cool night air.

"I can't believe this." Luci looked angry. "Just when things had a chance of being normal." Her mom put an elegant hand on her shoulder. "See you later," Luci said unhappily.

The West family slipped off into the night.

"Walk with me," Mr. Kawkazi rumbled.

Casey found himself wondering if that was a great idea.

"It's ok," Robert said. "Standard procedure after a public death threat. I'll come too."

"Now wait just a second." Despite his torn shorts, Dad looked formidable in his jet-black button-up and scowl, even though he was a head shorter than Kawkazi. "That was a prank, not a death threat. Let's not blow this out of proportion."

"Pierce misspoke," Kawkazi said. "But if you don't mind, I'd like to escort you to the border, just the same."

Robert frowned and prodded his carefully spiked hair.

"An escort would be wonderful," Mom said.

Casey glanced at her. So did Dad and Gloria. Casey remembered the attacking swarm of monsters, the mangled frying pan and broken weed whacker. He was pretty sure they were all picturing the same thing.

"An escort it is," Dad said.

The massive, well-dressed teacher extended one hand. His silver fingers gleamed in the moonlight. "Shall we?"

CHAPTER 8
THE CROW

MR. KAWKAZI DID NOT TRY to murder them on their hike to the border. But he did put a damper on things. When Dad asked him what he taught, Mr K. said Fireside Cookery.

"Ooh," Mom said. "Do you ever make s'mores?"

"No, ma'am." He looked like she'd suggested cooking boy scouts.

They crunched down the path in silence. Casey felt tense and breathless. He hadn't even started classes. Was he already done? Mr. K. might be taking him home for good. But that was ridiculous. Ms. Crake wouldn't let that happen. Calm down, he told himself. You have rights in Sylvan Woods now. You're a citizen. They can't just take that back...can they?

He forced himself to pay attention to his surroundings. Monsters were staying away and Casey didn't blame them. Kawkazi was scary. But that didn't mean the whole hike had to feel like a funeral procession. In fact, he was desperate for it not to.

"I've got it," he whispered to Robert.

"Got what?" Robert's head swiveled right and left as he scanned the shadows. Gloria paced next to the fierce boy, copying his scouting technique. Her mania for Robert had faded a little as his pink eye socket healed, but she still admired him greatly.

"A nickname," Casey said. "Aren't you tired of saying 'Kawkazi?'"

"No," Gloria whispered. "Kacrazy, Kacrazy—it's fun to say."

"Lay it on me," Robert said.

"Mr. Kawkazi becomes...The Crow—*caw caw*."

"Not bad, maybe a little obvious, but not bad."

"Please," Casey said. "Like 'The Craken' isn't obvious."

"You win," Robert said. "The Crow it is."

Pierce being so agreeable made things weird. Casey felt relieved when they said good night under the Old Oak. Robert and The Crow vanished into the woods like a pair of mismatched phantoms, and Casey looked up through massive, starlit branches.

You got me into this, he thought. He wished he could scale the giant tree—ancient, immovable, aware of his presence. Wished he could chat with Luci from the compass deck and see the world stretch away and fall asleep in the moonlight. But there wasn't time.

"What a night," Dad said.

A little later, they crossed their backyard.

"Trickery seems like a very *special* school," Mom said.

Casey shot her a glance. She was hobbling along gracefully in her one trail shoe.

"I've been thinking..." Dad hitched up his shorts, which now looked like a Hawaiian grass skirt. "Maybe I should invest in a nice mace like yours, Casey. You could advise me on the good brands."

That was about the last thing he'd expected Dad to say. It was much better than, "Son, our legs were almost chewed off by little monsters."

"Sure," Casey said. "We can hike to the Sylvan Shops sometime —they're supposed to be really cool. And you can borrow my mace if you want to try one. I could show you how to swing it without smashing your kneecaps. I have a sword too."

He didn't mention the sword was a priceless antique even Robert coveted.

"Deal." Dad smiled at him as they tromped up the stairs.

"I'll need something too." Mom kicked her orphaned shoe across the deck. "What do ladies wield around here?"

"Luci has a scythe-staff," Gloria said. "It's super deadly."

"Oh! I like the sound of that." Mom slid open the door. "Hot chocolate, showers, and straight to bed. You've got a big day tomorrow."

"Sorry about earlier," Dad said. "We'll be better prepared next time."

Preparedness, Casey thought. Secrecy. Magic. Maybe the less popular virtues were just as important as the big ones.

"Don't worry about that banner," Mom said. "Someone's jealous, that's all."

They drank their hot chocolate and got cleaned up. A horrified shout came from the master bath as Dad saw himself in the mirror. Casey snuggled into bed, smiling. He was proud of his parents. They were coping with Sylvan Woods better than he'd hoped. But as he lay there, his smile faded. Why would anyone say he was a traitor?

CHAPTER 9
HUMAN TARGET

FORTUNATELY, TRICKERY SCHOOL didn't begin at the crack of dawn. That was because most kids put in an hour or two of weapons practice before breakfast.

Out on the back deck, Casey did a few half-hearted mace moves as Gloria slashed the air with her small, pink-handled sword. Casey preferred the ancient blade he'd retrieved from the Old Oak, but carrying around a priceless, legendary sword hooked to his shorts made him a little jumpy. For now, it rested on a plush red towel under his bed.

"Ok, come on in," Mom called through the open door.

Gloria sheathed her sword. Casey clipped the mace to his backpack. It was a high-tech 127-Spiker on loan from Robert. "Most points of contact anyone's been able to cram on a mace so far," Pierce had said happily. Casey stepped inside. Breakfast was available at the cafeteria, but he and Gloria had agreed to eat at home on their first day of school.

"Close your eyes and count to ten," Mom said.

A rich, savory smell filled the kitchen as Mom slid plates across the counter.

"Breakfast pizza!" Gloria squealed.

"Wow," Casey said. "Is that skrabbit sausage?" He took a bite. "This is great!"

"Oh, it was nothing." Mom dusted flour off her hands, trying not to let her smile split her face. She and Dad grabbed slices, and everyone drank orange juice toasts.

"To Trickery School," Dad said.

"To getting more Sylvanish," Mom said.

"To unicorn class," Gloria said.

"To strength and honor." It was a line Casey'd stolen from a tattered copy of the old *Sylvan Handbook*, which later disintegrated when he sat on it. What he really felt like saying was, "To avoiding secret enemies."

He and Gloria shrugged on their packs, waved goodbye and set off down the trail. Crossing into Sylvan Woods was less dangerous in the day. If you kept on the right paths, your chances of sighting a monster were practically zero.

Before they knew it, they were slipping through the evergreens at Trickery's entrance. Modern-medieval spires brushed the clouds, spiderwebbed by platforms, ladders and catwalks. The famous Amber Tower shone gold in the morning sun.

Like always, the sight took Casey's breath away. Trickery was awe-inspiring. But it didn't always make you feel calm.

"Excited, Gloria?"

"No." For once, she looked serious.

"Oh." Casey felt better about his burbling stomach.

"I'm *super* excited!" She threw her arms in the air, pigtails flying.

"Yeah, me too." Casey hesitated. "Just a little nervous about that thing with the banner."

Gloria took one of his hands in both of hers. "Don't worry about that." She gazed into his eyes. "It's not true and I'll get whoever did it and everything will be great."

He actually felt better. Gloria was very truthful.

They hiked down Artemis Way and paused in the shade of a

brass orb the size of a house. Twenty feet off the ground, it hung in a web of cables like a giant gold spider.

"From here you go to...let's see..." Casey pulled their class schedule from his pocket.

"The Trident Garden and Splash Fountain!" Gloria hugged herself. "I know the way. See you at lunch, Casey!" She hooked her thumbs under her pack straps and skipped off down the trail. Passing kids watched her go.

"Hey, isn't that the kid who out-dueled the teacher?" someone said.

"Ohmigosh, she's *too* cute..."

With a sinking feeling, Casey realized he had no idea where his first class was being held. Or rather, he did, but...hmm. He consulted his Hall & Trail Guide. Where the heck was the Rondure Arena? The place should be right here. Trails moved around on the borders of Sylvan Woods, but he'd never known an entire building to disappear.

Casey turned in a slow circle. There were several treetop battlegrounds nearby, but none of them were called Rondure. He wished Luci and Robert hadn't tested out. A stream of students parted around him, staring as they hurried by. He felt his face get hot.

Someone tapped him on the shoulder, and Casey whirled to see a pale face topped with carefully mussed-up hair. Dressed stylishly in charcoal leggings and a fatigue hoody, Fiera Laurent might have been intimidating if not for the huge pack, tugging her nose skyward.

She gave him a thin smile. "Lost your bearings? Tell you what, I'll help you find your class, but in exchange I want you to—"

"Grimes, is that you?" A kid with a springy cloud of hair jogged over. "Holy creeps, man, good to see you back on campus!"

Seeing him up close, Casey realized Jake McGusty had grown a couple inches—but a poodle on its hind legs would still give him a run for his money. Luckily, he had more than enough confidence to make up for his missing height. It served him well as head reporter for Trickery News.

Casey grinned. "Good to see you too."

"We've got to talk," Jake said. "Where's your first class? Oh, hi Fiera."

Fiera looked down her nose at him. "Imagine seeing you here."

"The Rondure Arena," Casey said hopefully.

"Perfect," Jake said. "Mind if I walk you over? Then I can take my usual shortcut through the elevated toad garden and sneak into Intermediate Subterfuge."

"Perfect," Casey said.

Fiera gritted her teeth as they walked away. Ten feet away. To a spiral staircase.

"Been up before?" Jake asked. "Probably not, huh? From the top, you'll swing over. See what I mean? Try to stick the landing. Make sure your hands are dry. I've seen kids lose their grip and bounce off the sides."

They stood on a leafy, screened platform overlooking the huge metal globe.

"That?" Casey said. "But I thought–"

"Oh, it's definitely an arena."

From above, Casey saw rings of color at the top of the metal ball —red, yellow and blue circles—where the north pole would've been if it had represented any planet known to humankind. Slowly he realized what he was seeing.

"Aim for the center of the bullseye," Jake said. "Less chance of flopping off. We need to polish your persona, man. I can help. No one takes shots at Bootman, not on my watch."

"Bootman" was a nickname Casey had earned the previous semester when he'd tried to fight Sebastien Drooce, one of Trickery's nastiest. Casey hadn't exactly won, but in a bizarre chain of events, Drooce had gone down and Casey had triumphed—albeit with a knobby boot print on his chest.

Casey barely noticed the nickname.

He was staring at the huge globe that was somehow an arena. The rings of color at the top formed a target. *A human target.*

"Your image needs help after that banner," Jake continued. "Front page news, if we spin it right. Between you and me, I'm the guy you want to talk to. That Fiera girl is sharp, but I'm still making up my mind about her. Ok, now I've really gotta run. Catch you later, Bootman."

He hurried down the stairs.

"See you," Casey said.

Someone stomped onto the platform behind him.

"A rondure is a ball," Fiera said brattily. She pronounced it *ron-jer* —and Casey guessed she was probably saying it right. "Also, a *rondure* is a graceful arc. Like, an optimal weapons pathway. Get it?"

Casey seized a dangling cable, stepped to the guardrail, and prepared to launch himself into space.

"I would've told you where it was. You know that, right?" Fiera's voice lost some of its cool. "Wait, don't jump. All I want is a comment or two!"

Casey smiled grimly. Fiera's thin fingers tap-tapped his arm as he leaned back, gauged the distance, and surged forward.

"Casey, don't! Wait! Nooo!"

He swooshed through the dappled air. At the far side of his arc he let go, dropping in the center of the bullseye. To his relief, the target area was padded. You couldn't take that for granted in Sylvan Woods.

Muffled clapping reached his ears. Standing on the sphere, he realized the walls were mirrored glass. Students smiled up through thick, gold-tinted panes. Casey was reaching for a handle set into the glass when something smacked down behind him like a bucket of wet pasta. Under his feet, kids winced.

When he spun around, Fiera was facedown on the edge of the bullseye, trying to suction herself to the glass with every square inch of her body. Her skin squeaked like a toddler's rear on a hot metal slide. Casey covered his ears. As her pack dragged her toward the equator, Fiera looked up. Her eyes changed from icy to horrified.

"These *ron-jers* can be tricky," Casey said.

Fiera let out a shriek as she picked up speed.

"Oh, beast it." Casey bounded over the bullseye, threw himself flat, and snagged the top of her pack just before she disappeared.

CHAPTER 10
SHARK SIGHTING

FIERA DIDN'T LOOK AT CASEY as he helped her to the center of the globe. Her forehead was red from where she'd pressed the glass. Her eyes were stuck on extra-wide.

There's no reason to feel guilty, Casey told himself. It wasn't your idea for her to splat herself on the arena like a human jellyfish.

"Why'd you follow me?" he said.

"Pathetic...I know, I know." Fiera let out a shaky laugh. For a second she sounded almost human. Then she pulled herself together. "You could've taken a second to answer my question," she said. "'Any tips on swinging over?' *That's* what I was going to ask you."

"Wait, what?" Casey felt confused.

"I'm taking this class too," Fiera said. "Unless I just flunked out."

Now he felt bad. "Sorry, I thought—"

"It's ok, I get it." Fiera probed her hair, which was no longer fake-messy. "When I'm in reporter mode, I can be a little pushy."

And snotty, Casey thought. *And your hair is ridiculous.*

He grabbed the handle and swung the hatch door open.

Fiera scrubbed at her pinkish forehead. "Hey, not that you need to hear this, you being a big deal and all, but...thanks. For scraping me off that ronj—um, that big ball." She met his eyes. "Really embarrassing, but I know when a thank you is needed, so...thank you."

She smiled.

It was a little frightening. Maybe she didn't do it very often.

"It's ok," he said. "Maybe later I can answer a question or two."

"Wow, really? That would be *so* great."

They hurried inside, down a short flight of stairs. Fiera was annoying. Man, was she ever. But being a new kid was hard. It couldn't hurt to help her out.

Casey found himself in an enormous, echoey space. The arena's tinted glass gave it an extra-vivid glow. A couple dozen kids milled around, looking disappointed, on a big platform that didn't touch the rounded walls. "Why'd you have to save her?" someone whined.

Casey sighed. He had to admit, with Fiera's snobby face pressed against the glass, the view of her doom would've been spectacular. Peering over the edge, Casey saw a fully furnished level with chairs and carpets. And below that...

Clap, clap, clap. Casey straightened up as weak applause rang across the platform.

A path opened for a bony, elderly lady, students diving away like swimmers who'd spotted a great white shark. Oh no. It was Ms. Steele. Casey would never forget that toothy grin. Or her triple-decker slingshot, blasting him down the aisle. The last time he'd seen her, she'd been wearing a leather vest and black fedora. Today, she'd traded those in for a desert commando outfit, complete with bandana.

"First impressions are over," Ms. Steele said threateningly. "A few of you have already made your mark. While others..." She glanced at Fiera Laurent. "Were less fortunate." She stalked along the platform's edge. "A knee in midair—a flying elbow—a whirling headbutt—is a delightfully lethal thing. *Be* the weapon. Your lives and your grades depend on it. Obviously you'll all be fighting monsters eventually, especially those who aspire to one of Trickery's

War concentrations. Battlefield Command, Woodland Security, Sylvan Subterfuge, Prodigiumology, Monster Specializations, all the rest. There is no higher calling."

Kids elbowed each other wordlessly.

"Two bullseyes today." Steele frowned. "Rare for an incoming class. Well done, Matt Rhiannon. And well done...Casey Grimes." She gave a little shudder. "Let me be clear—magic has no place in my classroom. Get that, Grimes?" Her voice rose to a screech. "You got lucky today, but you'll be judged like everyone else, on cold, hard survivalism. Here's my advice. Get good at staying alive!"

Casey forced himself to hold still.

I'm already good at that, he thought.

Whispers began in the middle of the platform and rustled outward. "Grimes...he's here...which one?...can't believe he came to class..."

The whispers swarmed him like biting insects.

Thin fingers clutched his elbow.

"Grimes," Fiera hissed. "Neither of us is looking great. How 'bout we help each other out. Can I get that statement for Trickery News?"

CHAPTER 11
DIFFICULT PEOPLE

WHAT DO YOU WANT TO KNOW?" Casey ran a hand through his hair, already wishing he hadn't told Fiera yes. Kids were leaving the arena, grabbing cables and swinging back across. No one wanted a piece of the Grimes-Laurent meet-up. No one except one kid.

"Hey, brilliant landing, Grimes." A boy with close-cropped reddish hair gave Casey a nod as he slipped past, gripped a cable and swung away.

"Let's start with the magic stuff." Fiera's backpack juddered down. Stuff clinked inside as she ripped open the top.

"Well, I–"

Floosh. A burst of light caught him with his mouth open.

"These greenish shadows are tricky," Fiera said. "You need a colossal flash to get a decent exposure. Ok, continue."

Casey glared. "What was the question?"

Floosh.

"Put that camera down!" Aside from Robert, he didn't have much practice dealing with abrasive people, and Pierce was nothing compared to this.

"Ok, ok." Fiera dragged a tablet out and hovered her fingers over the screen. "I'll just take a few notes. Oh, and I'll record you." She dug into her pack again.

"Look," Casey said. "Everyone's gone but us." Ms. Steele stalked onto the bullseye, grabbed a cable and whistled away, her bony shape barely moving the air.

"Right, let's just get to it." Fiera leaned in uncomfortably close. "So, how would you describe your stance on magic?"

"Um, it's real."

"Good stuff." She nodded, hair ends flipping. "And can it change things?"

"Of course."

"You've seen that firsthand, have you?"

"Yeah."

"Would it be safe to say...you like magic?" She stuck her tongue in the corner of her mouth.

"Yes. I do." Casey remembered the entire sky lighting up over Sylvan Woods, blazing purple and orange, gold flames whirling like a thousand fireflies. "Magic saved my life," he said. "Without it I wouldn't be here and neither would Sylvan Woods, and everyone I care about would be dead." He swallowed.

"Cool." Fiera frowned. "Ok, changing gears..." She glanced at her screen. "Why would you betray Trickery?" She arched an eyebrow.

"I wouldn't!" Casey's stomach gave a lurch. "Time for me to go."

"Of course you wouldn't," Fiera said. "But I had to ask—you know, the banner accusations and all."

Casey grabbed a cable.

"Wait, we haven't talked about how fame has changed you!"

"I'm not famous, remember?" Casey sailed away. When he looked back, Fiera was stuffing equipment back in her pack with a watery smile on her face. She didn't seem too worried about getting back across. *Good, I don't want to help her.*

Casey ran down the spiral staircase. No doubt there was a high-level shortcut to his next class, but he didn't have time to experiment. Of course, there was the tunnel under the Green Field...but he didn't feel like getting covered in dirt.

He picked up his pace, jogged down Artemis Trail, and wound up the rocky hillside toward the bath caves. The last time he'd come this way, he and Gloria had been running for their lives, Butcher Beasts screaming overhead.

Horns blared from the woods nearby.

Uh oh. Casey picked up the pace, sweat trickling down his back.

Holy creeps, why had he given Fiera so much time?

He left the wooded hillside, glanced longingly at the baths, and charged down the gravel path by the Green Field. His lungs began to burn as he chugged past the orchard on his left. He was definitely slowing down. It would be a miracle if he wasn't late—like he needed more attention. Maybe not many kids would show up. It wasn't a Trickery core class and—*gasp*—wasn't being held in a very accessible place.

Casey had mixed feelings about it, actually.

He was in no hurry to return to the BeastWoods.

CHAPTER 12
THE SPECTRAL TRAIL

MAGIC CLASS, *THIS WAY*. Following the signs, Casey staggered into the fringes of the BeastWoods, holding his side and gasping. He found himself behind a cluster of kids facing the inner woods, where a round-faced young man with short, bristly hair stood on a crate.

"Welcome to Nonviolent Magic—An Introduction—I'm Mr. Peterson." The guy spoke in choppy bursts like he was getting paid by the words per minute. His tucked-in camo button-up seemed to say, *Of course I love the outdoors, and here's the shirt to prove it!*

But he still looked like the kind of person you'd meet in a government building. How did someone like this end up at Trickery?

"Hey there Casey Grimes—I see you in the back." A hint of energy snuck into the young man's voice. "Didn't expect you tardy the first day—we'll look past it. Can't kill the goose that lays the golden egg." He chuckled.

Casey wasn't sure what he appreciated less, being called a goose or being singled out the moment he set foot in class. He shouldered forward and stood next to the only person who hadn't turned to stare.

"Hubba hoy, Casey."

"Hey, Luci." He couldn't quite bring himself to return her ancient Sylvan greeting, even though he knew she was trying to bring it back.

"Quick hand for Casey Grimes." The teacher put his palms together. *Thwap, thwap, thwap.* One or two kids joined in, but mostly they stared like they were trying to see into Casey's dark, treacherous heart. Their eyes felt like tiny knives.

"Without Grimes's exploration of magic—this class wouldn't exist—and I wouldn't be here," Mr. Peterson said.

That's not fair, Casey thought. Don't blame yourself on me.

Luci gave him a sideways look that said, Ooo, look what you created.

"On to the good stuff," Peterson said. "This isn't one of those ultra-popular War-category classes, obviously—more a Woods or Work emphasis if you're wondering—but it's beast-guts-ing brilliant just the same." He paused to chuckle. "Imagine Forest Exploration with no security needed—a Metallurgy or Horticulture lab without monster infiltration! You may be wondering why this class meets in the BeastWoods. No better place to test—no, prove—the effectiveness of *magic.*"

Casey leaned forward in spite of himself.

"What if magic could open up a new, nonviolent era in Trickery?"

Wow, that was unexpected.

Kids studied Mr. Peterson like he was a silly birthday clown.

Except for Luci. She gave an interested nod, and she didn't appear to be flushed or greenish. Her breathing seemed normal...

"Stop staring at me," she whispered. "What if we don't have to be constantly chopping and slashing? What if there's a better way?"

Casey was surprised how stupid this sounded. Maybe Sylvan thinking had rubbed off on him more than he'd realized. Or maybe he'd spent too much time with Robert.

Ignoring the class's confusion, Mr. Peterson continued. "In

Nonviolent Magic we'll tap into organic and self-sustaining enchantments—maintenance-free once they're in place."

"Kinda like the Sentries," Luci whispered.

"They *need* attention," Casey said. "And didn't get it. That was the whole point."

"Don't nitpick." She folded her arms.

"So what are we going to do?" asked a kid in the front row.

Peterson stepped off his crate. "Glad you asked. Let's get started on our first project—a spectral trail through the BeastWoods. We'll use obsidian—a natural resource with a remarkably powerful aura —to walk safely through—all this." He gestured vaguely at the trees.

Casey remembered the vicious monsters that had stalked them last semester. Nightmarish creatures, each with its own awful appetites and mode of attack. Did Peterson realize how clueless he sounded?

Luci took in Casey's expression. "Let's give him a chance."

What in beast-guts had gotten into her?

"Out there is—an important Sylvan location." Peterson scratched his head. "Name escapes me but you've probably heard of it. A tree, a well?" He shrugged. "Who cares. Anyway, last semester a few kids took a field trip out there led by Mr. Grimes—fought off some beasties to verify an important magical theory. Now follow me."

Casey's mouth fell open.

Luci appeared shocked. Finally.

He shot her a look.

"Don't start," she said.

The crowd seemed smaller than it had a few minutes before. As Mr. Peterson led the way to the trailhead, a couple more kids sneaked away. Casey was tempted to follow, but it seemed wrong to ditch a Trickery class. At least there was a trail to the Sentry now. Not like last time, when the Butcher Brigade had hacked their way through the woods, following a trail of death-loving mushrooms. Smells of decay and monster scat still hung over everything.

Something big and dark glimmered through the trees.

"Aha!" Peterson said. "Our obsidian."

The heap of gleaming black gravel towered twenty feet high and wide. A row of wheelbarrows stood nearby.

"Obsidian has a powerful anti-beast aura," Peterson said. "After we deploy it, our trail to the important location will have an active spectral forcefield—keep it totally monster-free."

"I can't believe this," Casey muttered.

"Sir." Luci held up a hand. "This is probably a dumb question, but we're not really gonna spread all that gravel by hand. I mean..." She gave a shaky laugh. "Surely not."

"Don't worry." Peterson beamed proudly. "We've got the entire semester."

CHAPTER 13
WHAT YOU LEARN MAY SHOCK YOU

THE CAFETERIA RANG WITH CHATTER and laughter, but not at Casey's table. He poked at his bacon-potato salad. Luci sawed her asparagus like she had a vendetta. Robert had devoured an enormous steak and slipped away on some secret mission. Gloria was the only bright spot.

"First grade is wonderful!" She spooned up chocolate pudding. "We splashed our feet in the fountain and we learned the different kinds of monsters with flash cards. Of course, I already knew them mostly..." She nibbled an enormous strawberry. "But there was an angry Frog-Shrew in the fountain, trying to eat our toes, so I learned a new one!"

"That's great, Glo." Luci gave her a weak high five. "I can't believe how useless our magic class was."

"*Now* you admit it," Casey said.

"I didn't *not* admit it," Luci said. "I just wanted to give nonviolence a chance."

Casey wished Robert was here. Giving nonviolence a chance was against everything he stood for. Listening to him and Luci fight would've lifted the mood.

"I'd give nonviolence a chance," Casey said. "But not Mr.

Peterson."

Luci stirred her green juice with a carrot stick. "That didn't seem like magic at all. No poetry, no rhythm, no music. Magic is supposed to feel like–"

"Grimes!" Jake slid in next to Luci, giving her a bump that slopped juice everywhere. "What's this I'm hearing about you and Fiera?" He snatched a pencil from his hair and twirled it between his fingers. Casey hadn't seen him this worked up since...well, ever. Jake was the most unflappable kid he'd ever met.

"You seriously gave her an exclusive?"

Casey felt his face tingling. "Did I—what, with Fiera? No, I'd never do *anything* like that. I don't even like her!"

"He means an interview." Luci eyed him closely, drying off her dripping fingers. "You actually talked to that nit-witch?"

Casey wiped at his hot face. "Well, I answered a few questions..."

Luci flicked her eyebrows up. "Wow, whatever she did worked on you I guess."

"No, she didn't—I didn't..." *Probably better to ignore Luci.* "I still want to talk to you, Jake. I didn't realize it was a big deal."

McGusty massaged his thundercloud hair. "I get it, man, you didn't know what you were doing. But this isn't good. First to press wins at chess."

"What?"

Jake tapped the side of his head. "Strategy, Bootman. Strategy."

"Fiera Laurent is a piece of work, but she's smart," Luci said. "Got a reputation, transferring in from Moraine Gulch."

Casey pictured Fiera splatting face-first onto the Rondure Arena. "Maybe you're giving her a little too much credit."

"Let's hope so." Jake tapped his pencil on his teeth. "We'd better talk about your feature story, the *official* one."

"Umm, ok." Casey's insides jittered around.

"I'm thinking, lead off with the Butcher Brigade, the near death bits—thread in something about the Skewers if you don't mind—then the explosion incinerating all those bugs mid-flight. Talk about an awesome lead-in. And we have plenty of credible sources...well, I guess we have Bones, at least. And Luci."

Luci looked down.

"And me!" Gloria raised her hand.

"Yeah, hmm...too bad Robert was trapped in the tree and the rest of us were fighting our way through the Beast Woods. Anyway, at the end we'll mention in passing that you're a special Civilian transfer student. Hmm." Jake rubbed his chin. "Or maybe we shouldn't mention that."

"They need to know I'm not a traitor," Casey said.

"Absolutely." Jake's hair jounced as he nodded. "But here's the thing, Bootman. Everyone who actually knows you...me, Luci, Glo, Robert, the Skewers...we think you're great. But to everyone else..."

Luci groaned. "You're trouble."

"I would've said you're a complicated character, full of intrigue, easily misunderstood," Jake said. "But you get the point."

"Ohh." Casey's chest twisted into a knot. "I get it. Magic. Civilians... I'm a combination of stuff people don't like."

Luci gave a little twitch.

"So maybe we shouldn't write a story after all?" Casey said.

"No, we gotta," Jake said. "That was inevitable after Back to School Night."

The leaf-shaped speakers in the corners of the room gave a warning crackle. "Happy first day, everyone," said a snooty voice. "Hopefully you've had an exciting morning of combat and wilderness lore, with no lacerations." For someone wishing others happiness and excitement, Fiera sounded bored.

"That little shin-snip," muttered Luci.

Jake looked down, shaking his head.

"Since nothing much has happened, we don't have announcements. Just a few reminders from our *fearless leader*, Ms. Crake."

Casey imagined Fiera rolling her eyes as she said, "fearless leader."

"Don't be shy, say hi to someone new," she continued in a singsong tone. "Consider one of our exciting new magical electives." Finally, some energy entered her voice. "And be sure to read my interview with Mister Magic himself, Casey Grimes, in tomorrow's print edition. What you learn may shock you. For Trickery News, this is Fiera Laurent, over and out."

Jake threaded his pencil behind one ear as the lunchroom buzzed to life. "I don't like the sound of that."

"Dried out spider-squid." Luci speared a cherry tomato.

Casey barely heard them. He was trying to think what he'd told Fiera that could possibly be considered shocking.

CHAPTER 14
PINK AND DEADLY

CASEY HADN'T EXPECTED TO KILL anything in his first session of Land Creature Defense. He'd brought his mace, handle retracted, in case a skrabbit or Bog Creep got loose, like they had when he'd visited LCD last semester.

Posing as Luci's cousins, he and Gloria had been unprepared for the total chaos when a substitute teacher freed a whole zoo of monsters. The devious Hyena Toad still stalked him in his dreams.

Now he and a partner stared down at a squirming Pink Recluse.

"Do you want the first jab or should I?" Casey said. "Watch out, it's sneaking your way, Jenni."

He and Jenni Tompkins both held scalpels. Casey had been careful to learn her name, because his Biology partner at Vintage Woods Middle School had never learned his, the entire semester. It hadn't been a good feeling. Luckily, Jenni wasn't mostly invisible.

She flounced her straight brown hair and made a face at the venomous worm. "Ooh, that's awfully kind of you to offer, Case. But you can have the first slice."

Case. That was clever.

"Are you sure?" The Pink Recluse wriggled up the side of its container.

She narrowed her hazel eyes, pretending to get serious. "Deal with that pinkie *right now*."

Casey made a face and sliced down.

"Oh, gross," they said at the same time.

Casey had expected Land Creature Defense to be more nerve-wracking. But with a qualified teacher in charge, it wasn't bad. Mr. Chandler, with his all-black outfit, serious face and clear directions, made Casey feel confident things wouldn't get out of control. It was hard to imagine someone more opposite from Carrots, the panicky botanist who'd filled in last time. And Casey even had a good partner.

Jen—he was gathering his nerve to call her that—took a refreshing, light-hearted approach to monster attacks. She wore pink lip gloss, which he found kind of daring. Except for eyeshadow, makeup wasn't popular at Trickery, since it didn't help you blend in with the forest. Maybe styles were changing. Or maybe she was trying to start a new trend. Either way, Jen was fun, and she didn't make a big deal about him maybe being a traitor.

For the first time since setting foot on campus that morning, he felt himself relax a little. By the time they'd dissected their Pink Recluse and extracted its poison gland for full credit, Casey was beginning to think his first Sylvan semester might go ok after all.

"Later, Case. Don't go slicing up anything without me."

"Wouldn't think of it...Jen."

She wrinkled her nose at him.

He clattered down the suspension bridge away from the LCD barn with a smile on his face. Birds were singing away. The sun felt great, de-mustifying his skin. He gauged its position in the sky. Mr. Chandler had let them go a little early. If he moved fast, he could give his Shortest Sylvan Distance Theory another try.

Casey took the first corkscrew stairway up, up, up, to the top of the forest. By the time he reached falcon level, a hundred feet high, his breath was coming in ragged gasps.

Don't overdo it, man. He'd had more than his share of exercise that morning. He stood in a wide crow's nest, overlooking the tossing sea of green. Other platforms and elevated paths were close by, but it was amazing how well the leaves hid them. *Let's see...the Legbreak Slopes are due north.* A thick rope with guide wires shot off in that direction.

Casey took a deep breath and stepped on. Then he stopped, listening.

Thump, thump, thump. A sound like footsteps, faint but nearby. Someone climbing stairs. He waited, but the sound didn't repeat itself. Maybe just a woodpecker. Nothing to worry about. According to Luci, all the ones with serrated beaks and a taste for bone marrow had been hunted down long ago.

Casey set off across the thick, twisted cord. He slid his hands along the guide wires, swaying in the breeze. Rope treeways were his favorites. With just braided cable under your feet, your ties to earth got super thin. The views and adrenalin took his breath away.

Treetops disappeared and Casey really *was* walking through air. A misty streamer of cloud floated over him, dampening the sun. It felt like moving through a cotton tunnel. A watery rumble reached his ears, and he figured he must be crossing the Roaring River ravine, where whitewater raged and churned before it dove into Deep Down, the cave system that ran under the rocky Legbreak Slopes. Except for the cries of an unseen bird, the sky was eerily quiet.

The rope wobbled under his feet.

Strange, he hadn't felt the wind pick up.

Casey glanced over his shoulder but all he saw was mist. Just the same, he moved a little faster. Tips of giant evergreens brushed his legs, then his shoulders. A few steps later, the ropeway ended in a towering fir, massive bolts sunk in the tree. Casey stepped through a V of living wood and onto a stairway. The solid timber felt reassuring.

It's no big deal, he told himself.

A side effect of Sylvan Woods' magic was that sometimes you felt like you were being watched when there was no one there, unless you counted trees. If you *did* count trees, well, you were never really alone.

"You've got my back, right?" he said to the enormous evergreen. The tree nodded gently in the wind. Casey shot one more look over his shoulder, down the rope bridge.

It was empty, of course.

CHAPTER 15
RING THE BELL

DESPITE HIS UNUSUAL METHOD of arrival, Casey found Extreme Climbing without any trouble. A string of colorful pennants wove along the ridge top. Meant to catch the eyes of kids on the main lift, they were impossible to miss as he descended from his private route, high overhead. He couldn't help feeling a little proud.

Voices rang from the lift, but no one else was in sight.

Yes! He pumped his fist as he followed the streamers. How much time had he saved, coming from Land Creature Defense? Ten minutes, maybe more. His heart thumped happily. Shortest Sylvan Distance Theory actually worked!

"Gear up! First to ring the bell gets bonus points."

Casey's heart gave a double-thump. Where was the voice coming from?

Oh, of course.

A coffee-skinned woman in an emerald tank top swung from a giant pine, twenty feet off the ground. Casey immediately liked her. Mom would wear that shade of green, foresty enough to be considered Sylvan, bright enough to be fun.

"What are you waiting for, Grimes?" Her black eyes gleamed.

"Trying to make a race outta this?" Her accent sounded foreign, but Casey couldn't place it.

He wondered how she knew his name as he shrugged off his pack and pulled a harness from a pile of equipment. His fingers felt buttery under the teacher's gaze. *C'mon, you're good at this.* He pulled the harness tight and hurried to clip himself in. Dozens of ropes hung from the giant evergreen, vibrating in the breeze.

"Where's the bell?" he said.

The teacher gave him an easy shrug.

"Hello!" she called to a group of new arrivals. "First to ring the bell gets bonus points."

Casey released his rope and felt the familiar upwards tug as his counterweight began to sink. The bark was bumpy, plenty of knots and whorls, so he shot up the trunk like nothing.

"Quick, after him!" someone yelled.

"He's getting a head start!"

Bonus points were a big deal. It made a lot of sense, since most Trickery classes could send you to the infirmary without warning. He'd better take this seriously.

Casey jumped from branch to branch, gaining altitude, the climbing weight tugging his shoulders like wings. The heavy silver disk sunk past him, meaning he'd reached the tree's halfway point, around raccoon height. The *biggest* trees in Sylvan Woods, like the Old Oak, bottomed out even higher, and for a moment he paused, thinking about his tree. His friend, really. The one who'd lured him into Sylvan Woods. He owed the Sentry Oak a lot. Sometime soon, he needed to pay his favorite tree a visit.

Shouts rose from below. Aromatic needles brushed his shoulders, and sap clung to his hands. He started to climb again. Where was that bell? The teacher looked like a serious climber so it had to be near the top, right? Unless she had a tricky side.

Casey groaned.

Everyone at Trickery had a tricky side.

He clambered into thinner branches approaching hawk height

and craned his neck. Nothing gleamed or caught the light. Nothing broke the tree's down-sloping profile. What had the teacher said? *Whoever rings the bell*...that meant she'd have to hear it.

Twigs snapped below. Pulleys whirred overhead. Soon the crown of the pine would be crawling with kids...but Casey let go and sank back down.

Nothing was ever straightforward around here.

A boy with red-brown hair surged past, defying gravity with his upward leaps. Surprise flashed over his face when he saw Casey. In a few seconds, the main route would be total chaos.

"Creeps, help me out here," he told the tree. A moment later, his hands found a curving branch, and he yanked himself out of the way as a crowd of kids hurtled by, crunching and stomping everything in their path.

Casey traced every limb with his eyes as he sunk earthward.

Where in beast-guts was that bell?

Nothing at squirrel height. Raccoon height came up empty. As the trunk thickened, he got more worried. New arrivals were still shooting past, unaware of the kids already swarming the treetop. If the bell was up there, he'd never find it now.

Casey sank to tree frog height. Now he was level with the teacher. She swung in her climbing harness, sipping from a water bottle. Was this a prank? There was no point in climbing lower. The trunk below was totally exposed.

A copper gleam caught his eye. In the shadows...a few feet above the teacher's close-cropped head. The bell wasn't big. But it was definitely close enough to hear.

No way.

Casey stepped onto a path-sized limb and walked outward, pushing through needles. Directly over the teacher's swing, he knelt, reached down and...*ding, ding, ding*. She smiled up at him. It was like being hit with a camera flash, but in a good way. He teetered on the edge of the branch.

"Nice work, Grimes," she said. "The bonus points are yours. Also, accept my gratitude for your service to Trickery. Last semester was no coincidence."

He gripped the pine, his palms hot and sticky. Teachers being nice wasn't something he was used to, unless you counted Ms. Crake —and her *nice* was kind of scary.

"I'm Ms. Chantelle," the lady said. "A friend of Ms. Crake. I hear you guys call her The Craken, which is pretty funny. Keep your head up, ok?" She raised her water bottle and gave him another smile. "You're free to go, since you found the bell. By the way, I'm sure you're considering all your options, but I for one would like to keep you in the *Woods* program of study. Canopy Mapping, Treeway Design, Forest Planning—that's where it's at."

"Yes!—I mean, yes ma'am. Me too!—I mean, nice to meet you." Casey rappelled back to the ground in a daze, unclipped himself, and staggered over to his pack. He pulled it on, pointed himself toward the streamers, and glanced over his shoulder.

Swinging at tree frog level, Ms. Chantelle gave him a wave.

Casey's knees felt weak as he hiked off. OPOW had seemed like an awful class, and he didn't know what would happen next. But after his good experience in LCD and now this, Trickery was feeling more like home by the minute.

CHAPTER 16
CIVILIAN WITH A SECRET MISSION

CASEY HAD TIME TO TRY ANOTHER shortcut, but things had started going well. Why press his luck? He hiked along the top of the ridge, enjoying the feeling of fitting in, of being good at something.

For old time's sake, he took the moving rope lift over Legbreak Slopes. The *squeak, squeak* of the enormous pulley brought back memories. Sweaty flip-flops. Gloria on his back. Luci screaming as they ran from Old Knock, a savage Security officer and PE teacher. After their terrifying escape, kids had realized the lift went somewhere useful. Now it got lots of use.

Casey half-closed his eyes as he soared down the slope, wind fanning his face.

You could've been killed or deported, he thought. Instead, you're here. Making the most of your Sylvan life. Of course, it won't be all sunshine and smiles. It will get hard, but if you do your best—

Fwap. All of a sudden, he couldn't see. Casey pulled a sheet of paper off his face. The lift was approaching the Air Creature Defense platform, and he was surprised to see dozens of leaflets caught in the trees, rustling over the deck. He'd never seen even an empty soda can in Sylvan Woods. People had too much respect for the forest. What was going on?

He stepped off the lift, crumpling the trash. Then he noticed big, blocky letters.

EVERYONE'S HEARD OF CASEY GRIMES.

Wait. This had to be a joke. He spun around but no one jumped out, laughing. No one was hiding on the stairs. Nothing moved down below, except for all the blowing paper. Casey got a weird, unsettled feeling in his gut.

EVERYONE'S HEARD OF CASEY GRIMES.
BUT HAVE YOU HEARD THIS?
GRIMES IS A CIVILIAN.
A CIVILIAN SPY.
HE HAS A SECRET MISSION.
A MISSION TO MAKE SYLVANS BLEED.
DO NOT TRUST HIM.
SIGNED, A CONCERNED SYLVANITE

Casey picked up another sheet.

EVERYONE'S HEARD OF CASEY GRIMES...

"Noo..."
And another.

BUT HAVE YOU HEARD THIS?

Every flyer was the same. His chest felt tight and itchy. He ran around the platform, grabbing leaflets and stuffing them in his pockets. He tore his pack open, grabbed armfuls, rammed them in.

Now Air Creature Defense was mostly clear, but...he looked over the edge and felt like crying. More paper blew away, tangled in bushes and trees, hundreds of white splotches, all along the trail.

The rope lift hummed behind him. Any minute, students would stream down Legbreak Slopes. He'd never have enough time.

"GRIMES! Are you up there?"

His first impulse was to hide, jump on a lift and disappear into the woods. Run home, hide in his room and never come out. But he knew that voice. Casey stood up shakily.

"Hey, I've been looking for you everywhere." Robert stood at the bottom of the stairs, face dark. "Quick, let's go."

Casey trudged down the stairs.

"Faster," Robert said.

"Did you read one?" Casey swept his arm around the clearing.

"Of course." Robert put a hand on Casey's shoulder. "Listen, man. They are everywhere. Someone left stacks in high, windy places all over Trickery. Let's go."

Casey's stomach melted away. It was like sinking in quicksand. Being pulled back into a nightmare you thought you'd left for good. Familiar, awful feelings washed over him.

"Robert," he said. "Do you believe it?"

"Of course not." The dangerous boy grabbed Casey's shoulders. "Don't even ask me that, man!" His eyes gleamed dangerously. "When I find whoever did this..." He trailed off. "Of course, it's *kinda* true, just a few months late. Remember when you were a Civilian with a secret mission?"

Casey nodded. "Yeah, the Butcher Brigade."

Robert smiled. "You don't have anything to prove to me, Grimes. This is a stupid bluff. And between you and me, there's not another kid at Trickery I trust more...except maybe Gloria. Now shut up and start walking."

CHAPTER 17
WHAT'S WRONG WITH KNOCKING SKULLS?

WELL HEY THERE," Luciana said. "My favorite Civilian spy. And to think, I was the first to uncover your dark designs."

Casey tried to smile.

They waited in a small room at the top of the Mythic History building. Not quite an attic, with its polished floors and hand-carved ceiling. From the ground or even the trees, you wouldn't guess the place existed. Maybe that was the point. Robert had brought Casey down side paths and back treeways. They'd entered through a trap-door in the roof.

Luci leaned forward in her chair, pushing back her wavy hair. "I'm actually not in a good mood. *At all.* I just want to grab my scythe-staff and hunt down who's responsible and twist it in their—"

An enormous shadow filled the doorway. It was Gloria...followed by Robert...followed by Mr. Kawkazi, The Crow. Casey huddled deeper in his chair. What was the enormous Fireside Cookery teacher doing here?

"I'm sooo mad!" Gloria flung herself onto an ottoman. "I can't believe we're not supposed t'trust you." Her cheeks looked flushed and damp. "Everyone should trust you!"

Casey pictured her sounding out the big block letters on the flyer. He took her hand.

"It's ok, Glo."

"It's not! Whoever did this, I'll get them!"

Leaning in the doorway, Robert gave her an approving nod.

The Crow put one foot up on a wingback, probably all of him the chair could support.

Luci dug her fingernails into upholstery. "Grrrr."

Casey wasn't sure who they were waiting on, but he hoped they got here fast, before Luci—and her hair—got any wilder. Her locks seemed extra swirly. She kept flicking them out of her face. Now that she'd stopped trying to act all cool, her eyes were flames.

Casey felt angry too. But it was the punched-in-the-stomach kind that left you struggling to breathe. He wished he felt more fierce.

Two more figures slipped inside. Jake. And Ms. Crake.

Casey sat upright.

When he'd last seen Crake in person, eating cake on his twelfth birthday, he hadn't realized what a big deal she'd become at Trickery. Her role in the Butcher Beast War had changed a lot of things. Now that she was Headmaster, Casey wasn't quite sure how to act around her. He glanced at Robert and Luci to see if they were saluting or bowing or anything. No, just sitting up straight, looking polite.

The Crow set his foot down and towered by the doorway, providing shade.

"West, Kawkazi, Pierce, baby girl Grimes." Ms. Crake nodded around the room, landing on Casey. "Sorry Grimes, you deserve better than this." She reached out and awkwardly touched his shoulder like he was on fire and her hand was made of wax. Casey appreciated the gesture.

"I know what you're probably thinking, but you can't solve this with your swordsmanship," she said. "No brawling your way out this time. Wish it was as simple as knocking a few skulls together..."

Casey held back a groan. Would she ever stop thinking he was lethal?

She shrugged, black cloak bunching. "Instead, we need a strategy."

Robert cleared his throat. "But Headmaster...what's wrong with knocking skulls? All we need to do is figure out who's doing this."

Crake's face took on the girlish expression she got when she was thinking hard, the one that made Casey wonder how old she actually was. Maybe the harder the problem, the younger she looked. He hoped not. At the moment, she looked about eighteen.

The headmaster sighed. "I've been overly-optimistic, Grimes. I thought we handled your Civilian transition well. Kept it hush-hush. I thought your difficulties were over, but I now see that I've made you vulnerable." She put a hand to her forehead. "Please believe me when I say the opposite was what I wanted."

"And now," Kawkazi rumbled, "so much depends on him not dying."

"Yes." Crake nodded. "Let's try to keep him alive."

Casey blinked. "Wait, hang on a—"

"I've already started the front page story," Jake said.

"Excellent." Crake touched her chin. "Hold nothing back, we need to get ahead of this." She frowned. "It's not going to be easy for you either, West. You know that?"

Luci pinched the hem of her t-shirt. "Yes, I know."

"We're clear on assignments then. Jake, you write. Robert and K, do what you do. West, better make it Tuesdays. Baby girl Grimes, pay attention to your teacher, especially during Swordplay."

"Wait." Head spinning, Casey raised a hand. "What's going on?"

"Someone doesn't like what you stand for," Ms. Crake said. "Great heroes cast long shadows. Can I give you a word of advice, Grimes?" Her turquoise eyes burned into his. "Brace yourself."

CHAPTER 18
GLASS BRIDGES

THEY SLIPPED ONTO THE STONE ROOF and hurried across a glassy footbridge onto a hidden platform. It would take eyes like a hawk to catch someone coming or going from the secret room, shrouded in leafy shadows. Translucent treeways looped away into the gloom.

"Why didn't I get an assignment?" Casey said. "Everyone else did, even Gloria."

Robert glanced at him and looked away.

"Speaking of which," Jake said, "I've gotta pound out this story." He moved off, cables shimmering under his hands and feet.

"I wish my assignment was different," Gloria said. "I already pay close attention."

A breeze tugged Luci's hair and she tucked loose strands behind her ears.

"Your assignment is to let us do our assignments," The Crow said.

That didn't seem fair.

"Sorry Grimes." Casey caught the sympathy in Crake's voice, but only because he sort of knew her. "Mr. K. is right. Our assignments depend on you doing what you're supposed to do. So keep going to class, acting normal. Not too normal, though." She winked. "No picking fights."

"Right," Casey said.

"Wonderful." She half-extended an arm, like she was going to touch him again, but thought better of it. "Ok! I've got to be in a dozen places. Good luck, everyone. Bye, baby girl. Bye, hon."

She disappeared down a transparent treeway, more graceful in the air than on the ground.

Bye, hon. It was like being patted by a cactus, but Casey felt a little better, knowing Crake cared. At least he *did* feel better, until he caught Luci rolling her eyes.

"What?"

"Hon? Next thing you know, she'll be calling you sugarplum."

"Give it a rest, you never liked her."

"I think you've got it backward," Luci said. "My little dumpling."

"Robert," Casey said desperately. "How come you're acting like someone's going to–"

But Robert had disappeared. The Crow stood on the edge of the platform, watching them with his eyebrows raised. *Don't look at me,* his expression said.

"Where'd he go, Gloria?" Casey asked.

Gloria shrugged. "He's the best at sneakiness."

Casey sighed.

"Come on, sweetie-pie," Luci said. "Let's head home."

Casey knew better than to argue.

They took a glass treeway, swung over to a woven footpath, and climbed down a ladder to a hanging garden. From there, they struck off on one of the numerous owl-height paths, doing their best to avoid other students.

"Wish we could take the Old Oak route," Luci said. From there, straight shot to your backyard."

"I still want to visit," Casey said. "Even though they locked it down."

"Picnic!" Gloria said.

"What's a little broken protocol?" Luci shrugged. "I mean, I get it, we've got to guard our magical air defenses, but if anyone should be able to visit, we should."

"Hey, maybe I could ask Crake for special clearance." Casey winced as the words left his mouth. He'd set himself up big time, like roast Razor-Wing on a platter. Teacher's pet! He waited for the insult, but Luci didn't pounce. Instead, he almost bumped into her as she stopped and turned.

"Do you know," she said, "this semester isn't going at all the way I hoped? Not what I pictured when we were in your kitchen, eating cake. And laughing. Remember, you said you couldn't possibly be ready in time for Trickery, and I said you'd be kind of famous. I said everything would be fine. I thought...thought we'd..." She turned away.

"I thought we'd play more games," Gloria said. "And have sleepovers."

Luci wiped at her face. "Me too, Glo. I pictured us doing home-work and kidding around, maybe running away from Old Knock for fun. I even thought, Hey, if I get a B this semester, it won't be a big deal. I thought things would be...normal."

"Maybe they still will," Casey said. But his words stuck in his throat. A dark, heavy mood pulled him down into a swamp of heart-sick. It felt like the moment he'd learned he wasn't welcome in Sylvan Woods. The feelings time-traveled through the summer in an instant. They landed on him with the same crushing weight they'd had when he first saw Trickery through the pines.

Casey took a shuddering breath.

"Are you ok?" Luci said.

"Yeah, I'm good."

Of course he wasn't—but neither was Luci. Normal wasn't something she'd had much of. Now, just when she'd earned her chance to belong, everything was at risk again. Everything she'd earned. Thanks to Casey Grimes, the most unpopular kid in Sylvan Woods.

At least she didn't seem to be running away.

CHAPTER 19
A LITTLE LIKE OLD TIMES

THEIR ALTERNATE ROUTE TO Casey's house dropped them into a rickety elm that had seen better days. The ladder wobbled. The bark was flaky. The Elderly Elm was quite a comedown from the Old Oak.

"We need a treeway in our backyard," Gloria said.

She'd been the only one talking during the hike.

Luci cleared her throat. "I have one, and it's very convenient." She paused, and Casey heard the hint of a smile when she said, "You should ask your parents to move to the right side of the border. No offense."

"None taken," Casey said. "Wait, you have a dedicated treeway?"

"An ancient willow," Luci said. "Up a spiral staircase or out a second story window."

"Oh man. I've got to see this."

"That could be arranged," Luci said. "We could even play a board game while we're at it."

"Yay!" Gloria said.

Casey smiled.

They tromped into the backyard.

"Watch out for our Sylvan trap," he said. "We reactivated it recently."

"Hahaha," Luci said.

The inside joke made it feel a little like old times, when Luci believed all sorts of ridiculous things about Civilians. When Mom invited her inside, she arched her eyebrows at Casey and Gloria.

"I'd love to stay a little while...but only if you all come visit me."

"Oh!" Mom said.

"Seriously," Luci said. "For dinner. How about tonight?"

"Have you run this past your parents?" Mom said.

"They're very adaptable," Luci said. "And they already like you."

Mom looked pleased. "Well, we'll certainly visit *some* night."

They drank lemonade at the dining room table. "Now I give my mom a nudge and we wait," Luci whispered. "They'll get it figured out."

"It takes Mom a whole year to plan my birthday," Gloria said doubtfully.

"I'd better go," Luci said. "Air Creature Defense isn't gonna prep itself." She stood up. "Thanks for the lemonade, Mrs. Grimes."

"You're very welcome, honey—and you can call me Claire," Mom said.

Casey walked Luci to the door. The sunlight gave her face a rosy glow, lighting up her freckles.

"See you, Casey."

"Bye, Luci."

He watched her fade into the woods. The achy feeling in his heart had softened, but it was in there, lurking. Like Luci's smile... there was something weighing down the edges. They were both just doing their best.

He found Gloria and Mom in the living room on the love seat overlooking the woods. Gloria had her head on Mom's shoulder. Mom was reading her a book. The afternoon sun washed them white-gold. They were so cute that he stood there watching.

"'Now sir,' said the bulldog in his business-like way. 'Are you a animal, vegetable, or mineral?'" Mom used a gruff voice and Gloria giggled.

All of a sudden, sadness landed on Casey's shoulders. Gloria didn't deserve what was happening. Neither did Mom or Dad.

Casey went upstairs. He slid books out of his pack, wondering if a graphing calculator would help with Optimal Pathways of Weapons. The Nonviolent Magic class didn't seem to have a textbook. *Monsters of the Pacific Northwest & Their Weaknesses* was a thick one, but Mr. Chandler had given them a list of predators to focus on for LCD. "I'll be choosing a representative sample," he'd said.

Extreme Climbing Without Fear was more of a field guide, with lots of sketches and techniques. The section on finger and toe exercises looked really useful. There was even a *Challenging Scenarios* section, with bullet point suggestions for survival. He checked, but there wasn't a scenario where you were attacked by Butcher Beasts while climbing a Sentry Tree. Casey felt a little disappointed. Maybe next edition.

He didn't have the rest of his books yet. Something to look forward to. As he jostled stuff around on his bed, making room to sit, something in his pack made an unfamiliar *clunk*. Casey reached in. His fingers closed on a narrow, hard-edged shape.

Holy beast hash.

He pulled out a wicked curved dagger.

Good thing it was sheathed, or he might have lost a finger. When he slid it out, the blade gleamed darkly above a black bone handle. High class. A small square of paper fell to his comforter.

Take care of yourself, Grimes.

The note wasn't signed, but Casey knew Robert's handiwork when he saw it. Thanks man, he thought. And for a few minutes, he felt better.

CHAPTER 20
GREATER AND LESSER BITTERBIRDS

AT DINNER, CASEY TOLD HIS PARENTS about the campaign to make everyone at Trickery hate him. Just the facts, because he didn't want to talk about how it made him feel.

"The papers said not to *trust* Casey." Gloria clashed her fork down. It seemed to really bother her, more than his being accused of spying or being a Civilian.

"Someone has it in for you." Dad's mouth was a straight line. "That someone is a coward."

"I'm so sorry, honey." Mom came over to hug him.

Casey appreciated it, even though it made his chest tight.

"Maybe a word about this to Ms. Cake," Dad said.

"I agree," Mom said. "I don't understand these distinctions. So what if you live outside Sylvan Woods? Do kids really think that makes you a different kind of person?"

"Sort of," Casey said.

Gloria raised her hand. "Well, because, well, they think we're *lesser*," she said. "Like a Lesser Bitterbird. They *look* a lot like Greater Bitterbirds, but they're not as dangerous, and the greater ones don't like the lesser ones. I learned that in school today."

Dad and Mom beamed at her.

"Sounds about right," Casey said.

Dad pushed back his chair. "Well, I guess the answer is to become more dangerous and show those Greater Bitterbirds what's what."

"Jack Lewis Grimes!" Mom said. "Don't encourage that!"

Dad shrugged and started clearing plates.

Casey thought it was a little scary how right Dad was without even knowing it. You got dangerous...or the danger got you. He put some condiments away and went upstairs to finish his homework. He'd already read about Tiger Rats and the Moles of Eternal Twilight. It looked like they wouldn't cover skrabbits, which was ok since he already knew how to deal with them.

Baby ones, anyway.

He read more *Extreme Climbing Without Fear* than he needed to. That just left his OPOW pages, which he'd been putting off. There was no question he'd lucked out the first class. Once they got down to calculations on paper, things would get ugly, especially if he had to show his work. It was also lucky they hadn't discussed the place-ment test. Hopefully Ms. Steele would handle that tactfully—but tact didn't seem to be a strength of hers.

Casey groaned, picked up his pencil, and forced himself to get to work.

"The wind is blowing from the south, hard enough to move your hair. At what angle should you throw your spear to stop the Death Dog on the left?"

He hated these problems. Faced with multiple Death Dogs, you'd be running for your life, not doing sums in your head. And the math was precise, totally unlike his battles where he flailed away, hoping he'd hit something. Casey felt his eyelids getting heavy.

Robert could help him with this. Or maybe not, since he'd prob-ably memorized all this stuff in pre-school and hadn't thought about it since. Luci was the one to go to for OPOW tips. Or maybe Jen in LCD...

Casey dozed off. When he jerked awake, someone had dimmed

the light and cleared the junk off his bed, except for the OPOW book his face was planted in. He wiped off his drool with an old sock and undressed before flopping back in bed. The moon was a bright sliver outside his window. He wondered if magic floated down on the silver rays, telling the trails to twist and tangle, to lose anyone who didn't know them by heart. Or maybe the magic rose from the darkness at the forest's roots... Off in the woods, something howled.

For a moment, everything felt right.

He snuggled in and fell asleep.

CHAPTER 21
BAD OMENS

THE FIRST SIGN THE DAY WAS probably not going to go well was the dead monster they found on the back deck.

"What do you think?" Dad stretched a foot out and prodded the big-nosed, spiky-furred beast with his flip-flop. "One of those pig-wolf things?—and kind of a big one. I guess someone was asleep on the job."

Casey admired Dad's calm, even though he couldn't remember a discussion about pig-wolf monsters. He felt weirdly guilty, like it was his fault this thing had crawled out of the woods and died behind their house. After all, Dad was right. The mission of Sylvan Woods was keeping monsters away from suburban homes. This wasn't supposed to happen.

"We don't have a trash bag big enough." Mom held a knuckle to her lips. "We're not supposed to call Animal Control, right?"

"Right," Dad said. "It would cause a panic. I won't tell any of my Civilian friends, will you?"

Mom smiled. "I won't if you won't."

They both started laughing.

Casey stared. They were so weird. They seriously needed to get out more. Maybe they'd hit it off with Luci's parents.

Dad dropped to one knee, inspecting the big-bellied, bristly dead thing. "Casey, I need a real weapon in this house. Those tusks look dangerous."

"Yeah," Casey said. "For sure."

"Help me drag this thing off the deck, would you?"

They grabbed the pig-wolf by its hind legs and yanked, thunking it down the stairs and across the yard. Dad glanced back.

"She went inside. What do you say we toss it in the woods?"

"Quick," Casey gasped. Stuffing it in the garbage can would be a nightmare.

They staggered across the yard and into the trees, a good ways off the path.

"Hope our house is upwind," Dad said.

"Scavengers will get it," Casey said. They turned, brushing bristles off their hands, and that's when he noticed a dull black dart, buried in the pig-wolf's neck. Easy to miss in the thick fur. He pointed it out to Dad.

"Hmm..." Dad said noncommittally.

Weird. But then, monsters didn't usually drop dead for no reason. It made sense. The only part that didn't make sense was why it was on their deck.

"Grab Gloria and get out of here," Dad said. "You'll be late."

Gloria waited on the deck, tossing her ponytail. They waved goodbye, made a beeline for the Elderly Elm, and took the treeway from the day before.

"I wonder how Luci goes to school," Gloria said. "It would be fun to meet her. Or Robert."

"True..." Casey pictured Robert waving goodbye to his own parents and smiled. Hard to believe Pierce had ever been tucked in at night. But as they moved through Lesser Trick 'n' Trap, Casey's smile faded. The big block letters from the day before appeared behind his eyes.

GRIMES IS A CIVILIAN SPY.

His pack was feeling extra heavy. He shrugged it around and forced himself to breathe normally, but it wasn't easy.

Just words on paper, he told himself. People here aren't stupid. They'll realize anyone can make up threats. Anyone at Trickery can be targeted.

But he really *was* a Civilian—or had been. And maybe he didn't have a secret mission, but he *did* like magic, which a lot of kids would see as the same thing. Magic was mysterious, ancient—and tough to control. In a society obsessed with control, especially *monster* control, it was no wonder people didn't like it. Even though they were missing out.

It was enough to make him nervous, almost as nervous as the first day he'd entered Trickery. Then he and Gloria arrived on campus and things really fell apart.

CHAPTER 22
MISTER MAGIC

THEY PAUSED ON AN OVERLOOK with great views of central campus, all spires, smoke and shining windows. If Trickery had brochures to attract new students, they'd take the pictures here. Casey scanned the woods below for paper trash, but he didn't see any. The grounds crew must have worked fast.

He and Gloria zig-zagged down to owl height, and she took off to meet her class. Casey unfolded his schedule. His first class was Magical Blasts, one he and Luci'd both chosen. Even Robert had seemed interested, although Casey doubted he'd actually signed up. As Casey knew from his frayed class schedule, Magical Blasts met in the Secret Sunken Garden.

He traced his route across the map.

It seemed straightforward.

Reluctantly, Casey took a stairway to the ground. Everything was taking a little longer this morning, with his cramped lungs and tired shoulders. Turning his map, he got the compass points aligned. That's when he noticed someone staring. Not even trying to hide it. Just gaping in the middle of the trail. A gnat buzzed into her open mouth—hopefully not a carnivorous one. When she saw him staring back, she held a textbook in front of her face.

Okaaay... He edged away.

The Secret Sunken Garden was northwest on his map. As he walked down the trail, he noticed a second kid inspecting him. Then a third. A fourth held up a copy of the *Trickery Times,* shaking his head. For a second, Casey didn't understand.

Then he remembered.

Fiera Laurent's article! In her know-it-all voice she'd said it would be in print today. Casey kept moving. He felt eyes poking him but he didn't look up, didn't slow, until he saw a copy of the *Times* folded over a stone bench. He grabbed the paper and flung it open. As promised, the article splashed across the front page.

MEET CASEY GRIMES: MR. MAGIC'S UNTOLD STORY

By Fiera Laurent, staff reporter

Most Trickery students have heard of Casey Grimes, but few have actually met him. Fewer still have heard a detailed account of his role in the events of last semester. Events that papers like the *Glacier Gorge Gazette* are calling, "The Magic Revolution." *The Times* believes that as students, we owe it to ourselves to learn the truth about this boy who has done so much to shape Trickery's future.

"I love magic," Mr. Grimes told me. "It's as important to me as breathing. Once I got to Trickery, I decided to do everything I could to get it back on the curriculum."

Casey screwed his eyes shut. There was no way he'd said that. Once he'd sneaked onto campus, he'd immediately become very busy—fighting, hiding and running for his life.

Fiera was twisting his words. He forced himself to keep reading.

By his own admission, Casey Grimes played a central role in the mysterious incident that got magic reinstated at Trickery. But what exactly was that role?

"Magic was the only thing that could save Trickery," Mr. Grimes said. But in our interview, he didn't clarify why Trickery needed saving. Was it Butcher Beasts, the monsters rumored to have been seen last semester? (This reporter has been unable to find a single trace.) Was it a decline in enrollment? Or maybe Mr. Grimes was just bored.

Casey scrubbed at his eyes. Was he really reading this?

Because you see, Mr. Grimes arrived in Trickery only months ago. Without an invitation. Before that, he wasn't a Unified Wilderness Alliance citizen. Where *was* Mr. Grimes? you ask. Well, he wasn't living overseas. He wasn't taking a gap year. No, Casey Grimes was living a Civilian life in Vintage Woods, Oregon.

Sweat broke out on Casey's forehead.

That's right.

Up until a few days ago, Mr. Grimes was officially a Civilian.

The Times will not stop digging until these nagging questions are answered. We deserve to know the full story about Mr. Magic, the boy who is singlehandedly shaping *our* future. His personal preferences are dragging us back into the dark ages. We ought to know who he is working with. And why.

At the end of our interview, *The Times* asked Casey Grimes why he would betray Trickery. "No comment," he replied. Then he rushed away.

But that's not good enough, is it? We need more. We need the truth.

The investigation is ongoing.

Casey let the paper drop from his nerveless fingers. Maybe worst of all, the article had a picture. His mouth half open, one hand outstretched, looking annoyed. He remembered the moment. Fiera had blasted away with her huge flash. He'd played right into her plans.

Now everyone at Trickery would know him on sight.

And to think, he'd wanted to help her. Everyone would've been happy to watch her plummet into the shrubbery. Instead, he'd saved her. And in return, she'd done this.

That's what you got for being kind.

Casey jumped to his feet. He threw down the *Trickery Times* and stomped it into the gravel. His heart pounded in his ears.

CHAPTER 23
MAGICAL BLASTS

C'MON, LET'S GO BLOW STUFF UP."

Casey blinked. If it had been anyone else, saying anything else, he might have taken a swing. But green flames danced in Luci's eyes, trying to take over. She held a copy of the *Trickery Times*, mostly torn to shreds. She looked like she was about to kill someone while wiping away tears.

"We'll be late, but who cares." She held out her hand.

He took it, and she pulled him off the stone bench.

They walked down the twisting path. Trudged through a marshy patch. Veered onto a wooden bridge. The air smelled wet and earthy. The clunk of their trail shoes bounced off water lapping below. High cattails sprang up on either side. A minute later, they stepped onto firm, upward-sloping turf and followed a thin trail over a grassy hill. Slabs of green-gray limestone rose on either side as they started back down. A murmur of voices came from below.

"Let's hope this class is good," Luci said.

"Yeah," Casey said.

They walked through a gap in the rocks. The Secret Sunken Garden felt a little like being trapped. The limestone formed twenty-foot cliffs on all sides. A few small trees provided shade, but mostly the garden grew moss and ferns. About twenty students huddled in the middle.

Luci and Casey joined them as quietly as they could.

"You're pioneers," a willowy, oldish lady was saying. "Brave. A little stubborn. And pyromaniacs, if I had to guess."

A few kids tittered nervously.

"I'm happy each of you chose this class. I know it was a tough decision. You're probably wondering how this fits with your courses in Woods, Work and War, and here's what I say: Magic is the magnet that holds them all together. Like the force that keeps our atoms from falling apart. You'll never have to apologize for caring about it here." Her brown hair, streaked with silver, was pulled back in a bun. "Of course, we've got a lot of magical catching up to do." Then her eyes caught Casey's like a hook and she stopped short. "How many of you read the paper this morning?"

All the kids raised their hands.

Casey kept his down, fists clenched.

Luci shot him a look. *Hold it together.*

"Let me just say, I've seen a lot of mucky journalism," the teacher said. "But that front page article was absolutely, one hundred percent...pure scat."

The class gave a happy little buzz.

"I'm Ms. Vaughn, and we magickers have to stick together. Ms. Crake says hi."

That got a few handclaps.

"She's talking to you," Luci whispered.

Casey let himself relax, a little.

"I like her," Luci said.

"Is that a first for you?"

Luci gave him a half-hearted glare that said, *Well, sort of...*

Students queued up to get materials from a table stacked with boxes. When Casey tried to take his box, Ms. Vaughn didn't let go.

"I wasn't sure you'd turn up, Casey."

He didn't know what to say.

"You're being targeted," Ms. Vaughn said. "It's not fair, and I'm sorry. This is bigger than you, but that doesn't keep it from feeling very personal."

The icy anger in Casey's chest thawed at the edges. *She's right,* he thought. *It isn't fair, and I can't force people to like me. But a few people, at least, can see what's going on.*

Ms. Vaughn was still talking. "...anything you'd like to say to the class?"

"Oh. Wow." Casey was about to say no, because speeches weren't his thing. But he *did* have something to say. Something he *had* to say. He swallowed and pointed at the table in the middle of the garden. "Could I?"

"Of course."

Luci's eyes widened as he climbed up.

He cleared his throat. "Um, hello. I'm Casey Grimes." Kids around the sunken garden stopped opening their boxes. "Yeah, that guy. Listen, don't believe everything you read." He hesitated. "Here's the true part. I used to be a Civilian, on the outside looking in—and I saw how special this place was. I saw what a lot of people don't see anymore—that Sylvan Woods is full of magic. Moving the paths, guarding the borders, burning in the Sentries. It's everywhere."

He took a breath. "Now that I'm finally here, I like magic and you should too, 'cause Trickery is a magical place...and magic really *can* save your life and you shouldn't be afraid of it, even if it's dangerous and kind of scary and not popular 'cause it's so old"—he gulped air—"and, well, I love Trickery and I'm not going anywhere."

He jumped down, sweat pouring off his face.

CHAPTER 24
THE SPECIAL INVITATION

MS. VAUGHN GAVE HIM A LONG, embarrassing round of applause and half the class joined in. A few kids met his eye. More drifted by as Casey and Luci sorted their blast kits.

"Gutsy move, Grimes."

"Hey, I remember you from last semester. You gave Drooce the boot and now you're doing crazy stuff again."

"I liked your speech, Casey. That was *so* brave."

The weight on his shoulders felt lighter.

Ms. Vaughn talked about safety procedures as they looked through their kits. No random mixing of explosive powders, no horseplay, no juggling, et cetera. It was easy to get the gist:

Don't blow each other up.

Casey's blast box contained a half dozen powders in waterproof containers with labels like Lingering Phosphorescence, Violet Whoosh, Voracious Moonlight and Campfire Inferno. There were also spools of shiny black twine and several small devices Casey guessed were launchers or detonators.

"Smoldering Straitjacket sounds promising," Luci said. "Holy creeps, no wonder this stuff hasn't been on the curriculum for a while. What do you think?"

"I like the Bouncing Blaze," Casey said. "You know, for skrabbits or Hyena Toads."

"Right," Luci said. "Or Mangleroos. There's a surprisingly large number of monsters that hop, skip and jump." She smoothed back her hair.

Ms. Vaughn quieted the class a few minutes later. "Magical Blasts will be outcomes-focused," she said. "In other words, we won't be using microscopes, but you'll need to become familiar with the bits and pieces of your arsenal. Most important, you'll need to become comfortable, very comfortable...with fire."

Casey didn't consider himself a pyro, but he didn't think that would be a problem. He remembered the enormous bonfire in the Big Beech where he'd first encountered a Butcher Beast. The tree had nudged him awake, and without the white-hot blaze, his glowing skewer wouldn't have sliced the monster's wings. It had been perfect in an awful kind of way.

"Something on your mind?" Luci asked.

"It's good to have fire on your side," Casey said. "Especially magical fire."

"Can't argue with that," Luci said. "Here's hoping we're elite at this."

Near the end of the period, Ms.Vaughn handed out medical release forms for students to take to their parents. "Bring these back signed and we'll get crackling and snapping." Then the teacher nodded to Luci. "Go ahead, dear."

Luci started handing out slips of paper too.

Way to go, Luciana, Casey thought. This had to be a first. As snarky as she was toward authorities, being a teacher's aide would be good for her.

She returned to their boulder and pressed a slip into his hands. "New club, you're invited." She looked away. "No pressure. Don't come if you don't want to."

He gave her a look and read the invitation.

MAGIC HAS RETURNED TO TRICKERY AT LAST. PLAY A PART IN THE REVO-

LUTION! JOIN THE FIRST EVER TRICKERY MAGIC CLUB. MEETING TODAY, ON THE VERANDA OF THE AMBER TOWER, DURING STUDY HALL. LIGHT REFRESHMENTS AND A SPECIAL GUEST PROVIDED.

"Well, I'm sure you're going, so of course I'll come." Casey watched Luci scrape moss off their boulder with a thumbnail. "Did you think I wouldn't?"

"Oh, you know," Luci said. "I didn't want to assume that you—I mean, of course. I knew you'd come. I just thought you'd like to be invited anyway." She gave him a sickly smile.

"These invitations are cool," he said. "Pretty classy. I hope no one tries to eat the special guest, though." He smiled. "Almost sounds like he'll be the main course, don't you think?"

Instead of saying teehee or grinning wickedly, Luci snatched the invitation back.

"Oh great, why didn't I see that? Urgh." She pressed a hand to her forehead.

"It's ok," Casey said. "You can't always be the one who thinks of the jokes."

A clarion call of bugles rang through the trees, and they got to their feet, brushing off lichen.

"I wonder who Ms. Vaughn got for a special guest," Casey said.

Luci rummaged in her pack as Casey turned in his blast kit.

"Coming?"

"Yeah, of course." She adjusted her pack straps, shoved back her hair, and knelt to tug her shoe laces.

Holy hash, was there anything she didn't need to adjust?

Finally, Luci handed over her explosives box. She studied her feet as they left the garden. They'd almost reached the gap in the limestone cliffs when Ms. Vaughn called after them.

"Oh, Ms. West."

Luci froze.

"Afraid I won't be able to make it today, dear, but I'll look forward to attending a club meeting very soon." She smiled after them.

"Wonderful," Luci said. "I'll look forward to seeing you." Her chin drooped.

"Wait," Casey said. "Whoa, hang on. Does that mean—"

"Yes, it's true." Luci looked miserable. "I'm the one starting the club. I've been handing out these invitations all over, and I've never done anything like this before, so I know it will go horribly. I mean, who wants to come to a club started by me? But Ms. Crake asked me to. And I didn't plan it this way, but..." She looked even more wretched, as if she'd taken a gulp of vinegar and it had reached her stomach.

"But what?"

"Don't be mad." She looked up. "You're the special guest."

CHAPTER 25
FUTURISTIC FORESTRY

AFTER AN AWKWARD GOODBYE, Casey bolted for the nearest treeway. If there was ever a time for Shortest Sylvan Distance Theory, this was it. He had fifteen minutes to be in Futuristic Forestry, but more important, he had to pull himself together.

He didn't want to be a special guest. He wanted to fit in. Well, he did want to be noticed, but not because he was infamous or some kind of mascot. But he *did* want magic to be popular. So what did he actually want? His mind felt like a color wheel, the feelings whirled together so all you got was grey.

Casey slumped in a wicker love seat in the very top of a giant cottonwood. It was a nice spot, looking west into the rolling hills of Greater Trick 'n' Trap. If you were here when the sun went down, the sky would light up like a valentine, pink and purple and gold. The darkness would wrap you like a blanket, stars close enough to touch.

It would be magical.

"Best spot for...hmm...catching up with yourself." Casey kept a running list of all the special places he'd discovered in Sylvan Woods' forgotten corners. He'd forced himself to give them names so he didn't just call them Magical Spot #1, #9, #17... There was Deepest Shade, Best Bird Songs, Most Swamp-Smelling, Best Homework

Spot, A Dance Floor (shudder), Most Likely To Be Undisturbed, and more. He'd have to put them down on paper soon, to keep everything straight.

For a few minutes, he let the sunlight melt across his skin. I need to visit the Bath Cave, he thought. A swim under the waterfall would be good. But not yet.

He sighed, got up, and got moving.

This time, he knew exactly where he was headed. Futuristic Forestry was held in the Amber Tower, the scientific center of campus, also home to Dueling classes. Everyone thought combat and science were crucial to Trickery's future.

Magic deserves a chance too, Casey thought as he trotted along a footbridge, grabbed a rope and swung over to a catwalk. *Magic is our future as much as anything.*

It made him feel good to say *our.*

By the time he reached the Amber Tower, Casey felt less paralyzed. He stepped off the treeway onto a terrace and pushed through a swinging door. Inside, everything was lit by golden light. He caught a whiff of peanuts in the air and frowned, remembering the Wild West fiasco last semester. If there was a way to work combat into a Forestry class, Trickery's faculty would do it. Probably with axes and hand saws.

But that wasn't how Futuristic Forestry went.

There were no black hats, no white hats, no violence at all. Just a roomful of bark samples, root system diagrams, and gorgeous, leaf-colored textbooks. True, the clashing of weapons and a few screams reached them from the second floor, but no one acted like it was a big deal. The class really *was* about Dendrology, the science of trees.

Casey could hardly believe it.

His teacher, Mr. Chroamwell, was obviously a genius. Usually, when Trickery students talked about what they wanted to do when they grew up, Woods came in a distant third behind the War and Work programs—but here was a guy who made trees seem cool. He lounged in his captain's chair, lecturing passionately about chlorophyll and photosynthesis, and Casey admired his walnut-colored vest, complimenting a spruce-green shirt and oaky tie.

Maybe I could dress like that, he thought.

Every few minutes, Chroamwell bounded to his feet to make a point, stunning the class into absolute silence. And three times (Casey counted) he gave Casey a *nailed it* sign when he was the only one to raise his hand. Chroamwell's opening lecture on The Consequences of Neglected Forests was totally brilliant. There could be no question about it. The class was going to be amazing. Combine the study of trees with a love for magic, and you've got the future of Sylvan Woods, Casey thought.

And I can help figure it out.

Maybe this was what it felt like to be Robert in one of his weapons classes. Or Luci, in just about all her classes—minus the feeling the teacher was out to get you. Because he was sure he and Mr. Chroamwell were going to get along great. As the rest of the class rushed off to lunch, Casey took his time gathering his things so he could catch Chroamwell's eye on the way out.

"Great class, sir."

"Grimes!" The teacher stopped tidying his desk and grinned at him. "Glad you're here. The Woods need people of your caliber."

"Thanks, sir." Casey felt his face get hot as he smiled and left the room.

But taking his time turned out to be a mistake.

When he stepped outside, the amber terrace was empty. His classmates were long gone.

A low, sneering voice said, "Oh no. Help, I'm so afraid. It's Casey Grimes."

CHAPTER 26
OUR LITTLE SECRET

CASEY HADN'T SEEN SEBASTIEN Drooce for months. He and Tonya Cortland, his icy blonde partner in crime, had tried to ambush Casey twice before and failed, thanks to Robert's weapon skills and a scary level of fierceness from Luci.

When she'd sent Drooce and Cortland screaming into the night, it was the first real evidence of something Casey already suspected —Luci wasn't a normal girl. He had a picture of her in the back of his mind: Blazing eyes. Swirling hair.

Unfortunately, this time she wasn't here.

Lounging on the terrace, Drooce looked bigger, like he'd spent the summer pushing wheelbarrows of rock and mucking out gryphon pens. It was possible, because summer detentions at Trickery were a thing. Drooce hadn't abandoned his artfully floppy hair, though. It made him look like he was auditioning for a heart-throb tv role, except he had a pale diagonal scar under one eye.

Could Luci have put it there? Casey backed away, easing his pack down. Without taking his eyes off Sebastien, he unclipped the 127-Spiker on loan from Robert.

If only his friends were here now.

"I know what you're thinking." Drooce grinned, showing his

bleached white teeth. "Too bad Robert's not here, or your snaky little sidekick. Just you and me and our secret."

"Look," Casey said. "I never said I beat you up. It was a misunderstanding."

"Oh, that." Sebastien crossed his arms and leaned against the tower. His biceps were definitely bigger. "I haven't given that a second thought. No, I'm talking about your pal with the crazy eyes. And the wild hair." He tugged his own locks so they stood on end. "Your number one witch friend."

Casey's mouth felt dry. "No idea what you're talking about."

Drooce's smile was like a trapdoor creaking open. "That's cute, Grimes. Pretending you don't know. But now you know..." he tapped his chest. "That I know."

"Who cares!" Casey felt his temperature rising. "What's your point?"

"Don't be stupid," Drooce said. "I'm threatening you, obviously. Now you'll do what I want or, oops, word gets out that darling Luci is a–"

"Shut up!" Casey yelled. "Go ahead and tell. No one will care and then everyone will know she carved you up all by herself."

Drooce laughed. "I keep forgetting you're a total idiot. That's not how things work around here, Grimes. Not even close."

Casey fought to keep his chin up and his eyes hard as his heart sank down, down, down. All of a sudden, he knew Sebastien was right. Fiera's article proved it. All it took was a rumor to ruin your life, and Luci had switched schools before. He knew how hard she'd fought to keep her secret. A secret they'd never openly discussed. A secret he'd kind of hoped was all made up that day in the hospital, in his tired, drug-blurred mind.

The totally real secret. That Drooce would tell everyone.

Casey gritted his teeth. "What do you want?"

The bully nodded. "That's right, Grimes, I knew you'd get there. Let's see, what do I want...oh, so many things. I'd like that mace, for example—maybe later." He pushed off the tower and sidled closer.

"I'd like to PUNCH YOU!" He rammed a fist through the air, making Casey flinch.

"I'd like to know about your secret Civilian life." He prodded Casey in the chest. "But that can wait. What I want right now, today, this week...is for you to stay put. Everyone knows you wanna run like crazy, but *don't*. Don't run like the weak little civ-scat you are. Don't sneak away, don't hide, don't go anywhere. Just keep doing your Grimesy thing. I'll give you orders from here on in. I'll call the shots. I'll rule you."

Casey wanted to hit Drooce in the nose like he had that spring, even though he knew he'd never win the fight. Anger scorched his insides. But he couldn't. Not if the bully knew Luci's secret.

"I'm not afraid of you," he managed to say.

"Keep telling yourself that." Drooce smacked Casey on the back of the head as he turned. "Pretend to be as brave as you want, for dear, freakish Luci." He stepped onto the treeway and sauntered off.

CHAPTER 27
NOT ON MY WATCH

CASEY SANK TO HIS KNEES. The thick amber terrace felt cool under his sweaty hands. For a few seconds, he thought he'd throw up.

Instead, he picked up the mace and slowly clipped it to his pack. It would've been better if Drooce had attacked him. Things would've been simple. He would have fought back, and lost, and then he would've gone to the infirmary and got stitches, and eventually Drooce would've been caught and sent to the gryphon pens.

Now nothing was simple.

Casey wasn't sure what to do. He wasn't sure who to talk to. He didn't think he could even eat lunch. He pulled on his pack and sat on the terrace a few more minutes.

If he told Luci, she would go a little crazy, or she might lock herself in her room and never come out. They could never talk about this.

This secret.

Casey'd told her he didn't care, it wasn't a big deal, and he'd meant it, but...he'd been very groggy at the time. It was weird to think that Luci, a smart Sylvan girl, was also partly something else. Something fierce that might show up at any time—something that

Sylvan Woods existed to control, to police, to keep at bay. He couldn't imagine how it made Luci feel. Casey shook his head. No reason to think about it now.

He wished he could tell Robert. The dangerous kid was good with secrets, but if Pierce didn't already know, Casey couldn't tell him. And where had Robert been lately, anyway? Casey brought a fist down on the railing. If Robert was a little more present, maybe things like this wouldn't keep happening.

There had to be a way out.

Well, Drooce hadn't asked him to do anything bad. Stay where you are. Don't run away. It was a weird request. It didn't make sense. But it wouldn't be a problem, because he'd never run away.

At least...not since he'd considered it a couple hours ago at Magical Blasts.

Drooce thought he was a coward.

Well, Casey would show him how wrong he was. He walked down the treeway with short, jerky strides. He'd go to class. He'd fight the lies. And yeah, he'd be the special guest at Luci's magic club. He'd prove to everyone he wasn't afraid. Trickery was *his* school. Sylvan Woods was *his* home. When Drooce realized how stubborn Casey was, it would be too late.

He stomped to the cafeteria over empty treeways, planks shuddering under his feet. By the time he reached the wide stairs and yellow doors, he was hoarse from fuming.

"Not going anywhere," he muttered.

"Bootman, you ok?" Jake hurried up. "No worries, I talk to myself too, especially when I'm on deadline."

"Fine," Casey said.

"Fantastic." A pencil and notebook appeared in Jake's hands. "So, when I said 'deadline,' that was a cue, because I'm actually on deadline, man. I'm not a scat writer like Fiera, so this needs to be on point. Can I get a few quotes on the way to lunch? Been working on your story every spare minute."

"Oh, right, sure."

"Cool, so talk to me about the moment you decided to fight the butchers. Back when we thought you were Luci's cousin but you were really on the run, Old Knock breathin' down your neck."

"Wow." Casey paused on the stairs as he reached for the memories. "Let's see...Crake went down fighting, and I thought it was time to take Gloria home. But then...I couldn't leave Luci behind, or Robert or you and the Skewers—and I couldn't let Sylvan Woods be destroyed."

He just hadn't been able to walk away. "The trees, the magic," he said. "It really is the best place in the world. I had to fight the best I could, long as I could. Then Bones made me head of the Butcher Brigade..."

Jakes was scribbling like crazy. "That's what I like about you, Grimes. Lotsa other kids would've found moments to bail, even though we're supposed to be all combative and fierce and stuff—but you did the opposite. You found reasons to stay. When kids dropped their skewers and ran, you think they stopped to ask how the rest of us'd survive? Not for a second. But you just kept fighting."

"Yeah..." Casey said. "I had to. Even when I thought we'd all die. Especially then."

Jake chuckled. "Instead, you jumped on the butcher queen's back and battled her in the sky. How did you pull that off?"

"Well, I've always been good at trees." Casey winced. "I mean, I've got good balance and I'm not afraid of heights."

"Love the understatement," Jake said. "Any parting words?"

"Um, I'm grateful to be Trickery's first Civilian transfer student in...a really long time." Casey rubbed his neck. "Happy I got the chance to fight for Sylvan Woods and that the magic is real...in the woods, in the water—even in us, if we let it. And now I get to call this place home. Of course, I never could have done it without the Butcher Brigade...and the Skewers."

Jake beamed.

"And I'm happy we're true to our roots," Casey said. "Strength and honor and magic." He pictured the ink-stained pages in his crumbling *Sylvan Handbook*. "I hope Sylvan Woods will always be that kind of place."

Jake shut his notebook, shaking his head. "Nailed it, man. Gutsy take. Gives me plenty to work with."

"Hey Jake," Casey said as they shoved the doors open.

"Yeah man."

"You think I'll get through all this ok?"

Jake's brows came down. "You kidding me? My school's not gonna savage The Bootman, not while I'm around. Don't give it another thought. Everything's gonna be totally all right." But Jake had caught some of what Casey had.

He muttered under his breath as he hurried away.

CHAPTER 28
A BAD LUNCH

AS BAD AS THE MORNING HAD BEEN, it would've been nice if lunch had gone differently. Unfortunately, once someone spotted Casey in the cafeteria, a wave of hushed voices and sharp elbows moved across the room. He tried to ignore them as he marched through the lunch line, slopping this and that onto his plate.

"Hey look, it's Mister Magic."

"Guess he left his wand at home."

"Hey Grimes, where's your pointy hat?"

When he dropped into a seat across from Luci, she looked mad too. Somehow, he'd avoided all the food he liked. His plate was awash with pink jello, kale chips and unidentifiable brown mush, all if it soaking into cornbread. He checked out Luci's plate, but all she had were celery, tomatoes, and carrots she was rapidly snapping in half.

"Lots of veggies," he said.

"Yes." Luci broke the spine of a celery stalk. "I'm willing to try just about anything to make life better."

Robert materialized out of nowhere, jerked out a chair, and dropped into it, scowling. His eyes had dark circles. His normally perfect hair had loose wisps. He stabbed a cherry tomato with his fork and seedy red juice sprayed his black shirt. "Hell's bells!"

Casey had never seen him make a mental error like this before.

Luci didn't bother to correct Robert's language, something that normally gave her great joy. Instead, she gave him a smirk. "Really, you're surprised? Get them before they get you." She tore her vegetables into smaller and smaller bits.

Then, when it seemed the mood couldn't possibly get worse, Gloria climbed up next to Casey. Her face looked pink and creased as if she'd been awakened from a nap. She took a savage bite of leftover breakfast pizza.

"These kids are terrible. I want to shove them *all* in the sandpit."

Casey reached out to pat her hand. That's right, he thought. It's the only possible way to feel. He wished he had something encouraging to say, but he didn't. He could barely meet Luci's eyes. He was irritated with Robert for never being around. His problems were even ruining things for Gloria.

Casey took his frustration out on his lunch like everyone else.

When the leaf-shaped speakers came to life, even Jake McGusty sounded irritable. No wonder, he'd been working overtime on Casey's stupid story.

Everyone around me feels horrible. Everyone else feels wonderful and alive.

Trickery News updates were usually exciting. You learned about something awful going on, right under your nose. Or you got an update on how close you were to being exposed and caught, or a clue about Ms. Crake's new scheme. Today, the news sounded disorganized.

And angry.

"Good afternoon, Trickery." Jake didn't have his usual bounce. "I hope your second full day is off to a good start and that no one has slandered or defamed you." He coughed. "Let's see...we've got reports of kids floundering in the sandpit, triggering an outbreak of sand sprites, but I didn't have time to check those facts, so cool your engines. Not a great day for real journalism, kids..."

He paused, then sped up. "But when it comes to throwing muck —man, look out. I'm sure you read the feature in this morning's *Times*. As an employee, I don't have any comment on that, except to say IT'S A SMOKING PILE OF HASH AND NO ONE IN HER RIGHT MIND—"

The speakers went silent with a clatter.

"Good old McGusty, doing his part," Robert said.

The cafeteria doors flew open, thumping the walls. A familiar, shaggy-haired figure in a flannel shirt and gym shorts stalked inside. His eyes darted right and left.

Gloria slid off her chair and disappeared under the table.

With an effort, Casey stayed put. Even when you'd done nothing wrong, Old Knock was scary. And Casey'd broken plenty of rules... just not today. When Knock had chased him, Gloria and Luci all over Trickery in an awful game of cat and mice, Robert had compared their feat to playing with unquenchable fire. Casey was sure Knock hadn't forgotten, and *pretty* sure he'd solved the mystery of the flee-ing, screaming trio of shadows.

Casey studied his gloppy plate as the PE teacher and security guard moved past, thumping his axe handle and muttering. Luci stared at nothing. Robert threw a fry into his mouth and scowled at Gloria's empty place.

Then, like a foul odor fading in the breeze, Old Knock was gone.

A bright, adult voice came over the speakers. "That concludes our program, students. Have a wonderful day—full of Adventure, Courage and Fighting!"

As the static died, someone yelped on the far side of the cafeteria. "Ouch, stop hitting me!"

Robert tiredly got to his feet. "Gotta run, kids." He stuck his head under the table. "Bye Glo. I'll have a word with the witnesses at the sandpit."

Gloria slithered out, snatched a grape from Luci's plate and threw it at Robert's head.

He snatched it out of the air and squished it to pulp.

"You deserve to get graped." She pouted. "You're no fun anymore."

"Just so you know," Robert growled, "this isn't the semester I planned."

Any other day, watching Gloria and Robert fight would've made Casey laugh. But not today. Today, not even this was funny.

Robert glanced at them. "For the record, I was looking forward to dueling together...and strategizing about attacks...and doing combat homework with you all. This...*this*...isn't fun."

Casey and Luci nodded.

Gloria turned up her nose. "You should be stopping up all the mean kids."

Hard to know if she meant shutting up—or stomping.

Robert frowned at her. "Look, I wish I could–" He paused. "You're right, Glo. That *is* what I should be doing." His eyes darkened. "Casey, we'll talk soon, ok. Real soon."

Then he was gone, shoving chairs and kids out of his way.

"I liked him better when he had a pink eye," Gloria said.

CHAPTER 29
RETURN TO THE BATH CAVE

CASEY WANTED TO SKIP PUBLIC STORYTELLING, but it would be a really bad move the first day of class. His absence would be noted. At Trickery, being noted was not something you did lightly. Nevertheless, he slowed to a stop outside the cafeteria, where a collection of wooden signs pointed in a dozen directions.

No one cared if you showed up at Vintage Woods Middle School, he thought. You couldn't get in trouble, no matter how hard you tried. Other kids got yelled at and sent to the principal but no one ever noticed you. Maybe it was more awesome than you realized.

Kids streamed past, blinking and staring like he was a monster in the middle of a trout stream. He turned and walked in the opposite direction. He didn't use the enormous ramp that rose from the cafeteria clearing. He didn't test his Shortest Sylvan Distance Theory.

He just walked.

Dust puffed under his shoes as he wound around Mythic History, past the Amber Tower, under the Rondure Arena, past the Great Hall. He pushed through the pines and left campus.

On the sunny, rock-covered hillside, he ambled in the shade of birches and aspens. Halfway up the slope, he stopped to tie his shoe. No one bumped him from behind. No one elbowed him and pretended it was an accident.

He took the right fork into the boys' side of the bath house. Hot and cold fountains bubbled onto polished stone by pale stalagmites stacked with bath supplies. Mist swirled in warm curtains. The waterfall poured down the back wall with its dull, bass rumble. Not a single other kid was there.

It was perfect.

Casey felt so tired, it was a miracle he'd been able to walk here at all. He slumped on the floor, letting the mist envelop him. After a while he pulled off his clothes and stepped into a red rock fountain bubbling down from overhead. Oh man. He'd missed this. A shower at Trickery was better than a Civilian waterpark. So why did he feel so...

Head bowed in the mineral fountain, Casey wiped his eyes. "It wasn't supposed to go this way," he said into the splashing water. "Everything was supposed to change. But no one likes me. No one cares what I did. My friends are in trouble because of me. Gloria is having a bad time. It's all my fault."

He stepped out of the shower and dripped across to the blue-tiled pool where waves lapped like a tiny sea. He didn't have a cannonball in him, so he just waded deeper and deeper until the floor sloped under his feet.

"I don't even know why this is happening," he said. Then he ducked under and let the waterfall tumble over his head and shoulders, kneading his muscles, pushing him further and further down. His fingertips grazed the bottom. He held his breath and kept holding it until his lungs burned.

It was like a little death.

Everything that didn't really matter washed away.

When he came up, he knew who he was again.

He knew what he had to do.

"I've gotta get to magic club," he said. "Or Luci will kill me."

CHAPTER 30
THE NERDS OF TRICKERY

CASEY HADN'T PACKED A CHANGE OF clothes. Of course he hadn't. He never had in the past, splashing in swamps and stabbing creatures with black blood, so why start now?

"Smoking bones," he muttered. "Preparedness. How hard can it be?"

For a second, a millisecond really, he thought about running by Lost and Found. Instead, he pulled his sweaty t-shirt back on, scrubbed a towel through his hair, and tried to ruffle it stylishly in the mirror.

Hmm. Special guests weren't supposed to look like this. Standing in the misty cave, pulling on dirty clothes, wincing at his reflection, it all felt so familiar. The last time he'd done this, he'd been an illegal Civilian, stumbling cluelessly around Sylvan Woods. At least a few things had changed. For example, he wasn't wearing flip-flops.

He grabbed his pack and jogged out of the cave.

Shouts, laughter, and occasional cries of pain reached him from the woods. Class was out. He rushed back toward central Trickery, patting his damp hair and trying to think what would be expected from a special guest. Well, he'd be expected to show up for one thing. Casey quickened his pace.

A special guest would be polite. Chat with kids who showed up. Answer questions in a cool, humble kind of way.

As he neared the Amber Tower, a wrinkled old man clinging to a walker stumped toward him. It was hard to tell who was moving who along. A gold whistle dangled over his sunken chest. Kids said Bones had been a Sylvan soldier in the Civil War. Even if he *was* centuries old, he was someone you wanted on your side. Without Bones' vote of confidence last semester, Casey wouldn't have survived long enough to fight the Butcher Beasts.

"Get yer buttocks on that porch, Grimes." Bones glowered. "When I agreed t' supervise this club, didn't know I'd hafta hunt ya down and bring ya in."

"Yes sir!" Casey ran past as Bones spun the walker. Unlike Old Knock, Bones wasn't known for violence, but it was best to stay out of reach.

He bounded up three wide amber steps onto the veranda and slowed, his eyebrows tugging upward. A dozen kids loitered on the covered porch...but loitering required basic coordination. In Sylvan Woods it sometimes implied threat. This group implied a general squishiness. The amber veranda was a popular spot for class photos. The honeyed glow and textured backdrop were enough to make anyone look sophisticated and cool, with great skin.

Not these kids.

Some leaned against the tower, but not in a *Hey what's up* kind of way. Their arms and knees stuck out awkwardly. Cookie crumbs dotted their shirts. A chubby boy was crunching the last one, and Casey realized with shock, this was the first pudgy kid he'd seen in Sylvan Woods. Where had he been hiding?

A boy with pimples studied his reflection sadly. A spiky-haired girl with nose rings and too much blue eye-shadow stood nearby, doing the same. Less than a foot apart, they managed to ignore each other. A girl with waist-length pigtails polished her glasses on her yellow shirt. *Yellow,* like an Easter parade. A painfully thin kid worked out his biceps with a couple of pencils as a string-thin girl watched, clapping. A few more were talking about magic in squawky, nasal voices.

Casey knew what he was looking at.

These were the nerds of Trickery.

All of them.

Only one person in the group knew how to loiter properly. She sat on a bench, one leg crossed over the other, arms folded, eyes wide. *Why is this happening to me?* her expression said. *What did I do to deserve this?*

She stood slowly.

"Welcome to Magic Club," Luci said. "The cookies are gone. Our special guest is here. Shall we get started?"

CHAPTER 31
GIVE YOURSELF A HAND, MAGIC CLUB

YOU CAN DO THIS! CASEY WANTED to shout. Instead, he got ready to applaud at the first pause. It was obvious Luci was trying her best.

She put her hands behind her back like she had in Public Storytelling all those weeks before. "Hello, and welcome to the first Trickery Magic Club in two hundred years. Glad you could make it."

To their credit, the nerds stopped squawking, staring at themselves in the amber, and pumping pencils. They appeared to be paying attention.

"We're a rare kind of club." Luci forced a smile. "We have the full backing of Trickery's faculty—well, Ms. Crake at least—and we'll be meeting with their support instead of getting eaten by mosquitoes in the woods or crawling through dirty catacombs and stuff. So... that's cool."

She paused and Casey clapped as he thought, Sylvan Woods has catacombs?

A few other kids picked up his cue and put their hands together.

"Don't worry, we'll still use secret messages!" Luci said as the claps died away. "Our stated purpose is to investigate and discuss all things magical, whether magical defenses, like elixir, magical attacks, like blasts, or magic we use all the time but take for granted, like invisa-fade."

Casey had planned to clap some more, but his hands froze in midair. *Invisa-fade.* He and invisa-fade had a history, and not a good one. Luckily, the spiky-haired girl, now standing nearby, noticed what he'd intended to do. She put her hands together with a weak *pit-pit-pat.*

"Thank you." Luci gave her best modest smile. "Later, we'll have case studies to discuss from Sylvan history. We'll do some experiments and hopefully we'll talk about the reasons for magic, why it even exists. Today, we have a special guest who will say a few words about the return of magic to Sylvan Woods and, quite possibly, the whole Unified Wilderness Alliance. Please join me in welcoming Casey Grimes."

Pit-pit-pat. Clapitty clap clap.

Oh no, that's me. She means me. Casey stepped to the center of the terrace. *How could she do this to me?* His plan had been to support Luci and clap whenever there was silence.

There was definitely silence now.

"Give yourself a hand, Magic Club!" That bought him five more seconds as a few of the kids gave enthusiasm a try. "And let's have a hand for Luciana West as well. Great job, Luci." Now he was the only one clapping, but he drew it out for another ten seconds. Clap... clap...clap. Luci's face got rosy.

Those extra fifteen seconds really did help, though. Casey felt less panicky and rushed as he said, "Well, er, um, what would you like to know?"

There was a painful silence.

"Just talk," Luci whispered. "Like you did in Magical Blasts..."

That wasn't helpful. Casey tried to think of things you would say about yourself in a meeting. *I was born in...*well, he wasn't clear on that. *My hobbies are...*

"I've liked trees as long as I remember," he said.

Luci raised her eyebrows, smiled, and nodded, like he was a toddler taking shaky steps.

"And Sylvan Woods has the best trees ever. I mean, better than anywhere. They're A plus." Casey felt himself stalling out. He glanced around for inspiration. Luci looked panic-stricken. Leaning over his walker, Bones was shaking his head. The other kids looked puzzled.

The girl with the nose rings raised her hand. "Could you tell us what *really* happened the night the Butcher Beasts attacked?" With all the attention focused on someone else, she seemed quite articulate. "There's been so much disinformation..."

Sweat popped out on Casey's forehead. "Oh man. Yeah, there sure has." Did he want to talk about that? He found he sort of did, but it was like opening a scary attic door you'd left alone for ages. "Let's see... Well first off, there really were Butcher Beasts. Mr. Bones over there can tell you that. But it all began when we learned about the Sentry Trees..."

Fifteen minutes later, Casey brought his story to a close. "So I woke up in the hospital," he said. "Didn't know where I was until my friends came to visit me. But they told me everything would be ok." Of course, that wasn't really what had happened. Robert and Luci hadn't been sure they'd ever see him again.

And Luci had told him her secret.

But now, as Casey pictured the bright white lights and the vase of wild flowers and Luci's tear-streaked face, changing from sad to happy...the memory felt sour.

Because Drooce knew the secret too.

Clapping jarred him back to the amber veranda. Realizing he was done, Magic Club produced the most convincing round of applause in its short history.

"That article got it all wrong," said the girl in the yellow shirt. "It wasn't a publicity stunt, I knew it, I knew it!"

"You actually saved Trickery," said the pencil-thin kid.

"Magic is on the curriculum for a reason," said the chubby one.

"You're absolutely right." Luci stood up from her seat by the wall. "Casey is a true hero. Now you know the truth—and that adjourns our meeting for today. Thanks so much for coming, and feel free to tell your friends. All further messages about our meetings will be posted in code on the Trickery bulletin board, but you can assume we'll be here next week."

Casey exchanged awkward handshakes as the magic-lovers wandered off.

Luci sank back to her bench. "Well," she said. "That's over. You did a pretty good job for someone who hasn't taken Public Story-telling. Of course, you also showed up late and left me sitting here while everyone ate cookies with their mouths open. Never do that again."

"I'll try not to," Casey said.

They sat on the veranda, gathering their thoughts.

"Where to now?" Bones asked.

"Oh!" Casey had forgotten he was standing there.

"School's out, isn't it about time you went home?"

"I don't understand, Mr. Bones." Luci said. "Do you *want* us to go home?"

"Cut the act, girl. Of course I want you to go home. My shift lasts as long as your meeting. Once you leave, I'm done. Not to mention, this veranda is out in the open. Home is easier to defend."

"Got it," Casey said, although he didn't. The Sylvan obsession with security was something he hadn't wrapped his mind around. Especially when it popped up out of nowhere.

"Well Casey..." Luci said, stretching out on the bench. "I don't know, have you had enough discussion for today?" She snugged her shoulders back against the wall. "I'm kind of enjoying our little gathering. Maybe we should continue meeting a while longer?"

"What?" Luci could be evil around authorities. But despite her little smirk, she wasn't glaring at Bones. Was it possible she had a soft spot?

"You're as funny as rocks," Bones said. "Listen kid, just 'cause I put you on the Butcher Brigade, and just because I haven't revoked your library pass, that doesn't mean I like you. Now scram."

They sneered at each other as Luci scrambled off the porch. Casey wouldn't have believed it if he hadn't seen it with his own eyes. She had a teacher-friend.

"Stay outta trouble, Grimes." Bones gave him a whack on the shoulder as he passed. "And watch your back, I'd feel bad if you got eaten or eviscerated or somethin.'"

"Thanks," Casey said.

The old man watched them walk into the shade.

"What a weird, twisted old guy," Luci said admiringly.

Casey smiled.

"Hey, good news," Luci said. "My mom is going to talk to your mom about having you over for dinner. Maybe tomorrow or Saturday."

"Cool," Casey said. "That'll be fun."

He didn't realize it was the last good news he would hear for quite some time.

CHAPTER 32
WHERE THE HECK IS ROBERT?

WHEN CASEY GOT HOME, GLORIA was reviewing her monster flash cards at the dining room table. "Mr. Kacrazy walked me back," she said.

Casey wondered what they'd talked about. The Crow didn't say much, but if he'd been with Gloria, silence would not have been an option. Maybe he'd been lured into a chat about unicorns. Casey sat down across from his sister and grabbed a handful of cards. "Let's see what you've got here," he said. "Oh wow, a Bark Cheeper, haven't heard of those."

She gave him a serious look. "Don't be fooled by the inno... inno*cent* name, this monster gnaws arms and legs as well as tree limbs."

Casey turned the card over. "Wow, you memorized that word for word."

Gloria smiled. "Innocent means cute."

"What about this one?" He held up another.

"The Shin-Snip," Gloria said. "Despite their small, um, *stature*, Snips have dealt out some terrible injuries."

"Nailed it." Casey continued reading the back of the card and wished he hadn't. "Yikes," he said. "What about this one? The

Bloody Monster—is this a fake?"

"I wish it was but it's not," Gloria said.

"And the Bog Creek Vampire?"

"That's a weird one." Gloria wrinkled her forehead. "Prodigi—prodigi-umm-ologists are unsure of its origins."

"It looks like a bunch of monsters smashed together," Casey said.

"That's what I thought!" Gloria said. "I call it the Smash Monster for short."

Casey always enjoyed his talks with Gloria, and this time was no exception, even though their conversation was terrifying.

"So I guess you're feeling better," he said after they'd flipped through most of the deck.

"I'm still mad," Gloria admitted. "But we're going to Luci's house so I'm sort of better."

"We are?"

She pointed to a folded black parchment. Casey grabbed it. Most Sylvan homes had a computer or tablet, but Luci said they were only used in emergencies. "Everyone knows screens dull the senses," she'd said. "They weaken your connection to the perilous real world." The dinner invitation was written gracefully in silver ink.

"Did Mrs. West drop this off herself?" Casey said.

"Don't know," Gloria said. "Maybe she used the Sylvan Post."

"I wonder how that works."

"Maybe smart birds?" Gloria shrugged. "Like Lesser Bitterbirds?"

"Ha!" Casey said. "But for local messages, foxes would work just as well."

"Or maybe baby Shin-Snips," Gloria said.

Casey laughed.

He spent the rest of the afternoon reading his textbooks, playing Uno! and Clue with Gloria, and trying not to think about Trickery School. It wasn't easy, though. He kept on picturing the Back to School banner, the flyers blowing across campus, and Fiera's front page article. Then there was Drooce.

After dinner, he sat in an armchair with his OPOW textbook and pictured the bully's sneering face: "I'll give you orders from here on in. I'll call the shots. *I'll rule you.*" Casey didn't know what to do about that. So far, his only idea was telling Robert.

And where the heck *was* Robert anyway?

What was Pierce's deal?

Trickery School is off to a terrible start, Casey thought—and all his bad feelings came rushing back. So where's my friend, the most dangerous kid in Trickery? Nowhere to be found, except for five seconds at lunch. Casey felt annoyed. Then irritated. Then offended. *What's your problem, Robert? Too cool to be seen with me now?*

He said goodnight to his parents in the kitchen, patted Gloria where she snored on the couch, and went to bed feeling low. When he woke up Friday morning, bright sunlight pooled on his floor. His favorite backyard oak brushed his window, pale sky showing through its leaves. A perfect almost-weekend day. But he still felt grumpy.

He and Gloria had plans to eat at the cafeteria since Friday breakfasts were always kind of special. During mace exercises on the deck, Casey practiced his tactics for Tiger Rats in Land Creature Defense. He varied the timing on his swings. *Stomp-fwoosh-stomp. Stomp-fwoosh-fwoosh.* You had to keep the rodents guessing.

Gloria came out and practiced with her pink-handled sword for a while. She seemed focused, but her moves would've made more sense if she'd been wearing ballet shoes. A little later, Casey wiped his face with a towel, said bye to Dad and Mom, and headed down the trail with Gloria. If he'd known what the day held in store, he definitely would've stayed home.

CHAPTER 33
SUBSTITUTE SPEAKER

THE EARLIEST AND HUNGRIEST students had just started their rush to the buffet line when Casey and Gloria came in. He grabbed their favorite corner table by the window while she scurried off to load up on breakfast pizza. By the time he'd gone through line, choosing waffles, fried chicken, and a cheese and skrabbit omelet, Luci was there too.

They all smiled at each other.

Luci raised her glass of purple-brown juice.

"A toast," she said.

Here's to beets, Casey thought. Mixed with rich, nourishing dirt.

He and Gloria raised their glasses of hot chocolate and orange juice.

"To surviving your first week at Trickery."

They clinked glasses.

"None of us wanted school to start like this." Luci forked her spinach and mushroom scramble. "But at least the two of you are here, right? A couple months ago, I remember how bad I felt, sneaking out of Casey's hospital room..." She trailed off, and her face did something funny. "Oh, and another thing!" She smoothed her dark hair. "Have you thought about how lucky it was your house was treated with invisa-fade?"

Casey was about to say it was nice of her to look on the bright side. Instead, he paused with his fork halfway to his mouth. Maple syrup dripped onto his wrist. "What do you mean?"

Her eyebrows arched. "You *really* haven't thought about this? Wow."

Casey *had* thought about it. A lot. He still had dreams where he was invisible, and people looked through him, no matter what he did. He'd had these nightmares ever since Vintage Woods. But now the dreams included monsters. The shrieks and creeps were the only ones who could see him. Their toothy grins and gleaming eyes said *Why hello*. The nightmares weren't as common now, but Casey sounded snappish when he said:

"I've thought about it more than I want to."

"Being invidsible wasn't fun," Gloria said.

"I know, but that's not what I mean." Now Luci looked annoyed. "It must have been horrible, but without the invisa-fade, you wouldn't be here, would you?"

Casey looked at her blankly. Gloria took another bite of pizza.

"Ooo." Luci rolled her eyes as the speakers came to life. "Just think about it. You can thank me later."

Casey glared at her and took a bite of fried chicken.

"Uh, hey everyone, I mean, good morning, Trickery," said a dry voice. Fiera Laurent was never enthusiastic, but this morning she sounded like she'd been flattened by a rotten log. "You're probably wondering why I'm talking to you."

Always a fair question, Casey thought.

"Well, Jake's not here. Actually, he is here. I mean, he was...but he can't broadcast, because he's in so much pain."

They started paying attention.

"Well, probably not a *lot* of pain, since he's had injections, but it sure looked bad..." Her voice faded to a whisper. "They vandalized Trickery News and I don't want both my wrists broken. What if they come for me next? I want to live, I don't want to—" The transmission ended with a buzz.

"Trickery Programming will resume later," a cheerful adult voice said. "Have a great day of Adventure, Courage, and...well, have a great day!"

They stared at each other over the table.

"Oh no," Gloria said.

"She didn't sound like she was making that up." Casey pushed his plate away.

"If we leave right now, we can run by the infirmary." Luci was already scooting back her chair. Casey had two thoughts as they rushed through the carved yellow doors.

Please let Jake be ok.

Where in bloody creeps is Robert?

CHAPTER 34
THE MISCALCULATIONS OF FIERA LAURENT

IT WAS THE LAST THING CASEY wanted to do. But he had to admit, Fiera was right.

Jake McGusty did not look good.

Jake had fought off ravenous Butcher Beasts, founded the Skewers club, and escaped without a scratch. But someone or something had caught up with him this time. His face was badly bruised. Leaves and dirt stuck in his hair. Worst of all, his arms were encased in casts from his elbows down. Casey felt very weird, seeing his friend unconscious on an infirmary bed.

All Nurse Diaz could tell them was he'd been found in the woods near the Green Field.

Probably coming out of his favorite shortcut tunnel, Casey thought.

"Those don't look like claw marks." Luci pointed to the bruises on Jake's face. "Blunt trauma, I think someone attacked him. This was deliberate."

Gloria looked tearful.

"But who would do this?" Even as he asked the question, Casey had a sinking feeling.

Luci's mouth tightened as their eyes met.

Was she thinking what he was thinking?

"Time to go, kids. Please visit again later." Nurse Diaz was a formidable woman, even dressed completely in non-Sylvan white. Apart from her pouf of curly hair, her sharp black eyes were all you could see above her face mask. She was not someone you argued with.

"Thank you, Nurse Diaz," Luci said.

They left the infirmary.

"He'll be ok after a while." Casey squeezed Gloria's shoulder, even though he was talking to himself.

"I hope so," Gloria said. "He's the very best at news-ing."

"I'll see you next hour," Luci said. *We can talk then*, her eyes added. "Gloria, want me to walk you to your class?"

Gloria gratefully took her hand.

Casey watched them go, then hurried off to Optimal Pathways of Weapons.

This can't be a coincidence, he thought. Jake got attacked because of me. Everyone knew he was working on my story.

Fiera had sounded like she was falling apart on the broadcast, but he'd seen her put on an act before. She'd proved she couldn't be trusted. *Let's see how she acts in the arena. Someone didn't want my story printed. And who would benefit more than Fiera?*

His fingers tightened into fists as he moved down Artemis Way. He took the stairs to OPOW two at a time, grabbed a cable and swung across. *Bullseye.* Inside the brass and glass dome, everyone else had already arrived.

Ms. Steele stopped threatening the class to glare at him. "Nice of you to join us, Mr. Grimes. If you dare to show your face, be on time." Instantly, every eye in the arena was pinned on him. But no one whispered or shoved. Not with Ms. Steele watching.

He shrugged and joined the uneasy group.

"As...I...was...saying..." Ms. Steele looked disappointed when no one interrupted. "Preliminary results are in. Rarely have I seen a less promising class. Based on your assessments, it's obvious you grew up playing with magic wands."

Horrified gasps. Mouths dropped open.

Casey ignored the put-down.

"Let's not even talk about our first day," Ms. Steele said with obvious relish. "Students hitting the glass like baby birds."

Casey smiled grimly.

"We have our work cut out for us and it's not going to be pleasant." Steele rubbed her bony hands together. "And yet, amid all this failure, a few students have risen above the mediocrity. Of course, their success will not last. But at the moment..." She glanced down at her notes. "Well done, Matt Rhiannon. And..." She coughed as something caught in her throat. "Casey—*hack*—Grimes." Her sharky face sagged before she could tighten it back up.

Casey couldn't believe his ears.

"Now for some hands-on scenarios." Ms. Steele snapped her notebook shut. "Pair off and step forward to collect your gobsmackers."

Instantly, the group rearranged itself as kids grabbed partners they thought they had a chance of defeating. A slim, reddish-haired kid who looked familiar stepped toward Casey, but he was intercepted. Everyone else kept their distance. Casey found himself standing on the platform alone. Well, not exactly alone.

"Hi Fiera," Casey said.

"Oh, hi, didn't see you there." She twitched back a step.

Casey smiled. "Looks like it's us."

"Er, yes it does..."

"I'll get our gobsmackers," Casey said.

Ms. Steele led the class to the furnished middle floor of the arena and directed them to the outside edges. She paced an oriental carpet in the middle, weaving around chairs and ottomans.

"You are enjoying a quiet evening at home," she said, "When the front door crashes open. Instantly you recognize the fierce, malevolent face. It's your worst enemy, hunting you from your dark and tragic past." She smiled. "Finally, he's found you. And he's come for vengeance."

A few of the kids shuddered. The air of the arena felt cold on Casey's skin.

"Luckily," Steele intoned, "you are not without a weapon of your own. You have mere seconds to act. Without moving, you must dispatch your deadly foe—or be dispatched. At my signal..."

Casey clutched his gobsmacker tighter in spite of himself. The sleek, blob-headed weapon was squishy and scary at the same time. Stay calm, he thought. You've got this.

The students stood on the edges of the platform, facing each other over carpets dotted with armchairs and low tables. Add some newspapers and pipe tobacco and it could've been a scene from Sherlock Holmes. Except this is dark—so dark, Casey thought. Holy creeps, he told himself. Shake it off. Remember who you're facing.

He gauged the distance between him and Fiera. She glared back at him.

"I'm not afraid of you," she whispered. "And I'm *not* sorry."

"Good," Casey snapped. "I'm not sorry either."

"On your marks, get set, throw!" Ms. Steele screeched from overhead.

Casey caught a glimpse of Fiera's wide, chilly eyes as he bent his arm back, squinted, and whipped the gobsmacker forward. The sinister weapon sailed between two wingbacks and *splooshed* into Fiera's face with a sound like an exploding watermelon. Arms flailing, nose in the air, she dropped her weapon and spun off the platform with a thin wail.

Casey walked over to her empty spot. The bouncy, grapefruit-sized top of his gobsmacker had already regained its shape. The self-inflating slime gleamed darkly in the shadows. Casey was careful not to touch it.

"Man, that felt good," he said.

And he hadn't performed a single mental calculation.

"Nice shot, Grimes." The reddish-haired kid was standing next to Casey, holding out his hand. "I'm Matt Rhiannon."

They shook.

"Oh, hey," Casey said. "Trickery Spirit...Adventure, that was you."

"Thrilled to be here." Matt smiled. "I thought we could maybe team up, give ourselves a real challenge, but I was too slow and someone grabbed me. You know how it goes." He shrugged. "Hey, at least we both get winning marks this way, right?"

"Right." Casey wondered who Matt thought would win.

They both stared over the edge.

"Ha, look at them floundering like spider-squids," Matt said. "Who's the kid you gobsmacked?"

"Fiera Laurent, the one with her nose in the air."

She struggled toward a ladder through a sea of foam.

"The swim of shame," Matt said. "Hey, isn't she the reporter?"

"That's her."

"Serves the witch-snitch right," Matt said. "Hey, there's my partner, coming back for more. See you around, Grimes."

"See you."

The rest of OPOW went the same way. Casey gobsmacked Fiera three more times. She stopped screaming and disappeared silently, eyes blazing, arms flapping. Her hair got messier and messier—an improvement, Casey thought. Fiera finally managed to graze him with her gobsmacker. He didn't flinch as the dark blob wobbled past his ear. Another of her throws bounced off a coffee table and landed at his feet.

That was the closest she got.

He gave her a cold nod on the way out.

As he shouldered his pack, Casey knew one thing. Fiera's lack of coordination wasn't an act. She'd been gritting her teeth and squaring her thin shoulders, trying not to topple over backwards, but it hadn't done any good.

There was no way she could have hospitalized Jake.

So who had?

CHAPTER 35
MONSTER MEMORY

CASEY DIDN'T WASTE ANY TIME getting to Nonviolent Magic. This time he arrived with a clump of students—or about ten feet behind them, since they kept giving him suspicious glances. Mr. Peterson waited in their clearing, sitting on an upturned wheelbarrow, brushing dirt off his expensive-looking shoes.

He straightened a ridiculous khaki bow tie. "Shovels have arrived," he said happily. "Grab a partner and head to Obsidian Central."

Here we go again. Casey glanced around, just in case Luci was already there. The class did a shuffling dance as kids sorted themselves into pairs, careful to give Casey plenty of room.

"Hey Grimes. How 'bout a walk in the BeastWoods?"

Casey blinked. Where had Matt Rhiannon come from?

"I decided to give magic a try," the boy said as if reading Casey's mind. "Headmaster keeps mentioning it, so I dropped Enhanced Blacksmithery and picked this up. But I've gotta say, this class looks like..."

"Manual labor?" Casey lowered his voice. "Yeah, I know. Between you and me—"

"Into the woods you go," Mr. Peterson called, sipping from a thermos.

"Allow me to guide you, sir." Matt gestured to the path like he was the host at a fancy restaurant.

"Ha." Casey smiled and started for the trailhead.

"Casey, wait!" Luci rounded the tree line, hair flying, out of breath. It was weird to see her arrive late, let alone looking rumpled.

"Ha, look at her crazy hair," Matt said. "What a shriek. You know her?"

Casey licked his lips. For a second, he wished Luci had showed up a minute later. Or that she'd skipped class, just this once. "Yeah," he said. "I know her."

She jogged over. "Hey. Whew." She put her hands on her knees, drawing ragged breaths. "Sorry I'm late."

Matt raised his eyebrows as if to say, *You two, really?*

Casey shrugged. Matt was so cool that he couldn't help feeling disappointed.

"Well, catch you later," Matt said. *Good luck*, he mouthed at Casey as he strolled away.

Luci straightened up, pushing back her hair. "It was terrible," she said. "The kids from Magic Club kept popping up, like I'm their new best friend. Two of them trapped me in Fireside Cookery and started telling me their ideas for magical projects. I barely escaped."

"Oh wow." Casey watched Matt disappear into the trees.

"Heyy..." Luci said. "Were you and that kid paired up? No big deal, I could–"

"No," Casey lied. "I was waiting for you."

"Ah, good." She looked relieved.

He dragged a wheelbarrow upright and Luci grabbed two shovels.

"Wait a minute," he said. "Did you say Fireside Cookery?"

Luci looked slightly guilty. "There's nothing wrong with eating well. Besides, you know I like a good sleepover."

"True," Casey said. He'd never forget their sleepover in the Old

Oak. Or in the Big Beech or the Pavilion. Food was always involved, along with someone getting ambushed.

"Hopefully Crake will schedule a sleepover soon," Luci said. "After everything calms down." She slid the shovels into the barrow and Casey frowned. Now he was transporting *all* their equipment.

"Hope so," he said. "Who teaches Cookery? It can't really be The Crow."

"Oh, it's him all right." Luci smiled. "He's very accomplished in the culinary arts. Kids say he cut off his own hand and replaced it with steel to become more lethal, but let me tell you, it comes in handy at a campfire. You should see him stirring multiple sauces over a nice blaze."

"Wow," Casey said. Sometimes he felt like he had no idea at all what was going on. He shoved the wheelbarrow over a root and dropped the handles. They'd reached Obsidian Central. The pile of gravel towered above them like a black hole in the murky forest.

Luci sighed. Other kids were already shoveling obsidian, looking unhappy. She and Casey grabbed their spades and dug in. Grumbling and the clinking of gravel filled the clearing. Between the greenish shade, the musky smell of the forest and the midnight-colored stones, it was hard not to feel jumpy.

Casey thought about the deep, dark clearing in the heart of the BeastWoods where the final Sentry towered into the sky. He could almost imagine the Butcher Queen still waiting there, her horrible mandibles grating out almost-human speech.

So he was glad when Luci spoke.

"This is more like an easy detention than a class," she said.

"How do you know?" Casey asked.

"Um, I've talked to kids who had detentions."

"Uh huh," Casey said. "I just hope it works, that it really repels monsters."

"Well..." Luci stopped shoveling and half-closed her eyes. "I am feeling a little repressed, down in my bones or genes or something. And definitely irritated."

"Me too." Casey said. "What's your point?"

"Oh, no real point I guess." Luci dug back in with her shovel. The wheelbarrow was now quite full. "Should we try to move this down the trail?"

"Guess we have to, don't we?" Casey grabbed the handles. "Oh man," he said. "Too heavy."

"Let me try." Luci elbowed him aside. "Errrgh. Yeah, we over-filled it."

Casey rolled his eyes. "How much of a weakling do you think I am?"

"How about we each take a handle?"

Across the clearing Casey caught a glimpse of Matt Rhiannon, one foot on his shovel, grinning at him. *Creeps.*

The overloaded wheelbarrow wobbled dangerously as they rolled it into the leafy gloom. Each time they hit a rut or a root, they staggered, bumping into each other.

"Ouch, walk on your own feet," Casey said.

"Watch out for that groundwater," Luci said.

"What water?" But it was too late. Casey's feet slipped out from under him.

"Look out!"

"Let go, or it will smash us!"

The wheelbarrow hurtled away and crashed into a rotting tree, wheel spinning. Obsidian spilled everywhere. Casey stood up slowly, rubbing his damp behind. The puddle on the ground was dark and oily. No wonder he hadn't seen it. You never saw anything coming in the BeastWoods.

"Can you believe this class?" Luci said. "At least most of the obsidian is on the trail. And now we're finally alone."

He felt an odd twinge, like someone had strummed an off-key chord in his gut. It was a feeling he'd felt before. One he'd thought he was done with.

Luci tucked in a wavy strand of hair. "I thought we'd never get out of earshot. Seems like someone's always nearby."

"Do you think we should head back?" Now that they'd stopped moving, the beastly weight of the forest pressed in, reaching for him —and not in a friendly way.

"Of course not, dummy." She gave him an odd look. "Now we can finally talk about what's going on." She touched a knuckle to her bottom lip. "Jake wanted to print your story in a special edition of the *Times* today. Now, with him unconscious and the office smashed, that's not gonna happen. Add that to the other stuff..." She frowned. "This is serious. I mean, even *more* serious than people telling lies so your social life is ruined."

Casey pulled himself together. It's just a different kind of woods, he told himself. More fierce and wild than you're used to.

"Of course it's serious," he said. "Especially for Jake."

"Agreed, but no one is after him. He just got in the way."

Casey shifted uncomfortably. "He got hurt because of me."

"No," Luci said firmly. "He got hurt because someone is ruthless."

That didn't make Casey feel any better. "Listen," he said. "Are you sure you want to keep hanging out with me?"

"How dare you even ask that?" Her eyes flashed. "What kind of a person do you—waaiit..." She took a step back. "Maybe you'd *like* it if I left you alone."

"That's not what I meant," Casey said.

But hadn't he just been wishing that very thing?

"It's ok, be honest," Luci said. "I'm sure it's a real drag, seeing me so often."

"No," Casey said. "That's ridiculous."

He yanked the wheelbarrow out of a maze of vines and collected the shovels. They headed back up the trail in silence.

"I just don't want anyone else to get hurt," he said.

Luci bit her lip. "I guess I knew that."

A wheelbarrow rumbled toward them, pushed by a couple giggling kids. Casey and Luci stepped aside and watched it wobble around a bend. He wondered how the kids could be so light-hearted in this twisty, shadowed place.

"Um, I've been meaning to ask you something," Luci said.

Casey forced himself to stand still.

"Remember when you were in the hospital after surgery?"

He nodded.

"You were pretty druggy, weren't you?"

"Uh, yeah," Casey said. "The room didn't want to hold still."

"Yeah." She gave a laugh. "You seemed *very* out of it. So, I was just wondering...out of curiosity...if you remembered, um, what we talked about?"

"What we talked about..." Casey said. "Let's see..." He saw Luci leaping through the darkness toward the butcher queen—eyes flaming, hair writhing. Saw it instantly. Of course he did. He'd thought about it often, especially after yesterday.

The Secret.

In the Civilian hospital, under the bright lights of the operating room, Luci had told him she was part monster. "It kind of hangs around in your DNA," she'd said.

Man, had it ever.

And Casey had a crazy thought. Here was his chance to pretend he didn't know. If he acted like it'd never happened, they'd never have to talk about it again. Then he could be friends with Luci, close or *less* close, and she wouldn't have to wonder if it was all because of her monster blood. "Just a little," she'd told him. But he knew what happened when she let the monster out.

Flaming green eyes and snaky hair.

No, not snaky. Snakes. A headful of vipers.

Luci was staring at him.

There was only one thing to do.

"Well, I *was* pretty drugged up," he said. "The whole thing is blurry...but I'm pretty sure you brought me flowers."

Something flashed across her face and was gone. "Cool," she

said. "No worries. That's kind of what I thought. Creeps, you had a tough recovery ahead of you."

They started moving again, clinking and rumbling down the trail.

The woods were full of shadows. Huge spiderwebs hung overhead. Brambles twisted along the trail with thorns as big as fingers. Casey wondered if any of the Butchers had survived, if they were out there somewhere, a thought he'd never had before. Ridiculous, because the magic of the Sentries had killed them all. That gorgeous, wild, blazing magic.

"Hey...Luci."

She looked up with a sickly expression. "Nasty place, isn't it."

"Sure, but–"

He wanted to say something else, but they'd reached Obsidian Central. Barrows trundled back and forth. Most of the class was working right there, carting gravel just a few steps from the huge black pile before dumping it. The top of the trail would have a very strong protective aura.

Matt Rhiannon gave Casey a nod. Kind of like Robert, he had a knack for appearing out of nowhere.

"I was starting to think I'd have to go in after you," he said. "It *is* the BeastWoods, you know."

"Ha," Casey said. "Nope, everything's good."

He immediately felt bad for telling such a big lie.

CHAPTER 36
SHADOWS IN THE BEASTWOODS

HEY DUDE, I'M OUTTA HERE." Luci wiped sweat off her forehead.

"Dude?" Casey leaned on his shovel. "Since when do you speak Civilian?"

"Oh you know," she said. "It's fun to talk street once in a while. Plus I bet it's nice for you to remember your roots, the way you used to live before you got here. But seriously." She put a hand to her stomach. "I'm feeling a little weird. Maybe I'll see you later. Bye!" She handed him her shovel and fast-walked up the trail. Just before she was out of sight, she broke into a run.

Matt walked over. "She bailed on you?"

"No," Casey said. "Just not feeling well."

"This class is the worst," Matt said. "Where does the magic come in?"

It seemed like a fair question.

"After dark, I guess." Casey dropped Luci's shovel in their barrow. "The obsidian doesn't have much effect during the day."

"If it works at all." Matt leaned on his spade. "Tell you what, after carting rock all morning, I might go back to Enhanced Black-smithery. Ready to leave? The bugles are gonna blow any minute."

"Why not?" Casey said. "Let's get out of here."

He parked the wheelbarrow, rolled it on its side and put the shovels underneath in case it rained. It helped him feel better about sneaking out of a Sylvan class...something he'd never thought he'd do in a hundred years. But it was almost over, anyway. And Luci was gone.

"We'd better sneak through the woods and flank Peterson," Matt said. "Shouldn't be hard, since all he does is drink coffee."

"Makes sense," Casey said. "Think he'll notice we left?"

"Doubt it." Matt shrugged. "Half the class snuck off already."

They slipped into the dense thicket, circling the boles of mossy trees. The smells of leaf decay and monster musk swept over them as their feet sunk in the pathless soil.

"Have you been back here since it happened?" Matt asked.

"Since what happened?" Casey swiped at a spiderweb, trying to act calm. "Oh, you mean the Butcher Beasts." He glanced at Matt. "You don't think it was all fake?"

"Give me a break. I'm not that easily taken in."

"I haven't been back," Casey said. "Not into the deep woods. No hurry, although it would probably feel different with the Sentry back on its roots."

"Absolutely," Matt said. "Those Sentries changed everything. Wiped out the butchers, made magic a thing again. Who knows how far–"

"Hey." Casey held up a hand. "Did you hear that?"

Matt listened. A dagger filled his hand.

"Sorry, nothing," he said. "Unless you count giant mosquitoes."

"Let's get out of here," Casey said.

By now, the edge of the woods was in sight, streamers of sunlight burning through the crooked trees. They picked up their pace, weaving through vines and dodging marshy patches. By the time they burst into the sun, they were running.

Matt laughed. "Even in the day, it's a creepy place."

"Got that right," Casey said.

But he'd heard the careful footsteps, muffled in the leaves. Nearby but out of sight. Prowling alongside, keeping pace. It was too early in the day for monsters. Someone had tracked them through the Beast Woods.

CHAPTER 31
SHADOWS OF CROWS

CASEY WAS TEMPTED TO TELL MATT about his Shortest Sylvan Distance Theory. Rhiannon seemed like the kind of kid who'd appreciate it. But they'd only just met, and Casey didn't want to be labeled as a tree geek, so he held off. Being called Mister Magic was bad enough. They parted on the far side of the Green Field.

"See ya, Grimes. I've gotta make a stop before lunch."

"Later." Casey gave the woods a searching look as Matt struck off down a side trail. He hadn't seen or heard anything since the Beast-Woods, which made sense because they'd been out in the open. Looking for a stair or ladder, he wandered over the open slopes of Lesser Trick 'n' Trap east of the bath caves.

Finally he found a camouflaged climbing net and hauled himself to a lookout spot at owl height. Nothing crazy, but a nice vantage point on the thin trails twisting down into Trickery. A ropewalk stretched away, and Casey was thinking this could be a destination on his treetop tour, Best Bath Access or something, when his eyes caught movement below.

There then gone. He blinked.

The shadow hadn't been quite right. It hadn't fluttered or swayed. It had darted. And its size...way too big for a rabbit or squirrel. Casey stopped leaning against the tree trunk. He shaded his eyes and scanned the woods, but everything was still.

Despite the bright sunlight, he felt chilly. He stepped onto the ropewalk, moving through the air toward Trickery as fast as he could. Once or twice he looked back, but of course you'd have to be an idiot to try and shadow someone over a treeway. Unless. Unless the treeway was a mile long, stretching over the Roaring River—and covered in mist. How long had this thing been following him?

A blast of trumpets rang through the woods, and Casey welcomed the shouts of students leaving their classes. He floundered off the ropewalk near Mythic History, breathing hard. You're overreacting, he told himself. It's a little spooky, but that's it.

He had another fifteen minutes before lunch, but he didn't feel like spending it alone. Well, there was someone else who might appreciate company too.

He took a stairway down to Artemis Way and dodged toward the infirmary before anyone recognized him. Smells of flowers and antiseptic drifted out when he opened the door and stepped onto the polished flagstones. The triage area was empty, so Casey turned the corner and walked down the long, bright hall. He let himself into Jake's room as quietly as he could, but the door still creaked.

"Oh, hey Bootman." Propped up on pillows, Jake looked groggy but awake.

Casey dropped into the visitor's chair. "How you feeling?"

"Pretty good, man, pretty good. The bones're set cleanly and Diaz says I'll be able to go home for the weekend. Good thing, would've hated to miss Mom's pancakes."

McGusty was the only kid Casey knew who could break both wrists and say things were going well. "That's great to hear," he said. "We were worried about you."

"No big deal." Jake closed his eyes. "Just another day on the job."

Someone hummed outside the door as a broom whisk-whisked along the hall.

Jake blinked. "Really sorry about the story, man. Couldn't wait to print it, and now... I let you down."

"No you didn't," Casey said. "You didn't let anyone down." He wondered if he'd been this woozy in the Civilian hospital. Probably so, or worse. No wonder Luci wasn't sure if he remembered. But more important...

"Hey, Jake." Casey leaned in. "Did you see the person who did this?"

"Naw man." Jake was fading fast. "No one, then, *whack*. But..." He blinked. "After the hit, leaning over me...big guy." The light in his eyes faded.

"What big guy?"

"Forest..." Jake muttered. "Crow..." His chest rose and fell in a rhythm of deep breathing. Casey stared, frozen in his armchair. He reached out to squeeze Jake's arm but stopped himself. McGusty shouldn't be disturbed, but what he'd said made no sense.

It couldn't possibly be true.

If Casey could've chosen one person in Sylvan Woods to be on his side instead of out to get him, he would've chosen the person Jake had described.

Of all the warriors at Trickery, the one Casey never wanted to face.

Mr. K. The mountainous, silver-handed warrior with impeccable taste.

Kawkazi.

The Crow.

CHAPTER 38
WEIRD LUNCH

A FEW KIDS WHISPERED AND POINTED when Casey walked into the cafeteria, but most ignored him and kept their distance. The backlash was dying down to bored distrust. Maybe after a while they'd forget he was even there. He knew what that felt like.

Lunch was just him and Gloria. Not even she was having a good day—but luckily no one had connected her to the sandpit incident. At least not yet.

"Little...Miss...Magic." She crunched an apple slice with peanut butter. "Can you believe they're calling me *Little Miss Magic*—but they're doing it to be mean?"

"Sorry, Gloria." Casey stared into his bowl of tomato soup. He'd hoped it would soothe his stomach, but it looked a lot like blood. And blood made him think about...

Broken bones. Jake. The Crow. The soup was making his head swim. Then there was Fiera's article, Drooce's threats, the lies about him. All of it bloody-minded. Swirling around in his head like–

"I like the name," Gloria said. "But I don't like those kids."

"Huh?" Casey tore his eyes away from the soup and focused on Gloria. "Right, those kids. Little Miss Magic. You know they're calling me Mister Magic, right?"

"That's pretty good, but not as nice as Little *Miss* Magic."

"True," Casey said. "Your name is better. I think we should get t-shirts made and wear them around Trickery. That will show them."

Gloria smiled.

"What's up, mis amigos?" Luci slid in next to Gloria. Her plate had three celery stalks lined up neatly and one cherry tomato. She didn't look great. "Ready for a chill weekend?"

If "chill" meant resting quietly in bed, that's what Luci looked ready for.

"Why are you talking like that?" Gloria said.

"Yo, Glo," Luci said. "Sometimes I get on a Civilian riff. I thought Casey might enjoy some dialect from his past."

Casey spooned up soup. It was more orange than red, he decided.

"I like being Sylvan." Gloria tried a tiny bite of tapioca pudding. "But you know, I feel the same as I did when I was a Civilian."

"That's because you're the real deal, Glo-baby. What we see is what we get—unlike some."

Casey wondered why he felt so uncomfortable. It wasn't the soup, expertly seasoned with cheese and basil.

"Hi kids, hi Glo." Robert dropped into the seat by Casey like a sack of maces.

"Man, where you been?" Casey was ready to forgive Robert for barely being around, just so he had someone to talk to. But the dangerous boy looked even worse than he had that morning. Hair flopped onto his forehead as he took a sip of coffee, rubbing his eyes. He grabbed his knife and fork and attacked his steak.

"Can't wait for this to be over," he said as he chewed.

"What to be over?" Casey said. "This week? This semester? This lunch?"

They all seemed like good answers.

Robert groaned and ran a hand through his collapsing hair. "My assignments are kicking my tail. What are you doing tomorrow, Casey? Let's hang out and throw weapons around."

"Oh, hey! Great."

"It's been too long."

"That's for sure."

"Cool, gotta run." Robert's steak was gone. He'd wolfed it down in the time it would take a normal kid to eat a slice of watermelon. "Stay away from the sandpit for a while," he told Gloria. "Those first-graders aren't gonna snitch, but some of them want vengeance."

She sniffed as Robert walked away. "Maybe I'll go back to liking him."

And just like that, lunch was weird again.

No. Casey corrected himself.

It had been weird from start to finish. Like this day. Like this week.

Like his whole career at Trickery.

"Hey Luci," he said on their way out. "I hope you feel better."

"Oh, ok. Thanks, hombre. Hope ya get your flow back too."

For some reason, he found her really hard to deal with when she talked Civilian.

As he left, he made a mental note to watch out for The Crow.

CHAPTER 39
HEY BATTER BATTER

AS LUCK WOULD HAVE IT, THE FIRST class of the day without partners was also the first class where a partner could've saved your life. In Land Creature Defense, Casey chanted along with the rest of the students:

> *"We'll never stray from trees and sky.*
> *An urban life? We'd rather die.*
> *Our friendships happen face to face*
> *With feasts thrown in on special days.*
> *We fight the monsters in the woods*
> *To keep them from Civilian 'hoods.*
> *We'll guard the magic of the border*
> *To keep our bloodlines in good order.*
> *Fields and rivers we will tend,*
> *Forgotten trades and arts we'll mend.*
> *We build, we brew, we craft, we defend!"*

Reciting the Sylvan Pledge gave him a good feeling. It reminded him of what he'd loved about Sylvan Woods in the first place. Unfortunately, the feeling didn't last.

"Look out Casey!" Jenni Tompkins screamed a few minutes later. "Its beady eyes are staring at your neck!" Technically, he wasn't supposed to get help from anyone outside the protective glass barrier, but Jen was thoughtful like that. With shouts and screams echoing through LCD, there wasn't much Mr. Chandler could do.

And Jen was right.

The Tiger Rat *was* eyeing his neck. It scampered back and forth, an orange and black blur the size of a small house cat. Then it crouched on the slate floor, twisting its naked tail menacingly. According to the textbook, this meant the rat's voracious appetite had overcome its fear.

It was about to attack.

Casey spun the handle of his mace between his palms, wishing they were drier.

He hefted the spiky bat over his shoulder. *Balls of your feet, wrists loose.* There was no home plate, but timing was everything. He wouldn't get three strikes.

The rat was taking its time. Maybe it had played this game before...and won. *Uh oh, bad thought, don't go there.* The rat faked a lunge. Casey almost brought the mace around but checked his swing in time. *Oh no you don't, you vermin.*

Tired of the stalemate, the Tiger Rat launched itself with a shriek.

"NOO!" Casey swung the 127-Spiker in a desperate arc.

Whack. The striped rat hit the barrier with a wet smack. It slid to the floor.

"Yay, Case!" Jen yelled.

A few other kids joined her but most of the class had been rooting for the Tiger Rat. Grumbling and boos filled the vaulted room.

"Great work, Grimes." Mr. Chandler pushed back his hood. "You could've expedited that encounter, but once the T-rat came at you, you were ready. Level swing, good contact. The little brute didn't stand a chance."

"Thank you sir." Casey stepped over the barrier as it retracted into the floor.

"Who's next?" Mr. Chandler said. "You there, grab some glass cleaner. And no more booing. This is a supportive environment."

"That was great, Case." Jen grabbed his arm. Using a trident, she'd made short work of her rat without even tangling her hair. "If it hadn't been for the barrier, that thing would've flown a mile. I mean, home run!"

"Maybe a double or triple," Casey said modestly. "Wait, how do you know about baseball?"

Jen widened her eyes. "Baseball, what's that?" She giggled. "Seriously, Casey, not everyone is totally clueless about the outside world."

"Really?"

She spread her hands as if to say, *Ta-daa, look at me, I'm the proof.*

"I guess you must be right," Casey said. "Wow. That's sure not the impression I got..."

"Some of us know Civilian culture has things to offer." Jen watched another nervous kid step over the barrier. "Wow, I'm not sure about that weapons choice."

"Yikes," Casey said. "No, a bow and arrow is not going to end well."

"Look at the grin on the rat's little face. How long do you think, before Mr. Chandler jumps in?"

"Oh, probably a minute."

"I'll bet you a chocolate milk that kid doesn't last thirty seconds. Not everyone is as skilled as us, Casey."

"Ok, you're on."

By the time class was over, he owed Jen Tompkins at least five chocolate milks. She really did have better judgment when it came to assessing a fight. He'd tried harder and harder to predict what would happen, but it hadn't made any difference. It was uncanny how she knew who would get chewed, who'd lose her grip, who'd be a stomp too slow...

"Just admit it, Case. I'm better at this than you."

"Fine, I admit it."

"I'm sure you're better at other things, though. So what do you have next? You ran off last time without even telling me."

"I did?" He found that hard to believe.

"Yep. Ditched me, just like that." She snapped her fingers.

Bugles blasted outside.

"We all learned something today," Mr. Chandler yelled. "Some learned harder than others, but that's ok. If you have bites or claw marks, head to the infirmary. Ms. Diaz is expecting you. No cuts no guts no glory. See you Monday."

Casey and Jen headed for the door.

"You were saying?" Jen pulled on her pack, black with pink accents. It made Casey feel good to see someone besides Gloria wearing a Civilian color. Like they weren't such weirdos after all.

"Um, let's see." He forced himself to focus. "I go to Extreme Climbing from here."

"Are...you...serious?" A smile bloomed across her face. "Me too! I didn't know we both had that."

"Wow, neither did I." Casey grinned back. "The day just got better."

Had he said that out loud? He felt his face get hot.

"The day just *totally* did." Jen didn't seem to notice his color change. "C'mon, let's go. You're good at heights, right? So you've *got* to show me your very best secret route."

CHAPTER 40
TROUBLE WITH COMPLIMENTS

CASEY WAS TWO SECONDS FROM telling Jenni about his Shortest Sylvan Distance Theory. He even knew what she would say. "Wow Case, that's total genius!"

But then he pictured the long, silent walk through the mist, a mile above jagged rocks. They'd barely be able to see each other. And that narrow, windy rope would make it hard to chat.

Not to mention, a single misstep would be fatal, with the Roaring River and Deep Down rumbling under them like a stony throat. And he didn't know if Jen was good at climbing. She seemed superb at everything, though, so he was about to blurt it out, when he thought of one last thing:

Someone or something was tracking him.

He'd had so much fun in LCD, he'd forgot.

Someone had been on his trail. And Jake's message, not to mention his tomato soup, left Casey with a queasy feeling. He couldn't drag Jen into that. Not on a lonely, dangerous treeway.

"Yeah, I have a pretty good route," Casey said.

"I knew it." She gave him a smile.

They clattered over the bridge. Up ahead, Casey saw a familiar, snobbish face. Struggling with her pack, nose tilted skyward, Fiera

Laurent looked personally insulted to see Casey with another kid. She kept glancing between him and Jen. He could imagine the wheels turning in her head.

What in bog creeps? He's not supposed to have any friends. Not after my article. Doesn't she know he's a total loser? I mean, everyone should know, because I told them.

"See you in OPOW," he said as they walked past.

"Who peed in her porridge?" Jen asked. "Oops, sorry, that just slipped out."

"It's ok," Casey said. "She's not a friend."

"Good," Jen said. "That's a relief."

He took them up the spiral staircase, all the way to the weathered platform in the maple with the gorgeous view. Shouts and footsteps died away.

"Ooo," Jen said. "I knew you'd have a line on some elite spot. This is amazing. Wow, you know what this looks like, right?"

"Um...a dance floor?" Casey said.

"Great minds." She tapped her forehead. "I know we have to keep moving, but what do you say, sometime..." She pivoted into a twirl.

Now his face was burning up. Did all girls like to dance? He doubted it. That meant Luciana and Jenni would probably get along great. Then again, no, for some reason, he didn't think they would.

"Guess we should stop lollygagging, huh. Lead on." Jen swept an arm around the platform to show him she had no idea which way they were going.

Casey struck out on a northeasterly treeway that would drop them at Air Creature Defense. He'd glanced back to see how Jen was getting on, when he heard it—*scuff scuff,* then nothing. Cautious footsteps on the dance floor, so faint he could almost believe he'd imagined them. But he knew better.

"What?" Jen smiled, a couple feet back.

"Nothing." Casey started off again.

He wondered if they were in danger. If so, he was putting Jen in harm's way for no good reason. Whenever he looked back to check for movement, she gave him a nod or smile, which only made him feel worse. Branches swept the treeway like thick green curtains. It was impossible to tell if they were alone. When they stepped onto the three-story Air Creature Defense platform, crowded with kids, he took a deep, relaxing breath. No one would attack them now. Even if he *was* the least popular student at Trickery.

Kids were looking at him differently though, now that Jen was with him. Less muttering, fewer scowls. The two of them took their place in line and waited to step onto the automated lift that stretched over Legbreak Slopes.

"You got quiet," Jen said.

"Sorry," Casey said. "Too many things on my mind."

He instantly realized how jerky it sounded, but Jen didn't seem to notice.

"I'll bet." She sounded sympathetic. "Can't be easy for you, coming over from Civilian life. Out of the normal world into all this magic."

"It's been a big adjustment." He wondered how much she knew. She must have read Fiera's article. Was she a supporter of magic? Hey, you should come to Magic Club, he was about to say, but stopped himself. Because...Luci. And all the nerds. Somehow he couldn't see Jen fitting in with that crowd.

"You've got a knack for understatement, Case. I don't think many kids could've accomplished what you did in such a short period of time."

The creaking of the lift faded as they moved up the slope. Casey was grateful he'd got on first so Jen couldn't glance back and see him struggling for words. I guess I just need more practice with compliments, he thought. Speaking of which...how could he say this in a clear, concise way?

"Hey Jen..."

"Yup?"

"Um, you're really good at everything—all this Sylvan stuff I mean—and you fit right in at Trickery, and as you may have noticed, I'm not very popular...at all...so thanks for not treating me like everyone else, but actually being, well, nice."

He didn't dare turn around. A crow squawked overhead. Wind gusted past. Maybe she hadn't heard him.

"You're...totally welcome," she said.

Was it his imagination, or did she sound different? The fizz gone from her voice, like all the open space under her feet had gotten to her for a second.

"And I'm not just being nice, Case. I think you're a cool guy."

Ahh, now she sounded like herself. He risked a look over his shoulder. The wind was whipping her straight brown hair like ribbons, but she gave him a thumbs-up. He smiled back.

This was going to be a good day after all.

CHAPTER 41
BURNING BRIDGES

EVERYONE GETS THREE SHOTS with a tree harpoon," Ms. Chantelle called. "Your rope bridge must be able to hold your weight. For those of you interested in Treeway Design or Trailblazing, these principles are essential."

Ms. Chantelle had split the class in half and sent them into towering redwoods on opposite sides of the clearing. When everyone was fifty feet off the ground at owl height, she handed out the air-powered tree harpoons. As things got started, there was a lot of cheering and shouting followed by hiding behind branches as razor-sharp barbs shot past.

When it was his turn, Casey took his time, leveled the launcher, and...*crack!* The gleaming bolt whirred across the clearing, line unlooping behind it. *Whack!* It hit the opposite redwood, just a couple feet lower than he'd planned. His treeway would be slightly uphill in one direction.

Crack! Jen fired on his right. *Whack!* Her anchor sank home, four feet above his.

"Nice shot," Casey said. "We're operational."

She blew imaginary smoke off her fingers.

Once harpoons stopped whizzing back and forth, Casey and Jen spent the rest of the period tying off their temporary treeway, crossing it cautiously, and stretching a heavier foot rope into place. By the time the horns sounded, a half-dozen usable treeways hung between the redwoods. Just as many dangled crazily below like huge, failed knitting projects. No one had been dumb enough to try and cross those.

Ms. Chantelle took notes as kids packed away their climbing gear.

She gave them one of her brilliant smiles. "Casey and Jenni, nice work you two!"

They gave each other a high five on their very first try.

Casey was still glowing as they hiked along the ridge with everyone else. His classmates had stopped glaring at him. A few even seemed impressed.

The perfect ending to Friday.

Until they got on the lift.

Thin black smoke rose over Trickery in wisps. As they stepped onto Air Creature Defense, the smoke billowed up in a thick, dark column and kids milled around, unsure where to go. Casey instantly thought of Gloria.

"Gotta go, bye!" His shoes rang on the metal steps. He ran to the Splash Park and Fountain but no one was there, just a collection of small wooden chairs lined up in rows. Of course, Gloria's class would've been released an hour ago. She was probably safe at home, but he had to be sure. Casey charged down an alley, back onto Artemis Way. As he passed Mythic History, the upper air got dense. Smoke swirled above the Great Hall and shrouded the Rondure Arena, hiding the sun.

Students pressed around the Amber Tower and Casey slowed. A siren wailed nearby, getting closer. Ash drifted over the muttering crowd as he pushed his way forward. It was obvious why everyone was upset.

The golden base of the Amber Tower was blackened, a hole melted in one wall, big enough to fly a gryphon through. A classroom stood exposed to the forest like some kind of open air museum. The edges of the gaping hole still glowed. Casey wondered if the tower would start to lean. Would it ever be the same?

Then he realized that wasn't the worst part.

Words were painted on the veranda wall, untouched by flames. Right where the Magic Club had held its meeting.

WHO NEEDS SCIENCE? WE'VE GOT MAGIC. GO CASEY GRIMES!

Oh no. Casey stole sideways looks at the kids around him. No one had noticed him yet, but the crowd was still growing. He dropped his head and wove toward the edges, wishing he was wearing a hood. If only he could reach the shadows and get into the trees...

"Hey everyone, check this out! Grimes snuck back to enjoy his work!"

The crowd parted around him. Students stumbled away from him, grabbing for weapons.

Dozens of hot eyes tore at him.

Alone, in the center of an angry circle.

But only for a second.

The crowd parted again and Sebastian Drooce swaggered forward, brushing his hair out of his face. "Don't be afraid." He raised a reassuring hand to the crowd. "I'll take care of this."

Metal rasped as he drew a wicked-looking scimitar.

"Nice of you to stick around, Grimes." He grinned.

CHAPTER 42
THE 127-SPIKER

CASEY COULDN'T BELIEVE IT. Didn't anyone know who Drooce was? Sebastien's green eyes lit up as the students formed a circle, stomping and yelling at Casey.

"Way too far, Grimes!"

"Down with magic!"

"You're an embarrassment!"

"On guard, magicker," Sebastian said like he was playing the good guy in a stupid school play. Which he was, Casey realized... except the play was real. Only Casey was close enough to appreciate Drooce's sneer. The wicked light in his eyes.

Casey threw his pack to the ground, scrabbling to free the 127-Spiker.

Drooce made wide, lazy slashes with his scimitar. "Arm yourself, anti-realist filth!"

Casey stood up, clutching the mace.

He adjusted his grip on the leather-wrapped, fiberglass handle.

Shiish, shiish. Casey barely had time to dodge as the scimitar flashed past. Now Drooce was really trying. *Clang!* Casey parried a low, gut-level blow. *Shang!* He deflected a slice aimed at his head.

"Yeah! Cut him down to size!" The crowd was going crazy.

Shiish-shiish-shwick. Sebastien's scimitar wove a menacing pattern and then—*crunch.* The curved blade and mace collided, right in front of Casey's face. He struggled to hold steady, arms shaking.

Drooce yanked on his weapon. He looked puzzled, then angry.

The 127-Spiker's technology had done its job. Wedged between dozens of jagged points, the scimitar was going nowhere. Without meaning to, Casey had immobilized Drooce's weapon. This was the moment when a real fighter would take advantage and–

Oof. The breath rushed out of him as Drooce kicked him in the stomach.

Casey fell to his knees. His vision danced and sparkled.

Drooce yanked both weapons away.

The crowd got quiet.

There was a rasping clank as the bully freed his scimitar from the mace's clutches.

Casey felt something prick his throat.

"What do you say?" Drooce called to the mob. "Thumbs-up...or thumbs-down?"

"Don't do it," someone whispered.

"He deserves it!" shouted someone else.

"Smash him!"

Drooce nodded gravely. "The people have spoken." He grinned down at Casey.

He raised his blade. Then he flew away.

On his back in the leaves and dirt, Casey sucked in a deep, shuddering breath. The stars in the corners of his vision faded.

The space where Drooce had stood was empty.

Casey pushed himself up painfully. He stared.

Drooce hadn't flown very far. He hovered five feet away, flapping like a fish on a hook. His scimitar slipped from his hand and clanged to the ground. Thick, brawny fingers clutched the collar of his shirt. The fingers opened like a wrecking claw. Sebastian dropped with a thunk and groveled in the dirt.

"GET OUT OF HERE, RUNTS!" Mr. Kawkazi roared. Kids were

already slipping away. "I HAVE AN EXCELLENT MEMORY," he shouted. "I SEE YOU ALL!" The stream became a flood as students sprinted for trails and treeways, covering their faces. An armored vehicle shot out of the woods and bulky first responders jumped off, carrying hoses.

The Crow stared down at Drooce. He prodded him with his boot. "I'm making you my special project," he rumbled. "GO SHOVEL MUCK!"

Drooce clawed backwards like a crab, struggled upright, and ran crazily off in the direction of Security. Casey didn't want to look up and meet The Crow's fearsome glare.

But he did.

"On your feet," Mr. K. snapped. "What in beast's bane am I supposed to do with you? Always giving me the slip." He crossed his log-like arms. "I have a few ideas...once we get you somewhere quiet."

Casey wished he could scuttle away like Drooce, but he was still trying to breath.

"Do I need to help you up?" Kawkazi asked.

"No sir, I'm good." Casey grabbed his things and clutched them to his chest.

"March." Kawkazi pointed.

Casey marched.

CHAPTER 43
THE CROW

CASEY KNEW THIS WAS THE END. Like a fool, he'd obeyed Drooce's orders. Stayed put, gone to his classes, stayed out in the open. And now it was over.

They were deep in the woods on a trail he'd never seen. Grabby branches snatched at him. Spiderwebs brushed his face. Mr. K's hand fell on his shoulder like a collapsing tower.

Jake McGusty warned you this would happen.

A dark figure with messed-up hair and circles under his eyes stepped onto the path.

"I'll take it from here," Robert said.

"Are you sure?" The Crow's fingers made grooves in Casey's shoulder blade.

"Yep." Robert stretched, rubbing the back of his neck and rattling his weapons rack. "You're dealing with Drooce?"

"Obviously." Kawkazi looked offended.

"Fantastic," Robert said. "Tell you what, take the rest of the night off, huh? Ask Ms. Diaz out on that date."

The air felt thick and heavy. Or maybe that was Kawkazi's thumb, slowly crushing Casey's collarbone. At last, the pressure lifted.

Robert closed the distance, eyes alert.

The Crow had disappeared. Soundlessly.

"Probably shouldn't have given him friendly advice," Robert said. "I was just trying to lighten the mood."

Pierce, lighten the mood? Casey would've laughed if he hadn't been in pain.

"Anyway, sorry about him. Not thrilled with the organizational hierarchy."

"Ah," Casey said. "So...he wants to be Headmaster?"

"Oh, probably," Robert said. "Who wouldn't? But no, he respects The Craken—as he should."

"Ah," Casey said again.

"It's me, Grimes, me. He doesn't like that I'm in charge."

Casey opened his mouth. "Ah..."

"Walk with me." Robert flourished a hand and they started down the trail, murky with afternoon shadow. "First, Gloria's safe. I made sure of that myself. And after what just happened, I'm redacting your home from all public Trickery maps so no one can find you to firebomb your house or anything. Good thing the weekend's here. Campus will be on lockdown for a while. You got out just in time."

"Yeah..." Casey said.

"We're crossing the border now," Robert said. "Try to forget this trail since you're not authorized to know about it. Sylvan Watch, top secret. Better ice those bruises. And see you tomorrow. Things may look dark now, but believe me, this is far from over." He clapped Casey on the shoulder—his uncrushed one, luckily—and faded into the shadows.

Casey tried to piece his scattered thoughts together.

"Oh, hey!" Robert said.

Casey jumped.

"Sorry about the Porcus Lupus the other night. My espresso hadn't kicked in yet, so when it sneaked past me, I had to use a blow dart. Seemed like a monster on a mission, if y'know what I mean, but all's well that ends well. Bye."

This time Pierce was really gone.

Casey stood in the trail for a couple minutes. Porcus Lupus? Oh... that pig-wolf thing. What did it say about his life that he'd dumped the carcass in the woods and hadn't given it another thought?

His feet ached.

His brain ached.

Someone had burned the Amber Tower just to frame him.

"And I had to miss my favorite class," he said. "No Futuristic Forestry."

He jarred himself into motion when he noticed the woods were getting dark. Monsters were the last thing he needed. The trail crested a small ridge and Casey found himself in a familiar part of Lesser Trick 'n' Trap. He tried to remember the way, just to annoy Robert, but his mind was reeling.

Suddenly, he knew what he needed.

The Old Oak. Right now.

Just like that, he was running through the trees like Death Dogs were after him. Trails straightened their tangles and smoothed their bumps. Trees pulled their knotty roots out of the way. Or maybe he imagined it, but he didn't fall once, and then he was standing under the Oak, grabbing the ancient silver spikes, hauling himself up the craggy trunk as rough and warm as dinosaur skin.

Somehow—he couldn't have said exactly how—he found himself sprawled on the floor of the timber fortress where everything had started. No longer abandoned, every inch of the stronghold glowed like honey. He pressed his face against the golden planks.

"I can't do this," he told the oak. "Just can't."

The mighty tree swayed gently, sending a cool breeze down at him. The sinking sun brushed his skin, pouring from a lavender and tangerine sky. He stayed put.

"I have no idea what's going on," he said.

The tree groaned under him. Its branches nodded in the wind.

I know, I know, the oak was saying. Don't give up.

After a while Casey stood, rubbed his eyes, and went to the rail. To the east, roads were charcoal ribbons. Houses were neat little squares. To the west, the hidden world of Sylvan Woods was a rush of browns and greens and blue. He closed his eyes and saw the magic of the Sentries, winking like lazy stars, gathering in a brilliant blaze to burn the butchers from the sky. Swallowing their evil in a sea of color. Beautiful, wild, true.

"I can't leave," he said. "How could I?"

The great tree hummed, sap pulsing through its wooden heart.

"I've missed you," Casey said.

When he climbed down, security tape hung in tatters. Had he torn it in his hurry? He didn't think so. The Old Oak creaked in an offhand kind of way.

"It was you, wasn't it?" Casey said. "You took yourself off lockdown. Very tricky, since you'll never get the blame." He smiled as he headed home.

Through the woods, across his lawn, up the stairs. Inside.

"You're late," Dad said. "What's going on? Monster trouble, class trouble, just plain trouble?"

"Every kind," Casey said. He took a stool at the counter.

CHAPTER 44
A NORMAL FAMILY

AND THEN WE TOOK A SECRET trail away from Trickery," Casey finished, leaving out his visit to the oak. He didn't want to get the tree in trouble.

Dad's arms were crossed. "Beast guts," he said. "This is out of control."

Casey didn't correct him.

"I'm talking to the administration." Dad rubbed his jaw. "And I know you're excited to be at Trickery, but if it's a question of your safety..." He trailed off. "Tell me honestly, Casey. Do you still want to be there?"

Casey's chest tightened like The Crow was leaning on it.

"Yes." He thought of the Old Oak with its deep, deep roots. He thought of Luci and Robert and Jake. "I don't want to leave."

Dad sighed. "Mom and I like Sylvan Woods too," he said. "It feels like..." He blinked. "Well, whatever it feels like, we don't want to leave either. But we need to be realistic. Things are going pretty badly."

Casey nodded. They sat there, feeling sad.

We can't leave, Casey wanted to say. We just can't.

"We won't make a hasty decision," Dad said. "Mom and I will talk to Ms. Crake."

"Ok," Casey said. But he knew what that meant. Ms. Crake was blunt. Dad was honest. Mom was firm. There was only one decision they could make.

"Regardless, let's go weapon-shopping." Dad forced some cheerfulness into his voice. "Oh, and here's some good news. The Wests invited us to dinner tomorrow, something fun to take your mind off things."

"Oh cool. Thanks, Dad."

Dad squeezed his shoulder. A little later, Mom and Gloria arrived home with groceries. They fired up the grill and ate a big, late dinner as the moon came out.

Gloria told about her class's exploding water balloon exercise and how she'd barely gotten wet. Casey told about his fight with the Tiger Rat and building his first treeway.

Mom and Dad listened proudly.

"See," Mom said as they headed inside, "you're getting the hang of this."

Obviously, she hadn't talked with Dad yet. Casey's shirt hid the bruises from the fight with Drooce and he didn't want to ruin the moment. In bed he lay awake, wondering who was trying to get him. If they left Sylvan Woods, where would they go? Wherever they chose, it would feel like giving up, but Dad was right. Things were out of control. If only he could figure out what was going on.

Sometime after midnight, his brain gave up and shut itself off.

CHAPTER 45
PHASES OF ERADICATION

CASEY WAS POKING AT HIS EGGS and toast when someone rapped on the back door.

"Ooo, I'll get it!" Gloria jumped up. "Good morning, Black-and-Blue Eyes."

"Morning, Glo." Robert stepped inside. "Morning Casey, Mr. and Mrs. Grimes."

He looked better this morning, spiky hair on high alert. Gloria was right though, the bags under his eyes were big enough to pack for a weekend trip.

"Have you had breakfast?" Mom asked.

"Yes, thanks ma'am." He leaned wearily on a chair back. "But I'd take coffee if you don't mind." Mom slid him a mug.

Dad set his down. "Casey's been telling us about everything."

Robert took a gulp of coffee. "It escalated faster than expected," he admitted.

"What escalated?" Mom asked.

"And who expected it?" Dad followed up.

Casey drained his orange juice, interested to see what would happen. Pierce didn't usually respond well to questioning.

Robert crossed his arms. "It's sort of why I'm here." He seemed to be arguing with himself. "And it *does* involve you..." Truthful Robert was struggling to overcome Secret Robert. He drained his mug and clunked it down. Casey waited to see which Robert would speak.

"Saw it coming at Back to School Night," Robert said. "That banner had the telltale signs but Crake didn't want us jumping to conclusions so I kept it to myself." He shot a look at Casey. "Gave you a hint, though."

Casey stared back. Even Truthful Robert was hard to read.

"You know, be a little more careful than usual."

Casey shrugged.

"You're kidding me." Robert looked personally hurt. "And all week I've been telling myself not to worry because we're on the same page. You remember what I said, right?"

"Um..." Casey said.

Robert passed a hand across his eyes. "Only kid I know who could forget a death threat."

"What?" A small current jolted Casey's spine.

"Are you serious?" Mom asked.

He's always serious, Casey wanted to say.

"Someone did mention a death threat at Back to School night." Dad frowned. "It seemed ridiculous."

"That was me." Robert leaned in. "I thought you deserved a heads-up. And what do ya know, I was right, because now we're moving through all Machiavelli's Phases of Eradication, just as I expected." He ticked them off on his fingers. "Phase one, *discredit*. The banner, Fiera's article, those flyers. Phase two, *disable*. Jake goes down, the tower burns, and people start lining up to take a stab at you. We almost skipped straight to the final phase. *Destroy*."

"Oh my goodness." Mom looked pale.

"Kawkazi had to fight the crowd, hope you didn't stress too much," Robert said.

"Not at all," Casey said. "Totally cool."

"Good." Robert tapped his fingers on the rim of his mug. "Goes without saying, we've been shadowing you all week. And I've gotta say, those crazy treeway routes have been a real pain in the Achilles. Thanks for nothing."

"You've been watching me…" Casey said.

"We take it in shifts, obviously. Me, The Crow, Bones."

Casey tried to fit it all together.

"Should we still be worried?" Mom asked.

Robert frowned. "I wish I had a great answer, Mrs. Grimes. But it seems unlikely Drooce was working alone if he was part of this at all. He's not known for his scheming abilities."

Drooce is too dumb, Casey thought. Someone else is out there.

"For now, campus is closed," Robert said. "Headmaster Crake will decide what to do. She would've liked to speak to you herself, but we have to guard her, too, which doesn't make it safe for the two of you to be in the same place. Good news is, I don't have to sneak around anymore. We're escalated to full threat level. Me or Kawkazi will always be nearby."

Casey was pretty sure this was what you called *bad* news.

"Anyway," Robert said. "How 'bout some weapons practice. Seems appropriate, don't you think?"

CHAPTER 46
ROBERT GOES OFF

DAD AND MOM SAID YES, WEAPONS practice was a good idea. Then they disappeared and Casey was pretty sure he knew what they were doing. Deciding whether to enroll him in Vintage Woods Middle School. Or leave both the Woods immediately, Vintage and Sylvan, and move across the country. When Casey went outside, he felt hollow, like he was walking a thin line between real life and a dream.

On the deck he hefted the 127-Spiker.

"Why do people want to destroy Casey?" Gloria asked.

Casey felt sad she needed to ask a question like that.

"It's nothing personal," Robert said, and laughed grimly. "Stupidest expression ever. Everyone who's been in a fight knows it's always personal."

Casey nodded.

"It's not because Casey is a bad person, Glo. It's what he stands for—and you too, really."

Gloria paused her sword ballet. "What *do* I stand for?"

Casey leaned in.

Robert stopped an intricate rapier exercise and swiveled to face her. "Well, the two of you aren't exactly poster kids for combat, are you?"

Casey glanced down. He was gripping the mace the wrong way.

"Nope, and not subterfuge either," Robert said. "You stand for the other parts of Sylvan Woods, the ghostly forgotten parts. You didn't just fight the Butchers. You revived magic, dragged it onto the stage. Back then I was happy with how things were. Life was about strategy, cunning, weapons. Everything I'm good at. And there are lots of people like me, but now we know we aren't as tough as we thought. There are bigger things out there. Waiting."

Casey had the unpleasant thought that maybe Robert was about to cut his head off.

Robert looked down at his rapier. "It doesn't feel great," he admitted. "I like being in control. But magic means I'm not in control, not really. No matter how hard I practice, how great I get at fighting, there's always something stronger that I'll have to respect, maybe even be a little scared of. Something I'll never totally under-stand—even though it's real. And if that doesn't feel great to me, you know it doesn't feel great to other people, people with a lot more power and a lot less friendliness than me."

Casey couldn't believe his ears. *Robert needs to speak at Magic Club*, he thought. *Of course I'd have to drag him, kicking and scream-ing*. A second later he thought, *But I'll probably never go to Magic Club again*. And a second after that, he had to smile because Robert had just suggested that he, Trickery's most dangerous kid, was friendly.

Gloria held up her K-level sword. "We need to find all the bad kids."

Robert nodded. "Yeess."

She twirled, slicing ribbons in the air. "And march them to the sandpit!"

"Gloria!" Sometimes Casey wondered if all the emphasis on blood and combat was totally healthy for a six-year-old.

"You don't know anything about revenging," she told him.

Casey suspected she was right. He adjusted his grip on the 127-Spiker, knuckles lined up, index fingers spaced. Nice and limber, parallel to the ground. Yep, that's how you held a mace. He took a few swings, to work the knots out of his shoulders.

Someone wants you dead, he thought. No big deal.

Shwick, shwick, shwoock.

Someone cowardly, hiding in the shadows.

Shwoock, shwick.

Making it so you can't stay here anymore.

Shwick, ca-crack.

Oh great. He'd put a dent in one of the deck posts. Casey found he was breathing hard, cheeks hot, eyes damp. He wiped a hand across his face and lowered the mace.

Robert and Gloria were staring.

Casey flung himself on a bench. Someone should've told me sooner, he thought. Except I never would've believed it. How could anyone want me dead? Monsters are different. They're born bloodthirsty. But Robert's saying a person is out there, trying to kill me. Scheming to get me. Someone in Sylvan Woods. It's too horrible to believe.

Gloria put her sword down and squeezed his hand.

"Don't go to pieces on me, Grimes," Robert said. "What would I tell Crake? You know how much she likes you."

Casey took a deep, snuffly breath. "You seem to get along now."

"Oh, well yeah," Robert said. "I sold her short, man, between her limp and her magic obsession—I mean, her interest in magic. And I don't make a habit of telling other people's stories but let me say this: she didn't get that limp from falling off a cliff like some dumb novice." He whipped a figure eight in the air with his rapier. "I rated her too low, not proud of it. Give credit where it's due—that's part of my code, and The Craken deserves credit. So in case you've wondered, she's a lot more qualified than you might think."

Casey had wondered many things, but that wasn't one of them.

"But if she didn't fall off a—"

"She's been through more than you imagine."

"What actually happened to—"

"She's under my protection."

"Cool, great, I get it." Casey let it go, because he knew Ms. Crake was quality. She'd almost died fighting the butchers last semester. And after that, she'd taken a special interest in him and Gloria. She'd worked hard to get their Sylvan citizenship, and she'd done what she could to keep an eye on them.

Her interest in them was hard to comprehend, but sweet. Of course, with The Craken, you always wondered what she was up to. Where exactly her mind was headed. With her icy eyes and young chameleon face, it was impossible to tell.

At least *she* was on their side.

CHAPTER 47
THE SYLVAN SHOPS

YOU'RE SURE THE SYLVAN SHOPS are open?" Mom asked for the third time.

She didn't seem thrilled with them leaving and Casey got it. Part of him wanted to find a safe place and stay there, maybe under his bed. On the other hand, it made sense to hang out in a crowd and buy as many bludgeons, swords and pikes as they could afford.

"Let's play it safe over the weekend," Dad had said. "We'll get some brand new blades—while we decide what we're going to do."

Of course, Casey knew Dad and Mom had already decided.

"Believe me," Robert said. "The shops aren't closing their doors on a weekend. People want to upgrade their family weapon plans and throw feasts. Don't worry Mrs. Grimes, I'll keep a close eye on them."

Dad nodded. "Me too."

"Well, all right," Mom said. "Just call when you're on your way, ok? And maybe when you arrive? After you've shopped around a while. And when you're headed back."

Dad patted the phone in his pocket.

"No coverage," Robert said. "These woods eat signals. Literally."

"Ohh..." Mom said.

"Don't worry," Dad said. "We'll be careful."

They hiked away, Mom and Gloria waving from the deck. Casey had never been to the Sylvan Shops, but he'd heard kids talk about them. From the gravel trail by the Green Field, you could see their distant shapes. A collection of roofs, clustered on the southwest edge of Greater Trick 'n' Trap.

He'd imagined walking over with Luci and Gloria after school, pricing skrabbit steaks in the Local Beast, shopping for black designer t-shirts, seeing how far his allowance would stretch in a weapons shop. But that had never happened. And now it never would.

Instead, they were sneaking to the shops like spies.

Robert led them down a faint, straight trail through Lesser Trick 'n' Trap. The trail ended at the edge of the swamp, but Robert kept going, right across the marsh like it was made of brown glass. What in creeps? Casey put his foot down—on slippery rock. Stone columns waited just below the surface, impossible to see until you stood on them.

On a different day it would've been super cool.

They pushed through cattails on the far shore, hiked up a forested slope and traced the southern edge of the Green Field. Avoiding the BeastWoods on the left, they headed toward Greater Trick 'n' Trap.

As they zig-zagged around the forest's outermost point, Casey got his first real look at the famous shopping district. Even from a distance it was obvious the Sylvan Shops were open. Voices reached them over the turf. Figures streamed around the buildings—and he was shocked to see splashes of color. Dyed pennants waved over roofs. Painted signs swung above doors. The steady stream of customers, moving over cobbled streets, wore extreme earth-tones —azure, chartreuse and teal.

Casey could hardly believe it. Apparently Sylvans took a break from hunting and fighting after all. It was a side of the Woods he'd never seen. They strolled through a high wooden arch, carved with flowering vines:

WELCOME TO THE SYLVAN SHOPS

"Do people actually have fun here?" Casey said.

"Well...now and then," Robert admitted.

"I wasn't expecting *this*," Dad said.

As they walked down the central street, lined with covered boardwalks, Casey found it hard to feel dejected. Greenery twisted over rooftops. Shops with roll-up doors spilled diners and shoppers into the sun. People carried baskets and steered self-propelled wheelbarrows. Here and there, small kids were pulled along in wagons. It was like a miniature carnival, celebrating all the things he liked.

He saw Matt Rhiannon ducking into a candy shop. Ms. Chantelle stood under an awning, haggling over carabiners. In the Local Beast, Mr. Chroamwell from Futuristic Forestry ate steak and eggs with a book propped against his juice glass. Casey wanted to step over and say he was sorry they'd missed their second class because of the Amber Tower fire, but he realized that would be a little much.

Then he remembered.

I won't be here much longer. So what's the point?

Dad and Robert must've picked up on his mood, because no one talked much as they strolled past Roots & Leaves, an open air grocery. They passed Rare Contrivances, a pricy-looking hardware store. Then a tavern, a bakery, an apparel place, a blacksmith...

"This is crazy," Dad said. "Look, even a cafe."

"Ah yes," Robert said. "The espresso at Midnight Lynx is elite."

"So where do we buy weapons?" Dad said. "The blacksmith?"

"Not unless you want something custom-made," Robert said. "Do you?"

"Do we?" Dad looked at Casey.

"I guess not." Casey was sure he'd want a custom weapon *someday*, but by that time he'd be long gone from Sylvan Woods.

"Then it's the Baleful Blade," Robert said. "One of my favorites."

They walked through an arched stone doorway. Inside, the Blade looked like a cheerful, well-lit dungeon. It smelled of oil, leather and brand new steel.

"Amazing." Dad turned slowly, taking in racks of burnished weapons, clean-burning torches and a sand-strewn combat circle.

Despite his mood, Casey felt the excitement. Swords and spears and axes gleamed brightly, staged among monster hides, decorative whetstones, and a suit of Neo-Sylvan armor with clean, minimal lines. Any one of the shining blades could save your life. It made you feel like victory, against the worst odds, was always possible.

A young store associate stepped out from behind a cedar desk, trembling with eagerness. *Bryan*, his name tag said. He seemed highly aware of his important role at the Baleful Blade.

"Do you know what you're looking for today?" Bryan gave Robert a nod.

"Still figuring it out," Dad said. "I was thinking a mace, like Casey's here, but surrounded by all this...glorious metal...I'm not so sure."

"We get that reaction often." The associate beamed. "What's your favored attack style? And will this be a low-key backup or a statement piece?"

Dad stared into the middle distance. "Hmm." He glanced at Casey, took a breath and nodded decisively. "A statement piece. As to attack style..."

Casey had no idea what Dad would say. He had to admit, Dad was doing well. His clothing fit right in with the other weekenders. The store associate, Bryan, seemed to believe he was Sylvan. Just look at him, hanging on Dad's words.

"Well...I leave it all on the court," Dad said.

Bryan looked at him uncertainly.

"A go-for-the-jugular type," Robert said.

Bryan's face brightened. "Ah, very good. The Blade has a wide array of edge-first options. Swords, of course. Maces, like your son's. Some of our more exotic offerings have been very popular lately—assegais, khopeshes and such..."

Dad's eyes looked glazed.

"Maybe we'll just browse," Robert suggested.

"Excellent. You know your way around, Pierce. Just battle-shout when you need me."

Casey felt relieved as Bryan wandered off. They looked at a halberd, a claymore and a pike. Dad even took a hook-nosed cleaver down and gave it a few swings in a combat circle. Then he picked up a scythe-staff with a lovely, swirling blade. The slender handle wrapped in leather complimented it perfectly.

Dad blinked. "I need this."

"Um..." Casey said.

"For your mom."

"Ah, ok."

It took Dad a while longer to make his own choice. Casey began to think he'd handle every bladed weapon in the place.

"Aha," he finally said. "This is the one."

"Very classy," Robert said. "Those modified Gladius swords never go out of style."

The sword had a straight, tapered blade with three central grooves. It came to a leaf-shaped point. A hilt made of horn shone under a molded hand-guard.

Bryan hurried over. "Just look at the movement in that Damascus steel."

"I'll take these two," Dad said proudly.

"Wonderful choices." Bryan sheathed the blades and they followed him to the massive cedar desk. It took him an extra minute to process Dad's debit card. "Sorry, haven't run one of these in a while," he said.

Casey was just glad it worked.

As they left the Baleful Blade, Dad walked with extra swagger.

Shoulders squared, chin up. Well, it made sense. Carrying top-notch weaponry was good for your confidence. Just look at Robert. With a whole armory on his back, it was no wonder he came off as a jerk sometimes.

"Believe it or not," Dad said. "I was expecting to find a couple college kids selling maces out of a basement." He looked around the busy streets and sighed. "Well, we got what we came for. Anyone care for coffee before we go home?"

"Wouldn't say no to a double espresso," Robert said.

"I'll take a mocha...I guess," Casey said.

"That's the spirit," Dad said.

A few minutes later, they sipped their drinks at a boardwalk table by the Midnight Lynx. Dad kept the new weapons close as people streamed past under the awnings. He sipped his cappuccino. "This is excellent."

He sounded disappointed. Casey didn't need to wonder why. What could be more disappointing than a taste of something good just as you were leaving?

"Yessir." Robert had downed his espresso in two gulps. "The Midnight Lynx doesn't take alertness lightly."

"Or flavor," Dad pointed out.

"Well, that too."

There was a flurry of movement on the boardwalk.

"Hey Casey," someone said.

Robert leapt to his feet, knocking over their table as he swept a double-bladed dagger from his lap.

CHAPTER 48
IT TAKES ALL KINDS... OF WEAPONS

JEN TOMPKINS JERKED AWAY, eyes wide. Then her brows darted down. Her mouth made a hard line. "Get that haladie outta my face," she said. "What's your problem?"

Robert moved the two-bladed dagger half an inch. "Who are you?" he growled.

Jen clenched her fists next to her blue jeans. She looked about to explode.

"That's my friend Jen!" Casey flicked mocha off his fingers. "Leave her alone, Robert." He stepped between them as Dad righted the overturned table.

"Let's all calm down, ok?" Dad said.

Robert shrugged and put the dagger away.

There was a moment of tense silence.

"I was just going to–" Jen said.

"What are you–" Casey said at the same time.

"I didn't mean–"

"Sorry about–"

"You two are terrible," Robert said.

Dad set his empty mug on the table. "I'm Mr. Grimes. Nice to meet you, Jen."

"Nice to meet you, sir."

Jen and Dad shook, and Casey tried to think of something to say.

"Um...how's your day going?" Too late, he realized it probably wasn't the best question.

Jen crossed her arms over her pink and black tee, flipped back her hair and gave a little laugh. "Oh, not too bad. My parents are over there somewhere." She nodded down the boardwalk. "We were shopping for climbing gear and stew meat, nothing crazy...just thought I'd say hi. Almost getting stabbed was the biggest event of my day so far."

She darted a glance at Robert.

"Sorry, *not* sorry," he said. "You shouldn't have snuck up on us. At least you know your way around daggers."

Jen rolled her eyes. "Oh, so it's *my* fault for being quick on my feet. Anyone could identify a haladie when it's two inches from her face." She turned to Casey. "Well, I should probably get going. See ya, Case. Nice to meet you, Mr. Grimes." She strolled away.

If Robert minded being snubbed, he didn't show it.

"She seems nice enough," Dad said. "How'd you meet?"

"Land Creature Defense and Extreme Climbing," Casey said. "She's good at everything. What was that about, Robert?"

"It's nice we're having a good time," Robert said. "But the fun would end if I stopped doing my job. In case you're wondering, my job is making sure no one sneaks up on you and cuts your—"

"Ok, ok," Dad said. "You know, it's a relief having no cell phones out here. But we should probably get back before your mom starts to worry."

They marched down the boardwalk and crossed the cobbled street. Casey kept an eye out for Jen, but he didn't see her again, and that was probably for the best. Without the element of surprise he'd probably act all weird.

They took the same route home, along the Green Field, over the submerged swamp path, through Lesser Trick 'n' Trap. It was the most direct trail Casey had ever used. If he was going to say goodbye to Sylvan Woods, he'd need a lot more time.

Mom and Gloria were waiting on the deck under a big umbrella. When Casey got closer, he saw their Uno! game and Gloria's monster flash cards, spread around the table. Well, at least they weren't freaking out.

Mom jumped to her feet. "What took you so long?"

"Mom thought you got assass...assassined," Gloria said. "She wanted to call the police, but I told her not to worry."

"We're fine," Dad said. "And I got you something." He swept the scythe-staff from behind his back.

Mom looked at the paper-wrapped shape. "Is this something I'll like?"

Casey glanced back and forth.

"Well..." Dad said. "Yes. I think you'll be glad to have it."

Mom tugged at the paper. She took a little longer to unwrap the staff than she really needed to. When she saw what it was, she took a quick, deep breath. Then she nodded.

"Thank you," she said.

She and Dad looked at each other. Casey couldn't catch everything their eyes were saying. But he knew the message wasn't happy.

"It's so pretty!" Gloria said.

Robert's face broke into a tired grin.

Mom did her best to smile. "Hey, and look at that gorgeous sword," she said. "I guess nobody's gonna mess with us now, are they?"

"I should say not," Dad said.

"Let me just put this somewhere safe..." Mom led the way inside. Casey and Robert were sipping ice water at the kitchen counter when she reappeared.

"That came for you," she said, pointing.

A yellow envelope leaned against the coffeepot. It didn't have a postmark. Casey's name was scrawled across the front without an address.

"Your home is supposed to be a secret." Robert's eyes darkened. "You'd better let me open that." A knife appeared in his hands and before Casey could argue, he'd slit the envelope. He kept his dagger raised as he reached inside but nothing happened.

What *could* happen? Casey thought. What kind of danger lurks inside a letter? He realized it was a stupid question. This was Sylvan Woods.

Robert shrugged and handed him a splotchy sheet of paper:

It wasn't us. We're on your side. We'd never sabotage Trickery like that.
Love, the Magic Club

A dozen signatures were scrawled under the note. Casey was ashamed to realize he didn't know a single name. But he did know who they were, and he believed they hadn't set the Amber Tower on fire. He felt grateful they were trying to help.

"See, not everyone hates you." Robert put a hand on Casey's shoulder. "My shift is almost over, and I'd stick around, but I've hardly slept in seventy-two hours, so I'll be taking off as soon as Kawkazi gets here."

A heavy fist thumped the sliding door, making it shudder.

"Speak of the devil," Robert said.

"Great." Casey put his water glass to his forehead. "Hanging out with him is going to be a treat. I'll even have to take him to Luci's. Hey, are you sure about the Crow? I mean, you're sure he's on our side?"

Robert paused at the door.

Kawkazi stood outside, frowning.

"I'm not sure about anyone," Robert said. "Sometimes I'm not even sure about you."

"Not helpful," Casey said.

"Crake trusts him." Robert shrugged. "What more can you ask for?"

He slid the door open and Mr. K. stepped through, ducking. He smoothed his pin-striped vest. "Hello, Grimes. Ready for a night of fun and games?"

His smile was chilling.

CHAPTER 49
WEIRDNESS AT THE WESTS

HEY BRO, WELCOME TO MY CRIB," Luci said. "I invited Jake and Robert and that girl with the nose rings from Magic Club, but none of them could make it. Sucks, ya know."

Casey hated it when she talked like this. He was starting to think she knew that. Also, he hadn't known she was inviting other kids. He didn't much like that either, which was silly—everyone loves a party, right? But as he stepped inside, Casey felt more out of place than he'd expected.

After The Crow's stony presence invaded the Grimes home, Casey'd had just minutes to get cleaned up before it was time to leave again. As they hiked the outer edge of Lesser Trick 'n' Trap, he wondered how much time he'd have to say goodbye to Trickery.

Mom kept looking at a hand-made, birch-bark map Luci's mom had sent her. Scrawled across the top:

OUR SYLVAN HOMES... AREN'T FAR APART.

It would've made Casey smile a couple days before. Now it seemed like maybe their homes were very, very far apart after all. His heart felt so heavy that he hoped they'd get lost and miss dinner. Then he wouldn't have to pretend to be happy. It seemed like his wish might come true when they stumbled into a dry creek bed and through a patch of stinging nettles.

But Gloria led them back out.

Even Mr. K. started grunting directions, tired of thorns ripping his tailored slacks, and after a few more wrong turns, they reached Luci's house. Casey's dream of missing dinner was over, but his spirits rose in spite of himself. The woodland home was gorgeous.

Seriously, a dedicated treeway, he thought. Just look at that massive willow—and a catwalk, straight to the second story. So cool.

They'd knocked on the big green front door.

Luci opened it. Things had gone downhill from there.

"Welcome, Grimeses!" Luci's parents appeared behind her, ushering them in as she stepped aside, flicking her eyes to the tops of their sockets like she was marking off a list. *Overly welcoming parents, check.*

Casey ignored her and shook Mr. West's hand, doing his best to get a firm grip.

"Good to see you again, Casey."

"You too, sir." He smiled weakly.

Mrs. West gave his shoulder a squeeze. She had the same light brown skin and wavy hair as Luci. *Well, probably not exactly the same.*

Something inside him gave a little shudder.

After the hellos and handshakes, they headed to the middle of the house. The Wests acted like Mr. Kawkazi's presence was no big deal and mostly ignored him after introductions. Apparently they'd been warned about the extra security and didn't mind feeding someone as big as a tank. Standing in the cedar-paneled great room, Casey tried to catch Luci's eye, but she ignored him and kept talking to Gloria. He was admiring the thick, polished beams in the ceiling and the sunset glowing in the skylights when something licked his hand.

He almost yelped.

That would have been ironic because looking up at him was a fox.

"Hey, that's my line," the fox could have said.

Casey dropped to his knees and gave its huge ears a ruffle. The fox grinned. Casey felt a gloomy presence at his side, way too small to be Kawkazi.

"Hey Luci," he said. "This fox isn't from around here, is he?"

"Easy on his lobes." Her arms were crossed. "Woofles is an exotic Bat-Ear, an ideal messenger fox, very quick on his feet and *very* cute and *veerry* honest—aren't you Woofles?"

"Ha, messenger foxes," Casey said. "I knew it."

Luci's eyes flicked up again.

Casey taking credit for something dumb, check.

He decided to ignore her. "I'll bet he's good at delivering messages. But I don't see what honesty has to do with it."

"What a cute little foxy-woxy!" Gloria gave the fox a hug.

Woofles didn't seem to mind.

"What honesty has to do with *what*?" Luci said.

"Um...being a fox, I guess. Delivering messages."

Her eyes flicked up.

Casey being a total fool, check.

He looked down at Woofles, who seemed unaware of the tension crackling around him.

Why does Luci have to be this way? Casey thought. I'm making an effort.

"Foxes all have the same moral compass, Casey," Luci said. "But I think you'd probably agree, wouldn't you, that honesty has a lot to do with delivering messages."

He shrugged.

"Dinner's served, kids," called Mrs. West from the kitchen.

Just in time.

Except a few minutes later, Casey found Luci seated next to him. She didn't seem thrilled about it either, but she had Gloria on her other side, and they spent the meal chatting like besties by a campfire. Casey's parents were hitting it off with Mr. and Mrs. West. Everyone was getting along great—except for Kawkazi, who'd insisted on eating in the kitchen, on his feet.

And Casey.

He didn't get it. As he sat there in a bubble of quiet, eating gumbo with crawfish and red beans and rice, something untwisted in his chest—and started to squirm, struggling to get free. He couldn't ignore the feeling any longer. He had to say something. This couldn't go on.

"How's school, Luci?" Mom said.

"Oh, you know." Luci looked up from her untouched dinner. "Pretty great."

Mrs. West arched her brows. "Really, honey?"

Luci shot her mom a look.

"Oh, of course." Mrs. West put a finger to her lips.

Luci's dad passed Casey's dad the bread pudding. "Girls this age..." he said.

"Dad, Mom, would you please stop!"

Casey was paying close attention, but Mrs. West shrugged and turned to Luci. "Would you like to show Casey and Gloria your room, honey?"

"Ooo, yes!" Gloria bounced in her seat.

"Ok." Luci got up. "Come on, Glo."

Casey didn't get an invitation, but he tagged along. It would've been weird not to.

The second floor of the West house had a wide central hallway with doors on either side. At least one of them must open on the dedicated treeway, Casey thought, and he was tempted to go looking for it. But that would probably just offend Luci more.

Halfway down the hall, she opened a door. She and Gloria stepped inside.

Casey stuck his head in.

"Wow." He'd assumed her room would be nice, but he wasn't prepared for the high level of cool. Luci's bed stood in the middle, draped by a see-through canopy that hung from the angled ceiling. It was lit by twinkle lights like a stylish indoor campout.

The outer wall was one big window, with a glass door you could step through onto a deck that must connect to the treeway. The walls were lined with books and a silver rack that held Luci's scythe-staff, her Femme Fatale stiletto, and other equipment. There was an armchair with an orb lamp hanging overhead. She even had a big, glossy poster of her favorite Sentry, the Sighing Sycamore, with dim, spooky lights in its branches.

Casey was impressed. "This is really coo–"

Whupf. Something fluffy hit the side of his face. A stuffed lynx bounced to the floor.

"Oh, sorry," Luci said. "Just shifting a few things, didn't see you there."

Gloria giggled and bounced on the bed.

"Ok," Casey said. "Your room is really–"

Pluff. A stuffed owl got him in the nose.

"Gee whiz golly gee." Luci sat down next to Gloria, more stuffed animals in easy reach. "You seem to keep getting in the way, bud."

Her Civilian dialect was back. Obviously she was doing it to bother him. *Remember who you were, Casey,* she was saying. Or maybe, *Remember who you still are.*

Casey stepped away. When a fluffy fox shot toward him, he caught it. And the corduroy bloodhound that followed. So this is how it's going to be, he thought. Maybe you should just call it a night. She doesn't like you anymore.

"No, don't throw the unicorn!" Gloria said. "It's too cute."

For a second, Casey thought about swinging the window open, climbing out and heading home. But he couldn't do that. Not yet. The thing in his chest stood on its hind legs, refusing to be ignored.

"Look." He stepped to the doorway. "I'm leaving. But first I have to say something." He stepped aside as a wooly gryphon sailed past.

"See you later, alligator," Luci said.

He took a breath. "When you asked me about the hospital, the time you visited me... I lied."

Luci froze. A fuzzy platypus dangled from her hand.

"I *remember* what you said," Casey continued. "All of it. I thought it would be easier if I pretended not to know your secret—but that was dumb. I do know, and I won't forget. Ever."

"A secret?" Gloria's eyes got big.

Luci's face was expressionless.

Casey hovered a second longer. "Ok, bye."

He paused in the hallway under a glowing chandelier.

"Stupid," he said. *Stuffed animals shouldn't hurt your feelings.*

A door by the stairs was ajar and he peered through. The room on the far side was dark, except for weak light filtering through the windows. Huge windows—facing the forest and the giant willow. Hey...

He pushed the door open.

In most houses a mudroom would be on the first floor, but not in Sylvan Woods. Boots and trail shoes cluttered the flagstones. Umbrellas leaned in a flower pot along with a muddy sword-stick. Coats and hats and hoodies hung from pegs. This was probably the only messy room in the whole house, and it was unspeakably cool.

A stained glass portal stood in the center of the window wall, nicer than the door downstairs. The setting sun shone through it like a kaleidoscope.

"This is their *real* front door," Casey said.

He looked outside, along the catwalk floating above the yard. His hand was on the knob, ready to give it a try, when he saw something move, down in the shadows.

CHAPTER 50
BIG OR LITTLE, THIN OR WIDE

FOR A SECOND, CASEY THOUGHT about staying inside. But a flash of irritation changed that. *Go back to Luci's room where you're not wanted? Be a fifth wheel downstairs? Creeps no.* He eased the glass door open. Maybe he'd do a little monster-watching. If you lived inside Sylvan borders, the local species probably came right up to your house.

He set a foot down carefully on the black steel catwalk. Holding his breath, he peered over the handrails, down into the shadows. Nothing seemed to be moving now.

Shwick. Something flickered past his ear.

Casey jerked away. *Was that a bat?* It was sure moving fast. In the growing darkness, he remembered what Robert had said. "In case you're wondering, my job is to keep someone from sneaking up on you and cutting your—"

He threw himself down in a pool of shadow, inches from the deck. The metal smelled of leaves and dirt. The wind sighed past.

You're safe, he told himself. You're alone.

He pushed himself to his elbows, then to his feet.

But he was wrong.

A hooded figure stood at the far end of the catwalk.

Casey's mouth fell open, but no scream came out.

Moonlight gleamed on something rushing toward his face.

An irresistible force shoved him aside and down. *Cra-shing!* Sparks flew like shooting stars. The moon disappeared. This is it, Casey thought. I'm dead. Dead, just like that. Gloria laughing, Dad and Mom chatting, Luci still mad at me. This is how it all ends. Stars, pitch darkness...

The world sped up again. The catwalk shuddered as The Crow completed his acrobatic flip. A nasty barbed javelin gleamed in his silver hand. He roared and flung the weapon back. But the end of the catwalk was already empty. The javelin buried itself in the willow with a wet *thunk*. Kawkazi bounded after it, silent as a big cat.

A few moments later he was back.

Towering over Casey, his dark eyes smoldered.

"Can't track him because I can't leave *you* alone," Kawkazi growled. "Inform me next time you decide to take a death stroll. This isn't a game." The Fireside Cookery teacher glared down at him as the girls appeared at the mudroom door.

"What's going on?" Luci asked.

The Crow extended his silver hand. "After you, dear boy."

Casey walked inside. The night swayed around him even though the catwalk was solid. Kawkazi closed and locked the door behind them.

"What happened?" Luci said.

Gloria tugged Casey's elbow.

Kawkazi crossed his arms. "Tell me what you saw, Grimes."

Casey blinked. "I saw...nothing. No one was there, then someone. No face. I mean, just shadows in a hood."

"Big or little. Thin or wide. Man or woman. Tall or short." Mr. K. listed off the word pairs like he was talking to a kindergartener.

Casey hung his head. "It happened too fast."

The Crow bared his white teeth, spun on his heel and was gone.

Casey tried to think what to do. He turned to follow Kawkazi.

"Casey, wait." Luci had dropped her sassy tone.

When he glanced back, she looked concerned. *Well, about time. If it wasn't for The Crow, I'd be lying on my back on the catwalk, seeing nothing.*

"I should go," he said.

In the dining room the grown-ups were getting to their feet. Dad and Mom looked like they were in a bad dream. Luci's parents were furious.

"They'll regret this," Mr. West snapped.

"And in our house..." Mrs. West extended a hand to Mom. "I'm so sorry, Claire."

"Sweetheart!" Mom stepped to Casey.

"You're ok?" Dad asked.

"I'm fine," Casey lied.

The Crow was sorting through a rucksack. "If I might borrow your fox," he said, "I'll send my supervisor a message and we'll be on our way. Sorry to end your evening so abruptly."

Kawkazi didn't sound sorry. He sounded ticked off.

"Of course," Mr. West said. "And I'll come with you—don't argue."

Mr. K. inclined his head with the air of someone who didn't have time to mess around.

"I'd grab my rapier and come as well," Mrs. West said. "But I'd better stay with Luci."

The girls appeared at the bottom of the stairs.

"Do we really have to go?" Gloria said.

"Afraid so, honey." Dad took her hand. "Wish I'd brought my new Gladius."

"Let's get moving." Somehow, The Crow had already scrawled a message, folded it three or four times, and placed it in Woofles's eager jaws. The Bat-Eared Fox had appeared as if by magic.

"Sylvan Watch Command," Mr. K. said.

Woofles danced on his feet but kept his eyes on the huge man.

"Robert Pierce," Kawkazi muttered.

The fox gave a muffled yelp and flashed away.

"All right, let's go." Kawkazi herded them to the front door.

Mr. West joined them on the porch, carrying a glittering pole-axe. The Crow twisted a spherical object in the palm of his metal hand. Silvery light blazed, lighting up the yard with pale radiance.

"Excellent," Mr. West said. "Bet you don't even feel the star's heat."

"Not in the least." Kawkazi stepped forward. "Grimeses, follow me. West, if you'd bring up the rear, I'd appreciate it. Let's keep an eye on the forest."

They cut across the yard, straight to the trail. Casey guessed there'd be no wandering on the way back. When he looked over his shoulder past Mr. West, he saw Luci and her mom watching from the front door.

Casey had expected the evening to go badly, but not this badly.

Luci's eyes flashed in The Crow's star-lamp. She looked like she was about to cry or hit someone but couldn't decide which.

That was how Casey felt too.

CHAPTER 51
THE TERRIBLE TRUTH

SHADING HIS EYES FROM the radiance flooding the woods, Casey watched his shoes crunch through the leaves lit up by Kawkazi's star-glow. He wondered if the rumors were true and The Crow had cut off his own hand to become more lethal. It took a half mile of trail before he could start making sense of what had just happened.

Being attacked in Sylvan Woods wasn't a new thing. When he'd met Luci, she'd slapped him before they even shook hands. With Robert it had been war at first sight. Sebastian Drooce had tried to kill him at least three times.

But Sylvans always had something to say before they came at you. They wanted you to know *why* they were going to mangle you.

The shadow on the catwalk hadn't said a word. No boasts, no accusations, no insults. He or she'd tried to kill Casey as efficiently as possible. It was something new.

And horrible.

Robert had been right. He'd seen the pattern.

Discredit, Disable, Destroy.

It was happening too fast to keep up with.

Someone wanted him dead. Just, dead.

The question was—why? And who?

The answer was, he had no idea.

The most fearsome warrior at Trickery had just saved his life. Jake had seen The Crow in the woods but that had to be some kind of mistake. Surely he could remove Mr. K. from suspicion now. Even if he was lethal and not very friendly, he couldn't be in two places at once.

When Casey glanced up, he saw dozens of narrow eyes reflecting starlight on the edges of the glare. Just days ago, hungry little monsters had seemed horrifying. Now they seemed simple. You always knew what was on a Tree Shriek or Bog Creep's mind. Hunt, kill, eat. So uncomplicated. Casey wished his life was like that.

Let's see...who else disliked him?

Fiera Laurent detested him, but she had the agility of a box turtle. He pictured her backpack dragging her off a dark treeway as she shrieked. Printed words were her chosen weapons and she couldn't sneak up on anybody.

There was Ms. Steele. She despised magic and he *was* Mister Magic. But he couldn't see her draping a hoody over her old bones to stalk him through the woods.

Of course there was Drooce. Drooce would be the obvious choice, except he was out of play. With his own eyes, Casey had seen Kawkazi send him packing. Sebastian had headed to detention like half the BeastWoods were after him. At least, he'd *seemed* scared...

Casey frowned.

His theorizing was getting him nowhere. He had a sinking feeling that after all the lies, lots of people could hate him and he wouldn't even know their names. Of course, whoever was behind this had hated him before the banner unfurled on Back to School Night.

His frown deepened.

The only answer was to trust as few people as possible. He hoped Robert and Ms. Crake knew more than he did. They were the experts on Eradication Theory. In the meantime, he could trust Dad and Mom and Gloria, of course. And Luci, not that it mattered.

He stubbed his toe on the deck stairs even though they were brightly lit. The Crow held his palm high, lighting up the yard and a wide swath of Lesser Trick 'n' Trap. Nothing moved. The woods looked over-exposed and strangely ghostly in the glare.

Kawkazi twisted the sphere closed. They went inside, and the Crow took a post by the windows overlooking the yard. Mr. West wished them good night and disappeared into the dark, a small glow lighting his way. Mom put water on to boil. Dad disappeared upstairs, and Casey knew he was taking out his Gladius.

Gloria looked mad, but she was rubbing her eyes. "We'll find the bad person, Casey." She hugged his waist and leaned her head against him. "Right after I take a little nap."

"That's a good plan, Gloria." He took her hand and walked her upstairs.

"G'night, Casey." Her kiss smelled like cinnamon and raisins from the bread pudding at dinner. Gloria snuggled into bed and was asleep in seconds. Casey went back downstairs. He kindled a fire in the hearth for something to do. He felt shivery.

"Don't build it too big," The Crow said from his place at the window.

Casey didn't see why not. What was a small blaze after you'd lit up half the woods?

The kettle began whistling...and kept whistling. Casey took it off the heat and let the steam flow over his hands and face. He had a pretty good idea where Mom had gone. He wondered where she'd hidden her new scythe-staff.

"Well, goodnight," Casey said. "Maybe I'll come check on things in a while."

The Crow kept his massive back turned, scanning the darkness outside.

Casey went upstairs. He pulled the 127-Spiker out of his closet and leaned it against the wall. He opened his bedside table, took out the dagger Robert had given him, and slid it in his pocket. His throwing star (an earlier gift from Robert) he put under his pillow, just in case. On his hands and knees, he reached under his bed until his fingers found a fluffy towel. Carefully, he pulled it toward him. He folded back the soft red cotton.

A silver hilt gleamed at him. Cold but reassuring. A deadly friend.

He slid the Sylvan sword from its sheath.

CHAPTER 52
AWKWARD SILENCE

CASEY LOST TRACK OF TIME on the edge of his bed with the bare sword across his knees. He was careful to avoid the edges. Part of him wanted to put it away and go to sleep. Part of him wanted to push his window open and slip into the night, slashing left and right until he found whoever was out there.

Someone tapped on the door and Dad looked in. If he was surprised to see Casey holding a sword, he didn't show it. Dad's modified Gladius was belted at the waist of his jeans.

"How you doing, son?"

"I'm ok."

Dad stepped over and put a hand on Casey's shoulder. His jaw was set, his eyes stubborn. "We've put up with way too much for way too long, but it all ends tonight. Tomorrow, we're starting over, and I don't care if we have to move across the country—we'll find someplace right for you and Gloria. Someplace good. I know it's hard but try to get some sleep."

"Ok." Casey wished he could smile.

Mom came in to join them. "I love you." She kissed the top of his head.

"Love you, Mom."

Her brand-new scythe-staff was probably waiting in the hall. She and Dad said goodnight and closed the door, and Casey wondered where they'd wait. By the fireplace, maybe, with Kawkazi. Maybe they'd split up, cover the kitchen window and the second floor, but he hoped not. Maybe they'd pass the night drinking tea and coffee and when the sun rose, they'd find out the assassin had been hunted down. Maybe then they could stay here.

But he didn't think so. The dark, hollow feeling in his chest said No.

He kept an eye on his bedroom window. All he could see were twiggy fingers, swaying in the night. Now and then, one tapped the glass, letting him know he wasn't alone.

He wished he could sleep like Gloria.

He wondered if The Crow had moved a muscle.

He wondered what Luci was doing.

Outside his window, he could see the oak tree better.

Lit up by a pearly glow.

Had the moon come out?

Maybe I'll slip out onto the roof, he thought, and he was reaching for the window when a wild-eyed face appeared, hair blowing in the wind.

"Aaugh!" Casey stumbled backward.

Luci tapped the pane, holding up her pendant.

Casey froze, hands stretched toward the Sylvan Sword. Breathe, he told himself. *Holy creeps, my heart.* He sheathed the sword and slid the window open.

"About time." Luci climbed through, dragging her scythe-staff. "Been a while, right?" She shrugged her pack off. "Sneaking around after dark was all we ever used to do."

Casey slammed the window and frowned. "How'd you get here?"

"Easy, followed Kawkazi's light show. The entire forest knows where you are."

"Oh. Good point."

Luci looked around for a place to sit.

"Sorry." Casey shoved books and papers aside. He didn't have guests in his room very often. Now there was an understatement. He tried to think of something to say. "Do your parents know you're here?" What a dumb question.

Luci tucked a loose curl behind one ear. "They won't be happy, that's for sure. But I left them a note so they'll understand. You can't leave a friend alone when someone's trying to kill him."

The silence went on a while.

"Listen." Luci folded her hands on her lap, then unfolded them. "I'm sorry about earlier. I wasn't being very nice. All the Civilian slang and rudeness...well, I was trying to remind you of how you used to live—that you used to have a great, big secret."

"Oh," Casey said. "Ok."

She looked down. "Anyway, I had to come over, because I've been thinking, what if you died? What if I never saw you alive again?"

If she was trying to make him feel better, she was doing a terrible job.

"It's just that..." Her hands squeezed fistfuls of comforter. "I knew you lied about what happened in the hospital. I knew instantly. You're not good at lying, Casey. You should consider giving it up."

"Oh..." He could've asked what she was talking about, but he knew.

And she knew that he knew.

If only he could escape into the night.

"I was scared," he said. "No, not scared, I don't know why I said that." He didn't meet her eyes. "I thought if I said I didn't know—it would make things easier." He looked down at the bedspread she was squeezing into knots and wished he could pull it over his head.

When he made himself glance up, she looked pale.

"Did it work?" she asked.

"No." He swallowed. "Not at all."

"It didn't work for me either."

"I'm sorry I did that," he said. "Really sorry."

They studied opposite corners of the room.

"At first I was happy," Luci said, "when you didn't—allude to my monster blood. I thought you were being polite. Then I realized you were weirded out. Then you lied about it. But remember, back in the hospital..." Her voice fell to a whisper. "You were the one who asked. I wasn't going to tell."

Casey knew that was true. And he realized he'd done an awful thing. Luci had tried her best to keep her secret hidden and he'd pried it out of her—not only by asking but by dragging her into trouble. She'd let the secret out, protecting him and Gloria. Then, because the secret was a heavy one and awkward to carry, he'd pretended not to know.

"I've been a terrible friend," he said.

Luci examined the curtains.

"I wasn't weirded out," he said. "I was...lazy. I wanted things to be simple."

She turned her eyes on him. "But things *aren't* simple."

"I know...and it's ok." He wanted to say more, lots more. "I don't care about your monster DNA. You can't scare me off even if you try. I'll be a better friend. I haven't had a lot of practice, I mean, you're my first one, probably, but I'll—I'll do better, I promise."

Luci sighed, biting her lip.

He remembered that day in the hospital, or maybe it had been night, when she'd sneaked all the way from Sylvan Woods to check on him. He'd asked about her gorgon blood and said Who cares? and he'd meant it and she'd stopped crying. It had been the right thing then and it was the right thing now. It should have been obvious all along. Luci was the first person who'd seen him in Sylvan Woods and she hadn't just seen him, she'd *cared*.

If only he could put that into words, maybe she'd believe him.

But he didn't have time.

A shuddering crash came from the back deck and they jumped to their feet.

CHAPTER 53

THE BEGINNING OF THE END

THEY FLEW DOWNSTAIRS AS the crow stepped outside and slid the door shut behind him. He stood on the deck, feet squared, and swept a katana from his back. Something dark and scaly moved under the porch light, swooping forward and away like a reptilian manta ray or the head of an enormous cobra. Dad and Mom stood frozen in place.

"A Murklurker," whispered Luci. "They're not from around here."

"Are they bad?" Casey gripped his sword.

"The worst." Luci watched the monster sway back and forth, sizing up Mr. K. "Poisonous, and they can levitate."

"I'm going out," Dad said.

Mom put a hand on his shoulder.

Someone knocked on the front door.

All four of them stiffened. The showdown on the deck suddenly seemed like something they were watching on a screen.

Rat-a-tat-tat. The knock was light, teasing.

Clinka-chak-chak. Now it had a sharp, metallic edge.

Ka-thoom. The door shuddered on its hinges.

Casey took an involuntary step back. His hands flew up, and he forced them down, tearing at his sword hilt. It was happening. The killer was here, and they weren't ready.

Ka-thoom.

"Weapons out!" Dad shouted.

They swept their swords and scythe-staffs forward.

Ka-crunch. The lock broke and the door swung open.

A tall, dark figure took a step inside. Unhurried. Strangely graceful for someone so big. Mr. Chroamwell, Casey's Futuristic Forestry teacher, nodded pleasantly as if he'd been invited over for a nightcap.

Casey waited for him to say, "I'm here to help, and by the way, the alluvial soil in your yard is remarkable." Instead, a slow, nasty smile crept over his face. Up until that moment, Casey'd hoped deep in his heart and without logic that all the bad things were a terrible coincidence. Now he knew something horrible was about to happen.

"Good evening." Chroamwell's eyes swung right and left. "Must say I expected there to be more of you. I'm afraid I've brought a trident to a knife fight."

Behind him, two more figures stepped into the light.

Casey's jaw dropped. He squeezed his eyes shut, then opened them wide.

"You know where this is headed," Chroamwell said. "I need two Grimeses, the little ones. You big ones are no threat. No need for a bloody mess."

Dad stepped forward. "Get out," he growled.

Chroamwell shrugged. "Bloody mess it is then."

On Chroamwell's left crouched a boy with reddish hair. Matt Rhiannon. On his right, a girl pushed back her hood. Her straight brown tresses were pulled back tight, and her face was hard. Jen Tompkins wasn't smiling now.

There was a pitter-patter of feet as Luci turned and ran. Up the stairs, gone.

Casey couldn't believe it. Any of it.

Chroamwell laughed. "I like a girl who can read the odds." He drew twin short swords, enjoying the rasp of oiled metal. "Resist if you must, but realize that will only draw things out. Why make it *extra* painful?"

The assassin strolled forward, blades shredding the air. Jen and Matt stalked on either side like hungry cats trailing a giant predator. Jen held a trident. Matt a battle-axe. They'd laughed with Casey, joked, hiked trails together...

"Why are you doing this?" he said.

Something crashed heavily against the glass behind them.

"Ah, the eternal question," Chroamwell purred. "Magic is contagious, Grimes, and I'm here to stamp it out before it gets away." He clashed his swords together. "In the future we'll have full control— no wild untamed forces, no Sylvan backwaters—a red-blooded power structure full of gold. A new monopoly on monsters." He sneered at Casey. "That's the big picture, Grimes. So you understand how insulting it is—how intolerable—when a couple dumb kids bring magic back. Magic is a disease, and you and your sister are crawling with it."

Casey bit back a scream. Dad and Mom stood in front of him, brand new weapons raised. They were determined but they'd never been in a fight. He knew what was about to happen.

"Don't feel bad, Grimes." Chroamwell raised his swords. "It's nothing personal."

The killer stalked closer, Jen and Matt on either side. When Chroamwell gave the signal, they'd strike like forked lightning. There would be no thunder. Not a whisper of warning.

But it would rain blood.

Tap, tap, tap. Someone knocked on the splintered front door. Without waiting for an invitation, the person stepped inside. Chroamwell made a slightly-rushed half-swivel.

Dark eyes blazed under spiky hair.

"Anytime there's a fight," Robert said, "it's always personal."

CHAPTER 54
BLOOD AND SAND

UP UNTIL THAT MOMENT, everything had gone like a horrible choreographed meeting.

Now it became a wild, chaotic rush.

Robert sprang at the assassin, stabbing with a long-handled spear.

Matt and Jen froze, then came at the Grimes family. Casey found himself face to face with Rhiannon. The battle axe whistled past his gut and he jumped back, slicing down with his sword.

A thin wedge of metal fell to the floor.

Matt's eyes flicked to the notched axe-head, but he didn't stop. "Wish I'd caught you earlier," he snarled. His attack was a storm of two-handed chops. Casey dodged and parried desperately. He cut more slivers off the axe but not enough to make a difference.

Dodge, chop, jump back. He didn't have time to think—and that would hurt him in the end, because good fighters planned ahead. Matt was too fierce, too fast. One misstep and the axe would rip through skin and bone. Rhiannon showed a healthy respect for the Sylvan Sword, though. It was the only thing keeping Casey alive.

The kid assassin threw down a fierce chop that would've cracked

Casey's skull if he hadn't dodged. Matt yanked the axe out of the floor and Casey centered himself.

Balls of your feet, balance.

Out of the corner of his eye, he saw Dad and Mom holding off Jen Tompkins. Slashing and jabbing, she'd hemmed them in. His parents looked furious, but Casey knew the stalemate couldn't last. Pierce had taken Chroamwell off guard but now the boy was being beaten back, step by step, to the front door. The assassin's swords wove a net Robert's spear couldn't cut through.

Matt's axe bit into the dining room table, scattering splinters as Casey dove away. Stuck between the table and the counter, he could only move in one direction. He retreated before Rhiannon could split him from head to toe.

With a grinding crash, the deck doors shattered. Glass shards bit into Casey's back.

"Give me the big one," Kawkazi yelled.

Casey got a glimpse of his angry face as he lunged past. Through the jagged gap, an unmoving scaly shadow seemed to cover half the deck. Casey felt a surge of energy. Now the odds were changing.

"Make room, Pierce!" the Crow roared, but his voice sounded choked. He stumbled against the wall, pushed off, and came at Chroamwell.

Oh no, Casey thought. The odds aren't better after all.

Rhiannon smiled and Casey wondered how he'd never noticed the cruel twist in his lips. Then without warning, a spear blade split the air by Matt's head. Shock washed over his face.

"Let's see if you're on my level," Robert snarled. "Get Gloria!" he yelled at Casey.

Gloria. Casey started for the stairway.

But Jen had cornered his parents on the bottom stair. Only Mom's long scythe-staff was keeping her at bay. Casey ran across the splintered, glass-covered floor. By the time Jen saw him coming, it was too late. His shoulder sent her flying. She crashed to the floor but didn't let go of her trident. Her eyes burned like torches.

"Hit me from behind, will you?"

In the foyer The Crow sagged against a wall. He deflected Chroamwell's blows with the last of his strength.

"Dad, help Kawkazi," Casey gasped. "Mom, get Gloria out of here."

Clutching her scythe-staff, Mom ran up the stairs.

Dad flew at Chroamwell, who was standing over The Crow. Kawkazi's eyes were only half open. He slid down the entry wall, leaving streaks of blood. Chroamwell raised both his swords as Dad's elegant Gladius smashed them apart.

Jen stalked toward Casey.

Now he had her full attention—and it just might kill him.

She closed fast, feinting and jabbing. Barbed prongs flashed toward his face. Casey slashed desperately and one of the tines went spinning away. Jen gave a frustrated yell, but her next blow trapped his sword between the last two prongs. She gave her trident a twist and the sword flew from his fingers.

Casey reached but his fingers closed on air.

The Sylvan blade hit the far wall and clanked to the floor.

This was it.

Jen raised her broken trident, eyes flashing, breathing hard.

She leveled it at his throat and drew her elbow back.

Casey wanted to close his eyes but couldn't.

Her face was a mask under streaks of blood.

"I liked you," Casey said.

She paused mid-breath. Something flickered in her eyes.

It seemed like she was about to speak.

Fwoosh!

Jen flew backward in a fiery blast. Eyes stretched open, limbs flailing, she hit the far wall and crumpled to the floor. Her trident spun in a lazy circle, clanking across his sword.

Casey put his hands to his ears. Flames licked the floorboards at his feet. All he could hear was his heart, pounding wildly. The floor in front of him was a blackened circle.

A hand slapped his face. "Wake up!"

He turned, and Luci came into focus. Yells and crashing flooded his ears.

"I prepped one more Campfire Inferno," she shouted. "If we can get your dad away from Chroamwell..." Her hand flew to her mouth.

The Crow was down, stretched in a pool of blood.

That left only Dad, facing the assassin.

Flames flickered along the walls.

Near the shattered glass doors, Robert traded blows with Matt in a furious, intricate dance. "I'm coming!" he yelled. "Give me a minute." He'd thrown down his spear in favor of a longsword but showed no signs of breaking away.

Standing over the fallen Crow, Dad wielded the Gladius far better than Casey could've hoped, cutting and parrying with a vengeance. One edge of the sword was red. But Chroamwell had two swords and he was equally good with both. The assassin's eyes lit up. One of his blades caught Dad in the ribs.

No, no, that can't happen. Casey tore the dagger from his pocket and lunged forward but Luci grabbed his shoulder. "Casey, no!"

The assassin slashed again.

Dad slumped to the floor, his Gladius hitting the tiles.

Casey struggled to free himself. "Over here!" he shouted.

The assassin's head swerved hawkishly.

Casey threw the dagger through the smoky air. His practice in OPOW hadn't been wasted. The blade should've skewered Chroamwell's chest. Instead, the assassin snatched it and sent it hurtling back. The knife grazed Casey's shoulder and quivered in the wall.

"Now run!" Luci whispered. Her eyes swirled with green flame.

"Not without you." He grabbed her arm and yanked.

Chroamwell was halfway across the room when they turned and fled. Away from Robert, away from Dad...up the stairs. The second story was filling with smoke. Surely Mom and Gloria had escaped. Casey couldn't let himself believe they'd be here now.

He and Luci rushed down the hall and into his room. He gripped the 127-Spiker as she opened the window and gulped fresh air. Her hair swirled and darted, coming to life. She raised one arm shakily, poised to throw her Campfire Inferno. "When he comes in I'll–"

Chroamwell bounded through the door like a panther.

Luci's arm shot forward, but the assassin was already airborne.

The inferno burst under his feet.

His next blow was too fast for Casey to follow.

Luci flew against the wall and collapsed, her body too loose, the light in her eyes fading. The carpet snapped and crackled in an expanding ring of fire. Chroamwell towered over Casey, lit from behind like a nightmare.

Casey adjusted his grip on the mace.

The assassin moved closer—and Casey swung.

"I hate you!" he yelled.

Chroamwell knocked the 127-Spiker away like a feather. The thorny head hit the wall and stuck. Casey shielded his face from what was coming. If only he'd been better prepared. If only he was stronger.

The assassin flung his arms high in triumph. "I come with FIRE!" he announced—and laughed. His swords glittered as he let them fall, hissing in the flames.

Casey couldn't reach his throwing star but it wouldn't make a difference. Nothing could make a difference now. He stretched a hand out the window, brushing leaves and twigs. *If only I could reach your world.* Dry, clean bark touched his bloody knuckles.

"Goodbye," Casey whispered.

Chroamwell swept a dagger from his belt. The blade pricked Casey's throat.

"Blood and sand," Chroamwell whispered. "In the name of the Jabberwocky, I send you ahead into the darkness."

Something took Casey's arm. Rough, dry, incredibly strong—and yanked.

CHAPTER 55
LIVE OR DIE

GLASS SHATTERED. THE DAGGER scraped across Casey's clavicle as he flew out the window. He hung over the roof, feet kicking. The oak had wrapped a branch around him like a fist. Wood gripped him firmly but with care.

Now Chroamwell was on the roof, lurching over the slanting shingles. Not a trace of the sophisticated professor was left. Clothing in shreds, eyes gleaming, he'd become an animal.

"This is why I hate magic," he snarled.

Smoke drifted in Casey's eyes and nose. His mouth swam with the coppery taste of blood. He put his free hand on the oak that guarded his house. Words crawled over his teeth as Chroamwell's wolfish eyes found his.

"Save me," Casey said.

The tree groaned.

Chroamwell raised his dagger.

Tree limbs swept down like giant hands. The assassin tried to dodge but the oak caught him and flung him away with a thunderous *crack*. His hoarse shriek hung in the air, fading to a thin wail. Far off, something crashed into the woods.

Casey's heart knocked against his ribs, trying to get out.

His feet grazed the roof. He stood on the shingles.

Gently, the tree lifted away. The little oak bent close over his house, protecting it or maybe leaning on it for support. The rooftop became a forest. Leaves fluttered against his skin, checking how badly he was hurt.

"I'll never be able to thank you enough," Casey whispered.

His stomach felt dark and raw, a swirling angry hole. Smoke streamed from his shattered window. Through his sneakers, he could feel the heat of the roof.

Luci. Dad. Robert and The Crow.

Casey dove back through the window, glass skinning his knees and elbows. His bed was on fire, carpet blazing, flames crawling up the walls. The smoke blinded him and he dropped to the floor, feeling his way along until his hand brushed wavy hair. He found Luci's shoulder.

"Wake up Luci!"

She coughed as he shook her but didn't move.

He pulled her toward the window where rushing smoke left a patch of cooler air. Casey took a final breath, fumes burning his throat, and bent to lift her. Fire snapped at his heels. Cradling Luci, he shoved her through the shattered glass. Her head and shoulders lolled on the shingles, then her back. Her knees flopped onto the roof and he threw himself after her, slapping at his socks and shoes, the back of his shirt.

The leaves of the oak closed around them, smothering the flames.

Luci rolled onto her side. Her body jerked as she coughed, eyelids flickering.

"Be right back, Luci." *Take care of her*, he told the tree.

Through the window, his bedroom was a furnace. His throat seized up and his hair began to curl. But he had to get back in, he had to, because *Dad*. He scrambled down the roof and crouched on the edge.

"Don't jump, Grimes!"

His streaming eyes took a second to focus. A dark figure waved from below.

"Ok, *now* I'm ready," Robert yelled. "I'll catch you—and I got your dad out!"

The silence went on longer than it should have as Casey struggled to make sense of Pierce's words. Dad was out in the cool night air. But wait—Luci!

Tar bubbled under Casey's feet as he whirled to pry her off the burning roof. The side of her face had been pressed against the shingles. But he was too late. The place where she'd been resting was a blackened, fiery hole.

CHAPTER 56
TRIAGE

CASEY RUBBED HIS SOOTY EYES. "NO," he breathed. "No, no..."

The little oak gave a shuddering groan. Rough wooden arms bent to Casey, lifting him away as the housetop became a bonfire.

"Hell's bells!" Robert said.

Tears steamed on Casey's face. A breeze rushed over him, then his feet pressed earth. He collapsed in the grass, yanking off his melted shoes and smoking socks. His toes were already blistering.

"Get the t-shirt too," Robert said.

Casey grabbed his collar and yanked. The cotton smoldered with sparks. Behind him came a thunderous *CRACK* as the oak split down the middle. Half the tree collapsed on the burning roof. The other half sagged lower and lower until its leaves brushed Casey's shoulders.

"I'm sorry," he whispered to the dying tree.

"I've never seen anything like that." Robert sounded shocked.

"Where's Dad?" Casey said.

"Out front, safe." Robert pulled his eyes away from the oak. "Let's move Luci first—didn't even know she was here."

"What?"

"She's too close to the house."

"What?"

It took Casey a while to find her with his gritty eyes. Luci lay in the grass a few yards away. Her shoulders quivered and she sighed.

"She's alive," Casey whispered. "Robert, she's alive!" He stretched a hand toward Luci, got to his feet and stumbled toward Pierce. "Thank you, Robert, thank you."

"Whoa, man, it wasn't me. I found her lying there, so it must've been—ah, ok."

Robert carefully returned Casey's hug.

The stars were out, Casey noticed, high above his burning house. The constellations were dancing right and left. Swimming in circles. His knees gave way. Cool grass touched his painful back—*hush, hush.* The stars dissolved. The fire faded. He heard a voice that sounded like Gloria, small and wet with tears, and then the world went black.

†

"Ouch." Casey opened his eyes unwillingly. Someone was jabbing the bottom of his foot over and over. It felt insulting.

"I'd appreciate it," Nurse Diaz said, "if you'd stop injuring yourself so far away from Trickery. It puts extra pressure on the medical staff."

Sadness weighed down her professional tone.

"Sorry." He half-closed his eyes against the overhead lamp.

"Don't worry about it, baby. Bones may want to talk to you about the costs of emergency gryphon flights, though." She sprayed his feet with something that smarted.

"Ouch," he said again.

"All in all, very lucky." Diaz brushed her gloved hands together, stepping back. "First and second degree burns, none on your face. Forty-six stitches, none on your face. Momma's gonna be very happy."

"Wow," Casey said.

"Wish everyone were so lucky." Nurse Diaz pushed the lamp away. "Get up slowly and put on those sterile slippers." She took in his expression. "Price you pay for dancing on a burning roof." She took his elbow and helped him into the long, bright hall. She'd wrapped his feet in gauze, but even through the padded slippers, he winced his way along.

"Hold still while I get you a wheelchair," Diaz said.

But he didn't feel like waiting.

There was a little burst of applause as he stepped into the waiting room.

"Yeah, Grimes! Casey! My baby boy!"

Mom and Gloria were the quickest to their feet, rushing over to hug him. Dad stood up stiffly, a hand pressed to his side. The bandage wrapped around his head didn't keep him from grinning. Robert pushed off from the arms of his chair with an effort. It was the first time Casey'd seen him limp.

Mr. and Mrs. West stood up, clapping. Luci was curled up in an armchair next to them. One arm in a cast, her face bruised. But she was smiling too.

A shadow swirled in the doorway and Crake stepped forward crookedly. The fire-lit room became a secret council. A black cloth wrapped her throat, higher and tighter than a scarf.

"I'll keep this short," she said. "First, let's all congratulate ourselves on surviving the night. Special thanks to Robert—and Kawkazi."

Robert studied the floor.

Crake darted a look across the room. "Second, please accept my apologies. Despite the precautions we took, I was a step behind, and the cost was high. Unacceptably high. I thought more Sylvans would have our backs." She hung her head. "I was naive—and I know things won't ever be the same." She fingered the dark cloth at her neck. "I hope you can...forgive me."

Dad nodded.

"Yes," Mom said.

Mr. and Mrs. West inclined their heads.

Crake's uneven shoulders drooped. "There will be protocols to follow, a public statement. But I want you to know that I will not rest until we have an explanation." She paused, a hand on the door-knob. "In a few days or a week...I'll disappear. Something I've got to do, something I've put off far too long. I'm telling you now in case— well, in case you—might worry." She looked down at her shoes. "Goodnight."

The door swayed on its hinges.

Mom sighed. "Poor young lady."

Yes, Casey thought.

Then he realized he was still standing. It wasn't something he was used to thinking about. Getting off his feet and into a bed was suddenly the most important thing in the world.

CHAPTER 51
BENEFITS OF MELTED FEET

I CAN'T BELIEVE MY HOUSE IS GONE," Casey said.

Curled up on the Wests' window seat, his feet felt hot and itchy under their bandages. They'd made squishing sounds when he hobbled downstairs. Sleep had smoothed away his rage and shock, leaving him off balance. In the afternoon light, he felt like fire ants were crawling over his body, crowding his ankles, pricking his soles. He had to keep telling himself not to slap his burns.

"I'm really sorry," Luci said.

Slumped on the other side of the great room window, she showed little interest in moving either. Nurse Diaz had told her to take it easy after her concussion, and she wasn't arguing. On top of her broken arm, she had bruises from Chroamwell and stitches from Casey's shattered window. He wished he could've shoved her out more gently.

"I can't imagine how I would feel if..."

Luci trailed off, and Casey nodded to show he understood. No good reason to finish the sentence. He'd forced himself to get up for Sunday brunch, and the images kept right on coming, whenever the conversation faltered. The Murklurker's reptilian face. Kawkazi in a pool of blood. Dad going down. Luci on the burning roof. The little oak, dying to save him.

Burnt to ash overnight, Robert had told them. Including the house. And the bodies. Casey didn't want to think about that. "All my Trickery books," he said. "All my normal books. All my clothes. My favorite chair...my sword. Robert's mace, your scythe-staff..."

Luci lifted her head a half inch off the window frame. "Not that it will make you feel a whole lot better, but don't be so sure about the weapons. Maybe we'll find them in the wreckage."

Casey was quiet. "Maybe so."

He'd never imagined it was possible to fall asleep with your face smushed against a pane of glass, but when he woke up an hour later, he'd proved it. He heard voices upstairs, Mom, Dad and Gloria coming in from the treeway.

They tromped down into the vaulted great room, Dad with a hand on his side. Mr. and Mrs. West called hello from the kitchen. Casey's family looked exhausted except for Gloria, who gave him a thumbs-up and a smile.

Dad eased himself into an armchair. "How are you, son?"

"I'm...worn out," Casey said.

Luci appeared from the kitchen, sipping a mug of something hot and moving like she was on a tightrope.

"We were talking with the UWA liaison." Mom crinkled her eyebrows and Casey knew she was trying to remember the acronym. *Unified Wilderness Alliance.*

Casey got Luci's attention and made a drink-drink motion. She rolled her eyes and disappeared again in slow-mo. He felt a little bad, but hey, his feet *were* squishy.

"The liaison wasn't much fun," Dad said. "But with Ms. Crake backing us up, we got some things done."

"Like a forest scooter," Gloria said proudly.

"A what?"

"Kind of a military-grade Segway," Dad said. "Less dumb-looking though. Mr. Bones said WheelWraiths handle any terrain, although he doesn't trust 'em himself."

"He doesn't have melted feet," Mom pointed out.

"I didn't know Sylvan Woods allowed technology," Casey said.

"We have plenty of tech." Luci shuffled forward like someone who would spontaneously combust if she moved faster than a snail. "Just low key and local. We like to deploy it when needed instead of gluing it to our faces."

She pushed the mug into Casey's fingers. "How do you think we craft our weapons—tin foil and lucky guesses? Those WheelWraiths seem really cool. I've never had a good enough reason to sign one out, although I tried once, when I got a bad ankle sprain."

This was good. She was starting to sound more like herself.

The world felt a little less choppy and weird.

"But that's not the best part." Mom sat down next to Casey, hands in the pockets of her gray-blue hoody. The way she looked, it was hard to believe there *was* a best part. A weird part, maybe. A hard-to-believe part. Her eyes looked strained, like they were struggling to shrink back to normal size. "Should we tell him?" she asked Dad.

Dad leaned forward. "He doesn't look great. Maybe we should wait until–"

"We're moving to Sylvan Woods!" Gloria shrieked.

"What?" Casey looked from face to face.

"Yeah, that's right." Dad ran a hand across his ribs and pointed to his bandaged head. "At first we thought we'd had enough–"

"But when we met with Ms. Crake–" Mom said.

"We didn't say what we planned."

"It was weird," Mom whispered.

"Yes, it was." Dad took her hand. "But what happened last night and before that, what we did—you and Gloria and Mom and me— each of us, in our own way...we fought for our right to stay here."

"And we won." Mom sounded amazed.

"So we're staying." A tired smile worked across Dad's face. "You can't walk away from something you earned. Something you fought for, that you deserve to keep. But we'll stay on our own terms, no more being caught off guard. No more hoping for the best."

Casey couldn't believe it.

"Yeesss." Luci gently pumped her fist. "Now things will be better than ever. I mean...better than we thought they'd be...before school started..."

Casey took a sip of hot chocolate and closed his eyes. Mom put a hand on his shoulder, careful not to press his burns. "We're moving, honey. Leaving the Civilian world behind."

He felt tears on his face and held still, hoping no one else would notice.

But Casey heard the choky sound in Dad's voice when he said:

"High time, even if our house hadn't burned down. There's no feasting out there, no adventure."

"No real neighbors," Mom said.

"You can't sit on the edge forever," Dad said. "Waiting for something to happen."

"Isn't it wonderful?" Gloria nudged him.

When Casey gave up and opened his eyes, wiping his face, he noticed she was crying too. Crying and smiling. And so was Mom. And Dad. And Luci.

So it couldn't be all bad.

Mrs. West appeared and passed around a box of Kleenex.

"We're so glad," she said.

"You're most welcome." Mr. West put an arm around his wife's shoulder as she started sniffling. "Hey, this is contagious," he said, and took a tissue.

"What—happens next?" Casey managed to say.

"Ahem, the full treatment," Dad said, "Citizenship, relocation assistance, everything—but not official for a while. Remember how long it took them to sort out you and Gloria? I guess Mom and I were sort of tolerated as a favor, how awkward. But now we get remedial weapons training–"

"Although *he's* a natural," Mom said.

"*You're* the natural."

It was great to see them smile.

"This is so exciting." Luci dabbed her eyes.

"Yeah," Casey said. "I can't believe it's happening."

And then, without meaning to, he fell asleep.

CHAPTER 58
HELLOS AND GOODBYES

THE NEXT SEVERAL DAYS PASSED IN A flurry of Important Talks, careful rides on the Wheel Wraith and naps at the Trickery Guest Lodge. Robert and Luci came around when they could.

At first, Casey wondered how he'd get to class and keep up with his homework, but he soon realized how ridiculous that was. Taking a shower without shredding his scabs was a big enough challenge. Still, he worried about flunking out while he was napping or coasting down the residential trails of Sylvan Woods.

"Get a grip, Grimes," Ms. Crake told him when he mentioned his concerns. "Classwork is important but it won't be a problem. Not for a little-bit-lucky war hero like you." She stopped scribbling messages and looked up from her ebony desk long enough to give him a smile.

One afternoon that first week, he woke up on the picnic blanket where he'd fallen asleep. The combination of cool air, green-gold sunlight and lunch had been just right. The turf under the quilt felt good against his tender back.

Luci stared at him, frowning, as Gloria and his parents played a game of wiffle-bear. Gloria's giggles and the smack of the bat against the bear's plastic cranium rang through the clearing. The mushrooms surrounding the magical place were taller now than when Casey'd accidentally found them on Assessment Day.

"Did the oak by your house really come to life?" Luci watched him carefully.

He had the feeling he was being judged.

"Yes." Casey sat up slowly. "Yes it did."

"I could've sworn Robert was joking."

"Nope."

"I've never heard of anything like that. Of course, not many people even *try* to communicate with trees..."

"They're missing out."

"Yeah." Luci furrowed her brow. "Well, it wouldn't matter if they did. I just asked that willow to smack the back of your head and it didn't move an inch."

"Guess I'm special."

She smiled. "Oh, you're definitely that. By the way—did you ever figure out what I meant about invisa-fade, that day in the cafeteria?"

One of the weird things about Luci: When she asked you a question, she always seemed to know that *you* knew exactly what she was talking about before she even asked. Or maybe it was just him. Maybe she had his number.

Casey tried not to shiver. "Yeah," he said. "I've had a lot of time to think about it."

"And?" Luci said.

"If my house hadn't been accidentally treated with invisa-fade..."

"Yes?"

"I wouldn't have been invisible outside Sylvan Woods. So I would've stayed home. I never would've crossed the border and met you and fought monsters or done any of the other crazy things I did."

"Good job." She smiled, touching her thumb and index fingers together. "Took you awhile, but you got there."

Casey rolled his eyes.

"Makes you feel a little different, doesn't it?"

She already knew what he was going to say. Of course she did.

He nodded...and tried not to shiver.

†

He saw Ms. Crake a final time, in a sheltered cul-de-sac on a Sylvan Watch trail. Robert escorted him, walking ahead and to the right. He kept shooting looks over his shoulder, like Casey was going to lose control of the WheelWraith and run him down with its spiky treads. Casey thumbed the joystick. He was tempted to give it a try, but if he squashed Robert, he'd never find the meeting place.

"The assassins went all-out and failed." Crake limped in a circle of flattened brush. "That makes the eradication plot clear as writing on a cliff face. We'll make sure it's public knowledge, so there's no advantage in another attempt on your life—or Gloria's or mine. At least not for a while."

Her slender fingers clutched the dagger at her waist. "I'm bringing people in, professionals with proven magical track records." She sighed. "This would be so much easier if I had a—a wider circle of friends." She looked away, off into the trees, and Casey wanted to say something but the moment passed.

"It will be good to have you in the Woods, Grimes. Easier to keep an eye on." Crake studied him. "Listen to Robert. Go back to class when you're ready. And do one thing for me—make a basic report to Ms. Strick. She's a thorn in the hide, but we need to play the long game."

Casey nodded and shot Robert a confused look.

"I guess this is goodbye." Crake drew a long, deep breath. Her cloak swirled as she turned to leave. Then she pivoted, soundless like a phantom. Casey's nerves tingled. Her fingertips brushed the small of his back. A wisp of white-gold hair feathered his ear. She was even worse at hugs than Robert, which was saying a lot.

And then she really did disappear.

†

Robert came over one night to play cards on the guest lodge's long, polished veranda. He brought along a game called Bander-snatch. "It's a variation on that classic, Slapjack."

"I didn't know you liked fun!" Gloria squealed.

Figures, Casey thought. Pierce was probably a fan of Clubs as well.

"We can play Bandersnatch after we play Uno!" Gloria said generously.

"Sounds good, Glo."

They'd avoided talking about the fire. No one seemed eager to discuss it, not even Gloria, and Casey was grateful. A corpse in the woods. Blackened bones in the ashes. There could've easily been more. His heart hurt when he thought about it.

Luckily, they were having a games night.

Casey'd never seen Robert play a game unless you counted fisticuffs. He kept waiting for some kind of punchline. At the same time, a memory tugged the corner of his mind, something he couldn't quite put a finger on.

Seated at a split-log table, they played several rounds of Uno! Gloria kept winning, giggling and squealing, even though Robert was ruthless with his wild cards. Then Casey remembered.

"Jabberwocky," he said.

"The word is 'Uno,'" Gloria said.

"And you have a full hand." Robert flicked them.

"No." Casey put his cards down. "It's something Chroamwell said, 'in the name of the Jabberwocky.' I should've told Ms. Crake. He said some other things too..."

Robert nodded slowly. "I can send her a message. Who knows, maybe it's important."

Casey thought about it. Chroamwell had mentioned the Jabber-wocky just before he'd tried to shove a knife through Casey's throat, so maybe it *was* important.

"She's doing her best, you know," Robert said.

"Ms. Crake *is* the best," Gloria said.

"I know," Casey said. "Remember, I liked her first."

"True." Robert held up a finger. "But that was before I knew her origin story. Anyone who crawls into Sylvan Woods half-dead and makes a name for herself has my respect."

"Oh, so that's what happened?" Casey said.

Robert froze. His eyes sailed off across the porch and into the deep woods. It was the Pierce version of extreme embarrassment. "I thought you knew."

"Don't worry," Casey said. "I won't tell anyone."

Robert sighed. "Bandersnatch? I'm getting tired of losing. Here, I'll deal."

†

A day later, Casey discovered Crake had appointed someone to oversee Trickery in her absence. Apparently an Acting Headmaster was a kind of large-scale babysitter.

"Bones introduced her at lunch, along with some other new faces." Luci pushed back her rocking chair on the veranda. "I couldn't believe what I was seeing. I mean..." She put a hand to the side of her face, her eyes happy and far away. "We almost argued once—and she's kind of a big deal."

Casey could've pointed out Luci'd *almost argued* with everyone she'd ever met. Instead he leaned forward. "Ms. Jones, you're sure? The world's most highly qualified traveling babysitter?"

He'd never forget Ms. Jones. Not only had she cleaned the invisa-fade from their air ducts, ending his mostly-invisibility in the Civilian world—she'd done something even more unbelievable. She'd helped him and Gloria sneak into Sylvan Woods.

"There's no mistaking her, is there?" Luci said. "Not with those magnifying glasses for eyes, and that deceptively bland face. She's a pro all right. I get the idea babysitting isn't exactly what she does.

Her security clearance has gotta be off the charts. Reading the invisible ink, I'd say she oversees border safety. She must have had a *blast* at your place...oh."

Casey ate an apple slice to disguise the awkward silence.

"She'd better come say hi," Gloria said.

"No kidding," Casey said.

CHAPTER 59
THE DANGEROUS GAME

ONE OF THE FIRST THINGS MS. JONES did was hold a day-long memorial for The Crow. Everyone dressed in black and crowded inside the Great Hall as the Acting Headmaster read a statement. She looked small and strong on the faraway stage. Gasps and whispers filled the hall as people heard the official story.

"To our great disappointment," Ms. Jones said, "The origin of his silver hand will always be a mystery, but the nature of his heart, strong and brave and rare as diamond, is now as clear as a bright sunrise."

Robert passed a hand across his face. "Ms. Crake asked Jones to hold the memorial after she left," he said. "She didn't trust herself to do it."

Casey understood. As Ms. Jones' last words rang out, he shook hands with Robert and glided away on the WheelWraith before the crowds could swallow him.

But he couldn't outrun the sorrow.

†

Towards the end of the week, he met Jake McGusty at the *Trickery Times* office. On the eastern edge of campus, the modern-looking building stood inside the ruins of a former mansion or small castle.

Casey stopped to admire it after he chained the WheelWraith to a tree. A green terra cotta roof capped the gaping walls. Where the ancient stone had crumbled away, plate glass seamlessly filled the cracks. He could see Jake waving from the second story, timber ceiling glowing overhead.

Casey shook his head. People said you got tired of everything eventually. It was hard to believe he'd ever get tired of Sylvan architecture.

"Bootman." Jake gave him a warm handshake. His energy was back, along with the pencil stuck in his high-flying hair. "Just as I'm getting better, you go down—like a messed up game of tag-team combat. You got the better of yours though. Can't say I'm surprised, man."

Casey smiled back.

"No worries, we don't need to talk about that stuff right now. Crake told me to give you space, not that I wouldn't, although, if there's something burning a hole in your gut..." He gave Casey a second, waving him to a round birch table. "At least I was able to tip you off about Chroamwell, not that it *needs* to be in the full-length story, but it makes for a nice dramatic detail, doncha think?"

"Yeah." Casey still felt terrible about it. He didn't have the heart to tell Jake he'd totally blown the clue. Who knew what might've changed if he hadn't been so sure Kawkazi was the assassin? Maybe The Crow would still be with them. Maybe they would've got the jump on Chroamwell.

"Anyway, your feature story is ready to go. Or mostly ready. I'll have to update it with the pertinent details, but take a look."

Jake slid a mock-up across the table. "There's even a sidebar on Fiera Laurent. When I pressed her after the Assassin Inferno—sorry, that's what everyone's calling it—she saw the writing on the wall and spilled her guts. Guess who her sources were? Sebastian Drooce and, wait for it—her uncle."

Casey looked up.

"Old Knock's last name is Laurent." Jake looked smug.

"That's...crazy," Casey said absently. He was stuck on the story's headline.

A CIVILIAN IN A MILLION: THE TRUE CASEY GRIMES STORY

He had to read it a dozen times before he could move to the opening paragraph. Little birds fluttered in his stomach. They took flight, spiraling upward. A flock of little birds, soaring, chirping. Casey ran a finger along his cheekbone, one then the other.

"Um, why don't you take it with you." Jake moved off to one side and gave Casey's shoulder a punch. "You've been through a lot. Just happy to see some justice for you, Grimes."

"Thanks Jake," Casey managed to say.

McGusty gave him a grin and they shook again on the way out.

"Stay cool, Bootman."

Casey moved down the stairs as fast as he could with his hurting feet. He was out in the afternoon sun again before he really started crying.

†

True to Ms. Crake's final request, Casey searched out Ms. Strick, the UWA liaison. He found he didn't like her office much. Maybe it wasn't the office's fault.

The windows were shut, silencing the sounds of the Trident Garden and Splash Fountain. The curtains were drawn, shelves mostly bare. No plants, no books, no weapons (visible, anyhow), no color at all, except a slash of red lipstick that cut Strick's face in half. A huge computer monitor and a tiny keyboard were the only items on her beige metal desk.

"Ms. Crake asked me to come by," Casey said. "I'm Casey Grimes."

"Very good." Strick moved her mouth in what might be considered a smile if your face was frozen. Her fingernails gleamed red in the low light as she raised her hands to the keyboard. "I'll take your report."

"What kind?" Casey eyed the dusty chair in front of her desk.

"I'm sure I don't know, dear. Whatever you want to complain to the UWA about."

He decided to remain standing. "Maybe you've heard, someone tried to kill me. And my family. And Ms. Crake. It was all connected."

She flicked a few keys. "Sometimes our interactions with others take on a somber tone."

Casey frowned. "It started with lies and threats. Once the assassins decided no one would believe me anymore, and I couldn't fight back, they moved in."

"Peer learning can be *so* challenging." Strick patted her dyed-red hair and put her head on one side. "Thank you for sharing your perspective, Casey. You can be sure it will be passed on for consideration."

Casey stared at her. She didn't seem stupid. It was like they were both using English and speaking different languages at the same time.

"You don't understand." He put his hands down on her desk, harder than he meant to. "My house burnt down. People died—the assassins and The Crow, Mr. Kawkazi. And do you know why?"

Ms. Strick seemed mildly interested, as if he'd said there was skrabbit for lunch.

"It happened because of magic."

She winced, folding her hands.

"Do you understand?"

"All perspectives are given equal weight." Ms. Strick slid a desk drawer open. "I have the gist of your complaint. Threats, unpleasantness, physical assault." She uncapped her lipstick and refreshed her mouth.

"No," Casey said. "*No*. It wasn't some big accident. People died because other people hate magic—important people, powerful ones. Whoever was behind this didn't just hate me, they hated what I stand for." He felt like he was pleading. "My nickname is Mister Magic. Get it?"

She nodded and he felt a flash of relief.

"The UWA welcomes a diversity of perspectives," she said.

Casey narrowed his eyes.

"Magic is outdated and divisive, however," she said pleasantly. "It will not be *officially* noted in my report, although I appreciate your version of events *very* deeply. Good afternoon, Mr. Grimes." She smiled at his forehead and bent over her keyboard.

Casey took a last look around the dim, dry office. He was halfway down the hall, moving slowly, when he stopped. Turning, he stumbled back to the doorway. Ms. Strick did not look up. Casey clenched the knob and slammed the door. He stood there, breathing hard.

You can't get back here soon enough, Ms. Crake, he thought.

†

It was a good thing Ms. Jones came to dinner because he was about to lose it.

"Did you tell her people died?" Dad set down his fork.

"Maybe if I went over for a word..." Mom said.

Casey was about to throw his plate of spaghetti at the wall when someone knocked on the front door of their apartment.

Gloria ran to open it. "Ms. Jones," she gasped, "you came back!"

In moments, the famous traveling babysitter and Acting Headmaster had accepted a seat at the table and a glass of wine, eyes twinkling behind her spectacles.

"It's so wonderful to see you all again, dears."

If anything, she looked nicer and more mild than ever, gray hair pulled back in a professional ponytail. Casey had never seen someone eat spaghetti so neatly.

"I've heard about what happened." A shadow passed over her face. "When I helped you into Trickery, I hoped you'd find a place in Sylvan Woods, but I never expected you'd have to experience anything so dreadful."

"You're more than just a babysitter." Dad pointed his fork at her accusingly.

She blinked. "True, but let me assure you, I take the babysitting aspect of my vocation very seriously."

"Ms. Jones." Casey felt oddly hopeful. "You're here to sort things out, right? It's what you do, what you're good at. Because when I went to talk with Ms. Strick..."

Jones' eyes were soft. "Things will take their course, dear. Strick will regret her game, but we have to play along for now."

"Then she knows what she's doing?"

Her pupils sharpened to points. "Of course she knows, dear boy. She knows exactly how you feel, which is how she wants you to feel, how her employers want you to feel. Recognized into irrelevance. Confused into complacency." Ms. Jones set down her fork.

"Stay clear-headed, even if it makes you angry. The Unified Wilderness Alliance is a vast apparatus. Ms. Strick is a cog in a bad part of the machine. For now, we must tolerate her—even as we work to replace her." Ms. Jones twisted a forkful of spaghetti so aggressively that a spot of sauce plinked the table.

Her face brightened. "You have no idea what a treat it is to see you again, each one of you. And just so you know, in my capacity as Headmaster of the Moment, I've had some delightful conversations with your teachers, Casey." She winked. "Especially Ms. Steele. You'll be welcomed back with open arms—or at least a clean record, when you return."

Ever since Casey'd met Ms. Jones, she'd had a knack for making him feel better. Not by saying everything would be ok, quite the opposite. By pointing out how bad things really were, she helped him feel on point again. She paid such close attention that every time she opened her mouth, she said things most people wouldn't dare say. Things that were just right.

Casey felt very grateful.

†

Two weeks after his house burned to the ground, Casey rode the WheelWraith back. He stood on the slim, self-balancing platform between the two huge, dangerous-looking wheels. The joystick steering and acceleration took some getting used to, but Casey was quite good by now. He flashed along the edges of Trickery so he wouldn't run anyone down.

Robert was already in Casey's old yard when he arrived. The dangerous boy held up a notched and blackened battle-axe. "Handle didn't melt, good sign."

Casey stepped off the Wraith, dropping the semi-rigid control cord. The debris-filled lot felt like a place he'd never been. A rectangular blackened heap had replaced his house. He could look straight into Vintage Woods across the wreckage, onto his old street. The yard no longer felt like the edge of a mighty, ancient wood.

The small oak that had shaded his bedroom was a charred and twisted trunk. Running his eyes over what was left of the yard, he remembered aerating the grass with Ms. Jones' ice crampons.

Other memories from his home seemed to have happened in a different place. Mostly he remembered being tugged away into the woods. The horrible year at Vintage Woods Middle School. That final day of misery, when the Old Oak had risen from the gloom and coaxed him into the deep, dark forest.

He ducked under a long, fluttering ribbon of crime scene tape.

"I guess you got the better of that battle axe," Casey said.

He preferred to think of Matt Rhiannon as a weapon.

"Yeah, finally." Robert tipped the axe into the grass, like the memory made him tired. "He was devilish sticky, made it impossible to break away. Finally, he got overconfident. Or maybe rushed. I thought we'd still be fighting when the roof caved in."

Casey shoved a metal shelf aside. He didn't feel bad for Rhiannon, who had done his best to kill them. But he did feel bad for...

"No parents, if that's what you're thinking," Robert said. "Trust me, someone that vicious had no one."

"That's sad." Despite himself, Casey felt a twinge of sympathy for the fiery, agile kid.

"Yeah, I guess so." Robert shoved more charred wood aside. "Sad and deadly."

"What about–"

"Tompkins? Yeah, her too. Kid assassins, always orphans. Heartless, placeless—kinda how it works."

If Robert noticed Casey's numb expression, he didn't react. "Hey, look."

Something glimmered under a charred ceiling beam.

"Consider yourself lucky," Robert said.

Lucky. Hear that, Grimes, you're lucky.

Casey bent down, shoving and tugging.

The dark, sooty version of his Sylvan Sword slid free.

"Nothing some mineral oil from the Baleful Blade can't fix." Robert rubbed his hands together, nodding briskly.

"Hubba hoy!" Luci emerged from the tree line, eying the Civilian road across the burn site. "How's the search?"

It was strange to see her in Vintage Woods in full daylight. Of course she knew better than to believe in Sylvan traps now, but it had to make her nervous. Robert too, for that matter.

"Thanks for coming," Casey said. "Look." He held up the sword for Luci to see.

"Wonderful." She nodded. "Item A is recovered, let's move on to A1. Where would your bedroom have been? I want my scythe-staff back."

Robert scoffed.

They spent about an hour shoving wreckage, digging through the rubble. Luci gave a little cheer when they found her staff under a pile of blackened bedsprings. Further probing revealed Casey's antique dark lantern. Robert's 127-Spiker was nearby.

Goodbye, old room, Casey thought.

They were covered in sweat and charcoal by the time they unearthed Dad's Gladius and Jen's two-pronged trident.

"No point in keeping that," Luci said.

They never found Robert's spear. "Wasn't my favorite," he said. They didn't find Chroamwell's short swords either. Or Casey's dagger or his throwing star. But they did find a human leg bone, burned sad and black. Casey would never have picked it up, except at first, he thought it was a curved blade, carefully proportioned.

The slender femur fell through his trembling fingers.

Luci stared off across the street, pushing her hair back. She looked a little pale.

"You two had enough?" Robert said from the other side of the lot.

Casey wondered if he ever missed a thing.

Several cars had cruised down the Civilian road over the last hour, but now one slowed and stopped. A siren squawked. Casey appreciated the timing.

Luci gave him a relieved look as a policeman kicked the car door open.

"Get away from that crime scene!"

They were already running for the woods, carrying an arsenal of weapons.

Casey jumped onto the WheelWraith and woke it in one motion. A second later, he was rolling into the shadows of Lesser Trick 'n' Trap, sword gripped in his left hand, lantern knocking his elbow.

He'd never been more grateful for the Wraith's one-handed operation. Robert and Luci jogged ahead, running carefully with their arms full of weapons. Robert looked back to flash a grin, like this was the best feeling in the world.

"What the..." The police officer's words died in the weeds as they sped away.

CHAPTER 60
BACK TO OLD TRICKS

ALL BUT A COUPLE OF CASEY'S BURNS were healed. His deep cuts were scarring. A stack of replacement textbooks from Ms. Jones had arrived at the guest lodge, and he'd started reading them instead of taking naps. He went back to Trickery that week.

From there, the semester bumped and skidded along.

In Optimal Pathways of Weapons, he was still at the top of the class, even after he took the makeup tests. Later Ms. Steele figured out how he was getting so many right answers and made her quizzes less life-like. By then it was too late. He had a handle on the math.

Fiera Laurent went out of her way to avoid being his partner and he didn't force it. Having Old Knock for an uncle would be tough. When they did get paired up, however, Casey gobsmacked her into the guts of the Rondure Arena. Like Gloria would say, "Just because you don't like magic doesn't *mean* you have to be mean."

Nonviolent Magic was canceled, since the class's main theory was a flop, and the teacher was dead—killed by The Craken when he'd tried to cut her throat in her sleep. It was very ironic. Bog Creeps had been caught on camera, doing their business in the obsidian gravel. The entire class was a joke—and a cruel one.

"And we both knew it from day one, didn't we?" Luci said.

To replace Nonviolent Magic, Ms. Jones assigned them a magical library elective with a reading list and report due at the end of the semester. Their first research project was the recipe for Sentry Tree elixir.

Casey picked up where he'd left off in Land Creature Defense but it didn't feel the same. No one screamed "Yay Case! Go!" when he confronted the Hyena Toad. No one made chocolate milk bets and punched his shoulder. He found himself looking around for Jen Tompkins and had to remind himself she'd been a fake. The face he'd seen in his burning house was her real face. Hard, sharp, hungry. She'd been a killer. It was stupid that he missed her.

He still wondered, though. In her final moments, what had she been about to say?

Extreme Climbing was good. Ms. Chantelle was glad to see him. His face quivered, just a little, when she gave him a squeeze and said, "You got this, Grimes." And she was right. He moved the fastest, climbed the highest, and had a knack for treeways. He didn't hesitate when it was time to jump.

Now and then he talked to the trees. He knew they were listening, especially the oaks, but they rarely did what he asked—except when he was really serious. It was hard to be serious when only a grade was on the line. But they'd be there, waiting.

Magical Blasts was his most fun class, once he stopped thinking about the Fireside Infernos Luci had stolen. The peaceful, hidden garden in the limestone island was a perfect spot for screams and explosions. By the time he returned, everyone was wearing fire-retardant suits. Every inch of skin was covered, which made speaking difficult, but as Luci pointed out, nonverbal communication definitely increased.

Horrified gestures: *It's happening! When? Right now!—fwoosh!* Dramatic shrugs: *How in creeps was I supposed to know the fireball would levitate?* Three fingers, then two, then one... *Ka-bloosh!*

The fire suits didn't keep them from laughing themselves sick when their Bouncing Blaze hopped counterclockwise, against their clearly stated wishes, and blew Samantha and Luke across the clearing. Ms. Vaughn had smelling salts and ice packs. It was all in good fun. They didn't laugh quite as hard when Samantha and Luke unleashed a Violet Whoosh that blasted them into a small tree. "Oh well, accidents happen," Ms. Vaughn said.

When she smiled suddenly like that, Ms. Vaughn reminded Casey of Ms. Crake. He hoped, as he often did, that wherever The Craken was, whatever she was doing, she'd return to Trickery ok. He hoped there was someone watching her crooked back.

Futuristic Forestry was haunting for a while because Casey kept seeing Mr. Chroamwell lounging at the desk. Not the dapper, intellectual version, skimming a book over his latte. The wild-eyed killer on the rooftop was the version he remembered. He'd hear the shriek and the sickly crunch as the assassin flew into the night.

Casey imagined him unfurling wings and swooping away like a vampire, even though he knew the broken body lay somewhere in the woods. His oak had made sure of that. When Casey was finally able to focus on the new teacher, a serious young man with a trim goatee, he began to get better grades.

Public Storytelling was a total train wreck for weeks. Casey didn't know anyone and no one seemed interested in knowing him. He struggled to make up a tale that didn't involve dark, fiery places. Finally, he asked Ms. Jones for a special assignment, even though it felt like cheating. He and Jake McGusty met a few times and hammered out a story about the Assassin Inferno. Everything in the story was true, but some of the true parts were left out. He gave Jake permission to print a version with quotes in the *Trickery Times*.

Casey'd thought that maybe with The Crow gone Sebastian Drooce would terrorize Trickery again, but he was wrong. Ms. Jones had no trouble keeping Drooce in check. When Casey and Gloria visited Bones one weekend, he led them into the woods to see the gryphon enclosures, set back safely in the trees. "Look." He pointed. "Cleaner 'an ever before."

Magic Club stopped being Trickery's only official club and started meeting in secret like everyone else. Normal kids began sneaking through the woods to the Magical Toadstool Clearing. They were shocked to find themselves in a herd of nerds. But having come so far, they stuck around for at least one meeting, and Luci and Casey did their best to make everyone comfortable.

As the Club grew, some of the nerds began to change. Chewing with their mouths shut, coordinating their colors, looking people in the face and saying, "Hubba hoy!"

"This is blowing my mind," Luci said. "I guess they just needed to be noticed."

"Everyone deserves a chance," Casey pointed out.

He made it a point to learn kids' names and try to get to know them.

They tested their Sentry Elixir, Batch One, at a club meeting. The elixir worked, sort of. Due to a deployment problem, it caused an enormous Poison Ivy tree to overshadow the clearing, which they later destroyed with an Inward Collapsing Blast.

When Jake's feature story came out, A CIVILIAN IN A MILLION, Casey wished he'd stayed at the guest lodge, because his eyes kept watering. By the end of the day, he'd changed his mind. Trickery felt different. Kids had stopped ignoring him, frowning through him, or talking past him. It was like a bad spell had been lifted and he was real again. Surprise, interest, even regret—that's what he saw on their faces.

It felt better, even though it didn't feel right.

Over Fall Break, he took Robert, Jake, Luci and Gloria on his Treetop Tour of Trickery. It was too gorgeous to keep to himself. Oceans of leaves danced red and gold, a blazing celebration of wood fires, cider and smoked Razor-Wing. Gloria adored the Dance Floor. Jake wanted to print a fold-out map. Robert pretended he hadn't already traveled each treeway, shadowing Casey so assassins couldn't kill him. Luci's favorite spot was the Best for Catching Up With Yourself, and Casey didn't blame her.

And so, improving little by little, with plenty of extreme climbing, stargazing, and failed attempts at humor in Public Storytelling, the semester came to an end.

CHAPTER 61
THE MOST MAGICAL

AS ANOTHER SEMESTER COMES TO A close," Ms. Jones said, "It's time to acknowledge, as we do each year, that *dangerous* is not something one becomes by accident."

In the Great Hall, a hush fell over the packed-in crowd. Kids clenched their arm rests. Parents hid their nervousness by patting their children's heads. Casey's dad and mom were smiling and calm, but they didn't understand what was going on. He leaned forward, even though he knew he had no chance at Trickery's most prestigious trophy.

"Our Most Dangerous Awards are a highlight in the academic year," Ms. Jones said. "It would be more fitting if our own Headmaster, the most dangerous Ms. Crake, was here to give them out. Instead, let's wish her luck in her own risky endeavors, and pray for her safe return." She paused a moment, eyes closed. "And now, m'dears..." Ms. Jones adjusted her metal frame glasses. "The moment you've all been waiting for."

The hall, already quiet, became as silent as a grave.

Or maybe a forbidden glade.

"For outstanding ferocity in the face of great peril, Most Dangerous Boy goes to..." Jones darted her eyes around the hall, dragging out the moment longer than was really tasteful, Casey thought.

"Robert Pierce!"

"Yes! Yeah! Yay Robbie!" screamed Luci, Casey and Gloria.

"Hooray!" shouted the relieved and disappointed crowd.

Robert strode across the stage, allowing himself a fist pump.

"He was waiting stage right," Luci muttered. "Should've known he wasn't going to the bathroom."

"Well done, Mr. Pierce." Ms. Jones clapped Robert on the shoulder, handing him a ceremonial plaque and shiny dagger.

"Crusted with rubies, prolly," Luci said.

"You've proven yourself most dangerous," Ms. Jones said. "At noon and by moonlight, outnumbered and in single combat, your fierceness in defending your friends is unmatched, except by your loyalty and commitment. Trickery applauds you."

Robert inclined his head as Trickery applauded. With feeling.

Ms. Jones pushed her glasses to their proper height. "And now, just as coveted, for outstanding defiance toward all comers, it's my great honor to present—Trickery's Most Dangerous Girl!"

Kids squirmed and feet tapped as everyone fell silent again. Luci bit her lip.

"This year's award goes to...Camille Graham!"

Applause thundered. Luci looked stunned. A curly-haired girl sidestepped, whirled and parried across the stage. Even without a weapon, her footwork was impressive.

"I should've known they'd be notified beforehand," Luci said.

"Well done, Ms. Graham," said the Acting Headmaster. "You've proven yourself most dangerous, shattering records in Aquatic Creature Defense and One-On-Three Combat. Trickery applauds you!" Ms. Jones handed over another plaque and dagger to the smiling girl.

"Topazes on that one." Luci sighed.

"*You're* the most dangerous to me." Gloria tugged Luci's sleeve.

"You're the most hazardous to me, too," Casey said.

Luci's tender smile hardened into dagger eyes.

Chairs scraped the floor as people fumbled for cloaks, jackets and fang-proof vests.

"One more thing before our feast," Ms. Jones called. "This has been a magical semester at Trickery. Some would say the *most* magical, at least in recent memory, although, my goodness, it's been quite bloody, hasn't it? Our decision to reopen the book on magic, so to speak, was the right choice, but it wasn't easy." She polished her glasses. "Well, as the kids say, no cuts no guts no glory."

The kids in the crowd shouted their approval.

"Therefore, for the first time in a century, I present—Trickery's Most Magical."

The cheers ended abruptly.

"Casey and Gloria Grimes, come up here right now!"

Clapping began again, sparked by kids from Magic Club.

"Luciana West, you too!"

Luci looked shocked—again. A smile washed over her face.

"Yay!" Gloria squealed.

Casey found himself grinning.

As they headed down the aisle, the shrieks and awkward clapping from the Magic Club got the rest of the Great Hall on its feet. Gloria hopped and skipped. Luci walked with extra bounce. They reached the stage and Ms. Jones hugged them, beaming. The crowd was really getting into it now, as kids whispered to their parents and people put two and two together.

"CIVILIAN IN A MILLION!" someone yelled.

"GO MISTER MAGIC!"

"YEAH GLORIA! YEAH LUCI!"

Ms. Jones handed them their daggers and plaques. No one else could hear her over the applause when she said, "No one can possibly understand how much you deserve these." She dabbed at her glasses as they left the stage, high-stepping back to their parents.

"Mine's moonstone," Luci whispered. "It's perfect."

"Mine's perfect too," Casey said. "Fiery emeralds."

"I got the shiny purple kind!" Gloria said.

They laughed and gave out fist bumps as people streamed out the doors to the Hall of Feasting, reserved for the most special occasions.

Casey could hardly believe it wasn't a dream.

CHAPTER 62
EVE OF INTRIGUE

A COUPLE DAYS LATER WHEN CASEY got up in the morning, the ground was covered in snow. As he lounged by the front window, Robert Pierce passed The Trickery Guest Lodge, heading down Artemis Way. A minute later, a messenger fox wearing a red bow headed past in the opposite direction. It might have been Woofles, but its ears looked a little small.

"I wonder," Casey said.

He went to the cramped kitchen to find Mom.

A few minutes later, when he pulled on his coat and went outside, he could see his breath, gusting away like silver smoke. The snow crunched under his boots and flurries spiraled down. As expected, he found Robert going through the mail in Ms. Crake's official office on the first floor of Mythic History.

"Hey Grimes, doormat." When he was in The Craken's office, Robert was even more intense than usual. Or maybe just tense. Casey knew Robert worried about their missing headmaster, as he did. No one had expected her to be gone so long.

He wiped his feet. "What are you doing for Christmas, Rob?"

"Oh you know." Robert slit open an envelope with a letter opener that looked like a dagger. No, it *was* a dagger.

"I was wondering if you'd like to come over."

Robert froze with his hand on a decoder ring. "Umm..." He blinked. "I'll run it by my parents. They'll probably have plans, you know."

"Robert." Casey hesitated. "I know you don't have any parents, Robert."

Pierce jumped like someone had kicked him under the desk.

"It's ok, no one told me," Casey said. "Figured it out myself."

Snow whisked against the window.

For the first time Casey could remember, Robert looked taken off guard. His eyebrows hovered like he was plummeting into a bottomless Sylvan trap.

"Think about it." Casey zipped his coat all the way up and left, straightening the doormat on his way out.

†

"Merry night, Grimesies!" Luci sang out.

"Happy Christmas Eve," called her more polite parents.

"Good night, Merry Christmas!" they called back.

The Great Hall's archways were trimmed with evergreen and holly. The hushed interior glowed silver and gold in the candlelight, beautiful enough to take your breath away. And if that hadn't done it, the carols would have. Casey'd never tried to hold a note so long in his life. He grinned, a paper cup of cider warming his gloved hands. The hall hadn't been as packed as usual, Sylvans traveling for the holidays, and he hadn't minded. The smaller crowd had made him feel like they were celebrating a secret. A dark, shining magic that made them smile.

"'Night, Bootman, Pierce."

"Merry Christmas, Jake."

"Yeah, Merry Christmas," Robert said a second late. He wore a tiny sprig of holly at the collar of his long black coat. Other kids wore colorful scarves and hats, green dresses, crimson sweaters. Not the lead coordinator of the Sylvan Watch.

"So Grimes." He cleared his throat. "About tomorrow, I'm not sure–"

"Perfect." Casey waved to some Magic Club kids. "We've been planning on it."

"Planning what?" Robert looked mystified.

Gloria left a circle of her first grade friends and came over. "Merry Christmas, Mr. teeny-tiny holly leaf." She tugged his sleeve. "See you tomorrow for more Christmassing."

Robert smiled helplessly. "How'd you know I–"

"Ready to go, kiddos?" Dad took Mom's arm. "See you tomorrow, Pierce."

"Don't be late, Robert." Mom pressed a red envelope into his palm.

They walked away down the snowy trail. Mom put a hand over her mouth.

"Do you think he'll come?" Dad said.

"He will now," Casey said. "He can't resist intrigue."

They headed down Artemis Way, avoiding the drifts on either side.

"Umm, there's the lodge," Gloria said.

"It's a beautiful night," Dad said. "The stars are out."

"Mercedes West told me the icicles to the east are gorgeous," Mom said.

"I heard there was a frozen Razor-Wing, caught in a tree," Casey said.

"We've *got* to see that," Gloria said.

They crunched along Artemis Way and turned right, down Serpentine Trail, warm in their coats and hats. Mrs. West was right, the icicles in the trees were like carefully-hung blown glass, gleaming in the moonlight.

The Razor-Wing, too dumb to fly south for the winter, had frozen with its enormous wings outspread. Covered in glittering ice, it looked more noble in death than it ever had scaring kids in Lesser Trick 'n' Trap.

"I suppose we should head back," Mom said.

"I can feel the temperature dropping." Dad slapped his gloves together. "Hey, what's that?"

They'd wound away from Serpentine Trail, down one of the quiet side paths. Casey hadn't caught the name on the shadowy signpost. Now they stood in an evergreen clearing, their eyes drawn to a crackling blaze in a stone circle surrounded by benches and stumps. Behind the fire rose the roofline of a Sylvan cabin, a towering upside-down V.

"Picturesque," Mom said.

"Hey, anyone home?" Dad called. When no one answered, he shrugged. "Might as well get a little warmer before we start back."

They stepped to the fire, hands outstretched. The night had taken on a bite. Casey could feel the icy air swirling through his knit hat.

"Ooo, that's more like it." Gloria wriggled her green mittens.

"Don't catch yourself on fire," Dad said. "Kind of weird no one's out here, don't you think?"

Casey shrugged and tossed his empty cider cup into the blaze.

Mom tugged her scarf tighter, looking up at the dark house. "Maybe we should make sure everything's ok."

"Hmm." Dad stopped poking the fire with a stick. "Let's take a look."

"What?" Casey said.

Gloria looked doubtful.

Their parents were already striding toward the darkened home.

Casey and Gloria stared at each other.

"What're they thinking?" Casey braced himself for embarrassment.

Gloria pulled her red and pink hat down over her ears. "It's like we're the grown-ups—and they're the kids!"

They could hear Mom and Dad whispering on the porch. The

front door creaked open. Casey winced, waiting for angry voices. Instead, Mom gasped, and his blood temperature dropped a few degrees.

"Oh no," she said in a small, still voice.

As he and Gloria hurried up the hill, Casey loosened the emerald-studded dagger at his belt. What kind of monster would invade a home in the dead of winter? He took a last look at the stars—*Please let things be ok*—and rushed up the stairs onto the porch. Gloria's forehead crinkled in concern. They burst through the door, clutching their weapons.

"WHO'S THERE?" Casey yelled.

"PUT YOUR CLAWS IN THE AIR!" Gloria shrieked.

Casey searched the dark for movement. As if by magic, light flooded a high, narrow space. He blinked in the brilliance, then his mouth dropped open. The dagger fell from his fingers, just missing his foot, and clunked on a wooden floor.

Evergreen garlands twisted over fieldstone walls. Wreathing weapon racks and coat hooks, they spelled out leafy words:

MERRY CHRISTMAS GRIMESES

Casey turned as Dad's hand fell away from a light switch.

"What? Who?" Casey sputtered.

Gloria pinched herself. "I'm not asleep!" she breathed.

"Can you believe it?" Dad said to Mom. "I guess our plot succeeded, baby. We out-tricked the Trickery students!" He took her hand and let out a joyful whoop.

"Welcome home, Grimeses!" Mom started laughing—and maybe crying a little too.

Casey turned in a dazed circle. "This—can't be—ours?" Then Gloria hugged him so hard her coat buttons dug into his hips, and he knew it was real. And they were jumping up and down, laughter bouncing off the walls and ceilings of their new home.

CHAPTER 63
MOUNTAIN LAKES

CHRISTMAS MORNING DAWNED STILL and clear. A few minutes after sunrise, it got chaotic as Gloria ran up and down the stairs, slid over the flagstones in her footed pajamas, and put water on to boil that she forgot. The tea kettle screamed on and on like a happy banshee.

Casey shoved back his comforter, sliding his feet into warm shriek-skin slippers. Through his whole-wall window, the sun glimmered low over the trees. He slid open his personal portal and drew a deep breath of frosty air, smelling woodsmoke.

Ahh, now he was awake.

By the time Robert knocked shyly on the second-story treeway door, the great room was littered with wrapping paper. Dad and Mom had cleverly hidden the presents under their bed—the biggest piece of furniture in the mostly-empty house. A butter-basted Razor-Wing stuffed with savory skrabbit dressing was roasting in the oven. Gravy and cocoa and hot punch simmered on the stove, and a fire blazed in the enormous hearth. Good smells swirled and eddied under the massive timbers of the ceiling.

"Check it out," Casey said. "If you climb the barn-style ladder, there's a sentry ledge at the top. I tied my new rope to it so you can rappel down."

"Right into that pile of pillows," Gloria said.

"Holy creeps, step aside." Robert's shoulders relaxed as his hands touched the ladder. By the second or third time he'd slid down, spinning in midair, his tight expression had loosened and he cracked a smile.

They drank cocoa, roasted apples over the flames, and played Uno! and Bandersnatch as Dad and Mom sipped drinks and fought about where furniture would go. Robert had brought them their own set of Bandersnatch cards, carefully wrapped in black paper. By the time he opened his own gifts, he was relaxed and laughing.

"Hope you like the books," Casey said. "Doug at the Baleful Blade told us single-edged glaives are making a comeback and we thought about getting you one, but–"

"Already have one," Robert said.

"That's what we figured." Casey hoped the set of *Narnia* books had been a good choice. Robert seemed pleased, almost as happy as he'd been when Gloria had given him her poster splashed in pastel colors and glitter glue. "It's called 'Sylvan Woods at Sunset with a Hidden Unicorn and Watermelon Smells,'" she'd said.

Robert had already pulled on the anorak Mom had picked out for him, rated for sub-zero temperatures and coal-colored with grass-green accents. Casey had voiced his doubts, but Mom had insisted: "He can't wear all black *all* the time." If Robert minded the tiny streaks of color, he was hiding it well.

But then, he *was* trained in subterfuge.

By mid-afternoon, the roasting Razor-Wing smelled unbearably good. Knocks rang out from the mudroom as the West family arrived, kicking off their boots, hanging up their coats, handing over steaming dishes.

"I just looove your treeway," Luci said. "The way it winds through the pines? So mysterious and scary!"

A few minutes later, the McGusty family showed up, dusting off snow and sniffing the air.

"Oh man," Jake said. "And I thought I was already hungry."

Food covered the trestle table. An enormous smoked ham, seafood jambalaya, smashed potatoes, colorful salads, bacon-roasted beets. Even a loaded breakfast pizza. There were oohs and ahs as Dad slid the golden-brown Razor-Wing from the oven.

Mom put a hand to her mouth. "Oh no! I somehow overlooked the chair situation."

There were no chairs. But no one seemed to mind. They gathered around the table and raised their glasses over the enormous feast.

"To Christmas," Dad said.

"To all of you," Mom said.

"To...hang on a second," Casey said.

"That's a weird toast." Gloria wrinkled her nose.

He'd caught a glimmer of movement out the front window. With a houseful of friends and a rumbling stomach, that wouldn't normally have stopped him, but...Casey slipped around the table. Ruby-colored punch sloshed the flagstones as he reached the window and stopped in his tracks.

A dark figure glided down the trail. Graceful and deadly, a human-shaped hole in the snow. The figure paused. Strangely familiar. No, it couldn't be. Casey took a breath and turned the doorknob. The door made a half-circle on the snowy porch. The afternoon light was milky and dim.

"Ms. Crake?"

She froze. "Casey Grimes?"

It was hard to recognize her without the crooked shoulders and the limp. The Craken pushed back her furred hood. Her sapphire eyes shone against the snow and ice. Her white-blond hair was swept back from her face.

"I can't believe it's you," Casey said.

"So you finally have a home." In three steps she was on the porch. Casey gaped. No one, not even Robert, had ever moved so fast. The Craken smiled at the tiny dents her feet left in the snow. Close up, her eyes were frozen mountain lakes.

They stared at each other.

"I'm back." Crake's voice sounded brittle, like feet crunching over ice. "Really, truly back. Amazing what twenty-three surgeries can do for a girl." She gave him a tired smile.

For a moment, Casey felt deeply sad. Because for as long as he'd known her, she'd been limping, and *here's* how she should've been all along, quick and alive, age falling from her even shoulders. He stepped onto the porch, ice tingling through his socks.

"I've heard good things, Grimes." Her eyes glittered. "And *that's* a good thing, because you'll never guess what I've found out. Not the kind of news worth waiting for, but there you go. It's the Jabberwocky."

Casey smelled a burning roof.

He heard glass shattering and the groans of a dying oak.

He saw Luci's limp body and a bloody, twisted grin.

He swallowed.

"–not even supposed to exist," Ms. Crake was saying, "but it does. It does, and it's more horrible than you can imagine, hiding in the Civilian world, reaching across the border to stab us—a shadow agency. They're killers, Grimes. Destroyers. They want to gut the Wilderness Alliance, dismantle Sylvan life, crush magic, weaponize the monsters. If we don't push back with everything we've got, they'll–"

"Wait!" Casey held up his hands. His heart knocked against his ribs.

Crake pushed back her hair.

"This is horrible," Casey said. "Completely horrible. And—and it sounds complicated, but–" He gulped a breath. "It's Christmas. Don't you—don't you think you need a break?" He nodded to the rectangle of light behind him.

Crake sighed and tossed her head. "Christmas, ahh. Not on my agenda, Grimes. I just climbed off a copter. This is urgent. I can't possibly stop."

But Casey needed her to. Even for just one day. He didn't want to return to the burning roof and Chroamwell's wild eyes and two kids he'd thought were friends, hacking away at him.

Not the Jabberwocky. Not tonight.

"Please," he said. "Stop anyway. Come inside."

Ms. Crake's thin shoulders rose and fell. She took in the high, frosted eaves of the house. The stone chimney, blowing woodsmoke in the air. "Oh, very well," she said. "You've earned it, Grimes. As a favor."

Because he didn't know what else to do, Casey stretched out his arms. He wanted the darkness to flow backward, into the deep woods and winter sky—away from *them*. Crake's frozen cheek brushed his.

"C'mon," he said.

He pushed the door wider, but she hesitated on the porch until he took her hand and tugged her through. In the great room, laughter died. Stories ended mid-sentence. A fork clattered on a plate. Casey knew the effect Crake had on people but he didn't care. He wouldn't let it happen, not this time. He stepped to the table and raised his glass, trying to think of the right words.

Ms. Crake crept out from behind him and Mom handed her a glass. Dad held up his own, and everyone followed his example. The only sounds were *slish-sloshes* of wine and punch and cocoa.

Casey cleared his throat. The words came to him like they'd been waiting.

"To fighting hard," he said. "To be who you're supposed to be."

"HEAR! HEAR!" Everyone could drink to that. And they did, and then conversation and laughter broke out again, and Dad started carving up the Razor-Wing, and Gloria squeezed Ms. Crake's hand, and a few minutes later, Casey saw her smile—really smile—when Mom stepped over to give her a hug.

That's what she needed, Casey thought. *Maybe just as much as all those surgeries.* He took a deep breath and held it for ten seconds. Then he kicked Luci under the table and passed his plate for some skrabbit stuffing. It's Christmas, he thought. Nothing horrible counts tonight.

And in that moment, for the gathered friends and family in the firelight, everything was bright and good.

THANKS FOR READING TRICKERY SCHOOL.

If you're wondering what to read next, check out *Crooked Castle*, a standalone thriller that acts as book # 2.5 in the Casey Grimes universe:

For all the inside stuff on the Casey Grimes universe—including book news, tips on fighting monsters, and a free story—sign up for *The Sylvan Spy* at **b.link/TrickerySchool.**

ACKNOWLEDGMENTS

The team behind Casey Grimes is fierce in spirit and free. They crave adventure. They prefer underdogs. They call for special drinks. Creek-walking, glittery barrettes, and trash-talk are among their fields of expertise—but if *woods* or *mountains* of expertise were a thing, they'd choose those. Thanks for your wise and funny suggestions and for keeping me young.

For years now, I've been fortunate to work with a gifted editor whom I intend to keep to myself. Sorry, no free advertising for you, miss. Her eye for character arc, emotional resonance and pacing is uncanny, and I'll refer to her only as "Linds."

Thanks also to Kimberly and Daniel, whose encouragement made the experience of being published in a pandemic more tolerable. And to Peter, who is always in my corner.

I'd be remiss if I didn't give my Back Deck a mention. Those shady summer mornings, crisp fall afternoons, and all the hummingbirds—they were just right.

ABOUT THE AUTHOR

AJ Vanderhorst (that's me) has had many jobs, including journalist, paramedic, escape artist, and baby whisperer. One time in fifth grade, I built a traffic-stopping fort in a huge oak tree, using only branches and imagination, and slept there for a week.

Now my wife and I live in a woodsy house with our proteges and a ridiculous number of pets, including a turtle with a taste for human toes. This makes me an expert on wild, dangerous things—invisibility spells, butcher beasts, hungry kids, you get the idea.

I'm the only author in the world who enjoys pickup basketball and enormous bonfires, preferably not at the same time. My family has drawn up several blueprints for our future tree castle. Visit me online at **ajvanderhorst.com**

And hey, if you enjoyed the book, would you do me a favor? Head over to **b.link/ReviewTrickery** on your phone or laptop and leave an Amazon review. Casey, Gloria and their friends sure appreciate it!

CROOKED CASTLE

A TWISTY THRILLER FROM THE CASEY GRIMES FANTASY UNIVERSE

AJ VANDERHORST

Dedicated to people who are still looking for magic in hard places.

CHAPTER 1
AIRDROP

OUCH, the girl thought. *Stop shoving. Leave me alone.*

She kept her eyes shut tight because she didn't want to wake up and get involved in a stupid fight. "No thanks," she mumbled. "Go away." You learned to sleep through a lot at the Orphan Foundation, but this was crazy.

Kids were yelling and crashing. Fluorescent flashes zapped her eyelids, someone being an idiot with the light switch. And someone had dumped a cup of water on her—or maybe they'd lost their minds and pulled the fire alarm, turning on the sprinklers? But the noise and the lights and the dripping didn't explain why she felt so uncomfortable, like someone had put gravel under her sheets.

Great, now I'm awake.

Her eyelashes brushed cloth, and she tossed her head, but the sheets stayed put like some genius had wrapped them around her face. *Ok, now I'm mad.* She rolled onto her back in the dark—*ow*—shrugged her cramped shoulders, and tried to push the stuffy cotton off her face, but she couldn't. Her hands were stuck behind her back. No, not stuck, tied. Someone had knotted her wrists in rope—and it wasn't loose.

A feeling like scorched wire twisted in her chest. *Ok, ooh-kay.*

She thrashed around, trying to get to her knees. Then a sharp gust of air caught her, not the Foundation's stale AC, and she fell sideways onto stone, not a bed at all. A flash of lightning lit up the ceiling, but in the sharp glare through her blindfold, she realized there *was* no ceiling—and rain was pinging off her skin, not fire sprinklers, and there were no sheets, just her damp clothes and the cloth across her eyes.

The metal in her chest got icy as the heat drained out of her.

"No," she whispered.

There was only one place she could be.

The Foundation's gravel roof was four stories high. On the ground, miles of asphalt took bites out of kids when they played ball or got knocked down. This wasn't a prank, not anymore. This was out of control. She got ready to kick and scream and fight the second someone touched her.

Then something swept past with an angry roar—something huge. Wind howled like it was being shoved out of the sky, and she wished her hands were free to cover her ears. Was it a helicopter? Had someone called the police?

"Right here!" she yelled. "Help me!"

Rock gnawed at her knees and elbows as she struggled upright. Lightning flashed, making her blindfold paper thin, and in a split second she saw—

empty sky

sharp rocks

big waves

She froze, swaying on her knees. *Weed, California, doesn't have a coast. No ocean, no wild wind. Where'd the Foundation go? Where's the helicopter?* She tried to catch her scampering thoughts: *Where's everyone else? How'd I get here? Why?*

Off to her right, someone screamed, the sound fading fast. Falling down and down.

Her teeth began to chatter. This was bad.

This was the kind of situation you got out of at any cost. The kind that could only get worse, like angry kids on a corner, shouting and pointing guns. You didn't stop to figure out why they were fighting. You just got out of there.

"God, where am I?" she said.

An explosion rocked her backward. The sky glowed red through her blindfold and what she saw got stuck in her retinas: a snaky, winged shape, fire blasting from its mouth. The girl's wet hair flipped in her face and rock bit into her palms as she twisted away. Cold flooded back over her as the bellows of the giant creature faded.

A flying, fire-breathing creature.

On a strange coast.

Hunting her. Hunting them.

Kneeling in the drizzle, she wanted to fall asleep. Black out and pretend she was somewhere else. *Someone* else. Now and then it worked, and you woke up in your bed, nervous and stiff, and the crisis was over.

In the Foundation, she'd sometimes slammed awake on the floor, seeing stars, when she'd been shoved out of her top bunk. Most of them didn't have railings, and some kids took advantage— the ones who had gangs and liked to roam at night. If she'd thought there was the smallest chance of waking up now, of escaping from the nightmare, she would've thrown herself over the edge, onto the Foundation's concrete floor.

But she knew it wouldn't work. This wasn't a dream, even though she'd been dropped on a rocky coast by a dragon. Even though there was no ocean in Weed, California, and no dragons, anywhere. This was real.

Waves crashed far below, a watery rumble.

"I need my hands," she whispered.

She rolled onto her back, tucked her knees, and stretched her wrists toward her heels, gritting her teeth. Stone scraped her spine as she rocked back and forth, and one of her hips throbbed angrily: *Ow–ow–ow.* In the next flash of lightning, she saw the tips of her old canvas sneakers, and she wrestled her hands across. *Halfway free.*

Wincing, she tugged off her blindfold. Wind tore the knotted cloth away, and she knew she was somewhere high, far from any city. She'd never seen a sky so dark, and she wondered where the other kids were on the cliffs—and who they were, whether they were from the Foundation or if they could be trusted.

Holding up her wrists, she found the rope in the starless night and bit, gnawing and spitting out fibers. She was a good biter— she'd always taken care of her teeth. The knots frayed after a few minutes and the wind snatched the cord away.

She tucked her head against the salty gusts. For a minute she held perfectly still, forcing herself to take deep, regular breaths the way she did when she was angry or so scared she could barely think.

Don't let the wind steal all the oxygen. Some of it's yours.

Sounds poked through the pitch black storm like needles: Rock clattering, the dragon's roar, screams. A haunted feeling crept over her, the feeling she got when a person was around, part of the scenery, and then, without warning, gone. An empty bunk, an empty desk, an empty corner. There were nights in the Children's Foundation dorm when you woke up, not sure why, and knew there were fewer kids than before. You wondered how long they'd been gone and what secret they'd known that let them get away.

She sensed the cliffs getting less and less crowded. Kids were trying to cheat the wind and rocks and waves—but they were failing. She shoved her hands against the stone so hard her arms began to shake.

Stay calm, she thought. Stay calm, and you can get out of this, maybe.

She pulled her knees to her chest to muffle her wild heartbeat.

Thunder rumbled. When the lightning lit up the hungry cliffs, she froze. Huge chasms looked like dirty, jagged shower drains. Slimy stuff dangled like moldy hair. She looked away and pressed a hand to her stomach. Her soaking sneakers were inches from the edge. She wanted to run and put her back against a wall, but there were no walls. Just spiky rocks and dark open space where the shore must be.

The lightning moved off over the ocean. For a second she saw towering waves, then darkness rushed back in. It started to rain, really rain, and she realized she couldn't wait this out. Her best chance would be in the morning, but if the wind got any stronger, it would snatch her and toss her like a sack of trash.

A sliver of moonlight found its way through the clouds, and the faint glow showed her towers of rock like broken glass. Nothing that looked like a path. No one else was moving—if there was anyone else left. Only someone crazy or on drugs would try to climb this.

But that's what she had to do.

She started crawling, scraping her bare knees, skinning her palms. She realized she was shaking and told herself it didn't matter. Not as long as she was moving forward.

"Think with your fingertips," she whispered.

The holds she found had sharp edges.

It's just blood, she thought. You've got plenty.

The worst moments were when she had to stand up and fling herself to the next ledge. The wind yanked on her arms. The left side of her body ached, pain radiating from her hip. The rain plastered her shorts and t-shirt to her skin. She knew the waves were watching and waiting, churning under the cliffs like the acid in your stomach that eats whatever falls in.

When she made the final jump, hair flying, hands outstretched and dripping reddish rain, she was sobbing. It's ok, she told herself. Ok to cry as long as you're still calling the shots.

Wet sand clung to her hands and knees and slid into her shoes but she didn't stop crawling. High grass whipped her face so she had to half-close her eyes. When the sun finally rose, she was a long way inland, inching her way through sand dunes—but the sound of surf kept pounding in her ear drums.

She'd made it. Wherever *it* was.

As far as she could tell, she was the only one.

CHAPTER 2
THEY'D NEVER LET YOU GO

THE RAIN STOPPED, and the rising sun added dull browns and greens to the wet, gritty world. Reaching the top of the latest sand dune felt like climbing a mountain, but another rose ahead. She sat down in a patch of thin grass, tucked her knees, and blinked sand out of her eyes. *Just a short rest.* Maybe she could get the grains out easier if she closed her eyes entirely...

When she woke up, the sun had ghosted to the far side of the sky. It wasn't diving out of sight, but it was getting heavy, glowing with watery orange haze that made long shadows on the dunes.

Without meaning to, she'd fast-forwarded the whole day. The darkening sand felt like a video game that had blipped and sent her back to level one where everything was dark and scary. Her torn fingertips ached when she pressed them to her forehead.

For a minute she felt confused. The dream she'd been having— about a gang of girls moving toward her in the Children's Foundation basement—felt more real than wherever she was. Then she took a deep breath and smelled salt and mud and sweat and blood. She dug her fingers into the sand, cupping broken sea shells.

It felt...sandy. Really sandy, like real sand.

That's right, I made it, she thought. The cliffs and the dragon aren't a nightmare, even though they should be. I was left here to die. But I didn't. I escaped.

She searched the sky for movement and saw nothing, aside from clouds like shredded gauze. When she moved, her head pounded. Scrapes on her arms and legs had started scabbing, dried blood mixed with sand. Lifting her shirt, she saw bruises where she'd thunked into rocks, and an ugly gash on her left hip, still oozing blood. She wasn't sure when it had happened—maybe when she'd made her first desperate plunge toward the shore. Her toes were bruised, her shoes ripped. Even her face had cuts that she didn't remember getting.

And the daylight was fading, turning the beach-like place into a vague, murky landscape. Not a normal beach at all. She hadn't been to one in years, not since she was little and fun and cute—but you didn't need recent memories to know that where there's a beach, there ought to be an ocean, blue and shimmering, lapping at the sand, filling in your footprints when you dance out of the way. But this ocean was a hungry gap at the end of a long, dark hole.

Her stomach shuddered.

You won't fall, can't fall now, she thought.

And then, because there was no one to hear her, she said it out loud.

"You're safe. You got away."

Her next thought was, Am I the only one?

She'd rarely been alone, as long as she could remember. Always fighting for space, fighting to hold a place in line, fighting to keep her bunk, fighting for grades, for safety, for attention. And usually failing.

Maybe someone else had made it and they'd missed each other in the dark. Maybe that person was waking up on a different sand dune and having the same thoughts she was. Looking over her shoulder and thinking, If there's another person out there...do I really want to meet them?

"It depends..." she said out loud. Depended on who the other kid was. On whether she was a system kid too, on where she'd come from. What were the odds of meeting someone cool, not a thief or fighter or a liar, in a place like this?

Probably not great.

This seems like a horrible place, she thought, with kids from horrible places. Maybe my whole Foundation group got sent here. At the same time—look at all this room. All this sand, all these shells, all this sea grass. All this space.

The size of the beach washed over her. And she hadn't even stood up yet.

Finally she did, and walked slowly to the top of the dune to look back the way she'd come. Sand hills hugged the darkening sky in rolling, wet brown curves framed by sulky blue—still upset after the storm.

She could see her dented toe prints coming down then up, down then up, and the pointy scratches left by her fingers and the round imprints of her knees. There were wider drag marks where she'd flopped onto her stomach. Out beyond the dunes, the cliffs rose like broken project buildings full of violence.

There were no other prints in sight, and it made her feel totally alone.

She thought she should probably go back and look for survivors, but her gut slammed up at her heart like a closed fist, and she knew she couldn't. Just couldn't. At least not yet. If there were others, she'd have to find them later. Not that she had anything to offer.

Hi, it's me, a kid with zero assets just like you.

Could the rest of them really all be gone?

The dragon had dropped lots of them. At least a dozen, she was sure.

You learned to see a lot without sight, sleeping in shared dorms.

Her senses told her they were gone. Swept into the sea like rinds into a garbage disposal.

She swallowed and gave her shoulders a shake.

"You don't know for sure," she said. "Here's what you *do* know. Dragons exist. You're by the sea. No one cares if you die."

The first two bits were brand new pieces of information.

She wondered how long it had been since she'd stretched out in her top bunk, her toothbrush and a sharpened fork under her pillow. A day? Two days? A week? How much time had gone by since she'd woken up on the cliffs with the dragon roaring overhead?

She didn't feel older. She held up her hands and inspected her beat-up nails. They weren't especially long. So maybe it had just been a day or two. But that really didn't matter. What mattered was all this...

She looked inland, shading her eyes. Over the edge of the next dune, she caught a glimpse of waving, grassy fields, and in the distance something spiky and dark that might be trees. Maybe if she hiked far enough, she'd cross a protected wetland and stumble into a parking lot. People would stop walking their dogs to stare at her. "Sweetheart, are you ok? Here, take this blanket. Let's get you to a doctor." And she'd say, "Yes, please. And just so you know, there's a dragon out there, so stay close to your cars and keep your dogs on their leashes."

Once she made it back to civilization, she'd slip out of the doctor's office and down an echoey stairwell like people did in movies, and she'd hit the streets and keep her head down until she turned eighteen.

Eighteen. Hmm. She blinked and frowned. How long until that happened? Five years? Four? She chewed her lip. Well, she'd remember later, when her mind unfogged itself.

But who would let you wander the California coast? They'd keep marking you down on their lists as long as they possibly could. They'd keep adding more pages to your file. When would they ever set you loose? When would they ever let you you go? She frowned and answered herself out loud.

"Never. Absolutely never."

That's when she knew—or almost knew—she was on an island.

Even though she wanted to believe it wasn't true, and that she'd been dumped in a strange wildlife sanctuary by mistake. *A huge mistake involving a dragon. Yeah, that's believable.* She turned to look at the cliffs again. The black rocks caught the tired sun over the dunes and threw rays at her eyes like shards of glass.

"I'll make it work," she said. "I'm not going back to the Foundation, ever."

She turned back inland, thinking, How bad can island life be? People survive this kind of thing all the time, and some of them even—oh!

Her hand flew to her heart.

A boy stood waiting.

If her voice hadn't been raw from the saltwater and night air, she might've screamed, the absolute worst thing to do. Instead she groaned, a sound straight from her soul, and got ready to fight.

CHAPTER 3
THE FOX

THE BOY LOOKED like someone you didn't want to mess with. He studied her with dark eyes, his weight rocked back on one leg, a hand on his hip. His faded jeans were patched but in good shape. His shirt was a dull gray, sleeves rolled to the elbow. He didn't swagger too close, didn't mouth off, didn't try to touch her hair.

He's in control, she thought. He's dangerous.

Maybe she wouldn't win but she wouldn't roll up in a ball either. The important thing was to show that no one told her what to do. She got her balance in the sand, tightened her fists until they were white, and narrowed her eyes to slits.

He nodded. "Hope I didn't startle you."

She didn't move.

"I get it," he said. "I'd keep my distance too, but congratulations on making it." He ran a hand through rust-colored hair. "We used to rush to the cliffs and throw ropes when we heard the dragon roaring, but then the blindfolds started happening, and when kids heard our voices, they tried to walk toward us like they—what's the word?— like they, um, counted on us one hundred percent."

"Trust?" she said. "They trusted you?"

"Yeah, that must be it." He trailed off. "Anyway, it's suicide to sleep out by the cliffs at night. We don't want to, but we have to let the new arrivals go it alone."

New arrivals, she thought. This has happened before.

"Did anyone else make it?" the boy asked.

She didn't see what she had to lose by telling the truth. If she lied, he'd figure it out.

"I don't think so," she said.

"Ah, that's too bad." He sighed and touched his chin.

She thought of everyone out there on the cliffs. Wherever they'd come from, whether she'd have recognized their faces, they were probably all ghosts now.

All except her.

The boy was studying her. He didn't seem hostile, but he didn't make her feel relaxed. His eyes were friendly but sharp. He was a capped needle, a knife in a drawer.

You've got to be careful, she thought. Until you figure out how to handle him.

"So what's your name?" he asked.

"My name is..." She blinked.

Where had it gone? She shoved the darkness and the cliffs away and thought, Your name, your name is...but nothing came. A white blur rushed behind her eyes—and a single, quavering scream. The scream was a blue-black wisp of shadow, twisting through the empty whiteness. It left her breathless and confused.

She saw the look on his face.

"It's gone, huh? The names usually are, so there are a lot of us running around with made up ones. Some kids even call themselves 'Cliff.' Little inside joke, just until they remember their real names, except they never do—or until they think of something better, if they get enough time. Want me to call you Cliff for now?"

"Not a chance." Her torn nails bit into her palms. Cliff was a horrible name for someone who'd survived the Cliffs. You might as well say, Hi, I'm Drowning. Hi, I'm Blood Loss. Hi, I'm the Children's

Foundation. She tried to think of something better. Clean, safe, far from the sea.

"What's going on in there?" The boy said. "C'mon, talk to me."

She licked her lips, noticing how cracked they were. And salty. She needed water. Clear water, not the ocean. A creek, a stream.

"Brook," she said. "You can call me that."

The boy raised an eyebrow. "Nice to make your acquaintance, Brook. I'm very happy you're alive. I go by Fox." He rolled his eyes toward his scalp. "My hair, you know. The name just stuck." He extended his hand.

"Makes sense," she said.

After she made sure his palm was empty, she didn't hesitate.

Hesitation implied a lack of confidence.

They shook.

"It's a good thing I ran into you," Fox said.

"Why's that?" Brook wished she sounded more confident, the way she would've at school or on the street, where she was quick to prove she didn't need help, especially when someone offered it.

Fox smiled. "Maybe you've noticed, this is kind of a scary place."

She crossed her arms because she didn't have an answer to that. She didn't want the island to be a scary place. And she didn't want to ask too many questions, because questions showed how little you knew. But sometimes you could find out what you wanted if you played an angle. Circled around. Like the way you could sneak through the kitchen and steal a chocolate milk if you said you needed to see the nurse. But you never asked to visit the kitchen.

"Have you seen the dragon?" she said, taking a risk.

Fox didn't act surprised by the question, which was good.

"More times than I'd like," he said. "There's no killing a thing like that. Did you get a good look?"

She shook her head no. "But it was right above me. Breathing fire."

"Usually I only see its fire," Fox said. "At night, miles away. If you ever see it flying toward you, start running. Hide in the woods if you can. Even then, it'll get you if it wants to. Once it locks onto a kid, there's almost no chance." He frowned. "The only safe place is the castle."

"Castle?" Brook said before she could stop herself.

You dummy, she thought. You had him talking.

"Yeah." He swept an arm inland. "Do you know the word?"

Brook pictured a towering building made of stone.

"Like in movies," she said.

"That's right," he said. "Like Lord of the Rings. High walls, huge gate. It's where you want to be on this island, believe me."

So why aren't we walking there? Brook wanted to say. And did we go back in time? What is this, medieval Europe? Instead, she asked: "Is that where you live?"

The boy frowned. "If only. The blue-faces own the castle, and those kids don't share. They'd rather cut your throat than let you in, like their paint makes them better than the rest of us. You won't find them out here, scrapping in the dirt and rain, fighting to survive."

His eyes gleamed.

Brook thought he might actually snarl.

Fox took a breath. "They've owned the place as long as I've been here. The castle is closed to survivors like us."

Like us. She appreciated that.

"What do you do then?" She didn't want to sound like she was prying, but luckily Fox seemed happy to have someone to talk to. Well, she could be a great listener.

"Me?" he said. "Oh, nothing special. I do my best to keep my distance from the killers. I help where I can, but I try to steer clear of trouble, which can be a challenge. Sometimes I just think about better days." Fox glanced at the sky. "Speaking of trouble, I need to be getting back."

"Ah, ok," Brook said, wondering what he meant by *killers*.

They'd been chatting in the shelter of the dune, and it had been such a relief to talk with someone normal that she hadn't noticed the shadows getting long. On the inland side of the island, the sun was sinking behind the trees in a gold pool, spraying the sky with swooshes of creamsicle and grape. She stole a look at Fox. He was rolling his shoulders, watching the sun go down as well.

"You probably have a plan," he said. "You seem on top of things."

"Thanks," she said. "I do my best."

But I don't know a thing, she wanted to add. I don't know where I am.

"I'll see you around, Brook." He gave her a half smile and started away, following his own prints back along the dunes.

CHAPTER 4
SURVIVAL CHOICES

BROOK'S SHOULDERS twitched as she watched the boy go. She wanted to scream, *Wait! Let me come too.* She'd say, Our chances will be better together, against the dragon and the blue-faces and whatever.

But she couldn't say that. Because that's not what Fox would hear.

"Help, I'm trying to act tough, but if you shove me I'll crumble into pieces"—that's what he'd hear.

She couldn't stop her hands from shaking, so she put them behind her back. It's ok, she thought. As long as you're still in charge. She didn't say a word as Fox's shape got smaller.

Maybe she could dig a hole in the sand, just for tonight. Tomorrow she would figure something out. What did people do on desert islands? Eat berries, make fires with rocks, stay warm in caves? Maybe tomorrow she'd find some berries. Or she'd go looking for a cave. Yeah, that's what she'd do. Or maybe lightning would strike a dead tree and she'd grab a flaming branch and...who was she kidding?

Fox's shape looked about six inches tall in the distance. His legs were hidden by waist-high grass when he stopped moving and froze like a glitch in a video. A few seconds passed, then he turned and started back, a gray silhouette against the painted sky. Brook held her breath. What if he was taking a different trail? Maybe he'd walk all the way up to her, give her a nod and keep on going: "Sorry, Brook, I forgot something. Good luck."

Minutes went by.

Fox got closer. The backlight gave his head a coppery glow.

He stopped five feet away.

"No offense," he said. "But I realized maybe you hadn't had time to collect firewood or make plans to defend yourself. If you already have, just say so, I don't mean to be rude."

Brook took a quick breath through her nose. "I'm working on it," she said.

"Cool. Well." He nodded to the sunset. "You'd better move fast."

He started away again, but it was too much. Brook held out for five more seconds.

"Wait." At least she hadn't screamed.

When he turned, he looked curious but not surprised.

"If you don't mind, maybe I'll come too." It took all her self-control not to wince as the words left her mouth. She hadn't begged. But who was in charge now?

Fox didn't rub it in.

"That's great," he said. "I didn't want to be pushy. Everyone has to be careful out here, but you seem like one of the good ones. C'mon, we've got just enough time to get back before dark."

Brook fell into step beside him, looking away so her face could return to normal. Her skin tingled and she was pretty sure she'd gone pale.

"Is there any water?" She'd fallen this far, she might as well fall a little deeper into Fox's debt. Her mouth felt as dry as sand.

"Absolutely," he said. "And some food. I have enough to share."

"Cool, thanks," she said, and did her best to act all casual, so he wouldn't know she felt like crying—or cheering. Or maybe both.

They left the dunes and crunched through fields as the sun

dropped lower. Salty breezes streamed past, tossing the high grass. Brook couldn't hear the waves anymore or see the sharp, dark cliffs, and that helped her relax. Now the turf had some bounce under her feet. The forest loomed closer, inky-green and thick. They pushed through leafy bushes and little trees.

"The key is to stay out of the way," Fox said. "Let the bad stuff flow right past you like a train you don't have to take. It's why I like the edges of the forest. You don't want to go too far in, at least not at night. Some kids would say the woods are never worth it, but I disagree. It's not good to be out in the open when the sun goes down. It's even risky during the day."

"Yeah," Brook said. "Makes total sense."

She was actually thinking, Why so risky?

"Now we're halfway to camp," Fox said.

"Is that like halfway home?" Brook said.

"Um—sure, I guess."

They pushed into the woods on a thin dirt trail. At first the trees kept their distance, but as she and Fox got deeper and the sun got lost behind black, twisty branches, the plants got grabby, sticking their twigs into the trail and waving prickers near Brook's ankles. She had to keep ducking and sidestepping—which made it even harder to focus.

What's my name? she kept thinking. Who am I, am I, am I? She wanted to smack the side of her head, like maybe she could jar it loose. Meanwhile, there were big gaps in what Fox was telling her. She was happy he seemed talkative. It meant she was learning a lot. The problem was, he assumed she was smarter than she was, or that she'd caught on more quickly than she had.

Fox must've been dropped on the cliffs like her, so at some point his brain must have been going crazy too. Darting from thing to thing. Struggling to keep up. But apparently he'd forgotten what it felt like to wake up on the rocks knowing absolutely nothing, because he was giving her too much respect.

Too much respect. Ha.

"Now we're in the middle woods," Fox said. "Not the edges and not the deep dark part, kind of walking a line between the two. Other kids don't come in here at night."

"Cool," Brook said. Wait, what? she almost added. *Why are we in here then?*—but caught herself. Because *respect*. Respect was something you never gave back once you got it. Like being handed a wad of cash. As soon as the paper brushed your palm, you put it somewhere safe and didn't flaunt it, didn't give it away without a fight.

But she hoped there was a good reason they were twisting their way through dark, prickly woods as the sun went down.

CHAPTER 5
SNATCHED BY THE FOREST

"ACH!" Brook walked through a spiderweb and swallowed a gasp, then stuck out her bottom lip and blew, trying to float the stickiness off her face. When that didn't work, she half-closed her eyes and wiped her lashes. In the low light, she didn't see the spider. It had better not be riding in her hair.

"Watch out for spiderwebs," Fox said over his shoulder.

Brook wondered if he was grinning. "Thanks—I'll do that." She ran her tongue across her teeth and spit. She'd have to be more tuned in, like she was walking down an alley. But that was tough, the way her brain was buzzing.

Buzzing like a fly in a web, she thought. Ugh, that's gross.

She picked up a branch to hold in front of her face.

But she *was* stuck in a sticky place. If Fox had told her everything was going to be all right, or said, "Girl, you're too pretty to worry about details," she would've taken her chances by herself. She would've hit him and said, "Ok, what's up now?" Having his respect made things complicated. Questions she couldn't ask tumbled around her mind.

What do we drink?

What do we eat?

Who are we hiding from?

What happens at night?

Sure, there were other questions, like What is this place? and Why are we here? But those hardly even counted. Questions that big didn't get answered, never did. They didn't even get asked unless you were, hypothetically, talking with a friend.

Fox might be friendly, Brook thought, but he's hardly a friend. He seems like he knows what's going on, which is good, and maybe he's more trustworthy than most, but that's it. Take it for what it's worth. If I'm patient, things will start coming into focus and I'll figure out what's going on. So stay calm and play along.

"At least we get nice sunsets," she said, realizing she'd been quiet. When you were too quiet, people started giving you weird looks.

"We sure do." Fox paused to admire the sky. The trail was long gone, and they were shuffling through dead leaves and shoving their way through thick landscapes—thick forest-scapes, *thickets?* —whatever you called them, dodging the spiky fingers of the bigger trees.

"I sort of collect sunsets," Brook said so Fox would think she was the sharing type. "This one looks like rainbow sherbet with extra raspberry. I'd give it an seven point five out of ten."

"Seems about right," Fox said. "I should enjoy the sunsets more. Whatever happens, they're one thing no one can take away from you, right?"

Brook opened and closed her mouth. How did he know that? She remembered nights on the rusty fire escape, sitting by herself, when she'd thought the exact same thing. Hearing someone else say it out loud was crazy—and it made her think, Hey Fox, you're ok. But what she said was, "Hey Fox, you're kind of a philosopher."

He smiled over his shoulder.

She watched the colors melting into the spiky black nastiness of the forest, and thought, It *looks* like the same sky as Weed, CA—but you probably can't guess your location from a sunset. She thought of an ancient map she'd seen in one of her history books. The world looked flat like a magazine and if you sailed off the edges, the map said, Here be dragons. What if she and Fox had been dropped into some wild and forgotten corner of the world? Well, not a corner, more like a floating, abandoned lot.

Because there *was* a dragon.

She really, really wanted to ask:

Hey Fox, do you have any theories about, you know, all this?

Since you've got a philosophic streak and all?

Instead, she slashed at a spiderweb and took three deep, slow breaths to clear her mind. Then she hiked a little faster to catch up with Fox. The trees were bigger and more bristly now, stealing all her personal space. If these trees were human they'd be picking a fight. Browns and greens were fading to gray, and the ground felt rough and cluttered. Brook stole glances right and left as she scuffed over roots and rotting wood, trying not to twist an ankle. Hooky branches kept snatching at her clothes. Keeping track of all the prickly, sticky threats was a full-time job.

These woods are not the nice kind, she thought.

It made her forget to keep chatting up Fox.

"Doing ok back there?" he said.

"Oh, doing great," she said. "The spiders aren't winning!"

He glanced back, but the darkness had swallowed his face, like he was a villain who'd turned away—*surprise*—and pulled on a mask of shadow.

Brook flinched. If Fox *had been* a villain and *had* tried to scare her —and she knew he wasn't but if he *had* been—well, then it worked. She stopped walking. No one can see you, she thought. No one can hear you. You're not even carrying a sharpened fork. She let the space between them grow to a safer distance and pretended to pull leaves out of her hair. The open ground behind her had been eaten by trees and shadows. Fox said this was the middle forest, but it seemed deep and dark to her.

You're lost, she thought. Lost on a lost island. Of course you are.

If she turned and walked in a straight line, maybe she could get back to the fields, but she wouldn't bet on it. If she ran, she'd never find her way out. The sun was disappearing behind black, grabby branches and there weren't any obvious ways to escape. No wonder other kids didn't come here.

She wasn't sure she wanted to be close to Fox in the dark—especially when she couldn't see his face. Thinking about her options—turn and walk away; stop and hide; or keep following Fox—she took her eyes off the woods. A second later, she felt herself pulled up short. Her chin jerked to one side, her heart punched her chest, and her hands flew up to fight—but Fox was still in front of her, walking away. He hadn't touched her. When she turned her head, she saw a thorny vine twisted in her long, tawny hair. The forest had snatched her. Snuck in while she was spacing and said, *Gotcha*.

She took a handful of hair and yanked.

"Oww." Now the thorns were stuck deeper.

"Tangled up?" Fox appeared beside her. "Hey, you're only making it worse."

Brook tried to think of something to say as the woods and the night closed in like walls. "I got my name wrong, didn't I?" she gasped. "Rapunzel—that's what I should've called myself." She forced a smile.

"Here, let me," Fox said.

A sharp edge gleamed in his hand.

Brook froze. If she'd been at school or at the Foundation, she would've turned to run. But the forest was holding her down like bullies by the lockers.

Fox's knife shone in the dark like a razor.

CHAPTER 6
HIDDEN FIRE

BROOK JERKED AWAY but her hair snapped her back.

"Easy, Fox, easy." She held one hand in front of her chest and forced herself to keep talking. "Um, is that a knife? Cool, I'll bet it comes in handy." Her heartbeat drowned her words—THUMP, THUMP, THUMP—like music in a club, so loud you could hear it from the street. She tugged at her hair with her free hand, but she might as well have been tied down. She couldn't have trapped herself better if she'd tried.

"Seriously," Fox said.

THUMP.

"Stop moving," he said.

THUMP THUMP.

"That's not helping, Brook."

She let go of her hair and held up her palms like they were force shields that would blast Fox backward like Ironman. Of course, that wasn't how it worked when a blade met your skin. She curled her fingers into fists, then forced them to her sides and tried to put some laugh into her voice.

"Hey Fox, can I borrow that knife?"

"How much do you care about your hair?" Fox said at the same time.

Then *he* laughed and she joined in a second later, trying not to sound crazy.

"Seriously, though," Fox said. "Do you want me to chop the vine or your hair?" He glanced around the darkening woods, shadows pooling under trees like the night was about to flood upward from the ground. Wind whistled overhead. They could have been in a dead end alley or an empty basement.

Brook noticed he didn't offer her the knife.

"Um, cut the vine," she said. The further the blade stayed from her skin the better. She forced herself to hold still as Fox moved close. His arm brushed her elbow. She smelled the metal very near her face and held her breath because she wanted to grab for the knife or lash out with her elbows or knees—but it wouldn't work. She'd end up with sliced fingers and she'd still be trapped, and then Fox would pick himself up, brushing off dirt—and he'd be mad.

Please let him be a good person, she thought. Please please please.

With a crunch, the bramble released her.

"Thank you," Brook breathed.

"It's kind of a mess," Fox said, "but you can figure it out later. Let's go."

A wave of shuddery tension flowed out of her. She smoothed her hair against her shoulders and would've tucked it inside the collar of her t-shirt, but Fox was right. The vine had made a tangled knot, and she didn't want the thorns stabbing her back.

Thank God, she thought, Fox isn't a bad person.

Her feet felt lighter in her dirty shoes as she followed him through the shadows. A few minutes later, heavy shapes rose around them like an underpass, making the dark complete. Brook followed the sound of Fox's steps with her hands spread out, feeling the way. Her fingers brushed rough stone on either side as they moved down a narrow, maze-like path. Then she smelled woodsmoke, they turned a corner between two standing stones, and the darkness lifted. Reddish light glowed on smooth rock walls. They stood in a sunken hollow facing the glowing embers of a small campfire.

Brook felt like a door had swung shut on the darkness.

"Finally," Fox said. "That was pushing it, but we're safe now. Welcome to the best campsite on the island—not counting the castle, obviously." He smiled at her. "No one can sneak up on us. And nothing will see our fire either. This is as good as it gets."

"It's perfect," Brook said. Upright boulders disappeared into the blue-black night. When she looked up, the sky was mostly hidden by the branches of greedy trees. She would've liked to see more stars. But it was good the trees were there in case the dragon flew by.

A sound drew her to the far side of the hollow. At first she couldn't believe her ears, but sure enough, water trickled down a grooved boulder, splashing into a mossy pool. Maybe the campsite really was perfect.

Fox must have seen the longing on her face. "Go ahead," he said.

Brook threw herself down, cupped her hands, and gulped the cool, clear water. The drink was the best news she'd had since she'd woke up on the cliffs. Good news, the water said as it washed the salt off her lips, off her teeth, off her tongue. There's hope. Maybe, just maybe, something good will happen.

She sat up, wiping her face. "How long have you been here?"

"On the island, you mean?" Fox had added twigs to the embers and was prodding them with some kind of metal poker. "Or here?"

"Both." Brook smiled.

"Well..." He laid a stick on the coals. "I kept track of days at first. Then I kind of stopped counting, because it wasn't helping me. Just making me a little crazy." He touched his forehead. "You know what I mean?"

"Do I ever." She'd long ago stopped counting days at the Foundation.

"It was at least a couple months," Fox said. "I walked around the edges of the island, scoping things out. I hid from the dragon, met some other kids, and tried to get into the castle, but that went badly. Then I lost track until I found this place. After that, I started counting again. I've been here, let's see, eighteen days now. It's special."

"So you haven't been here years?" Brook said. "That's a relief."

He laughed. "Years, ha! Definitely not. But a few months, probably. I haven't seen a boat or a plane or anything. No one else comes here, no one but the dragon. You'll want to look for yourself, but you can't see land from any of the beaches."

Brook pushed the chunk of bramble off the back of her neck. It was pricking her skin like tiny claws. She wondered whether to risk another question.

"What do you think you'll do about your hair?" Fox asked.

The thorns were twisted in her locks like a little hair-destroying machine. There was only one choice, but it didn't make her happy.

"I think *I'll* have to cut it," she said, choosing her words. Fox could have killed her or hurt her in the forest and he hadn't, but she still didn't want him cutting her hair.

"Probably smart," Fox said. "The island is a prickly place."

"Understatement," she said, wondering if he was playing it cool on purpose.

"Here," Fox said.

Brook perked up, thinking he was about to hand her the knife, but instead he held out some dried meat. "Hey, thanks." The meat didn't smell bad, just smoky. Delicious, if she was being honest. She bit off a piece, her mouth swimming, and forced herself to chew it until it got soft, which meant about twenty times.

"Rabbit jerky," Fox said proudly. "Lots of them around. Of course I could kill something bigger, but rabbits, well, you don't waste anything, and they don't have fangs or talons or stingers to pull out, and they actually taste good."

"So good," Brook said. And she meant it. She found it hard to concentrate on much else as she tore at the jerky with her teeth, eating a shred at a time. Fox put two more sticks on the fire. The flames threw flickering lemon-gold light on the rock walls, making the camp seem warm and safe. And it *was* warm by the small fire, out of the wind. And if Fox was right, it was safe too. Safe from the sea, the cliffs, the dragon, and whatever else was out there.

CHAPTER 7
FIVE CAREFUL CUTS

"YOU CAN HAVE MORE rabbit if you want," Fox said. "I wouldn't recommend it, though. When you haven't eaten for awhile, it's smart to go easy on your stomach."

"Makes total sense," Brook said. The first hunk of jerky had mostly filled her up, but it was a nice gesture. Fox didn't have to give her food. Or let her drink his water. Or share his secret campsite. She didn't want to push it. He sat cross-legged in the dancing light of the fire, shoving it with the poker like he was trying to get the flames just right.

Now that Brook was no longer starving or dying of thirst, another sharp, twisty urge was rising in her chest. It wasn't a weird question about the meaning of life. It was an obvious one. She was getting the words ready when Fox held out his knife. She was so surprised her hand flew halfway to her mouth.

"Here you go," he said. "Hard to sleep with thorns in your hair."

She'd been wondering how the little drama would play out. Maybe she'd have to point out that her hair wasn't going to cut itself. Or ask if he had a pair of scissors lying around. She would've done both those things before she asked point blank to borrow his knife. Worse than asking a random kid for his address. Luckily it hadn't come to that.

She leaned forward on an elbow and reached, wondering if Fox would snatch the knife back at the last second. Instead she had the feeling, as she lifted it off his palm, that he'd put the moment off as long as he possibly could, and was forcing himself to let go. The knife felt heavy with Fox's mind hanging on to it. He kept his dark eyes pinned to her as she slid away to the far side of the fire.

Brook felt like a dog with a bone. For a split-second she could've jumped to her feet and sprinted into the night—but of course she'd just get lost. Instead, she touched her hair and sighed, and she wasn't faking. As she ran her fingers up her neck, she wished her hair had been twisted in a topknot, or pulled back in a ponytail or even braided.

Yeah, if only you could've been dropped on the cliffs with your hair done.

"This isn't going to be pretty," she said.

She'd never admitted it, but now she saw those Foundation kids were right, at least a little. Always on her case: "What's up, Shampoo Princess? When you gonna open your own salon?" She'd done her best to hide it, but she'd been proud of her hair, the whispery weight, the ways she could make it look good. Now she had to hack it off.

When she looked up, Fox was still watching.

"Wanna buy a ticket?" The words shot right out.

His eyebrows jumped and he looked into the fire.

"I mean, no big deal..." Maybe she'd been a little harsh.

"No, I get it." He kept his eyes on the blaze. "A haircut is personal."

Not to mention, Brook thought, this is a very sharp knife. She ran her thumb along the edge, glad he'd stopped staring so she could focus.

Then she swallowed and grabbed a handful. Dusky brown with amber streaks from the sun, now it smelled like the ocean. Pulling the hank away from her head, she raised the knife and sliced in a careful arc. At first she thought nothing had happened. Then the bramble bumped her wrist, dangling from the tangled mess in her hand. The knife was *really* sharp. It made her think of the hours she'd spent in her dorm, grinding away at her fork to give it razor edges. Her *shork*, she'd called it. Not a spork. Not a fork. A sharp-fork or even a *shark*-fork. A shork.

One of her better jokes, even though she'd kept it to herself.

She wanted to end the haircut right there, with the thorns sliced away, but she could imagine what she looked like and it would take a lot of product—and some dye and face piercings—to make it look like she'd done it on purpose.

Brook sighed and found another handful. The knife moved through it soundlessly. No sawing needed. Two more cuts and cool air swept the top of her spine. I wonder what I look like now, she thought, and frowned. *Short hair, don't care.*

She swept her left hand back and forth, collecting strands, and finished the job with a delicate swoop of the blade. She ran her thumb along her naked neck, feeling feathered edges. Her fingers found the hollow at the bottom of her skull, the place where your spine connects to your brain, a place you always keep safe. Now open to the air.

She shivered.

I look like a prank, she thought. She almost wished Fox had been watching, because seeing her now, changed all at once, it would hit him like a bad joke.

"Hey, what happened?" he'd say. "Where's that girl who was sitting there?"

She didn't like being laughed at. It made her tense inside. Then something slipped away from her like a breath of air. Her shoulders sagged. It doesn't really matter, she thought. Of course it doesn't. *There are no mirrors here, no combs or headbands.* Still, it was hard to let go of how she looked. To lose a part of herself to the island.

Maybe Fox sensed her lack of movement, because when she looked up, he was watching.

"Hey, you did a great job," he said. "You look good."

"Thanks," she said grudgingly. Was he lying? On this island, she'd never know. She stepped around the fire and gave him back the knife and he nodded up at her.

"Yeah, it's nice."

"Don't push it," she said, wishing she had a knife of her own.

He held up his hands in fake surrender. *Ok, ok.*

So she gave him a smile as she sat back down on the far side of the flames. And then, because they seemed to be getting along, she asked the question that was pricking her insides, irritating and unpleasant, the way the bramble had been pricking her neck.

CHAPTER 8
FOX'S BARGAIN

"WHERE IS EVERYONE ELSE?" Brook asked. When Fox didn't answer right away, she said, "I mean—why are you all alone?"

Fox played with the fire. She got the idea he was looking for words.

"You could say I'm not a very friendly person, but that's not quite it." He frowned. "It's not that I don't like people. I do, I'm pretty social."

"Yeah, you are." And good thing, Brook thought. Otherwise I'd still be on the beach.

"I wish I could share the campsite with other kids," Fox said. "But being friendly gets you in trouble around here. I tried it for a while and it didn't go well. We ended up fighting so much that it got dangerous to stay together." He hesitated. "Did you ever read *Lord of the Flies?*"

She swallowed and shook her head no, wondering what he'd say.

"Well, it's a story about a bunch of kids on an island. The island isn't terrible. You get the idea they could've all worked together and had a pretty good time, but that's not what happens. By the time help gets there, they've split into tribes and started killing each other. It's a fight for survival. That's kind of what living here is like—except this island *is* terrible." Fox met her eyes. "It kind of changes your outlook on life," he said, being philosophical again.

Brook nodded. She knew he was telling the truth. She'd known as soon as she woke up on the cliffs, even though she hadn't wanted to believe it. The island *was* a terrible place. She also knew what kids could be like. The Children's Foundation was a different kind of island. Her life in Weed was an urban version of *Lord of the Flies*.

She'd known that for a while, ever since she'd found a tattered copy of the book dumped in a corner of Language Arts. She hadn't told Fox because she'd wanted to hear his version of the story. And now she knew: The island was bad, and the kids were bad—but why? Forget the details. Why any of it? Why would anyone, or anything, work so hard to bring a nobody like her to–

"What about you?" Fox pushed his hair back from his forehead.

Brook froze. "Me?"

"Tell me something about you. It doesn't have to be a big thing."

"Um, well, let's see." She ground a clump of moss to bits behind her back and tried to look thoughtful. No one ever asked Brook about herself. It made her head spin because what could she possibly say that wouldn't sound like a total sob story?

"Well, I'm an orphan, or I was." She gave a little laugh. "Nothing special, just another numbered file...in a building stuffed with numbered files. It was a fun, exciting life."

"Uh huh," Fox said. "What could possibly be more fun than being a number?"

She hoped it was a good performance, but she got the idea he was wondering about her, which was the last thing she wanted—even though *she* was wondering about him too. Stuck in a bad story with someone she didn't understand.

Since he'd mentioned *The Lord of the Flies*, it made her curious who Fox thought he was. Did he see himself as the weak kid, Piggy, who got knocked off a cliff? Not likely. Maybe Rolf, Piggy's friend, who tried to help him and failed? She sure hoped not. Because who would that make her? But either of them would be better than the evil kid, Jack, who'd kill anyone who got in his way.

"You're cool, Brook," Fox said as if he could read her mind. "You're tough and smart, and I'm not flattering you, just calling it how it is. You seem like a what-you-see-is-what-you-get kind of girl. That's the only kind of friend worth having."

What you see is what you get? Brook thought. That's funny.

"Thanks," she said. "That's nice of you."

He spread his hands. "What I'm saying is, I—there's a word for it, but I forget—I—can *count on* you. Things are bad out there, and I'd like to have you on my team."

Brook pulled her knees to her chest. All at once she felt on edge, and it wasn't because of Fox's memory problems. "What does it mean to be on your team?" she said. You have the knife, she thought. You have the food and water and fire. What else will you want?

Fox nodded like he knew what she was thinking. "It means you have my back and I have yours. That's all. Two minds instead of one. We work together."

"Got it." Brook leaned back on her elbows, forcing herself to act casual. Stuck on an island, she thought, with a guy who probably thinks you're a weakling, and he wants you on his team. It's Rolf and Piggy all over again—except I'm not Piggy! The fire hissed and crackled at her feet. Fox was making sense, though. A team was a good idea.

Still, she might say no, because something about Fox said *caution*. But what kind of person would she want to team up with anyway? Someone who didn't make you nervous at all was probably a loser. Everyone worth knowing was a little dangerous. In a place like this, you *wanted* dangerous.

But that wasn't the real problem.

Brook saw the problem. Knew it inside and out.

She didn't want anyone.

Maybe she never had.

People weren't trustworthy. They said they loved you and

wanted you until one day, without warning—they didn't. The love stopped. The care disappeared. Parents were blurry memories who didn't meet your eyes. It turned out you were just too much, way too much, and you found yourself stuck in the Children's Foundation, repeating the pattern over and over like a bad habit.

That's why it was better to be alone.

When she glanced across at Fox, he dropped his eyes like he saw the darkness in her thoughts. He wasn't pushing her, which was smart of him. The fire threw off sparks as he twisted the poker.

Maybe it's my fault, she thought, because I never wanted anyone in the first place. At least, not like I should. Not after that first time— maybe not even then. Maybe that's why they decided I wasn't good enough. The *caring* part of my heart is cracked, and caring is hard to fake, even when you try.

A team could maybe help with that.

Right then she decided she'd do it, she'd team up with Fox—but she wouldn't tell him for a while. She had to get her nerve up first.

What I really want, she thought, is what he has. A place where you can sit in a pool of sunlight and be quiet. Ideally there would be a door with a big lock. And you'd never have to leave until you wanted.

If she had a secret campsite all to herself, would she invite someone else to share it? She didn't think so. It would have to be a pretty special kid. Maybe that made Fox a better person, because he was willing to share this hidden place.

Sharing was better than nothing.

Probably.

Maybe.

"Why don't you sleep on it?" Fox said.

She forced a smile to her lips. "Good idea. It's been a long day. Gosh, what a stupid thing to say. I mean, it's been awhile since I've been dumped by a dragon. I'm out of practice."

Fox laughed. "Pleasure meeting you, Brook."

"Thanks," she said. "You too, Fox."

"See you in the morning. The moss behind you is pretty soft."

She brushed crumbled dirt off her fingers. Hopefully she'd be able to sleep. The idea of being on Fox's team was floating her insides up and down.

He gave her a little salute, got to his feet and moved into the shadows. She could barely see him as he curled up by the far rock wall. Sounds from the night moved closer: birdcalls, scurrying noises, the wind in the trees. The island pressed in, reminding her she had no clue what she was doing. How long should I sit here? she wondered. Should I pretend to be thinking things over? The idea made her a little panicky. *What if I come up with a reason to change my mind?*

Then she noticed something startling. The metal poker shone in the firelight, sharp and hooked. Fox had left it leaning in the flames. Not a big deal, she thought. He just forgot it. He's tired. But she knew that was ridiculous. Someone like Fox, who could barely stand to loan her a four inch knife, would never leave a deadly weapon glowing in the embers. She put an elbow on her knees and leaned her chin in one hand.

He is *trusting* you. That word, that idea he has such a hard time with—he's trying it.

You could grab that poker.

Nothing he could do.

Brook nodded to herself. The poker was the sign she'd been waiting for.

She'd be on his team. She wouldn't change her mind.

CHAPTER 9
SCREAMS AND RUNNING

THE ANIMALS in the forest were crazy loud. If Brook heard this kind of noise in Weed, she'd think someone was dying. The screeches, hoots and shrieks sent her twisting to her knees in the night, digging at the moss for her shork until she remembered where she was. She could make out a few stars, pin-pricking the sky in the patches that showed through branches. Once she heard a rumbling roar and something flew past, erasing stars as it went.

The dragon.

She crossed her arms over her chest and squeezed. No ceiling inches from your face, she told herself. No lumpy mattress, no unwashed bodies. No one creeping toward your bed. This is better, it's better.

But still bad.

When she finally slept, the screams of the forest followed her. She felt herself falling, hitting the floor. Felt herself lash out—felt herself run. She was always running in her dreams. Heart pounding, sneakers smacking, breath coming in ragged gulps. Brook was quick on her feet but it never mattered.

She'd start sprinting in an alley or a school parking lot. Even a playground. In the first burst of speed, her pursuers would vanish.

But they always reappeared, moving closer without trying, like she was running in place while distance folded for them like a map so they could step across the city.

Her surroundings changed in a horrible, invisible way. She'd look over her shoulder or turn a corner and find herself in the one place she didn't want to be. Asphalt, linoleum, and grass melted to shadows, a room of locked closets, metal appliances and stained concrete. The chase always ended in the Children's Foundation basement.

The last place you'd ever want to be caught.

Brook came to, gasping. She pressed the back of her neck, smoothing away the tension, and huddled in the pitch darkness as something howled. Or maybe it was a wail. She didn't know her animal sounds. Maybe the dragon is circling, she thought. Who knows what sounds it makes? But he'll never find you here.

Over the dead fire, she couldn't make out Fox's shape in the dark. She put her cropped head back down on the moss and took slow, regular breaths. Pressing her shoulder into the ground, she tucked her knees and closed her eyes.

Remember where you are, she told herself.

Sharp golden sunlight hit her face. Her eyes snapped open on stone and moss and she sat up, blinking. Fox crouched by the fire, shoving charred wood to the center of the ring.

Giving her space.

Looking around in the light, she saw how hidden the camp was. If someone stood on the boulders overhead, he might still miss the sunken hollow. Leafy branches draped the tops of the rocks like a camouflage net. A couple of tree trunks stretched across like roof beams. Moss covered the ground like a thin green layer of memory foam, making things comfy. She didn't know if it was luck or hard work, but Fox's camp was perfectly tucked away.

She got to her feet feeling bruised and achy.

Fox gave her a nod. "Sleep ok? Sorry, bad question."

"Ha. You're right." She stepped to the spring-fed pool, knelt and cupped a drink, wishing she had her toothbrush. Her blurry outline in the water looked different, and she brushed her short hair with her fingertips. Her clothes were torn and dirty. Her shork was gone. So was her name.

Who are you? she thought.

It was like reaching for something, maybe a bird or butterfly, that always danced away. Effortless, not even trying, just out of reach. She knew her name was floating in her mind, but hidden so she'd never find it. She couldn't keep thinking about it, reaching for it. It would make her crazy.

She barely felt like herself at all.

"How hungry are you?" Maybe Fox sensed her mood because he didn't wait for an answer. "I've got more jerky, but today is a hunting day, so if you want to wait, we could cook something fresh. Or we could have a bite now and rabbit brunch."

Brook tried to pull her thoughts together. If she'd been alone, she would've pressed her back to the stone wall and slid down into the moss and held perfectly still until her mind and heart caught up. Instead, she took a breath through her nose and turned.

This was it.

"I'm in," she said. "About both things. What you said last night —let's be on a team. And also," she rushed on, "let's go hunting."

"Hey, excellent!" Fox grinned. "I'm happy you decided to stay. We'll make a good team—the best team, you'll see. And I love fresh rabbit."

A team! I'm on a team, she thought.

She smiled. Then she let herself laugh.

"Well of course you love fresh rabbits," she said, "I mean, haha, *every* fox would say that if foxes could talk."

Fox swept an arm out and dipped his head in a half bow. "I present to you the one and only talking fox."

Brook sighed. "Ah, laughing feels good."

"And it was just a little laugh," Fox pointed out.

That's as big as my laughs get, buddy, she could've said.

"I'll be ready in a minute." He shoved another chunk of smoking charcoal to the middle of the fire. The ash was deep and he was jabbing the poker around, searching for every last piece of glowing wood.

The poker.

Brook's eyes widened. What she'd mistaken for a poker in the night was really a long, serrated sword. The dark blade ended in a nasty hook. A loop of blackened twine was tied to the handle. It was hard to imagine a scarier-looking weapon. A kid could've ruled the Foundation with a thing like that.

Fox caught her staring. "Don't worry," he said. "It won't melt and I always clean it."

"Ah, that's a relief. It would be terrible if it got damaged." Brook looked away, then back at the sword. "Where did you get it? I mean —did the dragon give it to you or something?"

Fox hesitated.

Where are we? Brook thought. Did we travel back in time? If you put the clues together, would it be crazy to think we're stuck in the Dark Ages? Or back when pirates sailed the seas, burying treasure? She put a knuckle to her forehead.

Fox was watching her. "Actually," he said, "I found it."

She blinked. "You found it. Down a storm drain, buried in a dumpster, or what?"

He laughed and she felt relieved.

"I found it in the cliffs. Had to climb out on the rocks to get it."

Brook thought of the jagged, dirty rocks that ended in the belly of the sea. Kid-eating cliffs. Killer waves. She couldn't imagine someone climbing onto those rocks for anything.

Anything at all.

"I had to," Fox said. "Or someone else would have."

"That's impressive," she said after a minute.

You don't understand how bad this place is, she thought. Obviously you don't.

CHAPTER 10
RABBIT HUNT

BROOK PAID close attention as they walked through a tangle of boulders and springy bushes that waited to slap her in the face. She didn't need more scrapes and bruises. There has to be a way to map the woods, she thought, memorize them like sidewalks and fire escapes.

Was the forest less scary in the morning? She wasn't sure. The trees didn't openly threaten her. But they weren't the bright, happy forests you saw on school posters with slogans that made you want to puke.

These woods were not playing around.

Trees fought over the ground in twisted clumps. Some of their fights must have been going on for decades, because trunks shoved each other back and forth, twisting their way into the sky. Selfish shrubs grabbed every spare inch of soil, disguising their thorns with pretty leaves. The morning light filtered through it all in a greenish haze. Each time Brook looked down, there were more burrs on her clothes and shoelaces. Cutting her hair off had been the right choice. Scratches were appearing on her bare legs. No wonder Fox wore pants.

All she had were jean shorts, and she felt jealous.

When they shoved their way out of the brush, it felt like escaping. Brook pinched dozens of burrs off her clothes before she remembered they'd be coming back the same way. The woods would get another chance at them—so she gave up and took in the scenery.

Fields of high grass rolled away toward the sand, tossing and swirling in the wind. The sun was a golden ball, hanging over the far-off dunes. She was glad they couldn't see the cliffs. Now she just needed to stop thinking about them. It was like letting the island win. She could imagine it gloating:

Can't get me out of your head, Brook, can you?

"Rabbits love these fields," Fox said, breaking the silence. "I've got a dozen snares. A bow and arrows would give them more of a fighting chance, but when you're hungry it's hard to care about sportsmanship."

"Poor bunnies," Brook said. "At least they have big families."

Fox shaded his eyes and scanned the open ground. Nothing moved that Brook could see. He led the way onto the plain, and she was happy to find that walking was easier in the high grass. She stretched out her arms and let the stalks and seedpods brush her fingertips. After the claustrophobic woods, the blue sky seemed huge. She decided that aside from their campsite, the fields were her favorite place on the island. They were open, honest. Even friendly.

So this place wasn't one hundred percent bad. *Take that, island.*

"Here's my first snare," Fox said. "I put them in the rabbit runs, where the little guys go back and forth. Ah, no luck."

Brook leaned close. In an area of flattened turf, a loop of twine hung from a frame made of sticks. The lasso was empty.

"Do these actually work?" she asked.

"Of course they do," Fox said.

She realized she'd offended him. "How cool," she said. "Super resourceful."

Fox stared down at the trap. "Rabbits jump through the slipknot in the dark and...ahhk." He put a hand to his neck.

Brook thought about bunnies nibbling clover and felt a little guilty. But she also felt hungry. Getting hungrier.

"Have I mentioned this is genius?" she said.

Fox scoffed. Then he gave up and smiled.

But the next snare was empty too. And the third one.

"It's a numbers game," Fox said.

The fourth and fifth and sixth were empty. He muttered under his breath.

"It's ok," Brook said. "No rush."

Luckily, the seventh held a dead rabbit. A nice big one, Brook thought. And good thing. Fox's jaw had been getting harder, his eyes darker. She didn't want to see him lose his cool.

"About time," he said. "I usually do better than this." He rubbed his chin. "Makes you wonder if the rabbits are catching on."

The slipknot on the eighth trap had been jerked to one side, like something had struggled and pulled free. The ninth was empty again.

"It's just bad luck," Brook said.

Fox kicked at grass stems as he walked, making twice as much noise as usual. Brook hoped he wasn't mad about feeding her, because what was she supposed to do, volunteer to leave? Good thing we're officially on a team, she was thinking—when they rounded a bend in the faint path and Fox stopped short.

The jerky energy left his body. He got very still.

"What is it?" Brook whispered. "Did you catch another?"

She leaned around him to see. The rabbit run entered a patch of high red grass. Some kind of special edition grass like you'd see in a rich person's yard. Then she saw the broken snare—cracked sticks and snapped twine. The snare was red, and so was the dirt and everything, even the gravel. Brook realized she was looking at blood. It must've sprayed out from the trap or been wildly smeared around. For a second, she saw blood drip-drip-dripping onto a dirty concrete floor.

She shuddered and looked down, focusing on the trampled soil and bent grass.

Then she stepped away from the blood—and away from Fox.

Brook knew the signs. Anger can build and build inside you until even when you try to hold it in, you've hardly got a chance. When you see that coming in another person, you get out of the way if you have any brains at all. But Fox surprised her.

He didn't cuss or stomp on the broken trap or turn to yell at her. Instead, his hand dropped to his knife and he turned in a slow circle, searching the plain. It made the center of her stomach go very still. Fox glanced back the way they'd come. His eyes got narrow.

"We'd better get to the trees," he said.

Cold wind traced Brook's spine. "Ok," she said, and waited for him to move. She wasn't going to be left behind. Fox glided away from the bloody circle, and Brook lengthened her strides to keep up.

"What did that?" she asked, not caring if Fox was on edge. She felt exposed. Tricked. She'd thought the fields were pretty and bright, but now they felt deadly, a place you crossed as quickly as you could. Fox hadn't offered her a weapon. He had the sword *and* the knife. Maybe he'd thought they wouldn't need them, but now she felt almost naked, like she'd been dropped in a low-light parking garage without even a shiv or a winter coat.

"What did that?" she said again, drawing even with Fox.

"I'll tell you," he said, "when we reach the trees. Let's keep our voices down."

She didn't care for that answer, but she balled up her fists and kept pace, arranging her thoughts as they hurried through whispery, wind-tossed grass that was tall enough to hide an awful lot. Her left hip ached. Dry seedpods rattled like tiny, hollow drums.

Blood all over the place, she thought. Something shredded that rabbit like nothing. You're holding back things I should know and we're supposed to be on a team. You can't treat me that way, pal. No way. I'm not your little sidekick. You're angry, huh? Well, so am I.

I wish I had my shork.

CHAPTER 11
SPILLING GUTS

BY THE TIME they reached the edge of the forest, Brook's fingers had bit into her palms, leaving white half-circles. She couldn't afford to go crazy on Fox, but that didn't mean she'd let this slide. Not a chance. In the shadow of the trees, she slid her hands to her hips.

Fox looked back over the fields. A few clouds moved in the blue sky, but otherwise nothing had changed. When the boy turned to face her, she began counting down from ten. She'd give him a chance to tell her what was going on. Ten, nine, eight, seven, six, five, four...

"Death Dogs," Fox said.

She forgot her number.

"I don't think they're a normal species," he said. "Maybe you'd call them monsters. They're like wolves, with teeth and fur and they hunt in packs, but they also have stingers."

"How—do you know?" Brook said.

Fox turned and looked hard in her eyes. "Because I've seen them." He hesitated. "I've seen them kill. It's awful. They hunt at night, usually, but you can't be too careful. If they catch you in open country, it's over."

"So—we're safe now?" Brook said.

Fox gestured at the trees. "Yeah. Anyway, if they'd picked up our scent, they'd already be here."

Brook started another countdown, slower this time. She needed it for herself. Ten...nine...eight...seven...six...five...four... three...two...one.

Fox was staring across the fields like the conversation was over.

"Who do you think you are?" she said. "You acted like we were taking a walk in the park. That was a joke, a dirty joke. I could've been ripped apart by dogs and you didn't even warn me." *Or give me a knife.*

She put her hands behind her back. They were shaking—not with fear but with anger. If she wasn't careful, she'd say or do something she'd regret.

Fox crossed his arms and studied a patch of shadow.

"Ok," he said. "You've got a point, but here's the thing. I didn't expect Death Dogs this far inland. I haven't seen any signs and I didn't think I was putting you in danger, no more than waking up on this"—he scowled—"this hunk of rock. I thought the rabbits would be easy, and I didn't want to dump everything on you at once. It's a lot to handle, so believe it or not, I was trying to help."

She felt frustrated when she couldn't find any holes in his answer, but at the same time, she was pretty sure that when you were on a team, you didn't hold all kinds of secrets back.

"Maybe you shouldn't try so hard," she said. "Maybe I can handle more than you think. Anything else you were waiting to tell me?"

Fox's eyes burned into hers. He blinked. Then he sighed. "You know about the dragon," he said. "I mentioned the castle and the blue-faces. They're vicious but they keep to themselves. Why wouldn't they, when they have everything they need? There are probably other nasty creatures on the island, but the Death Dogs are the ones I know about. Other than that..." He shrugged, but Brook knew the look too well to be fooled.

"What else?"

"Just—other kids," Fox said. "Feral, I guess you could call them. Some of them are really dangerous. Luckily there are two of us now, but we'll keep an eye out."

"Oh," she said. "Fantastic."

No one ever spilled all their guts. There was always something left, and it was usually slimy. She looked at him, then away. Her stomach felt flat and achy.

"I'm sorry, Brook," Fox said. "I let you down. I should've known better because you're sharp, which is one reason I liked you in the first place. I shouldn't have treated you like a kid. Give me another chance, ok?"

When she looked up, his face had softened. She was almost surprised to hear herself say:

"Well, ok, I guess."

She couldn't help it. Apologies were rarer than birthday cards at the Foundation.

"Great." Fox let out a breath, rubbing his hands together. He pushed his hair off his forehead and turned in a half-circle. "Cool."

He may be a jerk but he's glad you're here, Brook thought, and had to keep herself from smiling.

"How about lunch, or brunch, whatever this is?" Fox said. "We could do something I hardly ever do, make a fire in the woods—a very small one, with hardly any smoke, you know? And cook this rabbit. Then I could make it up to you by showing you something cool, like one of the beaches—or even the castle."

His eyes always got a little bigger when he mentioned the castle.

"Yes, please," she said, putting some bounce in her voice. "That sounds amazing." She needed to get back on Fox's good side.

She watched him slice open the rabbit. It was gross but she'd seen worse things, and anyway, it was edible. She'd cut up raw chicken on kitchen duty in the Foundation, always closely super-vised, since God forbid that anyone steal a kitchen knife or mess up dinner, no matter what happened after curfew. The rabbit was cuter than a chicken, and it had more blood, but she was so hungry she didn't care.

She only looked away once, when Fox cut off its head.

"Nice and fresh," he said, stripping away the fur. "We'll roast it."

Fox handed her the knife like a peace offering, and she cut some thin branches off a tree and sharpened the ends to points. They slid chunks of raw rabbit onto the skewers and turned them over the small blaze Fox built. The meat took longer to cook than Brook would've liked.

"Can we eat it medium-rare?" she asked.

Fox laughed. "It's the best you can hope for, unless you like it black."

He showed her how to turn the meat slowly over the fire to keep it from going up in flames. As soon as the fire gave them embers, they used those.

"Steadier heat," Fox said. "Less likely to burn."

By the time the first pieces had cooled enough to eat, Brook's mouth was watering. The sizzling rabbit smelled wonderful. She and Fox tore off bites with their teeth. The meat was a little tough— "from running for its life," Fox said—but delicious. In fact, Brook felt like she'd eaten it before, many times. Usually baked, sometimes in soup with noodles, and once or twice fried with bread crumbs.

"I can't believe it tastes like chicken," she said. "But more earthy."

Fox nodded. "Kind of crazy, right?—certain things you can't escape from."

"Ha!" she said, because *escaping from chicken*. But he was right, certain things followed you wherever you went, and most of them were a lot worse than chicken. After they ate, Brook did her best to wipe the grease off her hands, but it was a losing battle. She hated feeling dirty, and it probably wasn't going to get better. At least her stomach was full. For now, anyway. They'd eaten the entire rabbit.

"What will it be?" Fox leaned against a tree trunk and picked his teeth with a little bone, somehow making it seem not-creepy. "The beach? A forest overlook? The castle?"

It was so obvious what he wanted that Brook smiled.

"Hmm, let's see. I was thinking it would be great to have a look at..." She studied the branches overhead, faking thoughtfulness. "How about the beeea—actually, no."

Fox looked relieved.

"I'd enjoy a nice overlook."

"Ok." He nodded sadly.

"Just kidding. Show me the castle."

His eyebrows shot up. "Really? Cool. Wait, am I that obvious?"

"Like an open book," Brook said, wishing it was true.

CHAPTER 12
THE CASTLE

THEY WOVE along the edges of the woods, dodging green plants that looked all innocent but were packing stingers. Brook had the Death Dogs in the back of her mind, and she was sure Fox did too. Otherwise, they would've just walked across the fields. Instead, they hugged the tree line for cover as they hiked, dodging the branches trying to claw them. Sunlight through the leaves left blotches on her skin like gray-green camo.

"This is like walking an invisible balance beam," Brook said.

It took Fox a second to get it, then he smiled. "This balance beam is heading north, in case you're wondering," he said. "Toward the center of the island."

"The heart of the mystery," Brook said.

Fox tapped his forehead as he dodged a thorn bush. "You've got a philosophical streak too."

"You're not wrong," Brook said. "I wonder about things, but it hasn't done me a whole lot of good."

"Tell me about it," Fox said.

They shared a smile—maybe even a smirk.

This guy's ok, Brook thought.

Balancing on the edges of the forest, they snuck along for a while.

A dozen football fields. Maybe a mile. Or even two.

Brook wasn't great at gauging distances. She wished she wasn't such a city girl. From the Children's Foundation to Weed Middle School was as good as her distance measurements got, and all she knew was how long it took her to make the trip. Eight minutes—five minutes if she fast-walked—always alone, with an eye out for trouble. She and Fox had been hiking for about fifteen minutes, mostly in silence, except for "watch that branch," and "look out, thorny thing," when Fox turned left, into the woods.

"The castle is in the woods?" Brook said.

"You'll see."

"Please don't tell me it's made of trees."

Back in the deeper shadow, the forest sloped up. The ground got rocky and after a few minutes their feet hit solid stone. Edging along boulders, watching her shins, Brook thought about how useless her thin sneakers were. Filthy, wet, falling apart. No protection, and they made her do everything in slow motion. Oh well. Going slow was better anyway.

There were kids who strutted around trying to prove themselves. *Hey, check me out.* Working hard to show they were just as dangerous as anyone else. And unless they had a gang behind them, those kids ended up with casts and stitches. No thanks. Calm, cool and in control was better—always.

Even so, she stole a glance at Fox's kicks as she skidded around. Tough-looking, with grippy treads for hiking. Even kind of stylish. Who was this guy, that he got such good stuff? She grabbed a boulder as her feet started to slide out from under her like they were covered in butter. Darn it, now she felt jealous. Some kids would kill for Fox's shoes, and if this went on much longer, she'd be one of them.

"Hey Fox, nice kicks," she said.

"Thanks, Brook. Hey, don't fall off the side, ok?"

"Ooo, great tip." *But I'm having so much fun on my roller skates.* She wondered how he'd lucked out with his shoes, and more important, what would happen to her when the rest of her clothes started falling apart like her flimsy canvas knockoffs. Maybe she should start saving rabbit skins.

Then she had to pay attention to the climb, searching for finger holds to keep herself from skidding down the giant slabs. Fox stayed within an arm's reach, keeping an eye on her. When she caught him hovering, he shrugged and raised his eyebrows.

"I'd hate to lose you on your first day."

"I'm *fine.*" Brook frowned at him, then toppled forward and grabbed a rock ledge as her feet shot out from under her with a squelching sound.

"Ok, you're fine." Fox held up his hands.

Brook pulled herself upright. "It's no different than gym class— or climbing a fire escape," she said through gritted teeth.

"Wow," Fox said. "Your gym classes must be wild. And your fire escapes must be covered in banana peels."

"Curse you," Brook said.

He really thinks I'm a klutz, she thought. *Great. These trash shoes, though!*

When she jumped off the last boulder and onto solid ground, she shoved her cropped hair out of her face, arched her arms in a stretch, and wriggled her battered fingers.

"Phew, glad that's over."

Fox's smile looked smug.

Let him think what he wants. Scuffing her feet over pine needles, she followed him through scratchy evergreens—and froze. They stood on the edge of a cliff. Sun-baked rock dove forty or fifty feet to the open plain below, where chunks of rock littered the ground. It would be a fatal fall—but at least this cliff didn't try to ambush you. Not like the coast with its slick and hungry teeth.

Looking down at the high brown grass, flattened here and there by rock, she realized that's where they'd be if they'd stuck to the open ground. Blocked from the woods by flat, unclimbable stone. It would've been like standing in a trashy courtyard with a project building at your back. Nowhere to run. Nowhere to hide.

Then she looked further out and saw the castle.

"Oh my—whoa."

Fox nodded. "Right?"

She shaded her eyes against the midday glare.

The castle sprawled huge and strong and dark against the plains, giving off a wealthy vibe, the kind of place that could never be built again because big blocks of stone were so expensive. It made her feel tiny, even standing miles away. She could make out arched windows that probably opened on pent houses or executive suites. The thick, regular notches at the tops of the walls had all kinds of swagger.

And the towers!—Brook let out a long, low breath. Five of them rose high and graceful into the blue sky, one on each corner and the fifth one in the middle. If you lived in one of *those*, you'd feel like you were someone.

She found herself staring with a hand over her mouth.

Yeah, I'm the biggest thing on this island, the castle seemed to say. I'm in charge and I'm not apologizing, so don't tick me off.

Brook loved it instantly. Maybe the killer cliffs and hungry ocean and the dragon didn't get the last laugh with everyone after all.

These walls are made to keep danger out, she thought. Not like the Children's Foundation, made to seal nastiness in. She'd assumed the castle would be a pile of stones, some kind of glorified hide-out.

Now she pictured herself throwing a—what did you call those clawed hooks?—one of those over a wall, and pulling herself up a rope in the moonlight. Then tiptoeing up tower stairs, winding higher and higher into the stars. She'd walk down a stone hall, turn into an open doorway, and there it would be.

A clean, quiet room with a view. She'd lock the door behind her and lower herself into a pool of moonlight, soft and silver. She'd rest. She'd think. She'd dream. All by herself, for as long as she wanted. After a while the sun would rise and the pool of moon would turn to warm, liquid gold and she'd–

"Amazing, isn't it," Fox said.

She gave a little twitch.

"Has to be at least two acres inside," he said. "Everything they need in there, a water source, gardens, shelter, even chickens. It's the perfect set-up."

Brook shook her head. "How do you know?"

"Those are the rumors," Fox said. "And look at the place. Can you imagine anything less? Besides, the blue-face kids never leave. The time I knocked on the door, they didn't even come out to fight. Just threw rocks down at me and laughed. They're self-sufficient."

They stared across the plain.

"How can we get in?" Brook said.

Fox had been tapping his knife on a stone. He turned to look at her.

"Wow, Brook. You don't mess around."

No joke, she thought. Look at us, we're on Death Island.

"But you're thinking the same thing, right?" she said.

Getting inside the castle was her one big goal. It had happened in a couple seconds, which made it a rushed decision, but she couldn't help it. The castle was the place for her—it was obvious, like a light clicking on in a dark room. She needed to get there. Whoever had put her on the island should never have let her see the castle, never even let the *idea* of the castle cross her mind, because now she'd do whatever she had to. She couldn't push Fox, though. She had to coax him along and help him see it her way.

"I don't know." Fox was staring out over the fields. "If we really want to try and get in, we'll have to do some serious thinking. Some serious planning. It would be like one of those heist movies where there's a billion dollars or some priceless blueprint in a safe, but if one little thing goes wrong, everyone dies. And in a movie, everyone's ok with that, but in real life—"

"I get it," Brook said. "But you don't think I'm crazy. Admit it, you want to get in there too, at least a little bit."

Fox licked his lips and turned to look her. "Well, sure I do. I mean, if you're stuck out here, how couldn't you? Once you got inside, you wouldn't have to worry about the dragon or the Death Dogs, or hunting—nothing. You do a few chores to keep things running, then you sit back and take it easy. But Brook—don't set your heart on it, ok?"

Brook smiled. She had a hard time seeing Fox taking it easy. She could definitely see him patrolling the walls or keeping an eye on the island from the top of a tower, though.

"Set my heart on it?" She laughed. "C'mon, Fox, I'm not a kindergartner asking for a lollipop."

"Good point. I guess you're not covered in sparkles."

"Nope," Brook said. "Not me." Although she wouldn't have minded a *few* sparkles. At the Foundation, wearing anything bright or glittery was asking to get slapped.

"Well, happy you like the castle," Fox said. "Alone, I never had a chance to get inside, but together—who knows, Brook, who knows? Maybe we'll figure something out. Those blue-faces have had everything their way for so long, they'll never see it coming. Maybe our luck is about to change."

"Lightning from a clear sky," Brook said. "That's us."

"Nice," Fox said. "Or like bats out of hell."

She sniffed and decided to lay it on thick. "Fox, has it ever occurred to you that hell is red, not black? Because—all that fire. Bats flying out of hell would be pretty easy to see. Maybe go with 'bats out of the dark' next time. Or 'bats out of the night.' Either one would be better."

"What the heck, Brook." Fox laughed. "You're over the top."

"Bats out of hell, seriously?"

They were both in a good mood, which was what she needed.

For this to work, Fox had to like her and take her seriously. She was glad he was coming around.

Because aside from being dropped into the castle out of a jet or using—what were they called, grapples? No, grappling hooks, crazy stuff that only worked in heist movies—she didn't see a single way to get inside.

CHAPTER 13
STRANGER ON THE PLAIN

"*SOOO*, have you seen any adults around?" Brook asked.

They crunched quietly along the edges of the woods, feeling pretty good after their chat about the castle. Brook was doing her best to keep feeling that way.

"Not a single one," Fox said. "If there were grown-ups, there'd be rules and some kind of escape plan. Huge bonfires, people building rafts. Believe me, there's none of that, makes it too easy to get picked off. No adults, no rules, no big plans. None."

Brook was relieved there were no grown-ups because if there were, they'd be creating schedules, putting kids on work teams, all that fake-important stuff. And it would be the Foundation all over again. The mean kids would kiss up and keep doing whatever they wanted. Meanwhile, the adults would kick back in the castle, gossiping and watching their soap operas while all hell broke loose. It was way better to have everything out in the open.

It meant Team Brook-Fox had a shot at the castle.

Brook was having a hard time getting the castle out of her head. She knew there was no point in imagining what the rooms would look like, or wondering how it would be to have a garden that didn't wilt and die in the city heat. But she couldn't seem to help herself. She swatted a low-hanging branch aside.

"Did you ever go swimming, Fox? You know, in a pool?"

"Don't think so. As far as I remember."

"Me either, pretty sure. Maybe the castle has one."

"Heck yeah, it's big enough."

She pictured a freshwater spring bubbling into an enclosure as big as an aquatic center—with a garden crowding the edges. Everyone knew vegetables were good for you. Maybe she'd like them if she got the chance. The only ones she'd tried were carrot sticks with ranch, slimy green beans and watery, tasteless lettuce.

"Hey Foxy, think there's a garden in there?"

"Gotta be with all that space...*Brooklyn*."

"Brooklyn? Very funny, but let's stick with Brook."

Brooklyn sounded like a girl who had a college fund and earrings by the time she could walk. Anyone named Brooklyn would get pulverized in Weed. And Brooklyn would definitely not get her hands and knees dirty, working in a castle garden. Brooklyn would not deserve this castle the way Brook did.

"So, do Foxes eat vegetables?"

"Is that a serious question?"

"Haha."

At the Foundation and Weed Middle School, there'd been plenty of junk to eat. A steady diet of rolled-up pizza and chocolate milk wasn't good for you, but it kept you going. Out here, the stakes were higher. Brook thought unlimited veggies and chicken—Fox said there were chickens—would be a huge advantage. She was ready to change her diet and never look back. Shoot, she was ready to change her life. All she needed was the castle to give her a fighting chance.

"Hey Fox, ever been inside a henhouse?"

"Nope, don't think I—oh my gosh, Brook, you've gotta stop." He chuckled.

She took a moment to enjoy her funniness as they circled a patch of thorns. The sun was over the forest now, casting spiky shadows on their skins.

Now let's see. The castle was more than just amenities. It would give them shelter when it stormed, like her first night on the cliffs. It would give them a bunker when the dragon came inland—no need to worry about a dragon when you've got a castle. No need to watch your back at all, except from about a mile in the air. Free time to relax in the pool or in a quiet corner.

But best of all...

She kept returning to the safe, bright room at the top of a tower. It seemed too good to be true. So much so that she couldn't even joke with Fox about it.

You're being dumb, she told herself. You don't even know that room exists.

But with Fox backing her up, maybe Team B-F could get inside. And maybe, just maybe, when she climbed the stairs, the room would be there, waiting.

You've never had a dangerous friend, she thought. Never had a friend other people would listen to. Wow, that would've changed things. Not that you and Fox are friends—at least not yet—but you're a team. People can't walk all over you now. They have to take you seriously, not talk down to you, not force you into situations.

All this time, they'd been weaving along the balance beam at the edge of the woods, walking a line between the salty, windswept grass and the greenish shade of the trees. Free to move but not too obvious. Hidden, but not attacked by leaves and twigs.

Brook tried to think of another Fox joke.

Whoa, slow down, she told herself. You had one good lunch and you saw a castle and just like that, you think the whole world is gonna change. Get a grip. But she couldn't help it if she felt good.

Then Fox stopped so suddenly she bumped into him. "Oof." She caught herself and slid away in case he took a swing. But he didn't even notice.

"Out there," he said, pointing toward the plain. "Look."

He crouched in the scrub and Brook got down beside him.

Sure enough, out in the sunlight and waving grass, she caught movement. Wind tossed her chopped hair against her chin as she shaded her eyes. Far out in the flatlands, light gleamed on a small upright figure. His legs, hidden by the grass, had to be moving fast.

"It's another kid," Brook said.

Fox nodded but didn't speak.

"Should we go out there and talk?" she said.

Fox shook his head no. "With any luck, he hasn't noticed us."

"If he has, so what?"

All the fun drained out of their conversation.

"I'm not sure you've been paying attention." Fox crossed his arms. "Just about anything you meet on this island will kill you, and that includes other kids."

"But—but we're together."

He didn't smile. "I took a calculated risk with you, Brook. It paid off, but I had the edge. I saw you before you saw me and I took a good long look to make sure you weren't a threat. Even after you woke up and we talked, it still took me a while to decide you were ok. You can't just walk up to people here."

She nodded, feeling offended but knowing it was true. She didn't like the idea of Fox spying on her while she slept. But she would've done the same, she guessed, if she'd come across his battered body. She might have even frisked him to see if he was carrying a weapon. Would that have made her a jerk?

"So we just let him wander around out there?" she said.

"Here's the thing," Fox said. "We don't know he's wandering. We don't know how long he's been on the island or whether he's working alone." He hadn't taken his eyes off the distant figure, steadily moving closer. "Let's get out of sight."

"And watch from the trees?" Brook said.

Fox was already sliding into the forest on his hands and knees. She blew hair out of her face and followed, trying to make sense of it.

If anything, the solitary kid in the tall grass had spooked Fox more than the Death Dogs. It didn't add up.

In the shadow of the forest, Fox stood behind a tree trunk, looking back.

"Heading right this way," he muttered. "Like he knows we're here."

"Would it hurt to yell? You know, from a distance?" Brook honestly wasn't sure. Fox was nervous and that made her nervous. Some kids were pure poison, it was true. You didn't want to mess with them, nod at them, get their attention in any way. Monique at the Foundation had been like that, with a posse waiting to follow her lead. Whoa, Monique—she'd remembered a name.

"Maybe we should leave," Brook said.

"Still coming our way," Fox said. "Let's lose him before he gets any closer, huh?"

"Yeah, let's."

When Fox trotted away, dodging trees and ducking under vines, she stayed right on his heels, even though her hip flared up and her shoes kept slipping. For another minute, if she looked over her shoulder, she could see flashes of the stranger getting closer to the edge of the sunny field. He didn't slow down at all, just kept coming like he'd been shot out of a gun.

It was creepy.

Then the leafy green maze of the forest took them out of sight. If the kid was trying to intersect them, they'd be long gone by the time he was in the woods.

Well, maybe not long gone.

But safely gone.

Gone enough.

She hoped.

CHAPTER 14
BROOK VERSUS WOODS

AS THEY BURROWED into the trees, the colors changed. Fresh greens faded to fatigue and olive. Shadows thickened from charcoal sketches to pools of oil. The forest got deep and dark faster than Brook would've liked.

As she plunged after Fox, she thought, *How many kids are on Death Island? And how many are bad and how can you know who is who?* Maybe the boy behind them was a survivor like her, and he needed help. Then a spider with mile-long legs swung past her face, and she told herself to snap out of it. She focused on the thorns and thickets, the filtered greenish light, and Fox's retreating back. He barely ever slowed, shoulders upright, legs pumping, light on his feet.

Well, he is called Fox, she thought. What did you expect? Then she thought, You need to get a handle on the forest too. Don't let it boss you. Right now, your only chance if you lost Fox would be to climb a tree and hug a branch all night. Is that what you want?

So she started to push herself in small ways. Keeping her pace the same as his, she veered a little to the right, a little to the left, and back—like he was an arrow, flying straight ahead, and she was a— well, something just as fast but with more freedom. Something learning the forest, something not afraid. Her path fluttered back and forth behind Fox. *Maybe a high-speed butterfly.* She swerved around bogs, jumped over knobby roots, sidestepped vines like they were partners in a dance. She did it quietly, and Fox didn't look back.

These woods, she decided, are the nasty kind, but I'm getting their number. All I need is a little more time. Fox is right, bad things happen in the open. Death Dogs, dangerous kids patrolling in fast straight lines. If you go out there, anyone can see you, and then there's the wind, whipping your smell around—yeah, I definitely smell now—and the Death Dogs can sniff you out. She did her best to *not* think about the dragon.

Then she realized she was tired of running. Her hip ached, her lungs burned—she had to stop fluttering around. As she struggled to keep Fox in sight, she imagined the island laughing at her, a hateful laugh that rumbled down the coast like crashing waves, echoing in hidden caves beneath her feet. Jagged slivers of light through the trees made her think the island was smiling.

Brook wiped her forehead with a dirty hand. "I'm fine," she whispered. A hollow knocking rang through the woods and she cocked her head, trying to locate the sound. *Hmm.* It sounded like the water pipes in the Foundation's walls. But there wasn't any plumbing in the–

"Eee-eee!" A red-headed bird swooped at her with an eerie cry.

Brook gasped and ducked, shielding her face as the bird shot past. She caught a glimpse of an open beak, serrated like a steak knife. Five heartbeats later, she was still hunched over, one hand hovering by her eyes.

Bloodthirsty birds, she thought. Are you kidding me? This place wants to get the jump on you. It's waiting for an opening. So stay awake, like you're on the streets in Weed. After a while your street smarts will turn into woods smarts, but it will take some work.

And she knew she wasn't ready for this yet. Without Fox she'd be totally clueless. *If I lose track of this guy, or if he gets tired of me, I'm as good as dead.*

I've gotta keep him close.

I have to. At least for now.

She didn't like the thought one bit. It made her frown as she scuffed through dead leaves, trying to catch her breath. And it made her wonder why he'd chosen her for his team. What if he wasn't as tough as she thought? *Because let's be real, him running from that boy in the field was weird.*

She hadn't expected that, not at all. Fox didn't seem like the retreating kind. Maybe she'd been wrong about him, maybe he wasn't so dangerous—even though he had a sharp knife and a scary sword, and seemed comfortable with both.

Ahead of her, Fox swerved right to avoid a thicket. She went left, showing the forest she wasn't scared, even though she was losing speed. When she reached an open patch of woods on the far side, Fox had ghosted ahead. *Does he ever slow down?*

Then she thought, He's dangerous all right, even if you haven't seen him do anything. When your hair was in the thorns and he held up the knife—you thought he might cut your throat. That's not how you feel about a nice, safe person.

She shoved another whip-thin branch away from her eyes and plunged through *another* patch of clingy plants. Her feet felt packed in dirt.

Nice and safe he is not, she thought. Dangerous and sort of honest, yes. So give it a rest. He knows all kinds of things you don't know yet, so if he wants to run into the woods, you run into the woods. You've only been here a day. And hey, it's always smart to avoid a fight if you can. She winced and forced herself into a jog. All of a sudden, her knees felt rusty.

Gritting her teeth, she sped up to close the distance between them. She jumped over a patch of marshy ground, but she came down in a sloppy skid, arms flailing. One of her feet glopped into wet mud, and when she pulled free, her shoe and half her shin were slimy black.

"Blech."

A second later, both her feet shot out from under her. "Aah!" She caught herself with her hands, her face inches from the dirt. Centipedes writhed from under her fingers like tiny monsters. *Yikes yikes yikes!*

Fox stepped from behind a tree as she thrashed around. He jogged back to her. "Hey, Brook." Very casual, like he wasn't watching her self destruct.

She struggled to her feet, flicking her fingers like a crazy person.

"You ok?" he asked.

Oh yeah, wrestling bugs in the mud is amazing, she wanted to say.

Instead she gulped a breath and gave him a thumbs-up. *Don't mind me. Doing great.*

He took a long look at her.

Slimy legs, dirty face, sorta-hyperventilating.

Perfect.

"Need to take a breather, Brook?"

She swallowed. "Nope, good to go."

"Ok." He moved forward at a walk.

She wondered if he was rolling his eyes.

A few minutes ago, she'd been cracking Fox jokes. Then the island had come after her, and the red-headed bird may as well have started pecking on her chest: Knock, knock, knock. Fox, fox, fox. Team Brook-Fox was really Team Fox-Brook.

Or maybe just Team Fox.

It was a good thing he'd decided to like her.

And maybe a little strange.

CHAPTER 15
UNWANTED

"PENNY FOR YOUR THOUGHTS, BROOK." Fox looked back. "I think it's safe to talk now."

Oh great. And at the same time, what a relief.

She shoved her hands in her shallow pockets and tried to pull herself together. "Cool," she said. "Umm." What could she say? *Well, Fox, since you asked, I've been thinking about* you. She reached for a joke, but she couldn't find one so instead she blurted out, "What do you think this place is?"

A big question. A dumb question. A philosophical, black hole of a question.

Fox gave a low whistle. "I wish I knew, Brook. I wish I knew."

She snapped off a fern leaf and fanned her burning face. It probably made her look stupid but she didn't care.

"I'm not sure where I'm from." Fox started hiking, politely acting like he hadn't noticed her little breakdown. "Don't have a lot of memories," he said, "so I don't have much to work with. For example, I'm not sure if the weather here is weird."

Brook fell into step behind him, willing her pulse back to normal. "I don't think the weather is weird." She was happy he'd picked an easy topic. "It feels like California."

"So we could be in America."

"We could be. Except."

"Except the dragon."

"Right." She brushed back her hair and instantly regretted it because her hands were so dirty. "And the castle." She dodged a black beetle as big as her fist, clicking its jaws and wobbling toward her ankles. Apparently the whole forest was coming after her now. But at least they'd stopped running. At least now they could talk, and she didn't have to be stuck in her head. She stepped up onto a dry log and walked on top, safe from creepy crawlies.

"My theory," she said, "since I know you'd love to hear it, is that we're a few hundred years in the past—the Dark Ages, when monsters roamed the earth."

"Nice," Fox said. "I like that theory. It explains the dragon." He stopped abruptly, like something inside him had twisted and turned into a hook. "Someone would still have to shove us in a time machine though," he said, "*after* they erased our memories—so it's still horrible on purpose. Nothing changes that."

"Horrible on purpose. Yeah." Brook took a few more steps, keeping her balance and thinking, *Well, of course it's on purpose.*

Fox laughed, but the laugh didn't sound quite right.

"What's wrong?" Brook finally said. If she pretended not to notice the awkward laugh, well, Fox *would* notice and store it away for the day when he took a close look at her and decided whether to keep her around.

"My old life," Fox said.

She waited.

"You don't remember your name," he said.

She shook her head.

"Neither do I. But in my case, I never had a name. No one gave me one. I was never wanted. Never wanted, ever. That's all I know about who I was. It hangs around in your bones."

Brook felt like all the air had been sucked out of the forest. Her feet felt heavy. She didn't ask how Fox knew he was never wanted.

That didn't matter. Instead she licked her dry lips and said, "I'm sorry." And she was. She knew what it felt like to be unwanted, except in her case, she'd been wanted once and then never again.

She wasn't sure which would be worse.

She jumped off her log to walk beside Fox. He didn't seem to mind.

Then her stomach jolted. *WAIT*. She forced herself to keep moving as her whole body tightened. *What if...what if that's who gets sent here? Rejects no one wants. What if the island is a place for kids like us? And the blue-faces in their castle, they're the only ones who belong. The island is theirs, but instead of helping people like me and Fox, they fight to stay in charge, to keep us out, to keep us...unwanted.*

The idea took her breath away. And it made her feel silly, because the truth was so obvious. She squeezed her fingers, making and unmaking fists.

Death Island is Reject Island.

As a rule, Brook tried not to feel sorry for herself, not if she could help it. But all of a sudden she felt sorry for Fox, and she had a sneaky feeling she was feeling sorry for herself at the same time.

I feel sorry for him. I feel sorry for us.

Being unwanted made you feel far away and too close at the same time. It made you numb and crazy and twisted up inside.

It was the worst feeling in the world.

CHAPTER 16
THERE'S NO NORMAL

BY THE TIME they made it back to the campsite, Brook's shoes were full of slime and leaf mold. In Weed, the cheap sneaks might have lasted months. Here they were used up in a few hours. She sat down in a bed of moss, leaned against the rock wall and yanked them off. Her socks were muddy brown. She pulled them off, holding her breath, and groaned.

Who knows how long I've had these on, she thought. Days for sure. Sorry, feet.

She wriggled her wrinkled toes in the gray-gold light, surprised how good it felt—and how tired she was. The sun still hovered over the trees, but she was ready to curl up. She wished she had a blanket, and that made her picture the castle again. The kids in there had blankets, blankets they didn't even need. The kids in there had everything, and they did their best to never share.

"Hungry?" Fox was digging at the cold fire, shoving coals around. He had a knack for finding embers in the ash. Brook had never kindled a fire in her life, and it was fascinating to watch him.

"Just a little hungry," Brook said. "No hurry." She wouldn't mind a piece of rabbit jerky, but she didn't want Fox to stop messing with the fire. The air was starting to get cold, and she felt the chill between her shoulder blades. The island was shutting down for the night, getting ready to wrap itself in dark and monsters. She scooted closer to the fire as wisps of smoke began to rise and inched her toes up to the very edge.

Flames licked at a log, and Brook breathed in the smell. She liked the scent of woodsmoke, she decided. Much better than trash burning in empty lots, cigarette smoke on the fire escapes, grease fires in the kitchen. Woodsmoke was rich and sweet, almost good enough to eat. It played nice with the salty tang in the air. Except... Brook wrinkled her nose.

"Sorry, Fox. That smell—I think it's my feet."

"Uh huh." His smile was pained. "I wasn't going to say anything but..."

"Ugh." Brook grabbed for her muddy socks.

"No, don't," Fox said. "I've smelled much worse, believe me, and anyway, your feet look like they could use some air."

"Ha," Brook said. "No argument there." She paused, then held up one foot and bobbed her toes at him. "Thank you," she said in a teensy voice.

Fox laughed and her toes gave him a regal nod. Brook was happy he seemed less tense. Maybe their talk had helped. Getting all that bad stuff out of his head.

"Hey!" She narrowed her eyes. "How come you don't smell bad? I mean, honestly, you smell pretty decent." Especially for a boy, she didn't add.

Fox prodded the fire and sighed.

Brook put her head on one side.

"I was hoping it wouldn't come to this," he said. "I was hoping I could keep this one secret for myself."

"Whaaat?" Brook said, "Ha-ha-ha. For your own sake, this is one secret you'd better share, buddy, or this whole place will smell like wet feet." Inwardly, she wasn't so cheerful.

Keep *one* secret for yourself, she thought. That's funny. I bet you're holding back dozens.

"Ok, you win." Fox grinned and gave the hooked sword a twist. A flurry of sparks spun upward like glowing bugs. "There's a nice pool in one of the creeks not far from here. Not too deep, so when it catches the sun, it gets less chilly. It never really gets warm, but hey." He shrugged. "The downside is that you have to use sand for soap."

"I'm in," Brook said. "Deal. It's on."

"I'll show you tomorrow," Fox said. "You'll like it."

Their conversation died away after that. Brook wanted to ask about the mystery kid in the field. Do you think he saw us? she'd say, starting with an easy question. Eventually she'd work up to, Why did you run? Was he tracking us? And if you're nervous, why don't you carry that sword and give me the knife?

She had a feeling that conversation wouldn't go well, and Team Brook-Fox was just getting back on track. In a situation like this, sharing a joke was almost as good as sharing a knife, she guessed. Anyway, pressing for answers kept you from finding out anything at all. As an orphan, if you learned nothing else, you definitely learned that.

After they each had some jerky, Brook took a long drink from the pool. She'd draped her socks over a rock by the fire where they steamed like huge earthworms. Huge *venomous* earthworms if they were from this island. Now there was a nasty thought. Brook didn't want to put her socks back on, but the evening chill made the decision for her, creeping down her bare arms and legs like invisible centipedes. *Yikes.*

She sighed and pulled on the brittle brown socks, tugging until they stretched halfway up her calves. Bits of dry mud fell off her legs. You're filthy, she thought. And you stink. And you look ridiculous, like a cheerleader for Team Dirt.

She shot Fox a side-eye to see if he was tracking her antics.

Of course he was.

"Stop judging," she said. "They're warm, like they just came out of the dryer."

He raised his brows and nodded.

Sitting by the blaze, she ran her fingers along her neck and pressed the hollow at the bottom of her skull. A day after her haircut, she still felt weird. At risk, like her long, glossy hair had been a good luck charm, keeping her safe. A charm she needed now more than ever.

You're still you, she thought. Without your hair, even without your name. How could you expect to feel normal? And what's normal anyway? Was your life at the Foundation normal? Of course not. Nothing that happened there was normal. There's no normal for you. You just stay alert. You pay attention. You keep yourself safe. That's it.

She gave Fox a little wave goodnight. He waved back and she curled up as close to the fire as she dared, angling her body so the heat would soak her face and legs and her arms, folded across her chest. She tilted her feet into the moss. Getting things arranged just right. It gave her a picture of herself, standing on her tiptoes in the Foundation dorm, tucking in the sheets on her top bunk, pulling the shabby blanket straight while someone hissed, "Loser! Goody two-shoes!"

She was glad Fox wasn't like that.

As she drifted off, she thought about the castle.

Maybe you've been looking for it a long time, without even knowing.

She woke up once, gasping for breath, fists clenched and feet jerking. The sounds of footsteps echoed in her head, and the dull, smoky light of the moon shone down like a bare light bulb. Her eyes darted right and left, then she realized the screams in her ears were night birds. The red-headed one was probably out there, looking for her and shrieking.

Brook pressed a hand to her heart and looked across the fire for Fox, but the shadows were deep. He didn't need the heat as much as she did. For a long minute, she watched the pitch dark spot where he slept, wishing she could see him. She pushed herself up on an elbow, thinking, Wait, did he leave? He's gone, isn't he? He sneaked away! Then she slumped back down.

No, he's right there, she told herself. And you're not going to wake him up. But maybe she wanted him awake, really, because she whispered, "It's just a dream." And she added, "No more cliffs that eat people. No more dragons. No more running, no more basements. You're safe now."

And she whispered louder than she needed to.

But Fox didn't take the bait.

Brook fell back asleep, trying not to think about how her whispers were lies.

CHAPTER 17
CAN I HAVE THAT KNIFE?

AT THE FOUNDATION, on the rare days you got to sleep in, school holidays or weekends when the dorm was quiet, you stayed in bed as long as you could. For a few hours you could pretend the world was different. When you got up and looked in the smudgy mirror, brushing your teeth, it was a treat to see a girl who didn't have darkish swoops under her eyes. A girl who looked like she might be going somewhere nice.

Brook lay on her back, eyes half shut, thinking, Everything's so soft and cool. And no one's screaming at me to get up. She wasn't sure why she'd been allowed to sleep in and she didn't want to ruin it.

After a while she narrowed her eyes. What was wrong with the ceiling? Something tiny crawled over her wrist. Since when were there ants in the dorms? When she turned to look over the edge of her bunk, she found herself staring at moss and a smoking fire. Her left hip ached. She blinked and rubbed her eyes until the cliffs, the dragon, and the island got solid in her mind.

And Fox.

"Morning, Brook," he said from somewhere by the pool.

"Morning," she croaked in his direction. Since he wasn't

messing with the fire, she sat up and scooted over to the stone ring, trying to remember why she felt so awkward. Oh, that was it. She'd woken up, stiff with terror, and started whispering in his direction. Luckily, Fox had slept through her kindergarten cry for help. Or had he? Maybe he'd heard her and was waiting to rub it in.

She groaned inwardly and looked at the fire-blackened sword, resting on a rock. Even coated with ash, it looked lethal. She sneaked a look at Fox, splashing water on his face. *If he didn't want me to touch it, he shouldn't have left it here.* She picked up the sword, hefted its hooked and deadly weight, and instantly stopped feeling silly.

Wow, she thought. This thing is for real. She wanted to give the blade a serious swing, slash it through the air, test its sharpness— but instead, she used it the way Fox did. What a waste, she thought. The hooked blade found an ember in the deep, warm ashes, then another. She prodded them to the surface, blew on them so they glowed, and dropped a scrap of bark on top. It felt like magic when the wood burst into flames.

"Nice work," Fox said behind her.

If he minded her touching the sword, he didn't show it. And how could he mind? He'd left it right beside her. If anything, it had been an invitation. Why don't you just hang onto that sword, Brook, he might say. Use it to protect yourself—or maybe you'd prefer this knife.

She almost smiled. *Yeah right.*

"Hunting, baths, firewood." Fox ticked them off on his fingers. "That's what I'm thinking we should do today. What do you want to tackle first?"

What about sitting by the fire and waking up? Brook thought. Or maybe you could step away for a few minutes so I can play with this very real sword.

When she didn't reply, Fox smiled. "No rush." He ran a hand through his tousled copper hair. "You don't sleep very well, do you? I think if I remembered my own past, I'd be up half the night too.

There are some scary things in your head, Brook. Something you're running from. Something that happened to you, maybe."

She realized he was watching her.

"Something you did?" he said.

Why not come out and say it, Fox? she thought. *Hey Brook, I heard you whispering last night and it was kind of freaky.*

Fox was quiet.

Normally, she would've resented his prying. A pointed question was a weapon, leveled at your chest. But Fox had a way of asking that let you know your response was optional. His questions felt like opportunities, and Brook decided to take this one. It was ok for Fox to know a little more about her. Not everything. Not a lot. Just the right amount of little.

"I dream about foster system stuff," she said. "Mean kids, bad situations, virtually no supervision. I've been in a group home for years. Do you know what those are?"

Fox blinked and rubbed his nose. "I can guess."

"You didn't miss anything." Brook tried to smile. "Not much happened inside the Foundation worth remembering. You're supposed to live there until someone wants you, but no one does—and no one wants you at the Foundation either. You just hang out with all these other unsolvable problems. Actually, I'm kind of jealous. I wish I could forget it all like you. Then maybe I could get some sleep." She sketched half-circles under her eyes.

"I hear you." Fox gave her a kind look and she thought, There, that wasn't so bad. It was about right. Now he knows where you're coming from, but he doesn't think you're a poor little baby. Good job, girl. She felt so pleased with herself that she said:

"Hey Foxy"—since they'd just been talking about their personal lives—"I was gonna ask—can I carry the knife?" She put a mildly hopeful expression on her face.

Fox blinked. "Oh, right, that would make sense. But the thing is, I hate carrying the sword through the woods. Gets heavy after a while, and I don't have a sheath—can't stick it in my pocket like the knife, you know—so it's always getting caught on stuff. But of course you're always welcome to borrow the knife if you want. We can kind of share it between us, ok?"

Brook smiled and blew her hair back from her face. "Cool."

Wow, she thought. He really doesn't want me to have that knife.

She wondered where he'd found it. Under a rock, up a tree? Maybe she'd find one too, but probably not, with all the kids Fox said were scavenging the island. She could volunteer to carry the sword, but that would be even more awkward. It was obvious how Fox felt. It was irritating but also hard to blame him, even though he had two weapons and she had nothing. How long had they known each other, a little over thirty-six hours?

If she was in his place, she wouldn't be eager to give a razor-sharp knife to a stranger who slept a few feet away. Without a weapon it was easier for Fox to trust her and that was good. She wanted him to trust her. She needed him to trust her. But she couldn't go on like this for too much longer.

"I vote we go hunting first," she said to break the silence.

"Perfect." Fox got up, slapping dust from his jeans. "I thought we could try the tide pools today. No reason to push our luck with rabbits yet."

Rabbits and luck, huh? Brook thought. That's all you want to say about that?

Fox had a way of smoothing things over that was kind of slippery. She'd been wondering if he'd mention them running from the kid yesterday. Apparently not—but surely she'd be able to bring it up at some point. Until then, she'd be sweet and agreeable.

"Tide pools," she said. "That means fish, right?"

"Or shellfish," Fox said. "Or starfish—but only if we're desperate. They're mushy." He made a face.

"No thanks," Brook said. "I don't care for mushy—but I hope I like seafood. I don't think I've ever had it. Unless, maybe that was another memory that got zapped." She half-closed her eyes like she was trying to remember.

"Yeah, probably." Fox nodded. "They took your name and your seafood history. Makes total sense."

"Don't joke around." Brook shook a fist. "It's a crippling loss."

"It's a big deal," Fox agreed.

"If I start puking everywhere, I'll try to point myself away from you," Brook said.

"Hey, I appreciate it."

She wrinkled her nose. "No guarantees though."

He smiled like he thought she was funny.

CHAPTER 18
SECRET IN THE DUNES

THEIR GOOD VIBES lasted about a mile.

After Brook rinsed out her mouth and took a drink, there was nothing else to do to get ready for the day, so they started walking. Their silence felt friendly, she decided. So for a while, she tried to think of what she might find that she could use as a toothbrush. Or a hair brush. They kind of overlapped. Even though her hair was short, it kept getting tangled.

As hard as she tried, she couldn't think of a single thing—except a hedgehog. She pictured herself holding one by its tiny feet and running its prickles through her hair. *Great idea, Brook. What could possibly go wrong?* But if she happened to find a hedgehog crawling around, she'd grab that cute little hairbrush.

For another couple minutes, she thought about how she was calling herself Brook and how strange it was to have no real name, just a dull spot in her mind that stayed empty no matter what. Every time she began the sentence, Hi, my name is...she expected she'd be able to finish it. But she never could.

Brook *could* be your name, she thought. It's not bad. Brooks are cool and clear. You could do a lot worse. About that time she realized the *friendly silence* had stretched into a kind of long silence as she tailed Fox through the woods, sliding through underbrush and dodging thickets. Any second now he'd say—

"What's on your mind, Brook?"

She smiled. He was getting predictable. "Do you keep track of how far you walk?" she asked. It was one of a few questions she'd stored away for moments like this.

"Hmm." Fox glanced over his shoulder. "Sometimes, but it's always approximate. I remember something about a seven minute mile—"

"That's running," Brook said before she could stop herself.

"Right," Fox said. "So I figure a hiking mile is about fifteen minutes, and that's how I figure distances."

"Smart," she said. "You just glance at your watch, or maybe your phone, and crunch the numbers."

"Exactly. I have several phones to choose from, actually."

"Of course," Brook said. "I left all *my* phones in our secret campsite, but guess I know how long ten minutes is. We're close to that now."

"Agreed," Fox said. "And heading toward the coast like we are, five more minutes will put us in the open."

"One mile to the ocean, neat and tidy," Brook said.

That's how she knew they'd walked a mile when it happened.

They'd left the woods, struggling through a prickly hedge as the sky bloomed indigo overhead, and Brook got more scratches, fighting the thorns. It was like they wanted to rip her clothes right off her.

"Fox, seriously!" she said.

"Sorry, the sea roses are everywhere. They love the coast."

She came *this* close to saying it was really too bad they didn't have something sharp, something with a long blade they could use to clear a path—you know, kind of like a machete. By the time they got out, Brook was irritable, rubbing her arms and sucking a pricked finger. Leaving the trees felt like an escape, which was weird, because diving into them felt the same way. The island made you feel like you were always looking for someplace safer, but once you got there, you realized you'd only put yourself in a different kind of danger.

"This is the south side of the island," Fox said.

"Cool," Brook said grudgingly. It *was* new information.

Her spirits began to lift as the dirt gave way to sand and grass. She saw something wide and glittering, stretched between dunes at the bottom of the sky. Her heart gave a little jump. For a second, she saw a small version of herself running and splashing through the waves.

The salty air grew even saltier, and Brook realized the sounds of the island had changed in just a few steps from the muffled, hidden sounds of the forest to a low bass rumble from the sea that crawled into your ears before you realized you were hearing it. The curve of a dune hid the ocean as they climbed, sliding in the white-brown sand, gulping breaths of tangy air. Big white gulls screamed overhead.

Brook felt excited and she couldn't help it. Wind flipped her hair around her face as they reached the top. The ocean crashed on a sandy beach a hundred feet away, and the waves rumbled even louder, like her eyes had turned up the volume. She wanted to run across the sand, kick off her shoes, and skip through the foam like that little girl.

The ocean's pull was so strong, she started to wriggle her toes in her flimsy shoes. She didn't know anything was wrong until Fox's whole body tightened. His arms flew out on either side like turnstiles to keep her from surging past. "Brook, wait!"

She felt confused as she stumbled against his elbow. Embarrassment washed the smile off her face. Why had Fox stopped her? What was wrong with pretending for just a few minutes that—

"Oh no!" Her hands flew to her mouth as she looked down the slope of the dune. In a small valley by the cold ashes of a fire lay a boy.

Brook went as tense as a coiled spring. No one moved. The boy in the sand was even more still than her and Fox.

"C'mon," Fox finally said. "We'd better take a look."

He stalked down the dune and into the hollow, and she followed, sliding in the sand, ready to fight or run. The wind died away as the hills rose over their heads and they came to a stop.

He must be dead, Brook thought. No one rests like that. Not even if they're hurt.

The side of boy's face was pressed to the sand, mouth half open. Legs bent, like he'd been sitting and had toppled over. Or maybe he'd tried to pull his legs to his chest for warmth.

They hovered over him, keeping their distance.

Not much blood, Brook thought. You expect a dying person to bleed a lot. But arrows don't slash you open I guess.

The arrow stuck out from between his shoulders, three feet long. The shaft was thin and straight. Tufted feathers lined the end. The whole scene was strange to look at. Weird, like the arrow and the death were not connected. The arrow could've been part of a costume for a middle school play, Pocahontas or something. Instead, it had killed him.

It was hard to believe arrows still killed people.

"It was a good shot," Fox said. "I'd say it got his heart. Look at the sand, no signs of struggle. When he got hit, he just fell over."

And died, Brook thought. Died here on the beach, alone.

She looked at the sand and saw what Fox meant. She also noticed the tiny grains of sand on the kid's skin from where he'd pressed his face to the ground, taking his last breaths. She looked away.

"Someone picked him off," Fox said. "Someone ruthless."

The boy's eyes were open—at least the one she could see. His eye was greenish, the pupil rolled to one side, looking toward the dunes from three inches away. The color was close to her own eyes, a hue between brown and green, something she hadn't thought about for days. But all the boy could see was sand. Empty sand, the last thing as he died.

"Someone has a real hunting bow and arrows," Fox said. "And this person can shoot." He paused. "A sniper."

"Yeah." Brook hugged herself, caught herself doing it and stopped. "Not much of a fight."

"It was murder," Fox said.

Instantly she thought of the knife, wrapped in dirty cloth in Fox's pocket. Not much good against a bow and arrows, but razor sharp and deadly nonetheless.

He was thinking about it right now too, she was sure.

She wished it was in her pocket.

CHAPTER 19
DEAD THINGS

WITHOUT PLANNING TO, Brook sat down. She felt as if something wonderful had been held out to her and yanked away. The sun, the sand, the big blue ocean. A few minutes splashing in the surf. She felt her shoulders tremble and bit her lip.

Death had ambushed her.

Fox looked over. Then he did something Brook never allowed anyone to do, ever.

He took her hand.

Her body stiffened like razor wire. With an effort, she made herself relax. Fox is your friend, sort of, she thought.

"Let's go," he said.

She let him tug her up the sandy hill. At the top, Brook scanned the shoreline and turned to search the field behind them. Nothing broke the flat, bright sand. If anyone was watching, he'd be a quarter mile back in the sea roses, or flat on his stomach in the waving grass. But she didn't have the feeling anyone was there.

Fox led her up a dune and down, between more hills, along a rocky string of tide pools near the glittering, angry sea. Waves pounded the beach in a battle that would never end. The same waves waited under the hungry cliffs. They didn't seem bright and lovely anymore.

"This is where I usually fish." Fox tugged her toward a little pool. The one he'd chosen was surrounded by sea-smoothed rocks. "Why don't you wait here? Check out the water if you want. I'll be right back."

She sat down on a boulder as Fox disappeared.

He's leaving, she thought. He won't come back. But she managed to stop her thoughts from running away. You already knew this was a terrible place, she thought. Lots of kids have died here—kids died the night you arrived. Gone in seconds, falling into the sea. And people die all the time. You just happened to find this body—and there wasn't a lot of blood. You can be happy about that. The kid died fast, and you didn't know him. Maybe he was a bad person. There are plenty of those.

The waves on the beach glittered. She realized the island was smirking at her again.

Surprise, surprise, it was saying. *I'll always get the jump on you.*

Brook turned away from the relentless surf. "You're still alive," she told herself. "So act like it."

She looked into the tide pool at her feet. The shallow water was colorful like a science poster. Thick grass waved on the bottom. Seaweed swirled like streamers. Tiny fish darted around like slivers of glass. She spotted a spiky brown fish, lurking by a rock. And aha! —a crab, a pretty big one, if she had to guess. She pulled her feet back from the edge, and noticed one of her big toes sticking out through battered canvas.

Great. Now her feet were crab bait—of course they were.

By the time Fox came back, she'd picked up a piece of driftwood and was herding the crab toward the shore. It kept waving its reddish pincers at her, snapping them open and shut. Neither of them had the upper hand.

"Where did you go?" she asked Fox.

He looked at her across the pool and she forced herself to keep her chin up.

"I needed a closer look." Fox held up a tangle of twine and a thin piece of metal, bent into a hook. "He didn't have much in his pockets. Maybe someone went through them." He paused and went on. "His shoes are in good shape if you're interested." He held them up, swinging from their laces.

Brook shook her head and Fox shrugged.

"I think they might fit you. Maybe he'd be happy someone had them."

"Who was he?" Brook asked. "Did you know him?"

"Never seen him before." Fox pulled off his own hikers and sat down by the pool. For a second she thought he'd try on the dead kid's shoes, but instead he stuck his toes in the water. "It's hard to keep track of who's on the island," he said. "Like I told you, a lot of these kids have gone feral. It's a mistake to get close to them—they're not even close with each other." He nodded back the way they'd come. "I guess you can see why."

Brook wanted to say, Why couldn't we all work together? But she'd lived in the Foundation. That wasn't how things went. People were always clumping into groups like paper clips stuck to a magnet. And if you weren't magnetized, and you weren't the magnet, well, it didn't matter how hard you tried to get along. You'd better watch your back. She'd learned that lesson and apparently Fox had too.

When she looked back into the pool, the crab had snuck away. She liked the feisty little thing. She was glad they wouldn't eat it.

Fox waded in, sea grass swirling under his feet.

"It's like *Lord of the Flies*," Brook said. She'd acted like she didn't know the story, and Fox probably remembered but she didn't care. "This is worse, though," she said. "Those kids kind of wind themselves up slowly, all the way to murder. It takes the entire book."

Heartless, she thought. Like Monique at the Foundation—but less headstrong than Monique, less wild-eyed and crazy. The bad kids here are more calculating.

"Here's what you've got to remember." The knife shone in Fox's hand, and Brook wondered if he wished he'd brought the sword. "Some of these kids, they've been here for an entire book. They're ready for the last chapter. They've figured out whatever they're gonna figure out and some of them are monsters. Take those blue-faces in the castle." He slashed the knife along an underwater rock, shaking his head, and Brook felt a stab of cold anger.

The blue-faces. Losers. Killers.

"Do you think they did this?" she asked.

Fox tossed a handful of lumpy black rocks to shore. "Hard to say. Normally they never leave the castle–"

"–because they don't have to," she said. "They have everything and they don't share."

"But you never know," Fox finished.

More rocks thudded into the sand at her feet. Why was he throwing rocks at her? Bending over, she realized they were rough oval shells crusted with tiny plants.

"Mussels," Fox said. "They take some getting used to but they're better than starfish, believe me—hey look, a crab."

Brook winced as the knife flashed down. She hoped Fox would miss but he didn't. The knife came back up with the crab on its tip, waving its legs and snapping its pincers. Fox stayed out of reach as its movements slowed.

Brook looked away and swallowed hard.

"There's something I don't understand," she said, forcing herself to think about something beside the tough little creature. "Where do these weapons come from?"

Fox stepped out of the pool. "You're smart, Brook. That's why you notice these things. Which means you probably know what I'm going to say."

Brook thought, Yeah, and you're smart too. Maybe too smart.

"Let me guess," she said, "you don't know, because where did the dragon come from? Why is there an island?"

"You got it." He dropped the crab in the sand to let it finish dying.

Brook waited to see if he'd give her one of his Fox monologues. He must have ideas or suspicions, no matter how crazy. But he didn't continue, so she carried on herself, looking away from the crab, which was making sad, jerky motions with its claws.

"This isn't an accident," she said. "We were brought to this place with monsters and a castle and weapons. Someone planned for this. Someone wants this place to be horrible. A dragon's island, littered with all kinds of nasty things..."

Brook trailed off. The crab had stopped moving.

"I hate them," Fox said, and her shoulders jerked at the anger in his voice. "Whoever's in charge," he said. "Whoever they are, I hate them."

When she looked up, his face was scary.

"Me too," she said. "I hate them so, *so* much." All the worst words she knew flew through her mind, but instead she said, "I hate those—killers." And she meant it, deep in her bones.

They collected the mussels. Brook stuffed hers in her pockets. Fox carried the dead crab. They'd reached the first dune on the trail home when Brook slowed and stopped. Her bruised toes were poking through her shoes. She sighed.

"Go ahead," Fox said. "It just makes sense."

The dead boy's shoes waited by the pool. Suede uppers. Rubber soles, almost as nice as Fox's. She didn't put them on but she took them. Dangling from springy laces, they bumped her leg as she walked. The crab looked like a wilted, spidery plant in Fox's hand. Both of them were carrying dead things—things she wished they didn't have.

Without warning, a sob rose in her chest and she fought it down, hoping Fox wouldn't notice. She took her time catching him, waiting for her face to stop scrunching up, working to get her breathing back.

Calm down, Brook. Stop being silly. It's just a crab.

It's just a boy.

CHAPTER 20
HIDDEN LITTLE WORLD

FOX HAD COVERED the body with sand, Brook noticed. It wouldn't stop a determined animal. Definitely not a pack of Death Dogs, based on what he'd said. But with the sand covering the scent, maybe the dogs wouldn't nose the body out. Fox had probably done it to make her feel better. She suspected that if he'd been alone, he would've left the dead kid lying where he found him after he'd gone through his pockets.

They moved fast. Fox was on high alert as they crossed the open ground, and Brook kept her head up, glancing right and left. She knew what Fox was thinking. The bow and arrows were still out there, and if someone wanted to shoot them, he could do it from a distance. Luckily there weren't a lot of hiding places in the dunes. And if the sniper was flat on his face, hugging the sand, he wouldn't be able to get a shot off.

As they left the high grass, Brook didn't see a thing. Not even a footprint. Of course, the wind had probably scrubbed those away. Then, finally, they reached the trees, and Fox started hacking at the sea roses, clearing the worst of them with the knife.

Brook didn't have the energy to be mad that he felt sorry for her. As they entered the woods, she slung the dead boy's shoes over one shoulder. They bumped her spine as she walked. They kicked her in the ribs when she shoved branches out of the way. The wet mussels in her pockets scraped her hips, making her gashed one hurt. *What I wouldn't give for a backpack.*

She didn't say anything as they hiked, and for once, Fox didn't either. Brook kept seeing the dead kid's greenish eye, staring at a floor of sand. She couldn't describe him, except for that one eye. She couldn't say how tall he'd been, or what color his hair was, or whether he was older or younger than her or about the same.

You don't know he was a good kid, she reminded herself. Not many are, and...

She tried to slow her thoughts but they ran on ahead.

...he could've died in lots worse ways.

Here she fought hard to stop, but failed.

He could've died slowly, she thought—stop it, Brook! Could've been attacked by animals or fallen off a cliff or—Get a grip!—he could've been cut, blood splashing all over, more and more until his life leaked out, gush-gush, drip-drip...dead.

Her mind stopped racing. Way too late, of course.

Talking to Fox would've been better than letting her thoughts run wild. They trudged into the boulders, down the narrow zig-zag passage to their camp. Brook dropped the shoes on her side of the fire and dug for the mussels wedged in her pockets. It felt like an ugly dance. Getting them out, she scraped a knuckle red and got black dirt under her nails. She couldn't remember ever feeling so dirty.

"Do you still want a bath?" Fox said.

How did he do that?

Brook realized she'd been staring at her dirty hands like they were objects of horror. She probably looked a little crazy. "Yes I do," she said. "I really do."

Fox nodded in a way that said, Thank goodness.

"Let's leave the mussels in the pool," he said. "I'll show you the way."

A couple minutes later, Brook hovered by the dead boy's shoes. She already knew what she would do, but she had to work herself up to it. The shoes were nicer than any she'd ever owned. Probably designed for the outdoors. She sighed, picked them up, and slung them over her shoulder again. She'd made the choice.

"Let's go," she said.

They started off through the woods in a direction she didn't think they'd tried.

"The creek runs across the forest north to south," Fox said. "We're heading west to intercept it. Not too far, and I've never seen anyone else here. It's our personal water source. One more reason to live in the trees."

"Absolutely," Brook said. "Our private creek club." She wasn't quite sure how the bath was going to work, but she had to try it. Anything to get clean. Anything up to a point.

"You're paying attention, right?" Fox said.

Brook nodded. Always, she thought.

"If you're ok with it, I'll leave you at the water and you can find your own way back," he said. "Don't worry about a trail—there's not one—but I think you'll be able to figure it out."

"Perfect," Brook said, and she meant it. If not for the dead boy, she might have actually cheered. Being alone meant she could relax, just for a little, and not have to worry about weirdness. She'd already picked out a few landmarks: rock formations, older trees, a stretch of boggy ground. It wouldn't be hard to find her way.

The woods ran downhill and the trees ahead grew thicker until Brook realized she was seeing the leafy outline of a stream. It was like seeing a rich person's lawn in summer, right next to a scraggly, brown one. The happy trees and shrubs hid the creek from the woods—like a green shower curtain, she decided.

"Push through the trees," Fox said. "Right ahead is a shallow sandy spot. Stay as long as you like. I'll see you back at camp, ok?"

"Thanks, Fox."

He nodded. Then he turned and hiked away, right on cue. Brook stood there enjoying the feeling of being alone. In the silence, she heard running water. No leaves rustled. Not a single twig snapped. She felt slightly embarrassed when she stepped behind a tree and waited for another couple minutes, just in case.

You can't be too careful, she thought.

Fox did not reappear.

See, you can trust him. At least about this...

She straightened her shoulders, blew hair out of her face, and pushed her way through the greenery. The creek bubbled over sand and gravel at the bottom of a smooth dirt bank. A few funny-looking, skinny insects skated on the surface. Other than that, she was alone. Alone—with clean, fresh water. Sun poured down on her from a patch of blue sky.

Safe. Quiet. In a place that was just hers.

Brook wished she could save the moment forever.

Then she realized something else:

"It's a brook," Brook said.

Seeing the thing she'd named herself after, and seeing how pretty it was, made her feel better than she'd felt since—well, since she could remember. She stood there awhile longer, feeling the sun on her face and taking in the magic.

It's not a bad name, she thought.

Then she kicked off her demolished canvas shoes. Threads and chunks of fabric hung off them, rubber soles sagging. The laces were shredded and covered in burrs. If she'd taken them to shop class and attacked them with a hammer and then carried them to lab and poured acid on them, she couldn't have made them worse.

Brook set the suede trail shoes beside her evil-looking sneakers. A second later, she picked the new shoes up and moved them further away—in case her old ones got any ideas. She pulled off her socks and stuck one foot in the stream. The current tugged brown wisps of dirt from her toes. Fox was right. The water wasn't bad. Not warm but not cold either. In the sunlight, it was refreshingly chilly. And who was she kidding? If it had floating chunks of ice, she'd still jump in.

She pulled the rest of her clothes off quickly and debated what to do with them. Her jean shorts were in the best condition. Thank God she hadn't been wearing gym shorts or something soft and knit. The forest would've scrubbed them off already. Her t-shirt was in sad shape, pre-shrunk cotton getting more ragged all the time. At least it was black and not sleeveless.

She folded her shorts on the bank—they were the least likely to dry fast—and clutched everything else to her chest as she stepped into the stream.

"Oh gosh, you're filthy," she said as dirt swirled off her legs.

Splashing water on herself in handfuls wasn't going to get it done, so she chose a sunny spot, took a quick breath, and sank in up to her neck. Sitting there was not bad at all. The current did its best to wash away the dirt, but the water turned clear again in moments, and her skin had never been this shade of brown, even in summer.

"That's just the top layer," Brook said. "What I need are some fish who like eating dirt." Except fish nibbling her was a gross idea. Luckily, nothing seemed interested in taking bites. The thin water bugs kept their distance and nothing else moved—except, as she was scrubbing her socks with sand, a small, brown lobster-looking thing crawled under a big stone.

"Keep your claws to yourself and we're good," Brook said.

Without warning, she found her shoulders shaking. She saw the crab, dying in the sand. She tried to make herself stop, gulping down big breaths and holding them in, but it didn't work. The sorrow kept bubbling in her lungs and throat. She put her face in her hands and let it all out.

The crab, the boy, the kids on the cliffs. Such a horrible place. And the Children's Foundation, another horrible place when it could've been so different. Sometimes she'd wanted to run around flicking ears and ball caps, saying, "Wake up! We don't have to treat each other this way. We could make things different. We could change it ourselves." But it never would've worked. It only would've made things worse.

"You've got to play the game in front of you," she said, and wiped her eyes.

She'd stopped cleaning up while she'd raised the water level with all those tears. Now she splashed cold water on her face, took a deep breath and got back to it.

After she'd scrubbed her socks and, very carefully, her shirt, she stepped out of the creek and dripped over to the trees to hang her clothes on branches. Then she splashed back in to scrub herself.

It took quite a while.

She was glad the creek felt like a hidden little world. Being naked was bad enough, and if she could've seen the whole forest rolling away, heavy with shadows, or even worse, the open, blazing plains —well, she would've had to just stay dirty. Instead, she sagged on the speckled gravel until the water touched her chin.

"How am I going to get in the castle?" she said.

She didn't know. But the next question that came to her, she knew the answer.

"Should I try to wash my hair?" she said. "Yes, I've gotta try."

It wasn't easy, using wet sand for shampoo. Combing sand through her locks with her fingers, she caught a memory of her own face, focused and serious, brushing her long brown hair in a cracked Foundation mirror. Then a hand smacked her reflection and someone sneered, "Watch out, shampoo princess."

Brook dunked her head to rinse.

After that, she spent some time with her eyes closed underwater, scrubbing her teeth with her index finger between coming up for breaths. She almost made herself laugh. By the time the bath was over, her skin tingled in a nice way except for the gash above her hip, still tender, and her scraped arms and legs, and a couple spots she'd rubbed too hard with sand.

One thing had become very obvious as she'd sat there with

nothing between her heart and lungs and guts and the island but softly rushing water.

"I need a weapon," she said. "Without one I'm naked all the time."

She'd take the knife from Fox. No more playing cute.

No more messing around.

CHAPTER 21
THE ON AND OFF SWITCH

BROOK HADN'T TRIED to keep track of time. Actually, she'd tried not to. Fox had said to take as long as she wanted and that's exactly what she did. No one yelled at her to get out of the shower. No one said, "Stop hogging water or I'll shut it off!" Of course the water wasn't hot, but she didn't mind.

By the time she stepped out of the stream a second time, the sun had swung across the sky and its rays had less heat. She shivered, hugged herself, and flicked water off her fingers so she could pick up her clothes.

Yes, they were dry! She gave a little cheer and stood there, realizing she was not. *Brilliant, Brook.* She sighed, draped her clothes back over the branches, and stood in the brightest patch of sun, swiping water off herself. She shook her head, drops flying from her hair and danced around, rubbing her arms for warmth. A few minutes later, she was damp but not dripping.

Good enough, she decided. You can dry off while you hike.

She pulled on her wrinkled clothes, enjoying the softness. Her socks were permanently stained brown, but they smelled neutral and felt good on her feet. She sat on a flat rock for a minute, looking at the two pairs of shoes on the bank. She picked up the dead kid's hikers. What if they didn't fit? The thought scared her enough that she stopped stalling. She gave the shoes a thwack to get the sand out and tried to pull one on.

Please, please, please, she thought.

Ahh, yes!

Her heel slid right in. Her toes even had some wriggle room. Fox had been right. The dead kid's shoes were a perfect fit. You couldn't have planned it better, she thought, and right away felt bad.

"Thank you, whoever you were." She pulled on the second shoe. "I hope you were a good person." She stopped. "Well, I guess I don't hope that. But whatever kind of kid you were, I'm sorry you died. I'll put these to good use, ok?"

She tied the laces snugly and walked back and forth over the gravel.

"Whoa," she said. The nicest shoes she'd ever owned had been thrift store skate shoes, and compared to the hikers, they'd been squishy slippers. Digging her treads into the dirt bank, she bounded into the trees in three big steps.

"Now my feet are invincible," she said.

She moved uphill with long steps, enjoying the traction. Maybe this is why people like camping, she thought. It wouldn't be so terrible with shoes like this, and a sleeping bag...and a towel and toothbrush and comb...and a pack to carry it all.

She paused near the top off the hilly stretch to remember how she and Fox had come. They'd pushed through a thicket on the right, but coming back, it wasn't obvious how to get back in. The army of shrubs and saplings looked like a woven security fence.

"Time for a detour." Brook hiked to the top of the rise, swiveling right and left on her heels and thinking about how good it would feel to sit by the fire as the sun went down. Her stomach felt empty, so hopefully she'd like seafood. It was nice to worry about something that didn't really matter. The thicket angled toward her, pushing her off course, but it wasn't a big deal. Once the scrub thinned out, she'd cut back to the right—let's see, that was probably south—and find the next–

Brook froze.

A huge shadow surged toward her, eating ferns and leaves. It twisted over the ground, reaching for her hungrily. She jumped away from the darkness like it was alive. Then she got hold of herself. She looked up through the branches and saw the dragon.

Its wings brushed the treetops, and its eyes were dark gashes as it tracked her through the canopy. Neck snaking out, it plunged toward her in a rush of cracking wood. Brook screamed as its jaws snapped shut, five feet away. Its breath smelled like rust. The dragon clawed and twisted, struggling to reach her. Its oil-dark body thrashed the trees as it snarled and tore free, lifting into the air on whooshing wings.

It's leaving, Brook thought. It's giving up.

But she was still frozen in place. And then–

"Don't move a muscle, sweetheart," the dragon rumbled.

"No!" Brook said. "Oh no!"

She wanted to move. She wanted to scream and run, but–

The dragon crashed into the canopy again, tearing the forest with its claws. Brook covered her face with her hands as tree trunks groaned and shattered. The dragon forced its way through layers of branches like a diver in a green-brown lake. Its massive forearms tore through trees like they were seaweed. Leaves whirled and darted like terrorized fish. The monster's jaws gaped open. Brook had never seen so many knives.

"Oh God, help," she said.

Stretching closer, the dragon tried to cup her in paws the size of manhole covers, studded with tire irons.

Her legs unlocked. She curled her toes. Something in her head clicked On.

"Let's get to know each other," the monster rumbled.

Brook screamed and went for it. Splinters needled her legs as the dragon made a grab and missed. She'd never run so fast. The hill ahead went up in flames, blazing like a furnace, but she dodged the burning trees. She flashed through gaps—blurred through the smoke like a ghost.

The whole time the dragon was after her, snatching for her like a forty foot cat.

But Brook escaped.

Twisting right and left, darting through cracks in the curtains of fire, she got away.

She won.

Fox never would've believed it.

She reached deep woods and plunged inside. She flew past the marshy ground. She circled the rock formation. By then the dragon was gone. When she crouched under a boulder, she saw it circling overhead, spitting flame and bellowing. She was glad she couldn't hear what it was saying.

Without warning, her mind flipped back to Off. Her lungs burned like they'd been scorched. Pain stabbed her hip. Her whole body started shaking. I'm stuck in a horror movie, Brook thought. I've got to get out. I've got to get out right now.

CHAPTER 22
THE INNER CIRCLE

THEIR CAMPSITE WASN'T FAR, but it took Brook another hour to get there. After she pulled the splinters out of her legs, she sat on the edge of a rock slab and kicked her feet. She'd known the dragon was real—it had dropped her on the cliff. It had flown over at night, breathing fire. But looking into its dark, dead eyes, watching it inch closer, hearing it talk–

Brook shuddered.

No wonder the dragon was the first thing Fox had warned her about.

Her hike turned into a stroll. She walked from the rocks to a big tree and stopped. "Don't move a muscle, sweetheart," the dragon had said. From the tree to a thicket. "Let's get to know each other." From the thicket to the maze of boulders, where she leaned her forehead against a rock.

Something that wants to eat you shouldn't be able to talk, she thought. It's horrible, horrible—but I got away. I tried to and I did. Fox doesn't even think that's possible. She pushed her hair back with both hands, brushed off her clothes, and ran into the labyrinth.

"Fox, I saw the dragon!" she yelled as she burst into their campsite.

His head snapped up. His eyes locked onto her face.

"It tried to get me," Brook said. "In the woods by the creek."

Fox jumped to his feet and glanced at the shimmering sky.

"What happened?" he said. "Did it follow you?"

"No," she said. "I got away."

She told him what had happened, sort of—as much as she could tell. As she talked, Fox got up and paced. She sat down by the fire, as close as she could get, and pulled the hooked sword over. Holding it made her feel better as she told him about the dragon's size, its eyes and teeth and claws. Fox probably already knew, but she didn't care. "Its scales shone," she said, "like oil under a car. Like a shiny shadow."

Nothing she said seemed to surprise him, but at the same time he looked ready to jump out of his skin. Finally, she told him the dragon's words. When she stopped, his shoulders sagged in relief.

"You didn't tell me it could talk." She bit the inside of her lip.

"I hoped you'd never have to know. And that's all it said, huh?"

"Yes. Just nasty threats."

He shook his head. "Brook—I don't know what to say."

"You don't have to say anything."

"I don't know what I would've done if it had got you."

"Well, you probably would've spent the next year sobbing," she said, enjoying the picture. "But it didn't get me and I'm not gonna give it another chance."

"Ha," Fox said. "Great to hear."

She didn't tell him what had really happened. She couldn't.

When the dragon lunged at her, she'd shot away with wings on her feet. The air in her lungs had turned to hope, pure hope, as she'd found a doorway through a wall of flame—and another and another. She'd outsmarted a dragon. Who knew what else was possible?

"How about dinner?" she said.

All of a sudden, she was tired of talking about the dragon.

Fox laughed. "Tell you what," he said. "Sit tight. The dragon is a big deal. You seem like you're doing ok, but dinner's on me."

Brook gave him a smile. She felt good, at least she thought she did, but she also felt used up. She wished she had a hoodie to snuggle in. And hot chocolate, the next best thing to chocolate milk. And...

"I wish I had a book," she said.

Fox didn't notice, pulling the mussels out of the pool.

A book. It was a strange thought, because books weren't safe at the Foundation. Movies were safe. Kids chattered in the common room while the movies played, and the volume was never loud, the lights never low.

Otherwise, let's say you were totally into a film, like the one with Frodo, who seemed to have real friends—but you hear all the words and it's dark, so you're paying close attention to the screen or worse, wiping your eyes—well, you'd never notice someone sneaking up behind you. But TV at the Foundation wasn't like that.

Books were different. They were dangerous. Reading was an invitation to get hurt, and Brook could only manage a few pages at a time, constantly looking over her shoulder. She'd tried *To Kill a Mockingbird* for school, but she'd had to turn it in before she finished. When she checked books out from the library, the same thing happened. *Lord of the Flies* was the exception. No one cared about the beat-up copy she'd found, so she kept it. While she'd read that one, anyone could've pranked her or stabbed her, except she'd finally found a decent hiding place.

"Hey Brook," Fox said, "can I borrow the sword?"

She stopped day-dreaming and looked up from the fire. Wow, Fox, she thought, so casual about a blade. Good for you, you're growing. She handed the weapon over, and he used the sword to make a bed of embers. He blew on them until they flared to life. Then he went to the rock wall where he kept the jerky and came back with a flat stone. Brook felt guilty doing nothing but watching until he gave her a sideways look.

"Enjoy it while it lasts, dragon girl."

She sniffed. "I intend to."

Fox put the stone on the fire and used an empty shell to carry water from the pool and pour it into the sunken center. A minute later, when the water was steaming, he set the mussels in.

"Aah." He rubbed his hands over the fire and sat. "Now we wait."

The water bubbled, jostling the mussels up and down.

Something had been bothering Brook.

"Hey Fox."

"Yeah."

She threaded hair behind one ear. "Why do you think the dragon came after me?"

He prodded the mussels with a stick, then looked at her across the fire. "I was wondering the same thing and, well—not quite sure how to say this, Brook." He paused. "I think we're in danger. I know, I know. Go ahead and laugh if you want."

She didn't laugh.

"That dead kid on the beach today? It looked planned, not accidental. It means people are getting picked off. And the dragon chasing you—well, it doesn't usually come crashing through the trees. Put those things together and it makes me think we're in trouble. Sometimes kids die here, you know that. But the way they die, well, it's usually not so targeted. Not so on purpose. When it feels like it was planned, it's not good. What I'm trying to say is, I think there's a list, Brook. And I'm starting to think we're on it."

Her mouth felt dry. The good feelings she had from escaping the dragon floated away.

"Sorry." Fox looked down. "This was supposed to be a good dinner."

Brook watched the shellfish juddering around. "Who do you think is after us?"

"Sure you want to talk about this now?"

She nodded.

He sighed. "I think there's an inner circle. Kids who know stuff we don't know, and kill whoever the dragon wants them to in exchange for privileges. I guess the most obvious group would be—"

"The blue-faces." Brook said it like a dirty word.

They watched the water boil.

"Yeah," Fox said.

CHAPTER 23
NEGOTIATIONS

"SO, how do we eat these things?" Brook asked.

Fox's knife appeared in his hand. "Let me open one for you. You let it cool down, then you kind of slurp it. And a few seconds after that...we'll know if you like seafood."

"Funny," Brook said.

They'd stopped talking about the dragon and the blue-faces, and Brook was glad. They had to figure out a plan—a survival plan—and just a little bit ago, she'd felt up to the challenge. But with every minute that went by, the island seemed more deadly, and the walls of the castle seemed higher. Death Island was closing in, reaching for them with its cliffs and thorns. The dragon and the island and the blue faces, working hand in hand.

Laughing at them. *You call yourselves a team? Two stupid kids? Just you wait and see.*

Trying to kill them. Literally. Trying to murder her and Fox.

Putting them on a list.

This place just kept surprising her with horrible feelings.

"Come on, Brook. Try one." Fox held an open mussel, revealing its creamy insides. "Only chew it if you like the flavor."

Their eyes met. Fox looked worried.

"Right," Brook said. "Thanks."

She tugged at the mussel—what was it, exactly?—and it came loose from its shell, wet and squishy. She tossed it in her mouth and chewed. Then she swallowed.

Fox raised his eyebrows. Whatever she'd seen on his face was gone.

"I think—I think it's delicious food from the ocean. And I think next time, I won't chew so much." She forced herself to smile.

It was tough to focus on the little bags of guts or whatever they were. She ate all hers because she was hungry, but she still couldn't say if she liked seafood. A little later, Fox handed her a crab leg. He insisted that she stay by the fire like she was a hero who needed to take it easy.

It was sweet of him, so she played along. But the crab made her mind flick back to the beginning of the horrible day. The beach, the boy—then the creek, the dragon. And now this. But the crab had died to give them dinner, so why waste it?

The white meat tasted tangy. Like the sea. Then all the food was gone and they were sitting back, rubbing their stomachs by the fire. Fox must be thinking the same thing I am, Brook decided. He has to be. Right? She wondered who was going to bring it up, her or Fox. She hoped it would be him. That would make things easier. Because even after the dragon's attack, she remembered the clear water of the creek—no, the brook. Her skin still smelled clean, scrubbed with sand and dried by sunshine. She wouldn't forget what she'd decided about the knife.

"You didn't throw up," Fox pointed out.

"I did not!" Brook said. "Guess I like seafood."

"That's a relief," he said. "Gotta admit, I was worried I'd have to scrub mussels out of my hair." He cleared his throat. Brook held her breath, but all he did was take the sword-poker and shove some embers around. Then he surprised her.

"So I've been thinking," he said. "It seems like we need to get inside the castle."

Her fingers curled in the moss. Yes yes yes, she thought. Here we go.

"Yeah," she said. "I mean, maybe..."

She wasn't sure how to read his face. Serious for sure. Hopeful, probably. Could he be nervous? Even Foxes had nerves, she guessed.

"I'm up for trying if you are," she said. That seemed about right. Keep him on track, thinking it's a good idea, but don't encourage him too much. Her heart gave a wild thump and she covered it with a hand because she didn't want Fox to know how much the castle meant to her. How badly she wanted to get in. "What have we got to lose?" she said.

Fox nodded slowly. The light had changed by now. In the shadows, his eyes reflected the fire. "Here's what I'm thinking," he said.

And he told her something about the middle of the night, and how the dragon wouldn't expect it in the darkness, and how the blue-faces had been on top so long they wouldn't see it coming. And how the front gate was suicide but there was a small back door, so–

Cool, Brook thought. Cool cool cool. You take care of all that Fox, and I'll take care of one other very important detail. We'll toss it in with all the others.

He'd stopped talking. He was prodding the fire, waiting for a reaction, but she didn't give him one. Finally, he looked her in the eye. "Well, what do you think?"

Brook's chin rested on one hand. She had the gesture planned. "I like it," she said. "It gives us a chance at winning. But here's the thing." She swallowed—not something she'd planned. "I'm not going to help you."

Fox's eyes got big.

"Not until I have a weapon." She forced the words out. "I'm not going out there without a weapon." She held her breath.

Fox's hands tightened on the sword. Then they relaxed. "Wow." He licked his lips. "Yeah, I can see how you'd feel that way, Brook. It makes total sense. Today was bad, really bad. And we have people trying to get us. Umm, how about this? What if I gave you the knife?"

Brook felt shocked. Could it have really been this easy? See, she thought. Sometimes you have to be blunt. Sometimes honesty works. Not usually—but sometimes it actually works! The knife. Wow, the knife.

"I'll think about it," she said to hide her confusion. "It's a very little knife."

Fox rubbed the back of his head. Maybe he was feeling surprised too.

Of course I'll take that knife, Brook thought. Of course I will. It's ridiculous I've had to wait so long. Well, too bad, Foxy, you finally found something you need more than an extra weapon. The castle, you gotta have it. And me, you need me! Did you think I was really gonna walk into a fight wearing nothing but pre-shrunk cotton? I hope you didn't think I'd play along. Yeah, Fox. Ok, Fox. Whatever you say, Fox. If you did, you're insane.

Her thoughts were starting to run away. She might say something biting. So instead she said, "It's a deal. I'm in."

She reached across the fire for a fist bump. And gave him what was probably a slightly crazy smile.

Fox smiled back.

CHAPTER 24
MAGICAL FIRE CIRCLE

AS THE SUN WENT DOWN, streaking the sky with a cherry and lemon watercolor that ranked about nine out of ten, Brook wondered if the silence felt a little tense. Fair's fair, she thought. Hopefully Fox isn't a sore loser. We're both getting what we want. She curled up on the moss, favoring her sore hip, and remembered the dragon reaching for her. Snapping trees like matchsticks. Incinerating her footprints just a step behind.

I'm not afraid of you, she thought. But now that she'd seen it up close, she never wanted to be that close again. The dragon stays in the sky at night, Fox said. Too hard to track us. Too hard to see us through the trees.

She hoped he was right.

For once, Brook's dreams didn't wake her. She slept like a rag doll, didn't open her eyes until morning, and didn't remember her dreams—not that she needed to, since nightmares happened on the island while you were wide awake. When she woke up, flat on her back with an arm flung over her face, a heaviness descended on her right away, sinking through the trees like smog.

What is it? she thought. What's wrong? Oh, that's right. A hit list. Not just dead kids. Not just cliffs, not just a dragon. A list, with someone checking off names, and you're on it. Why? Why would someone want to?—no, don't even start. You're on Death Island. And it's not the first time someone has come after you, is it?

But wait, she thought desperately. There was something good too. There's gotta be. You figured something out. You learned something. Oooh, that's it. You beat the dragon. You thought you could and you did. You ran, you jumped, you dodged. And today you get a knife, a wonderful knife. So the world's not over yet. Plus, you're still clean.

Sure, she smelled like woodsmoke, but that was as good as perfume out here.

Brook sat up, rubbed her neck and arched her back. For the first time, Fox wasn't around. She went to the pool, then back to the fire, hoping to see the knife waiting—maybe with a bow on top—but it wasn't there. Well, she'd get it soon.

She sat down by the fire and started to search for embers, prodding and digging with the long black sword. When she scooted closer, her knee knocked the handle, and the sword slid into the smoking ash...and kept sliding, until half the blade was underground, vanished like a weird illusion.

"What the heck." Brook stared.

It's like a magical portal to another dimension, she thought. No, let's be real, really soft dirt. But then her imagination kicked in. *Hey. Wait. What if it is magic? What if there's hidden magic twisting through this place, watching, just out of sight. It might be the only way the island makes sense, with the dragon and the blue-faces and the castle. And if there is magic, and it opened a door and brought you here...could it have brought you for a not-bad reason?*

The idea was ridiculous and sweet, like the smell of flowers in an icy urban winter. It took her breath away. If magic brought you to a horrible place, but did it for a good reason—the magic wouldn't *have* to be bad. Right? It could be shaking its fist at the badness. Giving it the finger. Maybe good magic was invading, fighting the evil of the island. Maybe it was hanging around, waiting...for just the right person to help.

Someone who would say, Ok, I'll be the hero in this story. I'll take on the bad even though it'll make me a target. I'll do what it takes to set things right. Here I am, choose me.

Brook pictured a portal shimmering in the air, leading to the place she was supposed to be. A castle wall dissolving as she stepped onto secret stairs. Or maybe the magic reached further, spiraling away through time and space, across the sea. A doorway would sparkle and fizz into existence and she'd arrive...someplace the opposite of the Foundation, the opposite of here—somewhere open and fresh, clean and free.

Someplace magical.

A few minutes later Brook was still sitting by the cold fire, staring at nothing. She gave her head a shake. *I can't just sit here. But I'd better be careful.* She got her legs under her, ready to jump away if something flared or *whooshed*, and she took the sword in both hands. Holding her breath, she moved it in a slow circle, and...

Clunk. The blade hit something. *Thunk,* it hit something else. The sword slithered around, bumping into stuff like she was stirring a big pot of dirt stew. Dust rose in wisps and floated toward Brook's face.

Nothing magical happened. At all.

The fire ring was a dirty old fire *pit*.

"Crap," Brook said. "Well, magic could still be out there, I guess." She sighed.

The ash-filled pit was interesting, but not compared to magic. If she had a shovel and she was bored, she might dig around. Who knew what could be down there? But the air was chilly and she wanted to get warm.

Then her mind made another sideways lurch. What if Fox had buried something? She touched a finger to her chin. *Now there's an idea. You know he loves secrets. What if he hid something like, hmm... treasure—yeah, buried treasure—and he dug it out of the sand and brought it here and put it back in the ground. And naturally, the treasure belongs to the dragon, and that's why the dragon is after us.*

Brook sighed. It wasn't very convincing. Anyway, Fox wouldn't care about gold and gems. No, Fox's treasure would be a survival pack, with a pot and utensils, a few more knives, string, hooks, a compass, all that boy scout stuff. But if he had it, he'd be using it. He wouldn't have stashed it in the dirt.

She shivered and rubbed her cold arms. "Idiot."

Brook pulled the sword free and started combing for embers. Maybe she'd dig around later when the ashes were cold, although they never really were. Fox kept them hot. You didn't want to be caught without a fire. She got some twigs smoking and was looking for larger branches when he tramped in, holding an armful of logs.

"Never got our firewood yesterday," he said.

"I'll get some too." Brook jumped to her feet and wove through the labyrinth. Helping with firewood was the least she could do after that seafood dinner. A few minutes later they had a nice blaze going. Brook warmed her hands, trying not to think about magic or treasure.

Fox handed her a piece of jerky.

"We need to go back to the rabbits, Brook."

"Oh—ok." So they weren't going to talk about the castle.

"We need more food. The Death Dogs are probably gone."

"Makes sense," she said, thinking, Give me the knife already!

She didn't have to wait much longer. After Fox had eaten his jerky, he banked the fire and picked up the sword. He spent a few minutes wiping it down with moss. "I'm taking your advice, taking better care of this thing," he said.

Stalling is what you're doing, Brook thought. She couldn't think of anything to say so she raised her eyebrows, and then–

"Here you go." Fox handed her the knife.

Oh wow. Where had it come from? Yay! She wanted to cheer, wave her hands in the air. Instead she said, "Cool, thanks Fox."

But her heart was racing, her brain screaming: *Now you've got a chance!* She wrapped the bright blade tenderly in its dirty cloth and slid it in her pocket. *No sudden movements. No tripping.*

Patting the metal at her hip, she wondered where Fox had found it. The dragon probably didn't drop weapons from the sky. Why would it arm its prisoners? So the knife and the sword and the bow that killed that kid had probably been here all along, like tokens on a game board. If there were other weapons out there, they were already taken. Well...taken until someone died.

Died. Oh no. That meant the murderers, the blue-faces and maybe the dragon, were collecting weapons.

God, what an awful thought. The killers have a weapons stash.

Why did she always follow these rabbit trails?

"Rabbits, Brook?" Fox stood at the exit, sword on one shoulder.

Her shoulders jerked. "How did you know I—Oh."

"You don't have to come if you don't want to," he said. "You can take it easy after yesterday."

"Are you kidding?" She got to her feet. "Of course I'm coming."

Hopefully for the last time, she thought. Hunt for rabbits, out in the open?

Not fun.

Get left in the woods, alone with my thoughts?

Not a chance.

CHAPTER 25
RACE TO THE WOODS

THEY STOPPED at the forest's edge and looked out over the grass. Brook shaded her eyes against the brightness. She didn't see a thing—but when did she ever? Around here, you never saw anything until it was too late.

She and Fox glanced at each other.

"Ready to take the field?" he said.

"Go team."

It was almost funny.

Fox set a quick pace, marching through the waist-high grass. Seedpods brushed Brook's elbows, and she glared at them. Stay off me, she thought. I'm still clean. Who knows when I'll make it back to the brook—or if I'll ever have the guts to go there again.

She remembered how mad Fox had been two days ago, resetting one empty snare after another as they followed the little paths. Right away, they had better luck. A fat rabbit dangled in the first trap, limp as a rag. Fox bent low in the rabbit run and Brook did too, even though she had nothing to do but watch him. Better to be out of sight, below the waving grass.

The second snare was sprung but empty. Fox replaced the sticks and loop of twine.

The third snare had another rabbit.

"Finally, a little luck," Fox said.

The fourth had one too.

"Jackpot," Brook said.

"This is more like it," Fox said.

The fifth and sixth were empty but the seventh was not.

"Four of them," Fox said. "Officially a great day. We'll be in jerky for a while. I'd stop now, but if there are more, we can't just leave them in the traps."

Without warning, Brook began to feel nervous. Things were going well. Too well. When things went better than they should, you knew something was about to fall apart. Also, she and Fox were getting close to the tenth snare where the Death Dogs had torn a rabbit to shreds. It wasn't a place she wanted to see again.

But they didn't get that far.

"Hey, what's that?" Brook said.

Something was moving on the plain, far off on their left.

Fox stiffened like he really was a fox, catching the scent of hunters.

They stared across the waving grasses.

"It's...another kid," Brook said.

Fox wheeled around. He pointed, sword tucked under his arm, dead rabbits dangling from his hands. "And another, coming from the south."

Insects whirred in the grass. The sun beat down. Brook's mouth felt dry.

She got the feeling the island was grinning.

"They're trying to cut us off." Fox's eyes were dark. "Stay close, Brook. It's a race to the woods." Then he was off and running, feet barely touching the ground. In the time it took her to draw a breath, he was twenty feet away.

This was serious.

With a rabbit in each fist, she took off after him, hair flying, trail shoes thudding. Back in middle school gym, she'd always run the laps—really ran—because the value of speed had been obvious to her for years. She flew after Fox, swishing through the grass. The knife in her pocket dug into her leg, and she hoped it wasn't cutting her.

Stay in your rag, she thought. Please don't hurt me.

Her breath came in gasps, her chest burned, and she knew one bad step would throw her ten or fifteen feet, scraping and bumping in the dirt. It would be the end. The other kids would catch her, and what could she do against a gang of them? Nothing good.

No, she thought. No, no, no.

The field was a blur on either side.

The wind made her eyes wet.

Branches whipped her arms and legs as she swerved blindly into the shade of the trees. Stumbling over roots, she threw her arms around a bumpy trunk to catch her balance. Bark scraped her face. The rabbits were squishy in her hands.

"Brook!" Fox called. "Keep moving."

Welts rose on her arms as she pushed away from the tree, but there was no blood spreading from her hip pocket.

"Good little knife," she whispered. "Stay where you are."

"They're close behind," Fox said.

She flinched when he took her elbow, but didn't pull away. She let him tug her forward, even though she'd got her legs back. He'd waited for her and he hadn't had to.

"Right behind you," she said. "I'm ok now."

His hand fell away. "We can lose them in the woods," he said.

"No you can't," said a shadow.

A tall, thick boy stepped into their path. "We knew you'd run this way," he said. "You're not the only one with brains." He looked at Fox, then Brook. "Once we deal with him..." He shrugged. "There aren't a lot of girls around. Maybe we'll keep you." His eyes flicked back to Fox and he raised his weapon, a wicked curved blade on the end of a staff.

Brook dug in her pocket for the knife.

"You've got this coming," the boy told Fox.

Then the stranger made a mistake. He glanced at Brook again.

She'd never thrown a weapon in her life. At the Foundation, you never let one out of your sight, let alone your hands. So when something dark flew past and the boy screamed and staggered, she froze. Had a bird attacked him?

Fox leapt forward. He kicked at the groaning stranger and bent over him.

Brook locked her fingers on the knife's hilt, wedged against her hip.

Fox picked up his dripping sword.

The boy stayed on his back, blood gushing from one leg.

Brook stared, then looked away. She flicked the switch in her head to On. On point, on alert, on guard. It's just blood, she told herself. It's what happens in a fight.

"Let's go," Fox said.

Branches snapped behind them and someone shouted, but Brook hesitated. She let go of the rabbits, straightened the knife in her pocket, and bent to grab the long, silver weapon the boy had dropped in the leaves. It felt cool and deadly in her hands.

Now it was hers.

"Brook!" Fox yelled.

She left the rabbits in the dirt and darted after him.

CHAPTER 26
RUNNING THROUGH TREES

CARRYING THE BLADED STAFF, Brook stayed right on Fox's heels. The shadowy woods yawned open like a puzzle, but with her new shoes and new weapon, she knew more of the answers than ever before. Now she was dangerous. If there was magic on the island, then maybe, just maybe, it had decided to be on her side.

Slim and silver, the staff trailed over her shoulder like featherweight death. She knew she'd never touched anything this lethal. Not here. Not in Weed, California. Not ever. If she turned and fought, she'd be scary. Even Fox would be impressed. But you never knew how a fight would end.

Fox didn't stop running and neither did she. They were moving so fast she couldn't waste a single breath. She couldn't miss a single step—and she didn't. Feet gliding, knees pumping, the staff slicing the air behind her, she stayed in rhythm.

She had the feeling she and Fox were leaving their pursuers behind. He must have sensed it too, because a few seconds ahead of her, he swerved away, off the straight line they'd been running. Brook skidded and made the turn. When Fox glanced back, he looked surprised to see her right behind him.

Then he slowed to fight through thick brush, the bristling, twisty kind of stuff they'd been avoiding. Brook shoved at vines and saplings, slashing with her staff. Fox was right, a big weapon was awkward in the forest—but the blade sure was sharp.

When she came out the far side of the thicket, leaves clinging to her clothes and hair, Fox was climbing an enormous slab of rock. She'd seen the leaning stones before. They'd run away from their campsite, cutting north through the woods toward the castle.

She scrambled up the angled rock, enjoying the way her shoes grabbed hold. Before, it had been like falling up a playground slide. Now it was an uphill jog. When she reached the top and jumped down next to Fox in the jumbled boulders, she saw why he'd brought them here. Looking back, there wasn't a trace of their escape. No scuffed leaves, no broken twigs. No footprints. Hiding behind the rocks and spying, they could watch the hillside without being seen.

Brook felt good, ready to run *or* fight.

If someone else threatened her, he'd regret it.

"Now we'll see if we've lost them." Fox set his rabbits down, then his sword, and slumped in the shade, chest rising and falling. The rabbits looked the worse for wear from being squeezed.

Brook wiped damp hair off her face, leaned against a boulder and slid a hand into her pocket. The knife was resting quietly, flat against her hip. Knowing what a razor edge like that could do, she felt grateful. She wanted to sit down like Fox, but she didn't want to set aside her bladed staff. The silver arc gleamed in the sun. It felt powerful in her hands.

Don't be silly, she told herself. No one's gonna snatch it. You're not in the Foundation. But still. She leaned it against a boulder, tugged the knife half-out of her pocket, and slid to the ground between Fox and the staff—just in case he made a grab.

"Why didn't we fight them?" she asked.

It seemed like such an obvious question.

Fox tilted his head back against the rock and closed his eyes.

"They were organized," he said. "And there were probably more of them—and they had weapons."

"Yeah, but..." Brook took a big swallow of air. "We do too."

Fox opened his eyes and looked at her. His gaze slid up and down the staff.

"True," he said, not giving much away.

She could imagine what he was thinking. Woo-hoo, Brook picked up a spiky staff-thing. She's been here four days and she's never touched a staff-thing in her life. But all of a sudden she thinks we're invincible. And she left behind her rabbits.

Maybe she was making up the part about the rabbits, but Fox had managed to hold onto his. She felt her face get hot and looked away, back down the long stone slab. The slope was empty in the sun.

She had the crazy urge to jump to her feet, grab her weapon, and show Fox she wasn't just a clueless girl. But she managed to catch her breathing as it started to speed up. She smoothed a hand across the front of her shirt. *Let him be.*

She checked the slope again. Still empty.

"It's a nice scythe-staff," Fox said. "In great shape, too. I'm jealous."

"Scythe-staff, huh? Cool name." Brook knew he was being polite. He had a knack for that. Well, it wasn't a bad quality. She crooked an arm around the staff and flashed a smile. "Don't tell me you want to trade," she said.

"Wow, seriously?" Fox narrowed his eyes, thinking about it. For a scary second, she thought he was about to say, Yeah, let's swap. Then he winked. "Naw, too pretty for me."

Brook smiled again, and this time she didn't fake it. The staff was hers. She was happy they'd nailed that down. *Scythe-staff.* It sounded good.

"I'm starting to think we lost them," Fox said.

"What if we didn't?"

"We'll see them coming and sneak away. By the time they get up here, we'll be halfway down." He pointed to the other side of the ridge, where boulders tumbled down to meet the trees. "And when they get up here, no trace of us."

Brook nodded. "That's pretty genius, Fox."

He shrugged, looking a little smug.

Slumping in the shadows of the rocks, she felt her muscles getting tight. Her lungs ached. Jumping and dodging through the woods, sprinting uphill, then this. Her gashed hip was smarting. Her stomach was unhappy. She should be walking it off and stretching her city muscles at the very least.

Brook stood up, half-crouching to stay below the rocks. She took her scythe-staff—she couldn't help herself—and crept forward to the castle overlook with the rock slide at her back. Fox didn't say a word, just watched her push through the evergreens.

The cliff fell away at her feet. She planted the staff like an explorer and looked out over the green and amber plains. The castle towered in the sun, even bigger than she remembered. A monument to safety and strength. Brook took a breath so big that her shoulders lifted. There really is magic here, she thought. Something good, waiting and watching. How else can you explain *that*?

"Gorgeous, isn't it?" Fox said behind her.

Standing there with a hip cocked, looking over the glowing fields, leaning on her scythe-staff with a certain swagger, Brook knew the castle was the right decision. The kids trying to kill them would never expect them to go there. Together, she and Fox could get exactly what they wanted.

CHAPTER 27
ISABELLA

THEY WALKED to their campsite through unfamiliar woods. Fox would've probably liked to talk—he usually did—and Brook felt like talking too, but she also felt giddy. The scythe-staff trailed over her shoulder like a sharp, curved streamer, making her think God was real—and hey, maybe God was behind the magic. Good things could still happen. Even with all the death.

She wanted to tell Fox, but she knew it would come out crazy:

"Fox, what if we're the good guys? What if we ended up here for a reason and we don't need to be afraid? We'll take over the castle and rule like a king and queen. We'll make a civilization with our own laws. Forget *Lord of the Flies*—we'll be *Lords of the Butterflies*! And later, we'll build a boat–"

Yeah, she was glad she wasn't saying this. It was over the top all right.

It just felt so good to win.

Yesterday she'd escaped the dragon. Today, the hit-kids. *You've got us on your list, so what? Eat our dust. And watch out, losers, we're coming for your castle. You blue-faces made a mistake coming after me and Fox.*

Hmm. Thinking about it, she couldn't remember if the big, tough hit-kid in the woods had been wearing face paint. Trying to recall his face now, she wasn't sure—so many shadows. But it was obvious which side he was on.

Once she calmed down, Brook tried to get her bearings in the forest. The trees were big and twisty with bark like alligator hide. It made walking easier, since the forest giants sucked in all the light and water for themselves. No rude vines, no grabby little shrubs. The ground was thick with rotting leaves.

She got the feeling they were being watched. Once, when she looked up, something twisted across a patch of sky. Her chest tightened. But it could've been just a broken branch, moving in the wind.

Later, something howled off to the west. Fox didn't comment but he moved a little faster. They'd walked at least an hour, about four miles, when he stopped and looked around. His face darkened. Brook got the idea he wanted to cuss. Instead, he lashed out with his sword, slicing splinters off a tree. Brook's hands tightened on her staff, but a second later he was calm again.

"Back we go," he said like nothing had happened. "I got off track."

They doubled back. Brook's muscles began to stiffen up, and her good spirits started to leak out. Maybe it was her fault for staying quiet, but she felt like Fox should've been happy too. A little cheerful at least, after their big escape. It made her feel silly. Maybe she wasn't thinking straight. Maybe the future wasn't bright if Fox didn't even see it.

No, she thought. He's in a bad mood. *I'm* right. Something good *can* happen.

But it made her irritable.

After they'd hiked two miles back the way they'd come, they stopped under a huge, pale tree with swooping branches and bark peeling off in big strips. *With our luck, it's probably haunted.* Fox chose a new angle—maybe southwest, Brook thought—and they set off, escaping the ghost tree. Their direction didn't seem very different from the way they'd gone before. But this time it worked.

When they found the creek, Fox looked at her and nodded. She checked his face for signs of anger, but he seemed ok. They followed the watercourse south, and long before they passed her bath spot, Brook knew where they were. When they reached the bottom of a wooded hill with the stream bubbling at their backs, her heart rate spiked.

"Um, Fox?" She paused, probably standing in her old footprints.

"We'll stay away from the burn area," Fox said.

She wasn't even surprised when he read her mind. She must be getting used to it. But she felt very nervous, creeping through the shadows. The scorched ground opened on their left as they wound through the thicket. Wisps of smoke rose from the blackened ground. Trees were snapped and broken like forty-foot toothpicks, and it was hard to believe anyone had survived. Fox looked at her and raised his eyebrows.

She kept an eye on the sky but it stayed empty.

The dragon was looking for them somewhere else.

By the time they wound through the standing stones and into their campsite, Brook's feet ached in her new hikers. Her scratched arms and legs had started itching.

"Camp sweet camp," Fox said.

"Not quite home, is it?" she said.

"Huh?" Fox itched behind one ear.

"Never mind."

"Ok. Gotta say, I'm sick of carrying these rabbits." He dumped them by the fire.

Brook got a drink, then leaned her staff against the rock on her side of the camp. She slumped beside it, and the cool, smooth stone soothed her back. Propping her chin on one hand, she studied her weapon. Its sculpted wooden handle rested in the moss. The dark, swirly blade shone against the granite. It could've been a weapon photo shoot.

"Not many blades like that," Fox said.

She turned. "Sorry I dropped my rabbits."

"It's ok, there's always more."

She nodded, happy he was being cool. She could tell he was tense, maybe angry, but he did a good job keeping it in check. That was something she understood. She wondered what he'd think of her if he got to know her better and saw that side of her. Well, it would happen eventually. And if anyone could understand, he should.

Fox got the fire going as Brook splashed water on her arms and legs. "Want me to skin the rabbits?" she asked. "I can pitch in."

"Thanks, but it's tricky," Fox said. "How about next time?"

So she handed him the knife and watched as he sliced the rabbits open, carved away the guts and peeled away the skins. She even made herself watch when he cut the heads off.

"I figure we can eat one and make jerky with the other," Fox said.

Since they'd skipped breakfast and lunch, they ate first. Brook took a turn with the knife, slicing one rabbit into chunks on a flat rock. They roasted them over the fire, licking their lips, and ate them almost too hot to chew.

"Wow." Brook said. "So good."

Fox smiled at her and some of her hope came back. *Look at us, sharing the knife like a couple good kids on kitchen duty.* She wondered if the two of them were friends. Whoa, she thought. Slow down, Brook. Take it easy.

"Hey," she said, "Do you ever feel like your head will explode?" She'd meant to go on, but instead she stopped on a dime and shut her mouth to see what Fox would say.

He kept slicing the second rabbit into strips. "Yeah, Brook. All the time."

"Seriously?" She waited.

"There's all these threads to keep track of," Fox said, "to hold together. Eating, hunting, planning, hiding. Gotta keep them tight and lined up, but you never know when your brain will surprise you and say something like, Man, I wish I'd had a chance to play baseball —I could've been really good. You know? And then everything twists into a tangled mess and starts burning, if you let it. I think my head's exploded a hundred times."

"Thank God, you get it." Brook touched her forehead. "I mean the island, the dragon, the castle, it all just whirls around in here. Why are we here? What's the point? If I'm not thinking about something else, it's like a firestorm in my head. The harder I try to figure it out, the worse it gets."

"That's why it's a good idea to stay busy." Fox handed her a skewer. "And if the bomb goes off, oh well. Maybe brains work better on fire."

"Maybe." Brook skewered chunks of rabbit. "Although I'm not sure I want my head on fire all the time. Sometimes I try to think about smaller questions instead, like—where does the dragon go when it's not flying? Where does it sleep?"

"That's a good one." Fox paused, the knife hovering. "Maybe a cave in the cliffs that can only be reached by air?"

"Probably," Brook said. "You think we should try to find it?"

"Probably not," Fox said.

"Right," Brook said. "Why die young? But it's the kind of thing I think about."

Fox tapped his own forehead. "You and me both."

She wanted to say something about magic, one of the explosive questions tumbling around her mind. "Hey Fox, what if good magic is carving out space on the island? What if the magic brought us here? What if the magic has a plan of its own?" But if she and Fox were friends—big IF—they weren't close enough for *that* talk.

Still it made her feel good, bringing more of her thoughts into the open.

They finished cutting up the second rabbit, and Fox showed her how to build a drying rack over the fire with Y-shaped upright branches and a center stick. After they hung the meat in the smoke, they sat by the blaze as the sun went down.

As soon as it was dark enough to feel like bedtime, Brook said goodnight. It made her seem like an eight-year-old but she didn't care. The wind and sun and running had made her bone tired. Before she curled up, she touched the handle of her scythe-staff.

"The island didn't want me to have you," she whispered. "But I got you anyway."

As she lay in the moss, she tried to think of a name for her weapon. She didn't know that many. Not her own. Not Fox's. Not many names at all. Monique, but that was the last name she'd give anything she liked. Names without faces fluttered around her mind like moths. Finally she settled on Isabella. She couldn't say where she'd heard it, but the staff deserved something nice. Something graceful. Isabella didn't sound especially deadly, but to make up for that...she would name the knife too. Maybe Fox would let her keep it, and then the knife and scythe-staff could balance each other out.

Hmm.

Demon-fang?

Dragon-tooth?

She fell asleep trying to think of something nasty.

That night she dreamed again. The gang of girls were on her tail, and the chase started by the bus stop, but she ran so fast and so far that she was on the cliffs, and the dragon came straight at her, roaring and snatching with its teeth, and she screamed and fell, down into the grinding mouth of the sea. But she landed in the woods, shoving through branches that exploded into splinters. Gasping, she ran deeper in, where the trees grew old and the silence was haunted. But somehow, even though she dodged and twisted, quick as a rabbit, the chase still ended in the basement.

It was the worst nightmare she'd ever had.

She woke up, shaking, when the dragon flew overhead. The real dragon. Soaring so close she could feel the rusty bass vibration of its roar. In her dream, the roar had been a city sound, an evil subway rumbling to life, and she didn't know how it would fit into the awful things that were happening, only that it would make them worse. Maybe the train would smash through the basement wall and she'd find herself on the tracks.

Her eyes flew open and she saw crimson flames eating up the night. The dragon could've seen her if it hadn't been for the screen of branches. The beast was flying low. She figured it could see in the dark since it had dropped her on the cliffs at night. She held her breath. She could have been a mannequin, lying on its back. The dragon wheeled and came around again. Fire burned behind the leaves, turning them blood red. Maybe the dragon smelled them.

Then it gave up and flew off toward the coast.

Thank God.

Brook lay awake for a long time. She could barely bring herself to move, to wipe her forehead and unbend her cramped legs on the moss.

"Fox," she gasped.

"I saw it too." He sounded hoarse. "But everything's about to change, Brook. Remember that."

She did her best to believe him.

CHAPTER 28
KILLER KIDS

THE HIT-KIDS FOUND them a little after dawn.

Brook came awake knowing something was wrong. Fox was on his feet in the gray light. The hooked sword was in his hands, but he hadn't touched the ashes of the fire. His head was on one side. Then she heard it too.

A rustle of leaves. Creaking branches.

It could've been the wind.

But it wasn't.

Brook jumped to her feet, ignoring her throbbing hip and aching legs. Her heart rattled her ribs—SLAM SLAM SLAM—as she snatched Isabella from the rock. In the second it took her to wheel around, a shadow had dropped into their hollow—and all her reflexes tightened to a razor point.

It's happening, she thought. They're still after us. Ok, ooh-kay.

Something flared to life in her chest and set the rest of her on fire.

The shadowy boy flicked his hand. A dagger ripped Fox's shoulder and clanged against the rocks. The boy moved closer. "Did you really think we'd let you—"

Fox didn't throw his sword this time. He yelled and threw himself.

Covering the distance, he brought his sword down in a fierce two-handed chop. Metal crashed on metal, and then the two boys were circling each other, hacking and dodging. The stranger had a gleaming spear-like thing with extra blades. Brook could hardly see it in the dark, but the kid kept using it to stop Fox's blows. She heard sounds on the path through the standing stones.

More killer kids were coming.

Go, Brook thought. Hit the switch.

She lowered her staff and ran at the shadowy boy. He saw her coming, and she didn't make it easy for him. To stop her, he'd have to turn away from Fox. Could he fight them both at once? Brook swiped with Isabella, just as quick and deadly as she'd thought. The stranger lashed out, their blades clashed, and she found her answer.

No, he couldn't fight them both. He knocked her blade away, but Fox cut at his legs and the boy went down with a scream. Fox's sword flashed again. He snatched the forked weapon from the kid's limp fingers and turned.

"Who's next?" he snarled.

More shadows spilled from the labyrinth, appearing as if by magic. One, two, three. Brook couldn't make out faces but their weapons glittered in the dawn.

Fox's arm whipped forward. The forky weapon shot through the air.

The first shadow made a choking sound and fell.

"Now it's two on two," Fox said like he was keeping score.

God, help, Brook thought. Here I go.

Fox stepped forward and she kept pace on his right. She held the scythe-staff level, hovering like a snake. The last two kids fanned out on either side. The third one lay twitching on the ground.

Fox laughed.

Then the two shadows did something Brook never expected. They split up. One went left, one right. The fight became two games of one-on-one, and Brook was ok with that, because if there was one thing she hated, it was multiple people coming at her at once.

Her attacker rushed in, closing fast with a spiky bat like Brook was a piñata, waiting to get cracked. *But I'm not.* She dodged the first swing and her attacker stumbled past. When the kid whirled, Brook realized she was fighting another girl—a girl with angry eyes and a bruise on one cheek. The girl took another swing, and Brook saw her opening. She snaked the scythe-staff under the bat and gritted her teeth when the blade hit something solid. The other girl screamed and staggered away, holding a bloody arm. Now her eyes looked wild.

That's what you get, Brook thought.

But her attacker still hadn't had enough. She pushed off from the rock wall, ready to come at Brook again—until she saw her weapon, pinned under Brook's foot. The girl's face changed and she made a dash for the labyrinth. *Go ahead and run*, Brook thought. *This isn't over.* Ahead of her, the killer bounced off a boulder, scuffled in the dirt, and made a wrong turn.

Brook smiled.

When Brook arrived at the dead end, the other girl had her back against the stone. Her face was a mask and her hands were in the air, saying Hey, don't hurt me, this was all a big mistake—but Brook knew what the killer kid would do if she lowered Isabella or looked away for even one second. The girl would jump at her, clawing and spitting like a dumpster cat.

Brook didn't give her the chance. She leveled the scythe-staff, gauged the distance, and pivoted on one foot to put her strength behind the blow.

"Don't!" The girl's hands started shaking. Her eyes widened until they took up her whole face. "I can tell you things! There's a plan, a reward! Please, I can–"

"Liar!" Brook spat. "You came here to kill us in our sleep. You can't tell me anything that'll keep me from–"

Wait, she thought. *Is this it—the way you're gonna choose? The you*

you want to be? Her whole body felt ready to plunge ahead. To cut, to stab, to end this, so she'd never have to see the girl again. Then her rage and the blood boiling behind her eyes crashed into something big and dark that flashed like lightning, and she thought, *But magic. You can't do this and have magic. Not both.* So she stepped back, never taking her eyes off the killer, who was holding up her hands like melted talons.

"Get out," Brook said through her teeth.

The girl shot past down the trail through the jumbled rocks. Cradling her bloody arm, she looked back once. Then she was gone —but still out there. Still dangerous. Half of Brook wished she'd ended the fight for good. *And the weird thing is, I don't even know if there* is *magic.* Brook's death grip on the scythe-staff weakened. "Well Isabella," she said, "at least it still makes sense for you to have that pretty name."

When she turned, Fox was coming to a stop behind her.

"Brook!" He dropped his sword and put his hands on her shoulders. "Are you ok?"

"Yeah. Are you?"

"I'm fine." He stepped back, taking her in. "Really, you're not hurt?"

"I'm great, Fox. I won."

He kept staring, probably checking for blood. Then he looked past her down the trail.

"I let her—she got away," Brook said. "But I cut her good."

"Maybe I'll show her to the door," Fox said.

And just like that he was gone.

Brook walked back to their campsite.

Standing by the fire, she caught herself breathing hard although she'd barely done a thing. Fox had done the real work, moving from weapon to weapon and fight to fight like it was nothing. It had been a performance.

"But I could've done more," she whispered.

One killer-kid was down by the standing stones. Fox had thrown the silver fork like a huge dart, straight to the bullseye. It had hit the kid in the neck. A second killer, the boy who'd jumped into their campsite, was crumpled in the moss like he'd dropped from the sky. The third kid Fox had fought lay face down near the fire, turning the ground red. Brook didn't need a closer look. Three less killers on the island.

So that was that. Seeing them now, cluttering their campground, she was happy with what Fox had done. She wasn't sure why she hadn't done it too. There wasn't any magic here. Just survival. *Just the most deadly wins.*

Brook yanked the fork-weapon free. Blood pounded in her ears.

She realized she was furious.

"How dare you," she said.

She kicked at the ground. She stalked back and forth between the three dead bodies.

"You thought you could kill us in our sleep," she said. "And now you're dead. How do you like that? Dead, you losers, dead." She was fighting for breath again. So she leaned her staff against the granite and stuck the fork-spear in the ashes so she could go to the pool, where she took a drink and splashed water on her face and hands.

"I need a toothbrush," she said.

Her mouth tasted awful.

She stood by the fire, looking around.

"They bled all over the moss." A sob caught in her throat.

Feeling sick, she sat in a clean patch by the embers and pulled her knees to her chest, digging through the ashes with the giant fork. It worked much better than the sword. She put a hand to her stomach. Things had just started to go well.

"It's ok," she gasped. "It's ok."

She was glad Fox didn't reappear.

After a while, she straightened up, wiping her eyes and nose, rubbing her hands in the moss. Her breathing had returned to normal.

"They deserved it," she said. "We didn't have a choice."

She focused on the smoking ashes. Usually they'd have the fire going by now. Usually they'd be waking up slowly (well, at least she would) and Fox would be saying what they needed to get done that day. It took more work than usual to dig for embers. She found a few small ones on the surface and jabbed the fork-thing deeper. It snagged a glowing, fist-sized chunk.

Brook pushed hair out of her face and dug in again, looking for more lava coals. The fork connected with a solid crunch, and she tried to lever it up. It quivered in her hands and didn't budge.

"What the heck," she said through gritted teeth.

She twisted and shoved and jerked. Sweat popped out on her forehead. The ashes of the fire swirled and collapsed like the the mouth of a volcano opening.

"Come—on!" Brook groaned and yanked.

The silver fork came up in a dusty cloud. Ash swirled into her eyes and nose. "Ack-blech!" She coughed, waving away the choking air. Before the dust could cover any more of her, she stumbled to the pool and splashed herself again. So much for being clean. Then she went back to the fire to see what she could salvage. Smoke rose from the dusty ruins.

Brook slid the forked weapon slowly from the ashes.

No more ash explosions, she thought. I've had enough–

"Oh God!" She dropped the weapon.

Looking up at her was a blackened, grinning skull.

CHAPTER 29
WEAPONS-RICH

WHEN FOX GOT BACK, the fire was cold and dead. Brook sat in her usual place, knees pulled up, arms around her shins. The skull sat next to her in the moss.

They stared at Fox, together.

"Whoa!" Fox put a hand on his heart. "That one rotted fast."

"Not funny." Brook forced herself to pat the skull. It had been sitting in the coals forever, so it had to be sterile, right? "Want to tell me about this?"

Fox came to stand by the ruined fire. Streams of ash were still trickling into the cavity Brook had opened underneath. It looked like the charred ruins of a tiny ancient city.

"Where else could I put it?" Fox said. "I didn't have a closet to hide it in."

"Why didn't you tell me about it?" Brook said.

"Why would I?" Fox crossed his arms. "Do you think I've told you about every horrible thing that's happened to me here? All kinds of things. Once I cut myself on a reef and Death Dogs smelled my blood and almost got me. Once the dragon chased me into the woods. I had to hide in the brush for days. And speaking of monsters, if you want to get really practical, do you think it's a good idea to leave a body in the forest by your campsite? Cremation made sense."

Brook crossed her arms.

"I've been attacked before," he said. "I may have mentioned it once or twice."

She waved a hand in the air. "I guess everyone just hates you."

"If you're not part of their little gang, then yeah, they hate you," Fox said. "We've talked about this. Something tells me you might know a little about it too."

Brook closed her mouth. He'd taken the wind right out of her. Fox was right, of course he was. He was the one living in reality. She was the one struggling to keep up.

Fox leaned several weapons against the rocks. One was the silver bat with spikes Brook had taken from her attacker. There was some kind of black axe and a gleaming spear with a leaf-shaped blade. Plus Isabella, and the huge barbed fork, and the little knife she hadn't named yet. Oh, and the knife the kid had thrown at Fox.

"Did you kill the last one?" Brook asked.

Fox shrugged. "Do you want me to tell you what happened?"

"Not really," she said.

"I bought us time," Fox said. "They won't come after us for a while. But we can't stay here much longer, Brook. If they can find us once, they can find us again."

"You're right," Brook said. "And then there's the dragon. Flying over, blasting flames around like fireworks—or signal flares. 'Hey everyone, here's where Fox and Brook are hiding.'"

Something wild flickered through Fox's eyes.

Panic? Rage? She couldn't tell. Brook looked around their secret campsite. Like the fire, it felt caved in on itself. Dirty with death and ash.

"Fox, can I ask you something?" She pointed at the three bodies. "Is this easy for you?" She took a good long look at him. There was blood on his shoulder from where the dagger had caught him. Other than that, he looked unhurt. Even relaxed.

"Is what easy for me?"

"This," Brook said. "Killing."

Fox blinked. She held her breath.

"No," he said. "It's not easy."

She waited.

"I hate this." All of a sudden, his face looked young—about her age, no older than fourteen. "I try not to think about what I'm doing," he said. "Because if I do, I'm dead." He pointed a finger at her. "And so are you. I'm a friendly guy, Brook, or I would be in normal life. I wish you could see that part of me. I'd rather be playing kickball or watching a movie or doing homework. I wish we were normal friends and we could work on a class project or walk to McDonald's. But we're not, are we?"

Brook felt bad. What did she expect from him? Definitely nothing normal.

"Sorry," she said.

Fox studied his feet. With his head down and his shoulders slumped, he looked less confident and more like a kid. Brook stepped closer. She held her breath as she put a hand on one of his shoulders and squeezed. He covered her hand with one of his. They stepped apart.

"Thanks," he said.

"I get it," Brook said.

Ash floated up the yellow sunbeams into bright green leaves. The morning was half over and they hadn't eaten and there were three dead bodies lying in the moss.

"At least we have a lot of weapons now," Brook said. She was trying to picture Fox in a McDonald's. Or playing kickball. It was tough.

"We're weapons-rich," Fox said. "Which one do you like best?"

Brook looked at the new ones he'd lined up. Strange, sharp lines gleamed bright and deadly. The slender spear was tempting. The axe and the spiky bat—a mace, Fox said—were on the heavy side and not as sleek.

She picked up the fork-spear from the fire. It had a brutal quality that she didn't love, even though it reminded her of her old Foundation shork. Maybe that was why she didn't like it. In the end, she decided to stick with Isabella. The scythe-staff was strangely pretty. Doing its job with all the style it could.

"Good choice." Fox smiled.

"What are you so happy about?"

"It's a gorgeous weapon."

"So?"

"It's kind of girly."

"Ah, I see." Brook put her hands on her hips. "So you're happy I didn't choose one you'd actually want. In that case..." She grabbed the fork-spear. "Mine!"

"No!" Fox pretended to be shocked. "I wanted that trident."

Brook narrowed her eyes and snatched the spear. "Also mine!"

"Hey! Stop being greedy!"

Brook wanted to keep grabbing weapons but her arms were full. "Hmm. Carrying all these is going to be tricky."

Fox hoarded up all the rest, pretending to be desperate.

They looked at each other and laughed.

"Let's eat something," he said. "Then we'll deal with these bodies. Then let's talk about the castle."

CHAPTER 30
KEY TO THE CASTLE

THEY STARED AT THE CORPSES. Brook was pretty sure that's what you called dead bodies—or was it cadavers? She preferred to call them Hit-Kids One, Two and Three, but no matter what she called them, when she looked at them she felt numb.

"I'm not sure what to do," Fox admitted.

Brook nodded. All their different problems smashed together made it hard to think.

"We could burn them," Fox said. "But believe me, you don't want to be here while that's happening. So we'd have to stay away from our campsite, and it's not a great time to be out hiking. We could drag them into the woods, but they'd attract—attention."

Death Dogs, Brook thought. Vampire birds. God knows what else. She pulled her eyes away from the bodies, feeling trapped, like the kids were still threatening them, holding them hostage with their flat, cold eyes. She wanted to stop thinking about it, but the hit-kids wouldn't let her. Her chest was tight. She needed the corpses gone.

"What if we move them into the woods," she gasped. "But we take them far enough away so..."

"So whatever finds them won't find us." Fox nodded. "It might work, for a while."

Brook found a patch of blue sky and studied it. "These kids—they're more trouble dead than alive." Her mind was in such a weird place, she didn't realize it might sound funny.

When Fox laughed, she tried to smile.

In the end, they dragged the bodies through the labyrinth by their feet. Brook looked at trees, rocks, spider webs—anywhere but down. She tried to act like she was dragging bags of laundry or trash. By the time they'd pulled the third body a quarter mile, she was flushed and sweaty, dirt sticking to her skin. She thought she might be sick. But what else can we do? she thought. We need them gone.

She inspected the forest's bright green ceiling as Fox covered the corpses in dead leaves and branches. "That'll buy us some time," he said.

"Good." She hoped they wouldn't need a lot, because she didn't think she could stay in the secret camp much longer. She wiped her forehead, rubbing her dirty skin, and stopped with a hand under one eye. "Wait," she said. "What happened to their face paint?"

Fox frowned. "They must take it off when they leave the castle," he said.

"Figures." She sighed.

They walked back to the campsite.

"How are you feeling?" Fox said.

Brook knew he didn't need to ask. She slumped in a blood-free patch of shade, hunching over her jerky, which seemed extra tough. The fresh rabbit and seafood had spoiled her.

"I'm great," she said.

I'm so angry, she thought. And I'm not even sure at who.

"I don't know about you." Fox was inspecting their weapons. "But I think we need to move." He waved a hand around the hollow, at the caved-in fire, the splashes of blood. "We can't stay here."

Brook blew out a long breath. "Yes, I'm with you. It's not secret anymore." Or safe or pretty, she thought. Not a place I want to read a book or sleep. It's ruined.

"You ready for the castle?" Fox said, using that knack of his.

"Sure, I'm ready." Yes oh yes, her heart said. *Now is the time.* Brook thought of *her room*, high in a tower, sunlight through the window, a lock on the door. Where she could sleep or think or just do nothing. "How are we gonna take over?" she asked. "Now that we're on a list, we'll have to fight every single blue-face, won't we?"

Fox smiled. "Here's the thing. The castle has a key."

"What?" Brook stopped looking at Isabella and turned to Fox. She narrowed her eyes. "But how is that going to–"

"The key hangs in the highest tower," Fox said. "That's where it's always kept. And if someone takes the key—he rules the castle."

"That doesn't make sense."

"It's weird." Fox nodded. "But you've gotta believe me. After a while you know where the tide pools are, where the rabbits run, and you know that only the best kids make it off the cliffs. You know that weapons are incredibly hard to find." He took a deep breath. "You figure out how things work, sort of."

"Why would there be a key?" Brook said.

"Why is there an island?" Fox ran a finger over the blade of the axe.

She saw his point. Then her shoulders twitched. *What if there's a key because—magic? So good can win. So the hero has a chance?* She didn't want to believe it after what had just happened, but she couldn't keep her heart from beating faster.

"The castle isn't supposed to be locked down." Fox picked up a handful of moss. "It belongs to whoever holds the key. But when the blue-faces took over, they shut everyone else outside. No one has a fighting chance. No one can challenge them. Seems wrong, doesn't it?" He squinted at the spear and started polishing.

"It does," Brook said. *Maybe,* she thought, *just maybe, the magic has been waiting for someone to make things right.* And if she let herself go that far, well...maybe that someone was her.

The blue-faces were like a posse that grabbed all the best things for itself—chocolate milk or donated clothes or a whole box of sparkle pens—as soon as they saw you wanted them. A vicious clique that worked to make your life miserable and worse.

She'd do anything to stop them.

Fox cleared his throat.

Brook raised her eyebrows.

"The key gives us a chance," Fox said. "I don't know what we'll find inside, but if we catch the blues off guard, we can climb the tower and grab that key, and then..." He spread his hands, eyes big.

"Anything is possible." Something in Brook's chest fluttered.

"We could run this place," Fox said. "We could rule the castle."

"Like a king and queen," Brook said.

And they might have laughed, except they were both dead serious.

CHAPTER 31
ONE LAST BATH BEFORE THE WAR

"WHAT WOULD you say to some weapons practice?" Fox said.

Brook thought it was a strange question for someone who didn't need to practice at all.

"Well, ok," she said.

"Just decide which of those weapons you favor, and let's spar," Fox said. "Mostly it's common sense."

Yeah right, Brook thought. Killing people like you're in a video game is not common sense. But I guess it's useful.

"I'll give you a few tips if I can," Fox said.

"*If* you can," she said. "Ha, thanks, Fox. You're so modest."

He gave a little bow. "By the way, how was that fight for you?"

"Uhh..." Brook said.

He wonders how you survived, she thought. Well!

"Guess I just got lucky," she said. "She tripped and I took a swing."

"Really?"

"Half of fighting *is* luck, don't you think?" she said to test her theory.

Fox didn't disagree, just raised one eyebrow. It could've meant anything.

Fine, Brook thought. I'll play it cool too if that's the way you're gonna be. You're not the only one who's good at games.

She picked up the scythe-staff. The handle tingled against her skin. Fox was touching everything in their weapons bank—a little theatrically, she thought.

"So many options!" Finally, he picked the axe. "Ok," he said. "Get ready."

Brook held the staff at waist height, hands loose, blade angled down to show she wasn't a threat. It made her think of a time, a moment, a memory—her holding her old Foundation shork loose in her fingertips, curled behind her wrist as she backed toward a wall —so no one would notice she was holding anything at all.

"You don't look very ready," Fox said.

"That's because you don't know how quick I–"

Wang!

"Ouch!" Brook yelped as the axehead connected with the top of her staff and sent vibrations through her hands. She snatched empty air as her weapon hit the moss.

"Gosh, my grip needs work, right?" She shook her fingers and laughed, trying to look just the right amount of embarrassed.

"See?" Fox said smugly.

"*You'll* see," Brook said. "When I kick your butt."

"Can't wait," Fox said.

She picked Isabella back up—now there's something she'd never reveal to Fox, that her weapon had a name—and tightened her grip. "Go ahead, try it again."

Fox swung the axe and this time she swooped her staff aside. He recovered and chopped again. She dodged a second time and smiled proudly.

"Good," Fox said, "Except–"

"Except what?" Brook frowned.

Fox threw down a flurry of two-handed chops. Brook jerked her staff right and left and managed to keep clear, but then she stumbled sideways and sat down hard.

"It's hard to fight from your rear," Fox said.

"Try not to be such a snot," Brook said.

They went a few more rounds, but things stayed about the same. Fox grinned. He was really enjoying this.

Look at him, Brook thought. So happy I proved him right, like a cocky little kid.

It almost made her smile.

"Well, you're not so good at weapons," Fox said. "But how could you be? Did you know, I was worried you might assassinate me at one point? Haw!"

"Stop gloating," Brook said from the ground. "Just because you're all quick and—and foxy—doesn't mean everyone else is."

"My bad." He leaned the axe on one shoulder and stuck out a hand to help her up. She gave him a look—*this isn't even fair*—as he pulled her to her feet.

"All about repetition," he said. "Training your reflexes, keeping your balance, and getting stronger wrists."

"Wow, that sounds like a lot of work—wait." Brook put her hands behind her back. "What are you saying about my wrists?"

"Nothing, they're great," Fox said. "But you're not much of a threat yet, are you?" He smiled.

"Whatever," Brook said. "Maybe I was holding back."

"I'm sure you were."

"So"—Brook shook her head—"do you have any tips for me, or are you going to stand there grinning until your head explodes for the hundredth time?"

"Of course I have tips," Fox said. "I'm happy to share."

Brook rolled her eyes and maybe Fox would have given her some good advice—about how to grip the staff or how to keep her balance —if she hadn't scooped water from the pool, moving a lot faster than she had been, and splashed him in the face.

Fox gaped at her. Water dripped off his nose. Brook pressed a hand to her mouth, but it did no good. She laughed and laughed. And after that, sputtering and stamping around, Fox seemed to forget about the fighting tips. When Brook looked at him and raised her eyebrows, he shook his index finger at her.

"Uh uh, no more lessons for you today."

She tossed her head and felt a little disappointed. But it was definitely worth it.

They ate more jerky. After that, the day slowed down to nothing as they waited for the sun to set.

Fox seemed absent-minded. Mostly he jabbed at the ruined fire, not bothering to relight it. His eyes kept veering off into space and she knew what he was struggling with.

The castle. How they'd get in. What would happen.

She wanted to interrupt. She wanted to splash more water in his face so she could laugh at his expression—but she didn't. What did she know? The castle was gorgeous and the blue-faces were killers, *and maybe possibly there was hidden magic that would give them a hand.* What did Fox know? A whole lot more than that. So she left him alone with his plans, but the silence made for an endless afternoon.

Brook picked up each of the weapons in turn, hoping Fox would take the bait. He only glanced at her. She realized she wasn't sure where Dragon-Claw was, or Shark-Tooth, whatever she was calling it, which would've been unthinkable just yesterday. She'd obsessed over the little knife for days. After she'd wandered back and forth awhile, she found it in a pile of leaves near a boulder.

"There you are, Snake-Tooth," she said, and bent to grab it.

Fox didn't even look up.

For crying out loud, she was talking to a knife. Brook sighed. The afternoon was hot, even in the shade, and her skin felt flushed and sticky. She was tired of thinking about the castle. She'd be dreaming about it all night. Monique and her mean girls would shove her out of her bunk, and she'd lash out with her shork and fly into the castle, where she'd run downstairs into a scary, low-lit basement, lined with washers and dryers where the dragon would be waiting.

Brook stopped playing with Viper-Fang. "I'm going to the creek. I need a bath."

"Mmhm," Fox said. "Oh, you're leaving? Be careful, Brook. Keep your eyes open. I can't afford to lose you. Actually, I could use a wash too. I'll come along. Don't worry, separate corners of the creek. You can have the one from last time."

"Fine," Brook said.

Whatever Fox was planning, it had better be good. She was getting tired of his schemy spaciness. They walked past the rock formation and around the swamp, then dove into the thicket without discussing the dragon-scorched hillside. When they shoved their way onto the open, Fox headed north.

"Yell if you need me," he said. "I'll be close enough to hear."

Brook sniffed.

He held his hands up as he walked away.

She scrambled through the leafy curtain and down the bank to the pebbled shore. Getting clean would be easier now that she had her system figured out. She slipped out of her clothes, waded into the stream and scrubbed them. She hung them up to dry and splashed back in to scrub herself. Then she started to shiver, but not because she was cold. The water was refreshing.

This could be my last bath, she thought. Tomorrow I could be dead.

Fox was good, very good, but they had no idea what they were getting into. All those blue-faces. Waiting in the castle like Pit Bulls. Did it really make sense? Maybe we could find another campsite, she thought. What if we kept on living the way we are?—except the way we're living is awful.

It wasn't like they'd been careless. Fox was the opposite of careless. And look at how close to death they'd come. Running and hiding, tracked and ambushed.

Kinda like her years at the Foundation.

Maybe this is hell, she thought. Maybe I'm being punished in a kind of endless loop.

Maybe I deserve to be here.

But no, hell wouldn't have a place like the castle. And she and

Fox were starting to be friends. She couldn't remember the last time she'd laughed without using the laughter to hide something else. You didn't laugh like that in hell. Not to mention, there wouldn't be even a hint of magic. Magic that opened a door and sent you to a bad place, but for a good reason, so that something happy had a chance of happening.

Please let there be magic, she thought.

"Please God, let there be magic," she whispered, and then because it seemed like the right thing: "Please God, send me magic, even though I don't deserve it."

She sat in the brook with water gurgling around her and wondered if God was listening.

It's worth fighting for, she thought. You have a chance at things you've never had your whole life, at least since your parents stopped loving you. It's worth the risk. And living on this island, surviving a day at a time, those aren't great odds anyway.

What's another day playing chicken with death?

Why not, if maybe something good could happen?

But it was hard to think of her life as something that could be used up. Poured out, a drop at a time. Emptied. And now the thought had crossed her mind, it kept creeping back in:

What if you deserve to be here, and not for a good reason?

What if you're being punished?

The water felt colder on her skin.

This brook leaks underground, she thought. It drips through rocks and caves and it touches the ocean—it must. So the sea, right now, is touching me. Trickling hungrily over my bones while I'm trying to get clean.

She knew the island was smiling again, teeth gleaming in the current, eyes watching from the darkness under rocks. Grinning at her.

It had never stopped.

CHAPTER 32
WHAT YOU DON'T KNOW CAN HURT YOU

BROOK PULLED her damp clothes back on and started back without looking for Fox.

Maybe there were more hit-kids out there, but it seemed unlikely they were searching the forest. She and Fox—well, mostly Fox—had crushed them. The rest of the blue-faces had to know something had gone badly wrong with their plan.

"Now they're nervous," Brook told the trees as she marched up the slope. She liked the way she sounded. Confident and deadly, a girl who could change a whole battle just by showing up. It wasn't at all the way she felt.

"I'm *soo* dangerous," she said in the same cool, breezy voice. "They'll never see it coming. Fox will get us inside, total stealth mode, and then, *Brook unleashed*. We'll take the key. If they get in our way, they'll wish they hadn't."

She stopped on the edge of the dragon scorch area, searching the sky. Five minutes went by, and when nothing moved except clouds, she gulped down a breath and shot into the open. Crunching through the ashes, she flew over blackened logs, dodging right and left until she reached the safe green shadows.

"Still got it," she gasped, brushing back her hair with her fingertips.

Brook found her way back to the campsite on autopilot. Inside their hollow she took a drink and stood there, admiring their weapons bank. Black and silver gleamed against the rocks. A row of spiky, razor-sharp death.

On this island it was worth a fortune.

Since Fox still wasn't back, she picked up the scythe-staff and did a few made-up drills, quick and quiet, focusing on her footwork. She stopped when she felt the first drop of sweat run down her back, because who knew when she'd get another bath?

She cut that thought off short.

By then she was hungry. At least her stomach was sending her signals, and she'd probably need the strength. She found the jerky easily, piled in a shady crack. Only a few dried strips of meat were left.

"Here's hoping our lives change fast," Brook said.

For a split second, she thought about heading to the rabbit runs or the coast to look for food. Then she pictured a gang of killer kids waiting on the edge of the forest, picking their teeth with their knives.

Being hungry would keep her alert.

Brook tore off a small piece of jerky and chewed slowly, pretending it was gum. She traced the grain of the stone wall with her eyes. The storage crack was a deep one. If they were staying, they could've stored their new weapons with the jerky. All those blades in the open were asking for trouble. She picked up Isabella and trailed the blade of her scythe-staff down the crack. It would easily fit inside.

The dark zig-zag in the rock face became a shallow cave. There was a lot of shade inside. Maybe raccoons or possums had lived there. If it had rained again like it had her first night, it would've been a good idea to crawl inside. She wondered if Fox knew the crack became a gap.

Clink went the blade of her staff.

She stopped with her head at an angle. Shading her eyes with one hand, she picked out a vague, pale gleam.

"Oh great," she said. "More bones."

When she'd found the skull under the fire, she'd guessed the rest of the skeleton was down there too. So what was this? Had Fox run out of room? How many feral kids had he burnt and buried?

She bit her lip and reached inside. If she came up with a rib or leg bone, she wouldn't scream. Fox wasn't stupid. The bones would be clean and sterilized. Her fingers closed on something cool to the touch and not as grainy as she'd expected. Cartilage? But cartilage would melt, wouldn't it?

What a gross question.

"No big deal," she said.

She pulled the slim bone into the light.

But it wasn't a bone.

The dagger had two blades, one on either side of a pale handle, and it was a good thing she'd grabbed the handle. The blades gleamed bluish-gray, like they'd been oiled moments before. She knew they'd slice her skin like she was made of paper.

A minute before, she'd been worried about sweating after her bath. Now ice-cold worms squirmed up and down her spine, wriggling like night crawlers after rain. Her fingers trembled. How could Fox have done this? And there was more. Leaning forward over the stone edge, she pulled weapon after weapon from the trove.

A brutal spiked hammer.

A pair of straight, two-edged knives.

A curvy sword.

A spear with a spiked blade on one side.

A bow and a bunch of arrows in a leather bag.

A whole zoo of gleaming, bladed death.

Fox, how could you? Her knees felt weak. He could've given her a weapon anytime, and instead he'd pretended they only had a sword —and a little knife. What was wrong with him? What had he been planning with all these weapons? Where had he found them and who had he taken them from?

She shuddered. Jumbled on the moss, they glittered in a lethal pile. She wondered if she should put them back. Could she hold it together when Fox walked in? Could she pretend this hadn't happened, that he wasn't a liar? That he wasn't...well, *what* was he? What had he done?

"I can do it," Brook said. "I can hold it together."

It will be better that way, she thought. You need to buy some time, decide what to do next, tease out what Fox is up to.

She picked up the spear on the top of the pile and slid it back into the cave.

A shadow fell across her back.

CHAPTER 33
MASTER OF EVERY SITUATION

BROOK TURNED SLOWLY.

Fox looked pale.

They stared at each other for a long moment. She took in his gray eyes, his damp, reddish hair. The mouth that could change so fast into a smile. The freckles on his nose. He always looked so confident, the master of every situation. Now he looked like someone had taken all his words away.

Fox sat down in a bed of moss, one of the few clean patches, and put his face in his hands. Brook slid one foot under a mace. She gave it a soccer lift and and caught it, squeezing the handle tight.

"Who are you?" She hadn't meant to whisper. She'd meant to sound strong and cool like she had in the woods. Instead, she clenched the mace even harder, until her knuckles turned white.

"I'm sorry, Brook," Fox croaked. "I'm sorry."

She stood there, wondering if he had a dagger in his lap. All he'd have to do was glance up, measure the distance, flick his wrist. She'd seen what he could do.

Still looking at the ground, he spread his hands. "You have a right to be angry."

Brook's face tingled like all the blood had drained away.

"Yeah," she said.

"I—I'm compulsive," Fox said. "I've been that way forever. I want all the weapons. I want all the angles. It makes me feel like I'm in charge."

"Not good enough," Brook said, since they were being honest. "You said you liked me. You said you wanted me on your team. Now I see that if I hadn't taken the scythe-staff, I'd probably still be begging you to let me carry the knife. 'Can I borrow it, Foxy?'"

She winced. "And if I'd known about all this, if I'd found it when I got here, I wonder what you would've said? 'Sorry, Brook, we need to keep you safe. I don't want you to cut yourself. Let's just keep all the swords and the spears and the hammer and the axe and the bow and the thing with two blades–"

"The haladie," Fox said.

"Right, let's hide all this stuff away in my weapons stash. And then, Brook, if you're very, very good—maybe I'll let you use a sword to poke the fire."

Fox finally looked up. His wet eyes flamed to life.

"Yeah," he said. "Ok. There's something not right with me, that holds on to every little thing. Even though I like you, it almost killed me to give you the knife, I admit it. My brain was screaming, *No no no!* when I handed it over. I'm even jealous of your scythe-staff because–" He blinked and took a breath.

"I've never been wanted, Brook. Never been wanted. I'm pretty sure I already told you but I lose track. I'm not supposed to be here, and I don't mean the island. I mean alive. I'm not supposed to be drawing breaths or taking up space. I don't remember anything about my past, but I know this one thing. It's in my bones. My parents tried to kill me."

He touched the spear he'd set down in the moss.

"Tried to kill me before they saw me. Crazy, huh? They hated me automatically. Can you believe that? There's a word for it, and you could probably tell me, but a few minutes later, I'd forget." He tapped his head. "Somehow, my parents didn't get to murder me. They must have been so disappointed! But I know they tried and I'll always know. I'll never, ever forget."

Fox was breathing hard. He looked like he'd run a race. Brook knew the word he was looking for but she didn't say it. She didn't say anything. What was there to say?

"I'm sorry," Fox said again. "I wish I was different. I wish I wasn't so on edge. I wish I didn't always expect to be attacked."

"This isn't right," Brook said. "What your parents tried to do to you—and this. This is horrible, just horrible. Someone like you should never be in a place like this."

Fox looked in her face. "No one should be in a place like this," he said. "You shouldn't be here either, Brook. You were abandoned too."

His voice became less shaky. He rubbed a wrist across his eyes, and when he took his hand away, they had dried back up.

"You're right, neither of us deserve this," Brook said. "Whoever did this will pay."

She'd been so angry with Fox and now she just felt sick. She set the mace down on top of the pile. All the weapons gleamed and shone. Spikes and blades and edges of all kinds. A shiny carnival of death. She felt like they were pointing at her and Fox. Maybe they'd been pointed at them their entire lives.

"We'll get the castle," Brook said. "Then we'll decide what to do. Maybe we need to go after the dragon."

Fox nodded. "Right. I don't think anyone's tried that yet."

They split the last of the jerky, barely a mouthful each.

"Maybe I'll go check the snares," Fox said.

"Do you think that's a good idea?"

"No." He smiled. "But we have a few hours and we need to eat. By tomorrow, we'll be inside the castle and everything will be different."

"I'll come with you," Brook said.

"Let me go. I'll be faster alone."

She didn't agree. A cool breeze skimmed the back of her neck, saying something bad would happen if they separated. But she nodded. She felt heavy and still inside, like she could lean back against the standing stones and maybe the granite would soak into her and she'd become part rock.

She wished she had the right words for Fox, words that would make things better, but those words didn't exist. Fox wanted to pull himself together. She'd never seen him cry before, and she couldn't imagine what he was feeling. He sure hid a lot behind that smile.

"I'll make a fire," she said.

"Sounds good." He grabbed a weapon from the pile, barely looking at it, and disappeared.

Brook leaned her head against the stone and coolness flowed through her cropped hair. The weight of the whole dark island pressed on her. How could a place like this exist? The worst possible place for people like her and Fox. The worst kind of place for anyone.

What do the blue-faces know? she wondered. *What have they figured out? Maybe there are secrets in the castle. Maybe the blues have promises from the dragon. Who knows what we'll discover when we get inside?*

But as hard as she tried to keep her mind busy, she couldn't stop thinking about Fox's words: Never wanted, Brook, never wanted.

Probably the worst words you could ever hear. And they weren't just true about Fox.

They are true about me.

It left her feeling weak, leaning on the rock until the emptiness in her chest flared up like dragon fire. Her parents, whoever they were, had made a mistake. The great mistake of their lives. If they ever met her, it would be too late. By then she'd have proved she was someone who mattered, someone tough and charming, a girl who impressed everyone, who everyone liked and wished they knew.

She and Fox would start with the castle.

They'd prove everyone wrong.

The blue-faces wouldn't know what hit them.

She wiped her eyes and gathered up some kindling.

By the time Fox got back with a rabbit, she'd kindled her own fire in the middle of their ruined campsite. Might as well be comfortable their final night.

CHAPTER 34
PLAN OF ATTACK

"HERE'S HOW IT WILL GO," Fox said.

He seemed to have recovered his confidence after his trip to the fields, and there wasn't a trace of choky wetness in his voice. Brook chewed her rabbit and listened. She thought about how angry she was and how things were going to go well.

"We'll cross the plains by moonlight," Fox said. "With a little luck, they won't see us coming. We'll reach the castle while it's still dark and find the door. Not the front door, the back one. Then I'll get somewhere out of sight and you'll knock."

"Why would they open for me?" Brook said.

"You'll pretend to be hurt so they won't think you're a threat."

"And?" She shrugged.

"And—you'll have a weapon with you. More than one."

"Ohhh." Brook almost smiled. "I'll carry some of your treasure as bait."

"Yeah." Fox didn't realize she was joking. "But it'll be worth it. Anyway, we'll get it back."

"So they see poor, sad, injured me, and more importantly, the weapons I'm carrying, and they open up?"

"That's right," Fox said. "Probably just one of them. It'll be early, so I don't expect too many will be up. Let's say one blue is on guard, and he sees you, a weak girl, acting all hurt, and he sees the weapons and his eyes light up. He's not going to call for help. He'll want them for himself."

"Uh huh," Brook said. "Me, a weak girl, thanks for clarifying that."

"That's what *he* thinks," Fox said. "But instead, we grab him."

"And we lock him outside." Brook pictured them slamming the door on the horrified blue-face, then turning to race up stone steps into the castle, higher and higher, into pale moonlight with just a trace of yellow in the eastern sky. "What if there's more than one guard?" she said.

"Even if there is, we'll have a chance," Fox said.

Brook thought about the bodies in the woods and knew he was right. *We'll always have a chance.*

"Then we're in, and it's still mostly dark, and maybe we'll find some face paint, but even if we don't, we start searching for the key."

"In the top of the highest tower," Brook said.

"Right."

"It's a plan I guess." She hugged herself and thought, What did you expect?

After they ate, Fox leaned all the weapons in a row against the rock face. The collection was scary and impressive. He lined them up on Brook's side, which was obviously an apology and possibly flattery, and she appreciated it, even though she couldn't bring herself to thank him.

With so many options in front of her, all she really needed was Isabella and maybe the little knife—Snake-Tooth or Viper-Fang, whatever she was calling it. She didn't need a whole arsenal like Fox seemed to think he did.

She sat by the fire, which probably had chalky bones under it, and stayed warm as the sun went down. Night birds began to shriek. Something howled far away and was joined by another howl, and another.

Death Dogs, talking to each other in the night.

"Do you think this will work?" she asked Fox.

The wall between them had mostly come down again.

He sat across the fire, feeding it small twigs and shoving it around with the sword. "Yes," he said. "It has to work and the two of us—we're unstoppable." He gave her a smile.

"Yeah. Unstoppable is us."

A few minutes later, she did her best to fall asleep. Thin lines of sunset dripped through crisscrossed trees, neon orange sinking in a pool of liquid cotton candy. The sunset was probably an eight point five, but she bumped it to a ten to show the island she wasn't scared. She told herself *this* sunset would always be one of her favorites.

Brook woke when it was still dark. Maybe Fox had touched her. Maybe it was just his movement nearby. She was instantly alert. Moonlight filtered through the trees like milky flashlight beams. She got up and stretched. Her mind was already racing.

Had they overslept? Did they have enough time to reach the castle?

"Ready when you are," Fox said in a hushed voice, like miles away the blue-faces might hear them. Water dripped off his chin, and Brook stepped over to take her turn at the pool. She rinsed her mouth and face and took a drink, then joined Fox by their shining row of weapons. The sharp edges gleamed under the moon.

Fox's face looked pinched, and she realized what was bothering him. There was no way they could carry everything. They'd have to leave some weapons behind. For him it was like leaving a pile of cash blowing in the wind.

Brook took Isabella and Dragon-Tooth from the moss. She'd kept them close while she slept. "Maybe we can come back for the rest," she said.

"Yeah," Fox said. "After we win."

He chose a battle-axe and a spear. "Better take something else for yourself," he said. "To make sure the blue-faces open the door."

"Oh," Brook said. "Right." She picked up a sword, realized how hard it would be to carry, and set it down. Instead she chose the trident. Less likely to slice her by mistake.

"I'm ready," she said. "Go team."

And just like that they set off, leaving the smoky wisps of their fire in the air. Brook didn't let herself look back. This is it, she thought. The chance to get everything you want. Quiet, safety, space. A high window. A locked door. You and Fox will take over, and everyone will see what you can do. Please God, let there be magic.

They stole through the woods like ghosts. Brook felt the cool night breeze on the back of her neck. She kept her eyes wide open as they crept under trees through pools of shadow. Before she knew it, they'd reached the plains. The sky lightened but there was no trace of the sun. A full moon hung like a big opal over the fields. In the distance, something howled.

Brook froze at the edge of the forest.

"It's ok," Fox said. "They're miles away. And it sounds like they're already on the hunt."

She nodded and followed him into the open. Fox began to jog, his spear and axe pressed to his shoulders. He wove toward the rabbit run.

"Hey!" Brook whispered loudly. "Where are you going?"

Fox's shadow swerved in the glimmering dark. She realized he was running backward, high-stepping like he was in track and field.

"Rabbits," he called in a low voice. "One last time."

That didn't make sense to Brook, but she didn't have Fox's compulsions. She picked up her pace, Isabella and the trident held against her shoulder blades, Snake-Tooth at her hip. Fox knew the fields by heart and by the time she caught him, he'd dodged down the worn run and bent over a snare. The blades of his weapons gleamed.

"Fox," she hissed, "what are you doing?"

He pulled a dead rabbit from the trap and glanced at her. It was hard to read his face in the shadow of the moon. "Sorry," he said.

"But we need a little blood to make this whole thing work. You need to look hurt, remember?"

"Ohh..." Brook said.

Of course. She was impressed by how carefully he'd planned this, and ticked off at herself for not thinking ahead. *Wake up, Brook. Stay on top of things.*

Fox pulled a knife from his pocket and slit the rabbit open.

"Do you really want to do that here?" She scanned the gently waving grass. Thanks to the moon, it was like standing in a sea of silver. The breeze smelled like the ocean and it wasn't a comforting smell. The salty tang made her think of hungry cliffs. Of the island watching. Of time ticking away.

"Better here than by the castle," Fox said through gritted teeth.

Blood drip-dripped in a dark puddle at his feet.

"I don't have free hands to carry it," he said. "So I'll have to tuck its paws into my pocket. Crap, this isn't easy."

Brook was turning in place by now. Grass rustled. A bird screamed in the night. Something squeaked in the grass.

"Fox, let's—" Then she heard the sound she was dreading. The one she didn't want to hear, the one that could ruin their plan, that could ruin everything.

A Death Dog howled. It was closer, she was sure.

"Give me that rabbit." Brook snatched it from him and the blood ran warm on her hands. She bit her lip and touched her face. No, not enough. She pulled her fingers down her cheeks, keeping it away from her eyes. She could smell the blood as well as feel it, slick and hot and coppery, coating her skin. She shook her fingers, flicking the stickiness away, happy she couldn't see herself.

"Ok, can we go now?"

Fox looked at her and nodded. "That should do it." He dropped the rabbit and moved away, shoes squishing in the grass. A Death Dog howled somewhere to the south, joined by another and another. Fox looked concerned.

"Now we'd better run," he said.

CHAPTER 35
CATCH ME IF YOU CAN

IN WEED, Brook had wanted to run track. No one had ever told her she was fast but she had a feeling, based on experience. Sports passes were really hard to come by, though. No one at the Foundation wanted to deal with the headache of a kid who stayed after school and whose movements would have to be documented when she practiced and traveled who knew where for track meets.

If only she'd been allowed to run track, maybe she could've run faster toward the castle, over the ghostly plains with the Death Dogs on her trail.

They'd barely even left their camp and nothing was going right. Nothing. The hard metal of Isabella and the trident jolted Brook's shoulders, sliding back and forth as she tried to keep them upright. Her face was hot and sticky, slick with sweat and blood. At the same time, the wind chilled her arms and legs, mocking her with memories of the cliffs.

You thought you got away, the island was saying. *Thought you could save your guts and bones from me. But it was just a small delay. I'll win, one way or another...*

Fox was pulling away and that was the last thing Brook wanted. Heart slamming her ribs, she made her feet move faster. Their journey had started as a jog and climbed quickly to a run. If they went any faster, it would be a sprint. When clouds floated over the moon, all she could do was keep moving in the same direction.

It's inevitable, the island whispered. *Whether it's the breakers or the rocks or the Death Dogs, you'll be mine...*

Her feet pounded over dead stalks and animal mounds. No matter how hard she tried, she couldn't catch her breath. Gasping, gasping. Would she ever breathe again?

The wind swirled and danced, grabbing the air right out of her mouth.

You can't outrun me, the island said. *I've had you since you crawled onto the sand. No one ever really gets away.*

She pictured the island smiling.

Its teeth were jagged coral. Its eyes were sunken caves.

Its belly was the bottom of the sea.

Maybe this is where it ends, Brook thought between gasps. You did your best—the best you possibly could—but now it's all caught up with you. Your knees will give out and you'll fall—maybe you'll hit your head—and the Death Dogs will get here—and you'll be dead.

Like those other kids, dead.

Then, somehow, they rounded the corner of the forest. The north side of the island opened in front of them, wide and pale, and the castle loomed into the sky. Huge. Impossibly big and black. Brook couldn't believe how close they were.

Her lungs decided not to collapse. Her legs agreed to keep working. She skimmed through the grass, flashing down rabbit runs, flying toward the castle's shadow. It got taller and taller, high notched walls and soaring towers. Brook wasn't aware of breathing anymore. Her lungs had stopped needing air. Now there was just the *thwack, thwack, thwack* of her feet over the fields and the weapons thunking against her bones, same as the pounding of her heart.

She blinked salt out of her eyes. Fox was just ahead.

Then the deep shade of the castle fell on her like a blanket.

They'd done it. They'd made it. Now everything would be ok. Brook realized her lungs were shriveling up, screaming for oxygen. She dropped the trident and put a hand to her side as pain knifed her ribs. "Ohhh—oww."

"C'mon, Brook." Fox was wheezing too. "Don't stop, we've gotta get inside." Juggling his own weapons, he groaned and bent to grab her trident.

Brook forced herself to take it. But when she touched the metal, her fingers were warm and wet. Oh no. When she looked down, the corner of her hip pocket was dark. Snake-Tooth had cut her. Snake-Tooth had *turned* on her. The little knife was supposed to be on her side. It was almost more than she could handle.

"Brook!" Fox's hands were on her shoulders. His smoky eyes burned into hers.

She knew he was doing everything he could to bring her along. Listen to him, she thought. Trust him completely, just this once.

"I'm coming," she said. "Show me."

An eerie howl drifted over the plains, broken by hungry, sharp-edged barks.

"They're close," Fox said. "But we're closer."

A massive front gate rose on their left, tall as trees, studded with metal bands and spikes. The moon gleamed on the timbers. On the right, the blue-black wall of the castle curved away.

Fox squeezed her cold hand. "Follow me."

The darkness was so thick, Brook felt like they were pushing through it. When she looked up, trying to slow her breathing, she saw black rectangles high on the giant walls. But down on the ground, in the high grass, night folded down on them. The dark side of the castle felt like the dark side of the moon.

Brook folded an arm across her chest and clasped her weapons awkwardly so she could slide a hand into her pocket. She prayed that Snake-Tooth hadn't bit too deep. She found the dagger's handle and pulled. A corner of its carrying cloth was torn and soaked with blood. But just a corner. The pain in her hip felt like a pin-prick and she hoped that's what it was, but she didn't have time to check.

Fox stopped under a jutting stone slab. At some point they'd turned a corner, because the moon was shining bright again. Stone steps rose from the grass, and Brook realized she was looking at a sheltered porch. Back in California, it was the kind of place homeless people would be sleeping. A metal-plated door stood at the top. In the center of the door was a thin slit.

"This is it," Fox whispered. "It's your time, Brook. Knock and tell them you're hurt. Don't think too hard, just do it."

Her heart was beating so loud, she wondered if she'd even need to knock. But she could hear the wind again, howling in the castle's towers. Except—no, that wasn't the wind. The howls were jagged and eager. Brook stumbled up the stairs and pounded on the door.

Doom, doom, doom. It echoed in the night like a rusty gong.

She took a breath and pounded again.

Doom, doom, doom.

"Keep knocking," Fox whispered from the shadows. She couldn't see him, but she pictured him clutching his spear and axe, staring at the door.

Brook raised her hand to knock again and almost screamed. A pair of wide eyes appeared in the narrow window. They got even bigger when they took in her bloody face.

"Are you hurt bad?" The boy's voice sounded squeaky from sleep.

Brook held up her weapons and leaned them against the wall, making sure the boy could see. She opened her mouth to say, Yes, yes, I'm hurt so bad I might not ever get better, but instead, a sob rose from her throat. She scrubbed at her face and her knuckles came away red and wet.

"Oh no." The kid's eyes looked horrified. "I'm not supposed to open this, ever."

Brook forced herself to look up as tears rolled down her face. She didn't understand what was happening. He wasn't reacting the way a blue-face should, even though she could see dark swirls of paint around his eyes. He wasn't staring greedily at her weapons. What was he doing? Why wasn't he taking the bait?

"Please help me," Brook said. "I can't run anymore."

His eyes flicked right and left. Surely he knew the weapons were worth a fortune—he had to, had to. The boy groaned and the thin strip of his face disappeared. Brook sagged against the wall in defeat. Now you've got to be deadly and smart, she told herself. Now you've got to fight the monsters.

Metal rasped on the far side of the door. Bolts sliding open, lots of them. Old hinges screamed in protest as the door scraped open

inch

after inch

after inch

until the boy looked through an opening barely wider that his head.

He held out one hand.

"Quick," he said. "What if he's out there, waiting for—"

Then everything happened.

CHAPTER 36
WHAT HAPPENED AT THE DOOR

THE BLUE-FACED BOY SCREAMED.

It made no sense. Brook hadn't tried to scare him. She hadn't lunged at him or made a grab for the door, even though she desperately wanted to get inside. Then she saw blood gushing from his upper leg—splashing on the stone at his feet. For a second, she couldn't make sense of it. She hadn't done this. This wasn't the Foundation basement, where there'd been a lot of blood—so much blood. Then the boy kicked Fox's spear away, and it fell clunking down the stairs.

"Fox, quick–" she started to say, but the blue-face was closing the door.

"No!" Brook threw herself forward, stuck her arm and shoulder through, and shrugged the door wider. Just like that, she was in.

Inside the castle. She couldn't believe it.

Thank God, she thought. Everything is about to change.

The boy backed away. His shoulders slumped, and when he held up his hands, they trembled. "Please, let me go." He turned and stumbled off, favoring his bloody leg.

This blue-face isn't fierce at all, Brook thought. *All the time he's spent getting everything his way has made him soft. Pitiful, and it will make things a lot easier.* She wasn't even holding Isabella.

"In," Brook breathed. "We're in, in, in!"

"Brook, hang on a second," Fox shouted.

She stuck her head through the door to grab her scythe-staff and laughed. "Are you crazy? Get in here!"

Fox could've been a silver statue in the moonlight. Then he moved toward her, sliding his weapons to one shoulder. "Hang on a second." He climbed the stairs. With his free hand, he reached for her through the doorway.

"No!" Brook stepped away. "Are you crazy?" She felt a flash of anger, more than a flash, because she'd almost died getting here. Death Dogs were closing in, and the door was open— against all odds, open!—and Fox was loitering in the dark.

"I'm going on," she said. "Something good just happened, something crazy good. Are you awake? Can you believe this? I'm going after the key, so stop trying to grab me."

She turned and shot away after the bleeding boy, holding Isabella at an angle to the stairs.

"Brook, wait!" Fox yelled.

She pretended not to hear him. Was he seriously gonna freeze up now? *Now*, when they had the edge, and he'd never been scared before? Well, she'd do it all then. It was her plan too, as much as his and maybe more. Getting in had been her idea first. She was the one who knew about the magic, who was ready to be a hero. She'd go alone.

She'd find the key herself.

The stones under her feet were wide and smooth. She flew up a long, straight flight of stairs like they were nothing. At the top, she stood on a wide landing where stars gleamed through a window. More stairs led off in three directions—and the place felt perfect, she thought, so huge and safe and strong.

She leaned on the windowsill, which—oh gross—was coated

with cobwebs, a thick layer of grime and tiny bones. All the luxury had made the blue-faces lazy. *She* wouldn't be lazy. Dirt could be scrubbed. Cobwebs swept away. Not a big job, just a bucket of water and a rag, a whole lot more rewarding than cleaning the cracked Foundation floors.

And now, onward!

Night wind brushed her face and swept her hair. She tossed her head, pushed a few strands behind one ear, and whispered, "This is who I am now. An adventurer. An explorer of castles. No, not castles —*my* castle."

She took another flight of stairs, up, up, up, searching for the highest tower. No one tried to stop her—the rest of the blue-faces were taking their time, which was perfect. She felt like she was racing over a rooftop while their heads were turned, her timing and her moves just right. She was about to get away with something *huge*. But as she went, she noticed a trail of drips and smears which she didn't like. It meant the injured blue-face was close by.

That made her think, Where's Fox? He should have caught up by now. But at the same time, she felt happy he wasn't there. Because now this was her heist. *Her* chance. Excitement hummed and darted in her chest like the tiny, shining birds that lived on nectar.

She was pulling off this crazy scheme alone.

It would make the castle *hers*. And let's be honest, she thought. This makes you really cool. If you pull it off, Fox will be so impressed. He'll know what you can do, no more wondering. No more secrets. You'll have proved your worth on Team Brook-Fox, helping him for once. After this, he'll like you even more. So do as much as you possibly can.

Get past the blue-faces.

Find the key.

Be the queen.

By the time Fox caught up, she'd be on a big throne, eating chicken and splashing her feet in clear, cold water. The blue-faces would be lined up, asking if there was anything else she needed. Queen of the castle. Hey Fox, you finally got here, she'd say. Good thing I saved you a seat.

That made her smile.

Then, without meaning to, she found the boy.

He crouched on the floor in the corner of another landing. A wooden torch flickered on the wall. The boy was struggling with his shirt, tugging it over his head, and he didn't look good. When he saw Brook, he froze in a huddled pile.

More good luck, she thought. He's not a threat at all.

"Why'd you do it?" he croaked. "Why'd you open the door for him?"

"You shouldn't have shut us out!" Brook shot back. *Here I am, ghosting up the stairs, conquering your castle like it's nothing, with magic opening doors for me. Why resist us?*

The boy was trying to wind the shirt around his bloody leg. He was having trouble knotting it. His fingers kept shaking.

"Not so tough now, huh?" she said. "Not when there's only one of you. Let me tie that, then you can show me the highest tower."

His eyes twitched toward her and away. "Why?"

"So I can get the key, of course," Brook said.

And look around and choose my room, she thought.

The boy shrugged. "Ok."

Wow, not even an argument. Handing her the castle, just like that. Brook hid a smile. She knelt beside him, wrapped the shirt around his leg and knotted it tight. The cut looked nasty and she stopped holding her breath once it was covered up.

"There you go," she said, and stood. "Sorry Fox did that, but you can't blame him, the way all of you have treated us."

The boy blinked. He started laughing, not a happy laugh.

And Brook noticed how skinny he was, skin and bones, really, and very dirty, covered in dust and stains. And he smelled bad too.

"Are you a servant for the real blue-faces or something?" she asked. "Do they make you do stuff they don't want to, like watch the door? Because–"

You don't look like the ruler of a castle, she wanted to say.

The kid looked up and finally met her eyes. "You're not kidding, are you?" The mask of blue paint was cracking and falling away in bits, and all at once it hit her: The paint wasn't supposed to cause fear. It was supposed to hide fear.

And it wasn't working.

Was she really that scary?

"Look," the boy said. "I don't know who you are, but you're really turned around. Go away. Run as fast as you can. Now that you've let him in, it's just a matter of time before he comes after all of us."

"What?" Brook stared down at him. "Who comes after us? You mean Fox?"

The boy smiled bitterly. "Around here we call him Wolf."

Brook took a sharp breath. So what if they do? she thought. Fox to his friends, Wolf to his enemies. A good kind of friend to have. She crossed her arms.

The boy didn't notice, pulling himself to his feet.

"Just point me to the highest tower," she said.

"You don't want to go there," the boy said.

"Where is it?" Brook snapped.

He pointed. "Up, always up. You'll get there sooner than you'd like." He paused. "I'm sorry for you."

Brook glared at him. *What a liar*, she thought. *Trying to trick me because he doesn't have the guts to fight. But some of his friends will, if I give them the chance.* Then she was flying up the stairs. Scuffling steps and a shout came from a side passage as she shot past. Another landing, another window. Outside, an open sea of black. And another landing and another—but something had changed.

Her grippy trail shoes scrabbled through trash. The shadows hid most of it, but what she saw made her feel sick. Crusty rags. Broken weapons. Fragments of bone. When wind sailed through the windows, it no longer felt clean. If felt hungry, like the wind out on the cliffs.

Her stomach twisted.

Then, without warning, she reached the highest tower.

CHAPTER 37
THE BASEMENT

BROOK SKIDDED TO A STOP, arms flailing, and half-fell backward. She stood on a dead-end balcony with no railings and a view to nowhere. The moon shone down through a huge stone silo, open to the sky. Empty walls rose another forty feet and plummeted down she couldn't say how far. No rooms, no stairs. No key hanging from a hook. Just hollow nothingness. Another step and she'd have fallen into the pitch-black pit—a man-made version of the cliffs. The castle's heart was an open elevator shaft.

A rotten hole. A giant trap.

No wonder the island was laughing.

Brook wanted to cry.

Standing there in the hushed emptiness, she felt her vision of the castle crumble and fall away. Roaches scuttled on the walls. Trash blew in the wind. She heard sounds above her, below her, behind the stone, and knew she was hearing rats. Hungry and hiding, living off scraps. The magnificent fortress in her mind was nothing but a ruin.

She thought she would suffocate.

Breathe, in and out, breathe.

She felt like she was back in Weed, under bare bulbs and a low, dirty ceiling. This time the memory from her dreams took over. She had nothing left to fight it with.

Pain shot up her spine, jarred the back of her skull as she hit the dormitory floor. Monique's gang stood over her, tossing her blanket and sheets—their way of showing they saw her trying to keep her head down—and it didn't work. They were cussing and searching for the shork that was somehow in her hand. She could've slid it in her waistband and lay there until her head stopped ringing. She could've closed her eyes and pretended to be somewhere else, *someone* else. Sometimes it worked, and when you woke up, the danger was gone.

But she was too angry and hurt to think.

When she lashed out with the shork, someone screamed and staggered back. Then Brook was up and running crookedly through the dorm, shoving off the double row of bunks with all the girls fake-sleeping. One hand on her head, she picked up speed as she ran down the low-lit hall. Curses and pounding feet came after her.

There was no one you could go to after dark, not with people hunting you, not in a hurry. She rushed down sticky corridors and creaky stairs, through the echoing rec room, shoving folding chairs out of the way—and then she made her great mistake.

She could've doubled back. She could've ducked into a closet. Instead, her head still ringing, she swerved into the darkness of the basement where she liked to hide, where she'd wedged herself between the washers and dryers to read *The Lord of the Flies*.

But no one had been chasing her then.

She'd barely hidden when Monique's gang crashed down the stairs. They found her in moments and closed in, cussing, one of them limping. Monique, big-boned and crazy, clenched a broken bottle.

"Hands over your head, Rapunzel," she hissed. "Always prepping, tidying, acting all better."

"No," Brook said. "No, I don't—"

"Did I say you could talk?" Monique sneered. "Let's make sure you don't act better anymore. Hands up."

No way, Brook thought. Not a chance—in the guts of the Foundation, on the stained concrete, under the bare lightbulbs. No one to hear me, no one to find me—no one to do a thing. She backed away.

"Ohh, you *do* think you're better."

A washing machine cut into Brook's back as the half circle closed in. Monique lunged, her eyes wild. Brook tried to dodge but there was no room. The bottleneck reached out like a jagged green mouth and bit her. She held back a scream. Panic pounded in her chest as hot blood trickled through her fingers. A red haze of pain spread under her hand when she pressed her hip.

Maybe now it's over, she thought. All I did was cut someone's leg.

Maybe now we're even.

"Gotcha." Monique's pupils glittered. "Not so lively now, are you?"

"Stop, I–"

Monique laughed and came at Brook again.

She never knew when to stop.

Palms pressed against the washer, Brook brought up her knees and drove her feet into Monique's stomach. The tall girl choked and doubled over. Brook pressed a hand to her burning side and tried to limp away. But no. The other girls were shaking their heads and scolding. No one stepped aside to let her go.

"Now you've done it," they said.

"Way too far, princess," someone leaned in and spat.

"Now she'll really kill you."

Monique straightened up, her face all twisted.

Brook believed them.

Monique bent to grab her broken bottle off the floor. It dripped in the low light.

That's my blood, Brook thought. You've got no right, no right at all.

The bigger girl grinned. "This was just for fun—but not anymore. If they ever find you, no one's even gonna recognize you. I'll take this broken glass and twist it—"

"NOO!" Brook screamed.

When Monique lunged, Brook spun on the balls of her feet and stabbed down blindly with the shork. And magic happened. Dark, horrible magic.

The broken bottle clanged off the washer.

The shork shivered in Brook's hand.

Soft as butter, even softer. The flat dent at the bottom of Monique's skull, where the shork slid down and stuck like it had hit a plate. Brook stepped back, staring.

Had she done this?

Monique dropped like a toy that had been turned off. Red was everywhere. Spraying, splashing, dripping red—and screaming, lots of screaming, but not from Monique.

Running feet. Then silence.

Everything wet and red under the bare lightbulbs.

It had been so easy. Brook hadn't even tried.

The shork fell from her shaking fingers. Her knees began to give way, but she grabbed a dryer for support and hauled herself up, away from the bloody floor. Knobs and dials dug into her back as she hugged her knees, rocking back and forth.

"I didn't mean to," she sobbed. "You should've let me go."

The shadows pressed in, red and black, and she closed her eyes against her tears. The darkness behind her eyelids was thick and gritty. The basement dripped and seeped its way inside.

Now the same darkness filled the tower as wind gusted her shoulders, whirling into the dark shaft. The dark clung to her, coated her skin and rustled against her insides. *Come on down, Brook. Lean over the edge.*

"I deserve to be here." Brook's voice was choked. "Because of what I did. And I guess I knew it the whole time, I just didn't want to..." She couldn't continue. So she inched her toes over the balcony.

The bottom was so far down she couldn't see it. Maybe there was no bottom at all, and she'd keep falling and falling until she fell asleep.

She leaned into the drafty dark. *That's right*, the island said. Then something caught her eye and froze her at the edge, knees bent, hands half covering her face.

Gold coins glowed in the shadows. Floating in the dark. Yellow and round, shining like a king had tossed them to a happy crowd of kids, and the wealth had paused to flash and shimmer in midair. The flock of golden coins hovered, waiting to swerve and dart away.

Magic.

Brook drew a long breath. She waited for the gold to rise into the sky and become part of a far-off sunrise. To leave her in the dark. But the magic stayed.

"Oh, thank you," she whispered.

Then she realized the coins were leaves—golden leaves on a stubborn, dark-defying vine. They were even better than coins because they were alive. She let out a sigh.

"You're beautiful," she said. "You're something that shouldn't be here. You're something good in a horrible, horrible place. And you're here"—she gasped—"for me."

The magic glowed softly in the shadows.

Brook stood up straight in the hungry silence.

"No," she told the island. "No, I won't. I'm not alone, and I can be someone different. There's magic helping me, so I know"—she shuddered—"things can change." Her whole body shook as she stepped back from the edge and the wind died with an angry *whuff.*

Then her stomach bent in on itself and crashed up and down like the ocean under the cliffs. She put her hands against the wall and puked off the edge. When she could breathe again, she felt another shadow at her elbow—but this one was human.

Fox stood behind her in the doorway.

Brook brushed at her eyes, flicking tears away, but they overflowed down her face and chin. "Fox, they ruined the castle," she said. "They trashed it and I couldn't find the key."

Death Dogs howled somewhere far below.

"I'm sorry, Brook." Fox sounded angry. "They're a bunch of cheaters."

"Maybe we could fix it..."

"Of course we can. We can still be king and queen—it'll just mean a lot of work."

Brook wiped her face and picked up Isabella. "What about the key?"

"Knowing the blue-faces–"

"They probably threw it away."

"Yeah. C'mon, Brook. Let's get out of here."

He turned to go and she followed him without question. The cold, dark stairs went on forever. How she'd climbed them so fast, she'd never know. When they crossed landings, she heard noises down side passages. A rasp of metal, footfalls, a muffled cough: The blue-faces were waking up. She was surprised they weren't moving faster.

She and Fox moved faster, though.

"Why are we going down?" she whispered.

"I was in a rush to find you," Fox said. "Now I've got to be sure about that door."

She nodded. *See, he cares.*

At the bottom Fox checked the locks, tugging on chains, moving bars right and left. "Hey, keep your eyes on the stairs," he said. "Stay on the lookout."

Brook turned to watch the stairway. "Do you think they'll all attack at once?"

"It's what I would expect," he said. "We have to do this exactly right."

"For sure. Hey, Foxy." She swallowed. "Thanks for coming to find me. I felt—all alone."

Fox stopped fiddling with the door. "Of course, Brook. Always."

And as awful as the night was, Brook felt better. The castle was horrible but they could improve it. Something good could happen.

And she wasn't by herself. She felt warm, even though the blue-faces were on the hunt and she was shut in by tons of stone.

She was about to tell Fox that maybe, just maybe, they had a chance, and that he could rely on her more than he thought. With her eyes still on the stairs, she said, "Hey, Fox"—when cold air hit her back. Wind rushed across the landing with a groan of hinges.

Brook spun around. "Oh no!"

The castle door stood open.

She stared. "Fox, what happened?"

They looked out side by side.

She took a step forward. "Let's get this closed before–"

"Sorry, Brook." She felt his hand on her arm, squeezing tight. "I really am." Then he shoved her through the doorway and out into the night.

CHAPTER 38
DEATH DOGS

BROOK SCREAMED as she fell down the stairs. She landed with a jolt, scraping her hands and knees as Isabella clattered on the stones. When she looked up, Fox stood in the doorway. For a few long moments, she didn't move. She couldn't. Her heart ached like she'd been stabbed and she felt hot tears brimming in her eyes *again*.

How could he have done that?

Was it supposed to be a joke?

She was about to run at Fox and hit him, hard, when she saw his face.

His grin twisted up at the corners.

Brook couldn't believe it.

"Move on down," he said. "I'll be right behind you."

"What are you doing?"

"Saving your life, so move. There's not a lot of room for error."

Brook picked up Isabella and squeezed her weapon tight. The weight of the night pressed down on her, and she thought she might sink into the ground. She felt like something incredibly valuable, a treasure, had been grabbed right out of her arms.

"It's you, isn't it," she said. "Not the blue-faces. It's you."

She'd never seen him look so happy.

Something tight and controlled inside him had got out.

Over her shoulder, green flames flashed close and sped away, then flashed close again.

The Death Dogs.

"You really ticked me off, you know," Fox said. "When you ran up the stairs. It could've ruined everything, but I like you, Brook, always have. So I came in after you, and luckily, like a good girl, you followed me right back out. And those gutless blues didn't attack us when they had the chance, and my dogs are still waiting. So—SO— the game is still on!"

The energy crackling from his eyes was crazy. "Here's how this will work, Brook. The dogs will empty the whole castle like a cleaning crew and I'll stroll in to pick up the pieces—and then I'll win. I'll be in charge! And I couldn't have done it without you. So thank you, Brook, I owe you. You're the secret sauce—you're the MVP. They would never, ever, in a million years, have opened that door for me."

So many things were rushing through her mind. She saw Fox finding her in the sand. Showing her the secret camp. Eating rabbit across the fire. Hiking with her through the woods. All that time acting as if he liked her—all of it leading to this.

It was too much. She couldn't make it work. Even now, after he'd thrown her down the stairs, she wanted to say, You're kidding, right Fox? We're still a team? But he wasn't kidding. They weren't a team. Nothing was like he'd said. The castle, their plan, the key. All of it, gone. And Fox was gone too. This Fox, grinning at her, she didn't know.

"You're a liar," she said. "All you do is lie, lie, lie. And we could've won together."

He shook his head no, looking smug and sad at the same time.

"Well, you're not throwing me away," Brook said. "You're losing me. I'm leaving." She leaned her scythe-staff gently against the wall and picked up the nasty-looking trident instead.

"You shouldn't have—what's the word?—leaned on me," Fox said. "You shouldn't have acted like I'd really carry your weight. Friends don't exist in real life, Brook. I think deep down, we both know that."

She held the handle of the trident to her forehead and gave herself five seconds, closing her eyes. This is the real Fox, she thought, the one you thought might be there and hoped was not. He tricked you—so no more hiding. Nothing to hold back now.

She leaned against the castle as hungry shadows gathered, circling and snapping under the moon. The massive stones felt like the safe walls of their secret campsite—another lie.

Even if you're surrounded by lies, you can still be you. So hush. Stay in charge. Do what you can. She thought about the open castle door and the terrified kids inside. And a safe, quiet room in a tower that didn't exist.

She stepped away from the stairs and into the cold, dark night.

The shapes of the Death Dogs stalked closer, jagged and bristling.

"Step aside," Fox said. "You don't need to get hurt. I'll handle them, and you can use that speed of yours and run away. You were great, Brook. You served your purpose. But now your part is over, so step off. Take a timeout or something."

"Don't tell me what to do," Brook said.

Fox glided down the stairs. At the bottom, he paused dramatically. "You know who the dogs are tracking, right? It's not me. It's you."

She stared at him. Her hand flew to her face, sticky with rabbit blood.

He'd pretended it was no big deal, like putting on make-up.

He'd made her the bait.

He'd lied. He'd liedliedlied.

Fox lifted his feet, tugging off his shoes. "I gave the dogs a little help," he admitted. "Stomped in rabbit guts, not that I needed to, and now we have that poor kid, bleeding all over inside. Death Dogs are basically land sharks, you know. Working themselves into a feeding frenzy. So get outta the way. Everything's falling into place."

She didn't move.

"Seriously, Brook, if I were you, I'd run—not now, not out there with the Death Dogs—but once they're inside, headed up the stairs, you'll have a chance. They'll be busy for a while. You can have the old campsite, I don't mind."

Until you come to take those weapons, she thought. Then you'll mind. You just want me out of the way now, so I don't confuse your pack of monsters.

Her whole body felt like fire.

Fox frowned. "Don't be stubborn, Brook."

She forced herself to look at the Death Dogs.

Eyes glowing, teeth snapping, they looked like hyenas on the nature channel. But they kept getting bigger, bigger than Rottweilers or Pit Bulls, bigger than the biggest dogs she'd ever seen. Saliva dripped from their teeth and Fox hadn't lied about their stingers. The gray-black fur gave way to barbs that swayed and jabbed like scorpion tails.

One of them lunged at her and she jerked away. Two more of them crept closer on her right and left. She couldn't fight them all. She couldn't stop them. So she did what Fox wanted. Stepped away from the stairs, out of the way.

"Good girl," Fox said. He rubbed his shoes together, still dripping rabbit blood, and the Death Dogs strained toward him, snarling. He tossed the shoes inside the castle. "Door's open, boys."

The first dog shot past in a spiny blur, claws scrabbling on the stone. When it reached the pool of the boy's blood, it tilted its long snout to the sky and howled. The other dogs rushed forward, parting around Fox like he was made of stone. A fight broke out on the stairs, dogs snarling and biting to get inside. More of them kept coming, pouring out of the dark like bats—*like bats out of the night*. Brook drew a quick, wet breath.

"It's like I'm one of them," Fox whispered, more focused on the dogs than her.

Hearing him talk like that helped.

And he didn't notice the Death Dogs parted around her too. They gave her space, even though her face and hip were streaked with blood. Even though they'd been tracking her over the plains. They wanted no part of her now that she was ready for a fight. Maybe they could smell her anger. Maybe they could smell her heart. She moved Snake-Tooth higher in her pocket. Hopefully he was on her side now that he'd got what he wanted.

"Now's the time," Fox said. "Aren't you going to run? I pulled you out of the castle on purpose, Brook. I'm giving you a chance. You earned it."

Brook shook her head. She noticed he'd picked up the spear from the bottom of the stairs. He had the axe over his shoulder, no big deal, like a baseball bat.

"I wish you would," Fox said. "I don't want to see them catch you. I like the idea of you being out there, Brook. Can't you see that?"

She wrapped her fingers around the trident.

Deadly and three-tined and razor-sharp. A familiar, hungry shape.

Welcome back, shork, she thought.

"Monsters don't always get what they want," she said.

CHAPTER 39
WHO WE REALLY ARE

WHEN SHE LEVELED the trident at Fox, it gleamed silvery-blue in the moonlight.

She flipped the switch in her head.

"Drop your weapons," she said.

Fox laughed. "Brook, c'mon. It's cute, but you really, really don't want to do this."

Brook slashed at him, a diagonal stroke from left to right, and he snapped his mouth shut and jumped back. She tried a straight jab, and he brought the axe down awkwardly to stop her, but one of the tines scraped a red line on his shin. She saw a question flicker in his eyes, and rocked another jab in hard and fast, the way you did when a bully gave you an opening.

The reach and speed of the trident took her breath away. It was as deadly as a hundred shorks. Fox swung the spear upright across his body, catching her next jab, but her blow tore the spear away and spun it into the grass. Brook snatched her weapon back and leveled it again.

"Magic brought me here," she said. "Good magic—and it's on my side. But don't worry. You still have the axe."

Now he was angry, and Brook took a deep breath and braced

herself. Ants crawled up her spine, rustling over the nape of her neck and turning to march back down. Up and down, up and down, dozens of ants with tiny, icy legs.

Fox stalked forward. "Who are you, Brook?" He swung the axe, a flashing arc, trying to smash the trident from her hands.

She stepped aside and made him jump back with a twisting jab. Letting loose all the quickness, all the rhythm, she'd done her best to bury since she'd arrived. She wasn't defenseless. She wasn't clueless. She was deadly. Now he'd find out.

"I thought I knew you," Fox said.

"And I thought I knew you," she said. "We were both wrong I guess."

The axe and trident met head-on with a grating crash that threw off sparks. It's an awkward match-up, Brook thought. Fox could've pinned me to the wall if he'd kept the spear. Instead, we both have to be cautious. The trident was quick—the axe was crushing. But she didn't think his cautiousness would last.

"Who taught you?" he snarled. "Where are you really from?"

"Try living in an orphanage for years," Brook snapped. "With people who hate you and who you hate back."

"I don't believe you." Fox chopped down at her, pivoted when she darted away, and swung the axe crosswise at her chest. The blow could've crushed a car door but she saw it coming and ducked. She snaked the trident out as the axe's breeze fanned her hair, and Fox jumped back like he'd been stung.

"Good job, shork," Brook whispered.

Fox spat into the grass. "They sent you, didn't they? To get close to me and take me out—that's even more twisted than the dragon." He didn't seem to care that one of his knees was bleeding.

"They?" Brook said. "Who's 'they?' Don't be an idiot. And don't pretend you trusted me—you didn't even like me!" Anger raced along her veins, melting all the ants. She cocked her right elbow and drove the trident forward, once, twice, three times. The axe wasn't made for defense. Fox knocked the first blow aside, dodged the second—then his upper arm was bleeding.

"Where—are—we?" she said through her teeth.

His eyes were shadows. Then he grinned. "You'd have to kill me before I told you, Brook. But that won't happen." He dropped the axe and her eyes widened. Fox snatched at his clothing, and she had the strange thought that he was on fire, trying to put himself out. Instead, something silver shot through the air.

Brook threw herself aside, but the knife still got her, ripping her t-shirt, slicing her shoulder, hitting the castle wall.

"I don't want to kill you, Brook—and I'm not lying when I say that." Now Fox was holding the spear. He'd marked its place in the grass. "Tell me all about yourself."

She bit the side of her cheek. Blood trickled from her shoulder. Inside the castle, someone screamed. How long had they been fighting? Just minutes that seemed like seconds that seemed like hours. And now the fight was almost over.

"Who are those kids?" she said. "The blue-faces."

Fox blinked. "Scared little brats, not a single one of them really dangerous. Not a single one of them highly rated. Keeping me out of my own castle, can you believe it? Locked outside, with all the ferals trying to hunt me down. But now I'm back in charge, and it's your turn, Brook. Who are you and why are you really here?"

CHAPTER 40
LAST DANCE

BROOK THOUGHT about making something up.

"I was sent here to spy on you, Fox," she could say. Even better, "I was sent here to sabotage you..." Something to keep him guessing, because she didn't see how she could stop the blood flowing from her shoulder while she held onto the new shork. If she kept bleeding, the pain would fade, and she'd get numb, and she'd take three steps to the castle and lean against the wall, or maybe sit on the stairs until she fell over.

Or maybe Fox would kill her first.

But she didn't have the heart to make something up. And who was supposed to have sent her? The dragon? The Foundation? Fox's parents, furious their baby wasn't dead? No, nothing made any sense.

"I'm supposed to be here," she said. "I deserve it. I killed a girl in the Foundation basement, so that's what it must be. Even though I thought—I thought..."

I thought there was magic. And I thought it could help me be a hero, and that it was waiting for me, waiting to make something good happen in a horrible place. But I'm so stupid. I was wrong.

Fox narrowed his eyes. "I don't get it," he said. "I don't see your play."

There were howls and shouts and crashing in the castle now. Behind the massive walls, raised voices sounded tinny and far away. Brook pictured Death Dogs racing down halls, bounding up stairs, hunting the blue-faces from room to room. She hoped the kids were organized, that they'd woken up fast and hadn't been surprised by hungry eyes staring down at them.

"I don't have a play." Brook took a hand off the trident and pressed her bleeding shoulder and she knew it was the truth. "That's who I am, just someone no one wanted, who decided to fight back. Otherwise, I'd be dead. Since I'm not dead, I'm here. That's the whole story." Anger rose in her again, but she could feel it seeping away like water as soon as it reached her heart.

"Oh." Fox passed a hand over his eyes. "That's all?" He sighed. "If that's really who you are, Brook, you have nothing to be ashamed of. Whoever you killed, she deserved it." He frowned. "I wasn't lying before, when you found all my weapons. I'm an orphan, too. I may have already said this—I lose track—but I was never wanted. They wanted to wipe me off the earth. Delete me, and they'd never even seen me, can you believe that? There's a word for it that I can't remember..."

Brook slid a little down the wall.

Fox trailed a finger under his eyes. "And you know what else? Half the time I wish they'd gotten away with it. Because then I wouldn't be here, would I? And I wouldn't feel so—rageful all the time." He cleared his throat. "I also didn't lie when I said I liked you, Brook. You're smart and a helluva better fighter than I thought. But I have to beat this island—burn it, break it, smash it—I have to win." A shadow moved over his face. "I can't let you ruin this. Not when I've waited so long."

He raised the spear.

Brook held her bloody hand against her shoulder. She wasn't sure what she could've ruined, what she could've possibly taken from Fox. He did whatever he wanted. She'd tried to stop him and failed.

"For once I wish I didn't have to do this," Fox said.

"Then don't." Brook felt darkness growing in her head. Blood ran down her elbow, making her feel cold. "You already won," she said. "You got what you wanted. No one can beat you, everyone's afraid of you—you got the castle. What if you never have to worry about me? I won't sneak up on you. I won't try to get you when you're not looking..."

She found herself sitting on the ground. Now there was black space behind her eyes, making her say things she wouldn't normally say. "We could be the king and queen, like we joked about, and we could change things. Fox, *we* could change. We could kill the Death Dogs and leave the other kids alone, at least the scared ones. Things could be different. We could become different people, like the good kids in the *Lord of the Flies*..."

She realized she was going on and on, and she was slipping sideways, grass brushing her face. She grabbed the trident to stay upright. Fox's shape was blurry against the brightening sky, and she squinted to bring him into focus. She had the idea he'd been listening, even leaning toward her. His spear was still raised, but resting on a bony shoulder. His other hand was touching his forehead. His eyes looked like the ashes of the fire in their secret campsite. When he finally spoke, his voice caught, like her hair in the thorns all those days ago.

"I can't, Brook. I wish I could do that but I can't. I don't think you can either. We'd be making promises we can't keep, and it would make us weak, and someone else would take advantage, and then—they'd all close in. They won't let us change like that. That's not how the island works. Not how anything works." He drew his knuckles across his eyes and when his hand came down, he looked fierce. "Anyway, I don't want to change."

Dawn glimmered on the long blade of the spear. Brook tried to lift the trident but she couldn't. Her arms felt like straws. She let them drop to her knees and the new shork fell against her shoulder. Her bloody fingers touched Snake-Tooth's handle. She forced herself to look at Fox as she tugged the knife from her pocket.

"Don't do that." He shook his head. "Don't."

She felt the familiar hilt in her palm, but she couldn't hold on. The knife slipped through her fingers and fell in the grass.

His spear blade hovered inches from her throat.

"Sorry, Brook," Fox said. "You're a good person."

She closed her eyes and turned away. She could've sworn he meant it.

Something like ice brushed her neck. She was so tired. Maybe it wouldn't be so bad.

God, I'm sorry, she thought. I wanted to be someone else.

CHAPTER 41
DRAGON

THE SKY WENT DARK. There was a roar and a flash of heat. Brook lost all sense of where she was. She had the feeling Fox had been suddenly snatched away, or she'd been grabbed away from him.

This is hell, she thought. This is death. And she wondered how much worse it got. There was no pressure at her neck. If her throat was cut, she couldn't tell, because it seemed like she was still breathing. A rough, cold surface pushed against her back, but the rest of her felt numb and floaty. There was pain but not too awful.

Someone was shouting and coming closer, more than one someone. There was a yell, metal scraping metal. Brook pictured angry devils, herding people with pitchforks. Oh no. Her mouth felt dry. *Devils carry shorks!* How had she never seen it?

She shuddered. Now it was too late. She was definitely in hell, and the bad part was about to start. With her eyes squeezed shut, she thought, Maybe if I hold very still, they'll leave me until later. Maybe they'll take me last.

But she knew they wouldn't, so she finally opened her eyes.

She saw the dragon.

Crouched on the edge of the eastern plain, wings folded, neck snaked low, the sunrise shimmered at the edges of its huge body. Even from where she slumped against the castle, Brook felt heat rising off the beast in waves. Human shapes were running past like they were racing—the ones she'd thought were devils—sprinting by, one after another, light gleaming off helmets and boots—and guns? They disappeared into the castle. Were these people on Fox's side?

But Fox didn't have anyone. That's why he was the way he was.

Brook's chest tightened as she scrabbled upright, catching herself on the stones. Her feet were like slippery bars of soap. She fell against the castle, pressed a hand to her shoulder and blinked. Could this be a rescue? Or were the soldiers running from the dragon? Nothing made sense.

She tried to focus her blurry vision. The dragon was in no hurry. Its blue-black scales glittered as it watched her, swaying in the yellow dawn. From time to time it hissed. Taking her in. Deciding what to do.

Because the dragon had to be in charge. It had sent the fighters in. Now it was making up its fierce and hungry mind, thinking, What should I do with this tiny girl? Brook knew she smelled like blood and exhaustion and death, which was bad. But maybe dragons weren't like Death Dogs. Maybe they liked a challenge.

Who knew what dragons liked?

Then the dragon twisted, and she flattened her palms against the stone—but it didn't lunge at her. Instead, it shifted its weight lazily, scales creaking with a *whush* of escaping smoke. Another shape moved toward her, stepping off the dragon's bent hind leg. Had he been riding on its back?

Someone big and dark stood over her. With the rising sun behind him, it was hard to see anything about him except that he was tall. She hunched against the wall, waiting to see what he would do.

"You were impressive," the man said. "We didn't see it coming, didn't think you'd stand a chance. He's lethal, the top dog, and we've known it for a while, but you're a close second. Or you were. Not much of a threat now are you?" He leaned in closer.

Brook made out dark eyes, a face used to being in charge.

She held as still as she could.

"You need medical attention," the man said. "You're worse than I thought."

"Is this...a rescue?" Brook whispered.

"Absolutely, sweetheart," the man said. "You've got all kinds of potential, and our favorite troublemaker had you hidden away. Of course we saw you—tried to scoop you up in the woods—but we had no idea what you could do. He tried to save you for himself, which is just like him. So much like him, I want to shake him until his teeth rattle. Maybe I will." He stood up. "I'm going to move you now."

"Oh, no, don't." Brook didn't like the sound of that. She was feeling more sleepy every second, and she didn't want to be touched, not by anyone. But maybe just this once, since it was a rescue...

"Try to relax." The man paused. "On second thought, you're relaxed enough. Try to stay awake. And no stabbing me with hidden weapons, that will go badly. I'm on your side."

Brook felt his fingers, hard and strong, slip behind her back. His other arm swept up her knees. As he lifted her easily, she tried not to flop. They stood by the back door of the castle as the man glared inside. Brook wondered what they were waiting for. She took the moment to look up at his face. Fierce eyes, a strong jaw, a calculating look on his face. This was someone you didn't want to cross.

The man shrugged, and Brook rose and fell with the movement of his shoulders. His clothing rustled in a stiff, plastic-like way. "Let's hope it's going well in there. Talk about a tactical nightmare. The whole island needs to be reset, picked up and shaken, everyone put on notice. We won't stand by and watch the population get liquidated. But you're my priority now. What do you call yourself?"

Nothing the man said had made her think their conversation was going to be two-sided, so Brook took a moment to think.

"Brook," she half-whispered.

He nodded down at her. "Ok Brook, don't be scared." He swiveled away from the shadows, and sunlight blinded her. She felt the man's footsteps, long and steady, crunching through the field, moving through the grass.

Brook twisted in his arms, but he was too strong.

She wanted to scream.

He was taking her to the dragon.

CHAPTER 42
BELLY OF THE BEAST

BROOK HAD EXPECTED to be dead already, slumped sideways against the castle wall. Now she suddenly knew the soldier —that's what he seemed to be—would shovel her into the dragon's mouth. This wasn't a rescue. He wasn't the rescuing type.

The soldier barely noticed she was struggling. As weak as she was, it probably felt like he was carrying a toddler. "Shush, shush," he said, tightening his grip. "You've come so far. Don't lose your head now."

She half-closed her eyes as they came even with the dragon's huge, triangular snout. Smoke rose from nostrils dark as gun barrels. Hungry yellow eyes watched them, flat and wicked like tinted glass. She was grateful its jaws were shut. The edges of its teeth gleamed like the wide ends of knives.

The soldier elbowed the dragon's monstrous head. Brook bit her lip to keep from screaming as its mouth gaped wider.

The soldier winked at her and snorted. "Stand down, beast," he told the dragon.

Brook tried to hold still as they walked past.

"I thought about snatching you from the air," the man said. "But things were complicated. Death Dogs on the hunt, kids running through the castle, your friend turning everything to hash. I think if we'd flown over and tried to pick you up, we might've just shredded you. Honestly, you look half-shredded already. I feel like I'm carrying hollow bones." He gave her a toss.

"Oww," Brook said.

Maybe he didn't know how strong he was. Or maybe he was showing off.

The soldier's feet creaked on the dragon's armored leg, which bent at a right angle, claws sunk in the turf. The soldier kicked the dragon's ribs, making it twitch and hiss, and Brook jerked in his arms. A door slid open in the monster's ribcage.

They stepped inside.

All the air drained from Brook's lungs and the blood ran away from her face. The beast's belly looked like the interior of a plane, the kind you saw in hero movies. Metal benches with grips and harnesses lined the walls. Rows of weapons rested in brackets. Lights glowed in a metal ceiling.

The soldier was watching her face. He let out a laugh. "Priceless. Absolutely priceless. If my hands were free, I'd snap a picture. You see, you've got nothing to worry about. Let's get you to the medical room."

Brook's brain couldn't keep up. She kept expecting to see light glowing redly through the walls, shining through dragon skin and arteries, revealing a huge reptilian skeleton. But all she saw were sleek, modern rooms with curving walls. It made her stomach twist and her brain thud against the sides of her skull. Every few steps, the man glanced down at her and smiled.

"I know," he said. "I know. And he didn't tell you. Of course he didn't, just like him."

When he set her on a long, white table, Brook's eyelids were fluttering. She couldn't seem to make them stop.

"Stay with me," the soldier said. "You're valuable—what's your name—Brook? You're valuable, Brook. I don't want to lose you. Don't get me wrong, everyone has *some* value—everyone who survives, obviously, everyone who makes it—but you're special. Let's start with an IV." She felt the needle prick her arm. "Give this a minute, then it's stitches. Nice thing about knife wounds, good clean edges. Easy to tie back together. A to B, B to A, like shoelaces. Nothing nasty for me to dig out inside."

He's honest, Brook thought. Not like Fox. But his honesty is not very nice.

When she felt the next needle bite into her shoulder, she gulped a deep breath, trying to stay awake, to keep an eye on the soldier. She couldn't help thinking about him digging around, cutting shreds of evil out. It was a horrible thought. He'd have to cut her open with a scalpel, wearing scrubs and a mask like in the ER shows.

Her chest would be folded open, flooded with white light as he carved at all the shards of darkness in her heart. What would be left of her when he was done? A pile of bones? She felt her fingers twitching. She bit her tongue and tasted blood.

"Noo," she groaned.

"Take it easy," the man said.

His needle poked her shoulder again.

She blacked out.

CHAPTER 43
THE FIRST OF MANY SECRETS

BROOK STARED at the ribbed silver ceiling and tried to match it to a place she knew. The bright, clean lines were new and expensive. A hooded lamp bent over her like it was worried about her health.

This wasn't Weed Middle School, with its dirty lockers and fluorescent lighting. It wasn't the Children's Foundation. The nurse there only gave out aspirin. Brook twitched a hand up from the table and put it on her stomach.

Instantly, her shoulder flared with pain. Her hip ached. Her head throbbed.

She wished she hadn't moved at all.

She wished it even more as she remembered she was on an island, and she'd had one friend but he had tried to kill her. The dragon had come down from the sky but it wasn't real. And that's where she was, inside the dragon. This bright, clean place where there was hardly room to move.

She wanted to get out and run across the plains and plunge into the forest. She'd give the Death Dogs the slip and build a fire in some hidden spot where she could fall asleep after a bath in the creek. But she knew those things would never happen.

The soldier wouldn't let her. The soldier—no, the commander, and his team of soldiers—they were the ones in charge. The dragon was a lie, just like the castle was a lie, and Fox. The whole island was a maze of lies that would kill you just as quickly as the truth.

Her body felt heavy. The hospital table pushed hard against her spine.

Brook knew she deserved to be there. She'd taken her shork and stuck it into Monique's brainstem and now, remembering it clearly, she couldn't allow herself to mind. Not one bit. Look at where caring had got her. If she cared, she might as well give up. She might as well be dead. No, she couldn't mind.

I don't mind, she told herself. I don't, I don't.

Brook sat up carefully and swung her legs over the side. Her heart was pounding hot and heavy like a monster trying to get out, because even though she knew this was her fault, there was nothing she could do about the way she felt. Her heart was like the fire in their ruined campsite, coals glowing under ash. Banked down, waiting for the moment it would roar to life. So angry. So, so angry.

She clenched her fists and pushed herself off the table. She was still wearing her bloody, tattered t-shirt, cut away at one shoulder, but there was a clean shirt folded on a chair. She pulled off the rags of her old shirt and threw them in a sterile-looking trash can.

The stitches in her shoulder were neat and dark like a lightning bolt with lots of zigs and zags. Her skin had closed right up. But the flesh below kept aching. She shrugged the clean black shirt over her head, wincing when she lifted her arm. It fit her snugly. The fabric was thick and stretchy, better than anything she'd ever owned.

No one seemed to be keeping an eye on her, but that was just another lie. Still, she was tired of waiting in the safe-seeming surgery. Outside the medical room, she found herself in a compact kitchen. Bright lights gleamed on chrome and white appliances. Brook stared at an industrial fridge. Her stomach ached, but she didn't want to eat. She wanted to dump food on the floor, splash it across the perfect kitchen—unless there was chocolate milk. But this was some kind of army plane, so there wouldn't be.

She moved unsteadily over the tile, lurching now and then. Her hip stung like someone was jabbing it with needles. She tugged at the waistline of her shorts and found more stitches. Of course. Snake-Tooth had bit deeper than she'd thought.

Why had she bothered naming him?

When she opened the fridge, cartons of milk lined the top shelf. Brook froze when she saw one row was chocolate. She picked up a quart, then flung her arm across the shelf and flailed. Containers smacked the polished floor. They bounced but didn't spill.

Brook wanted to scream. She waited for someone to come rushing through the door, but no one did. No one shouted at her. No one helped her make the mess she wanted. She let the fridge swing shut and moved along a table. The cold tiles seemed to tilt under her feet and she paused to catch her balance. Where were her shoes and socks?

When she shoved the next door open and stepped through, the first thing she noticed was the carpet. Soft to stand on, an expensive feel. When she looked up, she realized she'd walked into a meeting. The room was a thin lounge, lights glowing in the walls, a small table bolted to the floor. The soldier-commander sprawled across a chair. A bloody, angry-looking child sat upright in another.

The milk carton froze at Brook's lips when she realized it was Fox.

"Nice to see you're not leaking blood," the grown-up said. "Call me DaVinci. I was just making things clear to your friend here."

"Hi Foxy," Brook said. "I wish I could've killed you."

Fox didn't move or answer.

DaVinci raised his eyebrows. "I feel you," he said. "We'll both need massive self-control. The island has no rules"—he jabbed a finger at Fox—"and who would've thought you could ruin anarchy? But he found a way. Everything spiraling into chaos, the ecosystem trashed, the rankings totally shot. Top prospects dropping like flies.

Rising stars"—he nodded at Brook—"deceitfully hidden. Now we've got to empty the castle, bring new monsters in, reset the game."

DaVinci took a breath and clenched his fists. "Incredibly expensive, that's the point. All so we can have a proper free-for-all. This is your last chance, boy. You, on the other hand"—in a blink he was on his feet. Brook didn't have a chance to move as he wrapped a steely arm around her.

"You're in a different category, sweetheart. Your career is just beginning."

"You're lying," she said.

The man laughed and shot a look at Fox.

She thought how weird it was for Fox to be so quiet.

"Of course you think that," DaVinci said. "We've taught you well. But look around you. You've been rescued." He spread his hands. "You know the secret of the dragon—the first of many secrets. Everything's about to change. Good food, nice clothes, classes you'll be good at. If you play your cards right, you'll never see the island again."

"I don't believe you," Brook said. "Take me away from here if it's all true."

He laughed again and pushed a small white button in the wall. A section of the metal slid away, revealing tinted glass.

"Look out the window, honey."

CHAPTER 44
THE DEAL

BROOK STARED down at the ocean. Waves crashed as far as she could see. The dark, twisting tail of the dragon lashed the breakers. There was no island. No land of any kind. Nothing but a horizon and hungry water and distant purple clouds.

Her chocolate milk hit the floor, glugging from the open carton.

DaVinci picked it up and took a sip.

"It was all pretend," Brook said, knowing that wasn't even close to what she meant.

"You're too modest," the soldier said. "Despite *his* meddling, you moved through the survival funnel. Think about it. You escaped the cliffs. You survived the clans. You even crashed the castle and gave him—what did you call him, Foxy?—a serious scare. You're fearless, darling. You're deadly. The Jabberwocky really likes you. We've moved you to the top of our draft board." He frowned and Brook wondered if there was something about the draft board he didn't like. Then she thought of all the kids Fox had killed.

"What are you asking me to do?" she said.

"To live in the real world, where the odds aren't stacked against you." DaVinci's eyes burned into her. "To use your brains and your pretty face. To be the best."

"That makes no sense," she said.

DaVinci sighed. "To be a spy. There, I said it. I hate being so pedantic."

Waves lapped soundlessly outside the window.

Brook knew what it meant to be a spy. Sneaking around. Keeping an eye on everyone and giving away as little as you could. Stealing little moments for yourself. Expecting the worst and trusting no one. She'd been a spy her whole life and DaVinci was right. She was good at it. The problem was, she also hated it.

"What if I say no?" she finally said.

DaVinci smiled at her. Fox looked up and shook his head.

"I think you can probably guess," the soldier said.

"If you go back, everyone will hunt you," Fox said. "There will be a target on your back and you'll never get a chance to start a tribe or win the castle, even though you–"

"Shut up, Fox," Brook said. "I never want to hear your voice again."

DaVinci shrugged. "He knows what he's talking about, but have it your way." He held out the chocolate milk to her. "Before we continue, I need you to promise me you won't hurt Dog-Fox here."

Brook took the milk and felt her ears and face get hot. "Why would I promise that? From the moment I met him, all he's done is–"

"I won't hurt *you*," Fox said. "I thought I could, but when I tried to, I–"

"Stop!" It was more than she could take. Brook threw the milk carton at him. He ducked and it hit the wall. The attack was so weak she wanted to cry.

"Ha!" DaVinci said. "And why *would* you hurt her now that you're off the island? What could you possibly hope to gain?"

Fox shrugged. "I'm telling her so she knows–"

"STOP TALKING!" Brook yelled. *Breathe in, breathe out.* She wondered what the man would do if she ran at Fox and hit him. But she was hurt and couldn't move fast.

"There are no rules on the island," the commander said evenly.

"But once we leave the island, there are rules. Rules with penalties, aren't there, Dog?"

"Yes."

"So you need to understand this, Brook."

"Ok," she said. "I get it."

"Let me just finish my speech," he said. "You're being sent to a wonderful place. In fact, and you'll love this, some people call it *magical*. How cute, how ignorant—*magic*—so you'll be able to ride unicorns and talk to the trees. More to the point, you'll have nice clothes, good food, money, education, a tolerable amount of safety. Classes you'll enjoy and be good at. Chances to win awards or play around at making friends. Who knows where this will end if you don't blow your cover?"

"Magic," Brook said. "Great. And you'll be watching."

"Of course I will." DaVinci laughed. "Just like on the island but more so. I was going to save this for later, but since you mention it" —he grinned. "I'll be going with you. Education plus espionage is my sweet spot."

Fox's shoulders gave a little jerk.

"Everything will change for you, Brook," the soldier said. "You'll be the best, with connections in two different worlds. I expect great things from you. You'll thrive in a new situation." He uncrossed his legs and stood. "You'll absolutely love it in Sylvan Woods."

DaVinci hit buttons on a keypad and a door slid open. Brook saw the dragon's cargo area full of soldiers before he stepped through and the door slid shut behind him.

She and Fox stared at each other.

Brook stepped away and stood in the kitchen door. She wasn't sure where to go.

"You liar," she said. "You nasty, dirty–" She caught herself and brushed her hair back from her face. A few strands almost touched her shoulders now. "You will never fool me again," she said. "Never. Ever, ever."

"I hope you're right, Brook." Fox looked pale but she saw a trace of his old smile. It looked like fake jewelry to her now.

"You knew all along," she said. "About the island."

"I made a mistake." Fox sat up straight. "I admit it. We could've held them off, Brook. We could've hid inside the castle. The Death Dogs could've been our guard dogs. He"—they both glanced toward the door—"*He* would've had to leave us alone or burn the castle down. It could've worked. I didn't see it until too late. I'm sorry."

"We'll never know," Brook said. "Since you tried to kill me."

"I admit, I thought about it," Fox said. "But if I'd tried, really tried—do you really think you'd be here?" He traced a red slash across his face. She couldn't tell if it was his blood or someone else's —and she didn't answer his question.

"I wanted to burn everything down," he said. "Or get off that cursed island. The whole game was rigged against me when they sent me back, and I had to mess things up, make something happen." His fingers clenched the edges of his chair. "I wanted to ruin everything. Total chaos...or escape...I would've taken either one."

"Oh, I see" she said. "Then I guess you got what you wanted."

"Yeah." But this time he didn't smile. And in a stupid way, she wished he would, because it would be easier to hate him. And because at least someone would be happy.

"It's just that I'm so angry all the time," Fox said. "In my bones."

"Let me guess," Brook said. "It comes from never being wanted."

"So I told you?" he said. "I lose track."

"I feel it too," she said. "I snap my fingers and it's there. It comes from being treated like you're nothing. A no one. A thing no one wants. It makes you wonder what's wrong with you, but there's nothing wrong with me. Nothing wrong. Nothing."

"Of course there isn't," Fox said.

And she knew he felt the same way, but she still couldn't forgive him for everything he'd done. Because no matter how you felt, you still had choices.

Fox looked at the floor.

"Are you going," she asked. "Going to Sylvan Woods?"

"Of course I'm going," he said bitterly.

After a minute, Brook sat down in the second chair and looked out the window. Endless waves crashed under them, gray-green and capped with white and full of darkness underneath.

Somewhere out there, she thought, is a room with a big door and a lock, where warm sunlight spills in puddles on the floor. And I'll stay there for as long as I like and when I'm ready I will step outside and people will see there is more to me. Down here, right here, just waiting. I can be sweet and pretty. I can be tough and take care of myself.

I can be the best, just the best.

She half-closed her eyes.

And people will wish I was their girl, she thought, but I won't be. No one will be allowed to touch me. Maybe I'll have friends but probably not, since you can't trust anyone. And even though I'm fine by myself, people will wish they knew me—when I show them I am lovable.

"There's a word for us," Fox said.

Brook opened her eyes. He was looking at the sea.

"A word for the two of us," he said, "for what we could've had, if I hadn't ruined it. It's when you know someone, really know them, and when things go badly, you know that person will come, no matter what."

Brook tapped a rhythm on the arms of her chair.

"They'll crash in and do whatever they can," Fox said, "no matter how bad things are. And you know they will, you *know* it"— he touched the side of his head—"because they've proven it, proven they're solid, that you can count on them a hundred percent." He glanced up. "There's a word for it that I forget."

Brook dared him to meet her eyes. He didn't.

She tried to think of the missing word, and for the life of her she couldn't.

When she gave up, she brushed back the chopped ends of her hair.

She counted to ten. She counted to a hundred. Then a thousand.

Fox still hadn't met her eyes.

Waves flashed under the belly of the dragon as they sped across the sea.

THANKS FOR READING CROOKED CASTLE.

If you're wondering what to read next, check out *Twisting Trails*, book #3 in the Casey Grimes Series. You can learn more at **ajvanderhorst.com**.

For all the inside stuff on the Crooked Castle/Casey Grimes universe —including book news, tips on fighting monsters, and a free story— sign up for *The Sylvan Spy* at **b.link/Castle**.

ACKNOWLEDGMENTS

Big thank yous to the usual suspects at Lion & Co. Press. The more books I write, the more you pitch in. You're a gritty, glittery dream team full of passion, humor and (sometimes too much) drama. It's just a matter of time until you get notorious, and until then, I'm happy I get loads of your help. Some day we'll book a haunted castle for a ~~creative retreat~~ legendary party.

Thanks, **Gwen**, for all those morning coffees and pep talks.

Thanks, **Flannery**, for the after hours drinks and monster consultations.

Thanks, **Miles**, for the undying optimism and sales projections.

Thanks, **Ezra**, for the endless re-reads and notes on forest realism.

Thanks, **Asher**, for the concept sketches and drafting sessions.

Thanks, **Aidan**, for the frequent check-ins and knowing how to make a darn good cappuccino.

Thanks, **Lindsay**, for tugging on character arcs and plot lines until everything comes together.

Each of you help me remember that whether we find ourselves in Sylvan Woods or Crooked Castle, there's more magic in the world than we can see.

ABOUT THE AUTHOR

AJ Vanderhorst (that's me) lives in tornado country with his wife, kids, and a turtle with a taste for human toes. AJ especially likes hot sauce. His award-winning fantasy books for kids, *The Mostly Invisible Boy* and *Trickery School,* take place in an alternate USA where monsters stalk the suburbs. To learn more about how to survive a monster attack, visit AJ online at **ajvanderhorst.com**

And hey, if you enjoyed the book, would you do me a favor? Head over to **b.link/ReviewCastle** on your phone or laptop and leave an Amazon review. I sure appreciate it!

A FUNNY, SCARY AND DANGEROUS
SYLVAN WOODS TALE

"I LAUGHED... AND I FELT NERVOUS."
– 9YO MILES

THE
GHOST
OF
CREEPCAT

AJ VANDERHORST

*Dedicated to anyone
who's ever been scared in the woods
and to cats I have known.*

THE GHOST OF CREEPCAT

IT ALL STARTED when a raccoon ate our cat like barbecue chicken.

My twelfth birthday was on a Saturday, and I was trying to have a good attitude. I'd pulled my cinnamon hair back in a bouncy pony-tail, the kind that says, *good attitude.* And I'd put on a fun t-shirt: *Hedgehogs: Why Can't They Just Share the Hedge?* And I was wearing my favorite pair of skinny-but-not-death-grippy jeans.

Since I had no friends to celebrate with, I was looking for our cat, Orangesicle, while I waved a piece of bacon. My plan was to slip it to him before my parents noticed so maybe he'd hang around while I opened presents. Then I could throw balls of wrapping paper at him and watch him shred them in a crazy hissing fit like he was being attacked by monsters.

But Orangesicle wasn't in the house. Not even in his favorite lair, a stack of mostly-shredded moving boxes that smelled like some-thing had died—so I stepped outside. For a few seconds, the summer sun hit my skin and I thought, Hey, this could be a good day. Then I saw him.

Well, I saw what was *left* of him, actually, leaning against the house by the front porch. I ran back inside, squeezing the bacon so hard it greased all my fingers.

"Mom, Orangesicle is dead!" I yelled, and she jumped up with a strange, wild look in her eyes and followed me outside.

When she saw him she gave a little scream, and I felt better about the way my stomach had lurched sideways and folded over on itself. We stood there staring at the pile of bones—mostly bare with scraps of pink meat and pale tendons hanging off like someone had been a little too lazy to gnaw them clean.

A puffy raccoon tail lay nearby, so at least Orangesicle had put up a fight. You didn't want to think about what had happened after that, and I tried not to—but I pictured the raccoon eating an Orangesicle drumstick and licking his little paws.

Maybe Mom was picturing the same thing. I'd never seen her eyes so wide, and she must have seen the look on *my* face, because she put a hand on my arm. I swallowed. She sighed.

Then she pulled out her phone and held it up, *click*. She started tippy-tapping away on the screen—and our moment of sadness was over. The shock in her face drained away as she scanned what she'd written, smiled, and tapped a button. *Bling!* I looked over her shoulder at the photo caption:

Burn in hell, CreepCat! Guess you weren't as tough as you thought! :)

"Wow, Mom," I said. "Don't you know the internet's forever?"

"Who cares?" She giggled. "Can you believe he's finally gone?"

I grinned back at her. "It feels wrong to feel so good—but who cares? I'll get a trash bag!"

Ok, so Orangesicle wasn't a great cat. He was supposed to make me feel better about moving, but the best thing about him was his fur, which (surprise) was orange with shadowy stripes—but you never got to touch it. All his fur did was make him look dangerous and stuck up, like he was better than other cats.

And man, was he whiny. As a cute kitten he fuzzed up and hissed whenever he didn't get his way, which was every five minutes. Then without warning, he became a sulky teenage cat, hiding under tables and chairs to swipe at us when we walked past.

Once he bit my thumb to the bone just because I tried to pet him. As my blood dripped on the floor, he narrowed his eyes, licked his teeth and purred. Another time, when my aunt and uncle visited, we caught him trying to claw his way into their baby's pack 'n play. Let me tell you, that was an awful moment.

It's hard to like a cruel, mean-spirited CreepCat like that.

But we were stuck with him.

We tried to take him back to PetSpectacular and trade him in, but they said they'd stopped carrying his type of cat. "What kind is that?" I said. "Murder cats?"

The checkout lady got a weird look on her face and said it would violate their store policy to take him back, and he probably just needed a little more love—which is when I pounded my fists on the counter and Mom said we'd never shop at PetSucktacular again.

And of course, CreepCat sort of understood what we were trying to do. His yellow eyes gleamed through the slats of his carrier. He hated us even more after that.

Dad started carrying a SuperSoaker around the house at all times. Mom started wearing jeans tucked into snow boots, no skirts, so her ankles were protected. My aunt and uncle stopped visiting.

And I hate to tell you this, but I had a recurring dream where I woke up and wandered through the rooms of our house, and when I realized CreepCat was gone, I started dancing—twirling spins and big leaps like a ballerina, as butterflies swirled around me. Whenever I had that dream, I woke up smiling. (But I never told anyone about it.)

I swear that cat hated us all for trying to give him a good life. And he hated me a little extra because I worked harder to make him like me. *Now* maybe you understand how I could look at his gruesome remains and feel bad for about five seconds.

After that, I felt a ton of respect for the raccoon. I made a face, picked up its tail between my finger and thumb, and said, "Mom, can we make a trophy from the tail of this wonderful, magical animal?"

"Lila Banks, that's gross!" she said.

We both started laughing.

My birthday went well after that. With CreepCat gone, Mom and Dad and I relaxed and enjoyed ourselves. I got a new funny t-shirt—*If You Don't Love Tacos, I'm Nacho Type*—and a smartwatch and a pedicure-pocketknife with a tiny nail polish brush and file and everything.

We took our time with breakfast, kicking our legs under the table. For the first time I started to believe that when classes started at Vintage Woods Middle School, I'd fit in and be able to make friends.

Wow, having that cat gone made everything better.

Mom disappeared and returned a little later with her hands behind her back.

"Surprise!" she said, and held out one of my old ball caps. A bedraggled raccoon tail swung from the back. "I had to disinfect it first," she said. "But don't worry, it will get nice and puffy again—I think."

I covered my mouth with one hand.

"Wow," Dad said. "It's so..."

"So cute!" I said.

We all started laughing again. The raccoon cap was really awful, but I put it on anyway, because I felt good—and hey, I admired that raccoon.

After lunch Dad and Mom had some things to do, and I decided to take a hike in the woods. Maybe it was the hat's influence. I felt like I was wearing a charm that would bring good luck.

And let me say this, dear reader. I'd better warn you now. The fun, happy part of this story is over. (And remember, you already saw the bones of a dismembered cat.) Because let me tell you, I was very, very wrong.

At first, the woods seemed like just the kind of place you'd want to hike through. The trail looped around roots like muscly arms. Plenty of shade kept me from getting too hot. The air had a fresh, greenish tint, and the trees rocketed up like they wanted to reach the sun, big explosions of leaves splashing the sky.

I hoped I'd get a look at the raccoon, moving slowly after his huge dinner. I imagined us nodding at each other, and I'd say, "Hey bud, thanks for saving my birthday—and my ankles. That cat was a demon."

And he'd say, "For a demon, that thing sure tasted good."

And I'd say, "I hope you don't mind this hat—it's in your honor."

And he'd say, "You got it, girl. That tail looks way better on you than it did on me, although I miss it."

And I'd say, "Hey, I know you're wild and all, but we've got, well, some vacancy at my house in case you'd ever wanta–"

"Of course I'll hang out with you sometimes," he'd say. "You cool." Then we'd throw each other a peace sign and he'd fade into the shadows, my raccoon friend. And as he scampered off, I'd say–

Rawr!

I froze in the trail with my mouth half open. As I turned, the tight hairs at the back of my ponytail tugged my skin.

Orangesicle crouched in the middle of the trail with one paw shading his eyes. He'd never liked the sun very much, and seeing him there in the open, not sulking and slinking around the house, I realized how *big* he'd got before the raccoon ate him.

He shot his claws out—*shnick*—squinted his eyes half-shut, and started stalking me through the shade. His jaws gaped open in a slowly widening grin.

Betcha didn't know my mouth could get this big.

Oh no, I thought. Oh no oh no.

You know the feeling you get when something horrible happens that, in a thousand years, you never would've seen coming, even though you can think of all kinds of bad things that could happen?

Well, maybe you don't. But my chest got replaced by this sharp, shaking, silent scream. My heart and lungs and brain did somersaults in a dark, cold place. Then I trembled all over and backed away from the ghost of CreepCat.

"You're not real," I whispered. "You're dead. I'm not really here."

Of course I *was* really there—I got that part wrong because I was panicking. I was in a huge, strange forest: the kind of place where the ghost of my demon cat could come get me. And he'd probably heard me talking about him to the raccoon.

The raccoon! As I started running, I thought, If-I-can-just, *gasp*, find-my-friend, *gasp*, the-raccoon! And it made total sense. That raccoon had devoured Orangesicle once and he could do it again.

So I ran like crazy, and it turned out I was a pretty good runner—even though I was wearing my glittery *good attitude* sneakers. I skidded around curves and shot down every straight piece of trail I saw.

When the path broke up into two or three paths, I always chose the straightest one, so I could sprint faster. And I tried to keep my eyes up, looking for the raccoon, even though it meant I kept tripping.

Once my toes snagged a root, and I *thwapped* the ground like a cardboard cutout and crawled ten feet before I pulled myself up and kept running—because I wasn't gonna start crawling backward, sobbing, like the girls in those horror movies.

But it *was* a horror movie—it really was. The ghost of CreepCat was hunting me through the woods with his jaws unhinged so he could eat me.

I ran for as long as I could. It might've been twenty minutes. It might have been an hour—but I suddenly stopped and bent in half with my hands on my knees, because my lungs had stopped working. Huge, shuddering breaths that were half sobs made me shake all over and I couldn't help it.

Ok, I thought, ok. Now you've got to circle back the way you came.

That's what I started to do, because I'd given up on the raccoon.

He was probably asleep in his den. But I was sure if I could just get out of the woods, CreepCat's ghost would leave me alone.

At first, it worked. I walked as fast as I could, one hand pressing my ribs. With a stitch in my side, I kept gasping for air, but I wouldn't stand still and let Orangesicle catch me.

The trails seemed to lead toward my house, like the forest was trying to help. *Here's a path home, little girl—and another, and another. Your choice, any of them will work.*

And it *would've* worked, except CreepCat wouldn't let me take those paths. Every time I started down one, I'd hear his mocking, hungry yowl ahead of me—with a little slurp on the end as he licked his teeth.

And then the sun started to go down. And the paths stopped trying to help *me*, and they started helping him instead.

All those trails pointing back to Vintage Woods disappeared like they'd changed their minds. *Now* every path I followed curved deeper into the gloom.

Sometimes there'd be a homeward loop, and my heart would do a backflip—*I can do it, I can get back to Dad and Mom and my birthday cake*—and then the trail would swoop around again, like it had been waiting to trick me and make me cry.

I didn't cry though. Not one tear. All the water on my face was sweat, believe me. Every single drop. I mean, it was just darkness. It was just a haunted forest. It was only a ghost cat on my trail.

Ok, so maybe I cried, just a little. But I stopped crying when I realized I couldn't let CreepCat herd me deeper and deeper into the woods. I was probably miles from home and getting further away.

So I flipped my ponytail and felt the raccoon tail brush the back of my neck, and I thought, *You have to make your own luck.* I pulled my new pocketknife out of my pocket and opened every single tool, even the little brush. Then I put my back to a huge, bumpy tree and waited, trying to make myself stop shaking.

By now the woods were so dark that all I could see were

shadowy shapes. Trees looked like giants with twisted fingers. Ferns and bushes looked like hungry hands.

Orangesicle knew I had stopped running. I could hear it in his eager, high-pitched whine. A minute later I saw him coming down the trail. The sun was so far gone, now he looked like what he was: a ghost. His glowing eyes floated over a swirling, stripy shadow.

When he got closer, he slowed to a crawl, and I could see his bristling fur and hear the slurp in his snarl as he stretched his jaws.

"You're—you're just a—just a ghost," I said, trying to keep my voice from shaking. But I didn't do a very good job. If that cat could've talked, he would've said, Oh yeah? You think so, huh Lila? Can a ghost do this?

He launched himself at my neck.

You probably won't believe me, but I hadn't screamed all day until that second.

You've never heard a scream so loud and long and totally unlimited. It just went on and on, flying out across the night, as I did the only thing I could. I swung my fist up and stuck it in CreepCat's mouth as he crashed into me.

I wish I could call it a punch. It was a desperate, awkward shove, and as I fell to the ground, I kept shoving. I jammed my fist into his throat, up to my elbow—and the whole time I kept hearing my scream like it was someone else's voice, flying out over the forest like a radio frequency.

I knew I was about to die, I guess. But deep inside, I'd thought maybe CreepCat might take my hand as a sacrifice and let me go, and I'd jerk free from his mouth and stumble back home to my parents, holding my bloody wrist, while he crouched over my hand, chewing up my knuckles, *crick-crick-crack*—and swallowing them one by one.

At least, that would've bought me a little time.

But that's not what happened.

I felt his claws dig into my chest and my stomach, his muscles tightening for the big slash that would spill my heart and guts into the dirt. He didn't want just one hand—he wanted all of me. I knew it was the end.

Maybe I'd known all along it would end this way, ever since I'd seen him crouching in the trail behind me and slowly unhinging his jaws.

How did I ever think I'd get away? I was just a girl who put her hair in ponytails and talked to imaginary animals and wore silly, upbeat Ts and hoped for the best when she really shouldn't.

My scream faltered and broke like glass. It ended in a gasping hiccup. My arm was gone. My heart and guts were gone.

Stars rushed toward me through the trees.

I didn't even get to—was my last thought, and I could have ended that thought a hundred different ways, but I didn't have time.

The woods went black. Darkness wrapped itself around me in sheets.

I died.

In death, the night became thick, and hot, and furry. Then the darkness got gross and sticky—and no one can sleep through that.

I woke up.

When you think about it, dying from a monster attack would probably be a lot more painful.

It took me a minute to realize I wasn't dead. CreepCat lay on top of me like he'd finally become a snuggler and was trying to keep me warm. But his claws were hooked in my shirt, pricking my skin like needles, and even if he'd become all touchy-feely, I wanted him off me *right that second.*

So I tried to shove him off, but I couldn't. We were stuck together. My breath caught in my throat and my heart started hammering as I remembered CreepCat had eaten my arm.

I flopped onto my side and he rolled off me. He took my arm with him, which brought tears to my eyes, because now I'd have to go through life lop-sided. But then I winced as my shoulder twisted, and I realized I could feel his fangs digging into my elbow.

"Ow, ow, ow," I breathed. What happened next, to be honest,

was a lot more painful and disturbing than the moment when I'd died.

Slowly and stickily, I pulled my hand out of CreepCat's throat. It would've been a lot harder—maybe it would've taken a surgical operation—but one of the blades on my pocketknife, the mini nail-scissors, maybe, had stuck inside his gullet and opened him up like a fish.

You wanna know how gross this was, and how much blood I had on me, by the time it was over?

Well, I won't tell you—except to say that CreepCat's second mouth, the one in his neck, was bigger than his first one, and I thought there were huge worms squirming in his throat—and almost passed out again—until I realized I was looking at my own gooey fingers, slippy-sliding up toward his teeth.

I wriggled my fingers and gave myself a little wave.

It felt like someone else was waving, from inside CreepCat.

Sorry! I might've said too much, but I think maybe that's what happens when you go into shock. To me, can you believe it, it seems like I'm giving you just exactly the right amount of info!

When I got my arm out, I had red grooves running from my elbow to my wrist and several deep gouges where Orangesicle had tried to lock onto me as I'd shoved my fist past his teeth, slicing him open as I went.

I did my best to wipe all the blood on grass and leaves, but I still felt sticky. Then I sat down on a mossy rock and stared at Orangesicle, who had now died twice. My eyes kept sliding back to the big red gap that started under his chin and ran halfway down his chest. If I looked closely, I could actually see pieces of—well, you probably don't need to know that part.

Wonder if I'll have to kill him again, I thought.

And I wrapped my hand tighter around my pocketknife, although I didn't really have to, because it was basically stuck to my palm. The moon rose high over the woods. I felt like the trees were leaning down at me, reaching for me with twisty, pointed fingers, but they hadn't decided whether to pat my head or crush me.

And then the dangerous-looking boy showed up.

Why dangerous-looking, you ask? Well, there were dark circles under his eyes. There was his dark hair, *very* spikily spiked. There were his tight-fitting, army-looking clothes—all of them black. Oh, and also, he was carrying some kind of axe with a wicked blade and a long handle. The axe was black too, obviously. Lots of clues, you see, but I didn't especially care.

I giggled. "Isn't it a little late for chopping wood?"

The boy looked offended. Then he glanced at the bloody circle I was sitting in, and the ghost of Orangesicle beside me, and he said, "Hmm."

That's it. Hmm. Are you kidding me? I knew I deserved something better than *Hmm*. A funny t-shirt about killing ghosts would've made a lot of sense. A hug—heck yeah I deserved a hug—and a warm blanket and a whole box of bandaids. At the very least, a smile.

I felt a tear drip down my cheek.

The dangerous-looking kid looked uncomfortable, and for some reason that made me feel better, like I had a tiny bit of influence on the situation, so I kept right on crying.

"Ok, ok, ok." The kid put out his hand and kind of hovered it over my shoulder like I was a stove and he was checking the temperature. I grabbed it with my left hand, the one without the pocketknife, and squeezed.

He let me do that for about five seconds, his eyebrows darting toward the moon. Then he carefully unfolded my fingers, hesitated, and patted me on the head. That's right, he *patted me on the head* like I was six years old—and not even that really counted, since I was wearing my coonskin cap.

"I should probably knock you out and take you in for questioning," he said, "but I was wrong *one* time a while back, so I try to keep an open mind. Um..." He bit the inside of his cheek. "Guessing you don't know someone special who used to live in your neighborhood —or two special someones, one big and one little? The smaller one loves glitter glue and unicorns."

When I didn't answer he kept going.

"Well, looks like you did what you had to—but hell's bells, think you could've splashed any more blood around? I mean, I'm not sure there's enough."

I found that pretty insulting. Sure, maybe I looked like I'd been spray-painted red, but I'd killed the ghost of my demon cat, and anyone, absolutely anyone, should've found that impressive. I don't care how much black you wear.

The kid wrapped his hands around the top of his axe. "Here's the deal," he said. "I'm going to take you home. Maybe you were looking for us, maybe not—and if you were, well, you're right, we're out there, but I won't say another word about that. Now let's go."

When I realized he wasn't going to help me up, I got slowly to my feet.

"You're out there?" I said.

"Yeah." He'd already started down the trail.

"Who's out there?" I said. "Some kind of secret forest society?" I gave my best non-shaky laugh.

He frowned at me over his shoulder.

"And what does this secret society *do*?" I said brattily.

He turned with his hands on his hips, somehow still holding the axe. "Look," he said, "this is it. This is the last thing I'm saying, whether you're joking or you're really clueless or what. We do—we do—what you just did to that thing."

"Wait!" I said as I forced my legs to work. "You mean—you mean, you kill horrible, dangerous cats?" It was a weird idea, very weird, and kind of dark, but I have to admit...I liked it. I liked it a lot. What if Orangesicle came back?

"You're funny," the kid said. "Hey. I guess if you're meant to figure it out, you will."

And that was the last thing he said. Seriously. I asked him how I could get in touch if I needed help. I said, "Hey, by the way, my name's Lila Banks, what's yours?" I asked him if he ever lost track of himself in the dark, wearing all that black. I asked him how long he'd been killing horrible cats.

Anything to get him to talk, but he wouldn't. Not a word, not even a smile, until I saw the lemon-white glow of floodlights in my yard and the flashing blue strobes through the trees.

Know what he said to me then?

"Hubba hoy, Lila." He was right beside me when he said it, and when I turned to say, "What the heck is that supposed to mean?" he was gone. Gone without a "Take care, ok?" or a goodbye pat on the head. Gone with a *hubba hoy*.

What a weird, annoying, dangerous kid.

You can imagine what happened when I stepped into my back-yard. The whole place was lit up like it was noon. I looked like I was spray painted red, and I was holding a bloody pedicure-pocketknife.

You should've heard Mom scream. Hers was a good one, but it didn't even come close to my scream in the woods.

I told the police the truth: the ghost of our cat, Orangesicle, had lured me into the forest and tried to kill me but I'd killed it instead. They looked at me like I was crazy. One of them shrugged. Another covered his mouth. They told my parents, For God's sake, get this girl to bed. And I thought, Right? About time—thank you!

Mom sponged me off in the bathtub, crying over my cuts. She and Dad brought me birthday cake in bed and they told me, Sure, you can have a funny t-shirt about killing ghosts, but let's not talk about it right now, ok?

I found that really irritating, because *talk about it* was all I wanted to do.

It got even worse. For the next few days, they kept not-wanting-to-talk-about-it, and then I had to go to school. And here's some-thing weird. That kid—the dangerous, annoying one that I don't like? He was not there, even though I looked everywhere—just to make *sure* he wasn't there. And no one believed my story about the woods.

Of course, I should've known better. Looking back, I shouldn't have told them about my battle with the ghost of my dead cat.

And I really shouldn't have mentioned that somewhere out there in the woods is a secret society. A secret society that I might find my way back to, if it's meant to be.

And I definitely shouldn't have told Tony, who sits next to me in Math, that I sorta like to think I have what it takes to be part of a secret society that fights evil, killer cats.

And I really, definitely, shouldn't have asked him, "What do you think, Tony? Do you think I might have what it takes?"

Because he thought about it for a second. Then he said, "Yeah, Lila. I really, really do. I think you have what it takes."

By the next day, that's what everyone at Vintage Woods Middle School was saying to me. "Hey Lila, hey girl—you have what it takes!"

And that's who I am now. I'm that weird girl who wants to fight killer ghost cats—and everyone tells me I have what it takes.

Mom says, "Let's be honest, honey. You kind of brought this upon yourself."

Dad says, "Look sweetheart, *I* still like you—whatever other people say."

But I *did* follow the ghost of CreepCat into the woods, and I did meet a cool, dangerous-looking kid—I mean, not very cool—but he told me I'd find my way back if it was meant to be, and now not *only* do I not have friends, but I'm really struggling to concentrate on my studies.

But here's the good news: the ghost of Orangesicle hasn't returned.

I think I traumatized him even worse than that raccoon did—and wow, let me tell you, after fighting CreepCat myself, I've got even more respect for that animal. He made it look way too easy.

One of these days I'm sure I'll run into him, hiking through the woods, and we'll look at each other and *know.*

You're the real deal, girl.

You've got my respect, raccoon.

Peace.

But let me ask you a question.

It's important, so take your time.

And no fake answers please. This isn't a joke.

Somewhere out there in the woods is a secret society with dangerous-looking kids who are maybe sorta-cool, and they fight the ghosts of evil killer cats. And if it's meant to be, I might be able to find them.

But it's not for everyone, that's for sure.

So what do you think?

Be honest, ok.

Do you think I have what it takes?

THANKS FOR READING THE GHOST OF CREEPCAT.

For all the inside stuff on the Crooked Castle/Casey Grimes universe —including book news, tips on fighting monsters, and a free story— sign up for *The Sylvan Spy* at **ajvanderhorst.com**.

If you're wondering what to read next, it's probably time for another full-length Casey Grimes novel. To learn more about Casey Grimes #3 and #3.5, head to, you guessed it, **ajvanderhorst.com**.

THE END

READY TO READ A FREE STORY,
PICK A NEW T-SHIRT, OR
JOIN A SECRET MESSAGE RING?

HEAD OVER TO
AJVANDERHORST.COM

Made in the USA
Monee, IL
14 February 2023

27773680R00430